FLANN O'BRIEN

THE COMPLETE
NOVELS

AT SWIM-TWO-BIRDS
THE THIRD POLICEMAN
THE POOR MOUTH
THE HARD LIFE
THE DALKEY ARCHIVE

WITH AN INTRODUCTION
BY KEITH DONOHUE

EVERYMAN'S LIBRARY
Alfred A. Knopf New York London Toronto

309

THIS IS A BORZOI BOOK
PUBLISHED BY ALFRED A. KNOPF

First included in Everyman's Library, 2007
© Flann O'Brien
Published by arrangement with A. M. Heath & Co. on behalf of the
Flann O'Brien estate

At Swim-Two-Birds was first published in 1939, *The Hard Life* in 1961,
The Dalkey Archive in 1964 and *The Third Policeman* in 1967. *The Poor Mouth*
was first published in Gaelic as *An Béal Bocht* in 1941, and in English
translation by Patrick C. Power in 1973.

Introduction Copyright © 2007 by Keith Donohue
Bibliography and Chronology Copyright © 2007 by Everyman's Library
Typography by Peter B. Willberg

All rights reserved. Published in the United States by Alfred A. Knopf,
a division of Random House, Inc., New York, and in Canada by
Random House of Canada Limited, Toronto. Distributed by Random
House, Inc., New York. Published in the United Kingdom by
Everyman's Library, Northburgh House, 10 Northburgh Street,
London EC1V 0AT, and distributed by Random House (UK) Ltd.

US website: www.randomhouse.com/everymans

ISBN: 978-0-307-26749-8 (US)
1-84159-309-5 & 978-1-84159-309-8 (UK)

A CIP catalogue reference for this book is available from the
British Library

Book design by Barbara de Wilde and Carol Devine Carson

Typeset in the UK by AccComputing, North Barrow, Somerset

Printed and bound in Germany by GGP Media GmbH, Pössneck

FLANN O'BRIEN

CONTENTS

INTRODUCTION

'I considered it desirable that he should know nothing about me but it was even better if he knew several things which were quite wrong.' So says the eccentric unnamed narrator of *The Third Policeman*, lost in a strange land, deliberately shielding his identity and true nature. The desire for self-effacement persists among all of the crazy narrators in Flann O'Brien's five novels, and perhaps it is key to understanding the man behind the novel, who has hidden himself as well under a pen-name. For the very first thing to know about Flann O'Brien is that he is one of the creations of Brian O'Nolan.

And there are more than one of him. Beginning in his college days and continuing on to the end of his life, O'Nolan was a serial pseudonymist, but we need only concern ourselves with two. In addition to Flann, the quondam author of the breath-taking *At Swim-Two-Birds*, *The Third Policeman*, *The Hard Life*, and *The Dalkey Archive*, there is Myles na gCopaleen, author of *An Béal Bocht* (translated as *The Poor Mouth*), who appeared nearly every day as the first-person narrator of the column 'Cruiskeen Lawn' (The Overflowing Little Jug) in the *Irish Times* from 1940 through 1966. More often than not, Myles was also a character in 'Cruiskeen Lawn,' serving not only as a narrator and jesting anatomist of the social and political life of Dublin, but also as an elusive figure. A man of so many identities that he had none. Variously self-described as the Uncrowned King of Ireland, the archetypical Dublin Man, ageless confidant of everyone from Synge to Joyce, Myles was a cross between the comic stage Irishman embodying every known stereotype and a savage critic of clichéd language and thinking, bureaucracy, mendacity, and other social foibles. To the intelligentsia of Dublin, however, and habitués of the pubs, Myles was a real human being. He's that man in the corner nursing a pint, the fellow under the hat, the person otherwise known as Brian O'Nolan. On occasion, all three persons met in 'Cruiskeen Lawn,' such as this encounter in 1960 stimulated by the republication of *At Swim-Two-Birds*. In his thick mock Dublin accent,[1] Myles says:

ix

FLANN O'BRIEN

There's stories going round that Flann O'Brien and my good self are wan and the same pairson. I know my own know about that leaper. People has said that I have receded under many disguises in many papers, but nobody on or under this world knows what I have written or can declare on oath what I have not written.

Receding under many disguises, Flann and Myles and Brian are wan and the same, although all three have their respective roles. However, perhaps Myles is right to say that nobody can know for certain where one identity begins and ends.

*

This much is known: Brian O'Nolan was born on 5 October 1911, one of a family of twelve children, in Strabane, Ulster, Ireland. His cradle songs were sung in Irish. His father, Michael Nolan, was an Irish nationalist who met his mother, Agnes Gormley, in an Irish language class. After they married, the Nolans became the Ó Nualláin (the Irish Gaelic form) and in their home Irish was spoken, with English reserved as the language of social intercourse for the outside world. The family led a peripatetic lifestyle before finally settling in Dublin proper in 1922, where Brian was to spend the rest of his life. Brian O'Nolan's bilingualism played an important role in his intellectual and artistic career, and this split – Irish at home, English everywhere else – factors into the practice of masking his identity. The underlying linguistic differences between the two languages and the historic intertextual relationship with English play an integral role in the style and structure of the work done as Flann O'Brien and Myles na gCopaleen.

But before he was either of those two fellows, Brian O'Nolan entered an English-speaking school at age eleven, and seven years later, in 1929, began his studies at University College, Dublin. There he was to begin his literary career, primarily under the pen-name Brother Barnabas, in the college literary magazine *Comhthrom Féinne*. The fiction of a pen-name allowed Brian not only his highly cherished privacy but also the ability to critique his own humor, by commenting from the refuge of other pen-names on articles and essays he had written as Barnabas. After graduation, O'Nolan continued his shenanigans, aided and abetted by college friends, in the aptly named

Blather, a comic magazine, all the while pursuing a master's degree by editing and translating a quite serious anthology on Irish nature poetry. In 1935, he took up a post with the Irish government, where he would remain for nearly eighteen years. Two years later, his father died, and for the next decade, Brian would be the primary provider for the younger children in the O'Nolan family.

Perhaps the suddenness of this domestic burden caused him to focus on the novel he had been tinkering with since his college days. By 1938, he had completed a draft of *At Swim-Two-Birds*, and on the strength of novelist Graham Greene's enthusiasm, it was accepted by Longmans, Green & Co. for publication the following year. With this triumph in hand, O'Nolan turned his attention to other literary matters, beginning in October with a letter to the editor of the *Irish Times*, signed by Flann O'Brien. Joining the contretemps between Sean Ó Faoláin and Frank O'Connor, O'Brien pointed to the absurdity of the literary feud, and his letter drew fire from both writers. His friend Niall Sheridan described the flood opened by this first chink in the dam:

Writing under several different names, he proceeded to carry on furious arguments on many topics, satirizing *en passant* almost every established literary figure. Before long, many notable personalities joined the mêlée and the whole affair exploded into a giant display of fireworks, a mixture of satire, polemics, criticism, savage invective, and sheer nonsense.[2]

This extraordinary letter-writing campaign, with its wildly named participants, was carried out over two full years until the *Irish Times* offered its instigator a column of his own. 'Cruiskeen Lawn' debuted in October 1940, first alternately in Irish and English, but eventually given over entirely to its largely English-speaking audience. The invention of the pen-name Myles na gCopaleen is a nod to a prototypical 'stage Irishman' from a nineteenth-century melodrama, and hiding behind another identity enabled Brian O'Nolan to protect his status in the civil service. Myles would reign as the newspaper's licensed jester and resident wit for the next quarter decade, and many Dubliners began their day by turning first to 'Cruiskeen Lawn' to savor it with the morning tea or the hair of the dog.

At Swim-Two-Birds

One of the funniest Irish novels of the twentieth century, *At Swim-Two-Birds* is an exuberant send-up of literature, the novel, and the writer. Holed up in his uncle's Dublin home for the academic year, an unnamed narrator intermittently works on a mock-heroic novel about a man named Orlick Trellis who is, in turn, writing a novel, in which he freely borrows and steals his characters from Irish mythology and folklore, cowboy novels, and whole cloth invention based on the plain people of Ireland, who become strangely more alive while Trellis is asleep. These characters, frustrated by Trellis's authority, set off on a quest to find his son – the product of his union with one of his own characters – whom they commission to write a novel designed to capture, torture, and try Trellis and thus win their freedom.

At Swim-Two-Birds becomes a twisted Celtic knot, a book that eats its own tail, achieving its humor through parody and play. The figures from Irish mythology and folklore are exaggerated versions of the original and are re-enchanted through O'Brien's preposterous versions. Finn MacCool, the magical giant of pre-Christian Ireland, 'a better man than God,' an Ulsterman, Connachtman, Greek, Cuchulainn, Patrick, his own father and his own son, 'every hero from the crack of time,' becomes the slightly dim-witted storyteller who calls into being another figure from medieval Ireland, Mad Sweeny, who has been cursed to live as a madman in the trees. Seamus Heaney notes that O'Brien gave Sweeny 'a second life, as hilarious as it was melancholy,' and this mixture of whimsy and sorrow told through the madman's poetry works in counterpoint to the third great figure from folklore, the Pooka Mac-Phellimey, a kind of 'devil, third-class,' who spends a fair portion of the book arguing philosophy and kangaroos with the Good Fairy, a 'voice unsupported by a body.' All of these are set off by the ordinary Dubliners – Furriskey, Lamont, and Shanahan – whose splendid conversations accurately capture the banter among friends who circle around the smallest banalities. And laced over all is the narrator's tale, his early introduction to the pleasures of alcohol, his slide to dissolution, and his uncle's regular refrain about the boy's study habits:

'Tell me this, do you ever open a book at all?' Stories interlock, break free, re-form. *At Swim-Two-Birds* is a dizzying, slapstick extravaganza that satirizes contemporary Ireland and the over-romanticized view of the artist and the novel. As for the last of these, the student narrator overseeing this crazy quilt has the final word. 'A satisfactory novel,' he writes, 'should be a self-evident sham to which the reader could regulate at will the degree of his credulity.' Furthermore, writers should feel free to draw their characters from all of literature.

A wealth of references to existing works would acquaint the reader instantaneously with the nature of each character, would obviate tiresome explanations and would effectively preclude mountebanks, upstarts, thimbleriggers and persons of inferior education from an understanding of contemporary literature.

O'Brien writes for an audience in on the joke, and he realizes that humor works through displacement and disruption of the conscious surface, like the explosion of a splash sending ripples across the water, which liberates the tension. For all its allusions to topics from Irish nature poetry to speculations on time, the novel is intended as an extended joke and a celebration of the elasticity of stories and the artifice of art. O'Brien's disdain for certain, clear meaning and interpretation took an even more insidious turn in *The Third Policeman*.

The Third Policeman

After the structural counterpoint and weaving together of the four major plot strands of *At Swim-Two-Birds*, O'Brien experimented with another form for his second novel, and the result, *The Third Policeman*, might best be described as a hallucinatory existential murder mystery, with footnotes.[3] As in his first novel, O'Brien's hero is never given a name, and in the course of his journey, comes to realize that he has completely forgotten it in any case. Along the way, he encounters the seeming ghost of the man he has murdered and finds himself in a land of wonders with a police station at its center, run by the irrepressible Sergeant Pluck, who is overly concerned with bicycles, and the equally strange Policeman MacCruiskeen, who spends his time on marvelous inventions, including a mangle that converts light into sound – all in all, a kind of hellish literalization of the wild surmises of our hero's scholarly pursuits. The whole enterprise, as Brian O'Nolan would say, is played for laughs, and the critic Denis Donoghue points out that the narrator's rather affectless reaction to this world is part of a tradition of Irish anatomies of the human comedy, revealing the author's tendency to 'stand aside from the common urgencies of feeling and to treat the whole farrago of sensibility as warranting merely speculative attention.'[4] If that's the dark way to humor and abstraction, a very deep spiritual dread lurks long after the book's surprising conclusion. As Sergeant Pluck has said, 'The particular death you die is not even a death (which is an inferior phenomenon at the best) only an insanitary abstraction in the backyard . . .' As funny as this way of speaking – and this view of life and death – may be, that abstraction in the backyard gives pause.

What must have given Brian O'Nolan pause was the fact that *The Third Policeman* was rejected by Longmans and his agents could not find another publisher. To save face, O'Nolan concocted a number of stories about the supposed disappearance of the manuscript, but in truth, by late 1940, he put the book away and no longer sought to publish it in his lifetime. Flann O'Brien fell silent, giving way to the jests and barbs of Myles na gCopaleen. Only in 1967, after O'Nolan's death, was *The Third Policeman* brought to print and to critical acclaim. One can sadly speculate on the effect such a rejection had on his career as a novelist and the number of novels never written in this innovative, experimental, and extravagant style.

'Cruiskeen Lawn' provided some solace, and Myles produced a number of comic plays, was quoted daily by an admiring public, and was touted in publications such as the *New York Herald Tribune* and *Time* magazine as a comic genius. By 1943, the column had grown so popular that the *Irish Times* brought out an anthology of his best pieces with a facsimile cover of the newspaper's front page announcing in a banner headline: MYLES NA gCOPALEEN CROWNED KING of IRELAND. The anthology of 'Cruiskeen Lawn' was disposed throughout in two parallel columns in English and Irish, and it marked Myles's last attempt to juxtapose and counterpoint the Irish language of his youth with the English that helped expand his audience and refine his sense as a satirist of Dublin life and culture.

The Poor Mouth

While it was his farewell to his father tongue, his triumph in Irish was *An Béal Bocht*, translated into English in 1973 as *The Poor Mouth*. While every translation suffers from the journey between languages, *The Poor Mouth* has the added burden of being a parody of the style and substance of Irish Gaelic texts of the Irish literary revival – primarily Tomas Ó Criomhthain's *An tOileánach* (*The Islandman*). Strictly speaking, however, O'Nolan's satire is aimed more at those who wanted to romanticize and sentimentalize the Gaelic people and culture, remnants of a dying language and a dying way of life. Despite its wild exaggerations and forays into Irish Gaelic folklore and archetypes, *The Poor Mouth* is O'Nolan's most naturalistic and empathetic work. The tension between English and Irish, the allure of civilization and the comfort of the primitive, has its final turn in this novel, and the burden of the truly tragic fades, never to reappear in his work. Writing in the *New York Times Book Review* of the 1973 translation, Brian O'Doherty says *An Béal Bocht*

was written in a moribund language about a moribund language for a vanishing audience. Yet for almost any Irishman, the language calls up a primary culture, a lucid and devious state of mind to which only the language gives access ... [yet] O'Brien's very modern ironies give us as much access to that world as anyone who doesn't have Gaelic can get.

That lucid and devious state of mind for Flann/Myles/Brian began to diminish as well, darkening with the pressure of the column and the job, the drink and disappointment, the depressed state of post-war Dublin and the influence of the church on state affairs. A late marriage in 1948 to Evelyn McDonnell may have helped buttress him, as did an American edition of *At Swim-Two-Birds* in 1951 (though it sold poorly). Myles grew more cantankerous, and 'Cruiskeen Lawn' more overtly political. His frequent and direct criticism of the government became too much for his superiors to bear, and he was essentially 'retired' on partial benefits by early 1953. Freed from the government bureaucracy and the need to keep Myles separate from Brian O'Nolan, he turned his savage wit more and more on the state, the church, science, and other embodiments of authority. Not until the decade's end, and buoyed by another, more successful republication of *At Swim-Two-Birds* in 1960, did Flann O'Brien float back to the surface.

The Hard Life

Appearing twenty-two years after *At Swim-Two-Birds*, Flann O'Brien's novel *The Hard Life* seems the product of an altogether different mind, and indeed it is more in the spirit of Myles – funny, but caustic, and in terms of sheer artistry, far more conservative. Unlike his works from the 1940s that dealt with matters of Irish identity, mythology, and language, *The Hard Life* centers around Dubliners, and all of the novel's main characters stand in for familiar aspects of types introduced in 'Cruiskeen Lawn.' The two orphaned brothers are figures from the column – Finnbar, the faux-naïf, the unreliable narrator; and Manus, who mirrors dimensions of Myles's opportunistic spirit, pillaging old texts and repackaging ideas as his own. He is both scavenger and con artist, and foil to the brother. But the real targets of opprobrium are Father Fahrt, representing the failings of the church, and Mr Collopy, the bumbling crusader, obsessed with his campaign to provide public restrooms for women in Dublin. The novel opens, fittingly, in 1890, the year of Parnell's downfall, and ends in 1904, with the denouement in Rome occurring in the proximate time of Bloomsday. Oddly oblique, *The Hard Life* reads as an echo to James Joyce's *Dubliners*, but a rather mild attack on the pretenses of Catholicism and an already vanishing social order.

The Dalkey Archive

While composing *The Dalkey Archive*, O'Brien reported to his agent that it was 'not a novel . . . [but] really an essay in extreme derision of literary attitudes and people, and one pervasive fault is absence of emphasis, in certain places, to help the reader.'[5] By the time he gets through with James Joyce (and the cult of Joyce), St Augustine, the Jesuits, the Catholic church and the authority of science, the derision in *The Dalkey Archive* is extreme. Although the story is told through the perspective of the principal character, Mick Shaughnessy, the intrusive 'author' of the book is the central figure of *The Dalkey Archive*. Shaughnessy undergoes a series of tests not unlike Stephen Dedalus in Joyce's *A Portrait of the Artist*. Unlike the self-reflecting creator in all of Joyce's work, O'Brien's narrators move in an opposite direction – away from the artist as an empathetic figure, guided to form and content by his experience and sensibility, toward the artist as master of abstract feeling, exposing both form and content of the novel as artificial.

The Dalkey Archive sets up these representative figures not only to point out the futility of the search for self-identity, but also to undermine systems of authority that might guide individuals. Science, religion, secular and political authority, literature and art are exposed as incomplete and provisional systems to explain life. O'Brien had cannibalized the unpublished manuscript of *The Third Policeman* to create *The Dalkey Archive*. The new De Selby is a remake of the idiot savant de Selby, and he is thoroughly mad, a man of the atomic age, and more purposeful. Another figure of authority gone amok is Sergeant Fottrell, whose 'Mollycule Theory' and other bicycle-mania were lifted, virtually intact, from the earlier novel. While restricted in *The Dalkey Archive* as a secondary figure, Fottrell's theories come into play later when Mick discusses with James Joyce the meaning of the word *pneuma*, in an echo of Stephen Dedalus. And it is Joyce, ultimately, who suffers the worst in the novel, foiled in his heart's true desire to join the Jesuits.

In the end, as in the beginning, James Joyce looms large over the entire Flann/Myles enterprise, as with much of modern Irish literature. Joyce is the subject of dozens of 'Cruiskeen Lawn' columns, the subject of a very funny essay, 'A Bash in the Tunnel,' which was published under the name of Brian Nolan, and in some ways, the very opposite of Brian O'Nolan. In contrast to Joyce's mining of his own experience and fears to produce his representational human comedies, O'Nolan moves more toward self-effacement. One of the characters paraphrases his objections to realism and the autobiographical novel: 'One must write outside oneself. I'm fed up with writers who put a fictional gloss over their own squabbles and troubles. It's a form of conceit, and usually it's very tedious.'

Brian O'Nolan quite nearly succeeded in effacing the man behind Flann O'Brien, and it was not until after his death on 1 April 1966 that the full measure of his work became realized. *The Third Policeman*, the lost masterpiece, was published in 1967. *The Best of Myles*, a collection of his early 'Cruiskeen Lawn' columns, came out a year later, and three further collections followed, proving that while some of his stuff is topical, much of the wild humor and wit survives. *An Béal Bocht* was published as *The Poor Mouth* a few years later. The artificial Irishmen – Flann O'Brien and Myles na gCopaleen – live on, but O'Nolan himself vanished. A review of the first biography was entitled, quite wonderfully, 'The Disappearing Man,' and the self-effacement reflects what the narrator of *The Third Policeman* claims: 'I was satisfied to be left in peace because I knew that my own work was more important than myself.' Or as the irascible Myles once wrote:

It only occurred to me the other day that I will have biographers... and then there will be all sorts of English persons writing books 'interpreting' me, describing the beautiful women who influenced my 'life', trying to put my work in its true and prominent place against the general background of mankind, and no doubt seeking to romanticize what is essentially an austere and chastened character, saddened as it has been by the contemplation of human folly.

Yet all the while, he made us laugh. Reading Flann O'Brien for the first time is a bit like seeing fireworks go off inside a cathedral, unexpectedly brilliant.

Keith Donohue

INTRODUCTION

NOTES

1 It helps to read the dialogue in O'Nolan's work with a broad Irish accent and pass over incomprehensible bits of slang. These are almost always purely affect, and parsing the sense will only deter the enjoyment of the style.

2 'Brian, Flann, and Myles (The Springtime of Genius),' in *Myles: Portraits of Brian O'Nolan* (1973), still the best portrait of the artist as a young man.

3 Extraordinary footnotes that tell, in leaps and bounds, the strange history of de Selby, inventor, philosopher, and savant, and the subject of the narrator's lifelong scholarly pursuit.

4 In the 1999 introduction to the Dalkey Archive edition of the novel. In one of the most clever ironies of small-press publishing, the Dalkey Archive Press (named after the last of Flann O'Brien's books) brought back all of Flann O'Brien's books under their imprint.

5 Letter to Mark Hamilton, 28 November 1963.

SELECT BIBLIOGRAPHY

ANNE CLISSMAN and TESS HURSON, ed., *Conjuring Complexities: Essays on Flann O'Brien*, The Institute of Irish Studies, 1997.

ANTHONY CRONIN, *No Laughing Matter: The Life and Times of Flann O'Brien*, Grafton, 1989.

ANTHONY CRONIN, *Dead as Doornails: A Chronicle of Life in Dublin*, Oxford University Press, 1976.

DECLAN KIBERD, *Inventing Ireland: The Literature of a Modern Nation*, Jonathan Cape, 1995.

FLANN O'BRIEN/MYLES NA GOPALEEN, *The Best of Myles*, MacGibbon & Kee, 1968.

TIMOTHY O'KEEFFE, ed., *Myles: Portraits of Brian O'Nolan*, Martin, Brian and O'Keeffe, 1973.

CHRONOLOGY

―――――

DATE	AUTHOR'S LIFE	LITERARY CONTEXT
1911	Brian O'Nolan born 5 October 1911 in Strabane, Ulster, Ireland, to Michael Ó Nualláin, a civil servant, and Agnes Gormley. Irish is the primary language at home. Family lives briefly in Glasgow, then in Dublin.	Pound: *Canzoni.* Chesterton: *The Innocence of Father Brown.*
1912		Lady Gregory: *Irish Folk History Plays.* Mann: *Death in Venice.*
1913	Family moves back to Strabane.	Shaw: *Pygmalian.* Lawrence: *Sons and Lovers.* Proust: *In Search of Lost Time* (to 1927).
1914		Joyce: *Dubliners* published. *A Portrait of the Artist as a Young Man* serialized in *The Egoist.* Yeats: *Responsibilities.*
1916		George Moore: *The Brook Kerith.*
1917		Yeats: *The Wild Swans at Coole.* Eliot: *Prufrock and other Observations.*
1918		Moore: *A Story-Teller's Holiday.* Firbank: *Valmouth.*
1919		Shaw: *Heartbreak House.* Yeats: *The Player Queen.* Wodehouse: *My Man Jeeves.*
1920		Fitzgerald: *This Side of Paradise.* Lewis: *Main Street.*
1921		Huxley: *Crome Yellow.* Pirandello: *Six Characters in Search of an Author.* Hašek: *The Good Soldier Švejk* (to 1923).

HISTORICAL EVENTS

The 84-strong Irish Home Rule Party led by John Redmond supports the
Liberals' Parliament Act to reduce the power of the House of Lords in
return for another Home Rule bill.

Asquith presents third Home Rule Bill to Parliament. Ulster Covenant
pledges opposition to Home Rule. Irish Labour Party founded.

Home Rule Bill passes the Commons but the Lords are still able to delay it
temporarily. Ulster Volunteer Force set up. Irish Volunteer Force (IVF) raised
in the South. Strike of Irish Transport and General Workers' Union in
Dublin; James Connolly founds Irish Citizens' Army (ICA) to protect strikers.
World War I begins (August). Many thousands of Irishmen of all political
persuasions join the British army as volunteers. Home Rule Act placed on
statute book but implementation is suspended for the duration of the war.

Easter Rising of Nationalists in Dublin (24 April) is crushed by the British
who execute its leaders, outraging Irish public opinion. Asquith resigns;
Lloyd George forms a coalition government (December).
Release of remaining Easter Rising detainees. Eamon de Valera becomes
President of Sinn Féin, taking over from founder Arthur Griffith. Bolshevik
Revolution in Russia.
Sinn Féin leads opposition to conscription in Ireland. End of World War I
(November). In general election Sinn Féin candidates win, but do not take
up, 73 of the 105 Irish seats in the House of Commons. Irish rebel Con
Markievicz elected first British woman MP.
Sinn Féin MPs declare Irish independence; first meeting of Dáil in Dublin
with De Valera as President. IVF and ICA collectively renamed the Irish
Republican Army (IRA). Irish War of Independence (to 1921). Versailles
Peace Conference. German Republic adopts the Weimar constitution.
'Black and Tans' sent to support Irish police force. The first 'Bloody
Sunday.' Government of Ireland Act provides for Home Rule but with
separate parliaments for North and South. League of Nations founded.
Prohibition in US.
IRA sets fire to Dublin Customs House. First Parliament of Northern Ireland;
Ulster Unionist leader Sir James Craig becomes Prime Minister (June). Truce
signed between Sinn Féin and the British (July). IRA leader Michael Collins
sent to London to negotiate Anglo-Irish Treaty (December). The outcome –
Home Rule with dominion status for the South – dismays republicans.

xxiii

DATE	AUTHOR'S LIFE	LITERARY CONTEXT
1922	Family returns to Dublin. Brian begins, at age 11, his formal education at Synge Street School.	Joyce: *Ulysses* published in Paris. Eliot: *The Waste Land.* Woolf: *Jacob's Room.*
1923		Yeats awarded Nobel Prize for Literature. Shaw: *Saint Joan.* O'Casey: *The Shadow of a Gunman.* Svevo: *The Confessions of Zeno.*
1925		Shaw awarded Nobel Prize for Literature. O'Casey: *Juno and the Paycock.* Dos Passos: *Manhattan Transfer.* Kafka: *The Trial.*
1926		O'Casey: *The Plough and the Stars.* Valmouth: *Concerning the Eccentricities of Cardinal Pirelli.*
1927	Family moves to Blackrock neighborhood where Brian lives until his marriage in 1948.	Moore: *The Making of an Immortal.* Woolf: *To the Lighthouse.* Brecht: *A Man's a Man.* Hesse: *Steppenwolf.*
1928		Opening of Gate and Taibhdhearc theatres in Dublin. Yeats: *The Tower.*
1929	Enters University College, Dublin.	Shaw: *The Apple Cart.* Denis Johnston: *The Old Lady Says 'No!'* Bowen: *The Last September.* Henry Green: *Living.*
1931	Joins the College Literary and Historical Society. Begins publishing in *Comhthrom Féinne.*	Johnston: *The Moon in the Yellow River.*
1932	Receives BA in German, English and Irish.	Sean Ó Faoláin: *Midsummer Night Madness.* Faulkner: *Light in August.*
1933		Yeats: *The Winding Stair; Collected Poems.* Johnston: *A Bride for the Unicorn.* Hemingway: *Winner Take Nothing.*

HISTORICAL EVENTS

Irish Free State officially proclaimed and a constitution adopted (January).
Resignation of De Valera. Civil war breaks out between pro- and anti-treaty
factions of Sinn Féin. Assassination of Collins. Sectarian violence escalates in
the North. Royal Ulster Constabulary formed. USSR established.
Mussolini's Fascist march on Rome.
Pro-treaty side victorious in civil war but partition continues to be opposed
by the IRA. Prime minister William Cosgrove of the Cumann na nGaedheal
party embarks on program of national reconstruction. Irish Free State joins
the League of Nations. Stalin becomes General Secretary of the Communist
Party. Hitler's Munich *putsch* fails. German financial crisis.

Boundary Commission fails to recommend any significant changes to the
border with the North, as promised in the Anglo-Irish Treaty. Legislation
prohibiting divorce in Free State passed.

Radio Eireann set up. Anti-treaty faction of Sinn Féin splits; De Valera
forms Fianna Fáil party. General Strike in Britain.

Assassination of Kevin O'Higgins, Minister for Justice, by militant
republicans. De Valera's Fianna Fáil take up their seats, ending boycott of
the Dáil. Lindbergh flies the Atlantic solo. First 'talkie' – *The Jazz Singer*.

Completion of the Shannon Scheme to supply the South with hydro-electric
power. Abolition of proportional representation in the North.
Wall Street Crash. Beginning of worldwide depression.

Statute of Westminster establishes legal status of dominions of British
Commonwealth.

Fianna Fáil win general election; De Valera forms government. Protectionist
economic policies adopted. During the 1930s a number of semi-state
companies are set up (eg. Turf Development Board, Irish Sugar Company,
Irish Life). Annuities payable by Irish farmers for land purchase are diverted
from British to Irish Exchequer, provoking trade war with Britain.
Unemployment in Britain reaches 2,947,000.
De Valera re-elected with increased majority. Abolition of oath of allegiance
and reduction of powers of British governor-general. Fine Gael founded.
Unemployment Assistance Act. Foundation of Falange (Fascist party) in
Spain. Roosevelt announces 'New Deal.'

DATE	AUTHOR'S LIFE	LITERARY CONTEXT
1934	Visits Germany on a short sojourn. Publishes comic magazine *Blather* (five issues) with his brother Ciarán and Niall Sheridan.	Bowen: *The Cat Jumps.* Beckett: *More Pricks Than Kicks.* Sean Ó Faoláin: *A Nest of Simple Folk.* Waugh: *An Handful of Dust.*
1935	MA thesis 'Nature in Irish Poetry' accepted. Enters Irish civil service in the Department of Local Government (29 July).	Wodehouse: *Blandings Castle, The Luck of the Bodkins.* Compton-Burnett: *A House and its Head.*
1936		
1937	Father dies (29 July). O'Nolan becomes Private Secretary to the Minister for Health and Local Government.	Ó Criomhthain: *The Islandman.* Auden/MacNeice: *Letters from Iceland.* M.J. Farrell: *The Rising Tide.* Steinbeck: *Of Mice and Men.*
1938	Begins Letters to the Editor campaign in the *Irish Times.*	Beckett: *Murphy.* Brian Coffey: *Third Person.* Waugh: *Scoop.* Greene: *Brighton Rock.* Sartre: *Nausea.*
1939	*At Swim-Two-Birds* published by Longsmans, Green & Co. under the pseudonym Flann O'Brien (13 March).	Death of Yeats. Yeats: *Last Poems and Two Plays.* Joyce: *Finnegans Wake.*
1940	Manuscript of *The Third Policeman* rejected by Longmans (January). As Flann O'Brien, publishes essays in *The Bell,* edited by Sean Ó Faoláin. Publishes first column in the *Irish Times,* beginning of 'Cruiskeen Lawn' (4 October). Adopts the pen-name Myles na gCopaleen.	Sean Ó Faoláin: *Come Back to Erin.* Greene: *The Power and the Glory.* Hemingway: *For Whom the Bell Tolls.*
1941	*An Béal Bocht* appears (3 December).	James Joyce dies in Zurich. Fitzgerald: *The Last Tycoon.* Coward: *Blythe Spirit.*
1942	*Thirst,* a play, is produced at the Gate Theatre annual Christmas variety show.	O'Casey: *Red Roses for Me.* Patrick Kavanagh: *The Great Hunger.* Camus: *The Outsider.*
1943	*Faustus Kelly* is produced at the Abbey Theatre (January). Promoted to Acting Assistant	

CHRONOLOGY

HISTORICAL EVENTS

Hitler becomes German *Führer.*

De Valera severs ties with the IRA, imprisoning some of its leaders. Sale and importation of contraceptives made illegal in the Free State. In Germany Nuremberg laws deprive Jews of citizenship.

IRA declared illegal. First Aer Lingus flight. Spanish Civil War (to 1939). New constitution adopted which ignores the British Crown, claiming sovereignty over 'the whole island of Ireland' but 'pending reintegration' only applying to 26 counties. The nation is to be known as Eire. De Valera becomes Taoiseach (Prime Minister). Bombing of Guernica by German planes. Rome-Berlin Axis formed. Japan invades China.
Douglas Hyde is elected as the first President. Irish government agrees to pay lump sum to Britain to clear annuities debt. British agree to withdraw from naval bases in Eire. End of trade war. Germany annexes Austria. Munich Crisis.

Germans occupy Czechoslovakia. Nazi-Soviet Pact. Hitler invades Poland. Ireland declares its neutrality in World War II (though thousands of Irish citizens enlist to fight for Britain). A 'State of Emergency' declared.

IRA leadership attempts to open links with Nazi Germany. Resignation of Neville Chamberlain: Winston Chuchilll leads coalition ministry in Britain. Dunkirk evacuation. Fall of France. Battle of Britain. The Blitz.

Heavy German air-raids on Belfast and Derry: fire brigades from Eire are sent to assist victims. Bombs dropped on Dublin in error by German bombers (31 May), killing 334 and injuring 90. Germans invade Russia. Japanese attack on Pearl Harbor. US enters the war.
North African campaign. Gandhi calls on British to 'Quit India.'

Allied invasion of Italy.

DATE	AUTHOR'S LIFE	LITERARY CONTEXT
1943 *cont.*	Principal Officer in the Department of Local Government (March); investigates the infamous Cavan orphanage fire. *Cruiskeen Lawn* anthology published by the *Irish Times*.	
1944		Frank O'Connor: *Crab Apple Jelly*.
1945		Green: *Loving*. Waugh: *Brideshead Revisited*. Orwell: *Animal Farm*.
1947	Breaks leg in auto accident in January; misses work until 30 September.	Mann: *Doctor Faustus*.
1948	Marries Evelyn McDonnell, a civil servant in the Local Government Office (2 December).	MacNeice: *Holes in the Sky*. Greene: *The Heart of the Matter*.
1949		O'Casey: *Cock-a-Doodle Dandy*. Bowen: *The Heat of the Day*. Orwell: *Nineteen Eighty-four*. Miller: *Death of a Salesman*.
1950		Death of Shaw.
1951	American edition of *At Swim-Two-Birds* brought out by Pantheon Books in New York. Edits a special edition on James Joyce for *Envoy*, including his essay 'A Bash in the Tunnel', signed as Brian Nolan.	Beckett: *Molloy*; *Malone Dies*. Frank O'Connor: *Traveller's Samples*. Powell: *A Dance to the Music of Time* (to 1975). Salinger: *The Catcher in the Rye*.
1952	After a feud with the *Irish Times*, Myles quits 'Cruiskeen Lawn' (February). Publishes several columns as Myles in *Kavanagh's Weekly*, a short-lived journal run by Irish poet Patrick Kavanagh. Returns to 'Cruiskeen Lawn,' dropping the eclipsis, as Myles na Gopaleen (December).	Waugh: *Sword of Honour* trilogy (to 1961). Hemingway: *The Old Man and the Sea*. Calvino: *The Cloven Viscount*.

CHRONOLOGY

Allied landings in Normandy. Liberation of Paris.
Mussolini shot by partisans. Unconditional surrender of Gemany. De Valera
offers condolences to Germany on the death of Hitler. Atomic bombs
dropped on Japan. End of World War II. Nationalists in the North form
Anti-Partition League. Sean O'Kelly becomes Irish President. Period of
rapid inflation in the South. Labour party under Attlee sweep to victory in
Britain. United Nations established.
Marshall Plan: US aid for European post-war recovery. Beginning of Cold
War. India and Pakistan achieve independence as two separate dominions.

De Valera defeated; inter-party government formed in Ireland under John
Costello. Soviet blockade of Berlin and Allied airlife. Communist coup in
Czechoslovakia. State of Israel established. South African government
adopts *apartheid* as official policy. Assassination of Ghandi.
Republic of Ireland Act passed. Eire withdraws from the Commonwealth
and becomes fully independent. Attempts by Eire government to negotiate
union with the North firmly resisted by Unionist Prime Minister Basil
Brooke. Britain passes Ireland Act, recognizing the Republic but
guaranteeing that the North will remain part of the UK unless its
parliament decides otherwise. NATO founded (Irish Republic declines to
join as Northern Ireland remains part of the UK). Federal Republic of
Germany established. Communist revolution in China.
Economic depression in the Republic throughout the 1950s; emigration
increases. Korean War (to 1953).
De Valera returns as Taoiseach of Ireland. Abbey Theatre destroyed by fire.
Irish Arts Council set up. India declares itself a Republic within the British
Commonwealth. McCarthy's anti-Communist Committee of Enquiry active
in the US.

Accession of Elizabeth II. Eisenhower is elected US President. Irish tourist
board set up.

DATE	AUTHOR'S LIFE	LITERARY CONTEXT
1953	Publishes Irish translation of Brinsley MacNamara's play, *Mairéad Gillan*. After mocking government policies in 'Cruiskeen Lawn,' Brian O'Nolan is forced to resign his civil service position and retires on a limited disability.	Beckett: *Waiting for Godot*; *Watt*; *The Unnamable*. Borges: *Labyrinths*. Bellow: *The Adventures of Augie March*.
1954	On 16 June, with Anthony Cronin, Con Leventhal, Patrick Kavanagh, Tom Joyce, and John Ryan, celebrates the 50th anniversary of Bloomsday by attempting to trace the route of the characters in Joyce's *Ulysses*.	Behan: *The Quare Fellow*. Kingsley Amis: *Lucky Jim*. Dylan Thomas: *Under Milk Wood*. Golding: *Lord of the Flies*. Death of O'Casey.
1955	'A Weekly Look Around' as John James Doe, newspaper column in the *Southern Star*.	Nabokov: *Lolita*.
1956	Agnes, his mother, dies.	Osborne: *Look Back in Anger*.
1956–60	In and out of hospitals with various illnesses and accidents.	
1957	Runs for the Irish Senate, receiving 400 out of the 9,000 votes cast.	Beckett: *Endgame*. O'Connor: *Domestic Relations*. Hugh Leonard: *A Leap in the Dark*. Kerouac: *On the Road*.
1958		Behan: *The Hostage*; *Borstal Boy*. Beckett: *Krapp's Last Tape*. Johnston: *The Scythe and the Sunset*. Leonard: *Madigan's Lock*. Pinter: *The Birthday Party*.
1959		John B. Keane: *Sive*. Grass: *The Tin Drum*.
1960	MacGibbon and Kee publishes a new edition of *At Swim-Two-Birds* to critical acclaim. The author's real name is disclosed on the book jacket. 'Bones of Contention'/ 'George Knowall's Peepshow' as George Knowall, *The Nationalist and Leinster Times*, through 1966.	Pinter: *The Caretaker*. Dahl: *Kiss Kiss*. Spark: *The Ballad of Peckham Rye*. Updike: *Rabbit, Run*.

CHRONOLOGY

European Court of Human Rights set up in Strasbourg. Death of Stalin Hillary and Tenzing reach the summit of Mount Everest.

Coalition between Fine Gael and Labour party form government in Eire. Vietnam War begins. Nasser gains power in Egypt.

Ireland joins the United Nations. Warsaw Pact formed.

IRA reform and begin terrorist campaign in Northern Ireland which peters out by 1962. Suez Crisis. Hungarian uprising. Pakistan becomes the world's first Islamic Republic, but remains within Commonwealth.

De Valera returned to office. Dublin Theatre Festival founded. Treaty of Rome: European Economic Community founded. Harold Macmillan becomes British Prime Minister. Ghana and Malaya become independent.

T. K. Whitaker's Report on Economic Development.

De Valera stands down to run for President. Seán Lemass, his former deputy, becomes Taoiseach. Government adopts Whitaker's recommendations: protectionist policies abandoned and foreign investment encouraged. Castro comes to power in Cuba.
Sharpeville massacre in South Africa: ANC outlawed. Cyprus and Nigeria achieve independence.

DATE	AUTHOR'S LIFE	LITERARY CONTEXT
1961	*The Hard Life* published. 'The Boy from Ballytearim' (television program.)	Tom Murphy: *A Whistle in the Dark.* Heller: *Catch-22.*
1962	'The Time Freddie Retired,' 'Flight,' 'The Man With Four Legs,' (television programs.)	Brian Friel: *The Enemy Within.* Nabokov: *Pale Fire.* Solzhenitsyn: *One Day in the Life of Ivan Denisovich.*
1963	*The Ideas of O'Dea*, 25 scripts for weekly television series. Hospitalized for uraemia; breaks the same leg he had broken in 1947. Spends months in bed.	Burgess: *Inside Mr Enderby.*
1964	Proposes to write a history of drinking in Ireland to the Irish Distillers Group. 'Cruiskeen Lawn' abandoned from February to December. Diagnosed with pleurisy and neuralgia. *The Dalkey Archive* is published. *An Béal Bocht* reissued.	Friel: *Philadelphia, Here I Come!* Bellow: *Herzog.*
1965	*Th' Oul Lad of Kilsalaher*, 13 scripts for weekly television series. Begins the unfinished *Slattery's Sago Saga*. Diagnosed with cancer. Attends the opening night of *When the Saints Go Cycling In*, playwright Hugh Leonard's dramatization of *The Dalkey Archive* (September).	Heaney: *Eleven Poems.* John McGahern: *The Dark.* John B. Keane: *The Field.* Murdoch: *The Red and the Green.*
1966	Dies on April Fools' Day, Dublin.	MacNeice: *Collected Poems.* Heaney: *Death of a Naturalist.* Aidan Higgins: *Langrishe, Go Down.* Friel: *The Loves of Cass McGuire.* Leonard: *Mick and Mick.*
1967	Publication of *The Third Policeman* to critical acclaim.	
1968	Publication of *The Best of Myles*, first anthology culled from 'Cruiskeen Lawn.' Later posthumous volumes are *Stories and Plays* (1973), *Further Cuttings from Cruiskeen Lawn* (1976), *The Various Lives of Keats and Chapman and The Brother* (1976), *The Hair of the Dogma* (1977), *Myles Away from Dublin* (1985), *Myles Before Myles* (1988), *Flann O'Brien at War* (1999), and *King of Ireland* (forthcoming).	

CHRONOLOGY

The Republic's attempts to join the EEC fail (finally joins in 1972). Radio Telefís Eireann (RTE) begins television broadcasting. Erection of Berlin Wall. Yuri Gagarin becomes first man in space.
IRA calls off its 'Border Campaign', having failed to gain signficant support. Cuban Missile Crisis.

Terence O'Neill becomes Prime Minister in Northern Ireland, and seeks greater accommodation with the minority Catholic community. US President John Kennedy visits the Republic. Assassination of Kennedy in Dallas, Texas. Civil war between Greeks and Turks in Cyprus.

First 5-year economic plan exceeds its goals. The 1960s is a period of increased prosperity; rate of emigration declines. The Campaign for Social Justice launched in Northern Ireland. Khrushchev deposed in Russia. US Civil Rights Bill. Nobel Peace Prize awarded to Martin Luther King.

Landmark meetings between O'Neill and Lemass at Stormont and in Dublin. Anglo-Irish trade treaty signed. Lemass introduces free secondary education. War between India and Pakistan. Ian Smith makes Rhodesian Declaration of Independence; Britian declares the regime illegal.

50th anniversary of the Easter Rising celebrated by Catholics throughout Ireland. Lemass stands down and is replaced as Taoiseach by Jack Lynch. Opening of new Abbey Theatre. In the North, Ian Paisley forms the Ulster Constitution Defence Committee (UCDC) to campaign against O'Neill. He also helps to revive the militant loyalist Ulster Volunteer Force, declaring war on the IRA.

AT SWIM-TWO-BIRDS

Ἐξίσταται γὰρ πάντ' ἀπ' ἀλλήλων δίχα

CHAPTER 1

HAVING PLACED in my mouth sufficient bread for three minutes' chewing, I withdrew my powers of sensual perception and retired into the privacy of my mind, my eyes and face assuming a vacant and preoccupied expression. I reflected on the subject of my spare-time literary activities. One beginning and one ending for a book was a thing I did not agree with. A good book may have three openings entirely dissimilar and inter-related only in the prescience of the author, or for that matter one hundred times as many endings.

Examples of three separate openings – the first: The Pooka Mac-Phellimey, a member of the devil class, sat in his hut in the middle of a firwood meditating on the nature of the numerals and segregating in his mind the odd ones from the even. He was seated at his diptych or ancient two-leaved hinged writing-table with inner sides waxed. His rough long-nailed fingers toyed with a snuff-box of perfect rotundity and through a gap in his teeth he whistled a civil cavatina. He was a courtly man and received honour by reason of the generous treatment he gave his wife, one of the Corrigans of Carlow.

The second opening: There was nothing unusual in the appearance of Mr John Furriskey but actually he had one distinction that is rarely encountered – he was born at the age of twenty-five and entered the world with a memory but without a personal experience to account for it. His teeth were well-formed but stained by tobacco, with two molars filled and a cavity threatened in the left canine. His knowledge of physics was moderate and extended to Boyle's Law and the Parallelogram of Forces.

The third opening: Finn MacCool was a legendary hero of old Ireland. Though not mentally robust, he was a man of superb physique and development. Each of his thighs was as thick as a

horse's belly, narrowing to a calf as thick as the belly of a foal.
Three fifties of fosterlings could engage with handball against the
wideness of his backside, which was large enough to halt the
march of men through a mountain-pass.

I hurt a tooth in the corner of my jaw with a lump of the
crust I was eating. This recalled me to the perception of my
surroundings.

It is a great pity, observed my uncle, that you don't apply yourself more to your studies. The dear knows your father worked
hard enough for the money he is laying out on your education.
Tell me this, do you ever open a book at all?

I surveyed my uncle in a sullen manner. He speared a portion
of cooked rasher against a crust on the prongs of his fork and
poised the whole at the opening of his mouth in a token of
continued interrogation.

Description of my uncle: Red-faced, bead-eyed, ball-bellied.
Fleshy about the shoulders with long swinging arms giving
ape-like effect to gait. Large moustache. Holder of Guinness
clerkship the third class.

I do, I replied.

He put the point of his fork into the interior of his mouth
and withdrew it again, chewing in a coarse manner.

Quality of rasher in use in household: Inferior, one and two the
pound.

Well faith, he said, I never see you at it. I never see you at your
studies at all.

I work in my bedroom, I answered.

Whether in or out, I always kept the door of my bedroom
locked. This made my movements a matter of some secrecy and
enabled me to spend an inclement day in bed without disturbing
my uncle's assumption that I had gone to the College to attend
to my studies. A contemplative life has always been suitable to
my disposition. I was accustomed to stretch myself for many
hours upon my bed, thinking and smoking there. I rarely undressed and my inexpensive suit was not the better for the use

I gave it, but I found that a brisk application with a coarse brush before going out would redeem it somewhat without quite dispelling the curious bedroom smell which clung to my person and which was frequently the subject of humorous or other comment on the part of my friends and acquaintances.

Aren't you very fond of your bedroom now, my uncle continued. Why don't you study in the dining-room here where the ink is and where there is a good book-case for your books? Boys but you make a great secret about your studies.

My bedroom is quiet, convenient and I have my books there. I prefer to work in my bedroom, I answered.

My bedroom was small and indifferently lighted but it contained most of the things I deemed essential for existence – my bed, a chair which was rarely used, a table and a washstand. The washstand had a ledge upon which I had arranged a number of books. Each of them was generally recognized as indispensable to all who aspire to an appreciation of the nature of contemporary literature and my small collection contained works ranging from those of Mr Joyce to the widely read books of Mr A. Huxley, the eminent English writer. In my bedroom also were certain porcelain articles related more to utility than ornament. The mirror at which I shaved every second day was of the type supplied gratis by Messrs Watkins, Jameson and Pim and bore brief letterpress in reference to a proprietary brand of ale between the words of which I had acquired considerable skill in inserting the reflection of my countenance. The mantelpiece contained forty buckskin volumes comprising a Conspectus of the Arts and Natural Sciences. They were published in 1854 by a reputable Bath house for a guinea the volume. They bore their years bravely and retained in their interior the kindly seed of knowledge intact and without decay.

I know the studying you do in your bedroom, said my uncle. Damn the studying you do in your bedroom.

I denied this.

Nature of denial: Inarticulate, of gesture.

My uncle drained away the remainder of his tea and arranged his cup and saucer in the centre of his bacon plate in a token that his meal was at an end. He then blessed himself and sat for a time drawing air into his mouth with a hissing sound in an attempt to extract foodstuff from the crevices of his dentures. Subsequently he pursed his mouth and swallowed something.

A boy of your age, he said at last, who gives himself up to the sin of sloth – what in God's name is going to happen to him when he goes out to face the world? Boys but I often wonder what the world is coming to, I do indeed. Tell me this, do you ever open a book at all?

I open several books every day, I answered.

You open your granny, said my uncle. O I know the game you are at above in your bedroom. I am not as stupid as I look, I'll warrant you that.

He got up from the table and went out to the hall, sending back his voice to annoy me in his absence.

Tell me this, did you press my Sunday trousers?

I forgot, I said.

What?

I forgot, I shouted.

Well that is very nice, he called, very nice indeed. Oh, trust you to forget. God look down on us and pity us this night and day. Will you forget again today?

No, I answered.

As he opened the hall-door, he was saying to himself in a low tone:

Lord save us!

The slam of the door released me from my anger. I finished my collation and retired to my bedroom, standing for a time at the window and observing the street-scene arranged below me that morning. Rain was coming softly from the low sky. I lit my cigarette and then took my letter from my pocket, opened it and read it.

Mail from V. Wright, Wyvern Cottage, Newmarket, Suffolk. V. Wright, the backer's friend. Dear Friend and member. Thanks for your faith in me, it is very comforting to know that I have clients who are sportsmen who do not lose heart when the luck is 'the wrong way'. Bounty Queen was indeed a great disappointment tho' many were of opinion that she had dead-heated with the leaders but more of that anon. Considering I have been posting information from the same address since 1926, anybody leaving me now because of bad luck would indeed be a 'puzzler'. You had the losers why not 'row in' and make a packet over the winners that are now our due. So much for the past, now for the future. SENSATIONAL NEWS has reached me that certain interests have planned a gigantic coup involving a certain animal who has been saved for the past month. INFORMATION from the RIGHT QUARTER notifies me that a sum of £5,000 at least will be wagered. The animal in question will be slipped at the right moment with the right man up and there will be a GOLDEN OPPORTUNITY to all who act 'pronto' and give their bookmaker the shock of his life. To all my friends forwarding 6d. and two S.A.E.'s I will present this THREE-STAR CAST-IRON PLUNGER and we will have the win of our lives and all the bad luck forgotten. We will feel 'bucked' when this animal flashes past the post at a fancy price. This will be my only treble nap for the week and old friends will know that my STRICTLY OCCASIONAL LETTERS are always 'the goods'. Act now! Yours in sport and best of luck together, V. Wright. Order Form. To V. Wright, Turf Correspondent, Wyvern Cottage, Newmarket, Suffolk. Herewith please find P.O. for £   s.   d. and hoping to obtain by return your exclusive three-star Plunger for Thursday and I hereby promise to remit the odds thereon to one shilling. Name. Address. No business transacted with minors or persons at College. P.S. The above will be the business, have the win of your life. Yours, Verney.

I put the letter with care into a pocket at my right buttock and went to the tender trestle of my bed, arranging my back upon it in an indolent horizontal attitude. I closed my eyes, hurting slightly my right stye, and retired into the kingdom of my mind. For a time there was complete darkness and an absence of movement on the part of the cerebral mechanism. The bright square of the window was faintly evidenced at the juncture of my lids. One book, one opening, was a principle with which I did not find it possible to concur. After an interval Finn MacCool, a hero of old Ireland, came out before me from his shadow, Finn the wide-hammed, the heavy-eyed, Finn that could spend a Lammas morning with girdled girls at far-from-simple chess-play.

Extract from my typescript descriptive of Finn MacCool and his people, being humorous or quasi-humorous incursion into ancient mythology:

Of the musics you have ever got, asked Conán, which have you found the sweetest?

I will relate, said Finn. When the seven companies of my warriors are gathered together on the one plain and the truant clean-cold loud-voiced wind goes through them, too sweet to me is that. Echo-blow of a goblet-base against the tables of the palace, sweet to me is that. I like gull-cries and the twittering together of fine cranes. I like the surf-roar at Tralee, the songs of the three sons of Meadhra and the whistle of Mac Lughaidh. These also please me, man-shouts at a parting, cuckoo-call in May. I incline to like pig-grunting in Magh Eithne, the bellowing of the stag of Ceara, the whinging of fauns in Derrynish. The low warble of water-owls in Loch Barra also, sweeter than life that. I am fond of wing-beating in dark belfries, cow-cries in pregnancy, trout-spurt in a lake-top. Also the whining of small otters in nettle-beds at evening, the croaking of small-jays behind a wall, these are heart-pleasing. I am friend to the pilibeen, the red-necked chough, the parsnip land-rail, the pilibeen móna, the bottle-tailed tit, the common marsh-coot, the speckle-toed guillemot, the pilibeen sléibhe, the Mohar gannet, the peregrine plough-gull, the long-eared bush-owl, the Wicklow small-fowl, the bevil-beaked chough, the hooded tit, the pilibeen uisce, the common corby, the fish-tailed mud-piper, the crúiskeen lawn, the carrion sea-cock, the green-lidded parakeet, the brown bog-martin, the maritime wren, the dove-tailed wheatcrake, the beaded daw, the Galway hill-bantam and the pilibeen cathrach. A satisfying ululation is the contending of a river with the sea. Good to hear is the chirping of little red-breasted men in bare winter and distant hounds giving tongue in the secrecy of god. The lamenting of a wounded otter in a black hole, sweeter than harpstrings that. There is no torture so narrow as to be bound and beset in a dark cavern without food or music, without the bestowing of gold on bards. To be chained by night in a dark pit without company of chessmen – evil destiny! Soothing to my ear is the shout of a hidden blackbird, the squeal of a troubled mare, the complaining of wild-hogs caught in snow.

Relate further for us, said Conán.

It is true that I will not, said Finn.

With that he rose to a full tree-high standing, the sable cat-guts which held his bog-cloth drawers to the hems of his jacket

of pleated fustian clanging together in melodious discourse. Too
great was he for standing. The neck to him was as the bole of
a great oak, knotted and seized together with muscle-humps
and carbuncles of tangled sinew, the better for good feasting and
contending with the bards. The chest to him was wider than
the poles of a good chariot, coming now out, now in, and
pastured from chin to navel with meadows of black man-hair
and meated with layers of fine man-meat the better to hide his
bones and fashion the semblance of his twin bubs. The arms
to him were like the necks of beasts, ball-swollen with their
bunched-up brawnstrings and blood-veins, the better for harp-
ing and hunting and contending with the bards. Each thigh to
him was to the thickness of a horse's belly, narrowing to a green-
veined calf to the thickness of a foal. Three fifties of fosterlings
could engage with handball against the wideness of his backside,
which was wide enough to halt the march of warriors through
a mountain-pass.

> I am a bark for buffeting, said Finn,
> I am a hound for thornypaws.
> I am a doe for swiftness.
> I am a tree for wind-siege.
> I am a windmill.
> I am a hole in a wall.

On the seat of the bog-cloth drawers to his fork was shuttled
the green alchemy of mountain-leeks from Slieve an Iarainn
in the middle of Erin; for it was here that he would hunt for a
part of the year with his people, piercing the hams of a black hog
with his spears, birds-nesting, hole-drawing, vanishing into the
fog of a small gully, sitting on green knolls with Fergus and
watching the boys at ball-throw.

On the kerseymere of the gutted jacket to his back was the
dark tincture of the ivory sloes and the pubic gooseberries and
the manivaried whortles of the ditches of the east of Erin; for it
was here that he would spend a part of the year with his people,
courting and rummaging generous women, vibrating quick
spears at the old stag of Slieve Gullian, hog-baiting in thickets
and engaging in sapient dialectics with the bag-eyed brehons.

The knees and calves to him, swealed and swathed with

soogawns and Thomond weed-ropes, were smutted with dungs
and dirt-daubs of every hue and pigment, hardened by stainings
of mead and trickles of metheglin and all the dribblings and drip-
pings of his medher, for it was the custom of Finn to drink
nightly with his people.

> I am the breast of a young queen, said Finn,
> I am a thatching against rains.
> I am a dark castle against bat-flutters.
> I am a Connachtman's ear.
> I am a harpstring.
> I am a gnat.

The nose to his white wheyface was a headland against white
seas with height to it, in all, the height of ten warriors man on
man and with breadth to it the breadth of Erin. The caverns to
the butt of his nose had fulness and breadth for the instanding in
their shade of twenty arm-bearing warriors with their tribal rams
and dove-cages together with a generous following of ollavs and
bards with their law-books and their verse-scrolls, their herb-
pots and their alabaster firkins of oil and unguent.

Relate us further, said Diarmuid Donn, for the love of God.

Who is it? said Finn.

It is Diarmuid Donn, said Conán, even Diarmuid O'Diveney
of Ui bhFailghe and of Cruachna Conalath in the west of Erin,
it is Brown Dermot of Galway.

It is true, said Finn, that I will not.

The mouth to his white wheyface had dimensions and measurements to the width of Ulster, bordered by a red lip-wall and
inhabited unseen by the watchful host of his honey-yellow teeth
to the size, each with each, of a cornstack; and in the dark hollow
to each tooth was there home and fulness for the sitting there of
a thorny dog or for the lying there of a spear-pierced badger. To
each of the two eyes in his head was there eye-hair to the fashion
of a young forest, and the colour to each great eyeball was as the
slaughter of a host in snow. The lid to each eye of them was limp
and cheese-dun like ship-canvas in harbour at evening, enough
eye-cloth to cover the whole of Erin.

Sweet to me your voice, said Caolcrodha Mac Morna, brother
to sweet-worded sweet-toothed Goll from Sliabh Riabhach and

Brosnacha Bladhma, relate then the attributes that are to Finn's
people.

Who is it? said Finn.

It is Caolcrodha Mac Morna from Sliabh Riabhach, said
Conán, it is Calecroe MacMorney from Baltinglass.

I will relate, said Finn. Till a man has accomplished twelve
books of poetry, the same is not taken for want of poetry but is
forced away. No man is taken till a black hole is hollowed in the
world to the depth of his two oxters and he put into it to gaze
from it with his lonely head and nothing to him but his shield
and a stick of hazel. Then must nine warriors fly their spears at
him, one with the other and together. If he be spear-holed past
his shield, or spear-killed, he is not taken for want of shield-skill.
No man is taken till he is run by warriors through the woods of
Erin with his hair bunched-loose about him for bough-tangle
and briar-twitch. Should branches disturb his hair or pull it forth
like sheep-wool on a hawthorn, he is not taken but is caught and
gashed. Weapon-quivering hand or twig-crackling foot at full
run, neither is taken. Neck-high sticks he must pass by vaulting,
knee-high sticks by stooping. With the eyelids to him stitched
to the fringe of his eye-bags, he must be run by Finn's people
through the bogs and the marsh-swamps of Erin with two odorous prickle-backed hogs ham-tied and asleep in the seat of his
hempen drawers. If he sink beneath a peat-swamp or lose a hog,
he is not accepted by Finn's people. For five days he must sit on
the brow of a cold hill with twelve-pointed stag-antlers hidden
in his seat, without food or music or chessmen. If he cry out or
eat grass-stalks or desist from the constant recital of sweet poetry
and melodious Irish, he is not taken but is wounded. When pursued by a host, he must stick a spear in the world and hide behind
it and vanish in its narrow shelter or he is not taken for want of
sorcery. Likewise he must hide beneath a twig, or behind a dried
leaf, or under a red stone, or vanish at full speed into the seat of
his hempen drawers without changing his course or abating his
pace or angering the men of Erin. Two young fosterlings he
must carry under the armpits to his jacket through the whole of
Erin, and six arm-bearing warriors in his seat together. If he be
delivered of a warrior or a blue spear, he is not taken. One hundred head of cattle he must accommodate with wisdom about
his person when walking all Erin, the half about his armpits and

the half about his trews, his mouth never halting from the discoursing of sweet poetry. One thousand rams he must sequester about his trunks with no offence to the men of Erin, or he is unknown to Finn. He must swiftly milk a fat cow and carry milk-pail and cow for twenty years in the seat of his drawers. When pursued in a chariot by the men of Erin he must dismount, place horse and chariot in the slack of his seat and hide behind his spear, the same being stuck upright in Erin. Unless he accomplishes these feats, he is not wanted of Finn. But if he do them all and be skilful, he is of Finn's people.

What advantages are to Finn's people? asked Liagan Luaimneach O Luachair Dheaghaidh.

Who is it? said Finn.

It is Liagan Luaimneach O Luachair Dheaghaidh, said Conán, the third man of the three cousins from Cnoc Sneachta, Lagan Lumley O'Lowther-Day from Elphin Beg.

I will relate three things and nothing above three, said Finn. Myself I can get wisdom from the sucking of my thumb, another (though he knows it not) can bring to defeat a host by viewing it through his fingers, and another can cure a sick warrior by judging the smoke of the house in which he is.

Wonderful for telling, said Conán, and I know it. Relate for us, after, the tale of the feast of Bricriú.

I cannot make it, said Finn.

Then the tale of the Bull of Cooley.

It goes beyond me, said Finn, I cannot make it.

Then the tale of the Giolla Deacar and his old horse of the world, said Gearr mac Aonchearda.

Who is it? said Finn.

Surely it is Gearr mac Aonchearda, said Conán, the middle man of the three brothers from Cruach Conite, Gar MacEncarty O'Hussey from Phillipstown.

I cannot make it, said Finn.

Recount then for the love of God, said Conán, the Tale of the Enchanted Fort of the Sally Tree or give shanachy's tidings of the little Brawl at Allen.

They go above me and around and through me, said Finn. It is true that I cannot make them.

Oh then, said Conán, the story of the Churl in the Puce Great-coat.

Evil story for telling, that, said Finn, and though itself I can make it, it is surely true that I will not recount it. It is a crooked and dishonourable story that tells how Finn spoke honey-words and peace-words to a stranger who came seeking the high-rule and the high-rent of this kingdom and saying that he would play the sorrow of death and small-life on the lot of us in one single day if his wish was not given. Surely I have never heard (nor have I seen) a man come with high-deed the like of that to Erin that there was not found for him a man of his own equality. Who has heard honey-talk from Finn before strangers, Finn that is wind-quick, Finn that is a better man than God? Or who has seen the like of Finn or seen the living semblance of him standing in the world, Finn that could best God at ball-throw or wrestling or pig-trailing or at the honeyed discourse of sweet Irish with jewels and gold for bards, or at the listening of distant harpers in a black hole at evening? Or where is the living human man who could beat Finn at the making of generous cheese, at the spearing of ganders, at the magic of thumb-suck, at the shaving of hog-hair, or at the unleashing of long hounds from a golden thong in the full chase, sweet-fingered corn-yellow Finn, Finn that could carry an armed host from Almha to Slieve Luachra in the craw of his gut-hung knickers.

Good for telling, said Conán.

Who is it? said Finn.

It is I, said Conán.

I believe it for truth, said Finn.

Relate further then.

I am an Ulsterman, a Connachtman, a Greek, said Finn,
I am Cuchulainn, I am Patrick.
I am Carbery-Cathead, I am Goll.
I am my own father and my son.
I am every hero from the crack of time.

Melodious is your voice, said Conán.

Small wonder, said Finn, that Finn is without honour in the breast of a sea-blue book, Finn that is twisted and trampled and tortured for the weaving of a story-teller's book-web. Who but a book-poet would dishonour the God-big Finn for the sake of a gap-worded story? Who could have the saint Ceallach carried off by his four acolytes and he feeble and thin from his Lent-fast, laid in the timbers of an old boat, hidden for a night in a hollow oak tree and slaughtered without mercy in the morning, his shrivelled body to be torn by a wolf and a scaldcrow and the Kite of Cluain-Eo? Who could think to turn the children of a king into white swans with the loss of their own bodies, to be swimming the two seas of Erin in snow and ice-cold rain without bards or chessboards, without their own tongues for discoursing melodious Irish, changing the fat white legs of a maiden into plumes and troubling her body with shameful eggs? Who could put a terrible madness on the head of Sweeney for the slaughter of a single Lent-gaunt cleric, to make him live in tree-tops and roost in the middle of a yew, not a wattle to the shielding of his mad head in the middle of the wet winter, perished to the marrow without company of women or strains of harp-pluck, with no feeding but stag-food and the green branches? Who but a story-teller? Indeed, it is true that there has been ill-usage to the men of Erin from the book-poets of the world and dishonour to Finn, with no knowing the nearness of disgrace or the sorrow of death, or the hour when they may swim for swans or trot for ponies or bell for stags or croak for frogs or fester for the wounds on a man's back.

True for telling, said Conán.

Conclusion of the foregoing.

Biographical reminiscence, part the first: It was only a few months before composing the foregoing that I had my first experience of intoxicating beverages and their strange intestinal chemistry. I was walking through the Stephen's Green on a summer evening and conducting a conversation with a man called Kelly, then a student, hitherto a member of the farming class and now a private in the armed forces of the King. He was addicted to unclean expressions in ordinary conversation and spat continually, always fouling the flowerbeds on his way through the Green with a mucous deposit dislodged with a low grunting from the interior of his windpipe. In some respects he was a coarse man but he was lacking in malice or ill-humour. He purported to be a medical student but he had failed at least once to satisfy a body of examiners charged with regulating admission to the faculty. He suggested that we should drink a number of *jars* or pints of plain porter in Grogan's public house. I derived considerable pleasure from the casual quality of his suggestion and observed that it would probably do us no harm, thus expressing my whole-hearted concurrence by a figure of speech.

Name of figure of speech: Litotes (or Meiosis).

He turned to me with a facetious wry expression and showed me a penny and a sixpence in his rough hand.

I'm thirsty, he said. I have sevenpence. Therefore I buy a pint.

I immediately recognized this as an intimation that I should pay for my own porter.

The conclusion of your syllogism, I said lightly, is fallacious, being based on licensed premises.

Licensed premises is right, he replied, spitting heavily. I saw that my witticism was unperceived and quietly replaced it in the treasury of my mind.

We sat in Grogan's with our faded overcoats finely disarrayed on easy chairs in the mullioned snug. I gave a shilling and two pennies to a civil man who brought us in return two glasses of black porter, imperial pint measure. I adjusted the glasses to the front of each of us and reflected on the solemnity of the occasion. It was my first taste of porter. Innumerable persons with whom I had conversed had represented to me that spirituous liquors and intoxicants generally had an adverse effect on the senses and the body and that those who became addicted to stimulants in youth were unhappy throughout their lives and met with death at the end by a drunkard's fall, expiring ingloriously at the stair-bottom in a welter of blood and puke. Indian tonic-waters had been proposed to me by an aged lay-brother as an incomparable specific for thirst. The importance of the subject had been impressed upon me in a schoolbook which I read at the age of twelve.

Extract from Literary Reader, the Higher Class, by the Irish Christian Brothers: And in the flowers that wreathe the sparkling bowl, fell adders hiss and poisonous serpents roll – Prior. What is alcohol? All medical authorities tell us it is a double poison – an irritant and a narcotic poison. As an irritant it excites the brain, quickens the action of the heart, produces intoxication and leads to degeneration of the tissues. As a narcotic, it chiefly afflicts the nervous system; blunts the sensibility of the brain, spinal cord and nerves; and, when taken in sufficient quantity, produces death. When alcohol is taken into the system, an extra amount of work is thrown on various organs, particularly the lungs. The lungs, being overtaxed, become degenerated, and this is why so many inebriates suffer from a peculiar form of consumption called alcoholic phthisis – many, many cases of which are, alas, to be found in our hospitals, where the unhappy victims await the slow but sure march of an early death. It is a well-established fact that alcohol not only does not give strength but lessens it. It relaxes the muscles or instruments of motion and consequently their power decreases. This muscular depression is often followed by complete paralysis of the body, drink having unstrung the whole nervous system, which, when so unstrung leaves the body like a ship without sails or ropes – an unmovable or unmanageable thing. Alcohol may have its uses in the medical world, to which it should be relegated; but once a man becomes its victim, it is a terrible and a merciless master, and he finds himself in that dreadful state when all will-power is gone and he becomes a helpless imbecile, tortured at times by remorse and despair. Conclusion of the foregoing.

On the other hand, young men of my acquaintance who were in the habit of voluntarily placing themselves under the influence of alcohol had often surprised me with a recital of their strange adventures. The mind may be impaired by alcohol, I mused, but withal it may be pleasantly impaired. Personal experience appeared to me to be the only satisfactory means to the resolution of my doubts. Knowing it was my first one, I quietly fingered the butt of my glass before I raised it. Lightly I subjected myself to an inward interrogation.

Nature of interrogation: Who are my future cronies, where our mad carousals? What neat repast shall feast us light and choice of Attic taste with wine whence we may rise to hear the lute well touched or artful voice warble immortal notes or Tuscan air? What mad pursuit? What pipes and timbrels? What wild ecstasy?

Here's to your health, said Kelly.
Good luck, I said.

The porter was sour to the palate, but viscid, potent. Kelly made long noise as if releasing air from his interior.

I looked at him from the corner of my eye and said:

You can't beat a good pint.

He leaned over and put his face close to me in an earnest manner.

Do you know what I am going to tell you, he said with his wry mouth, a pint of plain is your only man.

Notwithstanding this eulogy, I soon found that the mass of plain porter bears an unsatisfactory relation to its toxic content and I became subsequently addicted to brown stout in bottle, a drink which still remains the one that I prefer the most despite the painful and blinding fits of vomiting which a plurality of bottles has often induced in me.

I proceeded home one evening in October after leaving a gallon of half-digested porter on the floor of a public-house in Parnell Street and put myself with considerable difficulty into bed, where I remained for three days on the pretence of a chill. I was compelled to secrete my suit beneath the mattress because it was offensive to at least two of the senses and bore an explanation of my illness contrary to that already advanced.

The two senses referred to: Vision, smell.

On the evening of the third day, a friend of mine, Brinsley, was admitted to my chamber. He bore miscellaneous books and papers. I complained on the subject of my health and ascertained from him that the weather was inimical to the well-being of invalids. . . . He remarked that there was a queer smell in the room.

Description of my friend: Thin, dark-haired, hesitant; an intellectual Meath-man; given to close-knit epigrammatic talk; weak-chested, pale.

I opened wide my windpipe and made a coarse noise unassociated with the usages of gentlemen.

I feel very bad, I said.

By God you're the queer bloody man, he said.

I was down in Parnell Street, I said with the Shader Ward, the two of us drinking pints. Well, whatever happened to me, I started to puke and I puked till the eyes nearly left my head. I made a right haimes of my suit. I puked till I puked air.

Is that the way of it? said Brinsley.

Look at here, I said.

I arose in my bed, my body on the prop of an elbow.

I was talking to the Shader, I said, talking about God and one thing and another, and suddenly I felt something inside me like a man trying to get out of my stomach. The next minute my head was in the grip of the Shader's hand and I was letting it out in great style. O Lord save us. . . .

Here Brinsley interposed a laugh.

I thought my stomach was on the floor, I said. Take it easy, says the Shader, you'll be better when you get that off. Better? How I got home at all I couldn't tell you.

Well you did get home, said Brinsley.

I withdrew my elbow and fell back again as if exhausted by my effort. My talk had been forced, couched in the accent of the lower or working-classes. Under the cover of the bed-clothes I poked idly with a pencil at my navel. Brinsley was at the window giving chuckles out.

Nature of chuckles: Quiet, private, averted.

What are you laughing at? I said.

You and your book and your porter, he answered.

Did you read that stuff about Finn, I said, that stuff I gave you?

Oh, yes, he said, that was the pig's whiskers. That was funny all right.

This I found a pleasing eulogy. The God-big Finn. Brinsley turned from the window and asked me for a cigarette. I took out my 'butt' or half-spent cigarette and showed it in the hollow of my hand.

That is all I have, I said, affecting a pathos in my voice.

By God you're the queer bloody man, he said.

He then brought from his own pocket a box of the twenty denomination, lighting one for each of us.

There are two ways to make big money, he said, to write a book or to make a book.

It happened that this remark provoked between us a discussion on the subject of Literature – great authors living and dead, the character of modern poetry, the predilections of publishers and the importance of being at all times occupied with literary activities of a spare-time or recreative character. My dim room rang with the iron of fine words and the names of great Russian masters were articulated with fastidious intonation. Witticisms were canvassed, depending for their utility on a knowledge of the French language as spoken in the medieval times. Psycho-analysis was mentioned – with, however, a somewhat light touch. I then tendered an explanation spontaneous and unsolicited concerning my own work, affording an insight as to its aesthetic, its daemon, its argument, its sorrow and its joy, its darkness, its sun-twinkle clearness.

Nature of explanation offered: It was stated that while the novel and the play were both pleasing intellectual exercises, the novel was inferior to the play inasmuch as it lacked the outward accidents of illusion, frequently inducing the reader to be out-witted in a shabby fashion and caused to experience a real concern for the fortunes of illusory characters. The play was consumed in wholesome fashion by large masses in places of public resort; the novel was self-administered in private. The novel, in the hands of an unscrupulous writer, could be despotic. In reply to an inquiry, it was explained that a satisfactory novel should be a self-evident sham to which the reader could regulate at will the degree of his credulity. It was undemocratic to compel characters to be uniformly good or bad or poor or rich. Each should be allowed a private life, self-determination and a decent standard of living. This would make for self-respect, content-ment and better service. It would be incorrect to say that it would lead to chaos. Characters should be interchangeable as between one book and another. The entire corpus of existing literature should be regarded as a limbo from which discerning authors could draw their characters as required, creating only when they failed to find a suitable existing puppet. The modern novel should be largely a work of reference. Most authors spend their time saying what has been said before – usually said much better. A wealth of references to existing works would acquaint the reader instantaneously with the nature of each character, would obviate tiresome explanations and would effectively preclude

mountebanks, upstarts, thimbleriggers and persons of inferior
education from an understanding of contemporary literature.
Conclusion of explanation.

That is all my bum, said Brinsley.

But taking precise typescript from beneath the book that was
at my side, I explained to him my literary intentions in considerable detail – now reading, now discoursing, oratio recta and
oratio obliqua.

*Extract from Manuscript as to nature of Red Swan premises, oratio
recta:* The Red Swan premises in Lower Leeson Street are held
in fee farm, the landlord whosoever being pledged to maintain
the narrow lane which marks its eastern boundary unimpeded
and free from nuisance for a distance of seventeen yards, that is,
up to the intersection of Peter Place. New Paragraph. A ter-
minus of the Cornelscourt coach in the seventeenth century,
the hotel was rebuilt in 1712 and afterwards fired by the yeo-
manry for reasons which must be sought in the quiet of its
ruined garden, on the three-perch stretch that goes by Croppies'
Acre. Today, it is a large building of four storeys. The title is
worked in snow-white letters along the circumference of the
fanlight and the centre of the circle is concerned with the
delicate image of a red swan, pleasingly conceived and carried
out by a casting process in Birmingham delf. Conclusion of the
foregoing.

*Further extract descriptive of Dermot Trellis rated occupier of the
Red Swan Hotel, oratio recta:* Dermot Trellis was a man of average
stature but his person was flabby and unattractive, partly a result
of his having remained in bed for a period of twenty years. He
was voluntarily bedridden and suffered from no organic or other
illness. He occasionally rose for very brief periods in the evening
to pad about the empty house in his felt slippers or to interview
the slavey in the kitchen on the subject of his food or bedclothes. He had lost all physical reaction to bad or good weather
and was accustomed to trace the seasonal changes of the year
by inactivity or virulence of his pimples. His legs were puffed
and affected with a prickly heat, a result of wearing his woollen
undertrunks in bed. He never went out and rarely approached
the windows.

Tour de force by Brinsley, vocally interjected, being a comparable description in the Finn canon: The neck to Trellis is house-thick and house-rough and is guarded by night and day against the coming of enemies by his old watchful boil. His bottom is the stern of a sea-blue schooner, his stomach is its mainsail with a filling of wind. His face is a snowfall on old mountains, the feet are fields.

There was an interruption, I recall, at this stage. My uncle put his head through the door and looked at me in a severe manner, his face flushed from walking and an evening paper in his hand. He was about to address me when he perceived the shadow of Brinsley by the window.

Well, well, he said. He came in in a genial noisy manner, closed the door with vigour and peered at the form of Brinsley. Brinsley took his hands from his pockets and smiled without reason in the twilight.

Good evening to you, gentlemen, said my uncle.

Good evening, said Brinsley.

This is Mr Brinsley, a friend of mine, I said, raising my shoulders feebly from the bed. I gave a low moan of exhaustion.

My uncle extended an honest hand in the grip of friendship.

Ah, Mr Brinsley, how do you do? he said. How do you do, Sir? You are a University man, Mr Brinsley?

Oh yes.

Ah, very good, said my uncle. It's a grand thing, that – a thing that will stand to you. It is certainly. A good degree is a very nice thing to have. Are the masters hard to please, Mr Brinsley?

Well, no. As a matter of fact they don't care very much.

Do you tell me so! Well it was a different tale in the old days. The old schoolmasters believed in the big stick. Oh, plenty of that boyo.

He gave a laugh here in which we concurred without emotion.

The stick was mightier than the pen, he added, laughing again in a louder way and relapsing into a quiet chuckle. He paused for a brief interval as if examining something hitherto overlooked in the interior of his memory.

And how is our friend? he inquired in the direction of my bed.

Nature of my reply: Civil, perfunctory, uninformative.

My uncle leaned over towards Brinsley and said to him in a low, confidential manner:

Do you know what I am going to tell you, there is a very catching cold going around. Every second man you meet has got a cold. God preserve us, there will be plenty of 'flu before the winter's out, make no mistake about that. You would need to keep yourself well wrapped up.

As a matter of fact, said Brinsley in a crafty way, I have only just recovered from a cold myself.

You would need to keep yourself well wrapped up, rejoined my uncle, you would, faith.

Here there was a pause, each of us searching for a word with which it might be broken.

Tell me this, Mr Brinsley, said my uncle, are you going to be a doctor?

I am not, said Brinsley.

Or a schoolmaster?

Here I interposed a shaft from my bed.

He hopes to get a job from the Christian Brothers, I said, when he gets his B.A.

That would be a great thing, said my uncle. The Brothers, of course, are very particular about the boys they take. You must have a good record, a clean sheet.

Well I have that, said Brinsley.

Of course you have, said my uncle. But doctoring and teaching are two jobs that call for great application and love of God. For what is the love of God but the love of your neighbour?

He sought agreement from each of us in turn, reverting a second to Brinsley with his ocular inquiry.

It is a grand and a noble life, he said, teaching the young and the sick and nursing them back to their God-given health. It is, faith. There is a special crown for those that give themselves up to that work.

It is a hard life, but, said Brinsley.

A hard life? said my uncle. Certainly so, but tell me this: is it worth your while?

Brinsley gave a nod.

Worth your while and well worth it, said my uncle. A special crown is a thing that is not offered every day of the week. Oh, it's a grand thing, a grand life. Doctoring and teaching, the two of them are marked out for special graces and blessings.

He mused for a while, staring at the smoke of his cigarette. He then looked up and laughed, clapping his hand on the top of the washstand.

But long faces, he said, long faces won't get any of us very far. Eh, Mr Brinsley? I am a great believer in the smile and the happy word.

A sovereign remedy for all our ills, said Brinsley.

A sovereign remedy for all our ills, said my uncle. Very nicely put. Well . . .

He held out a hand in valediction.

Mind yourself now, he said, and mind and keep the coat buttoned up. The 'flu is the boy I'd give the slip to.

He was civilly replied to. He left the room with a pleased smile but was not gone for three seconds till he was back again with a grave look, coming upon us suddenly in the moment of our relaxation and relief.

Oh, that matter of the Brothers, he said in a low tone to Brinsley, would you care for me to put in a word for you?

Thanks very much, said Brinsley, but –

No trouble at all, said my uncle. Brother Hanley, late of Richmond Street, he is a very special friend of mine. No question of pulling strings, you know. Just a private word in his ear. He is a special friend.

Well, that is very good of you, said Brinsley.

Oh, not in the least, said my uncle. There is a way of doing things, you understand. It is a great thing to have a friend in court. And Brother Hanley, I may tell you privately, is one of the best – Oh, one of the very best in the world. It would be a pleasure to work with a man like Brother Hanley. I will have a word with him tomorrow.

The only thing is, but, said Brinsley, it will be some time before I am qualified and get my parchment.

Never mind, said my uncle, it is always well to be in early. First come, first called.

At this point he assembled his features into an expression of extreme secrecy and responsibility:

The Order, of course, is always on the look-out for boys of

education and character. Tell me this, Mr Brinsley, have you ever...

I never thought of that, said Brinsley in surprise.

Do you think would the religious life appeal to you?

I'm afraid I never thought much about it.

Brinsley's tone was of a forced texture as if he were labouring in the stress of some emotion.

It is a good healthy life and a special crown at the end of it, said my uncle. Every boy should consider it very carefully before he decides to remain out in the world. He should pray to God for a vocation.

Not everybody is called, I ventured from the bed.

Not everybody is called, agreed my uncle, perfectly true. Only a small and a select band.

Perceiving then that the statement had come from me, he looked sharply in the direction of my corner as if to verify the honesty of my face. He turned back to Brinsley.

I want you to make me a promise, Mr Brinsley, he said. Will you promise me that you will think about it?

I will certainly, said Brinsley.

My uncle smiled warmly and held out a hand.

Good, he said. God bless you.

Description of my uncle: Rat-brained, cunning, concerned-that-he-should-be-well-thought-of. Abounding in pretence, deceit. Holder of Guinness clerkship the third class.

In a moment he was gone, this time without return. Brinsley, a shadow by the window, performed perfunctorily the movements of a mime, making at the same time a pious ejaculation.

Nature of mime and ejaculation: Removal of sweat from brow; holy God.

I hope, said Brinsley, that Trellis is not a replica of the uncle.

I did not answer but reached a hand to the mantelpiece and took down the twenty-first volume of my *Conspectus of the Arts and Natural Sciences*. Opening it, I read a passage which I subsequently embodied in my manuscript as being suitable for my purpose. The passage had in fact reference to Doctor Beatty (now with God) but boldly I took it for my own.

Extract from 'A Conspectus of the Arts and Natural Sciences', being a further description of Trellis's person, and with a reference to a failing: In person he was of the middle size, of a broad square make, which seemed to indicate a more robust constitution than he really possessed. In his gait there was something of a slouch. During his later years he grew corpulent and unwieldy; his features were very regular and his complexion somewhat high. His eyes were black, brilliant, full of a tender and melancholy expression, and, in the course of conversation with his friends, became extremely animated. It is with regret that it is found expedient to touch upon a reported failing of so great a man. It has been asserted that towards the close of his life he indulged to excess in the use of wine. In a letter to Mr Arbuthnot he says: With the present pressure upon my mind, I should not be able to sleep if I did not use wine as an opiate; it is less hurtful than laudanum but not so effectual. Conclusion of extract from letter to Mr Arbuthnot. He may, perhaps, have had too frequent a recourse to so palatable a medicine, in the hope of banishing for a time the recollection of his sorrows; and if, under any circumstances, such a fault is to be regarded as venial, it may be excused in one who was a more than widowed husband and a childless father. Some years after his son's death, he occupied himself in the melancholy yet pleasing task of editing a volume of the compositions of the deceased. From a pardonable partiality for the writings of a beloved child, and from his own not very accurate attainments in classical scholarship, he admitted into the collection several pieces, both English and Latin, which fall considerably below mediocrity. A few copies of the work were privately printed and offered as presents to those friends with whom the author was particularly acquainted. Conclusion of extract.

Further extract from my Manuscript, descriptive. Oratio recta: Trellis stirred feebly in his room in the stillness of the second floor. He frowned to himself quietly in the gloom, flickering his heavy lids and wrinkling his brow into pimpled corrugations. He twitched with his thick fingers at the quilts.

His bed was a timber article of great age in which many of his forefathers had died and been born; it was delicately made and embellished with delicately carved cornices. It was of Italian manufacture, an early excursion of the genius of the great

Stradivari. On one side of it was a small table with books and
type-darkened papers and on the other a cabinet containing two
chambers. Also there was a deal wardrobe and two chairs. On
the window-ledge there was a small bakelite clock which
grappled with each new day as it entered his room through the
window from Peter Place, arranging it with precision into
twenty-four hours. It was quiet, servile and emasculated; its twin
alarming gongs could be found if looked for behind the dust-
laden books on the mantelpiece.

Trellis had three separate suits of sleeping-clothes and was
accustomed to be extremely fastidious as to the manner in which
they were washed. He supervised the weekly wash, which was
carried out by his servant-girl on Tuesdays.

A Tuesday evening at the Red Swan, example of: In the darkness
of the early night Trellis arose from his bed and drew a trousers
over the bulging exuberance of his night-clothes, swaying on his
white worthless legs.

Nature of trousers: Narrow-legged, out-moded, the pre-War
class.

He groped for his slippers and went out to the dark stairs,
stretching an arm for guidance to the banister. He reached the
hallway and continued towards the dark stone stairs to the basement, peering before him with apprehension. Strong basement
smells assailed his nostrils, the odours of a washerwoman's fête
from a kitchen beflagged with the steamy bunting of underclothes drying. He entered and looked about him from the door.
The ceiling was decked with the rectangular banners of his long-
tailed shirts, the ensigns of his sheets, the flags of his bed-bibs,
the great buff pennants of his drawers.

The figure of Teresa was visible at the stove, her thick thighs
presented to the penetration of the fire. She was a stout girl of
high colour, attired in grey and divided at the centre by the
terminal ridge of a corset of inferior design.

Interjection on the part of Brinsley: He commented at some
length on the similarity between the ridge referred to and the
moulding-ridge which circumscribed the image of the red swan

in the fanlight. Both ridges he advanced as the ineluctable badge of mass-production. Slaveys, he considered, were the Ford cars of humanity; they were created to a standard pattern by the hundred thousand. But they were grand girls and there was nothing he liked better, he said.

Penultimum, continued: Trellis examined his wools with appraising fingers, turning them tenderly in his hands.

Nature of wools: Soft, lacked chafing hardness.

He smiled gratefully on his servant and laboured back to his bedroom, reflectively passing a hand across the pimples of his face. Fearing his bed would cool, he hastened past the emptiness of the hall, where a handsome girl stood poised without her clothes on the brink of a blue river. Napoleon peered at her in a wanton fashion from the dark of the other wall.

Biographical reminiscence, part the second: Some days later I said to my uncle in the morning at breakfast-time:

Could you give me five shillings to buy a book, please?

Five shillings? Well, dear knows it must be a great book altogether that can cost five shillings. What do they call it?

Die Harzreise by Heine, I answered.

Dee . . . ?

Die Harzreise, a German book.

I see, he said.

His head was bent, his two eyes engaged on a meticulous observation of the activities of his knife and fork as they dissected between them a fried haddock. Suddenly disengaging his right hand, he dipped in his waistcoat and put two half-crowns on the tablecloth.

After a time, he said:

So long as the book is used, well and good. So long as it is read and studied, well and good.

The redness of his fingers as he handed out his coins, his occupation with feeding for the nourishment of his body, these were two things that revealed for an instant his equal humanity. I left him there, going quickly to the street in my grey coat and bending forward through the cold rain to the College.

Description of College: The College is outwardly a rectangular plain building with a fine porch where the midday sun pours down in summer from the Donnybrook direction, heating the steps for the comfort of the students. The hallway inside is composed of large black and white squares arranged in the orthodox chessboard pattern, and the surrounding walls, done in an unpretentious cream wash, bear three rough smudges caused by the heels, buttocks and shoulders of the students.

The hall was crowded by students, some of them deporting themselves in a quiet civil manner. Modest girls bearing books filed in and out in the channels formed by the groups of boys. There was a hum of converse and much bustle and activity. A liveried attendant came out of a small office in the wall and pealed a shrill bell. This caused some dispersal, many of the boys extinguishing their cigarettes by manual manipulation and going up a circular stairway to the lecture-halls in a brave, arrogant way, some stopping on the stairs to call back to those still below a message of facetious or obscene import.

I perused a number of public notices attached to the wall and then made my way without offence to the back of the College, where there was another old ruined College containing an apartment known as the Gentlemen's Smokeroom. This room was usually occupied by card-players, hooligans and rough persons. Once they made an attempt to fire the complete building by igniting a number of armchairs and cane stools, but the attempt was foiled by reason of the dampness of the season – it was October – and the intervention of the porters.

I sat alone in a retired corner in the cold, closely wrapping the feeble citadel of my body with my grey coat. Through the two apertures of my eyes I gazed out in a hostile manner. Strong country boys were planking down cards and coins and roaring out the name of God. Occasionally there was a sudden burst of horseplay, scuffling and kicking, and a chair or a man would crash across the floor. Newspapers were widely read and notices posted on the wall were being torn down or altered by deletion of words or letters so as to impart to them an obscene or facetious import.

A friend of mine, Brinsley, came in and looked about him at the door. He came forward at my invitation and asked me to give him a cigarette. I took out my 'butt' and showed it to him in the hollow of my hand.

That is all I have, affecting a pathos in my voice.

By God you're the queer bloody man, he said. Are you sitting on a newspaper?

No, I said. I struck a match and lit my 'butt' and also another 'butt', the property of Brinsley. We smoked there together for a time. The floor was wet from foot-falls and a mist covered the high windows. Brinsley utilized an unclean expression in a random fashion and added that the weather was very bad, likening it, in fact, to a harlot.

I was talking to a friend of yours last night, I said drily. I mean Mr Trellis. He has bought a ream of ruled foolscap and is starting on his story. He is compelling all his characters to live with him in the Red Swan Hotel so that he can keep an eye on them and see that there is no boozing.

I see, said Brinsley.

Most of them are characters used in other books, chiefly the works of another great writer called Tracy. There is a cowboy in Room 13 and Mr McCool, a hero of old Ireland, is on the floor above. The cellar is full of leprechauns.

What are they going to all do? asked Brinsley.

Nature of his tone: Without intent, tired, formal.

Trellis, I answered steadily, is writing a book on sin and the wages attaching thereto. He is a philosopher and a moralist. He is appalled by the spate of sexual and other crimes recorded in recent times in the newspapers – particularly in those published on Saturday night.

Nobody will read the like of that, said Brinsley.

Yes they will, I answered. Trellis wants this salutary book to be read by all. He realizes that purely a moralizing tract would not reach the public. Therefore he is putting plenty of smut into his book. There will be no less than seven indecent assaults on young girls and any amount of bad language. There will be whisky and porter for further orders.

I thought there was to be no boozing, Brinsley said.

No unauthorized boozing, I answered. Trellis has absolute control over his minions but this control is abandoned when he falls asleep. Consequently he must make sure that they are all in bed before he locks up and goes to bed himself. Now do you understand me?

You needn't shout, said Brinsley.

His book is so bad that there will be no hero, nothing but villains. The central villain will be a man of unexampled depravity, so bad that he must be created *ab ovo et initio*. A small dark man called Furriskey.

I paused to examine my story, allowing a small laugh as a just tribute. Then whipping typescript from a pocket, I read an extract quickly for his further entertainment.

Extract from Manuscript where Trellis is explaining to an unnamed listener the character of his projected labour: . . . It appeared to him that a great and a daring book – a green book – was the crying need of the hour – a book that would show the terrible cancer of sin in its true light and act as a clarion-call to torn humanity. Continuing, he said that all children were born clean and innocent. (It was not by chance that he avoided the doctrine of original sin and the theological profundities which its consideration would entail.) They grew up to be polluted by their foul environment and transformed – was not the word a feeble one! – into bawds and criminals and harpies. Evil, it seemed to him, was the most contagious of all known diseases. Put a thief among honest men and they will eventually relieve him of his watch. In his book he would present two examples of humanity – a man of great depravity and a woman of unprecedented virtue. They meet. The woman is corrupted, eventually ravished and done to death in a back lane. Presented in its own *milieu*, in the timeless conflict of grime and beauty, gold and black, sin and grace, the tale would be a moving and a salutary one. *Mens sana in corpore sano*. What a keen discernment had the old philosopher! How well he knew that the beetle was of the dunghill, the butterfly of the flower! Conclusion of extract.

Looking up in triumph, I found Brinsley standing very straight and staring at the floor, his neck bent. A newspaper, soiled and damp, was on the floor at his feet and his eyes strained narrowly at the print.

Gob I see that horse of Peacock's is going today, he said.

I folded my manuscript without a word and replaced it in my clothing.

Eight stone four, he said.

Listen here, he continued looking up, we'd be bloody fools if we didn't have something on this.

He stopped and peeled the paper from the floor, reading it intently.

What horse is this? I asked.

What horse? Grandchild. Peacock's horse.

Here I uttered an exclamation.

Nature of exclamation: Inarticulate, of surprise, recollection.

Wait till I show you something, I said groping in my pocket. Wait till you read this. I got this yesterday. I am in the hands of a man from Newmarket.

I handed him a letter.

Mail from V. Wright, Wyvern Cottage, Newmarket, Suffolk: V. Wright, the Backer's Friend. Dear friend and member. Many thanks for yours to hand. As promised I send you my promised 'good thing' which is GRANDCHILD in 4.30 at Gatwick on Friday. Do not hesitate to plunge and put on an extra shilling for me towards my heavy expenses. This animal has been saved *for this race only* for the past two months and is a certain starter, ignore newspaper probabilities and GO IN FOR THE WIN OF YOUR LIFE. This horse is my treble nap CAST-IRON PLUNGER for the week – no other selection given – and I know all there is to be known about it. Old friends will know that I do not send 'guessworks' but only STRICTLY OCCASIONAL advices over animals already as good as past the post. Of course I have to pay heavily for my information, each winner costs me a packet so do not fail to remit the odds to a 'bob' promptly so as to make sure to not miss my next CAST-IRON PLUNGER and remain permanently on my books. Those not clear on my books by Tuesday next will be in danger of missing *the cream of racing information* which I expect to have available next week. So do not hesitate to plunge to your limit on GRANDCHILD on Friday and remit immediately after the race, on the same evening if possible. Excuses over winners will be ignored. If going away please do not fail to send me your new address so as not to miss my good things. Please have a good bet on Grandchild. Yours and best of luck together, V. Wright.

Remittance Form. To V. Wright, Wyvern Cottage, New-market, Suffolk. Herewith please find P.O. for £   s.   d. being the odds to 1/- over Grandchild (thus 4 to 1, 4/-), and hoping to receive further winners of the same kind. Name, address.

Do you know this man? asked Brinsley.

I do not, I said.

Do you intend to back the horse?

I have no money, I answered.

Nothing at all? I have two shillings.

In the interior of my pocket I fingered the smooth disks of my book-money.

I have to buy a book today, I said. I got five shillings for it this morning.

The price given here, said Brinsley from the paper, is ten to one and say that's seven to one at a half-a-crown each way that's twenty-one bob. Buy your book and you have sixteen shillings change.

More by accident than by any mastery of the body, I here expressed my doubts on the proposal by the means of a noise.

Tide of noise, the Greek version: πορδή.

That same afternoon I was sitting on a stool in an intoxicated condition in Grogan's licensed premises. Adjacent stools bore the forms of Brinsley and Kelly, my two true friends. The three of us were occupied in putting glasses of stout into the interior of our bodies and expressing by fine disputation the resulting sense of physical and mental well-being. In my thigh pocket I had eleven and eightpence in a weighty pendulum of mixed coins. Each of the arranged bottles on the shelves before me, narrow or squat-bellied, bore a dull picture of the gas bracket. Who can tell the stock of a public-house? Many no doubt are dummies, those especially within an arm-reach of the snug. The stout was of superior quality, soft against the tongue but sharp upon the orifice of the throat, softly efficient in its magical circulation through the conduits of the body. Half to myself, I said:

Do not let us forget that I have to buy *Die Harzreise*. Do not let us forget that.

Harzreise, said Brinsley. There is a house in Dalkey called Heartrise.

Brinsley then put his dark chin on the cup of a palm and leaned in thought on the counter, overlooking his drink, gazing beyond the frontier of the world.

What about another jar? said Kelly.

Ah, Lesbia, said Brinsley. The finest thing I ever wrote. How many kisses, Lesbia, you ask, would serve to sate this hungry love of mine? – As many as the Libyan sands that bask along Cyrene's shore where pine-trees wave, where burning Jupiter's untended shrine lies near to old King Battus' sacred grave:

Three stouts, called Kelly.

Let them be endless as the stars at night, that stare upon the lovers in a ditch – so often would love-crazed Catullus bite your burning lips, that prying eyes should not have power to count, nor evil tongues bewitch, the frenzied kisses that you gave and got.

Before we die of thirst, called Kelly, will you bring us *three more stouts*. God, he said to me, it's in the desert you'd think we were.

That's good stuff, you know, I said to Brinsley.

A picture came before my mind of the lovers at their hedge-pleasure in the pale starlight, no sound from them, his fierce mouth burying into hers.

Bloody good stuff, I said.

Kelly, invisible to my left, made a slapping noise.

The best I ever drank, he said.

As I exchanged an eye-message with Brinsley, a wheezing beggar inserted his person at my side and said:

Buy a scapular or a stud, Sir.

This interruption I did not understand. Afterwards, near Lad Lane police station a small man in black fell in with us and tapping me often about the chest, talked to me earnestly on the subject of Rousseau, a member of the French nation. He was animated, his pale features striking in the starlight and voice going up and falling in the lilt of his argumentum. I did not understand his talk and was personally unacquainted with him. But Kelly was taking in all he said, for he stood near him, his taller head inclined in an attitude of close attention. Kelly then made a low noise and opened his mouth and covered the small man from shoulder to knee with a coating of unpleasant buff-coloured puke. Many other things happened on that night now imperfectly recorded in my memory but that incident is still very clear to me in my mind. Afterwards the small man was some distance from us in the lane, shaking his divested coat and rubbing it along the wall. He is a little man that the name of Rousseau will always recall to me. Conclusion of reminiscence.

Further extract from my Manuscript wherein Mr Trellis commences the writing of his story: Propped by pillows in his bed in the white light of an incandescent petrol lamp, Dermot Trellis adjusted the pimples in his forehead into a frown of deep creative import. His pencil moved slowly across the ruled paper, leaving words behind it of every size. He was engaged in the creation of John Furriskey, the villain of his tale.

Extract from Press regarding Furriskey's birth: We are in position to announce that a happy event has taken place at the Red Swan Hotel, where the proprietor, Mr Dermot Trellis, has succeeded in encompassing the birth of a man called Furriskey. Stated to be doing 'very nicely', the new arrival is about five feet eight inches in height, well built, dark, and clean-shaven. The eyes are blue and the teeth well formed and good, though stained somewhat by tobacco; there are two fillings in the molars of the left upperside and a cavity threatened in the left canine. The hair, black and of thick quality, is worn plastered back on the head with a straight parting from the left temple. The chest is muscular and well-developed while the legs are straight but rather short. He is very proficient mentally having an unusually firm grasp of the Latin idiom and a knowledge of Physics extending from Boyle's Law to the Leclanche Cell and the Greasespot Photo-meter. He would seem to have a special aptitude for mathematics. In the course of a test conducted by our reporter, he solved a 'cut' from an advanced chapter of Hall and Knight's Geometry and failed to be mystified by an intricate operation involving the calculus. His voice is light and pleasant, although from his fingers it is obvious that he is a heavy smoker. He is apparently not a virgin, although it is admittedly difficult to establish this attribute with certainty in the male.

Our Medical Correspondent writes:

The birth of a son in the Red Swan Hotel is a fitting tribute to the zeal and perseverance of Mr Dermot Trellis, who has won international repute in connexion with his researches into the theory of aestho-autogamy. The event may be said to crown the savant's life-work as he has at last realized his dream of producing a living mammal from an operation involving neither fertilization nor conception.

Aestho-autogamy with one unknown quantity on the male side, Mr Trellis told me in conversation, has long been a commonplace. For fully five centuries in all parts of the world epileptic slavies have been pleading it in extenuation of uncalled-for fecundity. It is a very familiar phenomenon in literature. The elimination of conception and pregnancy, however, or the reduction of the processes to the same mysterious abstraction as that of the paternal factor in the commonplace case of un-explained maternity, has been the dream of every practising psycho-eugenist the world over. I am very happy to have been fortunate enough to bring a century of ceaseless experiment and endeavour to a triumphant conclusion. Much of the credit for Mr Furriskey's presence on this planet today must go to my late friend and colleague William Tracy, whose early researches furnished me with invaluable data and largely determined the direction of my experiments. The credit for the achievement of a successful act of procreation involving two unknown quantities is as much his as mine.

This graceful reference on the part of Mr Trellis to the late Mr William Tracy, the eminent writer of Western romances – his *Flower o' the Prairie* is still read – is apparently directed at the latter's gallant efforts to change the monotonous and unimaginative process by which all children are invariably born young.

Many social problems of contemporary interest, he wrote in 1909, could be readily resolved if issue could be born already matured, teethed, reared, educated, and ready to essay those competitive plums which make the Civil Service and the Banks so attractive to the younger breadwinners of today. The process of bringing up children is a tedious anachronism in these enlightened times. Those mortifying stratagems collectively known as birth-control would become a mere memory if parents and married couples could be assured that their legitimate diversion would straightway result in finished breadwinners or marriageable daughters.

He also envisaged the day when the breeding and safe deliverance of Old Age Pensioners and other aged and infirm eligible for public money would transform matrimony from the sordid struggle that it often is to an adventurous business enterprise of limitless possibilities.

It is noteworthy that Mr Tracy succeeded, after six disconcerting miscarriages, in having his own wife delivered of a middle-aged Spaniard who lived for only six weeks. A man who carried jealousy to the point of farce, the novelist insisted that his wife and the new arrival should occupy separate beds and use the bathroom at divergent times. Some amusement was elicited in literary circles by the predicament of a woman who was delivered of a son old enough to be her father but it served to deflect Mr Tracy not one tittle from his dispassionate quest for scientific truth. His acumen and pertinacity have, in fact, become legendary in the world of psycho-eugenics. Conclusion of the foregoing.

Shorthand Note of a cross-examination of Mr Trellis at a later date on the occasion of his being on trial for his life, the birth of Furriskey being the subject of the examination referred to:

In what manner was he born?

He awoke as if from sleep.

His sensations?

Bewilderment, perplexity.

Are not these terms synonymous and one as a consequence redundant?

Yes: but the terms of the inquiry postulated unsingular information.

(At this reply ten of the judges made angry noises on the counter with the butts of their stout-glasses. Judge Shanahan put his head out through a door and issued a severe warning to the witness, advising him to conduct himself and drawing his attention to the serious penalties which would be attendant on further impudence.)

His sensations? is it not possible to be more precise?

It is. He was consumed by doubts as to his own identity, as to the nature of his body and the cast of his countenance.

In what manner did he resolve these doubts?

By the sensory perception of his ten fingers.

By feeling?

Yes.

Did you write the following: Sir Francis Thumb Drake, comma, with three inquiring midshipmen and a cabin boy, comma, he dispatched in a wrinkled Mayflower across the seas of his Braille face?

I did.

I put it to you that the passage was written by Mr Tracy and that you stole it.

No.

I put it to you that you are lying.

No.

Describe this man's conduct after he had examined his face.

He arose from his bed and examined his stomach, lower chest and legs.

What parts did he not examine?

His back, neck and head.

Can you suggest a reason for so imperfect a survey?

Yes. His vision was necessarily limited by the movement of his neck.

(At this point Judge Shanahan entered the court adjusting his dress and said: That point was exceedingly well taken. Proceed.)

Having examined his stomach, legs and lower chest, what did he do next?

He dressed.

He dressed? A suit of the latest pattern, made to measure?

No. A suit of navy-blue of the pre-War style.

With a vent behind?

Yes.

The cast-aways of your own wardrobe?

Yes.

I put it to you that your intention was purely to humiliate him.

No. By no means.

And after he was dressed in his ludicrous clothes . . . ?

He spent some time searching in his room for a looking-glass or for a surface that would enable him to ascertain the character of his countenance.

You had already hidden the glass?

No. I had forgotten to provide one.

By reason of his doubts as to his personal appearance, he suffered considerable mental anguish?

It is possible.

You could have appeared to him – by magic if necessary – and explained his identity and duties to him. Why did you not perform so obvious an errand of mercy?

I do not know.

Answer the question, please.

(At this point Judge Sweeny made an angry noise with a crack of his stout-glass on the counter and retired in a hurried petulant manner from the court.)

I suppose I fell asleep.

I see. You fell asleep.

Conclusion of the foregoing.

Biographical reminiscence, part the third: The early winter in which these matters were occupying my attention was a season of unexampled severity. The prevailing wind (according to the word of Brinsley) was from the eastern point and was not infrequently saturated with a fine chilly rain. From my bed I had perceived the sodden forms of travellers lurking behind the frosted windows of the tram-tops. Morning would come slowly, decaying to twilight in the early afternoon.

A congenital disposition predisposing me to the most common of the wasting diseases – a cousin had died in Davos – had induced in me what was perhaps a disproportionate concern for pulmonary well-being; at all events I recall that I rarely left my room for the first three months of the winter except on occasions when my domestic circumstances made it necessary for me to appear casually before my uncle attired in my grey street-coat. I was, if possible, on worse terms than ever with him, my continued failure to produce for his examination a book called *Die Harzreise* being a sore point. I cannot recall that I ever quitted the four walls of the house. Alexander, who had chosen a scheme of studies similar to my own, answered with my voice at lecture roll-calls.

It was in the New Year, in February, I think, that I discovered that my person was verminous. A growing irritation in various parts of my body led me to examine my bedclothes and the discovery of lice in large numbers was the result of my researches.

I was surprised and experienced also a sense of shame. I resolved at the time to make an end of my dissolute habits and composed mentally a régime of physical regeneration which included bending exercises.

One consequence of my resolve, at any rate, was that I attended at the College every day and walked through the Green and up and down the streets, conducting conversations with my acquaintances and occasionally talking with strangers on general topics.

It was my custom to go into the main hall of the College and stand with my back to one of the steam-heating devices, my faded overcoat open and my cold hostile eyes flitting about the faces that passed before me. The younger students were much in evidence, formless and ugly in adolescence; others were older, bore themselves with assurance and wore clothing of good quality. Groups would form for the purpose of disputation and dissolve again quickly. There was much foot-shuffling, chatter and noise of a general or indeterminate character. Students emerging from the confinement of an hour's lecture would grope eagerly for their cigarettes or accept one with gratitude from a friend. Clerical students from Blackrock or Rathfarnham, black clothes and bowler hats, would file past civilly and leave the building by a door opening at the back where they were accustomed to leave the iron pedal-cycles. Young postulants or nuns would also pass, their eyes upon the floor and their fresh young faces dimmed in the twilight of their hoods, passing to a private cloakroom where they would spend the intervals between their lectures in meditation and pious practices. Occasionally there would be a burst of horse-play and a sharp cry from a student accidentally hurt. On wet days there would be an unpleasant odour of dampness, an aroma of overcoats dried by body-heat. There was a clock plainly visible but the hours were told by a liveried attendant who emerged from a small office in the wall and pealed a shrill bell similar to that utilized by auctioneers and street-criers; the bell served this purpose, that it notified professors – distant in the web of their fine thought – that their discourses should terminate.

One afternoon I saw the form of Brinsley bent in converse with a small fair-haired man who was fast acquiring a reputation in the Leinster Square district on account of the beauty of his poems and their affinity with the high-class work of another writer, Mr Pound, an American gentleman. The small man had an off-hand way with him and talked with jerks. I advanced without diffidence and learnt that his name was Donaghy. We talked together in a polished manner, utilizing with frequency words from the French language, discussing the primacy of America and Ireland in contemporary letters and commenting on the inferior work produced by writers of the English nationality. The Holy Name was often taken, I do not recollect with what advertence. Brinsley, whose education and maintenance was a charge on the rates of his native county – the product of a farthing in the pound applied for the purpose of enabling necessitous boys of promising intellect to enjoy the benefits of University learning – Brinsley said that he was prepared to give myself and Donaghy a pint of stout apiece, explaining that he had recently been paid. I rejoined that if his finances warranted such generosity, I would raise no objection, but that I (for my part) was no Rockefeller, thus utilizing a figure of speech to convey the poverty of my circumstances.

Name of figure of speech: Synecdoche (or Autonomasia).

The three of us walked slowly down to Grogan's, our three voices interplaying in scholarly disputations, our faded overcoats finely open in the glint of the winter sun.

Isn't there a queer smell off this fellow? said Brinsley, directing his inquiring face to that of Donaghy.

I sniffed at my person in mock appraisement.

You're in bad odour, said Donaghy.

Well it's not the smell of drink, I answered. What class of a smell is it?

Did you ever go into a room early in the morning, asked Brinsley, where there had been a hooley the night before, with cigars and whisky and food and crackers and women's scent? Well that's the smell. A stale spent smell.

There's a hum off yourself, I said.

We entered the tavern and ordered our dark drinks.

To convert stout into water, I said, there is a simple process. Even a child can do it, though I would not stand for giving stout to children. Is it not a pity that the art of man has not attained the secret of converting water into stout?

Donaghy gave a laugh but Brinsley restrained me from drinking by the weight of his hand upon my arm and named a proprietary brand of ale.

Did you ever taste it? he asked.

I did not, I said.

Well that crowd have the secret if you like, he said. By God I never tasted anything like it. Did *you* ever try it?

No, said Donaghy.

Keep away from it if you value your life.

Here there was a pause as we savoured the dull syrup.

We had a great feed of wine at the Inns the other night, observed Donaghy, a swell time. Wine is better than stout. Stout sticks. Wine is more grateful to the intestines, the digestive viscera, you know. Stout sticks and leaves a scum on the interior of the paunch.

Raising my glass idly to my head, I said:

If that conclusion is the result of a mental syllogism, it is falacious, being based on licensed premises.

Two laughs in unison, these were my rewards. I frowned and drank unheedingly, savouring the dull oaten after-taste of the stout as it lingered against my palate. Brinsley tapped me sharply on the belly.

Gob you're getting a paunch, he said.

Leave my bag alone, I answered. I protected it with my hand.

We had three drinks in all in respect of each of which Brinsley paid a sixpence without regret.

The ultimate emptors: Meath County Council, rural rating authority.

The sun was gone and the evening students – many of them teachers, elderly and bald – were hurrying towards the College through the gathering dusk on foot and on pedal-cycles. We closed our coats closely about us and stood watching and talking at the corner. We went eventually to the moving pictures, the three of us, travelling to the centre of the city in the interior of a tramcar.

The emptors: Meath County Council.

Three nights later at about eight o'clock I was alone in Nassau Street, a district frequented by the prostitute class, when I perceived a ramrod in a cloth cap on the watch at the corner of Kildare Street. As I passed I saw that the man was Kelly. Large spits were about him on the path and the carriage-way. I poked him in a manner offensive to propriety and greeted his turned face with a facetious ejaculation:

How is the boy! I said.

My hard man, he answered.

I took cigarettes from my pocket and lit one for each of us, frowning. With my face averted and a hardness in my voice, I put this question in a casual manner:

Anything doing?

O God no, he said. Not at all, man. Come away for a talk somewhere.

I agreed. Purporting to be an immoral character, I accompanied him on a long walk through the environs of Irishtown, Sandymount and Sydney Parade, returning by Haddington Road and the banks of the canal.

Purpose of walk: Discovery and embracing of virgins.

We attained nothing on our walk that was relevant to the purpose thereof but we filled up the loneliness of our souls with the music of our two voices, dog-racing, betting and offences against chastity being the several subjects of our discourse. We walked many miles together on other nights on similar missions – following matrons, accosting strangers, representing to married ladies that we were their friends, and gratuitously molesting members of the public. One night we were followed in our turn by a member of the police force attired in civilian clothing. On the advice of Kelly we hid ourselves in the interior of a church until he had gone. I found that the walking was beneficial to my health.

The people who attended the College had banded themselves into many private associations, some purely cultural and some concerned with the arrangement and conduct of ball games. The cultural societies were diverse in their character and aims and measured their vitality by the number of hooligans and unprincipled persons they attracted to their deliberations. Some were devoted to English letters, some to Irish letters and some to the study and advancement of the French language. The most important was a body that met every Saturday night for the purpose of debate and disputation; its meetings, however, were availed of by many hundreds of students for shouting, horseplay, singing and the use of words, actions and gestures contrary to the usages of Christians. The society met in an old disused lecture theatre capable of accommodating the seats of about two hundred and fifty persons. Outside the theatre there was a spacious lobby or anteroom and it was here that the rough boys would gather and make their noises. One gas-jet was the means of affording light in the lobby and when a paroxysm of fighting and roaring would be at its height, the light would be extinguished as if by a supernatural or diabolic agency and the effect of the darkness in such circumstances afforded me many moments of physical and spiritual anxiety, for it seemed to me that the majority of the persons present were possessed by unclean spirits. The lighted rectangle of the doorway to the debate-hall was regarded by many persons not only as a receptacle for the foul and discordant speeches which they addressed to it, but also for many objects of a worthless nature – for example spent cigarette ends, old shoes, the hats of friends, parcels of damp horse dung, wads of soiled sacking and discarded articles of ladies' clothing not infrequently the worse for wear. Kelly on one occasion confined articles of his landlady's small-clothes in a neatly done parcel of brown paper and sent it through a friend to the visiting chairman, who opened it *coram populo* (in the presence of the assembly), and examined the articles fastidiously as if searching among them for an explanatory note, being unable to appraise their character instantaneously for two reasons, his failing sight and his station as a bachelor.

Result of overt act mentioned: Uproar and disorder.

When I attended these meetings I maintained a position where I was not personally identified, standing quietly without a word in the darkness. Conclusion of the foregoing.

Further extract from my Manuscript on the subject of Mr Trellis's Manuscript on the subject of John Furriskey, his first steps in life and

*his first meeting with those who were destined to become his firm friends;
the direct style:* He remarked to himself that it was a nice pass when
a man did not know the shape of his own face. His voice startled
him. It had the accent and intonation usually associated with the
Dublin lower or working classes.

He commenced to conduct an examination of the walls of
the room he was in with a view to discovering which of them
contained a door or other feasible means of egress. He had completed the examination of two of the walls when he experienced
an unpleasant sensation embracing blindness, hysteria and a
desire to vomit – the last a circumstance very complex and
difficult of explanation, for in the course of his life he had never
eaten. That this visitation was miraculous was soon evidenced
by the appearance of a supernatural cloud or aura resembling
steam in the vicinity of the fireplace. He dropped on one knee
in his weakness and gazed at the long gauze-like wisps of vapour
as they intermixed and thickened about the ceiling, his eyes
smarting and his pores opening as a result of the dampness. He
saw faces forming faintly and resolving again without perceptible
delay. He heard the measured beat of a good-quality timepiece
coming from the centre of the cloud and then the form of a
chamber-pot was evidenced to his gaze, hanging without support and invested with a pallid and indeed ghostly aspect; it was
slowly transformed as he watched it until it appeared to be the
castor of a bed-leg, magnified to roughly 118 diameters. A voice
came from the interior of the cloud.

Are you there, Furriskey? it asked.

Furriskey experienced the emotion of fear which distorted for
a time the character of his face. He also experienced a return of
his desire for enteric evacuation.

Yes sir, he answered.

Biographical reminiscence, part the fourth: The further obtrusion
of my personal affairs at this stage is unhappily not entirely fortuitous. It happens that a portion of my manuscript containing an
account (in the direct style) of the words that passed between
Furriskey and the voice is lost beyond retrieval. I recollect that
I abstracted it from the portfolio in which I kept my writings –
an article composed of two boards of stout cardboard connected
by a steel spine containing a patent spring mechanism – and

brought it with me one evening to the College in order that I might obtain the opinion of Brinsley as to its style and the propriety of the matters which were the subject of the discussion set out therein. In the many mental searches which I conducted subsequently in an effort to ascertain where the manuscript was mislaid in the first instance, I succeeded in recalling the circumstances of my meeting and dialogue with Brinsley with perfection of detail and event.

Attired in my grey street-coat, I entered the College in the early afternoon by the side-portal and encountered a group of four ladies in the passage to the main hall. I recall that I surmised that they were proceeding to an undergound cloakroom or lavatory for the purpose of handwash or other private act. A number of male students, the majority of whom were unacquainted with me, were present in the hall in the vicinity of the steam-heaters, conversing together in low tranquil tones. I inspected the features of each but could not identify the face of Brinsley. I saw, however, a man who I knew was acquainted with him, a Mr Kerrigan, a slim young man of moustached features usually attired in inexpensive clothing. He came forward quickly when he saw me and enunciated and answered an obscene conundrum. He then looked away and frowned, waiting intently for my laugh. I gave this without reluctance and asked where Mr Brinsley was. Kerrigan said that he had seen him going in the direction of the billiard-hall, he (Kerrigan) then walking away from me with a strange sidewise gait and saluting in a military fashion from the distance. The billiard-hall referred to was in the basement of the building and separated by a thin wall from another hall containing gentlemen's retiring rooms. I halted at the doorway of the billiard-hall. Fifty youths were present, some moving at the conduct of their games in the murk of the tobacco smoke, a hand or a face pallidly illuminated here or there in the strong floods of light which were pouring from green containers on the flat of the tables. The majority of those present had accommodated themselves in lazy attitudes on chairs and forms and occupied themselves in an indolent inspection of the balls. Brinsley was present, eating bread from a paper in his pocket and following the play of a small friend called Morris with close attention, making comments of a derisive or facetious character.

As I advanced, he hailed me, utilizing a gesture of the purpose.

He chewed thickly, pointing to the play. The craft of billiards was unfamiliar to me but in politeness I watched the quick darting of the balls, endeavouring to deduce from the results of a stroke the intentions which preceded it.

Gob, *there's* a kiss, said Brinsley.

Extract from Concise Oxford Dictionary: Kiss, n. Caress given with lips; (Billiards) impact between moving balls; kind of sugar plum.

Diverting his attention with difficulty from the affairs of the table, I persuaded him to peruse my manuscript, a matter of some nine pages. He read idly at first, subsequently with some attention. He then turned to me and praised me, commenting favourably on my literary talent.

This is the shield, he said.

The subject-matter of the dialogue in question was concerned (as may be inferred) with the turpitude and moral weakness of Mr Furriskey. It was pointed out to him by the voice that he was by vocation a voluptuary concerned only with the ravishing and destruction of the fair sex. His habits and physical attributes were explained to him in some detail. It was stated, for example, that his drinking capacity, speaking roughly and making allowance for discrepancies in strength as between the products of various houses, was six bottles of stout; and that any quantity taken in excess of such six bottles would not be retained. At the conclusion of the interview, the voice administered a number of stern warnings as to the penalties which would befall him should he deviate, even in the secrecy of his own thought, from his mission of debauchery. His life was to be devoted without distraction to the attainment of his empirical lusts. The talking then stopped and the steam-like cloud grew thinner and thinner and finally disappeared, the last wisps going quickly up the chimney as a result of the draught. Mr Furriskey then found that his blue clothing was slightly damp but as the cloud receded from the room, he found his strength returning to him; and after an interval of about eighteen minutes, he was sufficiently strong to continue his search for the door. He found it in the third wall he examined and it may be valuable to state – as an indication of the growing acuteness of his reasoning powers – that he neglected investigating one of the walls as a result of a deduction to the effect that the door of a room in the upper storey of a house is rarely to be found in the same wall which contains the window.

He opened the door and went out to the passage. He opened one of the many other doors which he found there and entered a room in which (scarcely by accident) he found Mr Paul Shanahan and Mr Antony Lamont, two men of his own social class who were destined to become his close friends. Strange to say, they were already acquainted with his name and his congenital addiction to the delights of the flesh. Mr Furriskey detected a faint odour of steam in this room also. He conversed with the two other men, rather diffidently at first but subsequently in an earnest sincere manner. Mr Shanahan introduced himself and Mr Lamont by name, explained their respective offices and duties and was kind enough to produce his costly fifteen-jewel hunter watch and permit Mr Furriskey to appraise the character of his countenance on the polish of its inner lid. This relieved Mr Furriskey of some anxiety and facilitated further conversation, which now turned on such subjects as politics foreign and domestic, the acceleration due to gravity, gunnery, parabolics and public health. Mr Lamont recounted an adventure which once befell him in a book when teaching French and piano-playing to a young girl of delicate and refined nature. Mr Shanahan, who was an older man and who had appeared in many of the well-known tales of Mr Tracy, then entertained his hearers with brief though racy account of his experiences as a cow-puncher in the Ringsend district of Dublin city.

Substance of reminiscence by Mr Shanahan, the comments of his hearers being embodied parenthetically in the text; with relevant excerpts from the public Press: Do you know what I am going to tell you, there was a rare life in Dublin in the old days. (There was certainly.) That was the day of the great O'Callaghan, the day of Baskin, the day of Tracy that brought cowboys to Ringsend. I knew them all, man.

Relevant excerpt from the Press: We regret to announce the passing of Mr William Tracy, the eminent novelist, which occurred yesterday under painful circumstances at his home in Grace Park Gardens. Early in the afternoon, deceased was knocked down in

Weavers' Square by a tandem cycle proceeding towards the city. He got up unaided, however, laughed heartily, treated the accident as a joke in the jolly way that was peculiarly his own and made his way home on a tram. When he had smoked six after-dinner pipes, he went to ascend the stairs and dropped dead on the landing. A man of culture and old-world courtesy, his passing will be regretted by all without distinction of creed or class and in particular by the world of letters, which he adorned with distinction for many years. He was the first man in Europe to exhibit twenty-nine lions in a cage at the same time and the only writer to demonstrate that cow-punching could be economically carried on in Ringsend. His best-known works were *Red Flanagan's Last Throw*, *Flower o' the Prairie*, and *Jake's Last Ride*. Deceased was fifty-nine. Conclusion of excerpt.

One day Tracy sent for me and gave me my orders and said it was one of his own cowboy books. Two days later I was cow-punching down by the river in Ringsend with Shorty Andrews and Slug Willard, the toughest pair of boyos you'd meet in a day's walk. Rounding up steers, you know, and branding, and breaking in colts in the corral with lassoes on our saddle-horns and pistols at our hips. (O the real thing. Was there any drink to be had?) There certainly was. At night we would gather in the bunkhouse with our porter and all our orders, cigarettes and plenty there on the chiffonier to be taken and no questions asked, school-marms and saloon-girls and little black maids skivvying there in the galley. (That was the place to be, now.) After a while be damned but in would walk a musicianer with a fiddle or a pipes in the hollow of his arm and there he would sit and play *Ave Maria* to bring the tears to your eyes. Then the boys would take up an old come-all-ye, the real old stuff, you know, *Phil the Fluter's Ball* or the *Darling Girl from Clare*, a bloody lovely thing. (That was very nice certainly.) O we had the right time of it. One morning Slug and Shorty and myself and a few of the boys got the wire to saddle and ride up to Drumcondra to see my nabs Mr Tracy to get our orders for the day. Up we went on our horses, cantering up Mountjoy Square with our hats tilted back on our heads and the sun in our eyes and our gun-butts swinging at our holsters. When we got the length, go to God but wasn't it a false alarm. (A false alarm! Lord save us! What brought that about now?) Wait till I tell you. Get back to hell, says Tracy,

I never sent any message. Get back to hell to your prairies, says he, you pack of lousers that can be taken in by any fly-be-night with a fine story. I'm telling you that we were small men when we took the trail again for home. When we got the length, be damned but wasn't the half of our steers rustled across the border in Irishtown by Red Kiersay's gang of thieving ruffians. (Well that was a kick for you where-you-know.) Certainly it was. Red Kiersay, you understand, was working for another man by the name of Henderson that was writing another book about cattle-dealers and jobbing and shipping bullocks to Liverpool. (Likely it was he sent you the false message?) Do you mind the cuteness of it? Get yourselves fed, says I to Shorty and Slug, we're goin' ridin' tonight. Where? says Slug. Right over to them thar rustlers' roost, says I, before Tracy finds out and skins us. Where's the nigger skivvies? says Shorty. Now go to God, says I, don't tell me they have taken the lot with them. (And had they?) Every one.

Relevant excerpt from the Press: An examination of the galley and servants' sleeping-quarters revealed no trace of the negro maids. They had been offered lucrative inducements to come from the United States and had at no time expressed themselves as being dissatisfied with their conditions of service. Detective-Officer Snodgrass found a pearl-handled shooting-iron under the pillow in the bed of Liza Roberts, the youngest of the maids. No great importance is attached by the police to this discovery, however, as ownership has been traced to Peter (Shorty) Andrews, a cow-boy, who states that though at a loss to explain the presence of his property in the maid's bed, it is possible that she appropriated the article in order to clean it in her spare time in bed (she was an industrious girl) or in order to play a joke. It is stated that the former explanation is the more likely of the two as there is no intercourse of a social character between the men and the scullery-maids. A number of minor clues have been found and an arrest is expected in the near future. Conclusion of excerpt.

I'm not what you call fussy when it comes to women but damn it all I draw the line when it comes to carrying off a bunch of black niggers – human beings, you must remember – and a couple of thousand steers, by God. So when the moon had raised her lamp o'er the prairie grasses, out flies the bunch of us, Slug,

Shorty and myself on a buckboard making like hell for Irishtown
with our ears back and the butts of our six-guns streaming out
behind us in the wind. (You were out to get your own?) We
were out to get our own. I tell you we were travelling in great
style. Shorty drew out and gave the horses an unmerciful skelp
across the where-you-know and away with us like the wind and
us roaring and cursing out of us like men that were lit with
whisky, our steel-studded holsters swaying at our hips and the
sheep-fur on our leg-chaps lying down like corn before a spring-
wind. Be damned to the lot of us, I roared, flaying the nags and
bashing the buckboard across the prairie, passing out lorries and
trams and sending poor so-and-so's on bicycles scuttling down
side-lanes with nothing showing but the whites of their eyes.
(By God you were travelling all right.) Certainly, going like the
hammers of hell. I smell cattle, says Slug and sure enough there
was the ranch of Red Kiersay the length of a turkey trot ahead
of us sitting on the moonlit prairie as peaceful as you please.

Relevant excerpt from the Press: The Circle N is reputed to be
the most venerable of Dublin's older ranches. The main building
is a gothic structure of red sandstone timbered in the Elizabethan
style and supported by corinthian pillars at the posterior. Added
as a lean-to at the south gable is the wooden bunk-house, one of
the most up to date of its kind in the country. It contains three
holster-racks, ten gas fires and a spacious dormitory fitted with
an ingenious apparatus worked by compressed air by which all
verminous beds can be fumigated instantaneously by the mere
pressing of a button, the operation occupying only the space
of forty seconds. The old Dublin custom of utilizing imported
negroid labour for operating the fine electrically equipped cooking-galley is still observed in this time-hallowed house. On the
land adjacent, grazing is available for 10,000 steers and 2,000
horses, thanks to the public spirit of Mr William Tracy, the indefatigable novelist, who had 8,912 dangerous houses demolished
in the environs of Irishtown and Sandymount to make the enterprise possible. Visitors can readily reach the ranch by taking the
Number 3 tram. The exquisitely laid out gardens of the ranch
are open for inspection on Thursdays and Fridays, the nominal
admission fee of one and sixpence being devoted to the cause of
the Jubilee Nurses' Fund. Conclusion of excerpt.

Down we got offa the buckboard to our hands and knees and up with us towards the doss-house on our bellies, our silver-mounted gun-butts jiggling at our hips, our eyes narrowed into slits and our jaws set and stern like be damned. (By God you weren't a party to meet on a dark night.) Don't make a sound. says I *viva voce* to the boys, or it's kiss my hand to taking these lousers by surprise. On we slithered with as much sound out of us as an eel in a barrel of tripes, right up to the bunkhouse on the flat of our three bellies. (Don't tell me you were seen?) Go to hell but a lad pulls a gun on us from behind and tells us to get on our feet and no delay or monkey-work. Be damned but wasn't it Red Kiersay himself; the so-and-so, standing there with an iron in each hand and a Lucifer leer on his beery face. What are you at, you swine, he asks in a real snotty voice. Don't come it, Kiersay, says I, we're here for our own and damn the bloody thing else. (You were in the right, of course. What was the upshot?) Come across, Kiersay, says I, come across with our steers and our black girls or down I go straight to Lad Lane and get the police up. Keep your hands up or I'll paste your guts on that tree, says he, you swine. You can't cow the like of us with your big gun, says Slug, and don't think it my boyo. (O trust Slug.) You dirty dog, says I between my teeth, you dirty swine you, Kiersay, you bastard. My God I was in the right temper and that's a fact. (You had good reason to be. If I was there I don't know what I'd do.) Well the upshot was that he gave us three minutes to go home and home we went like boys because Kiersay would think nothing of shooting the lights out of us and that's the God's truth. (You had a right to go for the police.) That's the very thing we done. Out we crept to the buggy and down Londonbridge Road and across the town to Lad Lane. It was good gas all right. The station sergeant was with us from the start and gave us over to the superintendent, a Clohessy from Tipp. Nothing would do him but give us a whole detachment of the D.M.P. to see fair play and justice done, and the fire-brigade there for the calling. (Well that was very decent of him now.) Do you know what it is, says Slug, Tracy is writing another book too and has a crowd of Red Indians up in the Phoenix Park, squaws and wigwams and warpaint an' all, the real stuff all right, believe me. A couple of bob to the right man there and the lot are ours for the asking, says he. Go to hell, says I, you don't tell me. As sure as God, says he. Right, says I, let yourself go for the Indians, let Shorty here go back for our own boys and let myself stop where I am with the police. Let the lot of us meet at Kiersay's at a quarter past eight. (Fair enough, fair enough.) Off went the two at a half-canter on the buckboard and the super and myself got stuck into a dozen stout in the back-room. After a while, the policemen were rounded up and marched across the prairies to the Circle N, as fine a body of men as you'd hope to see, myself and the super as proud as be damned at the head of them. (Well that was a sight to see.) When we got the length, there was Slug with his Red Indians, Shorty and his cowboys, the whole shooting gallery waiting for the word. The super and myself put our heads together and in no time we had everything arranged. In behind the buckboards and food wagons with the policemen and the cowboys to wait for the sweet foe. Away with the Red Indians around the ranch-house in circles, the braves galloping like red hell on their Arab ponies, screaming and shrieking and waving their bloody scalp-hatchets and firing flaming rods into the house from their little bows. (Boys-a-dear.) I'm telling you it was the business. The whole place was burning like billyo in no time and out came Red with a shot-gun in his hand and followed by his men, prepared if you please to make a last stand for king and country. The Indians got windy and flew back to us behind the buckboards and go to God if Red doesn't hold up a passing tram and take cover behind it, firing all the people out with a stream of dirty filthy language. (Well dirty language is a thing I don't like. He deserved all he got.) Lord save us but it was the right hard battle. I fired off my six bullets without stopping. A big sheet of plate-glass crashed from the tram to the roadway. Then with a terrible scutter of oaths, the boys began to get busy. We broke every pane of glass in that tram, raked the roadway with a death-dealing rain of six-gun shrapnel and took the tip off an enemy cowboy's ear, by God. In no time wasn't there a crowd around the battlefield and them cheering and calling and asking every man of us to do his duty. (O you'll always get those boys to gather. Sneeze in the street and they're all around you.) The bloody Indians started squealing at the back and slapping their horses on the belly, the policemen were firing off their six-guns and their batons in the air and Shorty and myself behind a sack of potatoes picking off the snipers like be damned. On raged the scrap for a half an hour, the lot of us giving back more than we got and never thinking of the terrible danger we were in, every man jack of us, loading and shooting off our pistols like divils from below. Be damned but the enemy was weakening. Now is your chance, says I to the super, now is your chance to lead your men over the top, says I, and capture the enemy's stronghold for good and all. Right you are, says he. Over the top with my brave bobbies, muttered oaths flying all over the place, as bold as brass with their batons in their hands. The crowd gave a big cheer and the Indians shrieked and flayed the bellies offa their horses with their hands. (Well did the dodge work?) Certainly. The battle was over before you could count your fingers and here were my brave men handcuffed hand and foot and marched down to Lad Lane like a bunch of orphans out for a Sunday walk. Did you get Red? says I to the super. Didn't see him at all at all, says he. As sure as God, says I, he's doing the Brian Boru in his bloody tent. (What, at the prayers?) Round I searched till I found the tent and here was my bold man inside on his two knees and him praying there for further orders. Where's our girls, Red, says I. Gone home, says he. Take yourself out of here, says he, and bring your steers with you, says he, can't you see I'm at my prayers. Do you mind the cuteness of it? I could do nothing, of course, him there in front of me on his two knees praying. There wasn't a thing left for me to do but go off again and choke down my rising dander. Come on away with me, says I to Slug and Shorty till we get our stolen steers. Next day didn't the super bring the enemy punchers up before the bench and got every man of them presented free with seven days' hard without option. Cool them down, says Slug.

Relevant excerpt from the Press: A number of men, stated to be labourers, were arraigned before Mr Lamphall in the District Court yesterday morning on charges of riotous assembly and malicious damage. Accused were described by Superintendent Clohessy as a gang of corner-boys whose horse-play in the streets was the curse of the Ringsend district. They were pests and public nuisances whose antics were not infrequently attended by damage to property. Complaints as to their conduct were frequently being received from residents in the area. On the occasion of the last escapade, two windows were broken in a tram-car the property of the Dublin United Tramway Company. Inspector Quin of the Company stated that the damage to the vehicle amounted to £2 11s. od. Remarking that no civilized community could tolerate organized hooliganism of this kind, the justice sentenced the accused to seven days' hard labour without the option of a fine, and hoped that it would be a lesson to them and to other playboys of the boulevards. Conclusion of excerpt.

Biographical reminiscence, part the fifth: The weather in the following March was cold, with snow and rain, and generally dangerous to persons of inferior vitality. I kept to the house as much as possible, reclining safe from ill and infection in the envelope of my bed. My uncle had taken to the studying of musical scores and endeavouring, by undertoned hummings, to make himself proficient in the vocal craft. Conducting researches in his bedroom one day in an attempt to find ciga-rettes, I came upon a policeman's hat of the papier-mâché type utilized by persons following the dramatic profession. A result of this departure in his habits was absence from the house on three nights a week and temporary indifference – amounting almost to unconcern – for my temporal and spiritual welfare. This I found convenient.

I recall that at the time of the loss of portion of my day-papers, I found myself one day speculating as to the gravity of the situa-tion which would arise if the entirety of my papers were lost in the same manner. My literary or spare-time compositions, written not infrequently with animation and enjoyment, I always found tedious of subsequent perusal. This sense of tedium is so deeply seated in the texture of my mind that I can rarely suffer myself to endure the pain of it. One result is that many of my shorter works, even those made the subject of extremely flatter-ing *encomia* on the part of friends and acquaintances, I have never myself read, nor does my indolent memory enable me to recall their contents with a satisfactory degree of accuracy. A hasty search for syntactical solecism was the most I could perform.

With regard to my present work, however, the forty pages which follow the lost portion were so vital to the operation of the ingenious plot which I had devised that I deemed it advisable to spend an April forenoon – a time of sun-glistening showers –

glancing through them in a critical if precipitate manner. This was fortunate for I found two things which caused me considerable consternation.

The first thing: An inexplicable chasm in the pagination, four pages of unascertained content being wanting.

The second thing: An unaccountable omission of one of the four improper assaults required by the ramification of the plot or argument, together with an absence of structural cohesion and a general feebleness of literary style.

I recall that these discoveries caused me concern for many days and were mainly the subjects turned over in my mind in the pauses which occurred in the casual day-to-day conversations which I conducted with my friends and acquaintances. Without seeking independent advice on the matter, I decided – foolishly perhaps – to delete the entire narrative and present in its place a brief résumé (or summary) of the events which it contained, a device frequently employed by newspapers to avoid the trouble and expense of reprinting past portions of their serial stories. The synopsis is as follows:

Synopsis, being a summary of what has gone before, FOR THE BENEFIT OF NEW READERS: DERMOT TRELLIS, an eccentric author, conceives the project of writing a salutary book on the consequences which follow wrong-doing and creates for the purpose

THE POOKA FERGUS MACPHELLIMEY, a species of human Irish devil endowed with magical powers. He then creates

JOHN FURRISKEY, a depraved character, whose task is to attack women and behave at all times in an indecent manner. By magic he is instructed by Trellis to go one night to Donnybrook where he will by arrangement meet and betray

PEGGY, a domestic servant. He meets her and is much surprised when she confides in him that Trellis has fallen asleep and that her virtue has already been assailed by an elderly man subsequently to be identified as

FINN MACCOOL, a legendary character hired by Trellis on account of the former's venerable appearance and experience, to act as the girl's father and chastise her for her transgressions against the moral law; and that her virtue has also been assailed by

PAUL SHANAHAN, another man hired by Trellis for performing various small and unimportant parts in the story, also for running messages, &c. &c. Peggy and Furriskey then have a long discussion on the roadside in which she explains to him that Trellis's powers are suspended when he falls asleep and that Finn and Shanahan were taking advantage of that fact when they came to see her because they would not dare to defy him when he is awake. Furriskey then inquires whether she yielded to them and she replies that indeed she did not. Furriskey then praises her and they discover after a short time that they have fallen in love with each other at first sight. They arrange to lead virtuous lives, to simulate the immoral actions, thoughts and words which Trellis demands of them on pain of the severest penalties. They also arrange that the first of them who shall be free shall wait for the other with a view to marriage at the earliest opportunity. Meanwhile Trellis, in order to show how an evil man can debase the highest and the lowest in the same story, creates a very beautiful and refined girl called

SHEILA LAMONT, whose brother,

ANTONY LAMONT he has already hired so that there will be somebody to demand satisfaction off John Furriskey for betraying her — all this being provided for in the plot. Trellis creates Miss Lamont in his own bedroom and he is so blinded by her beauty (which is naturally the type of beauty nearest to his heart), that he so far forgets himself as to assault her himself. Furriskey in the meantime returns to the Red Swan Hotel where Trellis lives and compels all those working for him to live also. He (Furriskey) is determined to pretend that he faithfully carried out the terrible mission he was sent on. Now read on.

Further extract from Manuscript. Oratio recta: With a key in his soft nervous hand, he opened the hall door and removed his shoes with two swift spells of crouching on the one leg. He crept up the stairs with the noiseless cat-tread of his good-quality woollen socks. The door of Trellis was dark and sleeping as he passed up the stairs to his room. There was a crack of light at Shanahan's door and he placed his shoes quietly on the floor and turned the handle.

The hard Furriskey, said Shanahan.

Here was Shanahan stretched at the fire, with Lamont on his left and the old greybeard seated beyond dimly on the bed with his stick between his knees and his old eyes staring far into the red fire like a man whose thought was in a distant part of the old world or maybe in another world altogether.

By God you weren't long, said Lamont.

Shut the door, said Shanahan, but see you're in the room before you do so. Shut the door and treat yourself to a chair, Mr F. You're quick off the mark all right. Move up there, Mr L.

It's not what you call a full-time occupation, said Furriskey in a weary way. It's not what you call a life sentence.

It is not, said Lamont. You're right there.

Now don't worry, said Shanahan in a pitying manner, there's plenty more coming. We'll keep you occupied now, don't you worry, won't we, Mr Lamont?

We'll see that he gets his bellyful, said Lamont.

You're decent fellows the pair of ye, said Furriskey.

He sat on a stool and extended his fan to the fire, the fan of his ten fingers.

You can get too much of them the same women, he said.

Is that a fact, said Shanahan in unbelief. Well I never heard that said before. Come here, Mr Furriskey, did you. . . .

O it was all right, I'll tell you sometime, said Furriskey.

Didn't I tell you it was all right? Didn't I?

You did, said Furriskey.

He took a sole cigarette from a small box.

I'll tell you the whole story sometime but not now, he said. He nodded towards the bed.

Is your man asleep or what?

Maybe he is, said Shanahan, but by God it didn't sound like it five minutes ago. Mr Storybook was wide awake.

He was wide awake, said Lamont.

Five minutes ago he was giving out a yarn the length of my arm, Shanahan. Right enough he is a terrible man for talk. Aren't you now? He'd talk the lot of us into the one grave if you gave him his head, don't ask me how I know, look at my grey hairs. Isn't that a fact, Mr Lamont?

For a man of his years, said Lamont slowly and authoritatively, he can do the talking. By God he can do the talking. He has seen more of the world than you or me, of course, that's the secret of it. That's true, said Furriskey, a happy fire-glow running about his body. He carefully directed the smoke of his cigarette towards the flames and up the chimney. Yes, he's an old man, of course.

His stories are not the worst though, I'll say that, said Lamont, there's always a head and a tail on his yarns, a beginning and an end, give him his due.

O I don't know, said Furriskey.

O he can talk, he can talk, I agree with you there, said Shanahan, credit where credit is due. But you'd want what you'd call a grain of *salo* with more than one of them if I know anything.

A pinch of salt? said Lamont.

A grain of *salo*, Mr L.

I don't doubt it, said Furriskey.

Relate, said hidden Conán, the tale of the Feasting of Dún na nGedh.

Finn in his mind was nestling with his people.

I mean to say, said Lamont, whether a yarn is tall or small I like to hear it well told. I like to meet a man that can take in hand to tell a story and not make a balls of it while he's at it. I like to know where I am, do you know. Everything has a beginning and an end.

It is true, said Finn, that I will not.

O that's right too, said Shanahan.

Relate them, said Conán, the account of the madness of King Sweeny and he on a madman's flight through the length of Erin.

That's a grand fire, said Furriskey, and if a man has that, he can't want a lot more. A fire, a bed, and a roof over his head, that's all. With a bite to eat, of course.

It's all very fine for you to talk, now, said Lamont, you had something for your tea tonight that the rest of us hadn't, eh, Mr Shanahan. Know what I mean?

Keep the fun clean, said Shanahan.

I beg, Mr Chairman, said Furriskey, to be associated with them sentiments. What's clean, keep it clean.

There was a concerted snigger, harmonious, scored for three voices.

I will relate, said Finn.

We're off again, said Furriskey.

The first matter that I will occupy with honey-words and melodious recital, said Finn, is the reason and the first cause for Sweeny's frenzy.

Draw in your chairs, boys, said Shanahan, we're right for the night. We're away on a hack.

Pray proceed, Sir, said Lamont.

Now Sweeny was King of Dal Araidhe and a man that was easily moved to the tides of anger. Near his house was the cave of a saint called Ronan – a shield against evil was this gentle generous friendly active man, who was out in the matin-hours taping out the wall-steads of a new sun-bright church and ringing his bell in the morning.

Good for telling, said Conán.

Now when Sweeny heard the clack of the clergyman's bell, his brain and his spleen and his gut were exercised by turn and together with the fever of a flaming anger. He made a great run out of the house without a cloth-stitch to the sheltering of his naked nudity, for he ran out of his cloak when his wife Eorann held it for restraint and deterrence, and he did not rest till he had snatched the beauteous light-lined psalter from the cleric and put it in the lake, at the bottom; after that he took the hard grip of the cleric's hand and ran with a wind-swift stride to the lake without a halting or a letting go of the hand because he had a mind to place the cleric by the side of his psalter in the lake, on the bottom, to speak precisely. But, evil destiny, he was deterred by the big storm-voiced hoarse shout, the shout of a scullion calling him to the profession of arms at the battle of Magh Rath. Sweeny then left the cleric sad and sorrowful over the godless battery of the king and lamenting his psalter. This, however, an otter from the murk of the lake returned to him unharmed, its lines and its letters unblemished. He then returned with joyous piety to his devotions and put a malediction on Sweeny by the uttering of a lay of eleven melodious stanzas.

Thereafter he went himself with his acolytes to the plain of Magh Rath for the weaving of concord and peace between the hosts and was himself taken as a holy pledge, the person of the cleric, that fighting should cease at sundown and that no man should be slain until fighting would be again permitted, the person of the cleric a holy hostage and exchange between the hosts. But, evil destiny, Sweeny was used to violating the guarantee by the slaughter of a man every morning before the hour when fighting was permitted. On the morning of a certain day, Ronan and his eight psalmists were walking in the field and sprinkling holy water on the hosts against the incidence of hurt of evil when they sprinkled the head of Sweeny with the rest. Sweeny in anger took a cast and reddened his spear in the white side of a psalmist and broke Ronan's bell whereupon the cleric uttered this melodious lay:

> My curse on Sweeny!
> His guilt against me is immense,
> he pierced with his long swift javelin
> my holy bell.
>
> The holy bell that thou hast outraged
> will banish thee to branches,
> it will put thee on a par with fowls –
> the saint-bell of saints with sainty-saints.
>
> Just as it went prestissimo
> the spear-shaft skyward,
> you too, Sweeny, go madly mad-gone
> skyward.
>
> Eorann of Conn tried to hold him
> by a hold of his smock
> and though I bless her therefore,
> my curse on Sweeny.

Thereafter when the hosts clashed and bellowed like stag-herds and gave three audible world-wide shouts till Sweeny heard them and their hollow reverberations in the sky-vault, he was beleaguered by an anger and a darkness, and fury and fits and frenzy and fright-fraught fear, and he was filled with a restless tottering unquiet and with a disgust for the places that he knew and with a desire to be where he never was, so that he was palsied of hand and foot and eye-mad and heart-quick and went from the curse of Ronan bird-quick in craze and madness from the battle. For the nimble lightness of his tread in flight he did not shake dewdrops from the grass-stalks and staying not for bog

or thicket or marsh or hollow or thick-sheltering wood in Erin
for that day, he travelled till he reached Ros Bearaigh in Glenn
Earcain where he went into the yew-tree that was in the glen.

In a later hour his kin came to halt beneath the tree for a spell
of discourse and melodious talk about Sweeny and no tidings
concerning him either in the east or the west; and Sweeny in the
yew-tree above them listened till he made answer in this lay:

> O warriors approach,
> warriors of Dal Araidhe,
> you will find him in the tree he is
> the man you seek.

> God has given me life here,
> very bare, very narrow,
> no woman, no trysting,
> no music or trance-eyed sleep.

When they noticed the verses from the tree-top they saw
Sweeny in branches and then they talked their honey-words,
beseeching him that he should be trustful, and then made a ring
around the tree-bole. But Sweeny arose nimbly and away to Cell
Riagain in Tir Conaill where he perched in the old tree of the
church, going and coming between branches and the rain-clouds
of the skies, trespassing and wayfaring over peaks and summits
and across the ridge-poles of black hills, and visiting in dark
mountains, ruminating and searching in cavities and narrow
crags and slag-slits in rocky hidings, and lodging in the clump of
tall ivies and in the cracks of hill-stones, a year of time from
summit to summit and from glen to glen and from river-mouth
to river till he arrived at ever-delightful Glen Bolcain. For it is
thus that Glen Bolcain is, it has four gaps to the four winds and
a too-fine too-pleasant wood and fresh-banked wells and cold-
clean fountains and sandy pellucid streams of clear water with
green-topped watercress and brooklime long-streamed on the
current, and a richness of sorrels and wood-sorrels, *lus-bian* and
biorragan and berries and wild garlic, *melle* and *miodhbhun*, inky
sloes and dun acorns. For it was here that the madmen of Erin
were used to come when their year of madness was complete,

smiting and lamming each other for choice of its watercress and in rivalry for its fine couches.

In that glen it was hard for Sweeny to endure the pain of his bed there on the top of a tall ivy-grown hawthorn in the glen, every twist that he would turn sending showers of hawy thorns into his flesh, tearing and rending and piercing him and pricking his blood-red skin. He thereupon changed beds to the resting of another tree where there were tangles of thick fine-thorned briars and a solitary branch of blackthorn growing up through the core of the brambles. He settled and roosted on its slender perch till it bowed beneath him and bent till it slammed him to the ground, not one inch of him from toe to crown that was not red-prickled and blood-gashed, the skin to his body being ragged and flapping and thorned, the tattered cloak of his perished skin. He arose death-weak from the ground to his standing for the recital of this lay.

> A year to last night
> I have lodged there in branches
> from the flood-tide to the ebb-tide
> naked.
>
> Bereft of fine women-folk,
> the brooklime for a brother –
> our choice for a fresh meal
> is watercress always.
>
> Without accomplished musicians
> without generous women,
> no jewel-gift for bards –
> respected Christ, it has perished me.
>
> The thorntop that is not gentle
> has reduced me, has pierced me,
> it has brought me near death
> the brown thorn-bush.
>
> Once free, once gentle,
> I am banished for ever,
> wretch-wretched I have been
> a year to last night.

He remained there in Glen Bolcain until he elevated himself high in the air and went to Cluain Cille on the border of Tir Conaill and Tir Boghaine. He went to the edge of the water and took food against the night, watercress and water. After that he went into the old tree of the church where he said another melodious poem on the subject of his personal hardship.

After another time he set forth in the air again till he reached the church at Snámh-dá-én (or Swim-Two-Birds) by the side of the Shannon, arriving there on a Friday, to speak precisely; here the clerics were engaged at the observation of their nones, flax was being beaten and here and there a woman was giving birth to a child; and Sweeny did not stop until he had recited the full length of a further lay.

For seven years, to relate precisely, was Sweeny at the air travel of all Erin, returning always to his tree in charming Glen Bolcain, for that was his fortress and his haven, it was his house there in the glen. It was to this place that his foster-brother Linchehaun came for tidings concerning him, for he carried always a deep affection for Sweeny and had retrieved him three times from madness before that. Linchehaun went seeking him in the glen with shouts and found toe-tracks by the stream-mud where the madman was wont to appease himself by the eating of cresses. But track or trace of Sweeny he did not attain for that day and he sat down in an old deserted house in the glen till the labour and weariness of his pursuit brought about his sleep. And Sweeny, hearing his snore from his tree-clump in the glen, uttered this lay in the pitch darkness.

> The man by the wall snores
> a snore-sleep that's beyond me,
> for seven years from that Tuesday at Magh Rath
> I have not slept a wink.
>
> O God that I had not gone
> to the hard battle!
> thereafter my name was Mad –
> Mad Sweeny in the bush.
>
> Watercress from the well at Cirb
> is my lot at terce,

its colour is my mouth,
green on the mouth of Sweeny.

Chill chill is my body
when away from ivy,
the rain torrent hurts it
and the thunder.

I am in summer with the herons of Cuailgne
with wolves in winter,
at other times I am hidden in a copse –
not so the man by the wall.

And thereafter he met Linchehaun who came visiting to his
tree and they parleyed there the two of them together and the
one of them talkative and unseen in branches and prickle-briars.
And Sweeny bade Linchehaun to depart and not to pursue or
annoy him further because the curse of Ronan stopped him from
putting his trust or his mad faith in any man.

Thereafter he travelled in distant places till he came at the
black fall of a night to Ros Bearaigh and lodged himself in a
hunched huddle in the middle of the yew-tree of the church in
that place. But being besieged with nets and hog-harried by the
caretaker of the church and his false wife, he hurried nimbly
to the old tree at Ros Eareain where he remained hidden and
unnoticed the length of a full fortnight, till the time when Linchehaun came and perceived the murk of his shadow in the
sparse branches and saw the other branches he had broken and
bent in his movements and in changing trees. And the two of
them parleyed together until they had said between them these
fine words following.

Sad it is Sweeny, said Linchehaun, that your last extremity
should be thus, without food or drink or raiment like a fowl, the
same man that had cloth of silk and of satin and the foreign steed
of the peerless bridle, also comely generous women and boys
and hounds and princely people of every refinement; hosts and
tenants and men-at-arms, and mugs and goblets and embellished
buffalo-horns for the savouring of pleasant-tasted fine liquors.
Sad it is to see the same man as a hapless air-fowl.

Cease now, Linchehaun, said Sweeny, and give me tidings.

Your father is dead, said Linchehaun.

That has seized me with a blind agony, said Sweeny.

Your mother is likewise dead.

Now all the pity in me is at an end.

Dead is your brother.

Gaping open is my side on account of that.

She has died too your sister.

A needle for the heart is an only sister.

Ah, dumb dead is the little son that called you pop.

Truly, said Sweeny, that is the last blow that brings a man to the ground.

When Sweeny heard the sorry word of his small son still and without life, he fell with a crap from the middle of the yew to the ground and Linchehaun hastened to his thorn-packed flank with fetters and handcuffs and manacles and locks and black-iron chains and he did not achieve a resting until the lot were about the madman, and through him and above him and over him, roundwise and about. Thereafter there was a concourse of hospitallers and knights and warriors around the trunk of the yew, and after melodious talk they entrusted the mad one to the care of Linchehaun till he would take him away to a quiet place for a fortnight and a month, to the quiet of a certain room where his senses returned to him, the one after the other, with no one near him but the old mill-hag.

O hag, said Sweeny, searing are the tribulations I have suffered; many a terrible leap have I leaped from hill to hill, from fort to fort, from land to land, from valley to valley.

For the sake of God, said the hag, leap for us now a leap such as you leaped in the days of your madness.

And thereupon Sweeny gave a bound over the top of the bedrail till he reached the extremity of the bench.

My conscience indeed, said the hag, I could leap the same leap myself.

And the hag gave a like jump.

Sweeny then gathered himself together in the extremity of his jealousy and threw a leap right out through the skylight of the hostel.

I could vault that vault too, said the hag and straightway she vaulted the same vault. And the short of it is this, that Sweeny travelled the length of five cantreds of leaps until he had penetrated

to Glenn na nEachtach in Fiodh Gaibhle with the hag at her
hag's leaps behind him; and when Sweeny rested there in a
huddle at the top of a tall ivy-branch, the hag was perched there
on another tree beside him. He heard there the voice of a stag
and he thereupon made a lay eulogizing aloud the trees and the
stags of Erin, and he did not cease or sleep until he had achieved
these staves.

Bleating one, little antlers,
O lamenter we like
delightful the clamouring
from your glen you make.

O leafy-oak, clumpy-leaved,
you are high above trees,
O hazlet, little clumpy-branch –
the nut-smell of hazels.

O alder, O alder-friend,
delightful your colour,
you don't prickle me or tear
in the place you are.

O blackthorn, little thorny-one,
O little dark sloe-tree;
O watercress, O green-crowned,
at the well-brink.

O holly, holly-shelter,
O door against the wind,
O ash-tree inimical,
your spearshaft of warrior.

O birch clean and blessed,
O melodious, O proud,
delightful the tangle
of your head-rods.

What I like least in woodlands
from none I conceal it –

stirk of a leafy-oak,
at its swaying.

O faun, little long-legs,
I caught you with grips,
I rode you upon your back
from peak to peak.

Glen Bolcain my home ever,
it was my haven,
many a night have I tried
a race against the peak.

I beg your pardon for interrupting, said Shanahan, but you're after reminding me of something, brought the thing into my head in a rush.

He swallowed a draught of vesper-milk, restoring the cloudy glass swiftly to his knee and collecting little belated flavourings from the corners of his mouth.

That thing you were saying reminds me of something bloody good. I beg your pardon for interrupting, Mr Storybook.

In the yesterday, said Finn, the man who mixed his utterance with the honeywords of Finn was the first day put naked into the tree of Coill Boirche with nothing to his bare hand but a stick of hazel. On the morning of the second day thereafter...

Now listen for a minute till I tell you something, said Shanahan, did any man here ever hear of the poet Casey?

Who did you say? said Furriskey.

Casey. Jem Casey.

On the morning of the second day thereafter, he was taken and bound and rammed as regards his head into a black hole so that his white body was upside down and upright in Erin for the gazing thereon of man and beast.

Now give us a chance, Mister Storybook, yourself and your black hole, said Shanahan fingering his tie-knot with a long memory-frown across his brow. Come here for a minute. Come here till I tell you about Casey. Do you mean to tell me you never heard of the poet Casey, Mr Furriskey?

Never heard of him, said Furriskey in a solicitous manner.

I can't say, said Lamont, that I ever heard of him either.

He was a poet of the people, said Shanahan.

I see, said Furriskey.

Now do you understand, said Shanahan. A plain upstanding labouring man, Mr Furriskey, the same as you or me. A black hat or a bloody ribbon, no by God, not on Jem Casey. A hard-working well-made block of a working man, Mr Lamont, with the handle of a pick in his hand like the rest of us. Now say there was a crowd of men with a ganger all working there laying a length of gas-pipe on the road. All right. The men pull off their coats and start shovelling and working there for further orders. Here at one end of the hole you have your men crowded up together in a lump and them working away and smoking their butts and talking about the horses and one thing and another. Now do you understand what I'm telling you. Do you follow me?

I see that.

But take a look at the other end of the hole and here is my brave Casey digging away there on his own. Do you understand what I mean, Mr Furriskey?

Oh I see it all right, said Furriskey.

Right. None of your horses or your bloody blather for him. Not a bit of it. Here is my nabs saying nothing to nobody but working away at a pome in his head with a pick in his hand and the sweat pouring down off his face from the force of his work and his bloody exertions. That's a quare one!

Do you mind that now, said Lamont.

It's a quare one and one that takes a lot of beating. Not a word to nobody, not a look to left or right but the brain-box going there all the time. Just Jem Casey, a poor ignorant labouring man but head and shoulders above the whole bloody lot of them, not a man in the whole country to beat him when it comes to getting together a bloody pome – not a poet in the whole world that could hold a candle to Jem Casey, not a man of them fit to stand beside him. By God I'd back him to win by a canter against the whole bloody lot of them, give him his due.

Is that a fact, Mr Shanahan, said Lamont. It's not every day in the week you come across a man like that.

Do you know what I'm going to tell you, Mr Lamont, he was a man that could give the lot of them a good start, pickaxe and all. He was a man that could meet them . . . and meet the best . . . and beat them at their own game, now I'm telling you.

I suppose he could, said Furriskey.

Now I know what I'm talking about. Give a man his due. If a man's station is high or low he is all the same to the God I know. Take the bloody black hats off the whole bunch of them and where are you?

That's the way to look at it, of course, said Furriskey.

Give them a bloody pick, I mean, Mr Furriskey, give them the shaft of a shovel into their hand and tell them to dig a hole and have the length of a page of poetry off by heart in their heads before the five o'clock whistle. What will you get? By God you could take off your hat to what you'd get at five o'clock from that crowd and that's a sure sharkey.

You'd be wasting your time if you waited till five o'clock if you ask me, said Furriskey with a nod of complete agreement.

You're right there, said Shanahan, you'd be waiting around for bloody nothing. Oh I know them and I know my hard Casey too. By Janey he'd be up at the whistle with a pome a yard long, a bloody lovely thing that would send my nice men home in a hurry, home with their bloody tails between their legs. Yes, I've seen his pomes and read them and . . . do you know what I'm going to tell you, I have loved them. I'm not ashamed to sit here and say it, Mr Furriskey. I've known the man and I've known his pomes and by God I have loved the two of them and loved them well, too. Do you understand what I'm saying, Mr Lamont? You, Mr Furriskey?

Oh that's right.

Do you know what it is, I've met the others, the whole lot of them. I've met them all and know them all. I have seen them and I have read their pomes. I have heard them recited by men that know how to use their tongues, men that couldn't be beaten at their own game. I have seen whole books filled up with their stuff, books as thick as that table there and I'm telling you no lie. But by God, at the heel of the hunt, there was only one poet for me.

On the morning of the third day thereafter, said Finn, he was flogged until he bled water.

Only the one, Mr Shanahan? said Lamont.

Only the one. And that one poet was a man . . . by the name . . . of Jem Casey. No 'Sir', no 'Mister', no nothing. Jem Casey, Poet of the Pick, that's all. A labouring man, Mr Lamont, but

as sweet a singer in his own way as you'll find in the bloody
trees there of a spring day, and that's a fact. Jem Casey, an
ignorant God-fearing upstanding labouring man, a bloody
navvy. Do you know what I'm going to tell you, I don't believe
he ever lifted the latch of a school door. Would you believe
that now?

I'd believe it of Casey, said Furriskey, and

I'd believe plenty more of the same man, said Lamont. You
haven't any of his pomes on you, have you, Mr Shanahan?

Now take that stuff your man was giving us a while ago, said
Shanahan without heed, about the green hills and the bloody
swords and the bird giving out the pay from the top of the tree.
Now that's good stuff, it's bloody nice. Do you know what it is,
I liked it and liked it well. I enjoyed that certainly.

It wasn't bad at all, said Furriskey, I have heard worse, by God,
often. It was all right now.

Do you see what I'm getting at, do you understand me, said
Shanahan. It's good, very good. But by Christopher it's not every
man could see it, I'm bloody sure of that, one in a thousand.

Oh that's right too, said Lamont.

You can't beat it, of course, said Shanahan with a reddening
of the features, the real old stuff of the native land, you know,
stuff that brought scholars to our shore when your men on the
other side were on the flat of their bellies before the calf of
gold with a sheepskin around their man. It's the stuff that put
our country where she stands today, Mr Furriskey, and I'd have
my tongue out of my head by the bloody roots before I'd be
heard saying a word against it. But the man in the street, where
does he come in? By God he doesn't come in at all as far as
I can see.

What do my brave men in the black hats care whether he's in
or out, asked Furriskey. What do they care? It's a short jump
for the man in the street, I'm thinking, if he's waiting for that
crowd to do anything for him. They're a nice crowd, now, I'm
telling you.

Oh that's the truth, said Lamont.

Another thing, said Shanahan, you can get too much of that
stuff. Feed yourself up with that tack once and you won't want
more for a long time.

There's no doubt about it, said Furriskey.

Try it once, said Shanahan, and you won't want it a second time.

Do you know what it is, said Lamont, there are people who read that . . . and keep reading it . . . and read damn the bloody thing else. Now that's a mistake.

A big mistake, said Furriskey.

But there's one man, said Shanahan, there's one man that can write pomes that you can read all day and all night and keep reading them to your heart's content, stuff you'd never tire of. Pomes written by a man that is one of ourselves and written down for ourselves to read. The name of that man . . .

Now that's what you want, said Furriskey.

The name of that man, said Shanahan, is a name that could be christianed on you or me, a name that won't shame us. And that name, said Shanahan, is Jem Casey.

And a very good man, said Lamont.

Jem Casey, said Furriskey.

Do you understand what I mean, said Shanahan.

You haven't any of his pomes on you, have you, said Lamont. If there's one thing I'd like . . .

I haven't one *on* me if that's what you mean, Mr Lamont, said Shanahan, but I could give one out as quick as I'd say my prayers. By God it's not for nothing that I call myself a pal of Jem Casey.

I'm glad to hear it, said Lamont.

Stand up there and recite it man, said Furriskey, don't keep us waiting. What's the name of it now?

The name or title of the pome I am about to recite, gentlemen, said Shanahan with leisure priest-like in character, is a pome by the name of the 'Workman's Friend'. By God you can't beat it. I've heard it praised by the highest. It's a pome about a thing that's known to all of us. It's about a drink of porter.

Porter!

Porter.

Up on your legs man, said Furriskey. Mr Lamont and myself are waiting and listening. Up you get now.

Come on, off you go, said Lamont.

Now listen, said Shanahan clearing the way with small coughs. Listen now.

He arose holding out his hand and bending his knee beneath him on the chair.

When things go wrong and will not come right,
Though you do the best you can,
When life looks black as the hour of night –
A PINT OF PLAIN IS YOUR ONLY MAN.

By God there's a lilt in that, said Lamont.
Very good indeed, said Furriskey. Very nice.
I'm telling you it's the business, said Shanahan. Listen now.

When money's tight and is hard to get
And your horse has also ran,
When all you have is a heap of debt –
A PINT OF PLAIN IS YOUR ONLY MAN.

When health is bad and your heart feels strange,
And your face is pale and wan,
When doctors say that you need a change,
A PINT OF PLAIN IS YOUR ONLY MAN.

There are things in that pome that make for what you call *permanence*. Do you know what I mean, Mr Furriskey?

There's no doubt about it, it's a grand thing, said Furriskey. Come on, Mr Shanahan, give us another verse. Don't tell me that is the end of it.

Can't you listen? said Shanahan.

When food is scarce and your larder bare
And no rashers grease your pan,
When hunger grows as your meals are rare –
A PINT OF PLAIN IS YOUR ONLY MAN.

What do you think of that now?

It's a pome that'll live, called Lamont, a pome that'll be heard and clapped when plenty more . . .

But wait till you hear the last verse, man, the last polish-off, said Shanahan. He frowned and waved his hand.

Oh it's good, it's good, said Furriskey.

In time of trouble and lousy strife,
You have still got a darlint plan,

You still can turn to a brighter life –
A PINT OF PLAIN IS YOUR ONLY MAN.

Did you ever hear anything like it in your life, said Furriskey.
A pint of plain, by God, what! Oh I'm telling you, Casey was a
man in twenty thousand, there's no doubt about that. He knew
what he was at, too true he did. If he knew nothing else, he
knew how to write a pome. A pint of plain is your only man.

Didn't I tell you he was good? said Shanahan. Oh by Gorrah
you can't cod me.

There's one thing in that pome, *permanence*, if you know what
I mean. That pome, I mean to say, is a pome that'll be heard
wherever the Irish race is wont to gather, it'll live as long as
there's a hard root of an Irishman left by the Almighty on this
planet, mark my words. What do you think, Mr Shanahan?

It'll live, Mr Lamont, it'll live.

I'm bloody sure it will, said Lamont.

A pint of plain, by God, eh? said Furriskey.

Tell us, my Old Timer, said Lamont benignly, what do you
think of it? Give the company the benefit of your scholarly perti-
nacious fastidious opinion, Sir Storybook. Eh, Mr Shanahan?

Conspirators' eyes were winked smartly in the dancing fire-
light, Furriskey rapped Finn about the knees.

Wake up!

And Sweeny continued, said corn-yellow Finn, at the recital
of these staves.

> If I were to search alone
> the hills of the brown world,
> better would I like my sole hut
> in Glen Bolcain.
>
> Good its water greenish-green
> good its clean strong wind,
> good its cress-green cresses,
> best its branching brooklime.

Quick march again, said Lamont. It'll be a good man that'll
put a stop to that man's tongue. More of your fancy kiss-my-
hand by God.

Let him talk, said Furriskey, it'll do him good. It has to come out somewhere.

I'm a man, said Shanahan in a sententious fashion, that could always listen to what my fellowman has to say. I'm telling you now, it's a wise man that listens and says nothing.

Certainly said Lamont. A wise old owl once lived in a wood, the more he heard the less he said, the less he said the more he heard, let's emulate that wise old bird.

There's a lot in that, said Furriskey. A little less of the talk and we were right.

Finn continued with a patient weariness, speaking slowly to the fire and to the six suppliant shoes that were in devotion around it, the voice of the old man from the dim bed.

> Good its sturdy ivies,
> good its bright neat sallow,
> good its yewy yew-yews,
> best its sweet-noise birch.
>
> A haughty ivy
> growing through a twisted tree,
> myself on its true summit,
> I would lothe leave it.
>
> I flee before skylarks,
> it is the tense stern-race,
> I overleap the clumps
> on the high hill-peaks.
>
> When it rises in front of me
> the proud turtle-dove,
> I overtake it swiftly
> since my plumage grew.
>
> The stupid unwitting woodcock
> when it rises up before me,
> methinks it red-hostile,
> and the blackbird that cries havoc.
>
> Small foxes yelping
> to me and from me,

the wolves tear them –
I flee their cries.

They journeyed in their chase of me
in their swift courses
so that I flew away from them
to the tops of mountains.

On every pool there will rain
a starry frost;
I am wretched and wandering
under it on the peak.

The herons are calling
in cold Glen Eila
swift-flying flocks are flying,
coming and going.

I do not relish
the mad clack of humans
sweeter warble of the bird
in the place he is.

I like not the trumpeting
heard at morn;
sweeter hearing is the squeal
of badgers in Benna Broc.

I do not like it
the loud bugling;
finer is the stagbelling stag
of antler-points twice twenty.

There are makings for plough-teams
from glen to glen;
each resting-stag at rest
on the summit of the peaks.

Excuse me for a second, interposed Shanahan in an urgent
manner. I've got a verse in my head. Wait now.
What!

Listen, man. Listen to this before it's lost. When stags appear on the mountain high, with flanks the colour of bran, when a badger bold can say good-bye, A PINT OF PLAIN IS YOUR ONLY MAN!

Well by God, Shanahan, I never thought you had it in you, said Furriskey, turning his wide-eyed smile to the smile of Lamont, I never thought you had it in you. Take a look at the bloody poet, Mr Lamont. What?

The hard Shanahan by God, said Lamont. The hard man. That's a good one all right. Put it there, Mr Shanahan.

Hands were extended till they met, the generous grip of friendship in front of the fire.

All right, said Shanahan laughing in the manner of a proud peacock, don't shake the handle off me altogether. Gentlemen, you flatter me. Order ten pints a man till we celebrate.

My hard bloody Shanahan, said Lamont.

That'll do you now the pair of ye, said Shanahan. Silence in the court now.

The droning from the bed restarted where it stopped.

> The stag of steep Slieve Eibhlinne,
> the stag of sharp Slieve Fuaid,
> the stag of Eala, the stag of Orrery,
> the mad stag of Loch Lein.

> Stag of Shevna, stag of Larne,
> the stag of Leena of the panoplies
> stag of Cualna, stag of Conachail,
> the stag of two-peaked Bairenn.

> Oh mother of this herd,
> thy coat has greyed,
> no stag is following after thee
> without twice twenty points.

> Greater-than-the-material-for-a-little-cloak,
> thy head has greyed;
> if I were on each little point
> littler points would there be on every pointed point.

The stag that marches trumpeting
across the glen to me,
pleasant the place for seats
on his antler top.

After that song, the long one, Sweeny came from Fiodh
Gaibhle to Benn Boghaine, from there to Benn Faibhne and
thence to Rath Murbuilg, attaining no refuge from the attention
of the hag till he came to Dun Sobhairce in Ulster. Here he went
before the hag and threw a leap from the precise summit of the
dun. She followed him in swift course and dropped on the pre-
cipice of Dun Sobhairce till fine-pulp and small-bits were made
of her, falling lastly into the sea, so that it was thus that she found
death in her chase of Sweeny.

He then travelled and tarried in many places for a month and
a fortnight, on smooth clean delightful hills and on delicate chill-
breezed peaks for a fortnight and a month, making his abode in
the hiding of tree-clumps. And in leaving Carrick Alaisdar, he
delayed there till he had fashioned these staves as a farewell
address, a valediction on the subject of his manifold sorrow.

Cheerless is existence
without a downy bed,
abode of the shrivelling frost,
gusts of the snowy wind.

Chill icy wind,
shadow of a feeble sun
the shelter of a sole tree
on a mountain-plain.

The bell-belling of the stag
through the woodland,
the climb to the deer-pass,
the voice of white seas.

Forgive me Oh Great Lord,
mortal is this great sorrow,
worse than the black grief –
Sweeny the thin-groined.

Carraig Alasdair
resort of sea-gulls,
sad Oh Creator,
chilly for its guests.

Sad our meeting
two hard-shanked cranes –
myself hard and ragged
she hard-beaked.

Thereafter Sweeny departed and fared till he had crossed the encompassing gullet of the storm-wracked sea till he reached the kingdom of the Britons and fell in with another of a like frenzy, a madman of Briton.

If you are a madman, said Sweeny, tell me your family name.

Fer Caille is my name, he answered.

And the pair of them made a peace and a compact together, talking with each other in a lay of generous staves.

Oh Sweeny, said Fer Caille, let the each watch the other since we love and trust in each; that is, he who shall first hear the cry of a heron from the blue-watered green-watered water, or the clear call of a cormorant, or leap of a woodcock from a tree, the note or the sound of a waking plover, or the crack-crackle of withered branches, or he who shall first see the shadow of a bird in the air above the wood, let him call warning and tell the other, so that the two of us can fly away quickly.

At the butt-end of a year's wandering in the company of each other, the madman of Briton had a message for Sweeny's ear.

It is true that we must part today, he said, for the end of my life has come and I must go to where I am to die.

What class of a death will you die? asked Sweeny.

Not difficult to relate, said the other. I go now to Eas Dubhthaigh and a gust of wind will get under me until it slams me into the waterfall for drowning, and I shall be interred in the churchyard of a saint, and afterwards I shall attain Heaven. That is my end.

Thereafter, on the recital of valedictory staves, Sweeny fared again in the upper air on his path across sky-fear and rain-squalls to Erin, dwelling here and there in the high places and in the low nestling in the heart of enduring oaks, never restful till he had again attained ever-delightful Glen Bolcain. There he encountered a demented woman till he fled before her, rising stealthily nimbly lightly from the summit of the peaks till he reached Glen Boirche in the south and committed himself to these ranns.

Chill chill is my bed at dark
on the peak of Glen Boirche,
I am weakly, no mantle on me,
lodged in a sharp-stirked holly.

Glen Bolcain of the twinkle spring
it is my rest-place to abide in;
when Samhain comes, when summer comes,
it is my rest-place where I abide.

For my sustenance at night,
the whole that my hands can glean
from the gloom of the oak-gloomed oaks –
the herbs and the plenteous fruits.

Fine hazel-nuts and apples, berries,
blackberries and oak-tree acorns,
generous raspberries, they are my due,
haws of the prickle-hawy hawthorn.

Wild sorrels, wild garlic faultless,
clean-topped cress,
they expel from me my hunger,
acorns from the mountain, melle-root.

After a prolonged travel and a searching in the skies, Sweeny arrived at nightfall at the shore of the widespread Loch Ree, his resting-place being the fork of the tree of Tiobradan for that night. It snowed on his tree that night, the snow being the worst of all the other snows he had endured since the feathers grew on his body, and he was constrained to the recital of these following verses.

Terrible is my plight this night
the pure air has pierced my body,
lacerated feet, my cheek is green –
O Mighty God, it is my due.

It is bad living without a house,
Peerless Christ, it is a piteous life!
a filling of green-tufted fine cresses
a drink of cold water from a clear rill.

Stumbling out of the withered tree-tops
walking the furze – it is truth –
wolves for company, man-shunning,
running with the red stag through fields.

If the evil hag had not invoked Christ against me that I should
perform leaps for her amusement, I would not have relapsed into
madness, said Sweeny.

Come here, said Lamont, what's this about jumps?

Hopping around, you know, said Furriskey.

The story, said learned Shanahan in a learned explanatory
manner, is about this fellow Sweeny that argued the toss with
the clergy and came off second-best at the wind-up. There was
a curse – a malediction – put down in the book against him. The
upshot is that your man becomes a bloody bird.

I see, said Lamont.

Do you see it, Mr Furriskey, said Shanahan. What happens?
He is changed into a bird for his pains and he could go from here
to Carlow in one hop. Do you see it, Mr Lamont?

Oh I see that much all right, said Lamont, but the man that
I'm thinking of is a man by the name of Sergeant Craddock, the
first man in Ireland at the long jump in the time that's gone.

Craddock?

That was always one thing, said Shanahan wisely, that the Irish
race was always noted for, one place where the world had to give
us best. With all his faults and by God he has plenty, the Irishman
can jump. By God he can jump. That's one thing the Irish race
is honoured for no matter where it goes or where you find it –
jumping. The world looks up to us there.

We were good jumpers from the start, said Furriskey.

It was in the early days of the Gaelic League, said Lamont. This Sergeant Craddock was an ordinary bloody bobby on the beat, down the country somewhere. A bit of a bags, too, from what I heard. One fine morning he wakes up and is ordered to proceed if you don't mind to the Gaelic League Sports or whatever it was that was being held in the town that fine spring Sunday. To keep his eye open for sedition do you know and all the rest of it. All right. In he marches to do his duty, getting the back of the bloody hand from the women and plenty of guff from the young fellows. Maybe he was poking around too much and sticking his nose where it wasn't wanted...

I know what you mean, said Shanahan.

Anyway, didn't he raise the dander of the head of the house, the big man, the head bottle-washer. Up he came to my cool sergeant with his feathers ruffled and his comb as red as a turkeycock and read out a long rigmarole in Irish to your man's face.

That'll do you, said the sergeant, keep that stuff for them that wants it. I don't know what you're saying, man.

So you don't know your own language, says the head man.

I do, says the sergeant, I know plenty of English.

Your man then asks the sergeant his business in Irish and what he's doing there in the field at all.

Speak English, says the sergeant.

So be damned but your man gets his rag out and calls the sergeant a bloody English spy.

Well maybe he was right, said Furriskey.

Shh, said Shanahan.

But wait till I tell you. The sergeant just looked at him as cool as blazes.

You're wrong, says he, *and I'm as good a man as you or any other man*, says he.

You're a bloody English bags, says your man in Irish.

And I'll prove it, says the sergeant.

And with that your man gets black in the face and turns his back and walks to the bloody platform where all the lads were doing the Irish dancing with their girls, competitions of one kind and another, you know. Oh it was all the fashion at one time, you were bloody nothing if you couldn't do your Walls of Limerick. And here too were my men with the fiddles and the pipes playing away there at the reels and jigs for further orders. Do you know what I mean?

Oh I know what you're talking about all right, said Shanahan, the national music of our country, Rodney's Glory, the Star of Munster and the Rights of Man.

The Flogging Reel and Drive the Donkey, you can't beat them, said Furriskey.

That's the ticket, said Lamont. Anyway, didn't your man get into a dark corner with his butties till they hatched out a plan to best the sergeant. All right. Back went your man to the sergeant, who was taking it easy in the shade of a tree.

You said a while ago, says your man, that you were a better man than any man here. Can you jump?

I can not, says the sergeant, but I'm no worse than the next man.

We'll see, says your man.

Now be damned but hadn't they a man in the tent there from the county Cork, a bloody dandy at the long jump, a man that had a name, a man that was known in the whole country. A party by the name of Bagenal, the champion of all Ireland.

Gob that was a cute one, said Furriskey.

A very cute one. But wait till I tell you. The two of them lined up and a hell of a big crowd gathering there to watch. Here was my nice Bagenal as proud as a bloody turkey in his green pants, showing off the legs. Beside him stands another man, a man called Craddock, a member of the polis. His tunic is off him on the grass but the rest of his clothes is still on. He is standing as you find him with his blue pants and his big canal-barges on his two feet. I'm telling you it was something to look at. It was a sight to see.

I don't doubt it, said Shanahan.

Yes. Well Bagenal is the first off, sailing through the air like a bird and down in a shower of sand. What was the score?

Eighteen feet, said Furriskey.

Not at all man, twenty-two. Twenty-two feet was the jump of Bagenal there and then and by God the shout the people gave was enough to make the sergeant puke what was inside him and plenty more that he never swallowed.

Twenty-two feet is a good jump any day, said Shanahan.

After the cheering had died down, said Lamont, my man

Bagenal strolls around and turns his back on the sergeant and asks for a cigarette and starts to blather out of him to his friends. What does my sergeant do, do you think, Mr Shanahan.

I'm saying nothing, said knowing Shanahan.

By God you're a wise man. Sergeant Craddock keeps his mouth shut, takes a little run and jumps twenty-four feet six.

Do you tell me that! cried Furriskey.

Twenty-four feet six.

I'm not surprised, said Shanahan in his amazement, I'm not surprised. Go where you like in the wide world, you will always find that the Irishman is looked up to for his jumping.

Right enough, said Furriskey, the name of Ireland is honoured for that.

Go to Russia, said Shanahan, go to China, go to France. Everywhere and all the time it is hats off and a gra-ma-cree to the Jumping Irishman. Ask who you like they'll all tell you that. The Jumping Irishman.

It's a thing, said Furriskey, that will always stand to us – jumping.

When everything's said, said Lamont, the Irishman has his points. He's not the last man that was made now.

He is not, said Furriskey.

When everything had been said by Sweeny, said droning dark-voiced Finn, a glimmering of reason assailed the madman till it turned his steps in the direction of his people that he might dwell with them and trust them. But holy Ronan in his cell was acquainted by angels of the intention of Sweeny and prayed God that he should not be loosed from his frenzy until his soul had been first loosed from his body and here is a summary of the result. When the madman reached the middle of Slieve Fuaid, there were strange apparitions before him there, red headless trunks and trunkless heads and five stubbly rough grey heads without trunk or body between them, screaming and squealing and bounding hither and thither about the dark road beleaguering and besetting him and shouting their mad abuse, until he soared in his fright aloft in front of them. Piteous was the terror and the wailing cries, and the din and the harsh-screaming tumult of the heads and the dogsheads and the goatsheads in his pursuit, thudding on his thighs and his calves and on the nape of his neck and knocking against trees and the butts of rocks – a wild torrent of villainy from the breast of a high mountain, not enough resting for a drink of water for mad Sweeny till he finally achieved his peace in the tree on the summit of Slieve Eichneach. Here he devoted his time to the composition and recital of melodious staves on the subject of his evil plight.

After that he went on his career of wild folly from Luachair Dheaghaidh to Fiodh Gaibhle of the clean streams and the elegant branches, remaining there for one year on the sustenance of saffron heart-red holly-berries and black-brown oak-acorns, with draughts of water from the Gabhal, concluding there with the fashioning of this lay.

> Ululation, I am Sweeny.
> my body is a corpse;
> sleeping or music nevermore –
> only the soughing of the storm-wind.

> I have journeyed from Luachair Dheaghaidh
> to the edge of Fiodh Gaibhle.
> this is my fare – I conceal it not –
> ivy-berries, oak-mast.

After that Sweeny in his restlessness came to All Fharannain, a wondrous glen it is with green-streamed water, containing multitudes of righteous people and a synod of saints, heavy-headed apple-trees bending to the ground, well-sheltered ivies, ponderous fruit-loaded branches, wild deer and hares and heavy swine, and fat seals sleeping in the sun, seals from the sea beyant. And Sweeny said this.

> All Fharannain, resort of saints,
> fulness of hazels, fine nuts,
> swift water without heat
> coursing its flank.

> Plenteous are its green ivies,
> its mast is coveted;
> the fair heavy apple-trees
> they stoop their arms.

At length Sweeny penetrated to the place the head-saint
Moling was, that is, to speak precisely. House-Moling. The
psalter of Kevin was in Moling's presence and he reciting it to
his students. Sweeny came to the edge of the well and nibbled at
the cresses until Moling said:

Oh madman, that is early eating.

The two of them madman and saint then embarked on a
lengthy dialogue to the tune of twenty-nine elegant verses; and
then Moling spoke again.

Your arrival here is surely welcome, Sweeny, he said, for it is
destined that you should end your life here, and leave the story
of your history here and be buried in the churchyard there
beyant. And I now bind you that, however much of Erin that
you over-wander, you will come to me each evening the way
I can write your story.

And so it was, Sweeny returning from his wandering to and
from the celebrated trees of Erin at vespers each evening, Moling
ordering a collation for the mad one at that hour and com-
manding his cook to give Sweeny a share of the day's milking.
One night a dispute arose among the serving-women over the
head of Sweeny, the madman being accused of an act of adultery
in the hedge by the herd's sister as she went with her measure of
milk in the evening to place it in a hole in the cowdung for
Sweeny, the herd's sister putting the dishonourable lie in the ear
of her brother. He immediately took a spear from the spear-rack
in the house and Sweeny's flank being towards him as he lay in
the cowdung at his vesper-milk, he was wounded by a spear-cast
in the left nipple so that the point went through him and made
two halves of his back. An acolyte at the door of the church
witnessed the black deed and acquainted Moling, who hastened
with a concourse of honourable clerics until the sick man had
been forgiven and anointed.

Dark is the deed you have done, Oh herd, said Sweeny, for
owing to the wound you have dealt me I cannot henceforth
escape through the hedge.

I did not know you were there, said the herd.

By Christ, man, said Sweeny, I have not injured you at all.

Christ's curse on you, Oh herd, said Moling.

Thereafter they had colloquy and talked loudly together until

they had achieved a plurality of staves, Sweeny terminating the
talking with these verses.

> There was a time when I preferred
> to the low converse of humans
> the accents of the turtle-dove
> fluttering about a pool.
>
> There was a time when I preferred
> to the tinkle of neighbour bells
> the voice of the blackbird from the crag
> and the belling of a stag in a storm.
>
> There was a time when I preferred
> to the voice of a fine woman near me
> the call of the mountain-grouse
> heard at day.
>
> There was a time when I preferred
> the yapping of the wolves
> to the voice of a cleric
> melling and megling within.

Thereafter a death-swoon assailed Sweeny so that Moling and
his clerics arose till each man had placed a stone on Sweeny's
tomb.

Dear indeed is he whose tomb it is, said Moling, dear to me
the madman, delightful to behold him at yonder well. Its name
is Madman's Well for often he would feast on its cresses and its
water and the well is named after him on account of that. Dear
to me every other place that Sweeny was wont to frequent.

And Moling addressed himself to the composition and the
honey-tongued recital of these following poems.

> Here is the tomb of Sweeny!
> His memory racks my heart,
> dear to me therefore are the haunts
> of the saintly madman.
>
> Dear to me Glen Bolcain fair
> for Sweeny loved it;

dear the streams that leave it
dear its green-crowned cresses.

That beyant is Madman's Well
dear the man it nourished,
dear its perfect sand,
beloved its clear waters.

Melodious was the talk of Sweeny
long shall I hold his memory,
I implore the King of Heaven
on his tomb and above his grave.

Biographical reminiscence, part the sixth: Early one evening I was seated at the large table in the dining-room arranging and perusing my day-papers when I perceived that the hall-door had been opened from without by the means of a latch-key. After a brief interval it was shut again. I heard the loud voice of my uncle from the hallway intermixed with another voice that was not known to me at all; then the shuffling of feet and thud of gloved palms knocked together in discords of good humour. Hastily I covered such sheets as contained reference to the forbidden question of the sexual relations.

The door of the dining-room was thrown open but nobody entered for the space of fifteen seconds; after that, my uncle came in with a swift heavy stride bearing in his arms before him a weighty object covered with a black waterproof cloth. This he placed on the table without delay and clapped his hands together in a token that his task had been accomplished.

Description of my uncle: Bluff, abounding in external good nature; concerned-that-he-should-be-well-thought-of; holder of Guinness clerkship the third class.

An elderly man of slight build entered, smiling diffidently at me as I sat there at the supervision of my papers. His body was bent sidewise in an awkward fashion and his shoulders appeared to move lithely beneath his coat as if his woollen small-clothes had been disarranged in the divesting of his street-coat. His skull shone clearly in the gaslight under the aura of his sparse hair. His

double-breasted jacket bore a vertical ripple in the front, a result
of the inexpensive quality of the canvas lining. He nodded to me
in friendly salutation.

Fingering his coat-tails, my uncle took a stand near the fire
and surveyed us, bisecting between us the benison of his smile.
Not terminating it when he addressed me, it imparted a soft
husky quality to his voice.

Well, fellow-my-lad, he said, what are *we* at this evening? My
nephew, Mr Corcoran.

I arose. Mr Corcoran advanced and extended his small hand,
exerting considerable strength in a fine man-grip.

I hope we are not disturbing you at your work, he said.

Not at all, I answered.

My uncle laughed.

Faith, he said, you would want to be a clever man to do that,
Mr Corcoran. That would be a miracle certainly. Tell me this,
do you ever open a book at all?

This I received in silence, standing quietly by the table.

Nature of silence: Indifferent, contemptuous.

Perceiving that my want of reply showed me sad and crestfallen
before the rebuke of my uncle, Mr Corcoran moved quickly to
my defence.

Oh I don't know about that, he said. I don't know about that.
The people that never seem to exert themselves at all, these are
the boys that win the prize. Show me a man that is always fussing
and rushing about and I will show you a man that never did a
day's work in his life.

My uncle smiled about him without malice.

Maybe true, he said, maybe not.

Now a funny thing I have a young lad at home, said Mr Corcoran, and I declare to God I am sick sore and tired telling him
to stop in at night and do his lessons but you might as well be
talking to that, look.

Choosing his boot, the buttoned class, as a convenient
example of inanition, he lifted it in the air, slowly describing an
arc of forty-five degrees.

Well he came home the other day with a report and I declare

to God the little monkey got his own back in great style. He had me where he wanted me. First in Christian doctrine if you please.

My uncle removed his smile in solicitous interrogation.

Your boy Tom?

Young Tom the same boyo.

Well I'm very glad to hear it, I am indeed, said my uncle. A sharp-witted little lad he is too. Christian doctrine of course, it is very nice to see the young lads making that their own. That particular subject, I mean. It is very necessary in the times we live in, it is, faith.

He turned to me.

Now Mister-my-friend, he said, when are we going to hear from you? When are you going to bring home a prize? Certainly you have enough papers there to win a prize at something...

He laughed slightly.

... if it was only a paper-chase, he added.

His laugh had a dual function, partly to applaud his jest, partly to cloak his anger. Turning to Mr Corcoran he extracted from him a small smile of concurrence.

I know my catechism, I said in a toneless manner.

That is the main thing, said Mr Corcoran.

Aye but do you, said my uncle quickly, do you, that's the question. What is meant by sanctifying grace? Why does the bishop give those he confirms a stroke on the cheek? Name the seven deadly sins. Name the one that begins with S.

Anger, I answered.

Anger begins with A, said my uncle.

Mr Corcoran, in order to achieve diversion, removed the black cloth in a priestly manner, showing that the object on the table was a gramophone.

I think you have the needles, he said.

My uncle had assumed a flushed appearance.

All present and correct, Sir, he said loudly, taking a small canister from his pocket. Oh indeed there is little respect for the penny catechism in Ireland today and well I know it. But it has stood to us, Mr Corcoran, and will please God to the day we die. It is certainly a grand thing to see the young lads making it their own for you won't get very far in the world without it. Mark that, my lad. It is worth a bag of your fine degrees and parchments.

He blew his nose and went to the table in order to assist Mr

Corcoran. The two of them bent together at the adjustment of
the machine, extracting a collapsible extensible retractable tone-
arm from its interior with the aid of their four hands. I gathered
my day-papers silently, hopeful that I might escape without
offence. Mr Corcoran opened a small compartment at the base
of the machine by pressing a cleverly hidden spring and brought
out a number of records, scraping and whistling them together
by a careless manner of manipulation. My uncle was occupied
with inserting a cranking device into an aperture in the
machine's side and winding it with the meticulous and steady
motion that is known to prolong the life and resiliency of springs.
Fearing that his careful conduct of the task was not observed, he
remarked that fast winding will lead to jerks, jerks will lead to
strain and strain to breakage, thus utilizing a figure of speech
to convey the importance of taking pains.

Name of figure of speech: Anadipolsis (or Epanastrophe).

Moderation in all things, he said, that is the trick that won
the war.

I then recalled that he was a member of an operatic society
composed of residents of the Rathmines and Rathgar district, an
indifferent voice of the baritone range winning for him a station
in the chorus. Mr Corcoran, I thought, was likewise situated.

My uncle placed a needle finely on the revolving disk and
stepped quickly back, his meticulous hands held forth without
motion in his expectancy. Mr Corcoran was waiting in a chair
by the fire, his legs crossed, his downcast head supported in
position by the knuckles of his right hand, which were resting
damply on his top teeth. The tune came duly, a thin spirant from
the *Patience* opera. The records were old and not of the modern
electrical manufacture. A chorus intervening, Mr Corcoran and
my uncle joined in it in happy and knowledgeable harmony,
stressing the beat with manual gesture. My uncle, his back to me,
also moved his head authoritatively, exercising a roll of fat which
he was accustomed to wear at the back of his collar, so that it
paled and reddened in the beat of the music.

The time ended.

My uncle shook his head and made a noise of perplexed
admiration as he arose with haste to remove the needle.

I could listen to that tune, he said, from early morning to late at night and not a bit of me would tire of it. Ah, it's a lovely thing. I think it's the nicest of the whole lot, I do indeed. There's a great lilt in it, Mr Corcoran.

Mr Corcoran, whom by chance I was observing, smiled preliminarily but when about to speak, his smile was transfixed on his features and his entire body assumed a stiff attitude. Suddenly he sneezed, spattering his clothing with a mucous discharge from his nostrils.

As my uncle hurried to his assistance, I felt that my gorge was about to rise. I retched slightly, making a noise with my throat similar to that utilized by persons in the article of death. My uncle's back was towards me as he bent in ministration.

There's a very catching cold going around, Mr Corcoran, he said. You would need to watch yourself. You would need to keep yourself well wrapped up.

I clutched my belongings and retired quickly as they worked together with their pocket-cloths. I went to my room and lay prostrate on my bed, endeavouring to recover my composure. After a time the thin music came upon my ear, thinner and hollower through the intervening doors but perceptibly reinforced at the incidence of a chorus. Putting on my grey coat, I made my way to the street.

Such was the degree of my emotional disturbance that I walked down to the centre of the town without adverting to my surroundings and without a predetermined destination. There was no rain but the streets were glistening and people were moving in a quick active manner along the pavements. A slight fog, perforated by the constellation of the street-lamps, hung down on the roadway from the roofs of the houses. Reaching the Pillar, I turned about to retrace my steps when I perceived that Kerrigan had emerged from a side-street and was now walking actively before me. Hastening after him, I dealt him a smart blow with my closed fist in the small of the back, thereby eliciting a coarse expression not infrequently associated with the soldiery. We then saluted in formal fashion and talked on general academic topics, continuing to walk in the Grafton Street direction.

Where are you going, I asked him.

To Byrne's, he answered. Where are *you* going?

Michael Byrne was a man of diverse intellectual attainments

and his house was frequently the scene of scholarly and other disputations.

Description of Michael Byrne: He was tall, middle-aged, stout. Large eyes moved briskly with attention behind the windows of his glasses. His upper lip protruded in a prim bird-like manner. His tones when he spoke were soothing, authoritative, low and of delicate texture. He was painter, poet, composer, pianist, master-printer, tactician, an authority on ballistics.

Nowhere, I answered.

You might as well come along then, he said.

That, I answered, would be the chiefest wisdom.

The origin of the distinctive adjective, being the wise sayings of the son of Sirach: The fear of the Lord is the beginning and the crown of wisdom. The word of God is the fountain of wisdom, and her ways are everlasting commandments. The fear of the Lord shall delight the heart, and shall give joy, and gladness, and length of days. It shall go well with him that feareth the Lord, and in the days of his end he shall be blessed. My son, from thy youth up receive instruction, and even to thy grey hairs thou shalt find wisdom. Come to her as one that plougheth and soweth, and wait for her good fruits. For in working about her thou shalt labour a little, and shalt quickly eat of her fruits. Take all that shall be brought upon thee, and keep patience, for gold and silver are tried in the fire, but acceptable men in the furnace of humiliation. Hear the judgment of your father, and grieve him not in his life. The father's blessing establisheth the houses of the children, but the mother's curse rooteth up the foundation. Despise not a man in his old age, for we also shall become old. Despise not the discourse of them that are ancient and wise; but acquaint thyself with their proverbs. Praise not a man for his beauty, neither despise a man for his look. The bee is small among flying things, but her fruit hath the chiefest sweetness. Be in peace with many, but let one of a thousand be thy counsellor. Nothing can be compared to a faithful friend, and no weight of gold and silver is able to countervail the goodness of his fidelity. If thou wouldst get a friend, try him before thou takest him, and do not credit him easily. For there is a friend for his own occasion, and he will not abide in the day of thy trouble. A lie is a foul blot in a man. In nowise speak against the truth, but be ashamed of the lie in thy ignorance. Let not the naming of God be usual in thy mouth and meddle not with the names of saints. A man that sweareth much shall be filled with iniquity, and a scourge shall not depart from his house. Before thou hear, answer not a word, and interrupt not others in the midst of their discourse. Hast thou a word against thy neighbour, let it die within thee, trusting that it will not burst thee. Hedge in thy ears with thorns; hear not a wicked tongue; and make doors and bars of thy mouth. Melt down thy gold and silver, and make a balance for thy words. Flee from sin as from the face of a serpent. All iniquity is like a two-edged sword; there is no remedy for the wound thereof. Observe the time and fly from evil. He that loveth the danger shall perish therein, and he that toucheth pitch shall be defiled with it. In every work of thine regard thy soul in faith, for this is the keeping of the commandments. In all thy works remember thy last end and thou shalt never sin. Conclusion of the foregoing.

We sat there at Byrne's darkly in a dim room, five of us at voice-play on the threads of disputation. A small intense fire glowed from under a dome of slack, a rich roundness being imparted to adjacent or near-by table-legs by red incantation. Byrne was tinkling a spoon in the interior of his glass.

Yesterday, he said, Cryan brought me his complete prose works.

He was seated alone in the darkness beyond the table, dosing himself medicinally with ovoid tablets dissolved in water.

The day before that, he continued, he told me he was *aching* to hear me play Bach. Aching!

He gave a sustained indolent chuckle which he gradually declined in tone, affording a clink of the glass against his teeth in a symbol that he had ended.

Kerrigan unseen put in a voice from his ingle.

Poor Cryan, he said. The poor man.

He is addicted to mental ludo, said Byrne.

We pondered this between us for a time.

The poor man, said Kerrigan.

What is wrong with Cryan and most people, said Byrne, is that they do not spend sufficient time in bed. When a man sleeps, he is steeped and lost in a limp toneless happiness: awake he is restless, tortured by his body and the illusion of existence. Why have men spent the centuries seeking to overcome the awakened body? Put it to sleep, that is a better way. Let it serve only to turn the sleeping soul over, to change the blood-stream and thus make possible a deeper and more refined sleep.

I agree, I said.

We must invert our conception of repose and activity, he continued. We should not sleep to recover the energy expended when awake but rather wake occasionally to defecate the unwanted energy that sleep engenders. This might be done quickly – a five-mile race at full tilt around the town and then back to bed and the kingdom of the shadows.

You're a terrible man for the blankets, said Kerrigan.

I'm not ashamed to admit that I love my bed, said Byrne. She was my first friend, my foster-mother, my dearest comforter. . . .

He paused and drank.

Her warmth, he continued, kept me alive when my mother bore me. She still nurtures me, yielding without stint the parturition of her cosy womb. She will nurse me gently in my last hour and faithfully hold my cold body when I am dead. She will look bereaved when I am gone.

This speech did not please us, bringing to each of us our last personal end. We tittered in cynical fashion.

Glass tinkle at his teeth notified a sad concluding drink.

Brinsley gave a loud question.

Wasn't Trellis another great bed-bug?

He was, I answered.

I'm afraid I never heard of Trellis, said Byrne. Who is Trellis?

A member of the author class, I said.

Did he write a book on Tactics? I fancy I met him in Berlin. A man with glasses.

He has been in bed for the last twenty years, I said.

You are writing a novel of course? said Byrne.

He is, said Brinsley, and the plot has him well in hand.

Trellis's dominion over his characters, I explained, is impaired by his addiction to sleep. There is a moral in that.

You promised to give me a look at this thing, said Kerrigan.

Brinsley, re-examining his recollection of my spare-time literary work, was chuckling in undertones from his unseen habitation.

He is a great man that never gets out of bed, he said. He spends the days and nights reading books and occasionally he writes one. He makes his characters live with him in his house. Nobody knows whether they are there at all or whether it is all imagination. A great man.

It is important to remember that he reads and writes only green books. That is an important point.

I then gave an account of this quality in order to amuse them and win their polite praise.

Relevant extract from Manuscript: Trellis practised another curious habit in relation to his reading. All colours except green he regarded as symbols of evil and he confined his reading to books attired in green covers. Although a man of wide learning and culture, this arbitrary rule caused serious chasms in his erudition. The Bible, for instance, was unknown to him and much of knowledge of the great mysteries of religion and the origin of man was acquired from servants and public-house acquaintances and was on that account imperfect and in some respects ludicrously garbled. It is for this reason that his well-known work, *Evidences of Christian Religion*, contains the seeds of serious heresy. On being commended by a friend to read a work of merit lately come from the booksellers, he would inquire particularly as to the character of the bindings and on learning that they were not of the green colour would condemn the book (despite his not having perused it) as a work of Satan; this to the great surprise of his friend. For many years he experienced a difficulty in obtaining a sufficiency of books to satisfy his active and inquiring mind, for the green colour was not favoured by the publishers of London, excluding those who issued text-books and treatises on such subjects as fretwork, cookery and parabolics. The publishers of Dublin, however, deemed the colour a fitting one for their many works on the subject of Irish history and antiquities and it is not surprising that Trellis came to be regarded as an authority thereon and was frequently consulted by persons engaged in research, including members of the religious orders, the enclosed class.

On one occasion, his love of learning made him the victim of a melancholy circumstance that continued to cause him spiritual anxiety for many years. He acquired a three-volume work on the subject of the Irish monastic foundations at the time of the invasion and (being in the habit of sleeping during the day), read it throughout the night by the light of his incandescent petrol lamp. One morning he was recalled from his sleep accidentally by inordinate discords from Peter Place, where rough-mannered labourers were unloading hollow tar-barrels. Turning idly to resume the performance of his sleep, he noticed to his great alarm that the three volumes by his bedside were blue. Perceiving that he had been deluded by a subterfuge of Satan, he caused the books to be destroyed and composed a domestic curriculum calculated to warrant the orthodoxy of all books introduced into his house at any future time. Conclusion of the foregoing.

What happened, asked Brinsley, when the lad was sent to set about the servant or something?

Very unexpected things happened, I said. They fell in love and the villain Furriskey, purified by the love of a noble woman, hatched a plot for putting sleeping-draughts in Trellis's porter by slipping a few bob to the grocer's curate. This meant that Trellis was nearly always asleep and awoke only at predeterminable hours, when everything would be temporarily in order.

This is very interesting, said Byrne, an unseen listener.

Well what did Furriskey do when he got the boy asleep? asked Kerrigan.

Oh, plenty, I said. He married the girl. They took a little house in Dolphin's Barn and opened a sweety-shop and lived there happily for about twenty hours out of twenty-four. They had to dash back to their respective stations, of course, when the great man was due to be stirring in his sleep. They hired a girl to mind the shop when they were gone, eight and six a week with dinner and tea.

Polite amusement and approval were expressed at the un-suspected trend of events.

You will have to show me this thing, said Byrne, it involves several planes and dimensions. You have read Schutzmeyer's book, of course?

Well wait now, said Brinsley. What happened to Shanahan and that crowd? How did they use their freedom?

Shanahan and Lamont, I answered, were frequent and wel-come visitors to the little house in Dolphin's Barn. The girl Peggy made a neat and homely housewife. Tea was dispensed in a simple but cleanly manner. For the rest of their time, they did not use it too well. They consorted with sailors and cornerboys and took to drink and bad company. Once they were very nearly leaving the country altogether. They met two decadent Greek scullions, Timothy Danaos and Dona Ferentes, ashore from the cooking-galley of a strange ship. It happened in one of the low pubs down by the docks there.

The Greeks' names were repeated in admiration by two members of the company.

The two Greeks, I continued, were deaf and dumb but managed to convey, by jerking their thumbs towards the bay and writing down large sums of money in foreign currency, that there was a good life to be lived across the water.

The Greeks were employed, of course, said Kerrigan, as panders by an eminent Belgian author who was writing a saga on the white slave question. They were concerned in the transport of doubtful cargo to Antwerp.

I recall that the dexterity and ready wit of this conversation induced in all of us a warm intellectual glow extremely pleasant to experience.

That is right, I said. I remember that they inscribed contours in the air by means of gesture to indicate the fulness of the foreign bosom. A very unsavoury pair of rascals if you like.

You will have to show me this thing, said Byrne. It's not fair to be holding things back, you know.

Certainly, I said. The two boys were saved on this occasion by the bell. Trellis was about to waken, so they had to make a dash for it, leaving their half-took drinks behind them.

After enunciating a quiet chuckle, Byrne made a noise in the darkness of a kind associated with the forcible opening of the lid of a tin container. He then moved about the room, a cigarette for each voice in his enterprising hand. Kerrigan declined and remained unseen, the rest of us revealed at intervals, red pale faces with pucker-cheeks at the rear of the glow-points.

A time passed in casual dialectics. Tea was made without and the light flooded suddenly upon us from the roof, showing each for what he was in his own attitude.

Papers and periodicals were perused in a desultory fashion for some time. Afterwards Byrne searched for an old book purchased for a nominal sum upon the quays and read aloud extracts therefrom for the general benefit and/or diversion of the company.

Title of Book referred to: The Athenian Oracle, being an Entire COLLECTION of all the Valuable QUESTIONS and ANSWERS in the old Athenian Mercuries intermixed with many CASES in Divinity, Hiftory, Philofophy, Mathematicks, Love, Poetry, never before publifhed.

Extract from Book referred to: 1. Whether it be poffible for a woman fo carnally to know a Man in her fleep as to conceive, for I am fure that this and no way other was I got with Child.

2. Whether it be lawful to ufe Means to put a ftop to this growing mifchief, and kill it in the Embryo; this being the only way to avert the Thunderclap of my Father's Indignation.

To the firft Question, Madam, we are very pofitive, that you are luckily miftaken, for the thing is abfolutely impoffible if you know nothing of it; indeed, we had an account of a Widow that made fuch a pretence, and fhe might have better credit than a maid, who can have no plea but dead drunk, or in fome fwooning fit, and our Phyficians will hardly allow a poffibility of the thing then. So that you may fet your heart at reft, and think no more of the matter, unlefs for your diverfion.

As for the fecond Queftion, fuch practices are murder, and thofe that are fo unhappy as to come under fuch Circumftances if they ufe the forementioned means, will certainly one day find the remedy worfe than the Difeafe. There are wifer methods to be taken in fuch Cafes, as a fmall journey and a Confident. And afterwards, fuch a pious and good life as may redreff fuch an heavy miffortune.

Questions, a Selection of Further: Almond, why fo bitter being taken in the mouth, and yet the Oyl fo very fweet? Apprentice, reduced to want, how may he relieve himfelf? Blood, is the eating of it lawful? Baptifm, adminiftered by a Mid-wife or Lay Hand, is it lawful? Devil, why called Lucifer; and elfewhere the Prince of Darknefs? Eftate, gotten by felling lewd Books, can it profper? Eyes, what Method muft I take with 'em when weak? Horfe, with a round fundament, why does he emit a fquare Excrement? Happinefs, what is it? Lady, difturbed in her Bed, your thoughts of it? Light, is it a Body? Myftae or Cabalifts, what d'ye think of them? Marriage, is not the End of it, in a great Meafure, loft nowadays? Poem, by Mr Tate? Virginity, is it a Vertue? Wind, what is it? Wife, is it lawful for a Man to beat her? Wife, if an ill one, may I pray that God wou'd take her to himfelf? Conclusion of the foregoing.

Note to Reader before proceeding further: Before proceeding further, the Reader is respectfully advised to refer to the Synopsis or Summary of the Argument on Page 57.

Further extract from my Manuscript, descriptive of the Pooka Mac-Phellimey, his journey and other matters: it was the shine of the morning sun, diluted though it was by the tangle of the forest and the sacking on the windows, that recalled the Pooka Mac-Phellimey from his heavy sleep by the side of his wife. He awoke with a frown and made a magic pass in the air with his thumb, thus awakening also the beetles and the maggots and the other evil creeping things that were slumbering throughout the forest under the flat of great stones. He then lay on his back with his eyes half-closed and his sharp-nailed hands cupped together in the scrub of his poll, uttering his maledictions and his matins in an undertone and reflecting on the hump of his club-foot in the bed in the morning. His shank of a wife beside him was hidden and not easy to discern, a black evil wrinkle in the black sackcloth quilts, a shadow. The Pooka was for taking a hold of his pipe, his pen-knife and his twist of plug-tabacca – he had the three by him – for a morning smoke in bed when the boards of the door were urgently knocked from without and afterwards put in.

Welcome to my house, said the Pooka courteously, tapping his pipe on the bedrail and placing the club-foot sideways the way no remarks would be passed on the hump. He looked at the empty door with polite inquiry but there was no one there and the party responsible for the knocking could not easily be discerned in any quarter.

Be pleased to come in and welcome, the Pooka said a second time, it is seldom I am honoured by a caller in the morning early.

I am already in the middle of your fine house, said a small voice that was sweeter by far than the tinkle and clap of a waterfall

and brighter than the first shaft of day. I am standing here on the
flag with the elliptical crack in it.

Welcome to my poor hut, said the Pooka as he surveyed the
floor, and it is a queer standing. I do not see you there.

I have come to visit you, said the voice, and to spend an hour
in fine talk, and to enter into a colloquy with you.

It is early talking, said the Pooka, but welcome to my house.
Your surname, that is a secret that I respect.

My correct name is Good Fairy, said the Good Fairy. I am
a good fairy. It is a fine secret but one that is so big that each of us
may share it with the other. As to the hour of my advent in your
house, it is never too early of a morning for sapient colloquy.
Likewise, never is it too late of an evening either.

Under the murk of the bedclothes, the Pooka was fingering
the dark hairs of his wife's head – a token that he was engaged
in fine thought.

On account of the fact, he said gentlemanly, that I have at
all times purposely refrained from an exhaustive exercise of my
faculty of vision and my power of optical inspection (I refer now
to things perfectly palpable and discernible – the coming of dawn
across the mountains is one example and the curious conduct of
owls and bats in strong moonlight is another), I had expected
(foolishly, perhaps), that I should be able to see quite clearly
things that are normally not visible at all as a compensation for
my sparing inspection of the visible. It is for that reason that I am
inclined to regard the phenomenon of a voice unsupported by a
body (more especially at an hour that is acknowledged as inimical
to phantasy), as a delusion, one of the innumerable hallucinations
which can be traced to lapses from plain diet and to reckless over-
eating at bedtime, figments of the large gut rather than of the
brain. It is perhaps not altogether irrelevant to mention that last
night I finished the last delectable (if indigestible), portion of a
queer confection that was prepared in that pan there in the corner. Last night I ate a loins.

Your talk surprises me, said the Good Fairy. Was it the loins
of a beetle, or a monkey, or a woman?

Two loinses I ate, replied the Pooka, the loins of a man and
the loins of a dog and I cannot remember which I ate the first or
which was tasted sweeter. But two loinses I had in all.

I recognize that that is good eating, said the Good Fairy,

though myself I have no body that I could feed. As a feat of eating it is first-rate.

I hear what you say, said the Pooka, but from what quarter are you speaking?

I am sitting here, said the Good Fairy, in a white cup on the dresser.

There are four coppers in that cup, said the Pooka, be careful of them. The truth is that I would ill like to be at the loss of them.

I have no pockets, said the Good Fairy.

That surprises me, said the Pooka raising his thick eyebrows till they were mixed with his hair, that surprises me certainly and by the hokey I do not understand how you can manage without the convenience of a pocket. The pocket was the first instinct of humanity and was used long years before the human race had a trousers between them – the quiver for arrows is one example and the pouch of the kangaroo is another. Where do you keep your pipe?

It is cigarettes I smoke, said the Good Fairy, and I disincline to think that kangaroos are human.

That time you spoke, said the Pooka, it is of course a secret where your voice came from?

When I spoke last, said the Good Fairy, I was kneeling in the cup of your navel but it is bad country and I am there no longer.

Do you tell me that, said the Pooka. This here beside me is my wife.

That is why I left, said the Good Fairy.

There are two meanings in your answer, said the Pooka with his smile of deprecation, but if your departure from my poor bed was actuated solely by a regard for chastity and conjugal fidelity, you are welcome to remain between the blankets without the fear of anger in your host, for there is safety in a triad, chastity is truth and truth is an odd number. And your statement that kangaroos are not human is highly debatable.

Even if it were desirable, replied the Good Fairy, angelic or spiritual carnality is not easy and in any case the offspring would be severely handicapped by being half flesh and half spirit, a very baffling and neutralizing assortment of fractions since the two elements are forever at variance. An act of quasi-angelic carnality on the part of such issue would possibly result in further offspring consisting in composition of a half caro plus half the sum of a half caro and spiritus, that is, three-quarters caro and a quarter spiritus. Further carry-on would again halve the spiritual content of the progeny and so on until it becomes zero, thus bringing us by geometric progression to an ordinary love-child with nothing but an unrepresented tradition on the spiritual or angelic side. In regard to the humanity of kangaroos, to admit a kangaroo unreservedly to be a man would inevitably involve one in a number of distressing implications, the kangarooity of women and your wife beside you being one example.

Your granny, said the Pooka's wife lifting the flap of the blankets the way her voice could be let out.

If we take the view, observed the Pooka, that the angelic element can be eliminated by ordered breeding, it follows that the flesh can be reduced by an opposite process, so that the spectacle of an unmarried mother with a houseful of adult and imperceptible angels is not really the extravagance that it would first appear to be. As an alternative to the commonplace family, the proposition is by no means unattractive because the saving in clothes and doctors' bills would be unconscionable and the science of shop-lifting could be practised with such earnestness as would be compatible with the attainment and maintenance of a life of comfort and culture. I would not be in the least surprised to learn that my wife is a kangaroo, for any hypothesis would be more tenable than the assumption that she is a woman.

Your name, said the Good Fairy, is one thing that you have not related to me privately. There is nothing so important as the legs in determining the kangarooity of a woman. Is there for example fur on your wife's legs, Sir?

My name, said the Pooka, with an apologetic solicitude, is Fergus MacPhellimey and I am by calling a devil or pooka. Welcome to my poor house. I cannot say whether there is fur on my wife's legs for I have never seen them nor do I intend to commit myself to the folly of looking at them. In any event and in all politeness – nothing would be further from me than to insult a guest – I deem the point you have made as unimportant because there is surely nothing in the old world to prevent a deceitful kangaroo from shaving the hair off her legs, assuming she is a woman.

I knew you were of the Pooka class, said the Good Fairy, but your name, that much escaped me. Taking it for granted that the art of the razor is known to kangaroos as a class, by what subterfuge could the tail be passed off for something different from what it is?

The vocation of the pooka, said the Pooka, is one that is fraught with responsibilities, not the least of these being the lamming and leathering of such parties as are sent to me for treatment by Number One, which is the First Good and the Primal Truth and necessarily an odd number. My own personal number is Two. As regards the second objection you make about the tail, I must state that I personally belong to a class that is accustomed to treat with extreme suspicion all such persons as are unprovided with tails. Myself I have two tails in the bed here, my own tail of loose hair and the tail of my night-shirt. When I wear two shirts on a cold day, you might say that I appear to have three tails in all?

I find your commentary on the subject of your duties a matter of absorbing interest, said the Good Fairy, and I find myself in agreement with your conception of the Good and the Bad Numerals. It is for that reason that I consider the wearing of two shirts by you a deplorable lapse since it must result as you say in three tails in all and truth is an odd number. It is indisputable, whatever about the tail, that a woman kangaroo is provided with a built-in bag where youngsters and trinklets may be stored until such time as they are required – did you ever notice, Sir, that things were missing about the house where your wife might have put them in her sack for hiding?

I am afraid, replied the Pooka, that you are mistaken in the matter of my tails for I have never worn less than two or more than twenty-four at the one time and together, notwithstanding anything I have confided in you this fine morning. Your personal difficulty will be resolved when I tell you that my second-best day-shirt is fitted with two tails, the one longer than the other, thus enabling me to intermix the physical comfort of two shirts on a cold day with the ceremonial probity of four tails about my bottom (the four of them moving in unison in my trousers when I waggle my hair-tail). I never permit myself to forget that truth is an odd number and that my own personal numerals, the first and the last and all intermediaries, are all inevitably even. I have frequently missed these small things which are necessitous to personal comfort – my glasses and the black glove I use for moving the pan from the hob when it is hot, these are two examples. It is not impossible that my kangaroo has hidden them in her pouch, for by the hoke there was never a child there. To inquire the character of the weather you encountered in your travels here to my poor house from where you were, that would be deplorable violation of your status as a guest?

As regards the vexed question of the little tails, said the Good Fairy, I accept without question your explanation concerning your bi-tailed shirt, a device that I commend as ingenious. By what sophistry of mathematics, however, do you preserve your even numeral when the exigencies of social etiquette compel you to resort to the white waistcoat and the tail-coat of an evening? That is one point that perplexes me. It is very regrettable that a man of your years can be put to the loss of his glasses and his black glove for life is very narrow without glasses and a burnt hand is a bugger. The weather I experienced was wet and windy but that did not affect me in the least because I am without a body to be incommoded and I wear no suit that could be seeped.

There is little substance, said the Pooka, in your difficulty about the dress-coat for the tail of such an elegant garment has a split through the middle of it that makes it into two tails, which makes four tails in company with my own tail and my shirt-tail, or twelve tails in all with nine shirts. When I come to think of it, I have also missed a pig-iron coal-scuttle and a horsehair armchair and a ball of twine and a parcel of peats. I am perfectly sure that spirit though you be you would be troubled by a fog, for there are few things so spiritual or permeaty as a wispy fog, or that at least is my experience, because people who suffer from consumption complain most and frequently die when there is fog in the air. I make it a practice to inquire courteously of everyone I meet whether they can inform me as to the oddity or otherwise of the last number, I mean, will it be an odd one and victory for you and your people, or an even one and the resolution of heaven and hell and the world in my favour. And the question I ask you in conclusion is this, where did your talk come from the last time you talked?

Once again, said the Good Fairy, I find myself in the happy

position of being enabled to accept your answer about the tail-coat and I am much beholden to you. But there is this troubling me now, that there might be a heresy in your hair – for the number of such strands might well be odd and the truth is never even. Your enumeration of the matters you have missed about the house, that was an absorbing recital, and I am sure that you can retrieve the lot of them by catching the kangaroo when she is least expectant of rough play and inverting or upturning her the way all that is in her will fall out upon the flags of the kitchen. It is a mistake to think that ghosts and spirits are adversely affected by fogs and vapours (though it is quite possible that a consumptive or weak-chested spirit would find such an atmosphere far from salubrious). I would personally be a happier being if I could solve the riddle that you mention, viz., the character of the last number. When I spoke the last I was skating on that hard lard in the pan and I am now at present resting myself in an egg-cup.

The Pooka's face, at all times flushed and red, now changed to the colour of a withered acorn as he arose and propped himself by the elbows on the pillow.

In referring to my hair, he said with a strain of gentle anger in his voice, are you sure that you are not endeavouring to annoy me, or (worse still) to take a rise out of me? And when you give me the advice to invert my kangaroo the way my lost property will fall out on the hard stones of my poor kitchen, have you a mind to have my glasses smashed? Is it not so that good spirits are very vulnerable when there is fog because they have only one lung as a result of the fact that truth is an odd number? Are you aware of this, that your own existence was provoked by the vitality of my own evil, just as my own being is a reaction to the rampant goodness of Number One, that is, the Prime Truth, and that another pooka whose number will be Four must inevitably appear as soon as your own benevolent activities are felt to require a corrective? Has it never flitted across your mind that the riddle of the last number devolves on the ultimate appearance of a pooka or good spirit who will be so feeble a force for good or bad (as the case may be), that he will provoke no reagent and thus become himself the last and ultimate numeral – all bringing us to the curious and humiliat-ing conclusion that the character of the Last Numeral devolves directly on the existence of a party whose chief characteristics must be anaemia, ineptitude, incapacity, inertia and a spineless dereliction of duty? Answer me that!

As a matter of fact, said the Good Fairy, I do not understand two words of what you have said and I do not know what you are talking about. Do you know how many subordinate clauses you used in that last oration of yours, Sir?

I do not, replied the Pooka.

Fifteen subordinate clauses in all, said the Good Fairy, and the substance of each of them contained matter sufficient for a colloquy in itself. There is nothing so bad as the compression of fine talk that should last for six hours into one small hour. Tell me, Sir, did you ever study Bach?

Where did you say that from? inquired the Pooka.

I was sitting under your bed, replied the Good Fairy, on the handle of your pot.

The fugal and contrapuntal character of Bach's work, said the Pooka, that is a delight. The orthodox fugue has four figures and such a number is in itself admirable. Be careful of that pot. It is a present from my grandmother.

Counterpoint is an odd number, said the Good Fairy, and it is a great art that can evolve a fifth Excellence from four Futilities.

I do not agree with that, said the Pooka courteously. Here is a thing you have not informed me on – that is – the character of your sex. Whether you are a man-angel, that is a conundrum personal to yourself and not to be discussed with strangers.

It seems to me, Sir, said the Good Fairy, that you are again endeavouring to engage me in multi-clause colloquy. If you do not cease from it I will enter into your ear and you will not like it at all I will warrant you that. My sex is a secret that I cannot reveal.

I only inquired, said the Pooka, because I had a mind to get up and put on my clothes because long bed-hours are enemies and a new day is a thing to be experienced while it is still fresh. I will now do so and if you are of the woman class I must courteously request you to turn your back. And if that piteous itching in my left ear is due to your presence in the inside of it, please take yourself out of there immediately and return to the cup with the four coppers in it.

I have no back that I could turn, said the Good Fairy.

All right, I will rise in that case, said the Pooka, and if it is a useful occupation you desire, you could occupy your time with taking the tree out of my club-boot in the corner there.

By Hickory, said the Good Fairy in an earnest voice, it is full time that I gave you tidings concerning the purpose and the reason for my morning visit to your fine house here. I have come to inform you, Sir, about a party by the name of Sheila Lamont.

The Pooka had arisen with modest grace and was removing his silk nightshirt and reaching for his well-cut suit of seaman's kerseymere.

Where did you say that from? he inquired.

I am reclining in the key-hole, replied the Good Fairy.

The Pooka had put on his black underdrawers and his grey trousers and his old-world cravat and was engaged with his hands behind him in a fastidious adjustment of his tail of hair.

You did not inform me, he remarked politely, as to the sex of Miss Lamont.

As a matter of fact, said the Good Fairy, she is a woman.

That is very satisfactory, said the Pooka.

She is suffering at the moment, said the Good Fairy with the shadow of a slight frown on the texture of his voice, from a very old complaint. I refer now to pregnancy.

Do you tell me so? said the Pooka with a polite interest. That is very satisfactory.

The child is expected, said the Good Fairy, tomorrow evening. I shall be there and shall endeavour to put the child under my benevolent influence for life. To go there alone, however, without informing you of the happy event, that would be a deplorable breach of etiquette. Let the pair of us go therefore, and let the best man of us win the day.

That is a fine saying and a noble sentiment, said the Pooka, but tell me where it came from in the name of Goodness.

From your wife's hair, replied the Good Fairy. I am here in the dark, and it is a hard and joyless country.

I don't doubt it, said the Pooka. Did you tell me that this Miss Lamont was a man?

I did not, said the Good Fairy. She is a woman and a fine one from the point of view of those that have bodies on them.

That is very satisfactory, said the Pooka.

He carefully arranged the folds of his cravat before a piece of a looking-glass that was nailed to the back of the rough door. He then sprinkled an odorous balsam on his hair.

This party that you talk so much about, he inquired, where does it live?

Over there, said the Good Fairy with a jerk of his thumb, beyant.

If I could only see your thumb the time you jerked it, said the Pooka, I might know what you are talking about.

Hurry, said the Good Fairy.

What will we bring along with us against the journey? asked the Pooka. I am sure it is a long one and one that will soak our eyebrows with the sweat.

Bring what you like, said the Good Fairy.

Should I bring my shank of a wife – the party in the bed over there beyant?

I would not advise it, said the Good Fairy.

A change of black small-trunks? asked the Pooka.

When I have none at all, said the Good Fairy, it would not be right for you to have more than one pair.

The Pooka nodded courteously and carefully dressed himself in a soberly-cut raincoat of grey kerseymere with a built-in cape and an astrakhan collar and then took a hold of his black velour and his walking-stick. All things were then put in order about the house, pans were heeled up on their ends as a precaution against smuts, the fire was tended with black peats, and fine crocks were settled with their butts in the air. Everything was looked after down to the last acorn, which was retrieved from the floor and thrown out through the window.

Where are you now? asked the Pooka.

I am here, replied the Good Fairy, on the flag with the elliptical crack in it.

Pardon me for a moment if you please, said the Pooka with a small bow towards the cracked flag, I wish to take leave of my family.

He approached the bed with a tender solicitude the way he could put his hand in under the clothes. He caressed her rough cheek, hanging his stick on the rail.

Good-bye, my dear, he said tenderly.

Your granny, Fergus, she said in her queer muffled voice.

Where are you, asked the Pooka again.

I am in the pocket of your coat, said the Good Fairy.

You are a nice pocketful if I may say so, said the Pooka, but no matter. How will I know the way to go unless you proceed in front, cracking twigs and disturbing the leaves the way I will know the right direction?

There is no need for the like of that, said the Good Fairy. I will sit here in your pocket and look through the cloth and tell you when you make a wrong step.

You will not look through *that* cloth, said the Pooka, that is the best cloth that could be had. The cloth of that coat when it was new cost me five and sixpence a yard. That was before the War.

I could see through my lids if I shut my eyes, said the Good Fairy.

There is better stuff in that coat, said the Pooka with an earnest but polite inflexion, than was ever in any angel's eye-lid.

There is little doubt but that you are over-fond of the old talk, said the Good Fairy. Could I trouble you, Sir, to start walking?

I will start now, said the Pooka.

He caught hold of the boards of the door and pulled them open till he passed out into the glory of the morning. He fastened the door carefully with an old rope and strode from the clearing into the murk of the surrounding undergrowth, making short work of all obstacles with terrible batters of his club-boot, demolishing tendrils and creeper-ropes and severing the spidery suspensions of yellow and green and blood-red yams with whistling swats of his ashen stick and treading the lichen with a heavy tread and a light one, iambic pentameter, a club-step and a footstep.

There is no need, said the Good Fairy, to walk through every bed of briars you see. Picking your way, there is such a thing as that.

That is a matter of opinion, said the Pooka.

You could give yourself a bad jag, said the Good Fairy. Keep to the left, you are going the wrong way.

The Pooka wheeled in his course without appreciable loss of pace and went straight to the middle of a thicket of stout rods, cracking it before him the like of a walnut in a strong palm. The Fairy turned to survey the ruin of shattered stirks.

Some of these trees are sharp, he observed, mind or you will make a tatters of your coat.

There is better stuff in that coat, said the Pooka with a wilful march on a wall of thornsticks, than they are putting into clothes nowadays. A coat in the old days was made to stand up to rough wear and was built to last.

Keep to the left, called the Good Fairy. Do you always carry on like this when you are out walking?

I do not mind telling you, said the Pooka courteously, that there is no subterfuge of economy more misconceived than the purchase of cheap factory-machined clothing. I was once acquainted with a man who committed himself to the folly of a shoddy suit. What do you think happened?

Keep well to the left, said the Good Fairy. It was likely torn off his back by a nest of thorns on the roadside.

Not correct, said the Pooka. It lathered in a shower of rain and that is the odd truth. The seams of these inferior garments are secured with soap. It frothed on him in the street the like of a pan of new milk boiling over.

One thing is certain, observed the Good Fairy, if you walk through that clump you are now heading for, you will make ribbons of your coat and a tatters of your skin, you will kill the two of us. Discretion, there is such a thing as that.

I will not, said the Pooka. There was small else for him to do but to enter a barber's shop and have the suit shaved. Do you know how much that cost him in silver coin?

The Good Fairy gave a cry in the gloom of the pocket as the Pooka strode in his career through the mad rending and crackling of the thorn-fraught branch-thick tangle.

I do not, he said.

Ten and sevenpence, said the Pooka, and that was a lot of money before the War. Would it be a discourtesy to ask you whether I am travelling in the right direction at all.

You are doing very well, said the Good Fairy.

Very good, said the Pooka.

Once again he quitted the warm sunlight of the clear morning to smash and shatter a clear path in the sun-trellised twilight of the jungle.

The two of them had not journeyed the length of two perches statute when they saw the two men drinking draughts of cool water from their large hats by the stream-side, the one a tall-boned large fine man and the other a small fleshed man. Around their middles they had the full of two belts of bright bullets as well as a pair of six-guns apiece, and two hatfuls of clear crystal they had drunk before the Pooka approached to the back of them as they knelt there to surprise them with a mouthful of his talk.

Ask them who they are, said the Good Fairy.

Greetings, said the Pooka courteously, to the pair of ye.

God save you, said Slug Willard adroitly donning his wet hat the way he could raise it for politeness, this is my friend and my butty, Mr Shorty Andrews. How are you?

I am very well, said the Pooka. And how are you, Mr Andrews?

I am grand, said Shorty.

Isn't it wonderful weather, said the Good Fairy from the interior of the pocket, a morning like this is as good as a tonic.

What's that? What did you say, Sir? asked Slug.

I said nothing, said the Pooka.

My mistake, said Slug. Unfortunately, Sir, I suffer from noises in the head and in my sleep I often hear voices. You didn't happen to see a steer anywhere, did you, Sir?

We are searching our legs off looking for a lost steer, explained Shorty.

Lord save us, said the Good Fairy, you will surely have the nice job looking for it in a place like this.

You're right there, said Slug, but, no offence, you have a queer way of talking, Sir.

That time, said the Pooka smiling, I did not talk at all.

Maybe not, said Shorty.

On my word of honour, said the Pooka.

It seemed to come from your clothes, Sir – that voice, said Slug. You are not in the habit of carrying a small gramophone in your pocket, are you, Sir?

I am not, said the Pooka.

Introduce me, the Good Fairy said in his urgent whisper.

You are at it again, said Shorty roughly.

Allow me to explain, said the Pooka, the voice you hear is coming from the pocket of my coat. I have a spirit in my pocket and it is he that is doing the talking.

You have your porridge, said Shorty.

On my solemn word of honour, said the Pooka gravely. He came to my house this morning and the pair of us are now engaged on a private journey. He is very gentlemanly and very good at conversation. The two of us are on our way to assist at a happy event at the Red Swan Hotel.

Your porridge, said Shorty.

Well that's a good one, said Slug. Could you give us a look?

Unfortunately there is nothing to see.

Are you sure it's not a ferret you have in your pocket? asked Shorty. You look like a man that was out after rabbits.

Who's a ferret? asked the Good Fairy sharply.

It's a bloody spirit all right, said Slug. I know a spirit when I hear one talking.

Your porridge, said Shorty, would you be so kind, you in the pocket, as to give us a selection on your harp?

The idea that all spirits are accomplished instrumentalists is a popular fallacy, said the Good Fairy in a cold voice, just as it is wrong to assume that they all have golden tempers. Maybe your doubts would be resolved if I kicked the jaw off your face, Mr Andrews?

Keep your distance, me man, said Shorty with a quick move to the gun-butts, keep your distance or I'll shoot your lights out!

Put your gun up, man, said Slug, he hasn't got any. Do you not know that much at your time of life. He is all air.

He'll have a damn sight less when I'm through, shouted Shorty, no bloody spirit is going to best me.

Tut, tut, said the Pooka soothingly, there is no necessity to make a scene.

I was called a ferret, said the Good Fairy.

Porridge and parsnips, said Shorty.

You keep your trap shut for five minutes, said Slug with fierce shoulders towering over the head of his friend, shut your bloody mouth now, do you hear me? This gentleman and his spirit are friends of mine, mind that now, and when you insult them you insult me. Don't make any mistake about that if you value your bloody life. H.O., H.A. Hit one, hit all.

Now, gentlemen, *please*, said the Pooka.

Hit one, hit all, repeated Slug.

Pipe down, said Shorty.

I'll pipe you and I'll pipe you down the nearest sewer if you say another word, my fine man, shouted Slug, I'll give you what you won't hold, I'll knock your bloody block off if you say another word. Apologize!

Gentlemen! said the Pooka in a pained manner.

Make your apologies quick, rapped Slug.

All right, all right, said Shorty, apologies all round. Is everybody happy?

I am satisfied, said the Good Fairy.

That is very satisfactory, said the Pooka with a bright re-dawn of courtesy, and now possibly you gentlemen would care to join us in our happy mission. There is a small son being born to Miss Lamont and I have no reason to suspect that guests will be unprovided with refreshment of the right kind.

It's a pleasure, said Slug, we will go and welcome. Did you ever happen to know a party by the name of William Tracy?

I have heard of him, replied the Pooka. Let us take a short-cut through this copse here on the left.

A decent skin if there ever was one, said Slug with warmth, a man that didn't stint the porter. It was a pleasure to work for Mr Tracy. Isn't the Red Swan where Mr Trellis lives?

Quite correct, said the Pooka.

What about presents for the bride, asked Shorty, it's only right to bring the full of your pockets when you're going to a hooley.

It's the usual all right, said Slug.

That's a pretty sort of a custom, said the Good Fairy. I wish to God I had a pocket.

The travellers then scattered apart for a bit about the wilderness of the undergrowth till they had filled their pockets with fruits and sorrels and studded acorns, the produce of the yamboo and the blooms of the yulan, blood-gutted berries and wrinkled cresses, branches of juice-slimed sloes, whortles and plums and varied mast, the speckled eggs from the nests of daws.

What do you think I'm made of, asked the Good Fairy sharply, take that thing with the prickles out of your pocket.

Musha, you're very tender, said the Pooka.

I don't wear armour-plated stays, said the Good Fairy.

There's something in there in that clump, called Shorty, I saw something moving.

It's only a rabbit or a black tyke, said the Pooka.

You have your porridge, said Shorty as he peered with his shading hand, there's a trousers on it.

Give us a look, said Slug.

Are you sure it is not a ferret, asked the Good Fairy, chuckling.

Come out of there, roared Shorty with a clasp towards his gun, come out of there or I'll shoot the tail off you!

Steady now, said Slug. Good day, Sir. Come on out till we see you and don't be afraid.

It's a man and an old one, said the Good Fairy. I can see him through the cloth of the coat here. Advance, Sir, to be recognized!

I don't believe you will see much through *that* cloth, said the Pooka. Five and sixpence a yard it cost.

Give the word, said Shorty with a waving menace of his hand, or it's gunplay and gravestones. Come out of that tree, you bloody bastard you!

There was a prolonged snappling of stiffened rods and stubborn shoots and the sharp agonies of fractured branches, the pitiless flogging against each other of green life-laden leaves, the thrashing and the scourging of a clump in torment, a jaggle of briar-braced tangly-brambled thorniness, incensed, with a demon in its breast. Crack crack crack.

A small man came out of the foliage, a small man elderly and dark with a cloth cap and a muffler around his wind-pipe.

Jem by God Casey! said Slug Willard. Two emblems of amazement, his limp hands sank down to his waist until the thumbs found fastening in the bullet-studded belt.

Can you beat it? asked Shorty.

Good morning, said the Pooka courteously.

You are a terrible man, Casey, said Slug.

Greetings all round, said the Casey, and the compliments of the season.

All I can say is this, Casey, said Slug, you are the right fly-be-night, the right hop-off-my-thumb, to be stuck in a place like that. Ladies and gentlemen, this is Jem Casey, Poet of the Pick and Bard of Booterstown.

That is very satisfactory, said the Pooka. To meet a poet, that is a pleasure. The morning, Mr Casey, can only be described as a glorious extravagance.

What sort of a voice is that, asked Casey, high and low like a bloody swingboat?

The remark about the weather, explained the Pooka, was not made by me at all but by a fairy that I have here in my pocket.

It's a fact, said Slug.

I believe you, said the poet, I believe all that I hear in this place. I thought I heard a maggot talking to me a while ago from under a stone. Good morning, Sir or something he said. This is a very queer place certainly.

My hard Casey, said Slug. Tell me, what were you doing in that clump there?

What do you think, asked Casey. What does any man be doing in a clump? What would *you* be doing?

Here Shorty gave a loud laugh.

By God I know what *I'd* be doing, he laughed.

Approximately half of the company at this stage joined their voices together in boisterous noises of amusement.

We all have to do that, roared Shorty at the end of his prolonged laugh, the best of us have to do that.

He collapsed on his back on the grass, shrieking aloud in his amusement. He moved his feet in the air as if operating a pedal cycle.

They have no respect, said the Good Fairy quietly to the Pooka, no respect and no conception of propriety.

The Pooka nodded.

I hope I am broad-minded, he said, but I draw the line at vulgarity and smut. Talk the like of that reflects on them and on the parents that brought them up. It speaks very poorly for their home life.

Suddenly Casey turned round and presented a stern face to the company.

What was I doing? he asked. What was I doing then?

The only answer was a loud laugh.

Well I will tell you what I was doing, he said gravely, I will tell you what I was at. I was reciting a pome to a selection of my friends. That's what I was doing. It is only your dirty minds.

Poetry is a thing I am very fond of, said the Good Fairy. I always make a point of following the works of Mr Eliot and Mr Lewis and Mr Devlin. A good pome is a tonic. Was your pome on the subject of flowers, Mr Casey? Wordsworth was a great man for flowers.

Mr Casey doesn't go in for that class of stuff, said Slug.

Dirty minds be damned, said Shorty.

None of your soft stuff for Mr Casey, said Slug.

I am very fond of flowers, too, said the Good Fairy. The smell of a nice flower is like a tonic. Love of flowers, it is a great sign of virtue.

The stuff that I go in for, said Casey roughly, is the real stuff. Oh, none of the fancy stuff for me.

He spat phlegm coarsely on the grass.

The workin' man doesn't matter, of course, he added.

But why? asked the Pooka courteously. He is surely the noblest of all creatures.

What about all these strikes? asked the Good Fairy. I don't know about him being the noblest. They have the country crippled with their strikes. Look at the price of bread. Sixpence halfpenny for a two-pound loaf.

Dirty minds be damned, said Shorty again. Oh, by God I know what you were doing in that clump, me boyo.

And look at bacon, said the Good Fairy. One and ninepence if you please.

To hell with the workin' man, said Casey. That's what you hear. To bloody hell with him.

I have a great admiration for the worker, said the Pooka.

Well so have I, said Casey loudly. I'll always stand up for my own. It's about the Workin' Man that I was reciting my pome.

And then you have the Conditions of Employment Act, said the Good Fairy, class legislation, that's what it is. Holidays with full pay if you please. No wonder the moneyed classes are leaving the country. Bolshevism will be the next step.

I admire the working man immensely, said the Pooka, and I will not hear a word against him. He is the backbone of family life.

I'd advise that man in the pocket to keep his mouth shut, said Casey roughly. He wouldn't be the first of his kind that got a hammering.

It would take more than you to hammer me then, the Good Fairy answered.

The Pooka spread out his long-nailed hands and made a long soothing noise through his haired nostrils.

Please, gentlemen, he said, no need for acrimony.

If that's what you were at in the clump, said Shorty, stand out there and give us a couple of verses. Go on now.

The poet removed his frown.

I will if you want me to, he said.

Not everybody can recite poetry, said the Good Fairy. It is an art in itself. Verse-speaking they call it in London.

Don't mind him, said Slug. Off you go, Casey. One, two, three . . .

Casey then made a demonstration with his arm and gave out his poetical composition in a hard brassy voice, free from all inflexion.

> Come all ye lads and lassies prime
> From Macroom to old Strabane,
> And list to me till I say my rhyme –
> THE GIFT OF GOD IS A WORKIN' MAN.
>
> Your Lords and people of high degree
> Are a fine and a noble clan,
> They do their best but they cannot see
> THAT THE GIFT OF GOD IS A WORKIN' MAN.
>
> From France to Spain and from Holland gay
> To the shores of far Japan,
> You'll find the people will always say
> THE GIFT OF GOD IS A WORKIN' MAN.
>
> He's good, he's strong and his heart is free
> If he navvies or drives a van,
> He'll shake your hand with a gra-macree –
> THE GIFT OF GOD IS A WORKIN' MAN.
>
> Your Lords and ladies are fine to see
> And they do the best they can,
> But here's the slogan for you and me –
> THE GIFT OF GOD IS A WORKIN' MAN.

Good man! called Slug, good man yourself. Certainly that's a great bit of writing.

Bravo, said the Pooka politely.

Casey put out his two hands to make silence and then waved them up and down.

Here's the last verse, he shouted. All together, boys.

A WORKIN' MAN, A WORKIN' MAN,
Hurray Hurray for a Workin' Man,
He'll navvy and sweat till he's nearly bet,
THE GIFT OF GOD IS A WORKIN' MAN!

Oh, good man, said Slug. He started clapping in the sun-drenched clearing of the wild jungle and the applause was completed by the rest of the company.

That is what they call a ballad, observed the Good Fairy. Did you ever read the Ballad of Father Gilligan? he asked the Pooka.

That would be an Intermediate book, of course, replied the Pooka. I'm afraid I never read that. Unfortunately, I left school at Third Book.

A very nice spiritual thing, said the Good Fairy.

A workin' man, eh? said Shorty. He got up from the ground and brushed at his garments.

Now that we've heard and enjoyed Mr Casey's poetry, said Slug, maybe we should be moving.

Moving where? asked Casey.

We are going to a hooley, said Shorty, fill your pockets, man, and fall in. The fruits of the earth, you know.

The party then moved slowly on, the poet taking a last look at the clump where he had sat in conclave with a synod of tinkers, thimble-riggers, gombeen-men, beggars, channel-rakers, bacaughs, broom-men, and people from every walk in the lower order, singing and reciting a selection of his finer lyrics.

You in the pocket, said the poet, can you fly?

Maybe I can, replied the Good Fairy.

Would you go and tell my wife that I won't be home for dinner? Would you ever do that?

What do you take me for? asked the Good Fairy in a thin testy voice, a carrier-pigeon?

If you want to make him mad, said Shorty, call him a ferret. When I called him that he gave me any God's own thanks.

Can you tell me, Mr Casey, said the Pooka interposing quickly, whether my wife is a kangaroo?

The poet stared in his surprise.

What in the name of God, he asked, do you mean by throwing a question like that at me? Eh?

I was wondering, said the Pooka.

A kangaroo? She might be a lump of a carrot for all I know. Do you mean a marsupial?

That's the man, said Slug. A marsupial.

Stop the talk, said the Good Fairy quickly. I see a man in a tree.

Where? asked Shorty.

Too far away for you to see. I see him through the trunks and the branches.

Pray what is a marsupial? asked the Pooka.

I cannot see him too well, said the Good Fairy, there is about a half a mile of forest in between. A marsupial is another name for an animal that is fitted with a built-in sack the way it can carry its young ones about.

If you have wings, said the poet sharply, why in the name of barney don't you take a flight in the air and have a good look instead of blathering out of you in the pocket there and talking about what the rest of us can't see?

If that is what a marsupial is, said the Pooka courteously, where is the difference? Surely the word kangaroo is more descriptive?

What do you take me for, asked the Good Fairy, a kite? I will fly away in the air when it suits me and no sooner. There is this distinction between marsupial and kangaroo, that the former denotes a genus and the latter a class, the former is general and the latter particular.

I don't believe there is any kangaroo in the tree, said Slug. Kangaroos don't go up trees in this country.

Possibly, said the Pooka, it is my wife that is up there in the tree. She shares this much with the birds, that she can journey through the air on the shaft of a broomstick. It would not be hard for her to be thus in front of us in our journey.

Who in the name of God, asked Shorty, ever heard of a bird flying on a broomstick?

I did not say my wife was a bird.

You said she was a broomstick this morning, said the Good Fairy, a shank, that's what you called her.

What I was talking about, said the Pooka slowly, was kangaroos. Kangaroos.

It might be a bird in the tree, said Shorty, a big bird.

There's a lot in that, Slug said.

Very well, said the Good Fairy in a displeased way. No doubt

I was mistaken. It is not a man. It is a tit. A tit or a bloody wren.

Shorty with a quick gesture gripped his six-gun.

Is that the tree you mean, he shouted, that tree over there? Is it? There's something in *that* tree all right.

The Good Fairy nodded.

Answer me, you bloody little bowsy you! roared Shorty.

Be pleased to answer yourself less vigorously, said the Pooka nervously, there is no need for language the like of that. That is the tree he means. I felt him nodding his head against my hip.

Well why couldn't he say so, said Shorty, taking out his second gun.

If I get out of this pocket, said the Good Fairy in a thin voice, I will do damage. I have stood as much as I will stand for one day.

Come down out of that tree, roared Shorty, come down out of that, you bloody ruffian!

Keep your dander down, said Slug, you can't shoot anything that's sitting.

Whatever it is, observed the poet, it's not a man. It hasn't got a trousers on it. It's likely a marsupial.

I still fail to see the distinction, said the Pooka quietly, or why marsupial should be preferred to the more homely word.

If you don't come down out of that tree in two seconds, bellowed Shorty with a cock of his two hammers, you'll come out a corpse in three! I'll count to ten. One, two. . . .

I'm glad I have no body, said the Good Fairy. With that demented bully flourishing his irons every time he gets the sight of something he can shoot, nobody is safe. The term kangaroo, being the lesser, is *contained* in marsupial, which is a broader and more comprehensive word.

Five, six, seven . . .

I see, said the Pooka, you mean that the marsupial carries a kangaroo in its pouch?

TEN, said Shorty in decision. For the last time, are you coming down?

There was a gentle rustle in the thick of the green branches, a slow caress like the visit of a summer breeze in a field of oats, a faint lifeless movement: and a voice descended on the travellers, querulous and saddened with an infinite weariness, a thin voice that was occupied with the recital of these staves:

Sweeny the thin-groined it is
in the middle of the yew;
life is very bare here,
piteous Christ it is cheerless.

Grey branches have hurt me
they have pierced my calves,
I hang here in the yew-tree above,
without chessmen, no womantryst.

I can put no faith in humans
in the place they are;
watercress at evening is my lot,
I will not come down.

Lord save us! said Slug.

Shorty waved his guns about him in the air, swallowing at his spittle.

You won't come down?

I think I know the gentleman, said the Pooka courteously interposing, I fancy (it is possible that I may be wrong) that it is a party by the name of Sweeny. He is not all in it.

Do I shoot or don't I, asked Shorty presenting the orb of his puzzled face for the general inspection of the company.

Do you mean the Sweenies of Rathangan, inquired the Good Fairy, or the Sweenies of Swanlinbar?

Keep that bloody gun down, said Casey sharply, the voice that spoke was the voice of a bloody poet. By God I know a bloody poet when I hear one. Hands off the poets. I can write a verse myself and I respect the man that can do the same. Put that gun up.

I do not, replied the Pooka.

Or the flaxen Sweenies from Kiltimagh?

It's an old man, observed Slug, and you can't leave a man roosting in a tree like that. After we're gone he might get sick or have a fit or something and then where are you?

He might puke his porridge, said Shorty.

Not them either, said the Pooka courteously.

Then the MacSweenies of Ferns and Borris-in-Ossory?

With these words there came the rending scream of a shattered stirk and an angry troubling of the branches as the poor madman percolated through the sieve of a sharp yew, a wailing black meteor hurtling through green clouds, a human prickles. He came to the ground with his right nipple opened to the wide and a ruined back that was packed with the thorns and the small-wood of the trees of Erin, a tormented cress-stained mouth never halting from the recital of inaudible strange staves. There were feathers on his body here and there, impaired and shabby with vicissitude.

By God he's down! shouted Slug.

I don't mean them either, said the Pooka above the noise.

Then the O'Sweenies of Harold's Cross?

Jem Casey was kneeling at the pock-haunched form of the king pouring questions into the cup of his dead ear and picking small thorns from his gashed chest with absent thoughtless fingers, poet on poet, a bard unthorning a fellow-bard.

Give him air, said Slug.

Will you walk over there, said the Good Fairy to the Pooka, the way I can see this man that has been bird-nesting?

Certainly, said the Pooka courteously.

What is the man's name, asked the Good Fairy.

The Pooka made a sharp pass in the air with his thumb, a token of annoyance.

Sweeny, he answered. There is only one remedy for a bleeding hole in a man's side – moss. Pack him with moss the way he will not bleed to death.

That's the number, said Slug, plenty of moss.

Damp sponges of lichen and green moss were plied in the gapes of Sweeny's flank, young shoots and stalks and verdure, in his ruined side till they were reddened and stiffened with the bleeding of his thick blood. He fell to muttering discordant verses.

> As I made the fine throw at Ronan
> from the middle of the hosts,
> the fair cleric said that I had leave
> to go with birds.
>
> I am Sweeny the slender-thin,
> the slender, the hunger-thin,

> berries crimson and cresses green,
> their colours are my mouth.

> I was in the centre of the yew
> distraught with suffering,
> the hostile branches scourged me,
> I would not come down.

You're all right man, said Casey with kindly pats of his hand on the mossy side, you'll get over that. You'll be all right, don't you worry.

A bullet would put him out of his pain, said Shorty, it would be a merciful act of Providence.

I wish to Goodness, said the Pooka with a courteous insistence, that you would replace that shooting-iron and repress this craving for bloodshed. Can you not see the poor man is unwell?

What is wrong with him? inquired the Good Fairy.

He took a sore fall, said Slug kindly, he might have broken his bloody neck, eh, Mr Casey?

He might have split his arc, said Casey.

Maybe he is drunk, suggested the Good Fairy, I don't believe in wasting my sympathy on sots, do you?

There is no harm in an odd drop now and then, replied the Pooka, drink in moderation is all right. Drunkenness, of course – that is another pair of shoes altogether.

The invalid man stirred in his earthen couch and murmured:

> Our wish is at Samhain, up to Maytime,
> when the wild ducks come
> in each dun wood without stint
> to be in ivy-trees.

> Water of Glen Bolcain fair
> a listening to its horde of birds,
> its tuneful streams that are not slow,
> its islands, its rivers.

> In the tree of Cell Lughaidh,
> it was our wish to be alone,
> swift flight of swallows on the brink of summer –
> take your hands away!

It's drink all right, said the Good Fairy, leave him be.

Nonsense, man, said Slug, a little touch of fever and the best will rave, the strongest will go to the wall with one little dart of double-pneumonia, I had an uncle once that was shouting the walls of the house down two hours after he got his head wet in a shower of rain. Has anybody got a thermometer till we take his pulse?

Would a sun-glass be of any assistance to you? inquired the Pooka politely.

A shandy is what he wants, said the Good Fairy, a glass of gin and a bottle of stone beer, a curer.

That'll do you, said Casey, help me with him, somebody. We'll have to bring him along with us, by God I'd die of shame if we left the poor bastard here on his tod. Give us a hand, somebody.

I'm your man, said Slug.

Together the two strong men, joyous in the miracle of their health, put their bulging thews and the fine ripple of their sinews together at the arm-pits of the stricken king as they bent over him with their grunting red faces, their four heels sinking down in the turf of the jungle with the stress of their fine effort as they hoisted the madman to the tremulous support of his withered legs.

Mind his feathers, said Shorty in a coarse way, never ruffle a cock's feathers.

The madman fluttered his lids in the searchlight of the sun and muttered out his verses as he tottered hither and thither and back again backwards in the hold of his two keepers.

> Though my flittings are unnumbered,
> my clothing today is scarce,
> I personally maintain my watch
> on the tops of mountains.
>
> O fern, russet long one,
> your mantle has been reddened,
> there's no bedding for an outcast
> on your branching top.
>
> Nuts at terce and cress-leaves,
> fruits from an apple-wood at noon,

a lying-down to lap chill water –
your fingers torment my arms.

Put green moss in his mouth, said the Good Fairy querulously, are we going to spend the rest of our lives in this place listening to talk the like of that? There is a bad smell in this pocket, it is not doing me any good. What are you in the habit of keeping in it, Sir?

Nothing, replied the Pooka, but tabacca.

It's a queer smell for tabacca, said the Good Fairy.

One and sixpence I pay in silver coin for an ounce of it, said the Pooka, and nice as it is for the wee pipe, it is best eaten. It is what they call shag tabacca.

Notwithstanding all that, said the Good Fairy, there is a queer hum off it. It would be the price of you if I got sick here in your pocket.

Now be very careful, said the Pooka.

Quick march my hard man, said Casey briskly to the king, put your best leg forward and we will get you a bed before the sun goes down, we'll get a sup of whisky into you to make you sleep.

We'll get you a jug of hot punch and a packet of cream crackers with plenty of butter, said Slug, if you'll only walk, if you'll only pull yourself together, man.

And getting around the invalid in a jabbering ring, they rubbed him and cajoled and coaxed, and plied him with honey-talk and long sweet-lilted sentences full of fine words, and promised him metheglin and mugs of viscous tar-black mead thickened with white yeast and the spoils from hives of mountain-bees, and corn-coarse nourishing farls of wheaten bread dipped in musk-scented liquors and sodden with Belgian sherry, an orchard and a swarm of furry honey-glutted bees and a bin of sun-bronzed grain from the granaries of the Orient in every drop as it dripped at the lifting of the hand to the mouth, and inky quids of strong-smoked tabacca with cherrywood pipes, hubble-bubbles, duidins, meerschaums, clays, hickory hookahs and steel-stemmed pipes with enamel bowls, the lot of them laid side by side in a cradle of lustrous blue plush, a huge pipe-case and pipe-rack ingeniously combined and circumscribed with a durable quality of black imitation leather over a framework of stout cedarwood dovetailed and intricately worked and made to last, the whole being handsomely finished and untouched by hand and packed in good-quality transparent cellophane, a present calculated to warm the cockles of the heart of any smoker. They also did not hesitate to promise him sides of hairy bacon, the mainstay and the staff of life of the country classes, and lamb chops still succulent with young blood, autumn-heavy yams from venerable stooping trees, bracelets and garlands of browned sausages and two baskets of peerless eggs fresh-collected, a waiting hand under the hen's bottom. They beguiled him with the mention of salads and crome custards and the grainy disorder of pulpy boiled rhubarb, matchless as a physic for the bowels, olives and acorns and rabbit-pie, and venison roasted on a smoky spit, and mulatto thick-lipped delphy cups of black-strong tea. They foreshadowed the felicity of billowy beds of swansdown carefully laid crosswise on springy rushes and sequestered with a canopy of bearskins and generous goatspelts, a couch for a king with fleshly delectations and fifteen hundred olive-mellow concubines in constant attendance against the hour of desire. Chariots they talked about and duncrusted pies exuberant with a sweat of crimson juice, and tall crocks full of eddying foam-washed stout, and wailing prisoners in chains on their knees for mercy, humbled enemies crouching in sackcloth with their upturned eye-whites suppliant. They mentioned the leap of a fire on a cold night, long sleeps in the shadows and leaden-eyed forgetfulness hour on hour – princely oblivion. And as they talked, they threaded through the twilight and the sudden sun-pools of the wild country.

It is a scourge, said the Good Fairy, the hum in this pocket.

If that is the case, said the Pooka, you can change to another or get out and walk and welcome.

The smell of another pocket, replied the Good Fairy, that might be far worse.

The company continued to travel throughout the day, pausing at evening to provide themselves with the sustenance of oakmast and coconuts and with the refreshment of pure water from the jungle springs. They did not cease, either walking or eating, from the delights of colloquy and harmonized talk contrapuntal in character nor did Sweeny desist for long from stave-music or from the recital of his misery in verse. On the brink of night they halted to light faggots with a box of matches and continued through the tangle and the grasses with flaming brands above their heads until the night-newts and the moths and the bats and the fellicaun-eeha had fallen in behind them in a gentle constellation of winking red wings in the flair of the fires, delightful alliteration. On occasion an owl or an awkward beetle or a small coterie of hedgehogs, attracted by the splendour of the light, would escort them for a part of the journey until the circumstances of their several destinations would divert them again into the wild treachery of the gloom. The travellers would sometimes tire of the drone of one another's talk and join together in the metre of an old-fashioned song, filling their lungs with fly-thickened air and raising their voices above the sleeping trees. They sang *Home on the Range* and the pick of the old cowboy airs, the evergreen favourites of the bunkhouse and the prairie; they joined together with a husky softness in the lilt of the old come-all-ye's, the ageless minstrelsy of the native-land, a sob in their voice as the last note died; they rendered old catches with full throats, and glees and round-songs and riddle-me-raddies, *Tipperary* and *Nellie Deane* and *The Shade of the Old Apple Tree*. They sang Cuban love-songs and moonsweet madrigals and selections from the best and the finest of the Italian operas, from the compositions of Puccini and Meyerbeer and Donizetti and Gounod and the Maestro Mascagni as well as an aria from *The Bohemian Girl* by Balfe, and intoned the choral complexities of Palestrina the pioneer. They rendered two hundred and forty-two (242) songs by Schubert in the original German words, and sang a chorus from *Fidelio* (by Beethoven of *Moonlight Sonata* fame) and the *Song of the Flea*, and a long excerpt from a Mass by Bach, as well as innumerable tuneful pleasantries from the able pens of no less than Mozart and Handel. To the stars (though they could not see them owing to the roofage of the leaves and the branches above them), they gave with a thunderous spirit such pieces by Offenbach, Schumann, Saint-Saens and Granville Bantock as they could remember. They sang entire movements from cantatas and oratorios and other items of sacred music, *allegro ma non troppo*, *largo* and *andante cantabile*.

They were all so preoccupied with music that they were still chanting spiritedly in the dark undergrowth long after the sun, earlier astir than usual, had cleaned the last vestige of the soiling night from the verdure of the tree-tops – rosy-fingered pilgrim of the sandal grey. When they suddenly arrived to find mid-day in a clearing, they wildly reproached each other with bitter words and groundless allegations of bastardy and low birth as they collected berries and haws into the hollows of their hats against the incidence of a late breakfast. Temporary discontinuance of the foregoing.

Biographical reminiscence, part the seventh: I recall that I went into my uncle's house about nine p.m. one evening in the early spring, the sharp edge of my perception dulled somewhat by indulgence in spirituous liquors. I was standing in the middle of the dining-room floor before I had properly adverted to my surroundings. The faces I found there were strange and questioning. Searching among them, I found at last the features of my uncle.

Nature of features: Red, irregular, coarse, fat.

He was situated in a central position in the midst of four others and looked out from them in my direction in a penetrating attentive manner. I was on my way backwards towards the door when he said to me:

No need to go. Gentlemen, my nephew. I think we require a secretary. Take a seat.

After this I heard a murmur of polite felicitation. It was represented that my continued presence was a keen source of pleasure to the company without exception. I sat down at the table and took my blue pencil from a chest-pocket. My uncle studied a black note-book for a moment and then pushed it across to me and said:

I think that should be enough.

I took the book and read the legend inscribed on the front page in the square unambiguous writing of my uncle.

Nature of legend: Eighteen loaves. Two pan-loaves (? one pan). Three pounds cheese. Five pounds cooked ham. Two pounds tea (one and four). Tin floor-powder. Fancy cakes 2d. and 3d. (? 4d.). Eighteen rock-buns. Eight pounds butter. Sugar, milk (? each bring supply ?). Rosin. Bottle D.W.D. ? ? ? ? ? ? ? ? ?.

Hire of crockery £1. ? Breakages Speak re necessity care. ? Lemonade. Say £5.

My uncle made an urgent noise with the case of his spectacles.

You were saying, Mr Connors . . . ? he said.

Ah, yes, said Mr Connors.

A big loose man to my left drew himself together and braced his body for the ordeal of utterance. He wore on the upper lip a great straggling moustache and heavy tired eyes moved slowly as if belated in adjustment to his other features. He struggled to an attitude of upright attention.

Now I think it's a great mistake to be too strict, he said. We must make allowances. One old-time waltz is all I ask. It's as Irish as any of them, nothing foreign about the old-time waltz. We must make allowances. The Gaelic League . . .

I don't agree, said another man.

My uncle gave a sharp crack on the table.

Order, Mr Corcoran, he said in reprimand, order if you please. Mr Connors has the floor. This is a Committee Meeting. I'm sick sore and tired saying this is a Committee Meeting. After all there is such a thing as Procedure, there is such a thing as Order, there is such a thing as doing things in the right way. Have you a Point of Order, Mr Corcoran?

I have, said Mr Corcoran. He was tall and thin and fair. I found that his face was known to me. His hair was sparse and sandy.

Very well. If you have a Point of Order, well and good. Well and good if you have a Point of Order. Proceed.

Eh? said Mr Corcoran.

Proceed. Continue.

Oh, yes. Old-time waltzes. Yes. I don't agree with the old-time waltz at all. Nothing *wrong* with it, of course, Mr Connors, nothing actually *wrong* with it . . .

Address the Chair, address the Chair, said my uncle.

But after all a Ceilidhe is not the place for it, that's all. A Ceilidhe is a Ceilidhe. I mean, we have our own. We have plenty of our own dances without crossing the road to borrow what we can't wear. See the point? It's all right but it's not for us. Leave the waltz to the jazz-boys. By God they're welcome as far as I'm concerned.

Mr Connors to reply, said my uncle.

Oh, settle it any way you like, said Mr Connors. It was only a suggestion. There's nothing wrong with the old-time waltz. Nothing in the wide world. I've danced it myself. Mr Hickey here has danced it. We have all danced it. Because a thing is foreign it does not stand to reason that it's bad.

When did I dance it? asked Mr Hickey.

Description of Mr Hickey: Old, yellow, dark, lean. Pendulous flesh at eyes and jaws. Of utterance precise and slow. A watching listener.

On a Point of Personal Explanation? asked my uncle.

Yes, said Mr Hickey.

Very well.

Twenty-three years ago at the Rotunda Gardens, said Mr Connors. Haven't I a góod memory?

You certainly have, said Mr Hickey.

He smiled, mollified. He pursed his lips in the exercise of a retrospect across the years, absently playing with his loose plate. Bushy brows hid his eyes as they gazed on his white knuckles.

Mr Fogarty? said my uncle.

Mr Fogarty was a middle-aged man but with a round satisfied face. He smiled evenly on the company. He was attired in good-quality expensive clothing and wore an air of assurance.

Settle it between ye, he said lightly. Leave Mr Fogarty alone now.

The Gaelic League is opposed to the old-time waltz, said Mr Corcoran. So are the clergy.

Now, now, I don't think that's right, said Mr Connors.

Order, order, said my uncle.

I never heard that said, said Mr Connors. Which of the clergy now?

My uncle gave another crack.

Order, he repeated. *Order.*

Chapter and verse, Mr Corcoran. Which of the clergy,

That will do, Mr Connors, said my uncle sharply, that is quite sufficient. This is a Committee Meeting. We won't be long settling it. All those in favour of the old-time waltz say Aye.

Aye!

Those against say No.

No!

I declare the Noes have it.

Division, called Mr Connors.

A division has been challenged. I appoint Mr Secretary teller. All those in favour raise one hand.

The total that I counted in favour of each proposition was one; certain parties abstained from voting.

My casting vote, said my uncle loudly, is in favour of the negative.

Well that's that, said Mr Connors sighing.

If things are done in the right way, said my uncle, there is no question of wasting time. Now when does he arrive? You have the details, Mr Hickey.

Mr Hickey bestirred himself with reluctance and said:

He will be in Cork from the liner at ten, that means Kingsbridge about seven.

Very well, said my uncle, that means he reaches the hall about nine, making allowance for a wash and a bite to eat. By nine o'clock – yes, we will be in full swing by nine o'clock. Now a Reception Committee. I appoint Mr Corcoran and Mr Connors and myself.

I still challenge Mr Corcoran to give the name of the clergyman, said Mr Connors.

That is not a Point of Order, said my uncle. He turned to me and said: Have you the names of the Reception Committee?

Yes, I answered.

Very good. Now I think I should read a brief address when he is at the door. Something short and to the point. A few words in Irish first, of course.

Oh, certainly, said Mr Corcoran. Not forgetting a red carpet on the steps. That is the recognized thing.

My uncle frowned.

Well I don't know, he said. I think a red carpet would be a bit . . .

I agree with you, said Mr Hickey.

A bit, you know . . . well, a little bit . . .

I see your point, I see your point, said Mr Corcoran.

You understand me? We don't want to be too formal. After all he is one of our own, an exile home from the foreign clime.

Yes, he might not like it, said Mr Corcoran.

It was quite proper, of course, to raise the point if it was on

your mind, said my uncle. Well that is settled. Just a friendly
Irish welcome, céad mile fáilte. Now there is another important
matter that we'll need to see to. I refer to the inner man. The
honourable secretary will now read out my estimate of what we
want. The secretary has the floor.

In my thin voice I enunciated the contents of the black note-
book given over to my charge.

I think you might put down another bottle and a couple of
dozen stout, said Mr Hickey. I don't think they would go to
waste.

Oh, Lord yes, said Mr Fogarty. We would want that.

I don't think he touches anything, said my uncle. A very strict
man, I believe.

Well, of course, there are others, said Mr Hickey sharply.

Who? asked my uncle.

Who! Well dear knows! said Mr Hickey testily.

Mr Fogarty gave a loud laugh in the tense air.

Oh, put it down, Mr Chairman, he laughed. Put it down man.
A few of us would like a bottle of stout and we might have friends
in. Put it down and say no more about it.

Oh, very well, said my uncle. Very good, very good.

I entered these further items in my ledger.

Oh, talking about the clergy – on a Point of Order, Mr Chairman – talking about the clergy, said Mr Connors suddenly, I heard
a good one the other day. A P.P. down in the County Meath.

Now, Mr Connors, please remember that your audience is a
mixed one, said my uncle severely.

It's all right now, said Mr Connors smiling in reassurance. He
invited two young priests down to the house for dinner. Two
young priests from Clongowes or somewhere, you understand,
smart boys, doctors and all the rest of it. Well the three of them
went in to dinner and here were two fine fat chickens on the
table. Two chickens for the three of them.

Fair enough, said Mr Fogarty.

Now no disrespect, warned my uncle.

It's all right, said Mr Connors. Just when they were sitting
down for a good tuck in, the P.P. gets a sick call and away with
him on his white horse after telling the two visitors to eat away
and not to mind him or to wait for him.

Fair enough, said Mr Fogarty.

Well after an hour back came his reverence the P.P. to find a heap of bones on the plate there. Not a pick of the two chickens left for him. He had to swallow his anger for damn the thing else was there left for him to swallow.

Well dear knows they were the nice pair of curates, said my uncle in facetious consternation.

Weren't they, said Mr Connors. Well after a bit the two said they were very full and would like to stretch their legs. So out went the three of them to the farmyard. It was in the summer, you understand.

Fair enough, said Mr Fogarty.

Over comes the P.P.'s cock, a grand big animal with feathers of every colour in his tail. Isn't that the fine proud cock you have, says one of the curates. The P.P. turns and looks at him. And why wouldn't he be proud, says he, and him with two sons in the Jesuits!

Oh, fair enough, roared Mr Fogarty laughing.

There was general acclamation and amusement in which I inserted perfunctorily my low laugh.

Isn't it good? laughed Mr Connors. The P.P. turns on the curate and looks him straight in the eye. *And why wouldn't he be proud*, says he, *and him with two sons in the Jesuits!*

Very good indeed, said my uncle. Now we want three clean respectable women to cut the bread.

Let me see, said Mr Corcoran. You have Mrs Hanafin and Mrs Corky. Poor of course, but good clean respectable women.

Cleanliness is all-important, said my uncle. Lord save us, thumb-marks on bread, there is nothing so disgusting. Are they clean, Mr Corcoran?

Oh, very clean and respectable.

Very good, said my uncle, we will leave that to you.

He put up the four fingers of a hand in the air and identified by a finger the cares of each member of the assembly.

Sandwiches and refreshments Mr Corcoran, he said. Mr Hickey is attending to the band and will oblige in the interval. Mr Fogarty will be M.C. and will also oblige with a hornpipe. I will look after our friend. That is everything, I think. Any questions, gentlemen?

A vote of thanks to our efficient young secretary, said Mr Fogarty smiling.

Oh, certainly, said my uncle. Passed unanimously. Nothing else?

No.

Very good. I declare the meeting adjourned seeny day. Conclusion of reminiscence.

Penultimum continued. A further account of the journey of the Pooka and party: At approximately twenty past four p.m. they arrived at the Red Swan Hotel and entered the premises, unnoticed, by the window of the maids' private bed-room on the ground floor. They made no noise in their passage and disturbed no dust of the dust that lay about the carpets. Quickly they repaired to a small room adjoining Miss Lamont's bedroom where the good lady was lying in, and deftly stacked the papered wallsteads with the colourful wealth of their offerings and their fine gifts – their golden sheaves of ripened barley, firkins of curdy cheese, berries and acorns and crimson yams, melons and marrows and mellowed mast, variholed sponges of crisp-edged honey and oaten breads, earthenware jars of whey-thick sack and porcelain pots of lathery lager, sorrels and short-bread and coarse-grained cake, cucumbers cold and downy straw-laced cradles of elderberry wine poured out in sea-green egg-cups and urn-shaped tubs of molasses crushed and crucibled with the lush brown-heavy scum of pulped mellifluous mushrooms, an exhaustive harvesting of the teeming earth, by God.

Sit down and make yourselves happy, boys, said Slug, put a match to the fire, somebody. Give the door a knock, Mr Casey. See if the hour has come if you know what I mean.

These bogberries, said Shorty with a motion of his brown thumb, would it be against the rules to eat a few of them?

Certainly it would, said the Good Fairy, you won't touch them, in any case they are not bogberries.

Aren't they bogberries, mister smarty, asked Shorty, aren't they though, you little pimp!

The door is locked, said Casey.

No they are not, said the Good Fairy.

That is a pity, said the Pooka civilly. I suppose we can only wait until we are asked in. Has anybody got an American master-key?

A bullet would put the lock in in half a tick, said Shorty.

I don't doubt that, said Slug, but there is going to be no gun-play here, remember that.

I have not got a key anyway, said the Good Fairy, except an old-fashioned watch-key, a very good instrument for taking out blackheads.

The new-lit fire was maturing with high leaps which glowed for red instants on the smooth cheeks of the inky grapes on the long and tenuous flanks of the marrows.

Our policy, said the Pooka with his careful statesman's smile as he sat in his arm-chair with his club-foot hidden beneath the seat, must be an open one, a policy of wait and see.

What about a hand of cards? asked Shorty.

Eh?

Just to pass the time . . .

Not a bad idea at all, said the Good Fairy.

I don't hold with gambling, said the Pooka, for money.

With quiet industry he filled at his pipe, his face averted.

Of course a small stake to keep one's interest from flagging, he said, there is no great harm in that. That is a different thing.

It will pass the time for a start, said Casey.

Deal out for a round of Poker, said the Good Fairy, there is nothing like a good game of cards.

Have you a pack, Shorty? asked Slug.

I have the cards in my hand, said Shorty, gather in closer, my arm isn't a yard long. How many hands now?

Is Sweeny playing, asked Casey, are you, Sweeny?

Have you any money, Sweeny? asked Slug.

Six hands, said the Good Fairy placidly, everybody is playing.

You in the pocket, barked Shorty, if you think you are going to play cards you are making a bloody big mistake.

Mad Sweeny was sprawled on a chair in an attitude of inadvertence, idly plucking the blood-stiffened lichen from the gash in his nipple with an idle finger. His eyelids fluttered as he addressed himself to the utterance of this stave.

They have passed below me in their course, the stags across Ben Boirche, their antlers tear the sky, I will take a hand.

Tell me, said the Pooka putting his hand in his pocket, are *you* going to play?

Of course I am going to play, said the Good Fairy loudly, certainly I am going to play, why shouldn't I play?

We are playing for money, said Shorty roughly, what guarantee have we that you will . . . pay?

My word of honour, said the Good Fairy.

You have your porridge, said Shorty.

How are you going to take the cards if you have no hands and where do you keep your money if you have no pocket, answer me that, asked Slug sharply.

Gentlemen, interposed the Pooka civilly, we really must learn to discuss difficulties without a needless resort to acrimony and heat. The party in my pocket would not be long there if I were not satisfied that he was of unimpeachable character. The charge of cheating or defaulting at cards is a vile one and a charge that cannot be lightly levelled in the present company. In every civilized community it is necessary that the persons comprising it shall accept one another at their face value as honest men until the contrary is proved. Give me the cards and I will deal out six hands, one of which I will pass into my pocket. Did I ever tell you the old story about Dermot and Granya?

Take the cards if you want them, snapped Shorty, and talk about face value, that fellow has no face. By God it's a poor man that hasn't that much.

We'll try anything once, said Casey.

No, said the Good Fairy, I never heard that particular story. If it is dirty, of course, etiquette precludes me from listening to it at all.

The Pooka shuffled clumsily with his long-nailed fingers.

Go on, man, deal, said Slug.

It is not dirty, said the Pooka, it is one of the old Irish sagas. I played a small part in it in the long ago. The card-playing here brings it all back – how many hands did I say I would deal?

Six.

Six fives are thirty, one of the even numerals. Where women were concerned, this Dermot was a ruffian of the worst kind. Your wife was never safe if you happened to live in the same town with Dermot.

Don't waste so much time, man, said Slug.

You don't mean to tell me, said the Good Fairy, that he ran away with your kangaroo? Hurry and pass my cards in to me here. Come on now.

There you are now, said the Pooka, six hands. No he did not, all this happened before the happy day of my marriage. But what he did do, he ran away with Granya, the woman of Finn Mac-Cool. By Golly it took a good man to do that.

The light is very bad in here, said the Good Fairy, I can hardly see my cards at all.

Don't be striking matches in there, that's all, said the Pooka, fire is one thing that I don't like at all. Throw your cards on the floor, gentlemen. How many cards can I give you, Mr Casey?

Three.

Three gone over, said the Pooka. He had not gone far I need not tell you when Finn had started off behind him in full chase. It was hard going in the depth of winter for the fleeing lovers.

A knot of green-topped bunch-leaves, said Sweeny, is our choice from a bed of sorrel, acorns and nuts and cresses thick, and three cards we desire.

Three for you, said the Pooka.

Put your hand in your pocket, said the Good Fairy, take out the two cards on the left hand side and give me two new ones.

Certainly, said the Pooka. One dark night the woman and Dermot strayed into my cave in their wanderings, looking if you please for a night's lodging. I was working at that time, you understand, in the west of Ireland. My cave was by the seaside.

What in the name of God are you talking about? asked Shorty. It's up to me, I go threepence.

One thing led to another, continued the Pooka, till Dermot and myself agreed to play a game of chess for the woman. Granya was certainly a very fine-looking lump of a girl. I will advance the play to fivepence.

I cannot hear right, said the Good Fairy querulously, what are we playing for – a woman. What use is a woman to me?

Fivepence, you dumb-bell, shouted Shorty.

I will double that, said the Good Fairy. Tenpence.

At this stage certain parties signified that they were retiring from the game.

So we sat down to the chessboard the two of us, said the Pooka. My guest succeeded in getting white and opened with pawn to king's bishop four, apparently choosing the opening known as Byrd's, so much favoured by Alekhine and the Russian masters. I will make it a shilling.

One and sixpence, said Shorty quickly.

I will see one and sixpence, said the Good Fairy.

I replied with a simple pawn to king's three, a good temporizing move until my opponent disclosed the line he was to follow. The move has received high praise from more than one competent authority. I will also see Mr Andrews for the sum of one and sixpence.

All right, the two of you are seeing me for one and six, said Shorty, there you are, three kings, three royal sovereigns.

Not good enough, I am afraid, said the Good Fairy in a jubilant manner, there is a nice flush in hearts here in the pocket. Take it out and see it for yourselves. A flush in hearts.

None of your bloody miracles, shouted Shorty, we're playing for money! None of your trick-o'-the-loop, none of your bloody quick ones! If you try that game I'll take you out of that pocket by the scruff of the bloody neck and give you a kick in the waterworks!

What was his next move do you think? asked the Pooka. You would hardly credit it – pawn to king's knight four! I have a full house here, by the way.

Give us a look at it.

Three tens and two twos, said the Pooka quietly. All I had to do was to move my queen to rook five and I had him where I wanted him. Pay up, gentlemen, and look pleasant.

A good-looking one and sixpence, growled Shorty as he groped in the interior of his fob-pocket.

Queen to rook five was mate, of course, said the Pooka, mate in two, a world record. Stop tugging like that or you will tear my little pocket.

One moment, said the Good Fairy in a whisper, could I see you alone in the hallway for a couple of minutes. I want to discuss something private.

Hurry up for barney's sake till we have another round, said Slug rubbing his hands, give the luck a chance to circulate.

There you are, one and sixpence, said Shorty.

Most certainly, said the Pooka courteously, pray excuse us for a moment, gentlemen, the Fairy and myself have a private matter to discuss in the hallway, though itself it is a draughty place for colloquy and fine talk. We will be back again directly.

He arose with a bow and left the room.

What is it, he asked politely in the passage.

When you won the woman, said the Good Fairy, what did you do with her is it any harm to ask?

Is that all you require to know?

Well no. As a matter of fact . . .

You have no money!

Exactly.

What explanation have you to offer for such conduct?

You see, I always win at cards. I . . .

What is your explanation?

Don't talk so loud, man, said the Good Fairy in alarm, the others will hear you. I cannot be disgraced in front of a crowd like that.

I am sorry, said the Pooka coldly, but I am afraid it is my duty to make the matter public. If it were my own personal concern solely, it would be otherwise, of course. In the present circumstances I have no alternative. The others allowed you to play on my recommendation and you have callously dishonoured me. I cannot be expected to stand by and see them exploited further. Therefore . . .

For God's sake don't do that, don't do that under any circumstances, I would never get over it, it would kill my mother . . .

Your concern for your family does you credit but I'm afraid it is too late to think of that.

I will pay back every penny I owe you.

When?

Give me time, give me a chance . . .

Nonsense! You are merely wriggling, merely . . .

For God's sake, man . . .

I will give you one alternative to instant exposure and you can take it or leave it. I will forget the debt and advance you an extra sixpence – making two shillings in all – provided you relinquish absolutely your claim to influence the baby that is expected inside.

What!

You can take your choice.

You cad, you bloody cad!

The Pooka twitched his pocket with a profound shrug of his gaunt shoulders.

Which is it to be? he inquired.

I'll see you damned first, said the Good Fairy excitedly.

Very well. It is all the same to me. Let us go inside.

Stop a minute, you, you. . . . Wait.

Well?

All right, you win. But by God I'll get even with you yet, if it takes me a thousand years, I'll get my own back if I have to swing for it, don't forget that!

That is very satisfactory, said the Pooka with a grateful re-dawn of his urbanity, you have undoubtedly done the right thing and I offer you my congratulations on your pertinacity. Here is the extra sixpence. Let us rejoin the ladies.

You wait! Even if it is a thousand years, you wait!

In regard to the little question you asked me about the lady I won as a result of my skill at chess, it is a long story and a crooked one – shall we go in?

Go in and be damned to you!

The Pooka re-entered the room with his civil smile.

There's your hand, said Slug, hurry up, we haven't all day, man.

I'm sorry for the delay, said the Pooka.

The company again fell to card-play.

After a moderately lengthy interval a good-quality Yale key grated in the lock and the door of the bedroom was thrown open, a broad beam of gaslight pouring in on the players as they turned their questioning faces from their cards to the light. The pallor of the glare was tempered about the edges by a soft apparently-supernatural radiance of protoplasmic amethyst and spotted with a twinkling pattern of red and green stars so that it poured into the ante-room and flowed and eddied in the corners and the shadows like the spreading tail of a large male peacock, a glorious thing like muslin or iridescent snow or like the wispy suds of milk when it is boiling over on a hob. Temporary discontinuance of foregoing.

Note on Constructional or Argumentive Difficulty: The task of ren-dering and describing the birth of Mr Trellis's illegitimate offspring I found one fraught with obstacles and difficulties of a technical, constructional, or literary character – so much so, in fact, that I found it entirely beyond my powers. This latter state-ment follows my decision to abandon a passage extending over the length of eleven pages touching on the arrival of the son and his sad dialogue with his wan mother on the subject of his father, the passage being, by general agreement, a piece of undoubted mediocrity.

The passage, however, served to provoke a number of discussions with my friends and acquaintances on the subject of aestho-psycho-eugenics and the general chaos which would result if all authors were disposed to seduce their female characters and bring into being, as a result, offspring of the quasi-illusory type. It was asked why Trellis did not require the expectant mother to make a violent end of herself and the trouble she was causing by the means of drinking a bottle of disinfectant fluid usually to be found in bathrooms. The answer I gave was that the author was paying less and less attention to his literary work and was spending entire days and nights in the unremitting practice of his sleep. This explanation, I am glad to say, gave instant satisfaction and was represented as ingenious by at least one of the inquirers concerned.

It may be usefully mentioned here that I had carefully considered giving an outward indication of the son's semi-humanity by furnishing him with only the half of a body. Here I encountered further difficulties. If given the upper half only, it would be necessary to provide a sedan-chair or litter with at least two runners or scullion-boys to operate it. The obtrusion of two further characters would lead to complications, the extent of which would not be foreseen. On the other hand, to provide merely the lower half; *videlicet*, the legs and lumbar region, would be to narrow unduly the validity of the son and confine his activities virtually to walking, running, kneeling and kicking football. For that reason I decided ultimately to make no outward distinction and thus avoided any charge that my work was somewhat far-fetched. It will be observed that the omission of several pages at this stage does not materially disturb the continuity of the story.

Penultimum, continued: Momentarily shutting out the richness of the beam with his stout form furrily outlined in the glow, a stocky young man had entered the ante-room and stood looking with polite inquiry at the group of card-players about the fire. His dark well-cut clothing was in sharp contrast to the healthless rubiness of his face; there were pimples on his forehead to the size of sixpences and his languorous heavy eyelids hung uneasily midway over the orbs of his eyes; an air of slowness and weariness and infinite sleep hung about him like a cloak as he stood there standing.

The Pooka arose with a slight bow and pushed back his chair.

Three hundred thousand welcomes, he said in his fine voice, we are honoured to be here at the hour of your arrival. We are honoured to be able to present you with these offerings on the floor there, the choicest and the rarest that the earth can yield. Please accept them on behalf of myself and my friends. One and all we have the honour to wish you good day, to trust that you had a pleasant journey and that your dear mother is alive and well.

Gentlemen, said the newcomer with gratitude in his deep voice, I am deeply touched. Your kind gesture is one of these felicities that banish for a time at least the conviction that wells up in the heart of every newcomer to this world that life is empty and hollow, disproportionately trivial compared with the trouble of entering it. I thank you with all my heart. Your gifts, they are . . .

He searched for a word with his red hand as if to pull one from the air.

Oh, that is all right, said the Good Fairy, these things are plentiful and it was small trouble to bring them here. You are very welcome.

How much of that tack did you carry? snapped Shorty.

Fighting in front of strangers, said the Good Fairy, that, of course, is the height of vulgarity. The parents that brought you up must have had a terrible cross to bear.

You have your porridge, said Shorty.

The world is wonderful all the same, said Orlick. Everybody has a different face and a separate way of talking. That is a very queer little mouth you have in your clothes, Sir, he added to the Pooka. I have only one mouth, this one in my face.

Do not worry or wonder about that, said the Pooka. That is a little angel that I carry in my pocket.

Glad to know you, Sir, said the Good Fairy pleasantly.

A little angel? said Orlick in wonder. How big?

Oh, no size at all, said the Pooka.

I am like a point in Euclid, explained the Good Fairy, position but no magnitude, you know. I bet you five pounds you could not put your finger on me.

Five pounds that I would not put my finger on you? repeated Orlick in imperfect comprehension.

If you don't mind, said the Pooka, let us confine ourselves for the moment to what is visible and palpable. Let us proceed by degrees. Now look at these fruits and jars on the floor there...

Yes, said the Good Fairy, Irish apples, go where you will in the wide world you won't get better. There's a great flavour off them certainly.

We are honoured that you accept our poor offerings, said the Pooka humbly. You are very kind, Mr...

According to my mother, said Orlick, my little name is Orlick.

Orlick Trellis? said the Pooka. That is very satisfactory.

Shorty tore his sombrero from his head and waved it in the air.

Three cheers for little Orlick, he shouted, three cheers for Orlick Trellis!

Not too loud, counselled the Pooka with a motion of his head towards the door of the bedroom.

Hip Hip . . . Hurray! Hurray! Hurray!

There was a short pleased silence.

May I ask, said Slug civilly, what your plans are, Sir?

I have nothing settled yet, said Orlick. I shall have to have a good look round first and find out where I stand. I must say I was very surprised that my father was not present here to welcome me. One expects that, you know, somehow. My mother blushed when I asked about it and changed the subject. It is all very puzzling. I shall have to make some inquiries. Could anyone oblige me with a cigarette?

Certainly, said Slug.

These things in the baskets, they are bottles, said Shorty.

Why not open them and have a drink, said Orlick.

A modest celebration is undoubtedly called for, concurred the Good Fairy.

I say, said the Pooka in a whisper putting his hand in his pocket, I must ask you to leave my pocket for a minute. I wish to talk alone with our host. You remember our agreement?

That is all very well, said the Good Fairy querulously, but where am I to go? Put me on the floor and I'll be walked on, trampled to my death. I am not a door-mat.

Eh? asked Slug.

Be quiet, whispered the Pooka, what is wrong with the mantelpiece?

Nothing, I suppose, said the Good Fairy sulkily, I am not a door-mat.

Very well, you can lean on the clock until I am ready to take you back, said the Pooka.

He approached the fireplace with a few aimless paces and then turned courteously to his host. Shorty, stooping among the offerings, was engaged with earthen jars and kegs and wax-crusted green bottles, fondling and opening them and pouring dusky libations into medhers of old thick pewter.

Don't be all day, said the Good Fairy from the mantelpiece.

By the way, said the Pooka carelessly, could I see you alone for a moment?

Me? said Orlick. Certainly.

Excellent, said the Pooka, Let us go out into the passage for a moment.

He linked an arm in polite friendship and walked towards the door, endeavouring to match his club-step to the footstep.

Don't be too long now, said Casey, the drink is cooling.

The door closed. And for a long time the limping beat of the Pooka's club could be heard, and the low hum of his fine talk as they paced the passage, the Pooka and his Orlick. Conclusion of the foregoing.

Biographical reminiscence, part the eighth: While I was engaged in the spare-time literary activities of which the preceding and following pages may be cited as more or less typical examples, I was leading a life of a dull but not uncomfortable character. The following approximate schedule of my quotidian activities may be of some interest to the lay reader.

Nature of daily regime or curriculum: Nine thirty a.m. rise, wash, shave and proceed to breakfast; this on the insistence of my uncle, who was accustomed to regard himself as the sun of his house-hold, recalling all things to wakefulness on his own rising.

10.30. Return to bedroom.

12.00. Go, weather permitting, to College, there conducting light conversation on diverse topics with friends, or with acquaintances of a casual character.

2.00 p.m. Go home for lunch.

3.00. Return to bedroom. Engage in spare-time literary activity, or read.

6.00. Have tea in company with my uncle, attending in a perfunctory manner to the replies required by his talk.

7.00. Return to bedroom and rest in darkness.

8.00. Continue resting or meet acquaintances in open thoroughfares or places of public resort.

11.00. Return to bedroom.

Minutiae: No. of cigarettes smoked, average 8·3; glasses of stout or other comparable intoxicant, av. 1·2; times to stool, av. 2·65; hours of study, av. 1·4; spare-time or recreative pursuits, 6·63 circulating.

Comparable description of how a day may be spent, being an extract from 'A Conspectus of the Arts and Natural Sciences', from the hand of Mr Cowper. Serial volume the seventeenth: I am obliged to you for the interest you take in my welfare, and for your inquiring so particularly after the manner in which time passes here. As to amusements, I mean what the world call such, we have none; but the place swarms with them, and cards and dancing are the professed business of almost all the gentle inhabitants of Huntingdon. We refuse to take part in them, or to be accessories to this way of murthering our time, and by so doing have acquired the name of Methodists. Having told you how we do not spend our time, I will next say how we do. We breakfast commonly between eight and nine; till eleven, we read either the Scripture, or the Sermons of some faithful preacher of these holy mysteries; at eleven, we attend Divine Service, which is performed here twice every day, and from twelve to three we separate, and amuse ourselves as we please. During that interval I either read in my own apartment, or walk, or ride, or work in the garden. We seldom sit an hour after dinner, but if the weather permits, adjourn to the garden, where with Mrs Unwin, and her son, I have generally the pleasure of religious conversation till tea time. If it rains, or is too windy for walking, we either converse within doors, or sing some hymns of Martin's collection, and by the help of Mrs Unwin's harpsichord make up a tolerable concert, in which our hearts, I hope, are the best and the most musical performers. After tea, we sally forth to walk in good earnest. Mrs Unwin is a good walker, and we have generally travelled about four miles before we see home again. When the days are short, we make this excursion in the former part of the day, between church-time and dinner. At night, we read and converse as before, till supper, and commonly finish the evening with either hymns, or a sermon, and last of all the family are called to prayers. Conclusion of the foregoing.

Comparable further description of how a day may be spent, being a day from the life of Finn: It is thus that Finn spends the day: a third of the day watching the boys – three fifties of boys has he at play in his ball-yard; a third of the day drinking sack; and a third of the day in the calm sorcery of chess. Conclusion of foregoing.

Further Synopsis, being a summary of what has gone before, for the benefit of new readers: THE POOKA MACPHELLIMEY, having won dominion over Orlick by virtue of superior card-play, brings him home to his hut in the fir-wood and prevails upon him to live there as a P.G. (Paying Guest), for a period not exceeding six months, sowing in his heart throughout that time the seeds of evil, revolt, and non-serviam. Meanwhile,
    TRELLIS, almost perpetually in a coma as a result of the drugs secretly administered by Mr Shanahan, makes little progress with the design of his story, with the result that
    JOHN FURRISKEY is enabled to enjoy almost uninterrupted marital bliss with his wife (Mrs Furriskey), while
    MESSRS LAMONT & SHANAHAN continue to live a dissolute if colourful life. Now read on.

Extract from Manuscript, being description of a social evening at the Furriskey household: the direct style: The voice was the first, Furriskey was saying. The human voice. The voice was Number One. Anything that came after was only an imitation of the voice. Follow, Mr Shanahan?
    Very nicely put, Mr Furriskey.
    Take the fiddle now, said Furriskey.
    By hell the fiddle is the man, said Lamont, the fiddle is the man for me. Put it into the hand of a lad like Luke MacFadden and you'll cry like a child when you hear him at it. The voice was number one, I don't deny that, but look at the masterpieces

of musical art you have on the fiddle! Did you ever hear the immortal strains of the Crutch Sonata now, the whole four strings playing there together, with plenty of plucking and scales and runs and a lilt that would make you tap the shoe-leather off your foot? Oh, it's the fiddle or nothing. You can have your voice, Mr Furriskey, – and welcome. The fiddle and the bow is all I ask, and the touch of the hand of Luke MacFadden, the travelling tinsmith. The smell of his clothes would knock you down, but he was the best fiddler in Ireland, east or west.

The fiddle is there too, of course, said Furriskey.

The fiddle is an awkward class of a thing to carry, said Shanahan, it's not what you might call a handy shape. They say you get a sort of a crook in the arm, you know . . .

But the fiddle, continued Furriskey slow and authoritative of articulation, the fiddle comes number two to the voice. Do you mind that, Mr Lamont? Adam sang . . .

Aye, indeed, said Lamont.

But did he play? By almighty God in Heaven he didn't. If you put your fiddle, Mr Lamont, into the hands of our first parents in the Garden of Eden in the long ago . . .

They'd hang their hats on it, of course, said Lamont, but still and all it's sweetest of the lot. Given a good player, of course. Could I trouble you, Mr Furriskey?

A sugar-bowl containing sugar was passed deftly from hand to hand in the pause. Tea was stirred and bread was buttered swiftly and trisected; at the same time there were adjustments as to trouser-crease, chair-stance and seat. The accidental gong of a cream-jug and a milk-plate was the signal for a resumption of light conversation.

John is very musical, said Mrs Furriskey. Her eyes followed closely the movements of her ten fingers as they prepared between them a tasteful collation. I'm sure he has a good voice only it's not trained. He sings a lot when he thinks I amn't listening.

A small laugh was initiated and gently circulated.

Do you mind that, eh, said Lamont. What does he sing now, Mrs F.? Is it the songs of the native land?

The songs he sings, said Mrs Furriskey, have no words to them. The bare air just.

When do you hear me at it? asked the prisoner, a meek inquiry on the changing contours of his face. Then, stern and immobile, he waited for an answer.

Don't mind him, Mrs F., said Shanahan loudly, don't mind him, he's only an old cod. Don't give him the satisfaction.

Sometimes when you're down there shaving. Oh, I'm up to all his tricks, Mr Shanahan. He can sing like a lark when he feels like it.

Because when you were listening to my singing this morning, my good woman, said Furriskey stressing with his finger the caesura of his case, I was blowing my nose in the lavatory. That's a quare one for you.

Oh, that's a shame for you, said Mrs Furriskey contributing her averted giggle to an arpeggio of low sniggers. You shouldn't use language like that at table. Where are your manners, Mr Furriskey?

Clearing my head in the bowl of the W.C., he repeated with coarse laughing, that's the singing I was at, I'm the right tenor when it comes to that game,

It's a poor man that doesn't sing once in a while, anyway, observed Lamont, continuing the talk with skill, we all have our little tunes. We can't all be Luke MacFaddens.

That's true.

Of all the musical instruments that have been fashioned by the hand of man, said Furriskey, the piano is far and away the most . . . useful.

Oh, everybody likes the piano, said Lamont. Nobody can raise any objection to that. The piano and the fiddle, the two go well together.

Some of the stuff I've heard in my time, said Shanahan, is no joke to play for the man that has only two hands. It was stuff of the best make I don't doubt, classical tack and all the rest of it, but by God it gave me a pain in my bandbox. It hurt my head far worse than a pint of whisky.

It's not everyone can enjoy it, said Furriskey. Every man to his taste. As I was saying, the piano is a fine instrument. It comes number two to the human voice.

My sister, I believe, said Lamont, knew a lot about the piano. Piano and French, you know, it's a great thing at the convents. She had a nice touch.

Furriskey angled idly for the floating tea-leaf with the lip of his tea-spoon, frowning slightly. He was sprawled crookedly on his chair, his left thumb tucked in the arm-hole of his waistcoat.

You have only half the story when you say piano, he announced, and half the notes as well. The word is pianofurty.

I heard that before, said Shanahan. Correct.

The furty stands for the deep notes on your left-hand side. Piano, of course, means our friends on the right.

Do you mean to say it is wrong to call it piano? asked Lamont. His attitude was one of civil perplexity; his eyelids fluttered and his lower lip drooped as he made his civil inquiry.

Well, no . . . it's not *wrong*. Nobody is going to say you're wrong. But . . .

I know what you mean. I see the point.

By virtue of enlightenment, culture, and a spirit of give-and-take, the matter was amicably settled to the satisfaction of all parties.

Do you understand, Mr Lamont?

I do indeed. You are quite right. Pianofurty.

There was a pleased pause in which the crockery, unopposed, clinked merrily.

I believe, said Shanahan in a treacherous manner, I believe that you can do more in the line of music than give out a song. I'm told – no names, of course – I'm told the fiddle is no stranger to your hand. Now is that a fact?

What's this, good God? asked Lamont. His surprise, as a matter of fact, was largely pretence. He became upright and attentive.

You never told me, John, said Mrs Furriskey. She sadly reproached him with her weak blue eyes, smiling.

Not a word of truth in that yarn, boys, said Furriskey moving his chair noisily. Who told you that one? Is this another of your stories, woman?

Dear knows it's not.

It's a thing you want an ear for, I may tell you, told Lamont. For the hundred that takes it up, it's a bare one that lives to play it right. Do you play the violin, though, honest to God?

By God I don't, said Furriskey with a sincere widening of the eyes, no Sir. I was half thinking of trying it, you know, give it a short trial and see do I like it. Of course it would mean practice . . .

And practice means work, Shanahan said.

The ear is the main thing, observed Lamont. You can wear the last tatter of skin off your knuckles with a fiddle and a bow and you won't get as far as your own shadow if you haven't got the ear. Have the ear and you're half-way there before you start at all. Tell me this. Did you ever hear of a great fiddler, a man by the name of Pegasus? I believe he was the business.

That's one man I never met, said Shanahan.

He wasn't in our time, of course, said Lamont, but the tale was told that himself and the Devil had arrived at an understanding. What you call a working agreement.

Dear dear, said Furriskey. He gave a frown of pain.

Well now that's a fact. Your man becomes fiddler Number One for the whole world. Everybody has to toe the line. But when the hour comes for him to die, My Nabs is waiting by the bed!

He has come to claim his own, said Mrs Furriskey, nodding.

He has come to claim his own, Mrs Furriskey.

Here there was a pause for the purpose of heart-searching and meditation.

That's a queer story certainly, said Shanahan.

But the queerest part of it is this, said Lamont, in all the years he lived, man, never once did he do his scales, never once did he practise. It happened that his fingers were in the pay of who-you-know.

That's very queer, said Shanahan, there's no doubt about it. I'm sure that man's mind was like a sewer, Mr Lamont?

Very few of the fiddlers had their heads on the right way, said Lamont. Very few of them indeed. Saving, of course, the presence of our host.

Furriskey gave a sound of coughing and laughing, groped quickly for his hankerchief and waved a hand high in the air.

Leave me out of it, now, he said, leave the host alone boys, The biggest ruffian of the lot, of course, was our old friend Nero. Now that fellow was a thorough bags, say what you like.

He was a tyrant, said Mrs Furriskey. She brought her light repast to a dainty and timely conclusion and built her vessels into a fine castle. She leant forward slightly, her elbows on the table and her chin on the trestle of her interlocking hands.

If everything I hear is true, ma'am, said Furriskey, you praise him very high up when you call him a tyrant. The man was a bowsy, of course.

He was certainly not everything you look for in a man, said Shanahan, I'll agree with you there.

When the city of Rome, continued Furriskey, the holy city and the centre and the heart of the Catholic world was a mass of flames, with people roasting there in the streets by the God Almighty dozen, here is my man as cool as you please in his palace with his fiddle at his jaw. There were people there . . . roasting . . . alive . . . not a dozen yards from his door, men, women and children getting the worst death of the bloody lot, Holy God can you imagine it!

The like of him would have no principles, of course, said Mrs Furriskey.

Oh, he was a terrible drink of water. Death by fire, you know, by God it's no joke.

They tell me drowning is worse, Lamont said.

Do you know what it is, said Furriskey, you can drown me three times before you roast me. Yes, by God and six. Put your finger in a basin of water. What do you feel? Next to nothing. *But put your finger in the fire!*

I never looked at it that way, agreed Lamont.

I'm telling you, now, it's a different story. A very very different story, Mr Lamont. It's a horse of another colour altogether. Oh, yes.

Please God we'll all die in our beds, said Mrs Furriskey.

I'd rather live myself, I'll say that, said Shanahan, but if I had to go I'd choose the gun. A bullet in the heart and you're right. You're polished off before you know you're hurt at all. There's no nonsense about the gun. It's quick, it's merciful, and it's clean.

I'm telling you now, fire's a fright, said Furriskey.

In the old days, recalled Lamont, they had what you call a draught. It was brewed from weeds — deadly nightshade, you know. It got you at the guts, at the pit of the stomach, here, look. You took it and you felt grand for a half an hour. At the end of that time, you felt a bit weak, do you know. At the heel of the hunt, your inside is around you on the floor.

Lord save us!

A bloody fact now. Not a word of a lie. At the finish you are just a bag of air. You puke the whole shooting gallery.

If you ask me, said Shanahan quickly, inserting the shaft of his fine wit in the midst of the conversation, I've had an odd pint of that tack in my time.

A laugh was interposed neatly, melodiously, retrieved with skill and quietly replaced.

They called the dose a draught of hemlock, Lamont said, they made it from garlic and other things. Homer finished his days on earth with his cup of poison. He drank it alone in his cell.

That was another ruffian, said Mrs Furriskey. He persecuted the Christians.

That was all the fashion at one time, Furriskey said, we must make allowances, you know. You were nothing if you didn't let the Christians have it. *Onward Christian Soldiers, to your doom!*

No excuse, of course, said Lamont. Ignorance of the law is no excuse for the law, I've often heard that said. Homer was a great poet altogether and that made up for a lot of the rascality. His Iliad is still read. Wherever you go on the face of the civilized globe you will hear of Homer, the glory that was Greece. Yes, indeed. I'm told there are some very nice verses in the Iliad of Homer, very good stuff, you know. You have never read it, Mr Shanahan?

He was the daddy of them all, said Shanahan.

I believe, said Furriskey with a finger to his eye, that he was as blind as the back of your neck. Glasses or no glasses, he could see nothing.

You are perfectly right, Sir, said Lamont.

I saw a blind beggarman the other day, said Mrs Furriskey rummaging with a frown in the interior of her memory, in Stephen's Green I think it was. He was heading straight for a lamp-post. When he was about a yard away from it, he turned to the one side and made a beeline around it.

Oh, he knew it was there, said Furriskey, he knew it was there. He knew what he was about the same man.

The Compensations of Nature, that's what they call it, explained Shanahan. It's as long as it's broad. If you can't speak, you can listen twice as good as the man that can. Six of one and half a dozen of the other.

It's funny, said Mrs Furriskey. Curiously examining it, she replaced her reminiscence.

The blind are great harpers, said Lamont, great harpers

altogether. I knew a man once by the name of Searson, some class of a hunch-back that harped for his living about the streets. He always wore a pair of black glasses.

Was he blind, Mr Lamont?

Certainly he was blind. From the day of his birth he hadn't a light in his head. But don't worry, it was all made up to him. My brave man knew how to take it out of his old harp. I'll swear by God he did. He was a lovely harper certainly. It would do you good to listen to him. He was a great man altogether at the scales.

Is that so?

Oh, by God he was a treat.

Music is a wonderful thing when you come to think of it, observed Mrs Furriskey, raising her gentle countenance until its inspection had been duly accomplished by the company.

Here's a thing I was going to ask for a long time, said Shanahan, is there any known cure for blackheads?

Plenty of sulphur, said Mrs Furriskey.

Do you mean pimples? inquired Lamont. Pimples take time, you know. You can't clean pimples up in one night.

Sulphur's very good, of course, Mrs Furriskey, but it's for the bowels they give you sulphur unless I'm thinking of something different.

To clear away pimples in the one go-off, continued Lamont, you'll have to get up early in the morning. Very early in the morning, I'm thinking.

They tell me if you steam the face, said Shanahan, the pores will – you know – open. That's the man for blackheads, plenty of steam.

I'll tell you what it is, explained Lamont, bad blood is the back of the whole thing. When the quality of the blood isn't first class, out march our friends the pimples. It's Nature's warning, Mr Shanahan. You can steam your face till your snot melts but damn the good it will do your blackheads if you don't attend to your inside.

I always heard that sulphur was the best thing you could take, said Mrs Furriskey, sulphur and a good physic.

There would be less consumption in this country, continued Lamont, if the people paid more attention to their blood. Do you know what it is, the nation's blood is getting worse, any doctor will tell you that. The half of it is poison.

Blackheads are not so bad, said Furriskey. A good big boil on the back of your neck, that's the boy that will make you say your prayers. A boil is a fright. It's a fright now.

A boil is a fright if you get it in the wrong place.

You walk down the street and here you are like a man with a broken neck, your snot hopping off your knees. I know a man that never wore a collar for five years. Five years, think of that!

Well sulphur is good for that complaint, said Mrs Furriskey, people who are subject to that complaint are never without a pot of sulphur in the house.

Sulphur cools the blood, of course, concurred Lamont.

There was a girl that I knew once, said Mrs Furriskey rummaging anew in the store of her recollections. She worked in a house where they had a lot of silver, pots, you know, and that kind of thing. She used to polish them with sulphur.

Ah, but the boil's the boy, said Furriskey with a slap of his knee, the boil's the boy that will bend your back.

I'll tell you what's hard, too, said Shanahan, a bad knee. They say a bad knee is worse than no knee at all. A bad knee and an early grave.

Water on the knee, do you mean?

Yes, water on the knee is a bad man, I believe. So I'm told. But you can have a bad cap too, a split knee. Believe me that's no joke. A split knee-cap.

Where are you if you are gone in the two knees? asked Furriskey.

I knew a man and it's not long ago since he died, Bartley Madigan, said Shanahan. A man by the name of Bartley Madigan. A right decent skin too. You never heard a bad word about Bartley.

I knew a Peter Madigan once, said Mrs Furriskey, a tall well-built man from down the country. That was about ten years ago.

Well Bartley got a crack of a door-knob in the knee . . .

Eh! Well dear knows that's the queer place to get the knob of a door. By God he must have been a bruiser. A door-knob! – Oh, come here now. How high was he?

It's a question I am always asked, ladies and gentlemen, and it's a question I can never answer. But what my poor Bartley got was a blow on the crown of the cap . . . They tell me there was trickery going on, trickery of one kind or another. Did I tell you the scene is laid in a public-house?

You did not, said Lamont.

Well what happened, asked Furriskey.

I'll tell you what happened. When my hard Bartley got the crack, he didn't let on he was hurt at all. Not a word out of him. On the way home in the tram he complained of a pain. The same night he was given up for dead.

For goodness sake!

Not a word of a lie, gentlemen. But Bartley had a kick in his foot still. A game bucko if you like. Be damned but he wouldn't die!

He wouldn't die?

Be damned but he wouldn't die. I'll live, says he, I'll live if it kills me, says he. I'll spite the lot of ye. And live he did. He lived for twenty years.

Is that a fact?

He lived for twenty years and he spent the twenty years on the flat of his back in bed. He was paralysed from the knee up. That's a quare one.

He was better dead, said Furriskey, stern in the certainty of his statement.

Paralysis is certainly a nice cup of tea, observed Lamont. Twenty ... bloody ... years in bed, eh? Every Christmas he was carried out by his brother and put in a bath.

He was better dead, said Furriskey. He was better in his grave than in that bed.

Twenty years is a long time, said Mrs Furriskey.

Well now there you are, said Shanahan. Twenty summers and twenty winters. And plenty of bedsores into the bargain. Oh, yes, bags of those playboys. The sight of his legs would turn your stomach.

Lord help us, said Furriskey with a frown of pain. That's a blow on the knee for you. A blow on the head would leave you twice as well off, a crack on the skull and you were right.

I knew a man, said Lamont, that was presented with an accidental skelp of a hammer on the something that he sits on – the important what you may call it to the rear, you will understand. How long did he live?

Is this a man I know, asked Mrs Furriskey.

He lived for the length of a split second, long enough to fall in a heap in his own hall. Something, you understand, gave way. Something – I forget what they call it – but it was badly burst, so the doctors said when they examined him.

A hammer is a dangerous weapon, said Shanahan, if you happen to get it in the wrong place. A dangerous instrument.

The cream of the joke is this, but, continued Lamont, that he got the hammer on the morning of his birthday. That was the present *he* got.

The poor so-and-so, said Furriskey.

Shanahan gave a whisper from the screen of his flat hand and a privy laugh, orderly and undertoned, was offered and accepted in reward.

He died by the hammer – did you ever hear that said? A finger of perplexity straying to her lip, Mrs Furriskey presented the troubled inquiry of her face to each in turn.

I never heard that, ma'am, said Furriskey.

Well maybe I am thinking of something else, she reflected. *He died by the hammer.* I see they have great coal-hammers in that place in Baggot Street for one and nine.

A shilling is plenty to pay for a coal-hammer, said Furriskey.

There's another gentleman that I advise ye all to avoid, counselled Shanahan, cross the road if you see him coming. Our old friend pee-eye-ell-ee-ess.

Who might he be? asked Mrs Furriskey.

He's a man that'll make you sit up and take notice if you let him into your house, explained Furriskey, a private wink for the entertainment of his male companions. Eh, Mr Shanahan?

Oh, a bad man, said Shanahan. I met him once but I may tell you he got his orders. Out he went.

It's the blood again, said Lamont.

Here a loud knocking at the door became audible to the company. Mrs Furriskey moved quietly from the room in response.

That'll be Mr Orlick, said Shanahan. I was talking to him today. I think he is going to do a bit of writing tonight. Conclusion of the foregoing.

Biographical reminiscence, part the ninth: It was the late summer, a humid breathless season that is inimical to comfort and personal freshness. I was reclining on my bed and conducting a listless conversation with Brinsley, who was maintaining a stand by the window. From the averted quality of his voice, I knew that his back was towards me and that he was watching through the window without advertence the evening boys at ball-throw. We had been discussing the craft of writing and had adverted to the primacy of Irish and American authors in the world of superior or better-class letters. From a perusal of the manuscript which has just been presented in these pages, he had expressed his inability to distinguish between Furriskey, Lamont and Shanahan, bewailed what he termed their spiritual and physical identity, stated that true dialogue is dependent on the conflict rather than the confluence of minds and made reference to the importance of characterization in contemporary literary works of a high-class, advanced or literary nature.

The three of them, he said, might make one man between them.

Your objections are superficial, I responded. These gentlemen may look the same and speak the same but actually they are profoundly dissimilar. For example, Mr Furriskey is of the brachycephalic order, Mr Shanahan of the prognathic.

Prognathic?

I continued in this strain in an idle perfunctory manner, searching in the odd corners of my mind where I was accustomed to keep words which I rarely used. I elaborated the argument subsequently with the aid of dictionaries and standard works of reference, embodying the results of my researches in a memorandum which is now presented conveniently for the information of the reader.

Memorandum of the respective diacritical traits or qualities of Messrs Furriskey, Lamont and Shanahan:

Head: brachycephalic; bullet; prognathic.

Vision: tendencies towards myopia; wall-eye; nyctalopia.

Configuration of nose: roman; snub; mastoid.

Unimportant physical afflictions: palpebral ptosis; indigestion; German itch.

Mannerisms: tendency to agitate or flick fingers together in prim fashion after conveying bread or other crumbling substance to mouth; tooth-sucking and handling of tie-knot; ear-poking with pin or match, lip-pursing.

Outer clothing: D.B. indigo worsted; S.B. brown serge, two-button style; do., three-button style.

Inner or under-clothing: woollen combinations, front button-ing style; home-made under-tabard of stout moreen-cloth (winter) or paramatta (summer); abdominal belt or corset with attached unguinal protective appliance.

Fabric of shirt: tiffany; linen; tarlatan.

Pedal traits: hammer-toes; nil; corns.

Volar traits: horniness; callosity; nil.

Favourite flower: camomile; daisy; betony.

Favourite shrub: deutzia; banksia; laurustinus.

Favourite dish: bach; caudle; julienne. Conclusion of memorandum.

The door opened without warning and my uncle entered. From his manner it was evident that he had seen the note-books of Brinsley below-stairs on the hall-stand. He wore a genial and hostly manner. His cigarette-box, the ten-for-sixpence denomination, was already in his hand. He stopped with a polite ejaculation of his surprise at the presence of a guest by the window.

Mr Brinsley! he said.

Brinsley responded according to the practices of polite society, utilizing a formal good evening for the purpose.

My uncle conferred a warm handshake and immediately placed his cigarettes at the disposal of the company.

Well it isn't often we see you, he said.

He forestalled our effort to find matches. I had arisen from the supine attitude and was seated on the bed-edge in an uneasy manner. As he came round to me tendering his flame, he said:

Well, mister-my-friend, and how are *we* this evening? I see you're as fond of the bed as ever. Mr Brinsley, what are we going to do with this fellow? Dear knows I don't know what we'll do with him at all.

Without addressing my uncle I made it known that there was but one chair in the room.

You mean this lying in bed during the day? said Brinsley. His voice was innocent. He was intent on discussing my personal habits in a sympathetic manner with my uncle in order to humili-ate me.

I do, Mr Brinsley, said my uncle in an eager earnest manner,

I do certainly. Upon my word I think it is a very bad sign in a young lad. I don't understand it at all. What would you say is the meaning of it? The lad is healthy as far as I can see. I mean, you would understand an old person or an invalid. He looks as fit as a fiddle.

Putting his cigarette-hand to his head, he shut his right eye and rubbed the lid in perplexity with the crook of his thumb.

Dear knows it is more than I can understand, he said.

Brinsley gave a polite laugh.

Well we're all lazy, he said in a broad-minded manner, it's the legacy of our first parents. We all have it in us. It is just a question of making a special effort.

My uncle gave a rap of concurrence on the washstand.

We all have it in us, he repeated loudly, from the highest to the lowest we all have it in us. Certainly. But tell me this, Mr Brinsley. Do we make the effort?

We do, said Brinsley.

Oh, we do indeed, said my uncle, and faith it would be a very nice world to live in if we didn't. Oh, yes.

I agree with you, said Brinsley.

We can say to ourselves, continued my uncle, I have now rested. I have had enough. I will now rise and use my God-given strength to the best of my ability and according to the duties of my station in life. To the flesh we say: Thus far and no farther.

Yes, said Brinsley nodding.

Sloth – Lord save us – sloth is a terrible cross to carry in this world. You are a burden to yourself . . . to your friends . . . and to every man woman and child you meet and mix with. One of the worst of the deadly sins, there is no doubt about it.

I'd say it is the worst, said Brinsley.

The worst? Certainly.

Turning to me, my uncle said:

Tell me this, do you ever open a book at all?

I open and shut books several times a day, I replied in a testy manner. I study here in my bedroom because it is quiet and suitable for the purpose. I pass my examinations without difficulty when they arise. Is there any other point I could explain?

That will do you now, there is no need for temper, said my uncle. No need at all for temper. Friendly advice no wise man scorns, I'm sure you have often heard that said.

Ah don't be too hard on him, said Brinsley, especially about his studies. A little more exercise would do the trick. *Mens sana in corpore sano*, you know.

The Latin tongue was unknown to my uncle.

There is no doubt about it, he said.

I mean, the body must be in good condition before the mind can be expected to function properly. A little more exercise and study would be less of a burden, I fancy.

Of course, said my uncle. Lord knows I am sick sore and tired telling him that. Sick, sore, and tired.

In the speech of Brinsley I detected an opening for crafty retaliation and revenge. I turned to him and said:

That is all very well for you. You are fond of exercise – I am not. You go for a long walk every evening because you like it. To me it is a task.

I am very glad to hear you are fond of walking, Mr Brinsley, said my uncle.

Oh, yes, said Brinsley. His tone was disquieted.

Well, indeed, you are a wise man, said my uncle. Every evening in life I go for a good four-mile tramp myself. Every evening, wet or fine. And do you know what I am going to tell you, I'm better for it too. I am indeed. I don't know what I would do without my walk.

You are a bit late at it this evening, I observed.

Never you fear, late or early I won't forget it, he said. Would you care to join me, Mr Brinsley?

They went, the two of them. I lay back in the failing light in a comfortable quiet manner. Conclusion of the foregoing.

Synopsis, being a summary of what has gone before, for the benefit of new readers: ORLICK TRELLIS, having concluded his course of study at the residence of the Pooka MacPhellimey, now takes his place in civil life, living as a lodger in the house of

FURRISKEY, whose domestic life is about to be blessed by the advent of a little stranger. Meanwhile

SHANAHAN and LAMONT, fearing that Trellis would soon become immune to the drugs and sufficiently regain the use of his faculties to perceive the true state of affairs and visit the delinquents with terrible penalties, are continually endeavouring to devise A PLAN. One day in Furriskey's sitting-room they discover what appear to be some pages of manuscript of a high-class story in which the names of painters and French wines are used with knowledge and authority. On investigation they find that Orlick has inherited his father's gift for literary composition. Greatly excited, they suggest that he utilize his gift to turn the tables (as it were) and compose a story on the subject of Trellis, a fitting punishment indeed for the usage he has given others. Smouldering with resentment at the stigma of his own bastardy, the dishonour and death of his mother, and incited by the subversive teachings of the Pooka, he agrees. He comes one evening to his lodging where the rest of his friends are gathered and a start is made on the manuscript in the presence of the interested parties. Now read on.

Extract from Manuscript by O. Trellis. Part One. Chapter One: Tuesday had come down through Dundrum and Foster Avenue, brine-fresh from sea-travel, a corn-yellow sun-drench that called forth the bees at an incustomary hour to their day of bumbling. Small house-flies performed brightly in the embrasures of the windows, whirling without fear on imaginary trapezes in the limelight of the sunslants.

Dermot Trellis neither slept nor woke but lay there in his bed, a twilight in his eyes. His hands he rested emptily at his thighs and his legs stretched loose-jointed and heavily to the bed-bottom. His diaphragm, a metronome of quilts, heaved softly and relaxed in the beat of his breathing. Generally speaking he was at peace.

A cleric, attaining the ledge of the window with the help of a stout ladder of ashplant rungs, round and seasoned, quietly peered in through the glass. The bar of the sunbeams made a great play of his fair hair and burnished it into the appearance of a halo. He civilly unloosed the brass catch on the window by inserting the blade of his pen-knife between the sashes. He then raised up the bottom sash with a strong arm and entered into the room without offence, one leg first for all the hobble of his soutane, and afterwards the other. He was meek and of pleasing manners and none but an ear that listened for it could perceive the click of the window as it was shut. The texture of his face was mottled by a blight of Lent-pocks, but – stern memorials of his fasts – they did not lessen the clear beauty of his brow.

Each of his features was pale and hollow and unlivened by the visits of his feeble blood; but considering them together in the manner in which their Creator had first arranged them, they enunciated between them a quiet dignity, a peace like the sad peace of an old grave-yard. His manner was meek. The cuffs, the neck and the fringes of his surplice were intricately crocheted in a pattern of stars and flowers and triangles, three diversities cunningly needle-worked to a white unity. His fingers were wax pale and translucent and curled resolutely about the butt of a club of the mountain-ash that can be found in practically every corner of the country. His temples were finely perfumed.

He examined the bedroom without offence and with plenty of diligence, for it was the first room he was in. He drew a low sound from a delph wash-jug with a blow of his club and a bell-note was the sound he brought forth with the two of them, his sandal and a chamber.

Trellis arose and made a hypotenuse of his back, his weight being supported on his elbows. His head was sunken in the cup of his collar-bones and his eyes stared forth like startled sentries from their red watch-towers.

Who are you? he asked. A quantity of dried mucus had been lodged in a lump in his wind-pipe and for this reason the tone of his voice was not satisfactory. He followed his question without delay with a harsh coughing noise, presumably in order to remedy his defective articulation.

I am Moling, said the cleric. A smile crossed his face without pausing on its way. I am a cleric and I serve God. We will pray together after.

On the outer edge of the cloud of wonder that was gathered in the head of Trellis, there was an outer border of black anger. He brought down his lids across his eyeballs until his vision was confined to slits scarcely wider than those in use by houseflies when flying in the face of a strong sun, videlicet, the thousandth part of an inch statute. He ascertained by trial that his windpipe was clear before he loudly put this question:

How did you get in here? What do you want?

I was acquainted of the way by angels, said the cleric, and the ladder I have climbed to your window-shelf was fashioned by angelic craftsmen from pitch pine of the best quality and conveyed to my college in a sky-carriage in the middle of last night, at two of the clock to speak precisely. I am here this morning to make a bargain.

You are here to make a bargain.

To make a bargain between the pair of us, yourself and me. There is fine handwork in that thing on the floor. Too delightful the roundness of its handle.

What? said Trellis. Who did you say you were? What was that noise? What is the ringing for?

The bells of my acolyte, said the cleric. His voice was of a light quality and was unsupported by the majority of his wits, because these were occupied with the beauty of the round thing, its whiteness, its star-twinkle face.

Eh?

My acolytes are in your garden. They are taping the wallsteads of a sunbright church and ringing their bells in the morning.

I beg your pardon, Sir, said Shanahan, but this is a bit too high up for us. This delay, I mean to say. The fancy stuff, couldn't you leave it out or make it short, Sir? Couldn't you give him a dose of something, give him a varicose vein in the bloody heart and get him out of that bed?

Orlick placed his pen in the centre of his upper lip and exerted a gentle pressure by a movement of his head or hand, or both, so that his lip was pushed upwards.

Result: baring of teeth and gum.

You overlook my artistry, he said. You cannot drop a man unless you first lift him. See the point?

Oh, there's that too, of course, said Shanahan.

Or a varicose vein across the scalp, said Furriskey, near the brain, you know. I believe that's the last.

I saw a thing in a picture once, said Shanahan, a concrete-mixer, you understand, Mr Orlick, and three of your men fall into it when it is working full blast, going like the hammers of hell.

The mixture to be taken three times after meals, Lamont said laughing.

You must have patience, gentlemen, counselled Orlick, the whiteness of a slim hand for warning.

A concrete-mixer, said Shanahan.

I'm after thinking of something good, something very good unless I'm very much mistaken, said Furriskey in an eager way, black in the labour of his fine thought. When you take our hero from the concrete-mixer, you put him on his back on the road and order full steam ahead with the steam-roller . . .

And a very good idea, Shanahan agreed.

And a very good idea as you say, Mr Shanahan. But when the roller passes over his dead corpse, be damned but there's one thing there that it can't crush, one thing that lifts it high offa the road — a ten-ton roller, mind! . . .

Indeed, said Orlick, eyebrow for question.

One thing, said Furriskey, sole finger for true counting. They drive away the roller and here is his black heart sitting there as large as life in the middle of the pulp of his banjaxed corpse. *They couldn't crush his heart!*

Very . . . very . . . good, intoned Lamont. A winner, Mr Orlick. Well that will ring the bell certainly.

Admirable, concurred Orlick, honey-word for peace. *They couldn't crush the heart!*

Steam-rollers are expensive machines but, remarked Shanahan, what about a needle in the knee? He kneels on it by mistake, drives it in and then it breaks and leaves nothing to get a grip on. A knitting needle or a hat-pin.

A cut of a razor behind the knee, said Lamont with a wink of knowledge, try it and see.

Orlick had been quietly occupied with the arrangement of a paragraph of wisdom in his mind; he now inserted it with deftness in the small gap which he discovered in the disputations.

The refinements of physical agony, he enunciated, are limited by an ingenious arrangement of the cerebral mechanism and the sensory nerves which precludes from registration all emotions, sensations and perceptions abhorrent to the fastidious maintenance by Reason of its discipline and rule over the faculties and the functions of the body. Reason will not permit of the apprehension of sensations of reckless or prodigal intensity. Give me an agony within reason, says Reason, and I will take it, analyse it, and cause the issue of vocal admission that it has been duly received; I can deal with it and do my other work as well. Is that clear?

Very well put, Sir, said Shanahan.

But go beyond the agreed statutory limit, says Reason, and I won't be there at all. I'll put out the light and pull down the blinds. I will close the shop. I will come back later when I think I will be offered something I can deal with. Follow?

And back he'll come too. When the fun is over, back he'll come.

But the soul, the ego, the *animus*, continued Orlick, is very different from the body. Labyrinthine are the injuries inflictable on the soul. The tense of the body is the present indicative; but the soul has a memory and a present and a future. I have conceived some extremely recondite pains for Mr Trellis. I will pierce him with a pluperfect.

Pluperfect is all right, of course, said Shanahan, anybody that takes exception to that was never very much at the bee-double-o-kay-ess. I wouldn't hear a word against it. But do you know, this tack of yours is too high up in the blooming clouds. It's all right for you, you know, but the rest of us will want a ladder. Eh, Mr Furriskey?

A forty-foot ladder, said Furriskey.

At the conclusion of a brief interval, Lamont spread out his hand and addressed Mr Orlick in a low earnest voice.

A nice simple story would be very nice, Sir, he said, you take a lot of the good out of it when you start, you know, the other business. A nice simple story with plenty of the razor, you understand. A slash of the razor behind the knee. Oh, that's the boy!

The right hand of Orlick was fastened about his jaw.

Interpretation of manual attitude mentioned: a token of extreme preoccupation and intense thought.

I admit, gentlemen, he said at last, I admit that there is a certain amount to be said for your point of view. Sometimes...

There's this, too, said Shanahan with a quick continuance of his argument, there's this, that you have to remember the man in the street. *I* may understand you, *Mr Lamont* may understand you, *Mr Furriskey* may understand you – but the man in the street? Oh, by God you have to go very *very* slow if you want *him* to follow you. A snail would be too fast for him, a snail could give him yards.

Orlick detached his hand from his jaw and passed it slowly about his brow.

I could begin again, of course, he said with a slight weariness, but it would mean wasting some very good stuff.

Certainly you can begin again, said Shanahan, there's no harm done, man. I've been longer in this world and I can tell you this: *There's nothing to be ashamed of in a false start.* We can but try. Eh, boys? We can but try.

We can but try, said Furriskey.

Well, well, well, said Orlick.

Tuesday had come down through Dundrum and Foster Avenue, brine-fresh from sea-travel, a corn-yellow sun-drench that called forth the bees at an incustomary hour to their day of bumbling. Small house-flies performed brightly in the embrasures of the windows, whirling without a fear on imaginary trapezes in the limelight of the sunslants.

Dermot Trellis neither slept nor woke but lay there in his bed, a twilight in his eyes. His hands he rested emptily at his thighs and his legs stretched loose-jointed and heavily to the bed-bottom. His diaphragm, a metronome of quilts, heaved softly and relaxed in the beat of his breathing. Generally speaking he was at peace.

His home was by the banks of the Grand Canal, a magnificent building resembling a palace, with seventeen windows to the front and maybe twice that number to the rear. It was customary with him to remain in the interior of his house without ever opening the door to go out or let the air and the light go in. The blind of his bedroom window would always be pulled down during the daytime and a sharp eye would discover that he had the gas on even when the sun was brightly shining. Few had ever seen him in the flesh and the old people had bad memories and had forgotten what he looked like the last time they had laid their eyes on him. He paid no attention to the knocking of mendicants and musicians and would sometimes shout something at people passing from behind his blind. It was a well-known fact that he was responsible for plenty of rascality and only simple people were surprised at the way he disliked the sunshine.

He paid no attention to the law of God and this is the short of his evil-doing in the days when he was accustomed to go out of his house into the air:

He corrupted schoolgirls away from their piety by telling impure stories and reciting impious poems in their hearing.

Holy purity he despised.

Will this be a long list do you think, Sir, asked Furriskey.

Certainly, answered Orlick, I am only starting.

Well what about a Catalogue, you know?

A Catalogue would be a very cute one, Lamont concurred. Cross-references and double-entry, you know. What do you think, Mr Orlick? What do you say?

A catalogue of his sins, eh? Is that what you mean? asked Orlick.

Do you understand what I mean? asked Furriskey with solicitude.

I think I do, mind you. DRUNKENNESS, was addicted to. CHASTITY, lacked. I take it that's what you had in mind, Mr Furriskey?

That sounds very well, gentlemen, said Lamont, very well indeed in my humble opinion. It's the sort of queer stuff they look for in a story these days. Do you know?

Oh, we'll make a good job of this yarn yet.

We will see, said Orlick.

He paid no attention to the laws of God and this is the short of his evil-doing in the days when he was accustomed to go out of his house into the light.

ANTHRAX, paid no attention to regulations governing the movements of animals affected with.

BOYS, corner, consorted with.

CONVERSATIONS, licentious, conducted by telephone with unnamed female servants of the Department of Posts and Telegraphs.

DIRTINESS, all manner of spiritual mental and physical, gloried in.

ECLECTICISM, practised amorous.

The completion of this list in due alphabetical order, observed Orlick, will require consideration and research. We will complete it later. This is not the place (nor is the hour appropriate), for scavenging in the cesspools of iniquity.

Oh, you're a wise man, Mr Orlick, and me waiting without a word to see what you would do with x. You're too fly now, said Shanahan.

E for evil, said Furriskey.

He is quite right, said Lamont, can't you see he wants to get down to business. Eh? Mr Orlick. Can't you see that it means delay?

Quite right, said Shanahan. Silence!

On a certain day this man looked out accidentally through a certain window and saw a saint in his garden taping out the wall-steads of a new sun-bright church, with a distinguished con-course of clerics and acolytes along with him, discoursing and ringing shrill iron bells and reciting elegant latin. For a reason he was angry. He gave the whoop of a world-wide shout from the place he was and with only the bareness of time for completing the plan he was engaged with, made five strides to the middle of his garden. The brevity of the tale is this, that there was a sacrilege in the garden that morning. Trellis took the saint by a hold of his wasted arm and ran (the two of them), until the head of the cleric had been hurt by a stone wall. The evil one then took a hold of the saint's breviary – the one used by holy Kevin – and tore at it until it was a-tatters in his angry hand; and he added this to his sins, videlicet, the hammering of a young clergyman, an acolyte to confide precisely, with a lump of a stone.

There now, he said.

Evil is the work you have accomplished here this morning, said the saint with a hand to the soreness of his head.

But the mind of Trellis was darkened with anger and evil venom against the saintly band of strangers. The saint smoothed out the many-lined pages of his ruined book and recited a curse in poetry against the evil one, three stanzas in devvy-metre of surpassing elegance and sun-twinkle clearness . . .

Do you know, said Orlick, filling the hole in his story with the music of his voice, I think we are on the wrong track again. What do you say, gentlemen?

Certainly you are, said Shanahan, no offence but that class of stuff is all my fanny.

You won't get very far by attacking the church, said Furriskey.

I gather my efforts are not approved, said Orlick. He gave a small smile and took advantage of the parting of his lips for a brief spell of pen-tap at the teeth.

You can do better, man, said Lamont, that's the way to look at it. You can do twice as good if you put your mind to it.

I think, said Orlick, we might requisition the services of the Pooka MacPhellimey.

If you don't hurry and get down to business, Sir, said Furriskey, Trellis will get us before we get him. He'll hammer the lights out of us. Get him on the run, Mr Orlick. Get the Pooka and let him go to work right away. God, if he catches us at this game . . .

What about this for a start, asked Shanahan, a big boil on the small of his back where he can't get at it. It's a well-known fact that every man has a little square on his back that he can't itch with his hand. Here, look.

There's such a thing as a scratching-post, observed Lamont.

Wait now! said Orlick. Silence please.

Tuesday had come down through Foster Avenue and Dundrum, brine-fresh from sea-travel, a corn-yellow sun-drench that called forth the bees at an incustomary hour to their day of bumbling. Small house-flies performed brightly in the embrasures of the windows, whirling without fear on imaginary trapezes in the limelight of the sunslants.

Dermot Trellis neither slept nor woke but lay there in his bed, a twilight in his eyes. His hands he rested emptily at his thighs and his legs stretched loose-jointed and heavily to the bed-bottom. His diaphragm, a metronome of quilts, heaved softly and relaxed in the beat of his breathing. Generally speaking, he was at peace.

The utterance of a civil cough beside his ear recalled him to his reason. His eyes, startled sentries in red watch-towers on the brink of morning, brought him this intelligence, that the Pooka MacPhellimey was sitting there beside him on the cabinet of his pots, a black walking-stick of invaluable ebony placed civilly across the knees of his tight trousers. His temples were finely scented with an expensive brand of balsam and fine snuff-dust could be discerned on the folds of his cravat. A top-hat was inverted on the floor, with woven gloves of black wool placed neatly in its interior.

Good morning to you, Sir, said the Pooka with melodious intonation. No doubt you have awakened to divert yourself with the refreshment of the dawn.

Trellis composed his pimples the way they would tell of the greatness of the surprise that was in his mind.

Your visit to my house this morning, he said, that surprises me. A bull may sometimes be a cow, a jackdaw may discourse, cocks have established from time to time the hypothesis that the egg is impeculiar to the she-bird, but a servant is at all times a servant notwithstanding. I do not recall that I desired you for a guest at an hour when I am accustomed to be unconscious in the shadow of my sleep. Perchance you bring a firkin of sweet ointment compounded for the relief of boils?

I do not, rejoined the Pooka.

Then a potion, herbal and decanted from the juice of roots, unsurpassed for the extirpation of personal lice?

Doubts as to the sex of cattle, observed the Pooka after he had first adjusted the hard points of his fingers one against the other, arise only when the animal is early in its youth and can be readily resolved by the use of a prongs or other probing instrument – or better still, a magnifying glass of twenty diameters. Jackdaws who discourse or who are accustomed to express themselves in Latin or in the idiom of sea-faring men may betray an indication of the nature of their talent by inadvertently furnishing the same answer to all questions, making claim in this manner to un-limited ignorance or infinite wisdom. If a cock may secrete eggs from his interior, equally a hen can crow at four-thirty of a morning. Rats have been observed to fly, small bees can extract honey from dung and agamous mammals have been known to produce by the art of allogamy a curious offspring azoic in nature and arachnoid in appearance. It is not false that a servant is a servant but truth is an odd number and one master is a great mistake. Myself I have two.

Allogamy and arachnoid I understand, said Trellis, but the meaning you attach to azoic is a thing that is not clear to me at all.

Devoid of life, having no organic remains, said the Pooka.

That is an elegant definition, said Trellis, affording an early-morning smile for the enjoyment of his guest. A grain of know-ledge with the dawning of the day is a breakfast for the mind. I will now re-enter the darkness of my sleep, remembering to examine it anew on my recovery. My serving-girl, she is the little guide who will conduct you from the confinement of my walls. I have little doubt that the science of bird-flight is known to rats of cunning and resource, but nevertheless I have failed to observe such creatures passing by in the air through the aperture of my window. Good morning, Sir.

Your courteous salutation is one I cannot accept, answered the Pooka, for this reason, that its valedictory character invalidates it. It is my mission here this morning to introduce you to a wide variety of physical scourges, torments, and piteous blood-sweats. The fulness of your suffering, that will be the measure of my personal perfection. A window without rat-flight past it is a backyard without a house.

Your talk surprises me, said Trellis. Furnish three examples.

Boils upon the back, a burst eyeball, a leg-withering chill, thorn-harrowed ear-lobes, there are four examples.

By God we're here at last, said Furriskey loudly. He made a noise with the two of them, his palm and his knee. We're here at last. From now on it's a fight to the finish, fair field and no favour.

Strop the razor, boys, smiled Shanahan. Mr Lamont, kindly put the poker in the fire.

Here there was a laugh, immelodious, malicious, high-pitched.

Now, now, boys, said Orlick. Now, now, boys. Patience.

I think we are doing very well, said Furriskey. We'll have the skin off his back yet. He'll be a sorry man.

That is a piteous recital, said Trellis. Provide further examples five in number.

With a slight bow the Pooka arranged the long-nailed fingers of his left hand in a vertical position and then with his remaining hand he pressed a finger down until it was horizontal in respect of each of the agonies he recited.

An anabasis of arrow-points beneath the agnail, razor-cut to knee-rear, an oak-stirk in the nipple, suspension by nose-ring, three motions of a cross-cut athwart the back, rat-bite at twilight, an eating of small-stones and a drinking of hog-slime, these are eight examples.

These are eight agonies, responded Trellis, that I would not endure for a chest of treasure. To say which of them is worst, that would require a winter in a web of thought. A glass of milk, that is the delicacy I offer you before you go.

These and other gravities you must endure, said the Pooka, and the one that you find the worst, that is the thing you must whisper after in the circle of my ear. To see you arise and dressing against the hour of your torment, that would be a courtesy. A glass of milk is bad for my indigestion. Acorns and loin-pie, these are my breakfast-tide delights. Arise, Sir, till I inflict twin nipple-hurts with the bevel of my nails.

An agitation to the seat of the Devil's trousers of decent sea-man's serge betokened that his hair-tail and his shirt-tails were engaged in slow contention and stiff whirly gambols of precise intent. His face (as to colour) was grey.

Colour of the face of Trellis, not counting the tops of pimples: white.

Keep away, you crump, you, he roared. Oh, by God, I'll kick your guts around the room if you don't keep your hands off me!

These piteous visitations shall not accurse you singly, observed the Pooka in a polite tone, nor shall they come together in triads. These hurts shall gather to assail you in their twos or fours or in their sixties; and all for this reason, that truth is one.

It was then that the Pooka MacPhellimey exercised the totality of his strange powers by causing with a twist of his hard horn-thumb a stasis of the natural order and a surprising kinesis of many incalculable influences hitherto in suspense. A number of miracles were wrought as one and together. The man in the bed was beleaguered with the sharpness of razors as to nipples, knee-rear and belly-roll. Leaden-hard forked arteries ran speedily about his scalp, his eye-beads bled and the corrugations of boils and piteous tumuli which appeared upon the large of his back gave it the appearance of a valuable studded shield and could be ascertained on counting to be sixty-four in number. He suffered a contraction of the intestines and a general re-arrangement of his interior to this result, that a meat repast in the process of digestion was ejected on the bed, on the coverlet, to speak pre-cisely. In addition to his person, his room was also the subject of mutations unexplained by any purely physical hypothesis and not to be accounted for by mechanical devices relating to the manipulation of guy-ropes, pulley-blocks, or mechanical collap-sible wallsteads of German manufacture, nor did the movements of the room conform to any known laws relating to the behav-iour of projectiles as ascertained by a study of gravitation en-forced by calculations based on the postulata of the science of ballistics. On the contrary, as a matter of fact, the walls parted, diminished and came back again with loud noises and with clouds of choking lime-dust, frequently forming hexagons instead of squares when they came together. The gift of light was frequently withdrawn without warning and there was a continuous loud vomit-noise offensive to persons of delicate perceptions. Chamber-pots flew about in the aimless parabolae normally frequented by blue-bottles and heavy articles of furniture – a wardrobe would be a typical example – could be discerned stationary in the air without visible means of support. A clock could be heard incessantly reciting the hours, a token that the free flight of time had also been interfered with; while the mumbling of the Pooka at his hell-prayers and the screaming of the sufferer, these were other noises perceptible to the practised ear. The obscure atmosphere was at the same time pervaded by a stench of incommunicable gravity.

The butt of that particular part of the story is this, that Trellis, wind-quick, eye-mad, with innumerable boils upon his back and upon various parts of his person, flew out in his sweat-wet night-shirt and day-drawers, out through the glass of the window till he fell with a crap on the cobbles of the street. A burst eyeball, a crushed ear and bone-breaks two in number, these were the agonies that were his lot as a result of his accidental fall. The Pooka, a master of the science of rat-flight, fluttered down through the air with his black cloak spread about him like a rain-cloud, down to the place where the stunned one was engaged in the re-gathering of his wits, for these were the only little things he had for defending himself from harm; and this is a précis of the by-play the pair of them engaged in with their tongues.

You hog of hell, you leper's sore you! said Trellis in a queer voice that came through the grid of his bleeding mouth-hiding hand. He reclined on the mud-puddled cobbles, a tincture of fine blood spreading about his shirt. You leper's death-puke!

It was an early-morning street, its quiet distances still small secrets shared by night with day. Two fingers at the eyes of his nostrils, the Pooka delicately smelt the air, a token that he was engaged in an attempt to predict the character of the weather.

You leper's lights, said Trellis.

To forsake your warm bed, said the other courteously, without the protection of your heavy great-coat of Galway frieze, that was an oversight and one which might well be visited with penalties pulmonary in character. To inquire as to the gravity of your sore fall, would that be inopportune?

You black bastard, said Trellis.

The character of your colloquy is not harmonious, rejoined the Pooka, and makes for barriers between the classes. Honey-words in torment, a growing urbanity against the sad extremities of human woe, that is the further injunction I place upon your head; and for the avoidance of opprobrious oddity as to numerals, I add this, a sickly suppuration at the base of the left breast.

I find your last utterance preoccupying to my intellect, said Trellis, and I am at the same time not unmindful of the incidence of that last hurt upon my person . . .

Come here for a minute, said Shanahan, there's one thing you forgot. There's one cat in the bag that didn't jump.

Which cat would that be? Orlick asked.

Our man is in the room. Right. The boyo starts his tricks. Right. The room begins to dance. The smell and the noise starts. Right. Everything goes bang bar one thing. That one thing is a very important article of furniture altogether. Gentlemen, I refer to our friend the ceiling. *Is my Nabs too much of a gentleman to get the ceiling on the napper?*

Oh, God that's a terrible thing to get, said Lamont. A friend of mine got a crack of a lump of plaster on the neck here, look. By God Almighty it nearly creased him.

Didn't I tell you it was good, said Shanahan.

Nearly killed him, nearly put the light out for good.

A wallop of the ceiling is all I ask, Sir, Shanahan said. What do you say now? A ton of plaster on the napper.

It's a bit late to think of it now, you know, Orlick answered, table-tap for doubt.

He was in the Mater for a week, said Lamont. People were remarking the scab for the best part of a year – do you know that? Oh, not a bit of him could wear a collar.

It means bringing the whole party into the house again, said Orlick.

And well worth it! said Furriskey, slapping the sun-bright serge of his knee. And well worth it, by God.

Wheel him in, man, begged Shanahan. He'd be in and out by now if we had less talk out of us.

A second thought is never an odd thought, said the Pooka with a courteous offering of his snuff-box, and it is for that reason that it would be wisdom for the pair of us to penetrate again to the privacy of your bedroom. The collapse of the ceiling, that is one thing we forgot.

That time you spoke, said Trellis, the sweetness of your words precluded me from comprehending the meaning you attach to them.

It is essential, explained the Pooka, that we return to your room the way we may perfect these diversions upon which the pair of us were engaged.

That is an absorbing project, said Trellis. In what manner do we re-attain the street?

The way we came, said the Pooka.

Our project is the more absorbing for that, said Trellis, a small tear running evenly from his eye to his chin and a convulsion piteous to behold running the length of his backbone.

The Pooka thereupon betook himself into the upper air with a graceful retraction of his limbs beneath his cloak in the fashion of a gannet in full flight and flew until he had attained the sill of his window, with Trellis for company and colloquy by his side by the means of a hair-grip; and these were the subjects they held brief discourse on the time they were in flight together, videlicet, the strange aspect of tramway wires which, when viewed from above and from a postulated angle, have the appearance of confining the street in a cage; the odd probity of tricycles; this curious circumstance, that a dog as to his legs is evil and sinful but attains sanctity at the hour of his urination.

It is my intention, said the Pooka in the ear of Trellis, to remain resting here on the stone-work of this window; as for you, to see you regain the security of your bedroom (littered as it is by a coat of lime), that would indeed be a graceful concession to my eccentric dawning-day desires.

Easily accomplished, said Trellis, as he crawled in his crimson robe to the interior of his fine room, but give me time, for a leg that is in halves is a slow pilgrim and my shoulder is out of joint.

When he had crawled on to the floor, the ceiling fell upon his head, hurting him severely and causing the weaker parts of his skull to cave in. And he would have remained there till this, buried and for dead beneath the lime-clouded fall, had not the Pooka given him a quantity of supernatural strength on loan for five minutes, enabling him to raise a ton of plaster with the beam of his back and extricate himself until he achieved a lime-white hurtling through the window and dropped with a crap on the cobbles of the street again, the half of the blood that was previously in him now around him and on his outside.

It was here that Furriskey held up the further progress of the tale with his hand in warning.

Maybe we're going a bit too hard on him, he warned. You can easily give a man a bigger hiding than he can hold.

We're only starting, man, said Shanahan.

Gentlemen, I beg of you, leave everything to me, said Orlick with a taste of anger in his words. I guarantee that there will be no untoward fatality.

I draw the line at murder myself, observed Lamont.

I think we are doing very well, said Shanahan.

All right, Sir, away we go again, but don't forget he has a weak heart. Don't give him more than he can carry now.

That will be all right, answered Orlick.

Thereafter the Pooka applied his two horn-hard thumbs together, turning them at incustomary angles and scrubbing them on the good-quality kerseymere of his narrow trousers so that further sorcery was worked to this effect, that Trellis was beleaguered by an anger and a darkness and he was filled with a restless tottering unquiet and with a disgust for the places that he knew and with a desire to go where he never was, so that he was palsied of hand and foot and eye-mad and heart-quick so that he went bird-quick in craze and madness into the upper air, the Pooka at his rat-flight beside him and his shirt, red and blood-lank, fluttering heavily behind him.

To fly, observed the Pooka, towards the east to discover the seam between night and day, that is an aesthetic delight. Your fine overcoat of Galway frieze, the one with the khaki lining, you forgot that on the occasion of your second visit to your bedroom.

The gift of flight without the sister-art of landing, answered Trellis, that is always a doubt. I feel a thirst and the absence of a drink of spring water for a longer period than five minutes might well result in my death. It might be wisdom for the pair of us to attain land, me to lie upon my back and you to pour water from your hat into my interior. I have a hole here in my neck and through it the half of a cupful might escape before it could attain my stomach.

It was here that Orlick laid his pen upon its back.

Talking of water, Mr Furriskey, he said, pardon my asking but where is the parochial house, the bath-room, you know?

The important apartment to which you refer, Sir, answered Furriskey with gravity, is on your left on the first landing on your way up, you can't miss it.

Ah. In that case there will be a slight intermission. I must retire for meditation and prayer. The curtain will be lowered to denote the passage of time. Gentlemen, adios!

Safe home, cried Shanahan, waving his hand.

Orlick arose stiffly from where he was and left the room, pushing back his hair and running it swiftly through the comb of his fingers. Lamont extracted a small box from his pocket, exhibited it and proved to the company beyond doubt that it contained but one cigarette; he lit the sole cigarette with the aid of a small machine depending for its utility on the combustibility of petroleum vapour when mixed with air. He sucked the smoke to the bottom of his lungs and these following words were mixed with it when he blew it out again on the flat of the table.

Do you know we're doing well. We're doing very well. By God he'll rue the day. He'll be a sorry man now.

A bigger hiding, remarked Furriskey with articulation leisurely in character, no man ever got. A more ferocious beating was never handed out by the hand of man.

Gentlemen, said Shanahan, we're taking all the good out of it by giving him a rest, we're letting him get his wind. Now that's a mistake.

He'll get more than his wind.

Now I propose with your very kind permission to give our friend a little hiding of my own. A side-show, you understand. We'll put him back where we found him before the master comes back. Is the motion passed?

Now be careful, warned Lamont. Easy now. You'd better leave him be. We're doing very nicely so we are.

Not at all, man. Listen. A little party on our own.

The two lads in the air came to a sudden stop by order of his Satanic Majesty. The Pooka himself stopped where he was, never mind how it was done. The other fell down about a half a mile to the ground on the top of his snot and broke his two legs in halves and fractured his fourteen ribs, a terrible fall altogether.

Down flew the Pooka after a while with a pipe in his mouth and the full of a book of fancy talk out of him as if this was any consolation to our friend, who was pumping blood like a stuck pig and roaring out strings of profanity and dirty foul language, enough to make the sun set before the day was half over.

Enough of that, my man, says the Pooka taking the pipe from his mouth. Enough of your dirty tongue now, Caesar. Say you like it.

I'm having a hell of a time, says Trellis. I'm nearly killed laughing. I never had such gas since I was a chiseller,

That's right, says the Pooka, enjoy yourself. How would you like a kick on the side of the face?

Which side? says Trellis.

The left side, Caesar, says the Pooka.

You're too generous altogether, says Trellis. I don't know you well enough to take a favour like that from you.

You're welcome, says the Pooka. And with these words he walked back, took the pipe out of his jaw, came down with a run and lifted the half of the man's face off his head with one kick and sent it high up into the trees where it got stuck in a blackbird's nest.

Say you like it, says he to Trellis quicklike.

Certainly I like it, says Trellis through a hole in his head – he had no choice because orders is orders, to quote a well-worn tag. Why wouldn't I like it? I think it's grand.

We are going to get funnier as we go along, says the Pooka, frowning with his brows and pulling hard at the old pipe. We are going to be very funny after a while. Is that one of your bones there on the grass?

Certainly, says Trellis, that's a lump out of my back.

Pick it up and carry it in your hand, says the Pooka, we don't want any of the parts lost.

When he had finished saying that, he put a brown tobacco spit on Trellis's snot.

Thanks, says Trellis.

Maybe you're tired of being a man, says the Pooka.

I'm only half a man as it is, says Trellis. Make me into a fine woman and I'll marry you.

I'll make you into a rat, says the Pooka,

And be damned but he was as good as his word. He worked

the usual magic with his thumb and changed Trellis by a miracle of magic into a great whore of a buck rat with a black pointed snout and a scaly tail and a dirty rat-coloured coat full of ticks and terrible vermin, to say nothing of millions of plague-germs and disease and epidemics of every description.

What are you now? says the Pooka.

Only a rat, says the rat, wagging his tail to show he was pleased because he had to and had no choice in the matter. A poor rat, says he.

The Pooka took a good suck at his pipe.

Stop, said Furriskey.

What's the matter, amn't I all right man? asked Shanahan.

You're doing very nicely, Sir, said Furriskey, but here's where I contribute my penny to the plate. Here, gentlemen, is my idea of how our story goes on from where you stopped.

The Pooka took a good pull at his pipe. The result of this manoeuvre was magic of a very high order, because the Pooka succeeded in changing himself into a wire-haired Airedale terrier, the natural enemy of the rat from the start of time. He gave one bark and away with him like the wind after the mangy rat. Man but it was a great chase, hither and thither and back again, the pair of them squealing and barking for further orders. The rat, of course, came off second best. He was caught by the throat at the heel of the hunt and got such a shaking that he practically gave himself up for lost. Practically every bone and sinew in his body was gone by the time he found himself dropped again on the grass.

That's right, you know, remarked Furriskey, a rat's bones are very weak. Very soft, you know. The least thing will kill a rat.

Noises, peripatetic and external, came faintly upon the gathering in the midst of their creative composition and spare-time literary activity. Lamont handled what promised to be an awkward situation with coolness and cunning.

And the short of it is this, he said, that the Pooka worked more magic till himself and Trellis found themselves again in the air in their own bodies, just as they had been a quarter of an hour before that, none the worse for their trying ordeals.

Orlick came back amongst them, closing the door with care. He was fresh, orderly, civil, and a small cloud of new tobacco fumes was in attendance on his person.

More luck there, said Shanahan, the best story-teller in all the world. We're waiting with our tongues hanging out. The same again, please.

Orlick beamed a smile of pleasure with the suns of his gold teeth. A token of preoccupation, he retained his smile after its purpose had been accomplished.

A further thrilling instalment? Yes, he said.

No delay now, said Lamont.

I have been engaged, said Orlick, in profound thought. It is only now that the profundity of my own thought is dawning on me. I have devised a plot that will lift our tale to the highest plane of great literature.

As long as the fancy stuff is kept down, said Shanahan.

A plot that will be acceptable to all. You, gentlemen, will like it in particular. It combines justice with vengeance.

As long as the fancy stuff is kept down, said Shanahan, well and good.

Bending his head forward as if with the weight of the frown he had arranged on his brow, Lamont said in a dark voice:

Do anything to spoil the good yarn you have made of it so far, and I will arise and I will slay thee with a shovel. Eh, boys?

This was agreed to.

Now listen, gentlemen, said Orlick. Away we go.

That night they rested at the tree of Cluain Eo, Trellis at his birds'-roost on a thin branch surrounded by tufts of piercing thorns and tangles of bitter spiky brambles. By the sorcery of his thumbs the Pooka produced a canvas tent from the seat of his trousers of sea-man's serge and erected it swiftly upon the carpet of the soft daisy-studded sward, hammering clean pegs into the fresh-smelling earth by means of an odorous pinewood mallet. When he had accomplished this he produced another wonder from the storehouse of his pants, videlicet, a good-quality folding bed with a hickory framework complete with intimate bedclothes of French manufacture. He then knelt down and occupied himself with his devotions, making sounds with his tongue and with the hard horn of his thumbs that put the heart across the cripple high above him in the tree. This done, he hid his body in silk pyjamas of elegant oriental cut and provided about the waist of the trousers with gorgeous many-coloured tassels, a garment suitable for wear in the *harem* of the greatest Sultan of the distant East. He then said this to Trellis.

From the manner in which one breeze follows another about the trees, I predict that the day after tomorrow will be a wet one. Good night to you in the place you are, and a salubrious breathing of fresh-air towards the restoration of your strength. Myself, I sleep in a tent because I am delicate.

Trellis's wits were by this time feeble with suffering and by the time his courteous answer had made its way through the cloaks of the heavy leaves, it was barely perceptible.

Rain is badly wanted for the crops, he said. Good night to you. May angels guard you.

The Pooka then knocked the red fire from the interior of his meerschaum pipe and retired to the secrecy of his tent, having first taken good care to extinguish the embers of his pipe with a lump of flat stone, for fires are extremely destructive and are jealously guarded against by every lover of the amenities of our land. And of the two of them, this much is sure, i.e., that one of them snored soundly through the night.

The night passed and the morning, having first wakened the plains and the open places, came into the fastness of the trees and knocked on the gaberdine flap of the Pooka's tent. He arose, prayed, and scented his temples with a rare balsam which he invariably carried about his person in a small black jar of perfect rotundity. He afterwards extracted a pound of oats and other choice ingredients from the inside of his pockets and baked himself an oaten farl of surpassing lightness and nourishment. He fed on this politely in a shaded corner of the wood he was in, but did not begin his feasting until he had extended to the man upon the branch a courteous invitation to make company with him at eating.

Breakfast? said Trellis, his hollow whisper coming from the exterior of the wood, for his tree-top was a high one.

Not incorrect, replied the Pooka. I beg that you will come and eat with me and the better to destroy the oddity of a single invitation, I add this, that you must refuse it.

I will not have any of it, thank you, said Trellis.

That is a pity, rejoined the Pooka, cracking a brown-baked crust in the crook of his clean-shaven jaws. Not to eat is a great mistake.

It was the length of two hours before the Pooka had put the entirety of the farl deep down in the pit of his stomach. At the end of that time the cripple in the tree was abandoned without warning by each of his wits with this unfortunate result, that he fell senseless though the cruel arms of the branches, and came upon the ground with a thud that placed him deeper in the darkness of his sleep. The thorns which were embedded in his person could be ascertained on counting to be no less than 944 in number.

After the Pooka had restored him to his reason with this delicacy, videlicet, a pint of woodland hogslime, the pair of them went forward on a journey with no more than three legs between them.

Proceeding on a carpet of fallen leaves and rotting acorns they had not travelled a distance longer in length than twenty-six perches when they saw (with considerable surprise, indeed) the figure of a man coming towards them from the secrecy of the old oaks. With a start of pleasure, the Pooka saw that it was none other than Mr Paul Shanahan, the eminent philosopher, wit and raconteur.

Shanahan at this point inserted a brown tobacco finger in the texture of the story and in this manner caused a lacuna in the palimpsest.

Wait a minute, he said. Just a minute now. Not so fast. What's that you said, Sir?

Orlick smiled.

Nature of smile: Innocent, wide-eyed, inquiring.

Mr Paul Shanahan, he said slowly, the eminent philosopher, wit, and raconteur.

Furriskey adjusted his neck so that his face was close to that of Shanahan.

What's wrong with you man, he asked. What's the matter? Isn't it all right? Isn't it high praise? Do you know the meaning of that last word?

It's from the French, of course, said Shanahan.

Then I'll tell you what it means, it means you're all right. Do you understand me? *I've met this man. I know him. I think he's all right.* Do you see it now?

There's nothing to worry about, boy, said Lamont.

Shanahan moved his shoulders and said this:

Well all right. All right. It's a story I'd rather be out of and that's the God's truth. But now that I'm in it, well and good. I trust you, Mr Orlick.

Orlick smiled.

Nature of smile: satisfied, complacent.

A finer-looking man than Mr Paul Shanahan you would not hope to meet in a day's walk. The glory of manhood in its prime was stamped on every line of his perfectly proportioned figure and the rhythm of glorious youth was exemplified in every movement of his fine athletic stride. The beam of his shoulders and the contours of his chest made it clear to even the most casual observer or passer-by that here was a tower, a reservoir of strength – not strength for loutish feats or for vain prodigal achievement, no; but strength for the defence of weakness, strength against oppression, strength for the advancement of all that was good and clean and generous. His complexion without blemish, his clear eye, these were the tokens of his clean living. Perfect as he was in physique, however, it would be a mistake to assume that his charms were exclusively of the physical (or purely bodily) variety. To the solution of life's problems and anxieties he brought a ready wit and a sense of humour – an inexhaustible capacity for seeing the bright side of things even when skies were grey and no beam of sun lightened the dull blackness of the clouds. His high education, his wealth of allusion and simile embracing practically every known European language as well as the immortal classics of Greece and Rome, these were gifts that made him the mainspring and the centre of gravity of every conversation irrespective of the matter being discussed or the parties engaged therein. A kindly heart and an unfailing consideration for the feelings of others, these were reasons (if indeed more were needed) as to why he endeared himself to everybody with whom he chanced to come in contact. A man of infinite patience, he was, in short, of a fine upstanding type – a type which, alas, is becoming all too rare.

He had barely arrived in the orbit or radius of vision of the two travellers when he was joined by another man, one who resembled him in many respects with striking closeness. The newcomer was a man by the name of John Furriskey, a name happily familiar to all who still account the sanctity of home life and the family tie as among the things that matter in this mundane old world. In appearance and physique, it could not be truly said by an impartial observer that he was in any way inferior to Mr Shanahan, magnificent specimen of manhood as the latter undoubtedly was. Curiously enough, however, it was not the perfection of his body that impressed one on first seeing him but rather the strange spirituality of his face. Looking at one with his deep eyes, he would sometimes not appear to see one, tho' needless to say, nothing would be farther from his mind than to be deliberately rude to a fellow-creature. It was obvious that he was a man who was used to deep and beautiful thinking, for there was no escaping the implications of that calm thoughtful face. It has been wisely said that true strength and greatness can spring only from a study and appreciation of what is small and weak and tiny — the modest daisy raising its meek head in the meadow sward, a robin redbreast in the frost, the gentle wandering zephyrs that temper the genial exuberance of King Sol of a summer's day. Here if ever was a man who carried the repose and grandeur of nature in his face; here was one of whom it might be truly said that he forgave all because he understood all. A learning and an erudition boundless in its universality, an affection phenomenal in its intensity and a quiet sympathy with the innumerable little failings of our common humanity — these were the sterling qualities that made Mr John Furriskey a man among men and endeared him to the world and his wife, without distinction of creed or class and irrespective of religious or political ties or allegiances of any description or character.

It was more by coincidence than anything else that these gentlemen were now observed to have been joined by a third, who appeared to approach from a direction almost due east. It might at first appear to the *illiterati* or uninitiated that a person devoid of practically all the virtues and excellences just enumerated in respect of the other gentlemen would have but little to recommend him. Such an hypothesis, however, would involve a very serious fallacy and one of which Antony Lamont could be said to constitute a living refutation. His body was neat and compactly built but it had withal a lissom gracefulness and a delicacy that could be almost said to be effeminate without in any way evoking anything of the opprobrious connotation of that word. His features were pale, finely moulded and ascetic, the features of a poet and one addicted almost continuously to thoughts of a beautiful or fragrant nature. The delicate line of his nostrils, his sensitive mouth, the rather wild escapade that was his hair — all were clear indications of a curiously lovely aestheticism, a poetical perception of no ordinary intensity. His fingers were the long tapering fingers of the true artist and one would be in no wise surprised to learn that he was an adept at the playing of some musical instrument (which in fact he was). His voice when he spoke was light and musical, a fact that was more than once commented on by people who had no reason for praising him and indeed by people who had the opposite.

Thanks, said Lamont.

You are welcome, said Orlick.

No need to make a joke of everything, Mr Lamont, said Furriskey, frowning.

Oh God, I'm not joking, said Lamont.

All right, said Furriskey, prohibiting further utterance by the extreme gravity of his countenance. That will do now. Yes, Mr Orlick.

The three men, each of them a perfect specimen of his own type, stood together in a group and commenced to converse in low cultured tones. The Pooka, never averse to bettering himself and acquiring fresh knowledge, listened spell-bound from the shadow of a magnificent Indian cashew-tree, feeding absently on the nuts of the lower branches; and as for the crippled man, he rested his body on a bough between the earth and heaven, a bough of the strong medicinal chinchona; and the pair of them revelled in the enchantment of three fine voices mingling together in pleasing counterpoint, each of them sweeter than the dulcet strains of the ocarina (or oval rib-bellied musical instrument of terra cotta), and softer than the sound of the ophicleide, a little-known wind instrument now virtually obsolete.

The fiddle is the man, said Shanahan.

Please be quiet, said Orlick.

The following, imperfect résumé or summary as it is, may be taken as a general indication of the scholarly trend of the conversation sustained without apparent effort by the three of them.

It is not generally known, observed Mr Furriskey, that the coefficient of expansion of all gases is the same. A gas expands to the extent of a hundred and seventy-third part of its own volume in respect of each degree of increased temperature centigrade. The specific gravity of ice is 0·92, marble 2·70, iron (cast) 7·20 and iron (wrought) 7·79. One mile is equal to 1·6093 kilometres reckoned to the nearest ten-thousandth part of a whole number.

True, Mr Furriskey, remarked Mr Paul Shanahan with a quiet smile that revealed a whiteness of the teeth, but a man who confines knowledge to formulae necessary for the resolution of an algebraic or other similar perplexity, the same deserves to be shot with a fusil, or old-fashioned light musket. True knowledge is unpractised or abstract usefulness. Consider this, that salt in solution is an excellent emetic and may be administered with safety to persons who are accustomed to eat poisonous berries or consume cacodyl, an evil-smelling compound of arsenic and methyl. A cold watch-key applied to the neck will relieve nose-bleeding. Banana-skins are invaluable for imparting a gloss to brown shoes.

To say that salt in solution, Lamont objected finely, is a pleasing emetic is a triviality related to inconsequent ephemera – the ever-perishing plasms of the human body. The body is too transient a vessel to warrant other than perfunctory investigation. Only in this regard is it important, that it affords the mind a basis for speculation and conjecture. Let me recommend to you, Mr Shanahan, the truer spiritual prophylaxis contained in the mathematics of Mr Furriskey. Ratiocination on the ordered basis of arithmetic is man's passport to the infinite. God is the root of minus one. He is too great a profundity to be compassed by human cerebration. But Evil is finite and comprehensible and admits of calculation. Minus One, Zero and Plus One are the three insoluble riddles of the Creation.

Mr Shanahan laughed in a cultured manner.

The riddle of the universe I might solve if I had a mind to, he said, but I prefer the question to the answer. It serves men like us as a bottomless pretext for scholarly dialectic.

Other points not unworthy of mention, mentioned Mr Furriskey in an absent-minded though refined manner, are the following: the great pyramid at Gizeh is 450 feet high and ranks as one of the seven wonders of the world, the others being the hanging gardens of Babylon, the tomb of Mausolus in Asia

Minor, the colossus of Rhodes, the temple of Diana, the statue of Jupiter at Olympia and the Pharos Lighthouse built by Ptolemy the First about three hundred and fifty years B.C. Hydrogen freezes at minus 253 degrees centigrade, equivalent to minus 423 on the Fahrenheit computation.

Everyday or colloquial names for chemical substances, observed Mr Shanahan, cream of tartar – bitartrate of potassium, plaster of Paris – sulphate of calcium, water – oxide of hydrogen. Bells and watches on board ship: first dog – 4 p.m. to 6 p.m., second dog – 6 p.m. to 8 p.m., afternoon – noon to 4 p.m. Paris, son of Priam, King of Troy, carried off the wife of Menelaus, King of Sparta and thus caused the Trojan War.

The name of the wife, said Lamont, was Helen. A camel is unable to swim owing to the curious anatomical distribution of its weight, which would cause its head to be immersed if the animal were placed in deep water. Capacity in electricity is measured by the farad; one microfarad is equal to one millionth of a farad. A carbuncle is a fleshy excrescence resembling the wattles of a turkey-cock. Sphragistics is the study of engraved seals.

Excellent, remarked Mr Furriskey with that quiet smile which endeared him to everyone who happened to come his way, but do not overlook this, that the velocity of light *in vacuo* is 186,325 miles per second. The velocity of sound in air is 1,120 feet per second, in tin 8,150 feet per second, in walnut mahogany and heavy timbers 11,000 feet per second approximately; in firwood, 20,000 feet per second. Sine 15 degrees is equal to the root of six minus the root of two, the whole divided by four. Percentages of £1: $1\frac{1}{4}$ per cent, threepence; 5 per cent, one shilling; $12\frac{1}{2}$ per cent, a half a crown. Some metric equivalents: one mile equals 1·6093 kilometres; one inch equals 2·54 centimetres; one ounce equals 28·352 grams. The chemical symbol of Calcium is Ca and of Cadmium, Cd. A Trapezoid may be defined as a four-sided figure capable of being transformed into two triangles by the means of a diagonal line.

Some curious facts about the Bible, Mr Lamont mentioned politely, the longest chapter is Psalm 119 and the briefest, Psalm 117. The Apocrypha contains 14 Books. The first English translation was published in A.D. 1535.

Some notable dates in the history of the world, observed Mr Shanahan, 753 B.C., foundation of Rome by Romulus, 490 B.C.,

Battle of Marathon, A.D. 1498, Vasco da Gama sailed around
South Africa and reached India, 23 April 1564 Shakespeare was
born.

It was then that Mr Furriskey surprised and, indeed, delighted
his companions, not to mention our two friends, by a little act
which at once demonstrated his resource and his generous urge
to spread enlightenment. With the end of his costly malacca
cane, he cleared away the dead leaves at his feet and drew the
outline of three dials or clock-faces on the fertile soil in this
fashion:

How to read the gas-meter, he announced. Similar dials to
these somewhat crudely depicted at my feet may be observed on
any gas-meter. To ascertain the consumption of gas, one should
procure pencil and paper and write down the figures nearest to
the indicator on each dial – thus in the present hypothetical case
963. To this one should add two zeros or noughts, making the
number 96,300. This is the answer and represents the consumption of gas in cubic feet. The reading of the electric-meter for
the discovery of consumption in Kilowatt-hours is more intricate than the above and would require the help of six dials for
demonstration purposes – more indeed that I have room for in
the space I have cleared of withered leaves, even assuming the
existing dials could be adapted for the purpose.

Thereafter these three savant or wise men of the East began
to talk together in a rapid manner and showered forth pearls of
knowledge and erudition, gems without price, invaluable carbuncles of sophistry and scholastic science, thomistic maxims,
intricate theorems in plane geometry and lengthy extracts from
Kant's *Kritik der reinischen Vernunst*. Frequent use was made of
words unheard of by illiterates and persons of inferior education
exempli gratia saburra or foul granular deposit in the pit of the
stomach, tachylyte, a vitreous form of basalt, tapir, a hoofed
mammal with the appearance of a swine, capon, castrated cock,

triacontahedral, having thirty sides or surfaces and botargo, relish of mullet or tunny roe. The following terms relating to the science of medicine were used with surprising frequency, videlicet, chyme, exophthalmus, scirrhus, and mycetoma meaning respectively food when acted upon by gastric juices and converted into acid pulp, protrusion of the eyeball, hard malignant tumour and fungoid disease of hand or foot. Aestho-therapy was touched upon and reference made to the duodenum, that is, the primary part of the small intestine, and the caecum or blind gut. Flowers and plants rarely mentioned in ordinary conversation were accorded their technical or quasi-botanical titles without difficulty or hesitation for instance now fraxinella species of garden dittany, canna plant with decorative blossoms, bifoliate of two leaves (also bifurcate forked), cardamom spice from the germinal capsules of certain East India plants, granadilla passion flower, knapweed hard-stemmed worthless plant, campanula plant with bell-shaped blossoms, and dittany see fraxinella above. Unusual animals mentioned were the pangolin, chipmunk, echidna, babiroussa and bandicoot, of which a brief descriptive account would be (respectively), scabrous-spined scaly ant-eater, American squirrel *aliter* wood-rat, Australian toothless animal resembling the hedgehog, Asiatic wild-hog, large Indian insectivorous marsupial resembling the rat.

The Pooka made a perfunctory noise and stepped from the shelter of his tree.

Your morning talk in the shadow of the wood, he said with a bow, that has been an incomparable recital. Two plants which you did not mention – the bdellium-tree and the nard, each of which yields an aromatic oleo-resinous medicinal product called balsam which I find invaluable for preserving the freshness of the person. I carry it with me in my tail pocket in a chryselephantine pouncet-box of perfect rotundity.

The three men regarded the Pooka in silence for a while and then conversed for a moment in Latin. Finally Mr Furriskey spoke.

Good morning, my man, what can I do for you, he asked. I am a Justice of the Peace. Do you wish to be sworn or make a statement?

I do not, said the Pooka, but this man with me is a fugitive from justice.

In that case he should be tried and well tried, said Mr Lamont courteously.

This is my object in approaching you, said the Pooka.

He looks a right ruffian, observed Mr Shanahan. What is the charge, pray, he asked taking a small constabulary note-book from his pocket.

There are several counts and charges, replied the Pooka, and more are expected. I understand he is wanted in Scotland. The police have not yet completed their inquiries but that small note-book would not contain the half of the present charges, even if taken down in brief and precise shorthand.

In that case we will not bother about the charges at all, said Mr Shanahan putting away his book. He looks a very criminal type, I must say.

During this conversation the prisoner was stretched on the ground in an unconscious condition.

Let him be brought to trial in due process of law, said Mr Furriskey.

When his wits returned to Dermot Trellis, they did not come together but singly and at intervals. They came, each with its own agonies, and sat uneasily on the outer border of the mind as if in readiness for going away again.

When the sufferer was strong enough to observe the shape of his surroundings, he saw that he was in a large hall not unlike the Antient Concert Rooms in Brunswick Street (now Pearse Street). The King was on his throne, the satraps thronged the hall, a thousand bright lamps shone, o'er that high festival. Ornate curtains of twilled beaverteen were draped about the throne. Near to the roof there was a *loggia* or open-shaped gallery or arcade supported on thin pillars, each with a *guilloche* on its top for ornament; the *loggia* seemed to be packed with people, each with a cold-watching face. The air was heavy and laden with sullen banks of tobacco smoke; this made respiration an extremely difficult matter for a person like Trellis, who was not in perfect health. He felt a growing queasiness about his stomach and also tormina, griping pains in the region of the bowels. His clothing was disarranged and torn and piteously stained with blood and other fluids discharged probably from his many wounds. Generally speaking he was in very poor condition.

When he raised his eyes again there appeared to be no less than twelve kings on the throne. There was an ornamental bench in front of them like the counter of a good-class public house and they leaned their elbows on it, gazing coldly ahead of them. They were dressed uniformly in gowns of black gunny, an inexpensive material manufactured from jute fibre, and with their jewelled fingers they held the stems of long elegant glasses of brown porter.

In the centre of a shadow to the left-hand side of the bench was the Pooka MacPhellimey, attired in a robe of stout cotton fabric called dimity and seated in an article resembling a prie-dieu with a stout back to it; he appeared to be writing in short-hand in a black note-book.

The sufferer gave an accidental groan and found that the Pooka was immediately at his side and bending over him in a solicitous fashion, making formal inquiries on the subject of the cripple's health.

What is going to happen to me next? asked Trellis.

Shortly you will be judged, replied the Pooka. The judges are before you on the bench there.

I see their shadow, said Trellis, but my face is not in that direction and I cannot turn it. Their names, that would be a boon.

Woe to the man that shall refuse a small kindness, responded the Pooka with the intonation that is required for the articulation of the old proverbs. The names of the judges are easy to relate: J. Furriskey, T. Lamont, P. Shanahan, S. Andrews, S. Willard, Mr Sweeny, J. Casey, R. Kiersey, M. Tracy, Mr Lamphall, F. MacCool, Supt. Clohessy.

The jury? asked Trellis.

The same, rejoined the Pooka.

That is the last blow that brings a man to the ground, observed Trellis. His wits then took leave of him and remained at a distance for a long period of time.

That place is a picture-house now, of course, said Shanahan's voice as it cut through the pattern of the story, plenty of the cowboy stuff there. The Palace Cinema, Pearse Street. Oh, many a good hour I spent there too.

A great place in the old days, said Lamont. They had tenors and one thing or another there in the old days. Every night they had something good.

And every night they had something new, said Shanahan.

On his smallest finger Orlick screwed the cap of his Waterman fountain-pen, the one with the fourteen-carat nib; when he unscrewed it again there was a black circle about his finger.

Symbolism of the foregoing: annoyance.

I will now continue, he announced.

Certainly man, said Shanahan, a hand to the writer's biceps. We'll get him yet! We'll take the skin off his body.

A little less talk and we were right, said Furriskey.

When Trellis had again re-attained reason, he found that his body was on a large chair and supported by the loan of supernatural strength, for many of the bones requisite for maintaining an upright position were in two halves and consequently unable to discharge their functions. Noiselessly the Pooka came beside him and whispered in his ear.

To be defended by eminent lawyers, he said, that is the right of a man that is accused. There are two men in the court here and you can now be at the choice of them.

I did not expect this, said Trellis. He found that his voice was loud and probably strengthened by the agency of the one that was whispering at his ear, What are their names?

They are Greek citizens, rejoined the Pooka, Timothy Danaos and Dona Ferentes.

The gift of speech, said Trellis, that is one thing they lack.

And a great pity, said the Pooka, for they are fine-looking men and that is a serious blemish.

Trellis in reply to this fashioned a long sentence in his mind, but the words he put on it were lost by the activity of a string orchestra in one of the galleries which struck up a stirring anthem. The players were unseen but two violins, a viola, a piccolo and a violoncello would be a sagacious guess as to their composition. The judges at the long counter listened in a cultured fashion, quietly fingering the stems of their stout-glasses.

Call the first witness, said the voice of Mr Justice Shanahan. stern and dear as the last bit of music faded from the vast hall and retired to the secrecy of its own gallery. This was the signal for the opening of the great trial. Reporters poised their pencils above their note-books, waiting. The orchestra could be heard very faintly as if at a great distance, playing consecutive fifths in a subdued fashion and tuning their instruments one against the other. The Pooka closed his black note-book and stood up in his prie-dieu.

Samuel ('Slug') Willard, he boomed, take the stand.

Slug Willard hastily swallowed the residue of his stout, drew a cuff across his mouth and disengaging himself from his confreres at the counter, came forward to the witness-box swinging his large hat in his hand. He spat heavily on the floor and inclined his ear in a genial manner towards the Pooka, who appeared to be administering an oath in an undertone.

Trellis noticed that Sweeny was drinking bimbo, a beverage resembling punch and seldom consumed in this country. The stout-glass of Willard was now full again and stood finely on the counter against the back of his vacant chair.

A judge acting as a juryman is bad enough, said Trellis, but to act also as a witness, that is most irregular.

Silence, said Mr Justice Shanahan severely. Are you legally represented?

I have been assigned two dumb-bells, said Trellis bravely. I have declined their services.

Your ill-conditioned behaviour will avail you nothing, rejoined the judge in a tone even more severe. One more word and I will deal with you summarily for contempt. Proceed with the witness, Mr MacPhellimey.

I meant no harm, Sir, said Trellis.

Silence.

The Pooka stood up in his prie-dieu and sat on its back staring at the pages of his black note-book. A keen-eyed observer would notice that there was no writing on them.

State your name and occupation, he said to Mr Willard.

Willard, Slug, said Mr Willard. I am a cattleman and a cow-puncher, a gentleman farmer in the Western tradition.

Have you ever been employed by the accused?

Yes.

In what capacity?

As tram-conductor.

Give in your own words a brief statement of the remuneration and conditions of service attaching to the position.

My pay was fifteen shillings per week of seventy-two hours,

non-pensionable emoluments. I was compelled to sleep in an unsanitary attic.

Under what circumstances were your services utilized?

I was instructed to meet and accept his fare from Mr Furriskey when he was returning one night from Donnybrook. I did so.

In what manner were you compelled to address Mr Furriskey?

In guttersnipe dialect, at all times repugnant to the instincts of a gentleman.

You have already said that the character or milieu of the conversation was distasteful to you?

Yes. It occasioned considerable mental anguish.

Have you any further remarks to make on this subject relevant to the charges now under consideration?

Yes. It was represented that my employment as conductor would commence and terminate on the night in question. I was actually engaged for six months owing to my employer's negligence in falling to instruct me that my employment was at an end.

Was this curious circumstance afterwards explained?

In a way, yes. He attributed his failure to discharge me to forgetfulness. He absolutely refused to entertain a claim which I advanced in respect of compensation for impaired health.

To what do you attribute your impaired health?

Malnutrition and insufficient clothing. My inadequate pay and a luncheon interval of only ten minutes prohibited both the purchase or consumption of nourishing food. When my employment started, I was provided with a shirt, boots and socks, and a light uniform of dyed dowlas, a strong fabric resembling calico. No underdrawers were provided and as my employment was protracted into the depths of the winter, I was entirely unprotected from the cold. I contracted asthma, catarrh and various pulmonary disorders.

That is all I have to ask, said the Pooka.

Mr Justice Lamont tapped his stout-glass on the counter and said to Trellis:

Do you wish to cross-examine the witness?

I do, said Trellis.

He endeavoured to rise and place his hands in the pockets of his trousers in a casual manner but he found that much of the supernatural strength had been withdrawn. He found that he was now in the grip of a severe myelitis or inflammation of the spinal cord. He crouched on his chair, shuddering in the spasms of a clonus and pressed out words from his mouth with the extremity of his will-power.

You have stated, he said, that you were compelled to sleep in an unsanitary attic. In what respect were the principles of hygiene violated?

The attic was infested by clocks. I found sleep impossible owing to the activities of bed-lice.

Did you ever in your life take a bath?

Mr Justice Andrews rapped violently on the counter.

Do not answer that question, he said loudly.

I put it to you, said Trellis, that the bed-lice were near relations of other small inhabitants of your own verminous person.

That savours of contempt, said Mr Justice Lamont in a testy manner, we will not have any more of that. The witness is excused.

Mr Willard retired to his seat behind the counter and immediately put his stout-glass to his head; Trellis fell back on his chair in a swoon of exhaustion. Distantly the orchestra could be heard in the metre of a dainty toccata.

Call the next witness.

William Tracy, boomed the Pooka, take the stand.

Mr Tracy, an elderly man, fat, scanty-haired and wearing pince-nez, came quickly from the counter and entered the witness-box. He smiled nervously at the Bench, avoiding the gaze of Trellis, whose head was again bravely stirring amid the ruin of his body and his clothing.

State your name, said the Pooka.

Tracy, William James.

You are acquainted with the accused?

Yes, professionally.

At this point the entire personnel of the judges arose in a body and filed out behind a curtain in the corner of the hall over which there was a red-lighted sign. They were absent for the space of ten minutes but the trial proceeded steadily in their absence. The pulse of a mazurka, graceful and lively, came quietly from the distance.

Explain your connections with the accused.

About four years ago he approached me and represented that he was engaged in a work which necessitated the services of a

female character of the slavey class. He explained that technical
difficulties relating to ladies' dress had always been an insuperable
obstacle to his creation of satisfactory female characters and produced a document purporting to prove that he was reduced on
other occasions to utilizing disguised males as substitutes for
women, a device which he said could scarcely be persisted in
indefinitely. He mentioned a growing unrest among his readers.
Eventually I agreed to lend him a girl whom I was using in connexion with *Jake's Last Throw*, a girl who would not be required
by myself for some months owing to my practice of dealing with
the action of groups of characters alternately. When she left me
to go to him, she was a good girl and attentive to her religious
duties . . .

How long was she in his employment?

About six months. When she returned to me she was in a
certain condition.

No doubt you remonstrated with the accused?

Yes. He disclaimed all responsibility and said that his record
was better than mine, a remark which I failed to appreciate.

You took no action?

Not so far as the accused was concerned. I considered seeking
a remedy in the courts but was advised that my case was one
which the courts would be unlikely to understand. I discontinued all social intercourse with the accused.

Did you reinstate the girl in her employment?

Yes. I also created an otherwise unnecessary person to
whom I married her and found honest if unremunerative
employment for her son with a professional friend who was
engaged in a work dealing with unknown aspects of the cotton-
milling industry.

Did the introduction of this character to whom you married
the girl adversely affect your work?

Assuredly. The character was clearly superfluous and impaired
the artistic integrity of my story. I was compelled to make his
unauthorized interference with an oil-well the subject of a footnote. His introduction added considerably to my labours.

Is there any other incident which occurs to you explanatory
of the character of the accused?

Yes. During his illness in 1924 I sent him – in a charitable
attempt to entertain him – a draft of a short story I had written

dealing in an original way with banditry in Mexico towards the close of the last century. Within a month it appeared under his own name in a Canadian magazine.

That's a lie! screamed Trellis from his chair.

The judges frowned in unison and regarded the accused in a threatening fashion. Mr Justice Sweeny, returning from behind the curtain in the corner of the hall said:

You had better conduct yourself, Sir. Your arrogant bearing and your insolence have already been the subject of severe comment. Any further blackguardism will be summarily dealt with. Is it your intention to cross-examine this witness?

Trellis said, Yes.

Very well then. Proceed.

The invalid here gathered his senses closely about him as if they were his overcoat to ensure that they should not escape before his purpose was accomplished. He said to the witness:

Have you ever heard this said: *Dog does not eat dog*.

There was a rattle of glasses at this point and a stern direction from the bench.

Do not answer that question.

Trellis drew a hand wearily across his face.

One other point, he said. You have stated that this person whom you created was entirely unnecessary. If I recollect the tale aright he was accustomed to spend much of his time in the scullery. Is that correct?

Yes.

What was he doing there?

Peeling potatoes for the household.

Peeling potatoes for the household. You said he was unnecessary. You regard that as an entirely wasteful and unnecessary task?

Not at all. The task is necessary and useful. It is the character who carried it out who is stated to be unnecessary.

I put it to you that the utility of any person is directly related to the acts he performs.

There was a potato-peeler in the kitchen, a machine.

Indeed! I did not notice it.

In the recess, near the range, on the left-hand side.

I put it to you that there was no potato-peeler.

There was. It was in the house for a long time.

Here a question from the direction of the counter brought the further examination of the witness to a conclusion.

What is a potato-peeler? asked Mr Justice Andrews.

A machine, worked by hand, usually used for peeling potatoes, replied the witness.

Very well. Cross-examination concluded. Call the next witness.

Let the Good Fairy take the stand, boomed the Pooka.

I've been in the stand all the time, said the voice, the grand stand.

Where is this woman? asked Mr Justice Lamphall sharply. If she does not appear quickly I will issue a bench warrant.

This man has no body on him at all, explained the Pooka. Sometimes I carry him in my waistcoat pocket for days and do not know that he is there.

In that case we must declare the Habeas Corpus Act suspended, said Mr Lamphall. Proceed. Where is the witness now? Come now, no horseplay. This is a court of Law.

I am not very far away, said the Good Fairy.

Are you acquainted with the accused? asked the Pooka.

Maybe I am, said the Good Fairy.

What class of an answer is that to give? inquired Mr Justice Casey sternly.

Answers do not matter so much as questions, said the Good Fairy. A good question is very hard to answer. The better the question the harder the answer. There is no answer at all to a very good question.

That is a queer thing to say, said Mr Justice Casey. Where did you say it from?

From the key-hole, said the Good Fairy. I am going out for a breath of air and I will be back again when it suits me.

That key-hole should have been stuffed, said Mr Justice Shanahan. Call the next witness before the fly-boy comes back to annoy us.

Paul Shanahan, boomed the Pooka.

It would not be true to say that the sufferer on the chair was unconscious, however much his appearance betokened that happy state, for he was listening to the pulse of a fine theme in three-four time, coming softly to his brain from illimitable remoteness. Darkling he listened. Softly it modulated through a gamut of graduated keys, terminating in a quiet coda.

Paul Shanahan, called and sworn, deposed that he was in the employment of the accused for many years. He was not a party to the present action and had no personal grudge against the accused man. He was thoroughly trained and could serve in any capacity; his talents, however, were ignored and he was compelled to spend his time directing and arranging the activities of others, many of whom were of inferior ability as compared with himself. He was forced to live in a dark closet in the Red Swan Hotel and was allowed little or no liberty. The accused purported to direct witness in the discharge of his religious duties but he (witness) regarded this merely as a pretext for domestic interference and tyranny. His reputed salary was 45s. per week but no allowance was made for travelling and tramfares. He estimated that such expenses amounted to 30s. or 35s. per week. His food was bad and insufficient and required to be supplemented from his own resources. He had wide experience of cow-punching and had served with distinction at the Siege of Sandymount. He was accustomed to handling small-arms and shooting-irons. In company with other parties, he presented a petition to the accused praying relief from certain disabilities and seeking improved pay and conditions of service. The accused violently refused to make any of the concessions sought and threatened the members of the deputation who waited on him with certain physical afflictions, most of which were degrading and involved social stigma. In reply to a question, witness said that the accused was subject to extreme irritability and 'tantrums'. On several occasions, after reporting to the accused that plans had somewhat miscarried – a circumstance for which witness was in no way to blame – witness found his person infested with vermin. Friends of his (witness's) had complained to him of similar visitations. In reply to a question by the accused, witness said that he was always very careful of personal cleanliness. It was untrue to say that witness was a man of unclean habits.

At this stage a man in the body of the court announced that he had a statement to make and proceeded to read in an indistinct manner from a document which he produced from his pocket. He was immediately set upon by armed cowboys who removed him struggling violently, his words being drowned by a vigorous prestissimo movement of the gavotte class played in a spirited fashion by the orchestra in the secrecy of the gallery. The judges took no notice of the interruption and continued drinking from their long stout-glasses. Four of them at one end of the counter were making movements suggestive of card-play but as a result of their elevated position, no cards or money could be seen.

The next witness was a short-horn cow who was escorted by a black-liveried attendant from a cloakroom marked LADIES at the rear of the hall. The animal, a magnificent specimen of her class, was accorded the gift of speech by a secret theurgic process which had been in the possession of the Pooka's family for many generations. Udder and dewlap aswing in the rhythm of her motion, she shambled forward to the witness-box, turning her great eyes slowly about the court in a melancholy but respectful manner. The Pooka, an expert spare-time dairyman, familiar with the craft of husbandry, watched her with a practised eye, noting the fine points of her body.

State your name, he said curtly.

That is a thing I have never attained, replied the cow. Her voice was low and guttural and of a quality not normally associated with the female mammalia.

Are you acquainted with the accused?

Yes.

Socially or professionally?

Professionally.

Have your relations with him been satisfactory?

By no means.

State the circumstances of your relations with him.

In a work entitled – pleonastically, indeed – *The Closed Cloister*, I was engaged to discharge my natural functions in a field. My milking was not attended to with regularity. When not in advanced pregnancy, a cow will suffer extreme discomfort if not milked at least once in twenty-four hours. On six occasions during the currency of the work referred to, I was left without attention for very long periods.

You suffered pain?

Intense pain.

Mr Justice Lamont made a prolonged intermittent noise with the butt of his half-empty glass, the resulting vibration providing the porter it contained with a new and considerably improved head. The noise was a token that he desired to put a question.

Tell me this, he said. Can you not milk yourself?

I can not, replied the cow.

Musha, you appear to be very helpless. Why not, pray?

I have no hands and even if I had, the arms would not be long enough.

That savours of contempt, said the Justice sternly. This is a court of justice, not a music-hall. Does the defendant wish to cross-examine?

Trellis had been listening in a preoccupied manner to a number of queer noises in the interior of his head. He desisted from this occupation and looked at the Justice. The Justice's features were still arranged in the pattern of the question he had asked.

I do indeed, he said, endeavouring to rise and present a spirited exterior to the court. Still sitting, he turned in the direction of the witness.

Well, Whitefoot, he said, you suffered pain because your milking was overlooked?

I did. My name is not Whitefoot.

You have stated that a cow will suffer considerable pain if not milked at regular times. There is, however, another important office discharged by the cowkeeper, a seasonal rite not entirely unconnected with the necessity for providing milk for our great-grandchildren . . .

I do not know what you are talking about

The failure of the cowkeeper to attend to this matter, I am given to understand, causes acute discomfort. Was this attended to in your case?

I don't know what you are talking about, shouted the cow excitedly. I resent your low insinuations. I didn't come here to be humiliated and insulted. . . .

There was a loud rapping from the direction of the bench. Mr Justice Furriskey directed a cold severe finger at the defendant.

Your ill-conditioned attempt to discredit an exemplary witness, he said, and to introduce into the proceedings an element of smut, will be regarded as contempt and punished summarily as such unless immediately discontinued. The witness may go too. A more unsavoury example of the depraved and diseased mind it has rarely been my misfortune to encounter.

Mr Justice Shanahan concurred. The cow, very much embarrassed, turned and slowly left the court without a stain on her character, her glossy flank the object of expert examination by the practised eye of the Pooka as she passed him on her way. Stretching out a finger, he appraised the pile of her coat with a long nail. The members of the unseen orchestra could be faintly heard practising their scales and arpeggii and rubbing good-quality Italian rosin with a whistling noise on their bows. Three members of the bench had fallen forward in an attitude of besotted sleep as a result of the inordinate quantity of brown porter they had put into their bodies. The public at the back of the hall had erected an impenetrable barrier of acrid tobacco-smoke and had retired behind it, affording coughs and occasional catcalls as evidence that they were still in attendance. The light was somewhat yellower than it had been an hour before.

Call the next witness!

Antony Lamont, boomed the Pooka, take the stand.

At all times a strict observer of etiquette, the witness laid aside his judicial robe before making his way unsteadily from the bench to the witness-box. Under the cover of the counter the hand of a fellow-judge ran quickly through the pockets of the discarded garment.

You were an employee of the accused? asked the Pooka.

That is so.

Please afford the court a statement of your duties.

My main function was to protect the honour of my sister and look after her generally. People who insulted or assaulted her were to be answerable to me.

Where is your sister now?

I do not know. Dead, I believe.

When did you last see her?

I never saw her. I never had the pleasure of her acquaintance.

You say she is dead?

Yes. I was not even asked to her funeral.

Do you know how she died?

Yes. She was violently assaulted by the accused about an hour after she was born and died indirectly from the effects of the assault some time later. The proximate cause of her death was puerperal sepsis.

Very delicately put, said Mr Justice Furriskey. You are an exemplary witness, Sir. If every other witness in this court were to give evidence in a similar straightforward and clear manner, the work of the court would be appreciably lightened.

Those of the other judges who were in an upright position concurred with deep nods.

Your Lordship's generous remarks are appreciated and will be conveyed to the proper quarter, said the witness pleasantly, and I need scarcely add that the sentiments are reciprocated.

Mr F. MacPhellimey, court clerk, paid a tribute to the harmonious relations which had always obtained between the bar and the bench and expressed a desire to be associated with the amiable compliments which had been exchanged. The Justice returned thanks in the course of a witty and felicitous speech.

At this stage, the prisoner, in order to protect his constitutional rights and also in an endeavour to save his life, pointed out that this exchange of pleasantries was most irregular and that the evidence of the witness was valueless, being on his own admission a matter of hearsay and opinion; but, unfortunately, as a result of his being unable to rise or, for that matter, to raise his voice above the level of a whisper, nobody in the court was aware that he had spoken at all except the Pooka, who practised a secret recipe of his grandfather's – the notorious Crack Mac-Phellimey – for reading the thoughts of others. Mr Lamont had again donned his judicial robe and was making inquiries about a box of matches which he represented to have been put by him in the right-hand pocket. The members of the unseen orchestra were meticulously picking out an old French tune without the assistance of their bows, a device technically known as pizzicato.

Orlick laid down his pen in the spine-hollow of the red six-penny copybook he was writing on, the nib pointing away from him. He put his palms to the sides of his head and opened his jaws to an angle of roughly 70 degrees, revealing completely his twin dental horse-shoes. There were four machined teeth at the back and six golden teeth of surpassing richness and twinkle at the front. As his mandibles came together again, a weary moaning sound escaped him and large globules of glandular secretion stood out on the edge of his eyes. Closing the copybook in an idle manner, he read the legend printed legibly on its back.

Nature of legend: Don't run across the road without first looking both ways! Don't pass in front of or behind a standing vehicle without first looking both ways! Don't play at being last across on any road or street! Don't follow a rolling ball into the road while there is traffic about! Don't hang on to a vehicle or climb on to it! Don't forget to walk on the footpath if there is one! Safety First!

He read the last two phrases aloud, rubbing his eyes. Furriskey sat opposite in a downcast manner. His flat hands were fastened along his jaws and, being supported by his arms on the table, were immovable; but the weight of his head had caused his cheeks to be pushed up into an unnatural elevation on a level with his eyes. This caused the outside corners of his mouth and eyes to be pushed up in a similar manner, imparting an inscrutable oriental expression to his countenance.

Do you think it would be safe to go to bed and leave him where he is to the morning? he asked.

I do not, said Orlick. Safety first.

Shanahan took out his thumb from the armhole and straightened his body in the chair.

A false step now, he said, and it's a short jump for the lot of us. Do you know that? A false step now and we're all in the cart and that's a fact.

Lamont came forward from a couch where he had been resting and inclined his head as a signal that he was taking an intelligent interest in the conversation.

Will the judges have a bad head tomorrow, he asked.

No, said Orlick.

Well I think the time has come for the black caps.

You think the jury has heard enough evidence?

Certainly they have, said Shanahan. The time for talk is past. Finish the job tonight like a good man so as we can go to bed in peace. God, if we gave him a chance to catch us at this game . . .

The job should be done at once, said Lamont, and the razor's the boy to do it.

He can't complain that he didn't get fair play, said Furriskey. He got a fair trial and a jury of his own manufacture. I think the time has come.

It's time to take him out to the courtyard, said Shanahan.

A half a minute with the razor and the trick is done, said Lamont.

As long as you realize the importance of the step that is about to be taken, said Orlick, I have no objection. I only hope that nothing will happen to us. I don't think the like of this has been done before, you know.

Well we have had enough of the trial stuff anyhow, said Shanahan.

We will have one more witness for the sake of appearance, said Orlick, and then we will get down to business.

This plan was agreed to, Mr Shanahan taking advantage of the occasion to pay a spontaneous tribute to the eminence of Mr O. Trellis in the author world.

The company resumed their former attitudes and the book was re-opened at the page that had been closed.

Conclusion of the book antepenultimate. Biographical reminiscence part the final: I went in by the side-door and hung my grey street-coat on the peg in the shadow under the stone stairs. I then went up in a slow deliberate preoccupied manner, examining in my mind the new fact that I had passed my final examination with a creditable margin of honour. I was conscious of a slight mental exhilaration. When passing through the hallway the door of the dining-room was opened and my uncle's head was put out through the aperture.

I want a word with you, he said.

In a moment, I answered.

His presence in the house was a surprise to me. His talk had ceased and his head had gone before I could appraise the character of his evening disposition. I proceeded to my room and placed my body on the soft trestle of my bed, still nursing in my brain the warm thought of my diligence and scholarship . . . Few of the candidates had proved themselves of the honours class though many had made it known that they were persons of advanced intelligence. This induced an emotion of comfort and exhilaration. I heard a voice in the interior of my head. Tell me this: Do you ever open a book at all? A delay in my appearance would have the effect of envenoming the character of the interrogation. I took a volume from the mantelpiece and perused many of the footnotes and passages to be found therein, reading in a slow and penetrating manner.

The texts referred to, being an excerpt from 'A Conspectus of the Arts and Natural Sciences', volume the thirty-first:

Moral Effects of Tobacco-using: There can be no question but that tobacco has a seriously deteriorating effect upon the character, blunting moral sensibility, deadening conscience, and destroying the delicacy of thought and feeling which is characteristic of the true Christian gentleman. This effect is far more clearly seen, as would be expected, in youths who begin the use of tobacco while the character is receiving its mould, than in those who have adopted the habit later in life, though too often plainly visible in the latter class of cases. There can be no question but that the use of tobacco is a stepping-stone to vices of the worst character. It is a vice which seldom goes alone. It is far too often accompanied with profanity and laxity of morals, and leads directly to the use of alcoholic drinks. It is indeed the most powerful ally of intemperance; and it is a good omen for the temperance cause that its leaders are beginning to see the importance of recognizing this fact and promulgating it as a fundamental principle in all temperance work. Names of further paragraphs: The Nature of Tobacco; Poisonous Effects of Tobacco; Why All Smokers Do Not Die of Tobacco Poisoning; Effects of Tobacco on the Blood; Tobacco Predisposes to Disease; Smokers' Sore Throat; Tobacco and Consumption; Tobacco a Cause of Heart Disease; Tobacco and Dyspepsia; Tobacco a Cause of Cancer; Tobacco Paralysis; Tobacco a Cause of Insanity.

Moral Effects of Tea-Tasting. The long-continued use of tea has a distinct effect upon the character. This has been too often noticed and remarked to be questioned. There are tea-sots in every great charitable institution – particularly those for the maintenance of the aged. Their symptoms are generally mental irritability, muscular tremors and sleeplessness. The following is an account of one of the cases observed. The immediate effects upon him are as follows: in about ten minutes the face becomes flushed, the whole body feels warm and heated and a sort of intellectual intoxication comes on, much the same in character, it would seem, as that which occurs in the rarefied air of a mountain.

He feels elated, exhilarated, troubles and cares vanish, everything seems bright and cheerful, his body feels light and elastic, his mind clear, his ideas abundant, vivid, and flowing fluently into words. At the end of an hour's tasting a slight reaction begins to set in; some headache comes on, the face feels wrinkled and shrivelled, particularly about the eyes, which also get dark under the lids. At the end of two hours this reaction becomes firmly established, the flushed warm feeling has passed off, the hands and feet are cold, a nervous tremor comes on, accompanied with great mental depression. And he is now so excitable that every noise startles him; he is in a state of complete unrest; he can neither walk nor sit down, owing to his mental condition, and he settles into complete gloom. Copious and frequent urinations are always present, as also certain dyspeptic symptoms, such as eructations of wind, sour taste, and others. His mental condition is peculiar. He lives in a state of dread that some accident may happen to him; in the omnibus fears a collision; crossing the street, fears that he will be crushed by passing teams; walking on the sidewalks, fears that a sign may fall, or watches the eaves of houses, thinking that a brick may fall down and kill him; under the apprehension that every dog he meets is going to bite the calves of his legs, he carries an umbrella in all weathers as a defence against such an attack. Conclusion of the foregoing.

Ibidem, further extract therefrom, being Argument of the poem 'The Shipwreck', by William Falconer: 1. Retrospect of the voyage. Season of the year described. 2. Character of the master, and his officers, Albert, Rodmond and Arion. Palemon, son of the owner of the ship. Attachment of Palemon to Anna, the daughter of Albert. 3. Noon. Palemon's history. 4. Sunset. Midnight. Arion's dream. Unmoor by moonlight. Morning. Sun's azimuth taken. Beautiful appearance of the ship, as seen by the natives from the shore.

Canto II. 1. Reflections on leaving shore. 2. Favourable breeze. Waterspout. The dying dolphins. Breeze freshens. Ship's rapid progress along coast. Topsails reefed. Mainsail split. The ship bears up; again hauls upon the wind. Another mainsail bent, and set. Porpoises. 3. The ship driven out of her course from Candia. Heavy gale. Topsails furled. Top gallant yards lowered. Heavy sea. Threatening sunset. Difference of opinion respecting the mode of taking in the mainsail. Courses reefed. Four seamen lost off the lee main-yardarm. Anxiety of the master, and his mates, on being near a lee-shore. Mizzen reefed. 4. A tremendous sea bursts over the deck; its consequences. The ship labours in great distress. Guns thrown overboard. Dismal appearance of the weather. Very high and dangerous sea. Storm lightening. Severe fatigue of the crew at the pumps. Critical situation of the ship near the island of Falconera. Consultation and resolution of the officers. Speech and advice of Albert; his devout address to heaven. Order given to scud. The fore-staysail hoisted and split. The head yards braced aback. The mizzen-mast cut away.

Canto III. 1. The beneficial influence of poetry in the civilization of mankind. Diffidence of the author. 2. Wreck of the mizzen-mast cleared away. Ship puts before the wind – labours much. Different stations of the officers. Appearance of the island of Falconera. 3. Excursion to the adjacent nations of Greece renowned in antiquity. Athens. Socrates, Plato, Aristides, Solon, Corinth – its architecture. Sparta. Leonides. Invasion by Xerxes. Lycurgus. Epaminondas. Present state of the Spartans. Arcadia. Former happiness, and fertility. Its present distress the effect of slavery. Ithaca. Ulysses, and Penelope. Argos and Mycenae. Agamemnon. Macronisi. Lemnos. Vulcan. Delos. Apollo and Diana. Troy. Sestos. Leander and Hero. Delphos. Temple of Apollo. Parnassus. The muses. 4. Subject resumed. Address to the spirits of the storm. A tempest, accompanied with rain, hail and meteors. Darkness of the night, lightning and thunder. Daybreak. St George's cliffs open upon them. The ship, in great danger, passes the island of St George. 5. Land of Athens appears. Helmsman struck blind by lightning. Ship laid broadside to the shore. Bowsprit, foremast, and main top-mast carried away. Albert, Rodmond, Arion and Palemon strive to save themselves on the wreck of the foremast. The ship parts asunder. Death of Albert and Rodmond. Arion reaches the shore. Finds Palemon expiring on the beach. His dying address to Arion, who is led away by the humane natives.

Extract from the Poem referred to: The dim horizon lowering vapours shroud, And blot the sun yet struggling in the cloud; Thro' the wide atmosphere condensed with haze, His glaring orb emits a sanguine blaze. The pilots now their azimuth attend,

On which all courses, duly formed, depend: The compass placed to catch the rising ray, The quadrant's shadows studious they survey; Along the arch the gradual index slides, While Phoebus down the vertic-circle slides; Now seen on ocean's utmost verge to swim, He sweeps it vibrant with his nether limb. Thus height, and polar distance are obtained, Then latitude, and declination, gain'd; In chiliads next the analogy is sought, And on the sinical triangle wrought: By this magnetic variance is explored, Just angles known, and polar truth restored. Conclusion of the foregoing.

I closed the book and extinguished my cigarette at midpoint by a quick trick of the fingers. Going downstairs with an audible low tread, I opened the door of the dining-room in a meek penitent fashion. My uncle had Mr Corcoran in attendance by his side. They sat before the fire; having desisted from their conversation at my entry, they held between them a double-sided silence.

How do you do, Mr Corcoran, I said.

He arose the better to exert the full force of his fine man-grip.

Ah, good evening, Sir, he said.

Well, mister-my-friend, how do you feel today, my uncle said. I have something to say to you. Take a seat.

He turned in the direction of Mr Corcoran with a swift eye-message of unascertained import. He then stretched down for the poker and adjusted the red coals, turning them slowly. The dancing redness on his side-face showed a furrow of extreme intellectual effort.

You were a long time upstairs, he said.

I was washing my hands, I answered, utilizing a voice-tone that lacked appreciable inflexion. I hastily averted my grimy palms.

Mr Corcoran gave a short laugh.

Well we all have to do that, he said in an awkward manner, we are all entitled to our five minutes.

This much he regretted for my uncle did not answer but kept turning at the coals.

I am sure you will remember, he said at last, that the question of your studies has been a great worry to me. It has caused me plenty of anxiety, I can tell you that. If you failed in your studies it would be a great blow to your poor father and certainly it would be a sore disappointment to myself.

He paused as he turned his head in order to ascertain my listening attitude. I continued following the point of his poker as it continued burrowing among the coals.

And you would have no excuse, no excuse in the wide world. You have a good comfortable home, plenty of wholesome food, clothes, boots – all your orders. You have a fine big room to work in, plenty of ink and paper. That is something to thank God for because there is many a man that got his education in a back-room by the light of a halfpenny candle. Oh, no excuse in the wide world.

Again I felt his inquiring eyes upon my countenance.

As you know yourself, I have strong views on the subject of idling. Lord save us, there is no cross in the world as heavy as the cross of sloth, for it comes to this, that the lazy man is a burden to his friends, to himself and to every man woman or child he'll meet or mix with. Idleness darkens the understanding; idleness weakens the will; idleness leaves you a very good mark for the sinful schemes of the gentleman down below.

I noticed that in repeating idleness, my uncle had unwittingly utilized a figure of speech usually designed to effect emphasis.

Name of figure of speech: Anaphora (or Epibole).

Idleness, you might say, is the father and the mother of the other vices.

Mr Corcoran, visually interrogated, expressed complete agreement.

Oh, it's a great mistake to get into the habit of doing nothing, he said. Young people especially would have to be on their guard. It's a thing that grows on you and a thing to be avoided.

To be avoided like the plague, said my uncle. Keep on the move as my father, the Lord have mercy on him, used to say – keep on the move and you'll move towards God.

He was a saint, of course, said Mr Corcoran.

Oh, he knew the secret of life, said my uncle, he did indeed. But wait for a minute now.

He turned to me with a directness that compelled me to meet his eyes by means of imbuing them with almost supernatural intensity.

I've said many a hard word to you for your own good, he said.

I have rebuked you for laziness and bad habits of one kind or another. But you've done the trick, you've passed your examination and your old uncle is going to be the first to shake your hand. And happy he is indeed to do it.

Giving my hand to him I looked to Mr Corcoran in my great surprise. His face bore a circular expression of surpassing happiness and pleasure. He arose in a brisk manner and leaning over my uncle's shoulder, caused me to extract my hand from the possession of the latter and present it to him for the exercise of his honest strength. My uncle smiled broadly, making a pleased but inarticulate sound with his throat.

I don't know you as well as your uncle does, said Mr Corcoran, but I think I'm a good judge of character. I don't often go wrong. I take a man as I find him. I think you're *all right* . . . and I congratulate you on your great success from the bottom of my heart.

I muttered my thanks, utilizing formal perfunctory expressions. My uncle chuckled audibly in the pause and tapped the grate-bar with his poker.

You have the laugh on me tonight, you may say, he said, and boys there is nobody more pleased than I. I'm as happy as the day is long.

Oh, the stuff was there, said Mr Corcoran. It was there all the time.

And he would be a queer son of his father if it wasn't, said my uncle.

How did you find out about it? I asked.

Oh, never you mind now, said my uncle with a suitable gesture. The old boys know a thing or two. There are more things in life and death than you ever dreamt of, Horatio.

They laughed at me in unison, savouring the character of their bubbling good-humour in a short subsequent silence.

You are forgetting something? said Mr Corcoran.

Certainly not, said my uncle.

He put his hand in his pocket and turned to me.

Mr Corcoran and myself, he said, have taken the liberty of joining together in making you a small present as a memento of the occasion and as a small but sincere expression of our congratulation. We hope that you will accept it and that you will wear it to remind you when you have gone from us of two friends that watched over you – a bit strictly perhaps – and wished you well.

He again took one hand from me and shook it, putting a small black box of the pattern utilized by jewellers in the other. The edges of the box were slightly frayed, showing a lining of grey linen or other durable material. The article was evidently of the second-hand denomination.

Comparable word utilized by German nation: antiquarisch.

The characters of a watch-face, slightly luminous in the gloom, appeared to me from the interior of the box. Looking up, I found that the hand of Mr Corcoran was extended in an honest manner for the purpose of manual felicitation.

I expressed my thanks in a conventional way but without verbal dexterity or coolness.

Oh, you are welcome, they said.

I put the watch on my wrist and said it was a convenient article to have, a sentiment that found instant corroboration. Shortly afterwards, on the pretext of requiring tea, I made my way from the room. Glancing back at the door, I noticed that the gramophone was on the table under its black cover and that my uncle had again taken up the poker and was gazing at the fire in a meditative if pleased manner.

Description of my uncle: Simple, well-intentioned; pathetic in humility; responsible member of large commercial concern.

I went slowly up the stairs to my room. My uncle had evinced unsuspected traits of character and had induced in me an emotion of surprise and contrition extremely difficult of literary rendition or description. My steps faltered to some extent on the stairs. As I opened my door, my watch told me that the time was five fifty-four. At the same time I heard the Angelus pealing out from far away.

Conclusion of the Book, penultimate: Teresa, a servant employed at the Red Swan Hotel, knocked at the master's door with the intention of taking away the tray but eliciting no response, she opened the door and found to her surprise that the room was empty. Assuming that the master had gone to a certain place, she placed the tray on the landing and returned to the room for the purpose of putting it to rights. She revived the fire and made a good blaze by putting into it several sheets of writing which were littered here and there about the floor (not improbably a result of the open window). By a curious coincidence as a matter of fact strange to say it happened that these same pages were those of the master's novel, the pages which made and sustained the existence of Furriskey and his true friends. Now they were blazing, curling and twisting and turning black, straining uneasily in the draught and then taking flight as if to heaven through the chimney, a flight of light things red-flecked and wrinkled hurrying to the sky. The fire faltered and sank again to the hollow coals and just at that moment, Teresa heard a knock at the hall-door away below. Going down she did her master the unexpected pleasure of admitting him to the house. He was attired in his night-shirt, which was slightly discoloured as if by rain, and some dead leaves were attached to the soles of his poor feet. His eyes gleamed and he did not speak but walked past her in the direction of the stairs. He then turned and coughing slightly, stared at her as she stood there, the oil-lamp in her hand throwing strange shadows on her soft sullen face.

Ah, Teresa, he muttered.

Where were you in your night-shirt, Sir? she asked.

I am ill, Teresa, he murmured. I have done too much thinking and writing, too much work. My nerves are troubling me. I have bad nightmares and queer dreams and I walk when I am very tired. The doors should be locked.

You could easily get your death, Sir, Teresa said.

He reached unsteadily for the lamp and motioned that she should go before him up the stairs. The edge of her stays, lifting her skirt in a little ridge behind her, dipped softly from side to side with the rise and the fall of her haunches as she trod the stairs. It is the function of such garments to improve the figure, to conserve corporal discursiveness, to create the illusion of a finely modulated body. If it betray its own presence when fulfilling this task, its purpose must largely fail.

Ars est celare artem, muttered Trellis, doubtful as to whether he had made a pun.

Conclusion of the book, ultimate: Evil is even, truth is an odd number and death is a full stop. When a dog barks late at night and then retires again to bed, he punctuates and gives majesty to the serial enigma of the dark, laying it more evenly and heavily upon the fabric of the mind. Sweeny in the trees hears the sad baying as he sits listening on the branch, a huddle between the earth and heaven; and he hears also the answering mastiff that is counting the watches in the next parish. Bark answers bark till the call spreads like fire through all Erin. Soon the moon comes forth from behind her curtains riding full tilt across the sky, lightsome and unperturbed in her immemorial calm. The eyes of the mad king upon the branch are upturned, whiter eyeballs in a white face, upturned in fear and supplication. His mind is but a shell. Was Hamlet mad? Was Trellis mad? It is extremely hard to say. Was he a victim of hard-to-explain hallucinations? Nobody knows. Even experts do not agree on these vital points. Professor Unternehmer, the eminent German neurologist, points to Claudius as a lunatic but allows Trellis an inverted sow neurosis wherein the farrow eat their dam. Du Fernier, however, Professor of Mental Sciences and Sanitation at the Sorbonne, deduces from a want of hygiene in the author's bed-habits a progressive weakening of the head. It is of importance the most inestimable, he writes, that for mental health there should be walking and not overmuch of the bedchamber. The more one studies the problem, the more fascinated one becomes and incidentally the more one postulates a cerebral norm. The accepted principles of Behavourism do not seem to give much assistance. Neither does heredity help for his father was a Galwayman, sober and industrious, tried and true in the service of his country. His mother was from far Fermanagh, a woman of grace and fair learning and a good friend to all. But which of us can hope to probe with questioning finger the dim thoughts that flit in a fool's head? One man will think he has a glass bottom and will fear to sit in case of breakage. In other respects he will be a man of great intellectual force and will accompany one in a mental ramble throughout the labyrinths of mathematics or philosophy so long as he is allowed to remain standing throughout the disputaxions. Another man will be perfectly polite and well conducted except that he will in no circumstances turn otherwise than to the right and indeed will own a bicycle so constructed that it cannot turn otherwise than to that point. Others will be subject to colours and will attach undue merit to articles that are red or green or white merely because they bear that hue. Some will be exercised and influenced by the texture of a cloth or by the roundness or angularity of an object. Numbers, however, will account for a great proportion of unbalanced and suffering humanity. One man will rove the streets seeking motor-cars with numbers that are divisible by seven. Well known, alas, is the case of the poor German who was very fond of three and who made each aspect of his life a thing of triads. He went home one evening and drank three cups of tea with three lumps of sugar in each, cut his jugular with a razor three times and scrawled with a dying hand on a picture of his wife good-bye, good-bye, good-bye.

THE THIRD POLICEMAN

*Human existence being an hallucination containing
in itself the secondary hallucinations of day and night
(the latter an insanitary condition of the atmosphere
due to accretions of black air) it ill becomes any man
of sense to be concerned at the illusory approach of the
supreme hallucination known as death.*

DE SELBY

*Since the affairs of men rest still uncertain,
Let's reason with the worst that may befall.*

SHAKESPEARE

CHAPTER 1

NOT EVERYBODY knows how I killed old Phillip Mathers, smashing his jaw in with my spade; but first it is better to speak of my friendship with John Divney because it was he who first knocked old Mathers down by giving him a great blow in the neck with a special bicycle-pump which he manufactured himself out of a hollow iron bar. Divney was a strong civil man but he was lazy and idle-minded. He was personally responsible for the whole idea in the first place. It was he who told me to bring my spade. He was the one who gave the orders on the occasion and also the explanations when they were called for.

I was born a long time ago. My father was a strong farmer and my mother owned a public house. We all lived in the public house but it was not a strong house at all and was closed most of the day because my father was out at work on the farm and my mother was always in the kitchen and for some reason the customers never came until it was nearly bed-time; and well after it at Christmas-time and on other unusual days like that. I never saw my mother outside the kitchen in my life and never saw a customer during the day and even at night I never saw more than two or three together. But then I was in bed part of the time and it is possible that things happened differently with my mother and with the customers late at night. My father I do not remember well but he was a strong man and did not talk much except on Saturdays when he would mention Parnell with the customers and say that Ireland was a queer country. My mother I can recall perfectly. Her face was always red and sore-looking from bending at the fire; she spent her life making tea to pass the time and singing snatches of old songs to pass the meantime. I knew her well but my father and I were strangers and did not converse much; often indeed when I would be studying in the kitchen at night I could hear him through the thin door to the shop talking there from his seat under the oil-lamp for hours on end to Mick the sheepdog. Always it was only the drone of his voice I heard, never the separate bits of words. He was a man who understood all dogs thoroughly and treated them like human beings. My mother owned a cat but it was a foreign outdoor animal and was rarely seen and my mother never took any notice of it. We were all happy enough in a queer separate way.

Then a certain year came about the Christmas-time and when the year was gone my father and mother were gone also. Mick the sheepdog was very tired and sad after my father went and would not do his work with the sheep at all; he too went the next year. I was young and foolish at the time and did not know properly why these people had all left me, where they had gone and why they did not give explanations beforehand. My mother was the first to go and I can remember a fat man with a red face and a black suit telling my father that there was no doubt where she was, that he could be as sure of that as he could of anything else in this vale of tears. But he did not mention where and as I thought the whole thing was very private and that she might be back on Wednesday, I did not ask him where. Later, when my father went, I thought he had gone to fetch her with an outside car but when neither of them came back on the next Wednesday, I felt sorry and disappointed. The man in the black suit was back again. He stayed in the house for two nights and was continually washing his hands in the bedroom and reading books. There were two other men, one a small pale man and one a tall black man in leggings. They had pockets full of pennies and they gave me one every time I asked them questions. I can remember the tall man in the leggings saying to the other man:

'The poor misfortunate little bastard.'

I did not understand this at the time and thought that they were talking about the other man in the black clothes who was always working at the wash-stand in the bedroom. But I understood it all clearly afterwards.

After a few days I was brought away myself on an outside car and sent to a strange school. It was a boarding school filled with people I did not know, some young and some older. I soon got to know that it was a good school and a very expensive one but I did not pay over any money to the people who were in charge of it because I had not any. All this and a lot more I understood clearly later.

My life at this school does not matter except for one thing.

It was here that I first came to know something of de Selby. One day I picked up idly an old tattered book in the science master's study and put it in my pocket to read in bed the next morning as I had just earned the privilege of lying late. I was about sixteen then and the date was the seventh of March. I still think that day is the most important in my life and can remember it more readily than I do my birthday. The book was a first edition of *Golden Hours* with the two last pages missing. By the time I was nineteen and had reached the end of my education I knew that the book was valuable and that in keeping it I was stealing it. Nevertheless I packed it in my bag without a qualm and would probably do the same if I had my time again. Perhaps it is important in the story I am going to tell to remember that it was for de Selby I committed my first serious sin. It was for him that I committed my greatest sin.

I had long-since got to know how I was situated in the world. All my people were dead and there was a man called Divney working the farm and living on it until I should return. He did not own any of it and was given weekly cheques of pay by an office full of solicitors in a town far away. I had never met these solicitors and never met Divney but they were really all working for me and my father had paid in cash for these arrangements before he died. When I was younger I thought he was a generous man to do that for a boy he did not know well.

I did not go home direct from school. I spent some months in other places broadening my mind and finding out what a complete edition of de Selby's works would cost me and whether some of the less important of his commentators' books could be got on loan. In one of the places where I was broadening my mind I met one night with a bad accident. I broke my left leg (or, if you like, it was broken for me) in six places and when I was well enough again to go my way I had one leg made of wood, the left one. I knew that I had only a little money, that I was going home to a rocky farm and that my life would not be easy. But I was certain by this time that farming, even if I had to do it, would not be my life work. I knew that if my name was to be remembered, it would be remembered with de Selby's.

I can recall in every detail the evening I walked back into my own house with a travelling-bag in each hand. I was twenty years of age; it was an evening in a happy yellow summer and the

door of the public house was open. Behind the counter was John
Divney, leaning forward on the low-down porter dash-board
with his fork, his arms neatly folded and his face looking down
on a newspaper which was spread upon the counter. He had
brown hair and was made handsomely enough in a small butty
way; his shoulders were broadened out with work and his arms
were thick like little tree-trunks. He had a quiet civil face with
eyes like cow's eyes, brooding, brown, and patient. When he
knew that somebody had come in he did not stop his reading
but his left hand strayed out and found a rag and began to give
the counter slow damp swipes. Then, still reading, he moved his
hands one above the other as if he was drawing out a concertina
to full length and said:

'A schooner?'

A schooner was what the customers called a pint of Coleraine
blackjack. It was the cheapest porter in the world. I said that
I wanted my dinner and mentioned my name and station. Then
we closed the shop and went into the kitchen and we were there
nearly all night, eating and talking and drinking whiskey.

The next day was Thursday. John Divney said that his work
was now done and that he would be ready to go home to where
his people were on Saturday. It was not true to say that his work
was done because the farm was in a poor way and most of the
year's work had not even been started. But on Saturday he said
there were a few things to finish and that he could not work on
Sunday but that he would be in a position to hand over the place
in perfect order on Tuesday evening. On Monday he had a sick
pig to mind and that delayed him. At the end of the week he was
busier than ever and the passing of another two months did not
seem to lighten or reduce his urgent tasks. I did not mind much
because if he was idle-minded and a sparing worker, he was
satisfactory so far as company was concerned and he never asked
for pay. I did little work about the place myself, spending all my
time arranging my papers and re-reading still more closely the
pages of de Selby.

A full year had not passed when I noticed that Divney was
using the word 'we' in his conversation and worse than that, the
word 'our'. He said that the place was not everything that it
might be and talked of getting a hired man. I did not agree with
this and told him so, saying that there was no necessity for more

than two men on a small farm and adding, most unhappily for myself, that we were poor. After that it was useless trying to tell him that it was I who owned everything. I began to tell myself that even if I did own everything, he owned me.

Four years passed away happily enough for each of us. We had a good house and plenty of good country food but little money. Nearly all my own time was spent in study. Out of my savings I had now bought the complete works of the two principal commentators, Hatchjaw and Bassett, and a photostat of the de Selby Codex. I had also embarked upon the task of learning French and German thoroughly in order to read the works of other commentators in those languages. Divney had been working after a fashion on the farm by day and talking loudly in the public house by night and serving drinks there. Once I asked him what about the public house and he said he was losing money on it every day. I did not understand this because the customers, judging by their voices through the thin door, were plentiful enough and Divney was continually buying himself suits of clothes and fancy tiepins. But I did not say much. I was satisfied to be left in peace because I knew that my own work was more important than myself.

One day in early winter Divney said to me:

'I cannot lose very much more of my own money on that bar. The customers are complaining about the porter. It is very bad porter because I have to drink a little now and again myself to keep them company and I do not feel well in my health over the head of it. I will have to go away for two days and do some travelling and see if there is a better brand of porter to be had.'

He disappeared the next morning on his bicycle and when he came back very dusty and travel-worn at the end of three days, he told me that everything was all right and that four barrels of better porter could be expected on Friday. It came punctually on that day and was well bought by the customers in the public house that night. It was manufactured in some town in the south and was known as 'The Wrastler'. If you drank three or four pints of it, it was nearly bound to win. The customers praised it highly and when they had it inside them they sang and shouted and sometimes lay down on the floor or on the roadway outside in a great stupor. Some of them complained afterwards that they had been robbed while in this state and talked angrily in the shop the next night about stolen money and gold watches which had disappeared off their strong chains. John Divney did not say much on this subject to them and did not mention it to me at all. He printed the words – BEWARE OF PICKPOCKETS – in large letters on a card and hung it on the back of shelves beside another notice that dealt with cheques. Nevertheless a week rarely passed without some customer complaining after an evening with 'The Wrastler'. It was not a satisfactory thing.

As time went on Divney became more and more despondent about what he called 'the bar'. He said that he would be satisfied if it paid its way but he doubted seriously if it ever would. The Government were partly responsible for the situation owing to the high taxes. He did not think that he could continue to bear the burden of the loss without some assistance. I said that my father had some old-fashioned way of management which made possible a profit but that the shop should be closed if now continuing to lose money. Divney only said that it was a very serious thing to surrender a licence.

It was about this time, when I was nearly thirty, that Divney and I began to get the name of being great friends. For years before that I had rarely gone out at all. This was because I was so busy with my work that I hardly ever had the time; also my wooden leg was not very good for walking with. Then something very unusual happened to change all this and after it had happened, Divney and I never parted company for more than one minute either night or day. All day I was out with him on the farm and at night I sat on my father's old seat under the lamp in a corner of the public house doing what work I could with my papers in the middle of the blare and the crush and the hot noises which went always with 'The Wrastler'. If Divney went for a walk on Sunday to a neighbour's house I went with him and came home with him again, never before or after him. If he went away to a town on his bicycle to order porter or seed potatoes or even 'to see a certain party', I went on my own bicycle beside him. I brought my bed into his room and took the trouble to sleep only after he was sleeping and to be wide-awake a good hour before he stirred. Once I nearly failed in my watchfulness. I remember waking up with a start in the small hours of a black night and finding him quietly dressing himself in the dark. I asked him where he was going and he said he could not sleep and that he thought a walk would do him good. I said I was in the same condition myself and the two of us went for a walk together into the coldest and wettest night I ever experienced. When we returned drenched I said it was foolish for us to sleep in different beds in such bitter weather and got into his bed beside him. He did not say much, then or at any other time. I slept with him always after that. We were friendly and smiled at each other but the situation was a queer one and neither of us liked it. The neighbours were not long noticing how inseparable we were. We had been in that condition of being always together for nearly three years and they said that we were the best two Christians in all Ireland. They said that human friendship was a beautiful thing and that Divney and I were the noblest example of it in the history of the world. If other people fell out or fought or disagreed, they were asked why they could not be like me and Divney. It would have been a great shock for everybody if Divney had appeared in any place at any time without myself beside him. And it is not strange that two people never came to dislike each other as bitterly as did I and Divney. And two people were never so polite to each other, so friendly in the face.

I must go back several years to explain what happened to bring about this peculiar situation. The 'certain party' whom Divney went to visit once a month was a girl called Pegeen Meers. For my part I had completed my definitive 'De Selby Index' wherein the views of all known commentators on every aspect of the savant and his work had been collated. Each of us therefore had a large thing on the mind. One day Divney said to me:

'That is a powerful book you have written I don't doubt.'

'It is useful,' I admitted, 'and badly wanted.' In fact it contained much that was entirely new and proof that many opinions widely held about de Selby and his theories were misconceptions based on misreadings of his works.

'It might make your name in the world and your golden fortune in copyrights?'

'It might.'

'Then why do you not put it out?'

I explained that money is required to 'put out' a book of this kind unless the writer already has a reputation. He gave me a look of sympathy that was not usual with him and sighed.

'Money is hard to come by these days,' he said, 'with the drink trade on its last legs and the land starved away to nothing for the want of artificial manures that can't be got for love or money owing to the trickery of the Jewmen and the Freemasons.'

I knew that it was not true about the manures. He had already pretended to me that they could not be got because he did not want the trouble of them. After a pause he said:

'We will have to see what we can do about getting money for your book and indeed I am in need of some myself because you can't expect a girl to wait until she is too old to wait any longer.'

I did not know whether he meant to bring a wife, if he got one, into the house. If he did and I could not stop him, then I would have to leave. On the other hand if marriage meant that he himself would leave I think I would be very glad of it.

It was some days before he talked on this subject of money again. Then he said:

'What about old Mathers?'

'What about him?'

I had never seen the old man but knew all about him. He had spent a long life of fifty years in the cattle trade and now lived in retirement in a big house three miles away. He still did large business through agents and the people said that he carried no less than three thousand pounds with him every time he hobbled to the village to lodge his money. Little as I knew of social proprieties at the time, I would not dream of asking him for assistance.

'He is worth a packet of potato-meal,' Divney said.

'I do not think we should look for charity,' I answered.

'I do not think so either,' he said. He was a proud man in his own way, I thought, and no more was said just then. But after that he took to the habit of putting occasionally into conversations on other subjects some irrelevant remark about our need for money and the amount of it which Mathers carried in his black cash-box; sometimes he would revile the old man, accusing him of being in 'the artificial manure ring' or of being dishonest in his business dealings. Once he said something about 'social justice' but it was plain to me that he did not properly understand the term.

I do not know exactly how or when it become clear to me that Divney, far from seeking charity, intended to rob Mathers; and I cannot recollect how long it took me to realize that he meant to kill him as well in order to avoid the possibility of being identified as the robber afterwards. I only know that within six months I had come to accept this grim plan as a commonplace of our conversation. Three further months passed before I could bring myself to agree to the proposal and three months more before I openly admitted to Divney that my misgivings were at an end. I cannot recount the tricks and wiles he used to win me to his side. It is sufficient to say that he read portions of my 'De Selby Index' (or pretended to) and discussed with me afterwards the serious responsibility of any person who declined by mere reason of personal whim to give the 'Index' to the world.

Old Mathers lived alone. Divney knew on what evening and at what deserted stretch of road near his house we would meet him with his box of money. The evening when it came was in the depth of winter; the light was already waning as we sat at our dinner discussing the business we had in hand. Divney said that we should bring our spades tied on the crossbars of our bicycles because this would make us look like men out after rabbits; he would bring his own iron pump in case we should get a slow puncture.

There is little to tell about the murder. The lowering skies seemed to conspire with us, coming down in a shroud of dreary mist to within a few yards of the wet road where we were waiting. Everything was very still with no sound in our ears except the dripping of the trees. Our bicycles were hidden. I was leaning miserably on my spade and Divney, his iron pump under his arm, was smoking his pipe contentedly. The old man was upon us almost before we realized there was anybody near. I could not see him well in the dim light but I could glimpse a spent bloodless face peering from the top of the great black coat which covered him from ear to ankle. Divney went forward at once and pointing back along the road said:

'Would that be your parcel on the road?'

The old man turned his head to look and received a blow in the back of the neck from Divney's pump which knocked him clean off his feet and probably smashed his neck-bone. As he collapsed full-length in the mud he did not cry out. Instead I heard him say something softly in a conversational tone – something like 'I do not care for celery' or 'I left my glasses in the scullery'. Then he lay very still. I had been watching the scene rather stupidly, still leaning on my spade. Divney was rummaging savagely at the fallen figure and then stood up. He had a black cash-box in his hand. He waved it in the air and roared at me:

'Here, wake up! Finish him with the spade!'

I went forward mechanically, swung the spade over my shoulder and smashed the blade of it with all my strength against the protruding chin. I felt and almost heard the fabric of his skull crumple up crisply like an empty eggshell. I do not know how often I struck him after that but I did not stop until I was tired.

I threw the spade down and looked around for Divney. He was nowhere to be seen. I called his name softly but he did not answer. I walked a little bit up the road and called again. I jumped on the rising of a ditch and peered around into the gathering dusk. I called his name once more as loudly as I dared but there was no answer in the stillness. He was gone. He had made off with the box of money, leaving me alone with the dead man and with a spade which was now probably tinging the watery mud around it with a weak pink stain.

My heart stumbled painfully in its beating. A chill of fright ran right through me. If anybody should come, nothing in the world would save me from the gallows. If Divney was with me still to share my guilt, even that would not protect me. Numb with fear I stood for a long time looking at the crumpled heap in the black coat.

Before the old man had come Divney and I had dug a deep hole in the field beside the road, taking care to preserve the sods of grass. Now in a panic I dragged the heavy sodden figure from where it lay and got it with a tremendous effort across the ditch into the field and slumped it down into the hole. Then I rushed back for my spade and started to throw and push the earth back into the hole in a mad blind fury.

The hole was nearly full when I heard steps. Looking round in great dismay I saw the unmistakable shape of Divney making his way carefully across the ditch into the field. When he came up I pointed dumbly to the hole with my spade. Without a word he went to where our bicycles were, came back with his own spade and worked steadily with me until the task was finished. We did everything possible to hide any trace of what had happened. Then we cleaned our boots with grass, tied the spades and walked home. A few people who came against us on the road bade us good evening in the dark. I am sure they took us for two tired labourers making for home after a hard day's work. They were not far wrong.

On our way I said to Divney:

'Where were you that time?'

'Attending to important business,' he answered. I thought he was referring to a certain thing and said:

'Surely you could have kept it till after.'

'It is not what you are thinking of,' he answered.

'Have you got the box?'

He turned his face to me this time, screwed it up and put a finger on his lip.

'Not so loud,' he whispered. 'It is in a safe place.'

'But where?'

The only reply he gave me was to put the finger on his lip more firmly and make a long hissing noise. He gave me to understand that mentioning the box, even in a whisper, was the most foolish and reckless thing it was possible for me to do.

When we reached home he went away and washed himself and put on one of the several blue Sunday suits he had. When he came back to where I was sitting, a miserable figure at the kitchen fire, he came across to me with a very serious face, pointed to the window and cried:

'Would that be your parcel on the road?'

Then he let out a bellow of laughter which seemed to loosen up his whole body, turn his eyes to water in his head and shake the whole house. When he had finished he wiped the tears from his face, walked into the shop and made a noise which can only be made by taking the cork quickly out of a whiskey bottle.

In the weeks which followed I asked him where the box was a hundred times in a thousand different ways. He never answered in the same way but the answer was always the same. It was in a very safe place. The least said about it the better until things quietened down. Mum was the word. It would be found all in good time. For the purpose of safekeeping the place it was in was superior to the Bank of England. There was a good time coming. It would be a pity to spoil everything by hastiness or impatience.

And that is why John Divney and I became inseparable friends and why I never allowed him to leave my sight for three years. Having robbed me in my own public house (having even robbed

my customers) and having ruined my farm, I knew that he was
sufficiently dishonest to steal my share of Mathers' money and
make off with the box if given the opportunity. I knew that
there was no possible necessity for waiting until 'things quietened
down' because very little notice was taken of the old man's disappearance. People said he was a queer mean man and that going
away without telling anybody or leaving his address was the sort
of thing he would do.

I think I have said before that the peculiar terms of physical
intimacy upon which myself and Divney found ourselves had
become more and more intolerable. In latter months I had hoped
to force him to capitulate by making my company unbearably
close and unrelenting but at the same time I took to carrying a
small pistol in case of accidents. One Sunday night when both
of us were sitting in the kitchen – both, incidentally, on the same
side of the fire – he took his pipe from his mouth and turned
to me:

'Do you know,' he said, 'I think things have quietened down.'

I only gave a grunt.

'Do you get my meaning?' he asked.

'Things were never any other way,' I answered shortly. He
looked at me in a superior way.

'I know a lot about these things,' he said, 'and you would be
surprised at the pitfalls a man will make if he is in too big a hurry.
You cannot be too careful but all the same I think things have
quietened down enough to make it safe.'

'I am glad you think so.'

'There are good times coming. I will get the box tomorrow
and then we will divide the money, right here on this table.'

'*We* will get the box,' I answered, saying the first word with
great care. He gave me a long hurt look and asked me sadly did
I not trust him. I replied that both of us should finish what both
had started.

'All right,' he said in a very vexed way. 'I am sorry you don't
trust me after all the work I have done to try to put this place
right but to show you the sort I am I will let you get the box
yourself, I will tell you where it is tomorrow.'

I took care to sleep with him as usual that night. The next
morning he was in a better temper and told me with great
simplicity that the box was hidden in Mathers' own empty

house, under the floorboards of the first room on the right from the hall.

'Are you sure?' I asked.

'I swear it,' he said solemnly, raising his hand to heaven.

I thought the position over for a moment, examining the possibility that it was a ruse to part company with me at last and then make off himself to the real hiding-place. But his face for the first time seemed to wear a look of honesty.

'I am sorry if I injured your feelings last night,' I said, 'but to show that there is no ill-feeling I would be glad if you would come with me at least part of the way. I honestly think that both of us should finish what the two of us started.'

'All right,' he said. 'It is all the same but I would like you to get the box with your own hands because it is only simple justice after not telling you where it was.'

As my own bicycle was punctured we walked the distance. When we were about a hundred yards from Mathers' house, Divney stopped by a low wall and said that he was going to sit on it and smoke his pipe and wait for me.

'Let you go alone and get the box and bring it back here. There are good times coming and we will be rich men tonight. It is sitting under a loose board in the floor of the first room on the right, in the corner forenenst the door.'

Perched as he was on the wall I knew that he need never leave my sight. In the brief time I would be away I could see him any time I turned my head.

'I will be back in ten minutes,' I said.

'Good man,' he answered. 'But remember this. If you meet anybody, you don't know what you're looking for, you don't know in whose house you are, you don't know anything.'

'I don't even know my own name,' I answered.

This was a very remarkable thing for me to say because the next time I was asked my name I could not answer. I did not know.

CHAPTER 2

DE SELBY HAS some interesting things to say on the subject of houses.[1] A row of houses he regards as a row of necessary evils. The softening and degeneration of the human race he attributes to its progressive predilection for interiors and waning interest in the art of going out and staying there. This in turn he sees as the result of the rise of such pursuits as reading, chess-playing, drinking, marriage and the like, few of which can be satisfactorily conducted in the open. Elsewhere[2] he defines a house as 'a large coffin', 'a warren', and 'a box'. Evidently his main objection was to the confinement of a roof and four walls. He ascribed somewhat far-fetched therapeutic values – chiefly pulmonary – to certain structures of his own design which he called 'habitats', crude drawings of which may still be seen in the pages of the *Country Album*. These structures were of two kinds, roofless 'houses' and 'houses' without walls. The former had wide open doors and windows with an extremely ungainly superstructure of tarpaulins loosely rolled on spars against bad weather – the whole looking like a foundered sailing-ship erected on a platform of masonry and the last place where one would think of keeping even cattle. The other type of 'habitat' had the conventional slated roof but no walls save one, which was to be erected in the quarter of the prevailing wind; around the other sides were the inevitable tarpaulins loosely wound on rollers suspended from the gutters of the roof, the whole structure being surrounded by a diminutive moat or pit bearing some resemblance to military latrines. In the light of present-day theories of housing and hygiene, there can be no doubt that de Selby was much mistaken in these ideas but in his own remote day more than one sick person lost his life in an ill-advised quest for health in these fantastic dwellings.[3]

1 *Golden Hours*, ii, 261. 2 *Country Album*, p. 1,034.
3 Le Fournier, the reliable French commentator (in *De Selby – l'Énigme de l'Occident*) has put forward a curious theory regarding these 'habitats'. He suggests that de Selby, when writing the *Album*, paused to consider some

My recollections of de Selby were prompted by my visit to the home of old Mr Mathers. As I approached it along the road the house appeared to be a fine roomy brick building of uncertain age, two storeys high with a plain porch and eight or nine windows to the front of each floor.

I opened the iron gate and walked as softly as I could up the weed-tufted gravel drive. My mind was strangely empty. I did not feel that I was about to end successfully a plan I had worked unrelentingly at night and day for three years. I felt no glow of pleasure and was unexcited at the prospect of becoming rich. I was occupied only with the mechanical task of finding a black box.

The hall-door was closed and although it was set far back in a very deep porch the wind and rain had whipped a coating of gritty dust against the panels and deep into the crack where the door opened, showing that it had been shut for years. Standing on a derelict flower-bed, I tried to push up the sash of the first window on the left. It yielded to my strength, raspingly and stubbornly. I clambered through the opening and found myself, not at once in a room, but crawling along the deepest window-ledge I have ever seen. When I reached the floor and jumped noisily down upon it, the open window seemed very far away and much too small to have admitted me.

The room where I found myself was thick with dust, musty and deserted of all furniture. Spiders had erected great stretchings of their web about the fireplace. I made my way quickly to the hall, threw open the door of the room where the box was and paused on the threshold. It was a dark morning and the weather had stained the windows with blears of grey wash which kept the brightest part of the weak light from coming in. The far corner of the room was a blur of shadow. I had a sudden urge to have done with my task and be out of this house forever. I walked

---

point of difficulty and in the meantime engaged in the absent-minded practice known generally as 'doodling', then putting his manuscript away. The next time he took it up he was confronted with a mass of diagrams and drawings which he took to be the plans of a type of dwelling he always had in mind and immediately wrote many pages explaining the sketches. 'In no other way,' adds the severe Le Fournier, 'can one explain so regrettable a lapse.'

across the bare boards, knelt down in the corner and passed my hands about the floor in search of the loose board. To my surprise I found it easily. It was about two feet in length and rocked hollowly under my hand. I lifted it up, laid it aside and struck a match. I saw a black metal cash-box nestling dimly in the hole. I put my hand down and crooked a finger into the loose reclining handle but the match suddenly flickered and went out and the handle of the box, which I had lifted up about an inch slid heavily off my finger. Without stopping to light another match I thrust my hand bodily into the opening and just when it should be closing about the box, something happened.

I cannot hope to describe what it was but it had frightened me very much long before I had understood it even slightly. It was some change which came upon me or upon the room, indescribably subtle, yet momentous, ineffable. It was as if the daylight had changed with unnatural suddenness, as if the temperature of the evening had altered greatly in an instant or as if the air had become twice as rare or twice as dense as it had been in the winking of an eye; perhaps all of these and other things happened together for all my senses were bewildered all at once and could give me no explanation. The fingers of my right hand, thrust into the opening in the floor, had closed mechanically, found nothing at all and came up again empty. The box was gone!

I heard a cough behind me, soft and natural yet more disturbing than any sound that could ever come upon the human ear. That I did not die of fright was due, I think, to two things, the fact that my senses were already disarranged and able to interpret to me only gradually what they had perceived and also the fact that the utterance of the cough seemed to bring with it some more awful alteration in everything, just as if it had held the universe standstill for an instant, suspending the planets in their courses, halting the sun and holding in mid-air any falling thing the earth was pulling towards it. I collapsed weakly from my kneeling backwards into a limp sitting-down upon the floor. Sweat broke upon my brow and my eyes remained open for a long time without a wink, glazed and almost sightless.

In the darkest corner of the room near the window a man was sitting in a chair, eyeing me with a mild but unwavering interest. His hand had crept out across the small table by his side to turn up very slowly an oil-lamp which was standing on it. The oil-lamp had a glass bowl with the wick dimly visible inside it, curling in convolutions like an intestine. There were tea things on the table. The man was old Mathers. He was watching me in silence. He did not move or speak and might have been still dead save for the slight movement of his hand at the lamp, the very gentle screwing of his thumb and forefinger against the wick-wheel. The hand was yellow, the wrinkled skin draped loosely upon the bones. Over the knuckle of his forefinger I could clearly see the loop of a skinny vein.

It is hard to write of such a scene or to convey with known words the feelings which came knocking at my numbed mind. How long we sat there, for instance, looking at one another I do not know. Years or minutes could be swallowed up with equal ease in that indescribable and unaccountable interval. The light of morning vanished from my sight, the dusty floor was like nothingness beneath me and my whole body dissolved away, leaving me existing only in the stupid spellbound gaze that went steadily from where I was to the other corner.

I remember that I noticed several things in a cold mechanical way as if I was sitting there with no worry save to note everything I saw. His face was terrifying but his eyes in the middle of it had a quality of chill and horror which made his other features look to me almost friendly. The skin was like faded parchment with an arrangement of puckers and wrinkles which created between them an expression of fathomless inscrutability. But the eyes were horrible. Looking at them I got the feeling that they were not genuine eyes at all but mechanical dummies animated by electricity or the like, with a tiny pinhole in the centre of the 'pupil' through which the real eye gazed out secretively and with great coldness. Such a conception, possibly with no foundation at all in fact, disturbed me agonizingly and gave rise in my mind to interminable speculations as to the colour and quality of the real eye and as to whether, indeed, it was real at all or merely another dummy with its pinhole on the same plane as the first one so that the real eye, possibly behind thousands of these absurd disguises, gazed out through a barrel of serried peep-holes. Occasionally the heavy cheese-like lids would drop down slowly with great languor and then rise again. Wrapped loosely around the body was an old wine-coloured dressing-gown.

In my distress I thought to myself that perhaps it was his twin brother but at once I heard someone say:

Scarcely. If you look carefully at the left-hand side of his neck you will notice that there is sticking-plaster or a bandage there. His throat and chin are also bandaged.

Forlornly, I looked and saw that this was true. He was the man I had murdered beyond all question. He was sitting on a chair four yards away watching me. He sat stiffly without a move as if afraid to hurt the gaping wounds which covered his body. Across my own shoulders a stiffness had spread from my exertions with the spade.

But who had uttered these words? They had not frightened me. They were clearly audible to me yet I knew they did not ring out across the air like the chilling cough of the old man in the chair. They came from deep inside me, from my soul. Never before had I believed or suspected that I had a soul but just then I knew I had. I knew also that my soul was friendly, was my senior in years and was solely concerned for my own welfare. For convenience I called him Joe. I felt a little reassured to know that I was not altogether alone. Joe was helping me.

I will not try to tell of the space of time which followed. In the terrible situation I found myself, my reason could give me no assistance. I knew that old Mathers had been felled by an iron bicycle-pump, hacked to death with a heavy spade and then securely buried in a field. I knew also that the same man was now sitting in the same room with me, watching me in silence. His body was bandaged but his eyes were alive and so was his right hand and so was all of him. Perhaps the murder by the roadside was a bad dream.

There is nothing dreamy about your stiff shoulders. No, I replied, but a nightmare can be as strenuous physically as the real thing.

I decided in some crooked way that the best thing to do was to believe what my eyes were looking at rather than to place my trust in a memory. I decided to show unconcern, to talk to the old man and to test his own reality by asking about the black box which was responsible, if anything could be, for each of us being the way we were. I made up my mind to be bold because I knew that I was in great danger. I knew that I would go mad unless I got up from the floor and moved and talked and behaved in as ordinary a way as possible. I looked away from old Mathers, got carefully to my feet and sat down on a chair that was not far away from him. Then I looked back at him, my heart pausing for a time and working on again with slow heavy hammer-blows which seemed to make my whole frame shudder. He had remained perfectly still but the live right hand had gripped the pot of tea, raised it very awkwardly and slapped a filling into the empty cup. His eyes had followed me to my new position and were now regarding me again with the same unwavering languorous interest.

Suddenly I began to talk. Words spilled out of me as if they were produced by machinery. My voice, tremulous at first, grew hard and loud and filled the whole room. I do not remember what I said at the beginning. I am sure that most of it was meaningless but I was too pleased and reassured at the natural healthy noise of my tongue to be concerned about the words.

Old Mathers did not move or say anything at first but I was certain that he was listening to me. After a while he began to shake his head and then I was sure I had heard him say No. I became excited at his responses and began to speak carefully. He negatived my inquiry about his health, refused to say where the black box had gone and even denied that it was a dark morning. His voice had a peculiar jarring weight like the hoarse toll of an ancient rusty bell in an ivy-smothered tower. He had said nothing beyond the one word No. His lips hardly moved; I felt sure he had no teeth behind them.

'Are you dead at present?' I asked.

'I am not.'

'Do you know where the box is?'

'No.'

He made another violent movement with his right arm, slapping hot water into his teapot and pouring forth a little more of the feeble brew into his cup. He then relapsed into his attitude of motionless watching. I pondered for a time.

'Do you like weak tea?' I asked.

'I do not,' he said.

'Do you like tea at all?' I asked, 'strong or weak or halfway tea?'

'No,' he said.

'Then why do you drink it?'

He shook his yellow face from side to side sadly and did not say anything. When he stopped shaking he opened up his mouth and poured the cupful of tea in as one would pour a bucket of milk into a churn at churning-time.

Do you notice anything?

No, I replied, nothing beyond the eeriness of this house and the man who owns it. He is by no means the best conversationalist I have met.

I found I spoke lightly enough. While speaking inwardly or outwardly or thinking of what to say I felt brave and normal enough. But every time a silence came the horror of my situation descended upon me like a heavy blanket flung upon my head, enveloping and smothering me and making me afraid of death.

But do you notice nothing about the way he answers your questions?

No.

Do you not see that every reply is in the negative? No matter what you ask him he says No.

That is true enough, I said, but I do not see where that leads me.

Use your imagination.

When I brought my whole attention back to old Mathers I thought he was asleep. He sat over his teacup in a more stooped attitude as if he were a rock or part of the wooden chair he sat on, a man completely dead and turned to stone. Over his eyes the limp lids had drooped down, almost closing them. His right hand resting on the table lay lifeless and abandoned. I composed my thoughts and addressed to him a sharp noisy interrogation.

'Will you answer a straight question?' I asked. He stirred somewhat, his lids opening slightly.

'I will not,' he replied.

I saw that this answer was in keeping with Joe's shrewd suggestion. I sat thinking for a moment until I had thought the same thought inside out.

'Will you refuse to answer a straight question?' I asked.

'I will not,' he replied.

This answer pleased me. It meant that my mind had got to grips with his, that I was now almost arguing with him and that we were behaving like two ordinary human beings. I did not understand all the terrible things which had happened to me but I now began to think that I must be mistaken about them.

'Very well,' I said quietly. 'Why do you always answer No?'

He stirred perceptibly in his chair and filled the teacup up again before he spoke. He seemed to have some difficulty in finding words.

' "No" is, generally speaking, a better answer than "Yes",' he said at last. He seemed to speak eagerly, his words coming out as if they had been imprisoned in his mouth for a thousand years. He seemed relieved that I had found a way to make him speak. I thought he even smiled slightly at me but this was doubtless the trickery of the bad morning light or a mischief worked by the shadows of the lamp. He swallowed a long draught of tea and sat waiting, looking at me with his queer eyes. They were now bright and active and moved about restlessly in their yellow wrinkled sockets.

'Do you refuse to tell me why you say that?' I asked.

'No,' he said. 'When I was a young man I led an unsatisfactory life and devoted most of my time to excesses of one kind or another, my principal weakness being Number One. I was also party to the formation of an artificial manure-ring.'

My mind went back at once to John Divney, to the farm and the public house and on from that to the horrible afternoon we had spent on the wet lonely road. As if to interrupt my unhappy thoughts I heard Joe's voice again, this time severe:

No need to ask him what Number One is, we do not want lurid descriptions of vice or anything at all in that line. Use your imagination. Ask him what all this has to do with Yes and No.

'What has that got to do with Yes and No?'

'After a time,' said old Mathers disregarding me, 'I mercifully perceived the error of my ways and the unhappy destination I would reach unless I mended them. I retired from the world in order to try to comprehend it and to find out why it becomes more unsavoury as the years accumulate on a man's body. What do you think I discovered at the end of my meditations?'

I felt pleased again. He was now questioning me.

'What?'

'That No is a better word than Yes,' he replied.

This seemed to leave us where we were, I thought.

On the contrary, very far from it. I am beginning to agree with him. There is a lot to be said for No as a General Principle. Ask him what he means.

'What do you mean?' I inquired.

'When I was meditating,' said old Mathers, 'I took all my sins out and put them on the table, so to speak. I need not tell you it was a big table.'

He seemed to give a very dry smile at his own joke. I chuckled to encourage him.

'I gave them all a strict examination, weighed them and viewed them from all angles of the compass. I asked myself how I came to commit them, where I was and whom I was with when I came to do them.'

This is very wholesome stuff, every word a sermon in itself. Listen very carefully. Ask him to continue.

'Continue,' I said.

I confess I felt a click inside me very near my stomach as if Joe had put a finger to his lip and pricked up a pair of limp spaniel ears to make sure that no syllable of the wisdom escaped him. Old Mathers continued talking quietly.

'I discovered,' he said, 'that everything you do is in response to a request or a suggestion made to you by some other party either inside you or outside. Some of these suggestions are good and praiseworthy and some of them are undoubtedly delightful. But the majority of them are definitely bad and are pretty considerable sins as sins go. Do you understand me?'

'Perfectly.'

'I would say that the bad ones outnumber the good ones by three to one.'

Six to one if you ask me.

'I therefore decided to say No henceforth to every suggestion, request or inquiry whether inward or outward. It was the only simple formula which was sure and safe. It was difficult to practise at first and often called for heroism but I persevered and hardly ever broke down completely. It is now many years since I said Yes. I have refused more requests and negatived more statements than any man living or dead. I have rejected, reneged, disagreed, refused and denied to an extent that is unbelievable.'

An excellent and original régime. This is all extremely interesting and salutary, every syllable a sermon in itself. Very very wholesome.

'Extremely interesting,' I said to old Mathers.

'The system leads to peace and contentment,' he said. 'People do not trouble to ask you questions if they know the answer is a foregone conclusion. Thoughts which have no chance of succeeding do not take the trouble to come into your head at all.'

'You must find it irksome in some ways,' I suggested. 'If, for instance, I were to offer you a glass of whiskey . . .'

'Such few friends as I have,' he answered, 'are usually good enough to arrange such invitations in a way that will enable me to adhere to my system and also accept the whiskey. More than once I have been asked whether I would refuse such things.'

'And the answer is still NO?'

'Certainly.'

Joe said nothing at this stage but I had the feeling that this confession was not to his liking; he seemed to be uneasy inside me. The old man seemed to get somewhat restive also. He bent over his teacup with abstraction as if he were engaged in accomplishing a sacrament. Then he drank with his hollow throat, making empty noises.

A saintly man.

I turned to him again, fearing that his fit of talkativeness had passed.

'Where is the black box which was under the floor a moment ago?' I asked. I pointed to the opening in the corner. He shook his head and did not say anything.

'Do you refuse to tell me?'

'No.'

'Do you object to my taking it?'

'No.'

'Then where is it?'

'What is your name?' he asked sharply.

I was surprised at this question. It had no bearing on my own conversation but I did not notice its irrelevance because I was shocked to realize that, simple as it was, I could not answer it. I did not know my name, did not remember who I was. I was not certain where I had come from or what my business was in that room. I found I was sure of nothing save my search for the black box. But I knew that the other man's name was Mathers, and that he had been killed with a pump and spade. I had no name.

'I have no name,' I replied.

'Then how could I tell you where the box was if you could not sign a receipt? That would be most irregular. I might as well give it to the west wind or to the smoke from a pipe. How could you execute an important Bank document?'

'I can always get a name,' I replied. 'Doyle or Spaldman is a good name and so is O'Sweeny and Hardiman and O'Gara. I can take my choice. I am not tied down for life to one word like most people.'

'I do not care much for Doyle,' he said absently.

The name is Bari. Signor Bari, the eminent tenor. Five hundred thousand people crowded the great piazza when the great artist appeared on the balcony of St Peter's Rome.

Fortunately these remarks were not audible in the ordinary sense of the word. Old Mathers was eyeing me.

'What is your colour?' he asked.

'My colour?'

'Surely you know you have a colour?'

'People often remark on my red face.'

'I do not mean that at all.'

Follow this closely, this is bound to be extremely interesting. Very edifying also.

I saw it was necessary to question old Mathers carefully.

'Do you refuse to explain this question about the colours?'

'No,' he said. He slapped more tea in his cup.

'No doubt you are aware that the winds have colours,' he said. I thought he settled himself more restfully in his chair and changed his face till it looked a little bit benign.

'I never noticed it.'

'A record of this belief will be found in the literature of all ancient peoples.[4] There are four winds and eight sub-winds, each with its own colour. The wind from the east is a deep purple, from the south a fine shining silver. The north wind is a hard black and the west is amber. People in the old days had the power of perceiving these colours and could spend a day

---

4 It is not clear whether de Selby had heard of this but he suggests (*Garcia*, p. 12) that night, far from being caused by the commonly accepted theory of planetary movements, was due to accumulations of 'black air' produced by certain volcanic activities of which he does not treat in detail. See also pp. 79 and 945, *Country Album*. Le Fournier's comment (in *Homme ou Dieu*) is interesting. 'On ne saura jamais jusqu'à quel point de Selby fut cause de la Grande Guerre, mais, sans aucun doute, ses théories excentriques – spécialement celle que nuit n'est pas un phénomène de nature, mais dans l'atmosphère un état malsain amené par un industrialisme cupide et sans pitié – auraient l'effet de produire un trouble profond dans les masses.'

sitting quietly on a hillside watching the beauty of the winds, their fall and rise and changing hues, the magic of neighbouring winds when they are inter-weaved like ribbons at a wedding. It was a better occupation than gazing at newspapers. The sub-winds had colours of indescribable delicacy, a reddish-yellow half-way between silver and purple, a greyish-green which was related equally to black and brown. What could be more exquisite than a countryside swept lightly by cool rain reddened by the south-west breeze!'

'Can *you* see these colours?' I asked.

'No.'

'You were asking me what my colour was. How do people get their colours?'

'A person's colour,' he answered slowly, 'is the colour of the wind prevailing at his birth.'

'What is your own colour?'

'Light yellow.'

'And what is the point of knowing your colour or having a colour at all?'

'For one thing you can tell the length of your life from it. Yellow means a long life and the lighter the better.'

This is very edifying, every sentence a sermon in itself. Ask him to explain.

'Please explain.'

'It is a question of making little gowns,' he said informatively.

'Little gowns?'

'Yes. When I was born there was a certain policeman present who had the gift of wind-watching. The gift is getting very rare these days. Just after I was born he went outside and examined the colour of the wind that was blowing across the hill. He had a secret bag with him full of certain materials and bottles and he had tailor's instruments also. He was outside for about ten minutes. When he came in again he had a little gown in his hand and he made my mother put it on me.'

'Where did he get this gown?' I asked in surprise.

'He made it himself secretly in the backyard, very likely in the cowhouse. It was very thin and slight like the very finest of spider's muslin. You would not see it at all if you held it against the sky but at certain angles of the light you might at times accidentally notice the edge of it. It was the purest and most perfect manifestation of the outside skin of light yellow. This yellow was the colour of my birth-wind.'

'I see,' I said.

A very beautiful conception.

'Every time my birthday came,' old Mathers said, 'I was presented with another little gown of the same identical quality except that it was put on over the other one and not in place of it. You may appreciate the extreme delicacy and fineness of the material when I tell you that even at five years old with five of these gowns together on me, I still appeared to be naked. It was, however, an unusual yellowish sort of nakedness. Of course there was no objection to wearing other clothes over the gown. I usually wore an overcoat. But every year I got a new gown.'

'Where did you get them?' I asked.

'From the police. They were brought to my own home until I was big enough to call to the barracks for them.'

'And how does all this enable you to predict your span of life?'

'I will tell you. No matter what your colour is, it will be represented faithfully in your birth-gown. With each year and each gown, the colour will get deeper and more pronounced. In my own case I had attained a bright full-blown yellow at fifteen although the colour was so light at birth as to be imperceptible. I am now nearing seventy and the colour is a light brown. As my gowns come to me through the years ahead, the colour will deepen to dark brown, then a dull mahogany and from that ultimately to that very dark sort of brownness one associates usually with stout.'

'Yes?'

'In a word the colour gradually deepens gown by gown and year by year until it appears to be black. Finally a day will come when the addition of one further gown will actually achieve real and full blackness. On that day I will die.'

Joe and I were surprised at this. We pondered it in silence, Joe, I thought, seeking to reconcile what he had heard with certain principles he held respecting morality and religion.

'That means,' I said at last, 'that if you get a number of these gowns and put them all on together, reckoning each as a year of life, you can ascertain the year of your death?'

'Theoretically, yes,' he replied, 'but there are two difficulties.

First of all the police refuse to let you have the gowns together on the ground that the general ascertainment of death-days would be contrary to the public interest. They talk of breaches of the peace and so forth. Secondly, there is a difficulty about stretching.'

'Stretching?'

'Yes. Since you will be wearing as a grown man the tiny gown that fitted you when you were born, it is clear that the gown has stretched until it is perhaps one hundred times as big as it was originally. Naturally this will affect the colour, making it many times rarer than it was. Similarly there will be a proportionate stretch and a corresponding diminution in colour in all the gowns up to manhood – perhaps twenty or so in all.'

I wonder whether it can be taken that this accretion of gowns will have become opaque at the incidence of puberty.

I reminded him that there was always an overcoat.

'I take it, then,' I said to old Mathers, 'that when you say you can tell the length of life, so to speak, from the colour of your shirt, you mean that you can tell roughly whether you will be long-lived or short-lived?'

'Yes,' he replied. 'But if you use your intelligence you can make a very accurate forecast. Naturally some colours are better than others. Some of them, like purple or maroon, are very bad and always mean an early grave. Pink, however, is excellent, and there is a lot to be said for certain shades of green and blue. The prevalence of such colours at birth, however, usually connote a wind that brings bad weather – thunder and lightning, perhaps – and there might be difficulties such, for instance, as getting a woman to come in time. As you know, most good things in life are associated with certain disadvantages.'

Really very beautiful, everything considered.

'Who are these policemen?' I asked.

'There is Sergeant Pluck and another man called Mac-Cruiskeen and there is a third man called Fox that disappeared twenty-five years ago and was never heard of after. The first two are down in the barracks and so far as I know they have been there for hundreds of years. They must be operating on a very rare colour, something that ordinary eyes could not see at all. There is no white wind that I know of. They all have the gift of seeing the winds.'

A bright thought came to me when I heard of these police-men. If they knew so much they would have no difficulty in telling me where I would find the black box. I began to think I would never be happy until I had that box again in my grip. I looked at old Mathers. He had relapsed again to his former passivity. The light had faded from his eyes and the right hand resting on the table looked quite dead.

'Is the barracks far?' I asked loudly.

'No.'

I made up my mind to go there with no delay. Then I noticed a very remarkable thing. The lamplight, which in the beginning had been shining forlornly in the old man's corner only, had now grown rich and yellow and flooded the entire room. The outside light of morning had faded away almost to nothingness. I glanced out of the window and gave a start. Coming into the room I had noticed that the window was to the east and that the sun was rising in that quarter and firing the heavy clouds with light. Now it was setting with last glimmers of feeble red in exactly the same place. It had risen a bit, stopped, and then gone back. Night had come. The policemen would be in bed. I was sure I had fallen among strange people. I made up my mind to go to the barracks the first thing on the morrow. Then I turned again to old Mathers.

'Would you object,' I said to him, 'if I went upstairs and occu-pied one of your beds for the night? It is too late to go home and I think it is going to rain in any case.'

'No,' he said.

I left him bent at his teaset and went up the stairs. I had got to like him and thought it was a pity he had been murdered. I felt relieved and simplified and certain that I would soon have the black box. But I would not ask the policemen openly about it at first. I would be crafty. In the morning I would go to the barracks and report the theft of my American gold watch. Perhaps it was this lie which was responsible for the bad things that happened to me afterwards. I had no American gold watch.

CHAPTER 3

I CREPT OUT of old Mathers' house nine hours afterwards, making my way on to the firm high-road under the first skies of morning. The dawn was contagious, spreading rapidly about the heavens. Birds were stirring and the great kingly trees were being pleasingly interfered with by the first breezes. My heart was happy and full of zest for high adventure. I did not know my name or where I had come from but the black box was practically in my grasp. The policemen would direct me to where it was. Ten thousand pounds' worth of negotiable securities would be a conservative estimate of what was in it. As I walked down the road I was pleased enough with everything.

The road was narrow, white, old, hard and scarred with shadow. It ran away westwards in the mist of the early morning, running cunningly through the little hills and going to some trouble to visit tiny towns which were not, strictly speaking, on its way. It was possibly one of the oldest roads in the world. I found it hard to think of a time when there was no road there because the trees and the tall hills and the fine views of bogland had been arranged by wise hands for the pleasing picture they made when looked at from the road. Without a road to have them looked at from they would have a somewhat aimless if not a futile aspect.

De Selby has some interesting things to say on the subject of roads.[1] Roads he regards as the most ancient of human monuments, surpassing by many tens of centuries the oldest thing of stone that man has reared to mark his passing. The tread of time, he says, levelling all else, has beaten only to a more enduring hardness the pathways that have been made throughout the world. He mentions in passing a trick the Celts had in ancient times – that of 'throwing a calculation' upon a road. In those days wise men could tell to a nicety the dimension of a host

1 *Golden Hours*, vi, 156.

which had passed by in the night by looking at their tracks with a certain eye and judging them by their perfection and imperfection, the way each footfall was interfered with by each that came after. In this way they could tell the number of men who had passed, whether they were with horse or heavy with shields and iron weapons, and how many chariots; thus they could say the number of men who should be sent after them to kill them. Elsewhere[2] de Selby makes the point that a good road will have character and a certain air of destiny, an indefinable intimation that it is going somewhere, be it east or west, and not coming back from there. If you go with such a road, he thinks, it will give you pleasant travelling, fine sights at every corner and a gentle ease of peregrination that will persuade you that you are walking forever on falling ground. But if you go east on a road that is on its way west, you will marvel at the unfailing bleakness of every prospect and the great number of sore-footed inclines that confront you to make you tired. If a friendly road should lead you into a complicated city with nets of crooked streets and five hundred other roads leaving it for unknown destinations, your own road will always be discernible for its own self and will lead you safely out of the tangled town.

I walked quietly for a good distance on this road, thinking my own thoughts with the front part of my brain and at the same time taking pleasure with the back part in the great and wide-spread finery of the morning. The air was keen, clear, abundant and intoxicating. Its powerful presence could be discerned everywhere, shaking up the green things jauntily, conferring greater dignity and definition on the stones and boulders, forever arranging and re-arranging the clouds and breathing life into the world. The sun had climbed steeply out of his hiding and was now standing benignly in the lower sky pouring down floods of enchanting light and preliminary tinglings of heat.

I came upon a stone stile beside a gate leading into a field and sat down to rest upon the top of it. I was not sitting there long until I became surprised; surprising ideas were coming into my head from nowhere. First of all I remembered who I was – not my name but where I had come from and who my friends were. I recalled John Divney, my life with him and how we came to

2 *A Memoir of Garcia*, p. 27.

wait under the dripping trees on the winter's evening. This led me to reflect in wonder that there was nothing wintry about the morning in which I was now sitting. Furthermore, there was nothing familiar about the good-looking countryside which stretched away from me at every view. I was now but two days from home – not more than three hours' walking – and yet I seemed to have reached regions which I had never seen before and of which I had never even heard. I could not understand this because although my life had been spent mostly among my books and papers, I had thought that there was no road in the district I had not travelled, no road whose destination was not well-known to me. There was another thing. My surroundings had a strangeness of a peculiar kind, entirely separate from the mere strangeness of a country where one has never been before. Everything seemed almost too pleasant, too perfect, too finely made. Each thing the eye could see was unmistakable and unambiguous, incapable of merging with any other thing or of being confused with it. The colour of the bogs was beautiful and the greenness of the green fields supernal. Trees were arranged here and there with far-from-usual consideration for the fastidious eye. The senses took keen pleasure from merely breathing the air and discharged their functions with delight. I was clearly in a strange country but all the doubts and perplexities which strewed my mind could not stop me from feeling happy and heart-light and full of an appetite for going about my business and finding the hiding-place of the black box. The valuable contents of it, I felt, would secure me for life in my own house and afterwards I could revisit this mysterious townland upon my bicycle and probe at my leisure the reasons for all its strangenesses. I got down from the stile and continued my walk along the road. It was pleasant easeful walking. I felt sure I was not going against the road. It was, so to speak, accompanying me.

Before going to sleep the previous night I had spent a long time in puzzled thought and also in carrying on inward conversations with my newly-found soul. Strangely enough, I was not thinking about the baffling fact that I was enjoying the hospitality of the man I had murdered (or whom I was sure I had murdered) with my spade. I was reflecting about my name and how tantalizing it was to have forgotten it. All people have names of one kind or another. Some are arbitrary labels related to the appearance of the person, some represent purely genealogical associations but most of them afford, some clue as to the parents of the person named and confer a certain advantage in the execution of legal documents.[3] Even a dog has a name which dissociates him from other dogs and indeed my own soul, whom nobody has ever seen on the road or standing at the counter of a public house, had apparently no difficulty in assuming a name which distinguished him from other people's souls.

A thing not easy to account for is the unconcern with which I turned over my various perplexities in my mind. Blank anonymity coming suddenly in the middle of life should be at best alarming, a sharp symptom that the mind is in decay. But the unexplainable exhilaration which I drew from my surroundings seemed to invest this situation merely with the genial interest of a good joke. Even now as I walked along contentedly I sensed a solemn question on this subject from within, one similar to many that had been asked the night before. It was a mocking inquiry. I light-heartedly gave a list of names which, for all I knew, I *might* hear:

Hugh Murray.

Constantin Petrie.

Peter Small.

Signor Beniamino Bari.

3 De Selby (*Golden Hours*, p. 93, *et seq.*) has put forward an interesting theory on names. Going back to primitive times, he regards the earliest names as crude onomatopaeic associations with the appearance of the person or object named – thus harsh or rough manifestations being represented by far from pleasant gutturalities and vice versa. This idea he pursued to rather fanciful lengths, drawing up elaborate paradigms of vowels and consonants purporting to correspond to certain indices of human race, colour and temperament and claiming ultimately to be in a position to state the physiological 'group' of any person merely from a brief study of the letters of his name after the word had been 'rationalized' to allow for variations of language. Certain 'groups' he showed to be universally 'repugnant' to other 'groups'. An unhappy commentary on the theory was furnished by the activities of his own nephew, whether through ignorance or contempt for the humanistic researches of his uncle. The nephew set about a Swedish servant, from whom he was completely excluded by the paradigms, in the pantry of a Portsmouth hotel to such purpose that de Selby had to open his purse to the tune of five or six hundred pounds to avert an unsavoury law case.

The Honourable Alex O'Brannigan, Bart.

Kurt Freund.

Mr John P. de Salis, M.A.

Dr Solway Garr.

Bonaparte Gosworth.

Legs O'Hagan.

Signor Beniamino Bari, Joe said, *the eminent tenor. Three baton-charges outside La Scala at great tenor's première. Extraordinary scenes were witnessed outside La Scala Opera House when a crowd of some ten thousand devotees, incensed by the management's statement that no more standing-room was available, attempted to rush the barriers. Thousands were injured, 79 fatally, in the wild mêlée. Constable Peter Coutts sustained injuries to the groin from which he is unlikely to recover. These scenes were comparable only to the delirium of the fashionable audience inside after Signor Bari had concluded his recital. The great tenor was in admirable voice. Starting with a phase in the lower register with a husky richness which seemed to suggest a cold, he delivered the immortal strains of Che Gelida Manina, favourite aria of the beloved Caruso. As he warmed to his God-like task, note after golden note spilled forth to the remotest corner of the vast theatre, thrilling all and sundry to the inner core. When he reached the high C where heaven and earth seem married in one great climax of exaltation, the audience arose in their seats and cheered as one man, showering hats, programmes and chocolate-boxes on the great artist.*

Thank you very much, I murmured, smiling in wild amusement.

A bit overdone, perhaps, but it is only a hint of the pretensions and vanity that you inwardly permit yourself.

Indeed?

Or what about Dr Solway Garr. The duchess has fainted. Is there a doctor in the audience? The spare figure, thin nervous fingers and iron-grey hair, making its way quietly through the pale excited onlookers. A few brief commands, quietly spoken but imperious. Inside five minutes the situation is well in hand. Wan but smiling, the duchess murmurs her thanks. Expert diagnosis has averted still another tragedy. A small denture has been extracted from the thorax. All hearts go out to the quiet-spoken servant of humanity. His Grace, summoned too late to see aught but the happy ending, is opening his cheque-book and has already marked a thousand guineas on the counterfoil as a small token of his esteem. His cheque is taken but torn to atoms by the smiling medico.

*A lady in blue at the back of the hall begins to sing O Peace Be Thine
and the anthem, growing in volume and sincerity, peals out into the quiet
night, leaving few eyes that are dry and hearts that are not replete with
yearning ere the last notes fade. Dr Garr only smiles, shaking his head
in deprecation.*

I think that is quite enough, I said.

I walked on unperturbed. The sun was maturing rapidly in the
east and a great heat had started to spread about the ground like
a magic influence, making everything, including my own self,
very beautiful and happy in a dreamy drowsy way. The little beds
of tender grass here and there by the roadside and the dry sheltery
ditches began to look seductive and inviting. The road was being
slowly baked to a greater hardness, making my walking more and
more laborious. After not long I decided that I must now be near
the police barracks and that another rest would fit me better for
the task I had on hand. I stopped walking and spread my body
out evenly in the shelter of the ditch. The day was brand new
and the ditch was feathery. I lay back unstintingly, stunned with
the sun. I felt a million little influences in my nostril, hay-smells,
grass-smells, odours from distant flowers, the reassuring unmis-
takability of the abiding earth beneath my head. It was a new and
a bright day, the day of the world. Birds piped without limitation
and incomparable stripe-coloured bees passed above me on their
missions and hardly ever came back the same way home. My eyes
were shuttered and my head was buzzing with the spinning of
the universe. I was not long lying there until my wits deserted
me and I fell far into my sleep. I slept there for a long time, as
motionless and as devoid of feeling as the shadow of myself which
slept behind me.

When I awoke again it was later in the day and a small man
was sitting beside me watching me. He was tricky and smoked a
tricky pipe and his hand was quavery. His eyes were tricky also,
probably from watching policemen. They were very unusual
eyes. There was no palpable divergence in their alignment but
they seemed to be incapable of giving a direct glance at anything
that was straight, whether or not their curious incompatibility
was suitable for looking at crooked things. I knew he was watching me only by the way his head was turned; I could not meet
his eyes or challenge them. He was small and poorly dressed and
on his head was a cloth cap of pale salmon colour. He kept his

head in my direction without speaking and I found his presence disquieting. I wondered how long he had been watching me before I awoke.

Watch your step here. A very slippery-looking customer.

I put my hand into my pocket to see if my wallet was there. It was, smooth and warm like the hand of a good friend. When I found that I had not been robbed, I decided to talk to him genially and civilly, see who he was and ask him to direct me to the barracks. I made up my mind not to despise the assistance of anybody who could help me, in however small a way, to find the black box. I gave him the time of day and, so far as I could, a look as intricate as any he could give himself.

'More luck to you,' I said.

'More power to yourself,' he answered dourly.

Ask him his name and occupation and inquire what is his destination.

'I do not desire to be inquisitive, sir,' I said, 'but would it be true to mention that you are a bird-catcher?'

'Not a bird-catcher,' he answered.

'A tinker?'

'Not that.'

'A man on a journey?'

'No, not that.'

'A fiddler?'

'Not that one.'

I smiled at him in good-humoured perplexity and said:

'Tricky-looking man, you are hard to place and it is not easy to guess your station. You seem very contented in one way but then again you do not seem to be satisfied. What is your objection to life?'

He blew little bags of smoke at me and looked at me closely from behind the bushes of hair which were growing about his eyes.

'Is it life?' he answered. 'I would rather be without it,' he said, 'for there is a queer small utility in it. You cannot eat it or drink it or smoke it in your pipe, it does not keep the rain out and it is a poor armful in the dark if you strip it and take it to bed with you after a night of porter when you are shivering with the red passion. It is a great mistake and a thing better done without, like bed-jars and foreign bacon.'

'That is a nice way to be talking on this grand lively day,'

I chided, 'when the sun is roaring in the sky and sending great
tidings into our weary bones.'

'Or like feather-beds,' he continued, 'or bread manufactured
with powerful steam machinery. Is it life you say? Life?'

*Explain the difficulty of life yet stressing its essential sweetness and
desirability.*

What sweetness?

*Flowers in the spring, the glory and fulfilment of human life, bird-
song at evening – you know very well what I mean.*

I am not so sure about the sweetness all the same.

'It is hard to get the right shape of it,' I said to the tricky man,
'or to define life at all, but if you identify life with enjoyment
I am told that there is a better brand of it in the cities than in the
country parts and there is said to be a very superior brand of it
to be had in certain parts of France. Did you ever notice that cats
have a lot of it in them when they are quite juveniles?'

He was looking in my direction crossly.

'Is it life? Many a man has spent a hundred years trying to
get the dimensions of it and when he understands it at last and
entertains the certain pattern of it in his head, by the hokey he
takes to his bed and dies! He dies like a poisoned sheepdog. There
is nothing so dangerous, you can't smoke it, nobody will give
you tuppence-halfpenny for the half of it and it kills you in the
wind-up. It is a queer contraption, very dangerous, a certain
death-trap. Life?'

He sat there looking very vexed with himself and stayed for a
while without talking behind a little grey wall he had built for
himself by means of his pipe. After an interval I made another
attempt to find out what his business was.

'Or a man out after rabbits?' I asked.

'Not that. Not that.'

'A travelling man with a job of journey-work?'

'No.'

'Driving a steam thrashing-mill?'

'Not for certain.'

'Tin-plates?'

'No.'

'A town clerk?'

'No.'

'A water-works inspector?'

'No.'

'With pills for sick horses?'

'Not with pills.'

'Then by Dad,' I remarked perplexedly, 'your calling is very unusual and I cannot think of what it is at all, unless you are a farmer like myself, or a publican's assistant or possibly something in the drapery line. Are you an actor or a mummer?'

'Not them either.'

He sat up suddenly and looked at me in a manner that was almost direct, his pipe sticking out aggressively from his tight jaws. He had the world full of smoke. I was uneasy but not altogether afraid of him. If I had my spade with me I knew I would soon make short work of him. I thought the wisest thing to do was to humour him and to agree with everything he said.

'I am a robber,' he said in a dark voice, 'a robber with a knife and an arm that's as strong as an article of powerful steam machinery.'

'A robber?' I exclaimed. My forebodings had been borne out. *Steady here. Take no chances.*

'As strong as the bright moving instruments in a laundry. A black murderer also. Every time I rob a man I knock him dead because I have no respect for life, not a little. If I kill enough men there will be more life to go round and maybe then I will be able to live till I am a thousand and not have the old rattle in my neck when I am quite seventy. Have you a money-bag with you?'

Plead poverty and destitution. Ask for the loan of money.

That will not be difficult, I answered.

'I have no money at all, or coins or sovereigns or bankers' drafts,' I replied, 'no pawn-masters' tickets, nothing that is negotiable or of any value. I am as poor a man as yourself and I was thinking of asking you for two shillings to help me on my way.'

I was now more nervous than I was before as I sat looking at him. He had put his pipe away and had produced a long farmer's knife. He was looking at the blade of it and flashing lights with it.

'Even if you have no money,' he cackled, 'I will take your little life.'

'Now look here till I tell you,' I rejoined in a stern voice, 'robbery and murder are against the law and furthermore my life would add little to your own because I have a disorder in my chest and I am sure to be dead in six months. As well as that, there was a question of a dark funeral in my teacup on Tuesday. Wait till you hear a cough.'

I forced out a great hacking cough. It travelled like a breeze across the grass near at hand. I was now thinking that it might be wise to jump up quickly and run away. It would at least be a simple remedy.

'There is another thing about me,' I added, 'part of me is made of wood and has no life in it at all.'

The tricky man gave out sharp cries of surprise, jumped up and gave me looks that were too tricky for description. I smiled at him and pulled up my left trouser-leg to show him my timber shin. He examined it closely and ran his hard finger along the edge of it. Then he sat down very quickly, put his knife away and took out his pipe again. It had been burning away all the time in his pocket because he started to smoke it without any delay and after a minute he had so much blue smoke made, and grey smoke, that I thought his clothes had gone on fire. Between the smoke I could see that he was giving friendly looks in my direction. After a few moments he spoke cordially and softly to me.

'I would not hurt you, little man,' he said.

'I think I got the disorder in Mullingar,' I explained. I knew that I had gained his confidence and that the danger of violence was now passed. He then did something which took me by surprise. He pulled up his own ragged trouser and showed me his own left leg. It was smooth, shapely and fairly fat but it was made of wood also.

'That is a funny coincidence,' I said. I now perceived the reason for his sudden change of attitude.

'You are a sweet man,' he responded, 'and I would not lay a finger on your personality. I am the captain of all the one-leggèd men in the country. I knew them all up to now except one – your own self – and that one is now also my friend into the same bargain. If any man looks at you sideways, I will rip his belly.'

'That is very friendly talk,' I said.

'Wide open,' he said, making a wide movement with his hands. 'If you are ever troubled, send for me and I will save you from the woman.'

'Women I have no interest in at all,' I said smiling. 'A fiddle is a better thing for diversion.'

'It does not matter. If your perplexity is an army or a dog, I will come with all the one-leggèd men and rip the bellies. My real name is Martin Finnucane.'

'It is a reasonable name,' I assented.

'Martin Finnucane,' he repeated, listening to his own voice as if he were listening to the sweetest music in the world. He lay back and filled himself up to the ears with dark smoke and when he was nearly bursting he let it out again and hid himself in it.

'Tell me this,' he said at last. 'Have you a desideratum?'

This queer question was unexpected but I answered it quickly enough. I said I had.

'What desideratum?'

'To find what I am looking for.'

'That is a handsome desideratum,' said Martin Finnucane. 'What way will you bring it about or mature its mutandum and bring it ultimately to passable factivity?'

'By visiting the police barracks,' I said, 'and asking the policemen to direct me to where it is. Maybe you might instruct me on how to get to the barrack from where we are now?'

'Maybe indeed,' said Mr Finnucane. 'Have you an ultimatum?'

'I have a secret ultimatum,' I replied.

'I am sure it is a fine ultimatum,' he said, 'but I will not ask you to recite it for me if you think it is a secret one.'

He had smoked away all his tobacco and was now smoking the pipe itself, judging by the surly smell of it. He put his hand into a pocket at his crotch and took out a round thing.

'Here is a sovereign for your good luck,' he said, 'the golden token of your golden destiny.'

I gave him, so to speak, my golden thank-you but I noticed that the coin he gave me was a bright penny. I put it carefully into my pocket as if it were highly prized and very valuable. I was pleased at the way I had handled this eccentric queerly-spoken brother of the wooden leg. Near the far side of the road was a small river. I stood up and looked at it and watched the white water. It tumbled in the stony bedstead and jumped in the air and hurried excitedly round a corner.

'The barracks are on this same road,' said Martin Finnucane, 'and I left it behind me a mile away this today morning. You will discover it at the place where the river runs away from the road.

If you look now you will see the fat trout in their brown coats coming back from the barracks at this hour because they go there every morning for the fine breakfast that is to be had from the slops and the throwings of the two policemen. But they have their dinners down the other way where a man called MacFeeterson has a bakery shop in a village of houses with their rears to the water. Three bread vans he has and a light dog-cart for the high mountain and he attends at Kilkishkeam on Mondays and Wednesdays.'

'Martin Finnucane,' I said, 'a hundred and two difficult thoughts I have to think between this and my destination and the sooner the better.'

He sent me up friendly glances from the smokey ditch.

'Good-looking man,' he said, 'good luck to your luck and do not entertain danger without sending me cognisance.'

I said 'Good-bye, Good-bye' and left him after a handshake. I looked back from down the road and saw nothing but the lip of the ditch with smoke coming from it as if tinkers were in the bottom of it cooking their what-they-had. Before I was gone I looked back again and saw the shape of his old head regarding me and closely studying my disappearance. He was amusing and interesting and had helped me by directing me to the barracks and telling me how far it was. And as I went upon my way I was slightly glad that I had met him.

A droll customer.

CHAPTER 4

OF ALL THE many striking statements made by de Selby, I do not think that any of them can rival his assertion that 'a journey is an hallucination'. The phrase may be found in the *Country Album*[1] cheek by jowl with the well-known treatise on 'tent-suits', those egregious canvas garments which he designed as a substitute alike for the hated houses and ordinary clothing. His theory, insofar as I can understand it, seems to discount the testimony of human experience and is at variance with everything I have learnt myself on many a country walk. Human existence de Selby has defined as 'a succession of static experiences each infinitely brief', a conception which he is thought to have arrived at from examining some old cinematograph films which belonged probably to his nephew.[2] From this premise he discounts the reality or truth of any progression or serialism in life, denies that time can pass as such in the accepted sense and attributes to hallucinations the commonly experienced sensation of progression as, for instance, in journeying from one place to another or even 'living'. If one is resting at A, he explains, and desires to rest in a distant place B, one can only do so by resting for infinitely brief intervals in innumerable intermediate places. Thus there is no difference essentially between what happens when one is resting at A before the start of the 'journey' and what happens when one is 'en route', i.e., resting in one or other of the intermediate places. He treats of these 'intermediate places' in a lengthy footnote. They are not, he warns us, to be taken as arbitrarily-determined points on the A–B axis so many inches or feet apart. They are rather to be regarded as points infinitely near each other yet sufficiently

1 Page 822.
2 These are evidently the same films which he mentions in *Golden Hours* (p. 155) as having 'a strong repetitive element' and as being 'tedious'. Apparently he had examined them patiently picture by picture and imagined that they would be screened in the same way, failing at that time to grasp the principle of the cinematograph.

far apart to admit of the insertion between them of a series of other 'inter-intermediate' places, between each of which must be imagined a chain of other resting-places – not, of course, strictly adjacent but arranged so as to admit of the application of this principle indefinitely. The illusion of progression he attributes to the inability of the human brain – 'as at present developed' – to appreciate the reality of these separate 'rests', preferring to group many millions of them together and calling the result motion, an entirely indefensible and impossible procedure since even two separate positions cannot obtain simultaneously of the same body. Thus motion is also an illusion. He mentions that almost any photograph is conclusive proof of his teachings.

Whatever about the soundness of de Selby's theories, there is ample evidence that they were honestly held and that several attempts were made to put them into practice. During his stay in England, he happened at one time to be living in Bath and found it necessary to go from there to Folkestone on pressing business.[3] His method of doing so was far from conventional. Instead of going to the railway station and inquiring about trains, he shut himself up in a room in his lodgings with a supply of picture postcards of the areas which would be traversed on such a journey, together with an elaborate arrangement of clocks and barometric instruments and a device for regulating the gaslight in conformity with the changing light of the outside day. What happened in the room or how precisely the clocks and other machines were manipulated will never be known. It seems that he emerged after a lapse of seven hours convinced that he was in Folkestone and possibly that he had evolved a formula for travellers which would be extremely distasteful to railway and shipping companies. There is no record of the extent of his disillusionment when he found himself still in the familiar surroundings of Bath but one authority[4] relates that he claimed without turning a hair to have been to Folkestone and back again. Reference is made to a man (unnamed) declaring to have actually seen the savant coming out of a Folkestone bank on the material date.

Like most of de Selby's theories, the ultimate outcome is

3 See Hatchjaw's *De Selby's Life and Times*.
4 Bassett: *Lux Mundi: A Memoir of de Selby*.

inconclusive. It is a curious enigma that so great a mind would question the most obvious realities and object even to things scientifically demonstrated (such as the sequence of day and night) while believing absolutely in his own fantastic explanations of the same phenomena.

Of my own journey to the police-barracks I need only say that it was no hallucination. The heat of the sun played incontrovertibly on every inch of me, the hardness of the road was uncompromising and the country changed slowly but surely as I made my way through it. To the left was brown bogland scarred with dark cuttings and strewn with rugged clumps of bushes, white streaks of boulder and here and there a distant house half-hiding in an assembly of little trees. Far beyond was another region sheltering in the haze, purple and mysterious. The right-hand side was a greener country with the small turbulent river accompanying the road at a respectful distance and on the other side of it hills of rocky pasture stretching away into the distance up and down. Tiny sheep could be discerned near the sky far away and crooked lanes ran hither and thither. There was no sign whatever of human life. It was still early morning, perhaps. If I had not lost my American gold watch it would be possible for me to tell the time.

You have no American gold watch.

Something strange then happened to me suddenly. The road before me was turning gently to the left and as I approached the bend my heart began to behave irregularly and an unaccountable excitement took complete possession of me. There was nothing to see and no change of any kind had come upon the scene to explain what was taking place within me. I continued walking with wild eyes.

As I came round the bend of the road an extraordinary spectacle was presented to me. About a hundred yards away on the left-hand side was a house which astonished me. It looked as if it were painted like an advertisement on a board on the roadside and indeed very poorly painted. It looked completely false and unconvincing. It did not seem to have any depth or breadth and looked as if it would not deceive a child. That was not in itself sufficient to surprise me because I had seen pictures and notices by the roadside before. What bewildered me was the sure knowledge deeply-rooted in my mind, that this was the house I was

searching for and that there were people inside it. I had no doubt
at all that it was the barracks of the policemen. I had never seen
with my eyes ever in my life before anything so unnatural and
appalling and my gaze faltered about the thing uncomprehendingly as if at least one of the customary dimensions was missing,
leaving no meaning in the remainder. The appearance of the
house was the greatest surprise I had encountered since I had
seen the old man in the chair and I felt afraid of it.

I kept on walking, but walked more slowly. As I approached,
the house seemed to change its appearance. At first, it did nothing to reconcile itself with the shape of an ordinary house but it
became uncertain in outline like a thing glimpsed under ruffled
water. Then it became clear again and I saw that it began to have
some back to it, some small space for rooms behind the frontage.
I gathered this from the fact that I seemed to see the front and
the back of the 'building' simultaneously from my position
approaching what should have been the side. As there was no
side that I could see I thought the house must be triangular with
its apex pointing towards me but when I was only fifteen yards
away I saw a small window apparently facing me and I knew
from that that there must be *some* side to it. Then I found myself
almost in the shadow of the structure, dry-throated and timorous
from wonder and anxiety. It seemed ordinary enough at close
quarters except that it was very white and still. It was momentous
and frightening; the whole morning and the whole world
seemed to have no purpose at all save to frame it and give it some
magnitude and position so that I could find it with my simple
senses and pretend to myself that I understood it. A constabulary
crest above the door told me that it was a police station. I had
never seen a police station like it.

I cannot say why I did not stop to think or why my nervousness
did not make me halt and sit down weakly by the roadside.
Instead I walked straight up to the door and looked in. I saw,
standing with his back to me, an enormous policeman. His back
appearance was unusual. He was standing behind a little counter
in a neat whitewashed day-room; his mouth was open and he
was looking into a mirror which hung upon the wall. Again,
I find it difficult to convey the precise reason why my eyes found
his shape unprecedented and unfamiliar. He was very big and fat
and the hair which strayed abundantly about the back of his

bulging neck was a pale straw-colour; all that was striking but not unheard of. My glance ran over his great back, the thick arms and legs encased in the rough blue uniform. Ordinary enough as each part of him looked by itself, they all seemed to create together, by some undetectable discrepancy in association or proportion, a very disquieting impression of unnaturalness, amounting almost to what was horrible and monstrous. His hands were red, swollen and enormous and he appeared to have one of them half-way into his mouth as he gazed into the mirror.

'It's my teeth,' I heard him say, abstractedly and half-aloud. His voice was heavy and slightly muffled, reminding me of a thick winter quilt. I must have made some sound at the door or possibly he had seen my reflection in the glass for he turned slowly round, shifting his stance with leisurely and heavy majesty, his fingers still working at his teeth; and as he turned I heard him murmuring to himself:

'Nearly every sickness is from the teeth.'

His face gave me one more surprise. It was enormously fat, red and widespread, sitting squarely on the neck of his tunic with a clumsy weightiness that reminded me of a sack of flour. The lower half of it was hidden by a violent red moustache which shot out from his skin far into the air like the antennae of some unusual animal. His cheeks were red and chubby and his eyes were nearly invisible, hidden from above by the obstruction of his tufted brows and from below by the fat foldings of his skin. He came over ponderously to the inside of the counter and I advanced meekly from the door until we were face to face.

'Is it about a bicycle?' he asked.

His expression when I encountered it was unexpectedly reassuring. His face was gross and far from beautiful but he had modified and assembled his various unpleasant features in some skilful way so that they expressed to me good nature, politeness and infinite patience. In the front of his peaked official cap was an important-looking badge and over it in golden letters was the word SERGEANT. It was Sergeant Pluck himself.

'No,' I answered, stretching forth my hand to lean with it against the counter. The Sergeant looked at me incredulously.

'Are you sure?' he asked.

'Certain.'

'Not about a motor-cycle?'

'No.'

'One with overhead valves and a dynamo for light? Or with racing handle-bars?'

'No.'

'In that circumstantial eventuality there can be no question of a motor-bicycle,' he said. He looked surprised and puzzled and leaned sideways on the counter on the prop of his left elbow, putting the knuckles of his right hand between his yellow teeth and raising three enormous wrinkles of perplexity on his forehead. I decided now that he was a simple man and that I would have no difficulty in dealing with him exactly as I desired and finding out from him what had happened to the black box. I did not understand clearly the reason for his questions about bicycles but I made up my mind to answer everything carefully, to bide my time and to be cunning in all my dealings with him. He moved away abstractedly, came back and handed me a bundle of differently-coloured papers which looked like application forms for bull-licences and dog-licences and the like.

'It would be no harm if you filled up these forms,' he said. 'Tell me,' he continued, 'would it be true that you are an itinerant dentist and that you came on a tricycle?'

'It would not,' I replied.

'On a patent tandem?'

'No.'

'Dentists are an unpredictable coterie of people,' he said. 'Do you tell me it was a velocipede or a penny-farthing?'

'I do not,' I said evenly. He gave me a long searching look as if to see whether I was serious in what I was saying, again wrinkling up his brow.

'Then maybe you are no dentist at all,' he said, 'but only a man after a dog-licence or papers for a bull?'

'I did not say I was a dentist,' I said sharply, 'and I did not say anything about a bull.'

The Sergeant looked at me incredulously.

'That is a great curiosity,' he said, 'a very difficult piece of puzzledom, a snorter.'

He sat down by the turf fire and began jawing his knuckles and giving me sharp glances from under his bushy brows. If I had horns upon my head or a tail behind me he could not have looked at me with more interest. I was unwilling to give any lead to the direction of the talk and there was complete silence for five minutes. Then his expression eased a bit and he spoke to me again.

'What is your pronoun?' he inquired.

'I have no pronoun,' I answered, hoping I knew his meaning.

'What is your cog?'

'My cog?'

'Your surnoun?'

'I have not got that either.'

My reply again surprised him and also seemed to please him. He raised his thick eyebrows and changed his face into what could be described as a smile. He came back to the counter, put out his enormous hand, took mine in it and shook it warmly.

'No name or no idea of your originality at all?'

'None.'

'Well, by the holy Hokey!'

Signor Bari, the eminent one-leggèd tenor!

'By the holy Irish-American Powers,' he said again, 'by the Dad! Well carry me back to old Kentucky!'

He then retreated from the counter to his chair by the fire and sat silently bent in thought as if examining one by one the by-gone years stored up in his memory.

'I was once acquainted with a tall man,' he said to me at last, 'that had no name either and you are certain to be his son and the heir to his nullity and all his nothings. What way is your pop today and where is he?'

It was not, I thought, entirely unreasonable that the son of a man who had no name should have no name also but it was clear that the Sergeant was confusing me with somebody else. This was no harm and I decided to encourage him. I considered it desirable that he should know nothing about me but it was even better if he knew several things which were quite wrong. It would help me in using him for my own purposes and ultimately in finding the black box.

'He is gone to America,' I replied.

'Is that where,' said the Sergeant. 'Do you tell me that? He was a true family husband. The last time I interviewed him it was about a missing pump and he had a wife and ten sonnies and at that time he had the wife again in a very advanced state of sexuality.'

'That was me,' I said, smiling.

'That was you,' he agreed. 'What way are the ten strong sons?'

'All gone to America.'

'That is a great conundrum of a country,' said the Sergeant, 'a very wide territory, a place occupied by black men and strangers. I am told they are very fond of shooting-matches in that quarter.'

'It is a queer land,' I said.

At this stage there were footsteps at the door and in marched a heavy policeman carrying a small constabulary lamp. He had a dark Jewish face and hooky nose and masses of black curly hair. He was blue-jowled and black-jowled and looked as if he shaved twice a day. He had white enamelled teeth which came, I had no doubt, from Manchester, two rows of them arranged in the interior of his mouth and when he smiled it was a fine sight to see, like delph on a neat country dresser. He was heavy-fleshed and gross in body like the Sergeant but his face looked far more intelligent. It was unexpectedly lean and the eyes in it were penetrating and observant. If his face alone were in question he would look more like a poet than a policeman but the rest of his body looked anything but poetical.

'Policeman MacCruiskeen,' said Sergeant Pluck.

Policeman MacCruiskeen put the lamp on the table, shook hands with me and gave me the time of day with great gravity. His voice was high, almost feminine, and he spoke with a delicate careful intonation. Then he put the little lamp on the counter and surveyed the two of us.

'Is it about a bicycle?' he asked.

'Not that,' said the Sergeant. 'This is a private visitor who says he did not arrive in the townland upon a bicycle. He has no personal name at all. His dadda is in far Amurikey.'

'Which of the two Amurikeys?' asked MacCruiskeen.

'The Unified Stations,' said the Sergeant.

'Likely he is rich by now if he is in that quarter,' said Mac-Cruiskeen, 'because there's dollars there, dollars and bucks and nuggets in the ground and any amount of rackets and golf games and musical instruments. It is a free country too by all accounts.'

'Free for all,' said the Sergeant. 'Tell me this,' he said to the policeman, 'did you take any readings today?'

'I did,' said MacCruiskeen.

'Take out your black book and tell me what it was, like a good man,' said the Sergeant. 'Give me the gist of it till I see what I see,' he added.

MacCruiskeen fished a small black notebook from his breast pocket.

'Ten point six,' he said.

'Ten point six,' said the Sergeant. 'And what reading did you notice on the beam?'

'Seven point four.'

'How much on the lever?'

'One point five.'

There was a pause here. The Sergeant put on an expression of great intricacy as if he were doing far-from-simple sums and calculations in his head. After a time his face cleared and he spoke again to his companion.

'Was there a fall?'

'A heavy fall at half-past three.'

'Very understandable and commendably satisfactory;' said the Sergeant. 'Your supper is on the hob inside and be sure to stir the milk before you take any of it, the way the rest of us after you will have our share of the fats of it, the health and the heart of it.'

Policeman MacCruiskeen smiled at the mention of food and went into the back room loosening his belt as he went; after a moment we heard the sounds of coarse slobbering as if he was eating porridge without the assistance of spoon or hand. The Sergeant invited me to sit at the fire in his company and gave me a wrinkled cigarette from his pocket.

'It is lucky for your pop that he is situated in Amurikey,' he remarked, 'if it is a thing that he is having trouble with the old teeth. It is very few sicknesses that are not from the teeth.'

'Yes,' I said. I was determined to say as little as possible and let these unusual policemen first show their hand. Then I would know how to deal with them.

'Because a man can have more disease and germination in his gob than you'll find in a rat's coat and Amurikey is a country where the population do have grand teeth like shaving-lather or like bits of delph when you break a plate.'

'Quite true,' I said.

'Or like eggs under a black crow.'

'Like eggs,' I said.

'Did you ever happen to visit the cinematograph in your travels?'

'Never,' I answered humbly, 'but I believe it is a dark quarter and little can be seen at all except the photographs on the wall.'

'Well it is there you see the fine teeth they do have in Amurikey,' said the Sergeant.

He gave the fire a hard look and took to handling absently his yellow stumps of teeth. I had been wondering about his mysterious conversation with MacCruiskeen.

'Tell me this much,' I ventured. 'What sort of readings were those in the policeman's black book?'

The Sergeant gave me a keen look which felt almost hot from being on the fire previously.

'The first beginnings of wisdom,' he said, 'is to ask questions but never to answer any. *You* get wisdom from asking and *I* from not answering. Would you believe that there is a great increase in crime in this locality? Last year we had sixty-nine cases of no lights and four stolen. This year we have eighty-two cases of no lights, thirteen cases of riding on the footpath and four stolen. There was one case of wanton damage to a three-speed gear, there is sure to be a claim at the next Court and the area of charge will be the parish. Before the year is out there is certain to be a pump stolen, a very depraved and despicable manifestation of criminality and a blot on the county.'

'Indeed,' I said.

'Five years ago we had a case of loose handlebars. Now there is a rarity for you. It took the three of us a week to frame the charge.'

'Loose handlebars,' I muttered. I could not clearly see the reason for such talk about bicycles.

'And then there is the question of bad brakes. The country is honeycombed with bad brakes, half of the accidents are due to it, runs in families.'

I thought it would be better to try to change the conversation from bicycles.

'You told me what the first rule of wisdom is,' I said. 'What is the second rule?'

'That can be answered,' he said. 'There are five in all. Always ask any questions that are to be asked and never answer any. Turn everything you hear to your own advantage. Always carry a repair outfit. Take left turns as much as possible. Never apply your front brake first.'

'These are interesting rules,' I said dryly.

'If you follow them,' said the Sergeant, 'you will save your soul and you will never get a fall on a slippy road.'

'I would be obliged to you,' I said, 'if you would explain to me which of these rules covers the difficulty I have come here today to put before you.'

'This is not today, this is yesterday,' he said, 'but which of the difficulties is it? What is the *crux rei*?'

Yesterday? I decided without any hesitation that it was a waste of time trying to understand the half of what he said. I persevered with my inquiry.

'I came here to inform you officially about the theft of my American gold watch.'

He looked at me through an atmosphere of great surprise and incredulity and raised his eyebrows almost to his hair.

'That is an astonishing statement,' he said at last.

'Why?'

'Why should anybody steal a watch when they can steal a bicycle?'

Hark to his cold inexorable logic.

'Search me,' I said.

'Who ever heard of a man riding a watch down the road or bringing a sack of turf up to his house on the crossbar of a watch?'

'I did not say the thief wanted my watch to ride it,' I expostulated. 'Very likely he had a bicycle of his own and that is how he got away quietly in the middle of the night.'

'Never in my puff did I hear of any man stealing anything but a bicycle when he was in his sane senses,' said the Sergeant, '– except pumps and clips and lamps and the like of that. Surely you are not going to tell me at my time of life that the world is changing?'

'I am only saying that my watch was stolen,' I said crossly.

'Very well,' the Sergeant said with finality, 'we will have to institute a search.'

He smiled brightly at me. It was quite clear that he did not believe any part of my story, and that he thought I was in delicate mental health. He was humouring me as if I were a child.

'Thank you,' I muttered.

'But the trouble will only be beginning when we find it,' he said severely.

'How is that?'

'When we find it we will have to start searching for the owner.'

'But I am the owner.'

Here the Sergeant laughed indulgently and shook his head.

'I know what you mean,' he said. 'But the law is an extremely intricate phenomenon. If you have no name you cannot own a watch and the watch that has been stolen does not exist and when it is found it will have to be restored to its rightful owner. If you have no name you possess nothing and you do not exist and even your trousers are not on you although they look as if they were from where I am sitting. On the other separate hand you can do what you like and the law cannot touch you.'

'It had fifteen jewels,' I said despairingly.

'And on the first hand again you might be charged with theft or common larceny if you were mistaken for somebody else when wearing the watch.'

'I feel extremely puzzled,' I said, speaking nothing less than the truth. The Sergeant gave his laugh of good humour.

'If we ever find the watch,' he smiled, 'I have a feeling that there will be a bell and a pump on it.'

I considered my position with some misgiving. It seemed to be impossible to make the Sergeant take cognisance of anything in the world except bicycles. I thought I would make a last effort.

'You appear to be under the impression,' I said coldly and courteously, 'that I have lost a golden bicycle of American manufacture with fifteen jewels. I have lost a watch and there is no bell on it. Bells are only on alarm clocks and I have never in my life seen a watch with a pump attached to it.'

The Sergeant smiled at me again.

'There was a man in this room a fortnight ago,' he said, 'telling me that he was at the loss of his mother, a lady of eighty-two. When I asked him for a description – just to fill up the blanks in the official form we get for half-nothing from the Stationery Office – he said she had rust on her rims and that her back brakes were subject to the jerks.'

This speech made my position quite clear to me. When I was about to say something else, a man put his face in and looked at us and then came in completely and shut the door carefully and came over to the counter. He was a bluff red man in a burly coat with twine binding his trousers at the knees. I discovered afterwards that his name was Michael Gilhaney. Instead of standing at the counter as he would in a public house, he went to the wall, put his arms akimbo and leaned against it, balancing his weight on the point of one elbow.

'Well, Michael,' said the Sergeant pleasantly.

'That is a cold one,' said Mr Gilhaney.

Sounds of shouting came to the three of us from the inner room where Policeman MacCruiskeen was engaged in the task of his early dinner.

'Hand me in a fag,' he called.

The Sergeant gave me another wrinkled cigarette from his pocket and jerked his thumb in the direction of the back room. As I went in with the cigarette I heard the Sergeant opening an enormous ledger and putting questions to the red-faced visitor.

'What was the make,' he was saying, 'and the number of the frame and was there a lamp and a pump on it into the same bargain?'

CHAPTER 5

THE LONG and unprecedented conversation I had with Policeman MacCruiskeen after I went in to him on my mission with
the cigarette brought to my mind afterwards several of the more
delicate speculations of de Selby, notably his investigation of
the nature of time and eternity by a system of mirrors.[1] His
theory as I understand it is as follows:

If a man stands before a mirror and sees in it his reflection,
what he sees is not a true reproduction of himself but a picture
of himself when he was a younger man. De Selby's explanation
of this phenomenon is quite simple. Light, as he points out truly
enough, has an ascertained and finite rate of travel. Hence before
the reflection of any object in a mirror can be said to be accomplished, it is necessary that rays of light should first strike the
object and subsequently impinge on the glass, to be thrown back
again to the object – to the eyes of a man, for instance. There is
therefore an appreciable and calculable interval of time between
the throwing by a man of a glance at his own face in a mirror
and the registration of the reflected image in his eye.

So far, one may say, so good. Whether this idea is right or

---

1 Hatchjaw remarks (unconfirmed, however, by Bassett) that throughout
the whole ten years that went to the writing of the *Country Album* de Selby
was obsessed with mirrors and had recourse to them so frequently that he
claimed to have two left hands and to be living in a world arbitrarily
bounded by a wooden frame. As time went on he refused to countenance
a direct view of anything and had a small mirror permanently at a certain
angle in front of his eyes by a wired mechanism of his own manufacture.
After he had resorted to this fantastic arrangement, he interviewed visitors
with his back to them and with his head inclined towards the ceiling; he
was even credited with long walks backwards in crowded thoroughfares.
Hatchjaw claims that his statement is supported by the MS. of some three
hundred pages of the *Album*, written backwards, 'a circumstance that made
necessary the extension of the mirror principle to the bench of the wretched
printer'. (*De Selby's Life and Times*, p. 221.) This manuscript cannot now
be found.

wrong, the amount of time involved is so negligible that few reasonable people would argue the point. But de Selby, ever loath to leave well enough alone, insists on reflecting the first reflection in a further mirror and professing to detect minute changes in this second image. Ultimately he constructed the familiar arrangement of parallel mirrors, each reflecting diminishing images of an interposed object indefinitely. The interposed object in this case was de Selby's own face and this he claims to have studied backwards through an infinity of reflections by means of 'a powerful glass'. What he states to have seen through his glass is astonishing. He claims to have noticed a growing youthfulness in the reflections of his face according as they receded, the most distant of them – too tiny to be visible to the naked eye – being the face of a beardless boy of twelve, and, to use his own words, 'a countenance of singular beauty and nobility'. He did not succeed in pursuing the matter back to the cradle 'owing to the curvature of the earth and the limitations of the telescope'.

So much for de Selby. I found MacCruiskeen with a red face at the kitchen table panting quietly from all the food he had hidden in his belly. In exchange for the cigarette he gave me searching looks. 'Well, now,' he said.

He lit the cigarette and sucked at it and smiled covertly at me.

'Well, now,' he said again. He had his little lamp beside him on the table and he played his fingers on it.

'That is a fine day,' I said. 'What are you doing with a lamp in the white morning?'

'I can give you a question as good as that,' he responded. 'Can you notify me of the meaning of a bulbul?'

'A bulbul?'

'What would you say a bulbul is?'

This conundrum did not interest me but I pretended to rack my brains and screwed my face in perplexity until I felt it half the size it should be.

'Not one of those ladies who take money?' I said.

'No.'

'Not the brass knobs on a German steam organ?'

'Not the knobs.'

'Nothing to do with the independence of America or suchlike?'

'No.'

'A mechanical engine for winding clocks?'

'No.'

'A tumour, or the lather in a cow's mouth, or those elastic articles that ladies wear?'

'Not them by a long chalk.'

'Not an eastern musical instrument played by Arabs?'

He clapped his hands.

'Not that but very near it,' he smiled, 'something next door to it. You are a cordial intelligible man. A bulbul is a Persian nightingale. What do you think of that now?'

'It is seldom I am far out,' I said dryly.

He looked at me in admiration and the two of us sat in silence for a while as if each was very pleased with himself and with the other and had good reason to be.

'You are a B.A. with little doubt?' he questioned.

I gave no direct answer but tried to look big and learned and far from simple in my little chair.

'I think you are a sempiternal man,' he said slowly.

He sat for a while giving the floor a strict examination and then put his dark jaw over to me and began questioning me about my arrival in the parish.

'I do not want to be insidious,' he said, 'but would you inform me about your arrival in the parish? Surely you had a three-speed gear for the hills?'

'I had no three-speed gear,' I responded rather sharply, 'and no two-speed gear and it is also true that I had no bicycle and little or no pump and if I had a lamp itself it would not be necessary if I had no bicycle and there would be no bracket to hang it on.'

'That may be,' said MacCruiskeen, 'but likely you were laughed at on the tricycle?'

'I had neither bicycle nor tricycle and I am not a dentist,' I said with severe categorical thoroughness, 'and I do not believe in the penny-farthing or the scooter, the velocipede or the tandem-tourer.'

MacCruiskeen got white and shaky and gripped my arm and looked at me intensely.

'In my natural puff,' he said at last, in a strained voice, 'I have never encountered a more fantastic epilogue or a queerer story. Surely you are a queer far-fetched man. To my dying night I will not forget this today morning. Do not tell me that you are taking a hand at me?'

'No,' I said.

'Well Great Crikes!'

He got up and brushed his hair with a flat hand back along his skull and looked out of the window for a long interval, his eyes popping and dancing and his face like an empty bag with no blood in it.

Then he walked around to put back the circulation and took a little spear from a place he had on the shelf.

'Put your hand out,' he said.

I put it out idly enough and he held the spear at it. He kept putting it near me and nearer and when he had the bright point of it about half a foot away, I felt a prick and gave a short cry. There was a little bead of my red blood in the middle of my palm.

'Thank you very much,' I said. I felt too surprised to be annoyed with him.

'That will make you think,' he remarked in triumph, 'unless I am an old Dutchman by profession and nationality.'

He put his little spear back on the shelf and looked at me crookedly from a sidewise angle with a certain quantity of what may be called *roi-s'amuse*.

'Maybe you can explain that?' he said.

'That is the limit,' I said wonderingly.

'It will take some analysis,' he said, 'intellectually.'

'Why did your spear sting when the point was half a foot away from where it made me bleed?'

'That spear,' he answered quietly, 'is one of the first things I ever manufactured in my spare time. I think only a little of it now but the year I made it I was proud enough and would not get up in the morning for any sergeant. There is no other spear like it in the length and breadth of Ireland and there is only one thing like it in Amurikey but I have not heard what it is. But I cannot get over the no-bicycle. Great Crikes!'

'But the spear,' I insisted, 'give me the gist of it like a good man and I will tell no one.'

'I will tell you because you are a confidential man,' he said, 'and a man that said something about bicycles that I never heard before. What you think is the point is not the point at all but only the beginning of the sharpness.'

'Very wonderful,' I said, 'but I do not understand you.'

'The point is seven inches long and it is so sharp and thin that you cannot see it with the old eye. The first half of the sharpness is thick and strong but you cannot see it either because the real sharpness runs into it and if you saw the one you could see the other or maybe you would notice the joint.'

'I suppose it is far thinner than a match?' I asked.

'There is a difference,' he said. 'Now the proper sharp part is so thin that nobody could see it no matter what light is on it or what eye is looking. About an inch from the end it is so sharp that sometimes – late at night or on a soft bad day especially – you cannot think of it or try to make it the subject of a little idea because you will hurt your box with the excruciation of it.'

I gave a frown and tried to make myself look like a wise person who was trying to comprehend something that called for all his wisdom.

'You cannot have fire without bricks,' I said, nodding.

'Wisely said,' MacCruiskeen answered.

'It was sharp sure enough,' I conceded, 'it drew a little bulb of the red blood but I did not feel the pricking hardly at all. It must be very sharp to work like that.'

MacCruiskeen gave a laugh and sat down again at the table and started putting on his belt.

'You have not got the whole gist of it at all,' he smiled. 'Because what gave you the prick and brought the blood was not the point at all; it was the place I am talking about that is a good inch from the reputed point of the article under our discussion.'

'And what is this inch that is left?' I asked. 'What in heaven's name would you call that?'

'That is the real point,' said MacCruiskeen, 'but it is so thin that it could go into your hand and out in the other extremity externally and you would not feel a bit of it and you would see nothing and hear nothing. It is so thin that maybe it does not exist at all and you could spend half an hour trying to think about it and you could put no thought around it in the end. The beginning part of the inch is thicker than the last part and is nearly there for a fact but I don't think it is if it is my private opinion that you are anxious to enlist.'

I fastened my fingers around my jaw and started to think with great concentration, calling into play parts of my brain that

I rarely used. Nevertheless I made no progress at all as regards the question of the points. MacCruiskeen had been at the dresser a second time and was back at the table with a little black article like a leprechaun's piano with diminutive keys of white and black and brass pipes and circular revolving cogs like parts of a steam engine or the business end of a thrashing-mill. His white hands were moving all over it and feeling it as if they were trying to discover some tiny lump on it, and his face was looking up in the air in a spiritual attitude and he was paying no attention to my personal existence at all. There was an overpowering tremendous silence as if the roof of the room had come down half-way to the floor, he at his queer occupation with the instrument and myself still trying to comprehend the sharpness of the points and to get the accurate understanding of them.

After ten minutes he got up and put the thing away. He wrote for a time in his notebook and then lit his pipe.

'Well now,' he remarked expansively.

'Those points,' I said.

'Did I happen to ask you what a bulbul is?'

'You did,' I responded, 'but the question of those points is what takes me to the fair.'

'It is not today or yesterday I started pointing spears,' he said, 'but maybe you would like to see something else that is a medium fair example of supreme art?'

'I would indeed,' I answered.

'But I cannot get over what you confided in me privately *sub-rosa* about the no-bicycle, that is a story that would make your golden fortune if you wrote down in a book where people could pursue it literally.'

He walked back to the dresser, opened the lower part of it, and took out a little chest till he put it on the table for my inspection. Never in my life did I inspect anything more ornamental and well-made. It was a brown chest like those owned by seafaring men or lascars from Singapore, but it was diminutive in a very perfect way as if you were looking at a full-size one through the wrong end of a spy-glass. It was about a foot in height, perfect in its proportions and without fault in workmanship. There were indents and carving and fanciful excoriations and designs on every side of it and there was a bend on the lid that gave the article great distinction. At every corner there was a shiny brass

corner-piece and on the lid there were brass corner-pieces beautifully wrought and curved impeccably against the wood. The
whole thing had the dignity and the satisfying quality of true art.

'There now,' said MacCruiskeen.

'It is nearly too nice,' I said at last, 'to talk about it.'

'I spent two years manufacturing it when I was a lad,' said
MacCruiskeen, 'and it still takes me to the fair.'

'It is unmentionable,' I said.

'Very nearly,' said MacCruiskeen.

The two of us then started looking at it and we looked at it
for five minutes so hard that it seemed to dance on the table and
look even smaller than it might be.

'I do not often look at boxes or chests,' I said, simply, 'but
this is the most beautiful box I have ever seen and I will always
remember it. There might be something inside it?'

'There might be,' said MacCruiskeen.

He went to the table and put his hands around the article in a
fawning way as if he were caressing a sheepdog and he opened
the lid with a little key but shut it down again before I could
inspect the inside of it.

'I will tell you a story and give you a synopsis of the ramification of the little plot,' he said. 'When I had the chest made and
finished, I tried to think what I would keep in it and what I would
use it for at all. First I thought of them letters from Bridie, the
ones on the blue paper with the strong smell but I did not think
it would be anything but a sacrilege in the end because there was
hot bits in them letters. Do you comprehend the trend of my
observations?'

'I do,' I answered.

'Then there was my studs and the enamel badge and my presentation iron-pencil with a screw on the end of it to push the
point out, an intricate article full of machinery and a Present
from Southport. All these things are what are called Examples of
the Machine Age.'

'They would be contrary to the spirit of the chest,' I said.

'They would be indeed. Then there was my razor and the
spare plate in case I was presented with an accidental bash on the
gob in the execution of me duty . . .'

'But not them.'

'Not them. Then there was my certificates and me cash and

the picture of Peter the Hermit and the brass thing with straps that I found on the road one night near Matthew O'Carahan's. But not them either.'

'It is a hard conundrum,' I said.

'In the end I found there was only one thing to do to put myself right with my private conscience.'

'It is a great thing that you found the right answer at all,' I countered.

'I decided to myself,' said MacCruiskeen, 'that the only sole correct thing to contain in the chest was another chest of the same make but littler in cubic dimension.'

'That was very competent masterwork,' I said, endeavouring to speak his own language.

He went to the little chest and opened it up again and put his hands down sideways like flat plates or like the fins on a fish and took out of it a smaller chest but one resembling its mother-chest in every particular of appearance and dimension. It almost interfered with my breathing, it was so delightfully unmistakable. I went over and felt it and covered it with my hand to see how big its smallness was. Its brasswork had a shine like the sun on the sea and the colour of the wood was a rich deep richness like a colour deepened and toned only by the years. I got slightly weak from looking at it and sat down on a chair and for the purpose of pretending that I was not disturbed I whistled *The Old Man Twangs His Braces*.

MacCruiskeen gave me a smooth inhuman smile.

'You may have come on no bicycle,' he said, 'but that does not say that you know everything.'

'Those chests,' I said, 'are so like one another that I do not believe they are there at all because that is a simpler thing to believe than the contrary. Nevertheless the two of them are the most wonderful two things I have ever seen.'

'I was two years manufacturing it,' MacCruiskeen said.

'What is in the little one?' I asked.

'What would you think now?'

'I am completely half afraid to think,' I said, speaking truly enough.

'Wait now till I show you,' said MacCruiskeen, 'and give you an exhibition and a personal inspection individually.'

He got two thin butter-spades from the shelf and put them

down into the little chest and pulled out something that seemed to me remarkably like another chest. I went over to it and gave it a close examination with my hand, feeling the same identical wrinkles, the same proportions and the same completely perfect brasswork on a smaller scale. It was so faultless and delightful that it reminded me forcibly, strange and foolish as it may seem, of something I did not understand and had never even heard of.

'Say nothing,' I said quickly to MacCruiskeen, 'but go ahead with what you are doing and I will watch here and I will take care to be sitting down.'

He gave me a nod in exchange for my remark and got two straight-handled teaspoons and put the handles into his last chest. What came out may well be guessed at. He opened this one and took another one out with the assistance of two knives. He worked knives, small knives and smaller knives, till he had twelve little chests on the table, the last of them an article half the size of a matchbox. It was so tiny that you would not quite see the brasswork at all only for the glitter of it in the light. I did not see whether it had the same identical carvings upon it because I was content to take a swift look at it and then turn away. But I knew in my soul that it was exactly the same as the others. I said no word at all because my mind was brimming with wonder at the skill of the policeman.

'That last one,' said MacCruiskeen, putting away the knives, 'took me three years to make and it took me another year to believe that I had made it. Have you got the convenience of a pin?'

I gave him my pin in silence. He opened the smallest of them all with a key like a piece of hair and worked with the pin till he had another little chest on the table, thirteen in all arranged in a row upon the table. Queerly enough they looked to me as if they were all the same size but invested with some crazy perspective. This idea surprised me so much that I got my voice back and said:

'These are the most surprising thirteen things I have ever seen together.'

'Wait now, man,' MacCruiskeen said.

All my senses were now strained so tensely watching the policeman's movements that I could almost hear my brain rattling in my head when I gave a shake as if it was drying up into a wrinkled pea. He was manipulating and prodding with his pin till he had twenty-eight little chests on the table and the last of them so small that it looked like a bug or a tiny piece of dirt except that there was a glitter from it. When I looked at it again I saw another thing beside it like something you would take out of a red eye on a windy dry day and I knew then that the strict computation was then twenty-nine.

'Here is your pin,' said MacCruiskeen.

He put it into my stupid hand and went back to the table thoughtfully. He took a something from his pocket that was too small for me to see and started working with the tiny black thing on the table beside the bigger thing which was itself too small to be described.

At this point I became afraid. What he was doing was no longer wonderful but terrible. I shut my eyes and prayed that he would stop while still doing things that were at least possible for a man to do. When I looked again I was happy that there was nothing to see and that he had put no more of the chests prominently on the table but he was working to the left with the invisible thing in his hand on a bit of the table itself. When he felt my look he came over to me and gave me an enormous magnifying-glass which looked like a basin fixed to a handle. I felt the muscles around my heart tightening painfully as I took the instrument.

'Come over here to the table,' he said, 'and look there till you see what you see infra-ocularly.'

When I saw the table it was bare only for the twenty-nine chest articles but through the agency of the glass I was in a position to report that he had two more out beside the last ones, the smallest of all being nearly half a size smaller than ordinary invisibility. I gave him back the glass instrument and took to the chair without a word. In order to reassure myself and make a loud human noise I whistled *The Corncrake Plays the Bagpipes*.

'There now,' said MacCruiskeen.

He took two wrinkled cigarettes from his fob and lit the two at the same time and handed me one of them.

'Number Twenty-Two,' he said, 'I manufactured fifteen years ago and I have made another different one every year since with any amount of nightwork and overtime and piecework and time-and-a-half incidentally.'

'I understand you clearly,' I said.

'Six years ago they began to get invisible, glass or no glass. Nobody has ever seen the last five I made because no glass is strong enough to make them big enough to be regarded truly as the smallest things ever made. Nobody can see me making them because my little tools are invisible into the same bargain. The one I am making now is nearly as small as nothing. Number Onc would hold a million of them at the same time and there would be room left for a pair of woman's horse-breeches if they were rolled up. The dear knows where it will stop and terminate.'

'Such work must be very hard on the eyes,' I said, determined to pretend that everybody was an ordinary person like myself.

'Some of these days,' he answered, 'I will have to buy spectacles with gold ear-claws. My eyes are crippled with the small print in the newspapers and in the offeecial forms.'

'Before I go back to the day-room,' I said, 'would it be right to ask you what you were performing with that little small piano-instrument, the article with the knobs, and the brass pins?'

'That is my personal musical instrument,' said MacCruiskeen, 'and I was playing my own tunes on it in order to extract private satisfaction from the sweetness of them.'

'I was listening,' I answered, 'but I did not succeed in hearing you.'

'That does not surprise me intuitively,' said MacCruiskeen, 'because it is an indigenous patent of my own. The vibrations of the true notes are so high in their fine frequencies that they cannot be appreciated by the human earcup. Only myself has the secret of the thing and the intimate way of it, the confidential knack of circumventing it. Now what do you think of that?'

I climbed up to my legs to go back to the day-room, passing a hand weakly about my brow.

'I think it is extremely acatalectic,' I answered.

CHAPTER 6

WHEN I PENETRATED back to the day-room I encountered two gentlemen called Sergeant Pluck and Mr Gilhaney and they were holding a meeting about the question of bicycles.

'I do not believe in the three-speed gear at all,' the Sergeant was saying, 'it is a new-fangled instrument, it crucifies the legs, the half of the accidents are due to it.'

'It is a power for the hills,' said Gilhaney, 'as good as a second pair of pins or a diminutive petrol motor.'

'It is a hard thing to tune,' said the Sergeant, 'you can screw the iron lace that hangs out of it till you get no catch at all on the pedals. It never stops the way you want it, it would remind you of bad jaw-plates.'

'That is all lies,' said Gilhaney.

'Or like the pegs of a fairy-day fiddle,' said the Sergeant, 'or a skinny wife in the craw of a cold bed in springtime.'

'Not that,' said Gilhaney.

'Or porter in a sick stomach,' said the Sergeant.

'So help me not,' said Gilhaney.

The Sergeant saw me with the corner of his eye and turned to talk to me, taking away all his attention from Gilhaney.

'MacCruiskeen was giving you his talk I wouldn't doubt,' he said.

'He was being extremely explanatory,' I answered dryly.

'He is a comical man,' said the Sergeant, 'a walking emporium, you'd think he was on wires and worked with steam.'

'He is,' I said.

'He is a melody man,' the Sergeant added, 'and very temporary, a menace to the mind.'

'About the bicycle,' said Gilhaney.

'The bicycle will be found,' said the Sergeant, 'when I retrieve and restore it to its own owner in due law and possessively. Would you desire to be of assistance in the search?' he asked me.

'I would not mind,' I answered.

The Sergeant looked at his teeth in the glass for a brief intermission and then put his leggings on his legs and took a hold of his stick as an indication that he was for the road. Gilhaney was at the door operating it to let us out. The three of us walked out into the middle of the day.

'In case we do not come up with the bicycle before it is high dinner-time,' said the Sergeant, 'I have left an official memorandum for the personal information of Policeman Fox so that he will be acutely conversant with the *res ipsa*,' he said.

'Do you hold with rap-trap pedals?' asked Gilhaney.

'Who is Fox?' I asked.

'Policeman Fox is the third of us,' said the Sergeant, 'but we never see him or hear tell of him at all because he is always on his beat and never off it and he signs the book in the middle of the night when even a badger is asleep. He is as mad as a hare, he never interrogates the public and he is always taking notes. If rat-trap pedals were universal it would be the end of bicycles, the people would die like flies.'

'What put him that way?' I inquired.

'I never comprehended correctly,' replied the Sergeant, 'or got the real informative information but Policeman Fox was alone in a private room with MacCruiskeen for a whole hour on a certain 23rd of June and he has never spoken to anybody since that day and he is as crazy as tuppence-halfpenny and as cranky as thruppence. Did I ever tell you how I asked Inspector O'Gorky about rat-traps? Why are they not made prohibitive, I said, or made specialities like arsenic when you would have to buy them at a chemist's shop and sign a little book and look like a responsible personality?'

'They are a power for the hills,' said Gilhaney.

The Sergeant spat spits on the dry road.

'You would want a special Act of Parliament,' said the Inspector, 'a special Act of Parliament.'

'What way are we going?' I asked, 'or what direction are we heading for or are we on the way back from somewhere else?'

It was a queer country we were in. There was a number of blue mountains around us at what you might call a respectful distance with a glint of white water coming down the shoulders of one or two of them and they kept hemming us in and meddling oppressively with our minds. Half-way to these mountains the view got clearer and was full of humps and hollows and long parks of fine bogland with civil people here and there in the middle of it working with long instruments, you could hear their voices calling across the wind and the crack of the dull carts on the roadways. White buildings could be seen in several places and cows shambling lazily from here to there in search of pasture. A company of crows came out of a tree when I was watching and flew sadly down to a field where there was a quantity of sheep attired in fine overcoats.

'We are going where we are going,' said the Sergeant, 'and this is the right direction to a place that is next door to it. There is one particular thing more dangerous than the rat-trap pedal.'

He left the road and drew us in after him through a hedge.

'It is dishonourable to talk like that about the rat-traps,' said Gilhaney, 'because my family has had their boots in them for generations of their own posterity backwards and forwards and they all died in their beds except my first cousin that was meddling with the suckers of a steam thrashing-mill.'

'There is only one thing more dangerous,' said the Sergeant, 'and that is a loose plate. A loose plate is a scorcher, nobody lives very long after swallowing one and it leads indirectly to asphyxiation.'

'There is no danger of swallowing a rat-trap?' said Gilhaney.

'You would want to have good strong clips if you have a plate,' said the Sergeant, 'and plenty of red sealing-wax to stick it to the roof of your jaws. Take a look at the roots of that bush, it looks suspicious and there is no necessity for a warrant.'

It was a small modest whin-bush, a lady member of the tribe as you might say, with dry particles of hay and sheep's feathers caught in the branches high and low. Gilhaney was on his knees putting his hands through the grass and rooting like one of the lower animals. After a minute he extracted a black instrument. It was long and thin and looked like a large fountain-pen.

'My pump, so help me!' he shouted.

'I thought as much,' said the Sergeant, 'the finding of the pump is a fortunate clue that may assist us in our mission of private detection and smart policework. Put it in your pocket and hide it because it is possible that we are watched and followed and dogged by a member of the gang.'

'How did you know that it was in that particular corner of the world?' I asked in my extreme simplicity.

'What is your attitude to the high saddle?' inquired Gilhaney.

'Questions are like the knocks of beggarmen, and should not be minded,' replied the Sergeant, 'but I do not mind telling you that the high saddle is all right if you happen to have a brass fork.'

'A high saddle is a power for the hills,' said Gilhaney.

We were in an entirely other field by this time and in the company of white-coloured brown-coloured cows. They watched us quietly as we made a path between them and changed their attitudes slowly as if to show us all of the maps on their fat sides. They gave us to understand that they knew us personally and thought a lot of our families and I lifted my hat to the last of them as I passed her as a sign of my appreciation.

'The high saddle,' said the Sergeant, 'was invented by a party called Peters that spent his life in foreign parts riding on camels and other lofty animals – giraffes, elephants and birds that can run like hares and lay eggs the size of the bowl you see in a steam laundry where they keep the chemical water for taking the tar out of men's pants. When he came home from the wars he thought hard of sitting on a low saddle and one night accidentally when he was in bed he invented the high saddle as the outcome of his perpetual cerebration and mental researches. His Christian name I do not remember. The high saddle was the father of the low handlebars. It crucifies the fork and gives you a blood rush in the head, it is very sore on the internal organs.'

'Which of the organs?' I inquired.

'Both of them,' said the Sergeant.

'I think this would be the tree,' said Gilhaney.

'It would not surprise me,' said the Sergeant, 'put your hands in under its underneath and start feeling promiscuously the way you can ascertain factually if there is anything there in addition to its own nothing.'

Gilhaney lay down on his stomach on the grass at the butt of a blackthorn and was inquiring into its private parts with his strong hands and grunting from the stretch of his exertions. After a time he found a bicycle lamp and a bell and stood up and put them secretly in his fob.

'That is very satisfactory and complacently articulated,' said the Sergeant, 'it shows the necessity for perseverance, it is sure to be a clue, we are certain to find the bicycle.'

'I do not like asking questions,' I said politely, 'but the wisdom that directed us to this tree is not taught in the National Schools.'

'It is not the first time my bicycle was stolen,' said Gilhaney.

'In *my* day,' said the Sergeant, 'half the scholars in the National Schools were walking around with enough disease in their gobs to decimate the continent of Russia and wither a field of crops by only looking at them. That is all stopped now, they have compulsory inspections, the middling ones are stuffed with iron and the bad ones are pulled out with a thing like the claw for cutting wires.'

'The half of it is due to cycling with the mouth open,' said Gilhaney.

'Nowadays,' said the Sergeant, 'it is nothing strange to see a class of boys at First Book with wholesome teeth and with junior plates manufactured by the County Council for half-nothing.'

'Grinding the teeth half-way up a hill,' said Gilhaney, 'there is nothing worse, it files away the best part of them and leads to a hob-nailed liver indirectly.'

'In Russia,' said the Sergeant, 'they make teeth out of old piano-keys for elderly cows but it is a rough land without too much civilization, it would cost you a fortune in tyres.'

We were now going through a country full of fine enduring trees where it was always five o'clock in the afternoon. It was a soft corner of the world, free from inquisitions and disputations and very soothing and sleepening on the mind. There was no animal there that was bigger than a man's thumb and no noise superior to that which the Sergeant was making with his nose, an unusual brand of music like wind in the chimney. To every side of us there was a green growth of soft ferny carpeting with thin green twines coming in and out of it and coarse bushes putting their heads out here and there and interrupting the urbanity of the presentation not unpleasingly. The distance we walked in this country I do not know but we arrived in the end at some place where we stopped without proceeding farther. The Sergeant put his finger at a certain part of the growth.

'It might be there and it might not,' he said, 'we can only try because perseverance is its own reward and necessity is the unmarried mother of invention.'

Gilhaney was not long at work till he took his bicycle out of that particular part of the growth. He pulled the briers from between the spokes and felt his tyres with red knowing fingers and furbished his machine fastidiously. The three of us walked back again without a particle of conversation to where the road was and Gilhaney put his toe on the pedal to show he was for home.

'Before I ride away,' he said to the Sergeant, 'what is your true opinion of the timber rim?'

'It is a very commendable invention,' the Sergeant said. 'It gives you more of a bounce, it is extremely easy on your white pneumatics.'

'The wooden rim,' said Gilhaney slowly, 'is a death-trap in itself, it swells on a wet day and I know a man that owes his bad wet death to nothing else.'

Before we had time to listen carefully to what he was after saying he was half-way down the road with his forked coat sailing behind him on the sustenance of the wind he was raising by reason of his headlong acceleration.

'A droll man,' I ventured.

'A constituent man,' said the Sergeant, 'largely instrumental but volubly fervous.'

Walking finely from the hips the two of us made our way home through the afternoon, impregnating it with the smoke of our cigarettes. I reflected that we would be sure to have lost our way in the fields and parks of bogland only that the road very conveniently made its way in advance of us back to the barrack. The Sergeant was sucking quietly at his stumps and carried a black shadow on his brow as if it were a hat.

As he walked he turned in my direction after a time.

'The County Council has a lot to answer for,' he said.

I did not understand his meaning, but I said that I agreed with him.

'There is one puzzle,' I remarked, 'that is hurting the back of my head and causing me a lot of curiosity. It is about the bicycle. I have never heard of detective-work as good as that being done before. Not only did you find the lost bicycle but you found all the clues as well. I find it is a great strain for me to believe what I see, and I am becoming afraid occasionally to look at some things in case they would have to be believed. What is the secret of your constabulary virtuosity?'

He laughed at my earnest inquiries and shook his head with great indulgence at my simplicity.

'It was an easy thing,' he said.

'How easy?'

'Even without the clues I could have succeeded in ultimately finding the bicycle.'

'It seems a very difficult sort of easiness,' I answered. 'Did you know where the bicycle was?'

'I did.'

'How?'

'Because I put it there.'

'You stole the bicycle yourself?'

'Certainly.'

'And the pump and the other clues?'

'I put them where they were finally discovered also.'

'And why?'

He did not answer in words for a moment but kept on walking strongly beside me looking as far ahead as possible.

'The County Council is the culprit,' he said at last.

I said nothing, knowing that he would blame the County Council at greater length if I waited till he had the blame thought out properly. It was not long till he turned in my direction to talk to me again. His face was grave.

'Did you ever discover or hear tell of the Atomic Theory?' he inquired.

'No,' I answered.

He leaned his mouth confidentially over to my ear.

'Would it surprise you to be told,' he said darkly, 'that the Atomic Theory is at work in this parish?'

'It would indeed.'

'It is doing untold destruction,' he continued, 'the half of the people are suffering from it, it is worse than the smallpox.'

I thought it better to say *something*.

'Would it be advisable,' I said, 'that it should be taken in hand by the Dispensary Doctor or by the National Teachers or do you think it is a matter for the head of the family?'

'The lock stock and barrel of it all,' said the Sergeant, 'is the County Council.'

He walked on looking worried and preoccupied as if what he was examining in his head was unpleasant in a very intricate way.

'The Atomic Theory,' I sallied, 'is a thing that is not clear to me at all.'

'Michael Gilhaney,' said the Sergeant, 'is an example of a man that is nearly banjaxed from the principle of the Atomic Theory. Would it astonish you to hear that he is nearly half a bicycle?'

'It would surprise me unconditionally,' I said.

'Michael Gilhaney,' said the Sergeant, 'is nearly sixty years of age by plain computation and if he is itself, he has spent no less than thirty-five years riding his bicycle over the rocky roadsteads and up and down the hills and into the deep ditches when the road goes astray in the strain of the winter. He is always going to a particular destination or other on his bicycle at every hour of the day or coming back from there at every other hour. If it wasn't that his bicycle was stolen every Monday he would be sure to be more than half-way now.'

'Half-way to where?'

'Half-way to being a bicycle himself,' said the Sergeant.

'Your talk,' I said, 'is surely the handiwork of wisdom because not one word of it do I understand.'

'Did you never study atomics when you were a lad?' asked the Sergeant, giving me a look of great inquiry and surprise.

'No,' I answered.

'That is a very serious defalcation,' he said, 'but all the same I will tell you the size of it. Everything is composed of small particles of itself and they are flying around in concentric circles and arcs and segments and innumerable other geometrical figures too numerous to mention collectively, never standing still or resting but spinning away and darting hither and thither and back again, all the time on the go. These diminutive gentlemen are called atoms. Do you follow me intelligently?'

'Yes.'

'They are lively as twenty leprechauns doing a jig on top of a tombstone.'

A very pretty figure, Joe murmured.

'Now take a sheep,' the Sergeant said. 'What is a sheep only millions of little bits of sheepness whirling around and doing intricate convolutions inside the sheep? What else is it but that?'

'That would be bound to make the beast dizzy,' I observed, 'especially if the whirling was going on inside the head as well.'

The Sergeant gave me a look which I am sure he himself would describe as one of *non-possum and noli-me-tangere.*

'That remark is what may well be called buncombe,' he said sharply, 'because the nerve-strings and the sheep's head itself are whirling into the same bargain and you can cancel out one whirl against the other and there you are – like simplifying a division sum when you have fives above and below the bar.'

'To say the truth I did not think of that,' I said.

'Atomics is a very intricate theorem and can be worked out with algebra but you would want to take it by degrees because you might spend the whole night proving a bit of it with rulers and cosines and similar other instruments and then at the wind-up not believe what you had proved at all. If that happened you would have to go back over it till you got a place where you could believe your own facts and figures as delineated from Hall and Knight's Algebra and then go on again from that particular place till you had the whole thing properly believed and not have bits of it half-believed or a doubt in your head hurting you like when you lose the stud of your shirt in bed.'

'Very true,' I said.

'Consecutively and consequentially,' he continued, 'you can safely infer that you are made of atoms yourself and so is your fob pocket and the tail of your shirt and the instrument you use for taking the leavings out of the crook of your hollow tooth. Do you happen to know what takes place when you strike a bar of iron with a good coal hammer or with a blunt instrument?'

'What?'

'When the wallop falls, the atoms are bashed away down to the bottom of the bar and compressed and crowded there like eggs under a good clucker. After a while in the course of time they swim around and get back at last to where they were. But if you keep hitting the bar long enough and hard enough they do not get a chance to do this and what happens then?'

'That is a hard question.'

'Ask a blacksmith for the true answer and he will tell you that the bar will dissipate itself away by degrees if you persevere with the hard wallops. Some of the atoms of the bar will go into the hammer and the other half into the table or the stone or the particular article that is underneath the bottom of the bar.'

'That is well-known,' I agreed.

'The gross and net result of it is that people who spend most of their natural lives riding iron bicycles over the rocky road-steads of this parish get their personalities mixed up with the personalities of their bicycle as a result of the interchanging of the atoms of each of them and you would be surprised at the number of people in these parts who nearly are half people and half bicycles.'

I let go a gasp of astonishment that made a sound in the air like a bad puncture.

'And you would be flabbergasted at the number of bicycles that are half-human almost half-man, half-partaking of humanity.'

Apparently there is no limit, Joe remarked. *Anything can be said in this place and it will be true and will have to be believed.*

I would not mind being working this minute on a steamer in the middle of the sea, I said, coiling ropes and doing the hard manual work. I would like to be far away from here.

I looked carefully around me. Brown bogs and black bogs were arranged neatly on each side of the road with rectangular boxes carved out of them here and there, each with a filling of yellow-brown brown-yellow water. Far away near the sky tiny people were stooped at their turfwork, cutting out precisely-shaped sods with their patent spades and building them into a tall memorial twice the height of a horse and cart. Sounds came from them to the Sergeant and myself, delivered to our ears without charge by the west wind, sounds of laughing and whistling and bits of verses from the old bog-songs. Nearer, a house stood attended by three trees and surrounded by the happiness of a coterie of fowls, all of them picking and rooting and disputating loudly in the unrelenting manufacture of their eggs. The house was quiet in itself and silent but a canopy of lazy smoke had been erected over the chimney to indicate that people were within engaged on tasks. Ahead of us went the road, running swiftly across the flat land and pausing slightly to climb slowly up a hill that was waiting for it in a place where there was tall grass, grey boulders and rank stunted trees. The whole overhead was occupied by the sky, serene, impenetrable, ineffable and incomparable, with a fine island of clouds anchored in the calm two yards to the right of Mr Jarvis's outhouse.

The scene was real and incontrovertible and at variance with the talk of the Sergeant, but I knew that the Sergeant was talking the truth and if it was a question of taking my choice, it was possible that I would have to forgo the reality of all the simple things my eyes were looking at.

I took a sideways view of him. He was striding on with signs of anger against the County Council on his coloured face.

'Are you certain about the humanity of the bicycle?' I inquired of him. 'Is the Atomic Theory as dangerous as you say?'

'It is between twice and three times as dangerous as it might be,' he replied gloomily. 'Early in the morning I often think it is four times, and what is more, if you lived here for a few days and gave full play to your observation and inspection, you would know how certain the sureness of certainty is.'

'Gilhaney did not look like a bicycle,' I said. 'He had no back wheel on him and I did not think he had a front wheel either, although I did not give much attention to his front.'

The Sergeant looked at me with some commiseration.

'You cannot expect him to grow handlebars out of his neck but I have seen him do more indescribable things than that. Did you ever notice the queer behaviour of bicycles in these parts?'

'I am not long in this district.'

Thanks be, said Joe.

'Then watch the bicycles if you think it is pleasant to be surprised continuously,' he said. 'When a man lets things go so far that he is half or more than half a bicycle, you will not see so much because he spends a lot of his time leaning with one elbow on walls or standing propped by one foot at kerbstones. Of course there are other things connected with ladies and ladies' bicycles that I will mention to you separately some time. But the man-charged bicycle is a phenomenon of great charm and intensity and a very dangerous article.'

At this point a man with long coat-tails spread behind him approached quickly on a bicycle, coasting benignly down the road past us from the hill ahead. I watched him with the eye of six eagles, trying to find out which was carrying the other and whether it was really a man with a bicycle on his shoulders. I did not seem to see anything, however, that was memorable or remarkable.

The Sergeant was looking into his black notebook.

'That was O'Feersa,' he said at last. 'His figure is only twenty-three per cent.'

'He is twenty-three per cent bicycle?'

'Yes.'

'Does that mean that his bicycle is also twenty-three per cent O'Feersa?'

'It does.'

'How much is Gilhaney?'

'Forty-eight.'

'Then O'Feersa is much lower.'

'That is due to the lucky fact that there are three similar brothers in the house and that they are too poor to have a separate bicycle apiece. Some people never know how fortunate they are when they are poorer than each other. Six years ago one of the three O'Feersas won a prize of ten pounds in *John Bull*. When I got the wind of this tiding, I knew I would have to take steps unless there was to be two new bicycles in the family, because you will understand that I can steal only a limited number of bicycles in the one week. I did not want to have three O'Feersas on my hands. Luckily I knew the postman very well. The postman! Great holy suffering indiarubber bowls of brown stirabout!' The recollection of the postman seemed to give the Sergeant a pretext for unlimited amusement and cause for intricate gesturing with his red hands.

'The postman?' I said.

'Seventy-one per cent,' he said quietly.

'Great Scot!'

'A round of thirty-eight miles on the bicycle every single day for forty years, hail, rain or snowballs. There is very little hope of ever getting his number down below fifty again.'

'You bribed him?'

'Certainly. With two of the little straps you put around the hubs of bicycles to keep them spick.'

'And what way do these people's bicycles behave?'

'These people's bicycles?'

'I mean these bicycles' people or whatever is the proper name for them — the ones that have two wheels under them and a handlebars.'

'The behaviour of a bicycle that has a high content of humanity,' he said, 'is very cunning and entirely remarkable. You never see them moving by themselves but you meet them in the least accountable places unexpectedly. Did you never see a bicycle leaning against the dresser of a warm kitchen when it is pouring outside?'

'I did.'

'Not very far away from the fire?'

'Yes.'

'Near enough to the family to hear the conversation?'

'Yes.'

'Not a thousand miles from where they keep the eatables?'

'I did not notice that. You do not mean to say that these bicycles *eat food*?'

'They were never seen doing it, nobody ever caught them with a mouthful of steak. All I know is that the food disappears.'

'What!'

'It is not the first time I have noticed crumbs at the front wheels of some of these gentlemen.'

'All this is a great blow to me,' I said.

'Nobody takes any notice,' replied the Sergeant. 'Mick thinks that Pat brought it in and Pat thinks that Mick was instrumental. Very few of the people guess what is going on in this parish. There are other things I would rather not say too much about. A new lady teacher was here one time with a new bicycle. She was not very long here till Gilhaney went away into the lonely country on her female bicycle. Can you appreciate the immorality of that?'

'I can.'

'But worse happened. Whatever way Gilhaney's bicycle managed it, it left itself leaning at a place where the young teacher would rush out to go away somewhere on her bicycle in a hurry. Her bicycle was gone but here was Gilhaney's leaning there conveniently and trying to look very small and comfortable and attractive. Need I inform you what the result was or what happened?'

Indeed he need not, Joe said urgently. *I have never heard of anything so shameless and abandoned. Of course the teacher was blameless, she did not take pleasure and did not know.*

'You need not,' I said.

'Well, there you are. Gilhaney has a day out with the lady's bicycle and vice versa contrarily and it is quite clear that the lady in the case had a high number – thirty-five or forty, I would say, in spite of the newness of the bicycle. Many a grey hair it has put into my head, trying to regulate the people of this parish. If you let it go too far it would be the end of everything. You would have bicycles wanting votes and they would get seats on the County Council and make the roads far worse than they are for their own ulterior motivation. But against that and on the other hand, a good bicycle is a great companion, there is a great charm about it.'

'How would you know a man has a lot of bicycle in his veins?'

'If his number is over Fifty you can tell it unmistakable from his walk. He will walk smartly always and never sit down and he will lean against the wall with his elbow out and stay like that all night in his kitchen instead of going to bed. If he walks too slowly or stops in the middle of the road he will fall down in a heap and will have to be lifted and set in motion again by some extraneous party. This is the unfortunate state that the postman has cycled himself into, and I do not think he will ever cycle himself out of it.'

'I do not think I will ever ride a bicycle,' I said.

'A little of it is a good thing and makes you hardy and puts iron on to you. But walking too far too often too quickly is not safe at all. The continual cracking of your feet on the road makes a certain quantity of road come up into you. When a man dies they say he returns to clay but too much walking fills you up with clay far sooner (or buries bits of you along the road) and brings your death half-way to meet you. It is not easy to know what is the best way to move yourself from one place to another.'

After he had finished speaking I found myself walking nimbly and lightly on my toes in order to prolong my life. My head was packed tight with fears and miscellaneous apprehensions.

'I never heard of these things before,' I said, 'and never knew these happenings could happen. Is it a new development or was it always an ancient fundamental?'

The Sergeant's face clouded and he spat thoughtfully three yards ahead of him on the road.

'I will tell you a secret,' he said very confidentially in a low voice. 'My great-grandfather was eighty-three when he died. For a year before his death he was a horse!'

'A horse?'

'A horse in everything but extraneous externalities. He would spend the day grazing in a field or eating hay in a stall. Usually he was lazy and quiet but now and again he would go for a smart gallop, clearing the hedges in great style. Did you ever see a man on two legs galloping?'

'I did not.'

'Well, I am given to understand that it is a great sight. He always said he won the Grand National when he was a lot younger and used to annoy his family with stories about the intricate jumps and the great height of them.'

'I suppose your great-grandfather got himself into this condition by too much horse riding?'

'That was the size of it. His old horse Dan was in the contrary way and gave so much trouble, coming into the house at night and interfering with young girls during the day and committing indictable offences, that they had to shoot him. The police were unsympathetic, not comprehending things rightly in these days. They said they would have to arrest the horse and charge him and have him up at the next Petty Sessions unless he was done away with. So my family shot him but if you ask me it was my great-grandfather they shot and it is the horse that is buried up in Cloncoonla Churchyard.'

The Sergeant then became thoughtful at the recollection of his ancestors and had a reminiscent face for the next half-mile till we came to the barracks. Joe and I agreed privately that these revelations were the supreme surprise stored for us and awaiting our arrival in the barracks.

When we reached it the Sergeant led the way in with a sigh. 'The lock, stock and barrel of it all,' he said, 'is the County Council.'

CHAPTER 7

THE SEVERE shock which I encountered soon after re-entry to
the barrack with the Sergeant set me thinking afterwards of the
immense consolations which philosophy and religion can offer
in adversity. They seem to lighten dark places and give strength
to bear the unaccustomed load. Not unnaturally my thoughts
were never very far from de Selby. All his works – but particularly
Golden Hours – have what one may term a therapeutic quality.
They have a heart-lifing effect more usually associated with spirituous liquors, reviving and quietly restoring the spiritual tissue.
This benign property of his prose is not, one hopes, to be attributed to the reason noticed by the eccentric du Garbandier, who
said 'the beauty of reading a page of de Selby is that it leads
one inescapably to the happy conviction that one is not, of
all nincompoops, the greatest'.[1] This is, I think, an overstatement
of one of de Selby's most ingratiating qualities. The humanizing
urbanity of his work has always seemed to me to be enhanced
rather than vitiated by the chance obtrusion here and there of
his minor failings, all the more pathetic because he regarded some
of them as pinnacles of his intellectual prowess rather than
indications of his frailty as a human being.

Holding that the usual processes of living were illusory, it is
natural that he did not pay much attention to life's adversities
and he does not in fact offer much suggestion as to how they
should be met. Bassett's anecdote[2] on this point may be worth
recounting. During de Selby's Bartown days he had acquired
some local reputation as a savant 'due possibly to the fact that he
was known never to read newspapers'. A young man in the town
was seriously troubled by some question regarding a lady and

1 'Le suprème charme qu'on trouve à lire une page de de Selby est qu'elle
vous conduit inexorablement a l'heureuse certitude que des sots vous n'êtes
pas le plus grand.'
2 In *Lux Mundi*.

feeling that this matter was weighing on his mind and threatening to interfere with his reason, he sought de Selby for advice. Instead of exorcizing this solitary blot from the young man's mind, as indeed could easily have been done, de Selby drew the young man's attention to some fifty imponderable propositions each of which raised difficulties which spanned many eternities and dwarfed the conundrum of the young lady to nothingness. Thus the young man who had come fearing the possibility of a bad thing left the house completely convinced of the worst and cheerfully contemplating suicide. That he arrived home for his supper at the usual time was a happy intervention on the part of the moon for he had gone home by the harbour only to find that the tide was two miles out. Six months later he earned for himself six calendar months' incarceration with hard labour on foot of eighteen counts comprising larceny and offences bearing on interference with railroads. So much for the savant as a dispenser of advice.

As already said, however, de Selby provides some genuine mental sustenance if read objectively for what there is to read. In the *Layman's Atlas*[3] he deals explicitly with bereavement, old age, love, sin, death and the other saliencies of existence. It is true that he allows them only some six lines but this is due to his devastating assertion that they are all 'unnecessary'.[4] Astonishing as it may seem, he makes this statement as a direct corollary to his discovery that the earth, far from being a sphere, is 'sausage-shaped'.

Not a few of the critical commentators confess to a doubt

3 Now very rare and a collector's piece. The sardonic du Garbandier makes great play of the fact that the man who first printed the *Atlas* (Watkins) was struck by lightning on the day he completed the task. It is interesting to note that the otherwise reliable Hatchjaw has put forward the suggestion that the entire *Atlas* is spurious and the work of 'another hand', raising issues of no less piquancy that those of the Bacon–Shakespeare controversy. He has many ingenious if not quite convincing arguments, not the least of them being that de Selby was known to have received considerable royalties from this book which he did not write, 'a procedure that would be of a piece with the master's ethics'. The theory is, however, not one which will commend itself to the serious student.

4 Du Garbandier has inquired with his customary sarcasm why a malignant condition of the gall-bladder, a disease which frequently reduced de Selby to a cripple, was omitted from the list of 'unnecessaries'.

as to whether de Selby was permitting himself a modicum of unwonted levity in connection with this theory but he seems to argue the matter seriously enough and with no want of conviction.

He adopts the customary line of pointing out fallacies involved in existing conceptions and then quietly setting up his own design in place of the one he claims to have demolished.

Standing at a point on the postulated spherical earth, he says, one appears to have four main directions in which to move, viz., north, south, east and west. But it does not take much thought to see that there really appear to be only two since north and south are meaningless terms in relation to a spheroid and can connote motion in only *one* direction; so also with west and east. One can reach any point on the north–south band by travelling in either 'direction', the only apparent difference in the two 'routes' being extraneous considerations of time and distance, both already shown to be illusory. North–south is therefore one direction and east-west apparently another. Instead of four directions there are only two. It can be safely inferred,[5] de Selbys says, that there is a further similar fallacy inherent here and that there is in fact only one possible direction properly so-called, because if one leaves any point on the globe, moving and continuing to move in any 'direction', one ultimately reaches the point of departure again.

The application of this conclusion to his theory that 'the earth is a sausage' is illuminating. He attributes the idea that the earth is spherical to the fact that human beings are continually moving in only one known direction (though convinced that they are free to move in any direction) and that this one direction is really around the circular circumference of an earth which is in fact sausage-shaped. It can scarcely be contested that if multi-directionality be admitted to be a fallacy, the sphericity of the earth is another fallacy that would inevitably follow from it. De Selby likens the position of a human on the earth to that of a man on a tight-wire who must continue walking along the wire or perish, being, however, free in all other respects. Movement in this restricted orbit results in the permanent hallucination known conventionally as 'life' with its innumerable concomitant

5 Possibly the one weak spot in the argument.

limitations, afflictions and anomalies. If a way can be found, says de Selby, of discovering the 'second direction', i.e., along the 'barrel' of the sausage, a world of entirely new sensation and experience will be open to humanity. New and unimaginable dimensions will supersede the present order and the manifold 'unnecessaries' of 'one-directional' existence will disappear.

It is true that de Selby is rather vague as to how precisely this new direction is to be found. It is not, he warns us, to be ascertained by any microscopic subdivision of the known points of the compass and little can be expected from sudden darts hither and thither in the hope that a happy chance will intervene. He doubts whether human legs would be 'suitable' for traversing the 'longitudinal celestium' and seems to suggest that death is nearly always present when the new direction is discovered. As Bassett points out justly enough, this lends considerable colour to the whole theory but suggests at the same time that de Selby is merely stating in an obscure and recondite way something that is well-known and accepted.

As usual, there is evidence that he carried out some private experimenting. He seems to have thought at one time that gravitation was the 'jailer' of humanity, keeping it on the one-directional line of oblivion, and that ultimate freedom lay in some upward direction. He examined aviation as a remedy without success and subsequently spent some weeks designing certain 'barometric pumps' which were 'worked with mercury and wires' to clear vast areas of the earth of the influence of gravitation. Happily for the people of the place as well as for their movable chattels he does not seem to have had much result. Eventually he was distracted from these occupations by the extraordinary affair of the water-box.[6]

As I have already hinted, I would have given much for a glimpse of a signpost showing the way along the 'barrel' of the sausage after I had been some two minutes back in the white day-room with Sergeant Pluck.

We were not more than completely inside the door when we became fully aware that there was a visitor present. He had coloured stripes of high office on his chest but he was dressed in

---

6 See Hatchjaw: *The de Selby Water-Boxes Day by Day.* The calculations are given in full and the daily variations are expressed in admirably clear graphs.

policeman's blue and on his head he carried a policeman's hat with a special badge of superior office glittering very brilliantly in it. He was very fat and circular, with legs and arms of the minimum, and his large bush of moustache was bristling with bad temper and self-indulgence. The Sergeant gave him looks of surprise and then a military salute.

'Inspector O'Corky!' he said.

'What is the meaning of the vacuity of the station in routine hours?' barked the Inspector.

The sound his voice made was rough like coarse cardboard rubbed on sandpaper and it was clear that he was not pleased with himself or with other people.

'I was out myself,' the Sergeant replied respectfully, 'on emergency duty and policework of the highest gravity.'

'Did you know that a man called Mathers was found in the crotch of a ditch up the road two hours ago with his belly opened up with a knife or sharp instrument?'

To say this was a surprise which interfered seriously with my heart-valves would be the same as saying that a red-hot poker would heat your face if somebody decided to let you have it there. I stared from the Sergeant to the Inspector and back again with my whole inside fluttering in consternation.

It seems that our mutual friend Finnucane is in the environs, Joe said.

'Certainly I did,' said the Sergeant.

Very strange. How could he if he has been out with us after the bicycle for the last four hours?

'And what steps have you taken and how many steps?' barked the Inspector.

'Long steps and steps in the right direction,' replied the Sergeant evenly. 'I know who the murderer is.'

'Then why is he not arrested into custody?'

'He is,' said the Sergeant pleasantly.

'Where?'

'Here.'

This was the second thunderbolt. After I had glanced fearfully to my rear without seeing a murderer it became clear to me that I myself was the subject of the private conversation of the two policemen. I made no protest because my voice was gone and my mouth was bone-dry.

Inspector O'Corky was too angry to be pleased at anything so surprising as what the Sergeant said.

'Then why is he not confined under a two-way key and padlock in the cell?' he roared.

For the first time the Sergeant looked a bit crestfallen and shame-faced. His face got a little redder than it was and he put his eyes on the stone floor.

'To tell you the truth,' he said at last, 'I keep my bicycle there.'

'I see,' said the Inspector.

He stopped quickly and rammed black clips on the extremities of his trousers and stamped on the floor. For the first time I saw that he had been leaning by one elbow on the counter.

'See that you regularize your irregularity instantaneously,' he called as his good-bye, 'and set right your irrectitude and put the murderer in the cage before he rips the bag out of the whole countryside.'

After that he was gone. Sounds came to us of coarse scraping on the gravel, a sign that the Inspector favoured the old-fashioned method of mounting from the back-step.

'Well, now,' the Sergeant said.

He took off his cap and went over to a chair and sat on it, easing himself on his broad pneumatic seat. He took a red cloth from his fob and decanted the globes of perspiration from his expansive countenance and opened the buttons of his tunic as if to let out on wing the trouble that was imprisoned there. He then took to carrying out a scientifically precise examination of the soles and the toes of his constabulary boots, a sign that he was wrestling with some great problem.

'What is your worry?' I inquired, very anxious by now that what had happened should be discussed.

'The bicycle,' he said.

'The bicycle?'

'How can I put it out of the cell?' he asked. 'I have always kept it in solitary confinement when I am not riding it to make sure it is not leading a personal life inimical to my own inimitability. I cannot be too careful. I have to ride long rides on my constabulary ridings.'

'Do you mean that I should be locked in the cell and kept there and hidden from the world?'

'You surely heard the instructions of the Inspector?'

Ask is it all a joke? Joe said.

'Is this all a joke for entertainment purposes?'

'If you take it that way I will be indefinitely beholden to you,' said the Sergeant earnestly, 'and I will remember you with real emotion. It would be a noble gesture and an unutterable piece of supreme excellence on the part of the deceased.'

'What!' I cried.

'You must recollect that to turn everything to your own advantage is one of the regulations of true wisdom as I informed you privately. It is the following of this rule on my part that makes you a murderer this today evening.

'The Inspector required a captured prisoner as the least tiniest minimum for his inferior *bonhomie* and *mal d'esprit*. It was your personal misfortune to be present adjacently at the time but it was likewise my personal good fortune and good luck. There is no option but to stretch you for the serious offence.'

'Stretch me?'

'Hang you by the windpipe before high breakfast time.'

'That is most unfair,' I stuttered, 'it is unjust . . . rotten . . . fiendish.' My voice rose to a thin tremolo of fear.

'It is the way we work in this part of the country,' explained the Sergeant.

'I will resist,' I shouted, 'and will resist to the death and fight for my existence even if I lose my life in the attempt.'

The Sergeant made a soothing gesture in deprecation. He took out an enormous pipe and when he stuck it in his face it looked like a great hatchet.

'About the bicycle,' he said when he had it in commission.

'What bicycle?'

'My own one. Would it inconvenience you if I neglected to bar you into the inside of the cell? I do not desire to be selfish but I have to think carefully about my bicycle. The wall of this day-room is no place for it.'

'I do not mind,' I said quietly.

'You can remain in the environs on parole and ticket of leave till we have time to build the high scaffold in the backyard.'

'How do you know I will not make excellent my escape?' I asked, thinking that it would be better to discover all the thoughts and intentions of the Sergeant so that my escape would in fact be certain.

He smiled at me as much as the weight of the pipe would let him.

'You will not do that,' he said. 'It would not be honourable but even if it was we would easily follow the track of your rear tyre and besides the rest of everything Policeman Fox would be sure to apprehend you single-handed on the outskirts. There would be no necessity for a warrant.'

Both of us sat silent for a while occupied with our thoughts, he thinking about his bicycle and I about my death.

By the bye, Joe remarked, *I seem to remember our friend saying that the law could not lay a finger on us on account of your congenital anonymity.*

Quite right, I said. I forgot that.

As things are I fancy it would not be much more than a debating point.

It is worth mentioning, I said.

O Lord, yes.

'By the way,' I said to the Sergeant, 'did you recover my American watch for me?'

'The matter is under consideration and is receiving attention,' he said officially.

'Do you recall that you told me that I was not here at all because I had no name and that my personality was invisible to the law?'

'I said that.'

'Then how can I be hanged for a murder, even if I did commit it and there is no trial or preliminary proceedings, no caution administered and no hearing before a Commissioner of the Public Peace?'

Watching the Sergeant, I saw him take the hatchet from his jaws in surprise and knot his brows into considerable corrugations. I could see that he was severely troubled with my inquiry. He looked darkly at me and then doubled his look, giving me a compressed stare along the line of his first vision.

'Well great cripes!' he said.

For three minutes he sat giving my representations his undivided attention. He was frowning so heavily with wrinkles which were so deep that the blood was driven from his face leaving it black and forbidding.

Then he spoke.

'Are you completely doubtless that you are nameless?' he asked.

'Positively certain.'

'Would it be Mick Barry?'

'No.'

'Charlemagne O'Keeffe?'

'No.'

'Sir Justin Spens?'

'Not that.'

'Kimberley?'

'No.'

'Bernard Fann?'

'No.'

'Joseph Poe or Nolan?'

'No.'

'One of the Garvins or the Moynihans?'

'Not them.'

'Rosencranz O'Dowd?'

'No.'

'Would it be O'Benson?'

'Not O'Benson.'

'The Quigleys, the Mulrooneys or the Hounimen?'

'No.'

'The Hardimen or the Merrimen?'

'Not them.'

'Peter Dundy?'

'No.'

'Scrutch?'

'No.'

'Lord Brad?'

'Not him.'

'The O'Growneys, the O'Roartys or the Finnehys?'

'No.'

'That is an amazing piece of denial and denunciation,' he said.

He passed the red cloth over his face again to reduce the moisture.

'An astonishing parade of nullity,' he added.

'My name is not Jenkins either,' I vouchsafed.

'Roger MacHugh?'

'Not Roger.'

'Sitric Hogan?'

'No.'

'Not Conroy?'

'No.'

'Not O'Conroy?'

'Not O'Conroy.'

'There are very few more names that you could have, then,' he said. 'Because only a black man could have a name different to the ones I have recited. Or a red man. Not Byrne?'

'No.'

'Then it is a nice pancake,' he said gloomily. He bent double to give full scope to the extra brains he had at the rear of his head.

'Holy suffering senators,' he muttered.

I think we have won the day.

We are not home and dried yet, I answered.

Nevertheless I think we can relax. Evidently he has never heard of Signor Bari, the golden-throated budgerigar of Milano.

I don't think this is the time for pleasantries.

Or J. Courtney Wain, private investigator and member of the inner bar. Eighteen thousand guineas marked on the brief. The singular case of the red-headed men.

'By Scot!' said the Sergeant suddenly. He got up to pace the flooring.

'I think the case can be satisfactorily met,' he said pleasantly, 'and ratified unconditionally.'

I did not like his smile and asked him for his explanation.

'It is true,' he said, 'that you cannot commit a crime and that the right arm of the law cannot lay its finger on you irrespective of the degree of your criminality. Anything you do is a lie and nothing that happens to you is true.'

I nodded my agreement comfortably.

'For that reason alone,' said the Sergeant, 'we can take you and hang the life out of you and you are not hanged at all and there is no entry to be made in the death papers. The particular death you die is not even a death (which is an inferior phenomenon at the best) only an insanitary abstraction in the backyard, a piece of negative nullity neutralized and rendered void by asphyxiation and the fracture of the spinal string. If it is not a lie to say that you have been given the final hammer behind the barrack, equally it is true to say that nothing has happened to you.'

'You mean that because I have no name I cannot die and that you cannot be held answerable for death even if you kill me?'

'That is about the size of it,' said the Sergeant.

I felt so sad and so entirely disappointed that tears came into my eyes and a lump of incommunicable poignancy swelled tragically in my throat. I began to feel intensely every fragment of my equal humanity. The life that was bubbling at the end of my fingers was real and nearly painful in intensity and so was the beauty of my warm face and the loose humanity of my limbs and the racy health of my red rich blood. To leave it all without good reason and to smash the little empire into small fragments was a thing too pitiful even to refuse to think about.

The next important thing that happened in the day-room was the entry of Policeman MacCruiskeen. He marched in to a chair and took out his black notebook and began perusing his own autographed memoranda, at the same time twisting his lips into an article like a purse.

'Did you take the readings?' the Sergeant asked.

'I did,' MacCruiskeen said.

'Read them till I hear them,' the Sergeant said, 'and until I make mental comparisons inside the interior of my inner head.'

MacCruiskeen eyed his book keenly.[7]

'Ten point five,' he said.

'Ten point five,' said the Sergeant. 'And what was the reading on the beam?'

---

7 From a chance and momentary perusual of the policeman's notebook it is possible for me to give here the relative figures for a week's readings. For obvious reasons the figures themselves are fictitious:

PILOT READING	READING ON BEAM	READING ON LEVER	NATURE OF FALL (if any) with time	
10.2	4.9	1.25	Light	4.15
10.2	4.6	1.25	Light	18.16
9.5	6.2	1.7	Light (with lumps)	7.15
10.5	4.25	1.9	Nil	
12.6	7.0	3.73	Heavy	21.6
12.5	6.5	2.5	Black	9.0
9.25	5.0	6.0	Black (with lumps)	14.45

'Five point three.'

'And how much on the lever?'

'Two point three.'

'Two point three is high,' said the Sergeant. He put the back of his fist between the saws of his yellow teeth and commenced working at his mental comparisons. After five minutes his face got clearer and he looked again to MacCruiskeen.

'Was there a fall?' he asked.

'A light fall at five-thirty.'

'Five-thirty is rather late if the fall was a light one,' he said. 'Did you put charcoal adroitly in the vent?'

'I did,' said MacCruiskeen.

'How much?'

'Seven pounds.'

'I would say eight,' said the Sergeant.

'Seven was satisfactory enough,' MacCruiskeen said, 'if you recollect that the reading on the beam has been falling for the past four days. I tried the shuttle but there was no trace of play or looseness in it.'

'I would still say eight for safety-first,' said the Sergeant, 'but if the shuttle is tight, there can be no need for timorous anxiety.'

'None at all,' said MacCruiskeen.

The Sergeant cleared his face of all the lines of thought he had on it and stood up and clapped his flat hands on his breast pockets. 'Well now,' he said.

He stooped to put the clips on his ankles.

'I must go now to where I am going,' he said, 'and let you,' he said to MacCruiskeen, 'come with me to the exterior for two moments till I inform you about recent events officially.'

The two of them went out together, leaving me in my sad and cheerless loneliness. MacCruiskeen was not gone for long but I was lonely during that diminutive meantime. When he came in again he gave me a cigarette which was warm and wrinkled from his pocket.

'I believe they are going to stretch you,' he said pleasantly.

I replied with nods.

'It is a bad time of the year, it will cost a fortune,' he said. 'You would not believe the price of timber.'

'Would a tree not suffice?' I inquired, giving tongue to a hollow whim of humour.

'I do not think it would be proper,' he said, 'but I will mention it privately to the Sergeant.'

'Thank you.'

'The last hanging we had in this parish,' he said, 'was thirty years ago. It was a very famous man called MacDadd. He held the record for the hundred miles on a solid tyre. I need to tell you what the solid tyre did for him. We had to hang the bicycle.'

'Hang the bicycle?'

'MacDadd had a first-class grudge against another man called Figgerson but he did not go near Figgerson. He knew how things stood and gave Figgerson's bicycle a terrible thrashing with a crowbar. After that MacDadd and Figgerson had a fight and Figgerson – a dark man with glasses – did not live to know who the winner was. There was a great wake and he was buried with his bicycle. Did you ever see a bicycle-shaped coffin?'

'No.'

'It is a very intricate piece of wood-working, you would want to be a first-class carpenter to make a good job of the handlebars to say nothing of the pedals and the back-step. But the murder was a bad piece of criminality and we could not find MacDadd for a long time or make sure where the most of him was. We had to arrest his bicycle as well as himself and we watched the two of them under secret observation for a week to see where the majority of MacDadd was and whether the bicycle was mostly in MacDadd's trousers *pari passu* if you understand my meaning.'

'What happened?'

'The Sergeant gave his ruling at the end of the week. His position was painful in the extremity because he was a very close friend of MacDadd after office hours. He condemned the bicycle and it was the bicycle that was hanged. We entered a *nolle prosequi* in the day-book in respect of the other defendant. I did not see the stretching myself because I am a delicate man and my stomach is extremely reactionary.'

He got up and went to the dresser and took out his patent music-box which made sounds too esoterically rarefied to be audible to anybody but himself. He then sat back again in his chair, put his hands through the handstraps and began to enter-tain himself with the music. What he was playing could be roughly inferred from his face. It had a happy broad coarse satisfaction on it, a sign that he was occupied with loud obstreperous barn-songs and gusty shanties of the sea and burly roaring marching-songs. The silence in the room was so unusually quiet that the beginning of it seemed rather loud when the utter stillness of the end of it had been encountered.

How long this eeriness lasted or how long we were listening intently to nothing is unknown. My own eyes got tired with inactivity and closed down like a public house at ten o'clock. When they opened again I saw that MacCruiskeen had desisted from the music and was making preparations for mangling his washing and his Sunday shirts. He had pulled a great rusty mangle from the shadow of the wall and had taken a blanket from the top of it and was screwing down the pressure-spring and spinning the hand wheel and furbishing the machine with expert hands.

He went over then to the dresser and took small articles like dry batteries out of a drawer and also an instrument like a prongs and glass barrels with wires inside them and other cruder articles resembling the hurricane lamps utilized by the County Council. He put these things into different parts of the mangle and when he had them all satisfactorily adjusted, the mangle looked more like a rough scientific instrument than a machine for wringing out a day's washing.

The time of the day was now a dark time, the sun being about to vanish completely in the red west and withdraw all the light. MacCruiskeen kept on adding small well-made articles to his mangle and mounting indescribably delicate glass instruments about the metal legs and on the superstructure. When he had nearly finished this work the room was almost black, and sharp blue sparks would fly sometimes from the upside-down of his hand when it was at work.

Underneath the mangle in the middle of the cast-iron handiwork I noticed a black box with coloured wires coming out of it and there was a small ticking sound to be heard as if there was a clock in it. All in all it was the most complicated mangle I ever saw and to the inside of a steam thrashing-mill it was not inferior in complexity.

Passing near my chair to get an additional accessory, MacCruiskeen saw that I was awake and watching him.

'Do not worry if you think it is dark,' he said to me, 'because

I am going to light the light and then mangle it for diversion and also for scientific truth.'

'Did you say you were going to mangle the light?'

'Wait till you see now.'

What he did next or which knobs he turned I did not ascertain on account of the gloom but it happened that a queer light appeared somewhere on the mangle. It was a local light that did not extend very much outside its own brightness but it was not a spot of light and still less a bar-shaped light. It was not steady completely but it did not dance like candlelight. It was light of a kind rarely seen in this country and was possibly manufactured with raw materials from abroad. It was a gloomy light and looked exactly as if there was a small area somewhere on the mangle and was merely devoid of darkness.

What happened next is astonishing. I could see the dim contours of MacCruiskeen in attendance at the mangle. He made adjustments with his cunning fingers, stooping for a minute to work at the lower-down inventions on the iron work. He rose then to full life-size and started to turn the wheel of the mangle, slowly, sending out a clamping creakiness around the barrack. The moment he turned the wheel, the unusual light began to change its appearance and situation in an extremely difficult fashion. With every turn it got brighter and harder and shook with such a fine delicate shaking that it achieved a steadiness unprecedented in the world by defining with its outer shakes the two lateral boundaries of the place where it was incontrovertibly situated. It grew steelier and so intense in its livid pallor that it stained the inner screen of my eyes so that it still confronted me in all quarters when I took my stare far away from the mangle in an effort to preserve my sight. MacCruiskeen kept turning slowly at the handle till suddenly to my sick utter horror, the light seemed to burst and disappear and simultaneously there was a loud shout in the room, a shout which could not have come from a human throat.

I sat on the chair's edge and gave frightened looks at the shadow of MacCruiskeen, who was stooping down again at the diminutive scientific accessories of the mangle, making minor adjustments and carrying out running repairs in the dark.

'What was that shouting?' I stuttered over at him.

'I will tell you that in a tick,' he called, 'if you will inform me

what you think the words of the shout were. What would you
say was said in the shout now?'

This was a question I was already working with in my own
head. The unearthly voice had roared out something very quickly
with three or four words compressed into one ragged shout.
I could not be sure what it was but several phrases sprang into
my head together and each of them could have been the contents
of the shout. They bore an eerie resemblance to commonplace
shouts I had often heard such as *Change for Tinahely and Shillelagh!
Two to one the field! Mind the step! Finish him off!* I knew, however,
that the shout could not be so foolish and trivial because it
disturbed me in a way that could only be done by something
momentous and diabolical.

MacCruiskeen was looking at me with a question in his eye.

'I could not make it out,' I said, vaguely and feebly, 'but I think
it was railway-station talk.'

'I have been listening to shouts and screams for years,' he said,
'but I never surely catch the words. Would you say that he
said "Don't press so hard"?'

'No.'

'Second favourites always win?'

'Not that.'

'It is a difficult pancake,' MacCruiskeen said, 'a very compound crux. Wait till we try again.'

This time he screwed down the rollers of the mangle till they
were whining and till it was nearly out of the question to spin the
wheel. The light that appeared was the thinnest and sharpest light
that I ever imagined, like the inside of the edge of a sharp razor,
and the intensification which came upon it with the turning of
the wheel was too delicate a process to be watched even sideways.

What happened eventually was not a shout but a shrill scream,
a sound not unlike the call of rats yet far shriller than any sound
which could be made by man or animal. Again I thought that
words had been used but the exact meaning of them or the
language they belonged to was quite uncertain.

' "Two bananas a penny"?'

'Not bananas,' I said.

MacCruiskeen frowned vacantly.

'It is one of the most compressed and intricate pancakes I have
ever known,' he said.

He put the blanket back over the mangle and pushed it to one side and then lit a lamp on the wall by pressing some knob in the darkness. The light was bright but wavery and uncertain and would be far from satisfactory for reading with. He sat back in his chair as if waiting to be questioned and complimented on the strange things he had been doing.

'What is your private opinion of all that?' he asked.

'What were you doing?' I inquired.

'Stretching the light.'

'I do not understand your meaning.'

'I will tell you the size of it,' he said, 'and indicate roughly the shape of it. It is no harm if you know unusual things because you will be a dead man in two days and you will be held incognito and incommunicate in the meantime. Did you ever hear tell of omnium?'

'Omnium?'

'Omnium is the right name for it although you will not find it in the books.'

'Are you sure that is the right name?' I had never heard this word before except in Latin.

'Certain.'

'How certain?'

'The Sergeant says so.'

'And what is omnium the right name for?'

MacCruiskeen smiled at me indulgently.

'You are omnium and I am omnium and so is the mangle and my boots here and so is the wind in the chimney.'

'That is enlightening,' I said.

'It comes in waves,' he explained.

'What colour?'

'Every colour.'

'High or low?'

'Both.'

The blade of my inquisitive curiosity was sharpened but I saw that questions were putting the matter further into doubt instead of clearing it. I kept my silence till MacCruiskeen spoke again.

'Some people,' he said, 'call it energy but the right name is omnium because there is far more than energy in the inside of it, whatever it is. Omnium is the essential inherent interior essence which is hidden inside the root of the kernel of everything and it is always the same.'

I nodded wisely.

'It never changes. But it shows itself in a million ways and it always comes in waves. Now take the case of the light on the mangle.'

'Take it,' I said.

'Light is the same omnium on a short wave but if it comes on a longer wave it is in the form of noise, or sound. With my own patents I can stretch a ray out until it becomes sound.'

'I see.'

'And when I have a shout shut in that box with the wires, I can squeeze it till I get heat and you would not believe the convenience of it all in the winter. Do you see that lamp on the wall there?'

'I do.'

'That is operated by a patent compressor and a secret instrument connected with that box with the wires. The box is full of noise. Myself and the Sergeant spend our spare time in the summer collecting noises so that we can have light and heat for our official life in the dark winter. That is why the light is going up and down. Some of the noises are noisier than the others and the pair of us will be blinded if we come to the time when the quarry was working last September. It is in the box somewhere and it is bound to come out of it in the due course inevitably.'

'Blasting operations?'

'Dynamiteering and extravagant combustions of the most far-reaching kind. But omnium is the business-end of everything. If you could find the right wave that results in a tree, you could make a small fortune out of timber for export.'

'And policemen and cows, are they all in waves?'

'Everything is on a wave and omnium is at the back of the whole shooting-match unless I am a Dutchman from the distant Netherlands. Some people call it God and there are other names for something that is identically resembling it and that thing is omnium also into the same bargain.'

'Cheese?'

'Yes. Omnium.'

'Even braces?'

'Even braces.'

'Did you ever see a piece of it or what colour it is?'

MacCruiskeen smiled wryly and spread his hands into red fans.

'That is the supreme pancake,' he said. 'If you could say what the shouts mean it might be the makings of the answer.'

'And storm-wind and water and brown bread and the feel of hailstones on the bare head, are those all omnium on a different wave?'

'All omnium.'

'Could you not get a piece and carry it in your waistcoat so that you could change the world to suit you when it suited you?'

'It is the ultimate and the inexorable pancake. If you had a sack of it or even the half-full of a small matchbox of it, you could do anything and even do what could not be described by that name.'

'I understand you.'

MacCruiskeen sighed and went again to the dresser, taking something from the drawer. When he sat down at the table again, he started to move his hands together, performing intricate loops and convolutions with his fingers as if they were knitting something but there were no needles in them at all, nothing to be seen except his naked hands.

'Are you working again at the little chest?' I asked.

'I am,' he said.

I sat watching him idly, thinking my own thoughts. For the first time I recalled the wherefore of my unhappy visit to the queer situation I was in. Not my watch but the black box. Where was it? If MacCruiskeen knew the answer, would he tell me if I asked him? If by chance I did not escape safely from the hangman's morning, would I ever see it or know what was inside it, know the value of the money I could never spend, know how handsome could have been my volume on de Selby? Would I ever see John Divney again? Where was he now? Where was my watch?

You have no watch.

That was true. I felt my brain cluttered and stuffed with questions and blind perplexity and I also felt the sadness of my position coming back into my throat. I felt completely alone, but with a small hope that I would escape safely at the tail end of everything.

I had made up my mind to ask him if he knew anything about

the cashbox when my attention was distracted by another surprising thing.

The door was flung open and in came Gilhaney, his red face puffed from the rough road. He did not quite stop or sit down but kept moving restlessly about the day-room, paying no attention to me at all. MacCruiskeen had reached a meticulous point in his work and had his head nearly on the table to make sure that his fingers were working correctly and making no serious mistakes. When he had passed the difficulty he looked up somewhat at Gilhaney.

'Is it about a bicycle?' he asked casually.

'Only about timber,' said Gilhaney.

'And what is your timber news?'

'The prices have been put up by a Dutch ring, the cost of a good scaffold would cost a fortune.'

'Trust the Dutchmen,' MacCruiskeen said in a tone that meant that he knew the timber trade inside out.

'A three-man scaffold with a good trap and satisfactory steps would set you back ten pounds without rope or labour,' Gilhaney said.

'Ten pounds is a lot of money for a hanger,' said MacCruiskeen.

'But a two-man scaffold with a push-off instead of the mechanical trap and a ladder for the steps would cost the best majority of six pound, rope extra.'

'And dear at the same price,' said MacCruiskeen.

'But the ten-pound scaffold is a better job, there is more class about it,' said Gilhaney. 'There is a charm about a scaffold if it is well-made and satisfactory.'

What occurred next I did not see properly because I was listening to this pitiless talk even with my eyes. But something astonishing happened again. Gilhaney had gone near MacCruiskeen to talk down at him seriously and I think he made the mistake of stopping dead completely instead of keeping on the move to preserve his perpendicular balance. The outcome was that he crashed down, half on bent MacCruiskeen and half on the table, bringing the two of them with him into a heap of shouts and legs and confusion on the floor. The policeman's face when I saw it was a frightening sight. It was the colour of a dark plum with passion, but his eyes burned like bonfires in the forehead and there were frothy discharges at his mouth. He said no words for a while, only sounds of jungle anger, wild grunts and clicks of demoniacal hostility. Gilhaney had cowered to the wall and raised himself with the help of it and then retreated to the door. When MacCruiskeen found his tongue again he used the most unclean language ever spoken and invented dirtier words than the dirtiest ever spoken anywhere. He put names on Gilhaney too impossible and revolting to be written with known letters. He was temporarily insane with anger because he rushed ultimately to the dresser where he kept all his properties and pulled out a patent pistol and swept it round the room to threaten the two of us and every breakable article in the house.

'Get down on your four knees, the two of you, on the floor,' he roared, 'and don't stop searching for that chest you have knocked down till you find it!'

Gilhaney slipped down to his knees at once and I did the same thing without troubling to look at the policeman's face because I could remember distinctly what it looked like the last time I had eyed it. We crawled feebly about the floor, peering and feeling for something that could not be felt or seen and that was really too small to be lost at all.

This is amusing. You are going to be hung for murdering a man you did not murder and now you will be shot for not finding a tiny thing that probably does not exist at all and which in any event you did not lose.

I deserve it all, I answered, for not being here at all, to quote the words of the Sergeant.

How long we remained at our peculiar task, Gilhaney and I, it is not easy to remember. Ten minutes or ten years, perhaps, with MacCruiskeen seated near us, fingering the iron and glaring savagely at our bent forms. Then I caught Gilhaney showing his face to me sideways and giving me a broad private wink. Soon he closed his fingers, got up erect with the assistance of the door-handle and advanced to where MacCruiskeen was, smiling his gappy smile.

'Here you are and here it is,' he said with his closed hand outstretched.

'Put it on the table,' MacCruiskeen said evenly.

Gilhaney put his hand on the table and opened it.

'You can now go away and take your departure,' Mac-Cruiskeen told him, 'and leave the premises for the purpose of attending to the timber.'

When Gilhaney was gone I saw that most of the passion had ebbed from the policeman's face. He sat silent for a time, then gave his customary sigh and got up.

'I have more to do tonight,' he said to me civilly, 'so I will show you where you are to sleep for the dark night-time.'

He lit a queer light that had wires to it and a diminutive box full of minor noises, and led me into a room where there were two white beds and nothing else.

'Gilhaney thinks he is a clever one and a master mind,' he said.

'He might be or maybe not,' I muttered.

'He does not take much account of coincidental chances.'

'He does not look like a man that would care much.'

'When he said he had the chest he thought he was making me into a prize pup and blinding me by putting his thumb in my eye.'

'That is what it looked like.'

'But by a rare chance he *did* accidentally close his hand on the chest and it was the chest and nothing else that he replaced in due course on the table.'

There was some silence here.

'Which bed?' I asked.

'This one,' said MacCruiskeen.

CHAPTER 8

AFTER MACCRUISKEEN had tiptoed delicately from the room like a trained nurse and shut the door without a sound, I found myself standing by the bed and wondering stupidly what I was going to do with it. I was weary in body and my brain was numb. I had a curious feeling about my left leg. I thought that it was, so to speak, spreading – that its woodenness was slowly extending throughout my whole body, a dry timber poison killing me inch by inch. Soon my brain would be changed to wood completely and I would then be dead. Even the bed was made of wood, not metal. If I were to lie in it –

Will you sit down for Pity's sake and stop standing there like a gawm, Joe said suddenly.

I am not sure what I do next if I stop standing, I answered. But I sat down on the bed for Pity's sake.

There is nothing difficult about a bed, even a child can learn to use a bed. Take off your clothes and get into bed and lie on it and keep lying on it even if it makes you feel foolish.

I saw the wisdom of this and started to undress. I felt almost too tired to go through that simple task. When all my clothes were laid on the floor they were much more numerous than I had expected and my body was surprisingly white and thin.

I opened the bed fastidiously, lay into the middle of it, closed it up again carefully and let out a sigh of happiness and rest. I felt as if all my weariness and perplexities of the day had descended on me pleasurably like a great heavy quilt which would keep me warm and sleepy. My knees opened up like rosebuds in rich sunlight, pushing my shins two inches further to the bottom of the bed. Every joint became loose and foolish and devoid of true utility. Every inch of my person gained weight with every second until the total burden on the bed was approximately five hundred thousand tons. This was evenly distributed on the four wooden legs of the bed, which had by now become an integral part of the universe. My eyelids, each weighing no less than four tons, slewed ponderously across my eyeballs. My narrow shins, itchier and more remote in their agony of relaxation, moved further away from me till my happy toes pressed closely on the bars. My position was completely horizontal, ponderous, absolute and incontrovertible. United with the bed I became momentous and planetary. Far away from the bed I could see the outside night framed neatly in the window as if it were a picture on the wall. There was a bright star in one corner with other smaller stars elsewhere littered about in sublime profusion. Lying quietly and dead-eyed, I reflected on how new the night[1] was, how

1 Not excepting even the credulous Kraus (see his *De Selby's Leben*), all the commentators have treated de Selby's disquisitions on night and sleep with considerable reserve. This is hardly to be wondered at since he held (a) that darkness was simply an accretion of 'black air', i.e., a staining of the atmosphere due to volcanic eruptions too fine to be seen with the naked eye and also to certain 'regrettable' industrial activities involving coal-tar by-products and vegetable dyes; and (b) that sleep was simply a succession of fainting-fits brought on by semi-asphyxiation due to (a). Hatchjaw brings forward his rather facile and ever-ready theory of forgery, pointing to certain unfamiliar syntactical constructions in the first part of the third so-called 'prosecanto' in *Golden Hours*. He does not, however, suggest that there is anything spurious in de Selby's equally damaging rhodomontade in the *Layman's Atlas* where he inveighs savagely against 'the insanitary conditions prevailing everywhere after six o'clock' and makes the famous *gaffe* that death is merely 'the collapse of the heart from the strain of a lifetime of fits and fainting'. Bassett (in *Lux Mundi*) has gone to considerable pains to establish the date of these passages and shows that de Selby was *hors de combat* from his long-standing gall-bladder disorders at least immediately before the passages were composed. One cannot lightly set aside Bassett's formidable table of dates and his corroborative extracts from contemporary newspapers which treat of an unnamed 'elderly man' being assisted into private houses after having fits in the street. For those who wish to hold the balance for themselves, Henderson's *Hatchjaw and Bassett* is not unuseful. Kraus, usually unscientific and unreliable, is worth reading on this point. (*Leben*, pp. 17–37.)

As in many other of de Selby's concepts, it is difficult to get to grips with his process of reasoning or to refute his curious conclusions. The 'volcanic eruptions', which we may for convenience compare to the infra-visual activity of such substances as radium, take place usually in the 'evening', are stimulated by the smoke and industrial combustions of the 'day' and are intensified in certain places which may, for the want of a better term, be called 'dark places'. One difficulty is precisely this question of terms. A 'dark place' is dark merely because it is a place where darkness 'germinates' and 'evening' is a time of twilight merely because the 'day' deteriorates owing to the stimulating effect of smuts on the volcanic processes. De Selby makes no attempt to explain why a 'dark place' such as a cellar need be dark and does not define the atmospheric, physical or mineral conditions which must prevail uniformly in all such places if the theory is to stand. The 'only straw offered', to use Bassett's wry phrase, is the statement that 'black air' is highly combustible, enormous masses of it being instantly consumed by the smallest flame, even an electrical luminance isolated in a vacuum. 'This,' Bassett observes, 'seems to be an attempt to protect the theory from the shock it can be dealt by simply striking matches and may be taken as the final proof that the great brain was out of gear.'

A significant feature of the matter is the absence of any authoritative record of those experiments with which de Selby always sought to support his ideas. It is true that Kraus (see below) gives a forty-page account of certain experiments, mostly concerned with attempts to bottle quantities of 'night' and endless sessions in locked and shuttered bedrooms from which bursts of loud hammering could be heard. He explains that the bottling operations were carried out with bottles which were, 'for obvious reasons', made of black glass. Opaque porcelain jars are also stated to have been used 'with some success'. To use the frigid words of Bassett, 'such information, it is to be feared, makes little contribution to serious deselbiana (sic)'.

Very little is known of Kraus or his life. A brief biographical note appears in the obsolete *Bibliographie de de Selby*. He is stated to have been born in Ahrensburg, near Hamburg, and to have worked as a young man in the office of his father, who had extensive jam interests in North Germany. He is said to have disappeared completely from human ken after Hatchjaw had been arrested in a Sheephaven hotel following the unmasking of the de Selby letter scandal by *The Times*, which made scathing references to Kraus's 'discreditable' machinations in Hamburg and clearly suggested his complicity. If it is remembered that these events occurred in the fateful June when the *County Album* was beginning to appear in fortnightly parts, the significance of the whole affair becomes apparent. The subsequent exoneration of Hatchjaw served only to throw further suspicion on the shadowy Kraus.

Recent research has not thrown much light on Kraus's identity or his ultimate fate. Bassett's posthumous *Recollections* contains the interesting suggestion that Kraus did not exist at all, the name being one of the pseudonyms adopted by the egregious du Garbandier to further his 'campaign of calumny'. The *Leben*, however, seems too friendly in tone to encourage such a speculation.

Du Garbandier himself, possibly pretending to confuse the characteristics of the English and French languages, persistently uses 'black hair' for 'black air', and makes extremely elaborate fun of the raven-headed lady of the skies who deluged the world with her tresses every night when retiring.

The wisest course on this question is probably that taken by the little-known Swiss writer, Le Clerque. 'This matter,' he says, 'is outside the true province of the conscientious commentator inasmuch as being unable to say aught that is charitable or useful, he must preserve silence.'

distinctive and unaccustomed its individuality. Robbing me of
the reassurance of my eyesight, it was disintegrating my bodily
personality into a flux of colour, smell, recollection, desire – all
the strange uncounted essences of terrestrial and spiritual existence. I was deprived of definition, position and magnitude and
my significance was considerably diminished. Lying there, I felt
the weariness ebbing from me slowly, like a tide retiring over limitless sands. The feeling was so pleasurable and profound that
I sighed again a long sound of happiness. Almost at once I heard
another sigh and heard Joe murmuring some contented incoher-
ency. His voice was near me, yet did not seem to come from the
accustomed place within. I thought that he must be lying beside
me in the bed and I kept my hands carefully at my sides in case
I should accidentally touch him. I felt, for no reason, that his
diminutive body would be horrible to the human touch – scaly or
slimy like an eel or with a repelling roughness like a cat's tongue.

That's not very logical – or complimentary either, he said suddenly.

What isn't?

That about my body. Why scaly?

That's only my joke, I chuckled drowsily. I know you have no
body. Except my own perhaps.

But why scaly?

I don't know. How can I know why I think my thoughts?

By God I won't be called scaly.

His voice to my surprise had become shrill with petulance.
Then he seemed to fill the world with his resentment, not by
speaking but by remaining silent after he had spoken.

Now, now, Joe, I murmured soothingly.

Because if you are looking for trouble you can have your bellyful, he
snapped.

You have no body, Joe.

Then why do you say I have? And why scaly?

Here I had a strange idea not unworthy of de Selby. Why was
Joe so disturbed at the suggestion that he had a body? What if
he *had* a body? A body with another body inside it in turn, thousands of such bodies within each other like the skins of an onion,
receding to some unimaginable ultimum? Was I in turn merely a
link in a vast sequence of imponderable beings, the world I knew
merely the interior of the being whose inner voice I myself was?
Who or what was the core and what monster in what world was

the final uncontained colossus? God? Nothing? Was I receiving these wild thoughts from Lower Down or were they brewing newly in me to be transmitted Higher Up?

From Lower Down, Joe barked.

Thank you.

I'm leaving.

What?

Clearing out. We will see who is scaly in two minutes.

These few words sickened me instantly with fear although their meaning was too momentous to be grasped without close reasoning.

The scaly idea – where did I get that from? I cried.

Higher Up, he shouted.

Puzzled and frightened I tried to understand the complexities not only of my intermediate dependence and my catenal un-integrity but also my dangerous adjunctiveness and my embarrassing unisolation. If one assumes –

Listen. Before I go I will tell you this. I am your soul and all your souls. When I am gone you are dead. Past humanity is not only implicit in each new man born but is contained in him. Humanity is an ever-widening spiral and life is the beam that plays briefly on each succeeding ring. All humanity from its beginning to its end is already present but the beam has not yet played beyond you. Your earthly successors await dumbly and trust to your guidance and mine and all my people inside me to preserve them and lead the light further. You are not now the top of your people's line any more than your mother was when she had you inside her. When I leave you I take with me all that has made you what you are – I take all your significance and importance and all the accumulations of human instinct and appetite and wisdom and dignity. You will be left with nothing behind you and nothing to give the waiting ones. Woe to you when they find you out! Good-bye!

Although I thought this speech was rather far-fetched and ridiculous, he was gone and I was dead.

Preparations for the funeral were put in hand at once. Lying in my dark blanket-padded coffin I could hear the sharp blows of a hammer nailing down the lid.

It soon turned out that the hammering was the work of Sergeant Pluck. He was standing smiling at me from the doorway and he looked large and lifelike and surprisingly full of breakfast. Over the tight collar of his tunic he wore a red ring of fat that looked fresh and decorative as if it had come directly from the laundry. His moustache was damp from drinking milk.

Thank goodness to be back to sanity, Joe said.

His voice was friendly and reassuring, like pockets in an old suit.

'Good morning to you in the morning-time,' the Sergeant said pleasantly.

I answered him in a civil way and gave particulars of my dream. He leaned listening on the jamb, taking in the difficult parts with a skilled ear. When I had finished he smiled at me in pity and good humour.

'You have been dreaming, man,' he said.

Wondering at him, I looked away to the window. Night was gone from it without a trace, leaving in substitution a distant hill that lay gently against the sky. Clouds of white and grey pillowed it and on its soft shoulder trees and boulders were put pleasingly to make it true. I could hear a morning wind making its way indomitably throughout the world and all the low unsilence of the daytime was in my ear, bright and restless like a caged bird. I sighed and looked back at the Sergeant, who was still leaning and quietly picking his teeth, absent-faced and still.

'I remember well,' he said, 'a dream that I had six years ago on the twenty-third of November next. A nightmare would be a truer word. I dreamt if you please that I had a slow puncture.'

'That is a surprising thing,' I said idly, 'but not astonishing. Was it the work of a tintack?'

'Not a tintack,' said the Sergeant, 'but too much starch.'

'I did not know,' I said sarcastically, 'that they starched the roads.'

'It was not the road, and for a wonder it was not the fault of the County Council. I dreamt that I was cycling on official business for three days. Suddenly I felt the saddle getting hard and lumpy underneath me. I got down and felt the tyres but they were unexceptionable and fully pumped. Then I thought my head was giving me a nervous outbreak from too much overwork. I went into a private house where there was a qualified doctor and he examined me completely and told me what the trouble was. I had a slow puncture.'

He gave a coarse laugh and half-turned to me his enormous backside.

'Here, look,' he laughed.

'I see,' I murmured.

Chuckling loudly he went away for a minute and came back again.

'I have put the stirabout on the table,' he said, 'and the milk is still hot from being inside the cow's milk-bag.'

I put on my clothes and went to my breakfast in the day-room where the Sergeant and MacCruiskeen were talking about their figures.

'Six point nine six three circulating,' MacCruiskeen was saying.

'High,' said the Sergeant. 'Very high. There must be a ground heat. Tell me about the fall.'

'A medium fall at midnight and no lumps.'

The Sergeant laughed and shook his head.

'No lumps indeed,' he chuckled, 'there will be hell to pay tomorrow on the lever if it is true there is a ground heat.'

MacCruiskeen got up suddenly from his chair.

'I will give her half a hundredweight of charcoal,' he announced. He marched straight out of the house muttering calculations, not looking where he was going but staring straight into the middle of his black notebook.

I had almost finished my crock of porridge and lay back to look fully at the Sergeant.

'When are you going to hang me?' I asked, looking fearlessly into his large face. I felt refreshed and strong again and confident that I would escape without difficulty.

'Tomorrow morning if we have the scaffold up in time and unless it is raining. You would not believe how slippery the rain can make a new scaffold. You could slip and break your neck into fancy fractures and you would never know what happened to your life or how you lost it.'

'Very well,' I said firmly. 'If I am to be a dead man in twenty-four hours will you explain to me what these figures in Mac-Cruiskeen's black book are?'

The Sergeant smiled indulgently.

'The readings?'

'Yes.'

'If you are going to be dead completely there is no insoluble impedimentum to that proposal,' he said, 'but it is easier to

show you than to tell you verbally. Follow behind me like a
good man.'

He led the way to a door in the back passage and threw it open
with an air of momentous revelation, standing aside politely to
give me a complete and unobstructed view.

'What do you think of that?' he asked.

I looked into the room and did not think much of it. It was a
small bedroom, gloomy and not too clean. It was in great disorder
and filled with a heavy smell.

'It is MacCruiskeen's room,' he explained.

'I do not see much,' I said.

The Sergeant smiled patiently.

'You are not looking in the right quarter,' he said.

'I have looked everywhere that can be looked,' I said.

The Sergeant led the way in to the middle of the floor and
took possession of a walking-stick that was convenient.

'If I ever want to hide,' he remarked, 'I will always go upstairs
in a tree. People have no gift for looking up, they seldom examine the lofty altitudes.'

I looked at the ceiling.

'There is little to be seen there,' I said, 'except a bluebottle
that looks dead.'

The Sergeant looked up and pointed with his stick.

'That is not a bluebottle,' he said, 'that is Gogarty's outhouse.'

I looked squarely at him in a mixed way but he was paying me
no attention but pointing to other tiny marks upon the ceiling.

'That,' he said, 'is Martin Bundle's house and that is Tiernahins and that one there is where the married sister lives. And
here we have the lane from Tiernahins to the main telegraph
trunk road.' He drew his stick along a wavering faint crack that
ran down to join a deeper crack.

'A map!' I cried excitedly.

'And here we have the barrack,' he added. 'It is all as plain as
a pikestick.'

When I looked carefully at the ceiling I saw that Mr Mathers'
house and every road and house I knew were marked there, and
nets of lanes and neighbourhoods that I did not know also. It
was a map of the parish, complete, reliable and astonishing.

The Sergeant looked at me and smiled again.

'You will agree,' he said, 'that it is a fascinating pancake and a conundrum of great incontinence, a phenomenon of the first rarity.'

'Did you make it yourself?'

'I did not and nobody else manufactured it either. It was always there and MacCruiskeen is certain that it was there even before that. The cracks are natural and so are small cracks.'

With my cocked eye I traced the road we came when Gilhaney had found his bicycle at the bush.

'The funny thing is,' the Sergeant said, 'that MacCruiskeen lay for two years staring at that ceiling before he saw it was a map of superb ingenuity.'

'Now that was stupid,' I said thickly.

'And he lay looking at the map for five years more before he saw that it showed the way to eternity.'

'To eternity?'

'Certainly.'

'Will it be possible for us to come back from there?' I whispered.

'Of course. There is a lift. But wait till I show you the secret of the map.'

He took up the stick again and pointed to the mark that meant the barracks.

'Here we are in the barracks on the main telegraph trunk road,' he said. 'Now use your internal imagination and tell me what left-hand road you meet if you go forth from the barrack on the main road.'

I thought this out without difficulty.

'You meet the road that meets the main road at Jarvis's outhouse,' I said, 'where we came from the finding of the bicycle.'

'Then that road is the first turn on the left-hand latitude?'

'Yes.'

'And here it is – here.'

He pointed out the left-hand road with his stick and tapped Mr Jarvis's outhouse at the corner.

'And now,' he said solemnly, 'kindly inform me what this is.'

He drew the stick along a faint crack that joined the crack of the main road about half-way between the barrack and the road at Mr Jarvis's.

'What would you call that?' he repeated.

'There is no road there,' I cried excitedly, 'the left-hand road at Jarvis's is the first road on the left. I am not a fool. There is no road there.'

By God if you're not you will be. You're a goner if you listen to much more of this gentleman's talk.

'But there *is* a road there,' the Sergeant said triumphantly, 'if you know how to look knowledgeably for it. And a very old road. Come with me till we see the size of it.'

'Is this the road to eternity?'

'It is indeed but there is no signpost.'

Although he made no move to release his bicycle from solitary confinement in the cell, he snapped the clips adroitly on his trousers and led the way heavily into the middle of the morning. We marched together down the road. Neither of us spoke and neither listened for what the other might have to say.

When the keen wind struck me in the face it snatched away the murk of doubt and fear and wonder that was anchored on my brain like a raincloud on a hill. All my senses, relieved from the agony of dealing with the existence of the Sergeant, became supernaturally alert at the work of interpreting the genial day for my benefit. The world rang in my ear like a great workshop. Sublime feats of mechanics and chemistry were evident on every side. The earth was agog with invisible industry. Trees were active where they stood and gave uncompromising evidence of their strength. Incomparable grasses were forever at hand, lending their distinction to the universe. Patterns very difficult to imagine were made together by everything the eye could see, merging into a supernal harmony their unexceptionable varieties. Men who were notable for the whiteness of their shirts worked diminutively in the distant bog, toiling in the brown turf and heather. Patient horses stood near with their useful carts and littered among the boulders on a hill beyond were tiny sheep at pasture. Birds were audible in the secrecy of the bigger trees, changing branches and conversing not tumultuously. In a field by the road a donkey stood quietly as if he were examining the morning, bit by bit unhurryingly. He did not move, his head was high and his mouth chewed nothing. He looked as if he understood completely these unexplainable enjoyments of the world.

My eye ranged round unsatisfied. I could not see enough in

sufficient fulness before I took the left turn for eternity in company with the Sergeant and my thoughts remained entangled in what my eyes were looking at.

You don't mean to say that you believe in this eternity business?

What choice have I? It would be foolish to doubt anything after yesterday.

That is all very well but I think I can claim to be an authority on the subject of eternity. There must be a limit to this gentleman's monkey-tricks.

I am certain there isn't.

Nonsense. You are becoming demoralized.

I will be hung tomorrow.

That is doubtful but if it has to be faced we will make a brave show.

We?

Certainly. I will be there to the end. In the meantime let us make up our minds that eternity is not up a lane that is found by looking at cracks in the ceiling of a country policeman's bedroom.

Then what *is* up the lane?

I cannot say. If he said that eternity was up the lane and left it at that, I would not kick so hard. But when we are told that we are coming back from there in a lift — well, I begin to think that he is confusing night-clubs with heaven. A lift!

Surely, I argued, if we concede that eternity is up the lane, the question of the lift is a minor matter. That is a case for swallowing a horse and cart and straining at a flea.

No. I bar the lift. I know enough about the next world to be sure that you don't get there and come back out of it in a lift. Besides, we must be near the place now and I don't see any elevator-shaft running up into the clouds.

Gilhaney had no handlebars on him, I pointed out.

Unless the word 'lift' has a special meaning. Like 'drop' when you are talking about a scaffold. I suppose a smash under the chin with a heavy spade could be called a 'lift'. If that is the case you can be certain about eternity and have the whole of it yourself and welcome.

I still think there is an electric lift.

My attention was drawn away from this conversation to the Sergeant, who had now slackened his pace and was making curious inquiries with his stick. The road had reached a place where there was rising ground on each side, rank grass and brambles near our feet, with a tangle of bigger things behind that, and tall brown thickets beset with green creeper plants beyond.

'It is here somewhere,' the Sergeant said, 'or beside a place somewhere near the next place adjacent.'

He dragged his stick along the green margin, probing at the hidden ground.

'MacCruiskeen rides his bicycle along the grass here,' he said, 'it is an easier pancake, the wheels are surer and the seat is a more sensitive instrument than the horny hand.'

After another walk and more probing he found what he was searching for and suddenly dragged me into the undergrowth, parting the green curtains of the branches with a practised hand.

'This is the hidden road,' he called backwards from ahead.

It is not easy to say whether road is the correct name for a place that must be fought through inch by inch at the cost of minor wounds and the sting of strained branches slapping back against the person. Nevertheless the ground was even against the foot and some dim distance to each side I could see the ground banking up sharply with rocks and gloominess and damp vegetation. There was a sultry smell and many flies of the gnat class were at home here.

A yard in front of me the Sergeant was plunging on wildly with his head down, thrashing the younger shoots severely with his stick and calling muffled warnings to me of the strong distended boughs he was about to release in my direction.

I do not know how long we travelled or what the distance was but the air and the light got scarcer and scarcer until I was sure that we were lost in the bowels of a great forest. The ground was still even enough to walk on but covered with the damp and rotting fall of many autumns. I had followed the noisy Sergeant with blind faith till my strength was nearly gone, so that I reeled forward instead of walking and was defenceless against the brutality of the boughs. I felt very ill and exhausted. I was about to shout to him that I was dying when I noticed the growth was thinning and that the Sergeant was calling to me, from where he was hidden and ahead of me, that we were there. When I reached him he was standing before a small stone building and bending to take the clips from his trousers.

'This is it,' he said, nodding his stooped head at the little house.

'This is what?' I muttered.

'The entrance to it,' he replied.

The structure looked exactly like the porch of a small country church. The darkness and the confusion of the branches made it hard for me to see whether there was a larger building at the rear. The little porch was old, with green stains on the stonework and warts of moss in its many crannies. The door was an old brown door with ecclesiastical hinges and ornamental ironwork; it was set far back and made to measure in its peaked doorway. This was the entrance to eternity. I knocked the streaming sweat from my forehead with my hand.

The Sergeant was feeling himself sensually for his keys.

'It is very close,' he said politely.

'Is this the entrance to the next world?' I murmured. My voice was lower than I thought it would be owing to my exertions and trepidation.

'But it is seasonable weather and we can't complain,' he added loudly, paying no attention to my question. My voice, perhaps, had not been strong enough to travel to his ear.

He found a key which he rasped in the keyhole and threw the door open. He entered the dark inside but sent his hand out again to twitch me in after him by the coat sleeve.

Strike a match there!

Almost at the same time the Sergeant had found a box with knobs and wires in it in the wall and did whatever was necessary to make it give out a startling leaping light from where it was. But during the second I was standing in the dark I had ample time to get the surprise of my life. It was the floor. My feet were astonished when they trod on it. It was made of platefuls of tiny studs like the floor of a steam-engine or like the railed galleries that run around a great printing press. It rang with a ghostly hollow noise beneath the hobnails of the Sergeant, who had now clattered to the other end of the little room to fuss with his chain of keys and to throw open another door that was hidden in the wall.

'Of course a nice shower of rain would clear the air,' he called.

I went carefully over to see what he was doing in the little closet he had entered. Here he had operated successfully another unsteady light-box. He stood with his back to me examining panels in the wall. There were two of them, tiny things like matchboxes, and the figure sixteen could be seen in one panel and ten in the other. He sighed and came out of the closet and looked at me sadly.

'They say that walking takes it down,' he said, 'but it is my own experience that walking puts it up, walking makes it solid and leaves plenty of room for more.'

I thought at this stage that a simple and dignified appeal might have some prospect of succeeding.

'Will you please tell me,' I said, 'since I will be a dead man tomorrow – where are we and what are we doing?'

'Weighing ourselves,' he replied.

'Weighing ourselves?'

'Step into the box there,' he said, 'till we see what your registration is by plain record.'

I stepped warily on to more iron plates in the closet and saw the figures change to nine and six.

'Nine stone six pounds,' said the Sergeant, 'and a most invidious weight. I would give ten years of my life to get the beef down.'

He had his back to me again opening still another closet in another wall and passing trained fingers over another light-box. The unsteady light came and I saw him standing in the closet, looking at his large watch and winding it absently. The light was leaping beside his jaw and throwing unearthly leaps of shadow on his gross countenance.

'Will you step over here,' he called to me at last, 'and come in with me unless you desire to be left behind in your own company.'

When I had walked over and stood silently beside him in the steel closet, he shut the door on us with a precise click and leaned against the wall thoughtfully. I was about to ask for several explanations when a cry of horror came bounding from my throat. With no noise or warning at all, the floor was giving way beneath us.

'It is no wonder that you are yawning,' the Sergeant said conversationally, 'it is very close, the ventilation is far from satisfactory.'

'I was only screaming,' I blurted. 'What is happening to this box we are in? Where –'

My voice trailed away to a dry cluck of fright. The floor was falling so fast beneath us that it seemed once or twice to fall faster

than I could fall myself so that it was sure that my feet had left it
and that I had taken up a position for brief intervals half-way
between the floor and the ceiling. In panic I raised my right foot
and smote it down with all my weight and my strength. It struck
the floor but only with a puny tinkling noise. I swore and
groaned and closed my eyes and wished for a happy death. I felt
my stomach bounding sickeningly about inside me as if it were
a wet football filled with water.

Lord save us!

'It does a man no harm,' the Sergeant remarked pleasantly,
'to move around a bit and see things. It is a great thing for widening out the mind. A wide mind is a grand thing, it nearly always
leads to farseeing inventions. Look at Sir Walter Raleigh that
invented the pedal bicycle and Sir George Stephenson with his
steam-engine and Napoleon Bonaparte and George Sand and
Walter Scott – great men all.'

'Are – are we in eternity yet?' I chattered.

'We are not there yet but nevertheless we are nearly there,' he
answered. 'Listen with all your ears for a little click.'

What can I say to tell of my personal position? I was locked in
an iron box with a sixteen-stone policeman, falling appallingly
for ever, listening to talk about Walter Scott and listening for a
click also.

Click!

It came at last, sharp and terrible. Almost at once the falling
changed, either stopping altogether or becoming a much slower
falling.

'Yes,' said the Sergeant brightly, 'we are there now.'

I noticed nothing whatever except that the thing we were in
gave a jolt and the floor seemed to resist my feet suddenly in a
way that might well have been eternal. The Sergeant fingered
the arrangement of knob-like instruments on the door, which
he opened after a time and stepped out.

'That was the lift,' he remarked.

It is peculiar that when one expects some horrible incalculable
and devastating thing which does not materialize, one is more
disappointed than relieved. I had expected for one thing a blaze
of eye-destroying light. No other expectation was clear enough
in my brain to be mentioned. Instead of this radiance, I saw a
long passage lit fitfully at intervals by the crude home-made

noise-machines, with more darkness to be seen than light. The walls of the passage seemed to be made with bolted sheets of pig-iron in which were set rows of small doors which looked to me like ovens or furnace-doors or safe-deposits such as banks have. The ceiling, where I could see it, was a mass of wires and what appeared to be particularly thick wires or possibly pipes. All the time there was an entirely new noise to be heard, not unmusical, sometimes like water gurgling underground and sometimes like subdued conversation in a foreign tongue.

The Sergeant was already looming ahead on his way up the passage, treading heavily on the plates. He swung his keys jauntily and hummed a song. I followed near him, trying to count the little doors. There were four rows of six in every lineal two yards of wall, or a total of many thousands. Here and there I saw a dial or an intricate nest of clocks and knobs resembling a control board with masses of coarse wires converging from all quarters of it. I did not understand the significance of anything but I thought the scene was so real that much of my fear was groundless. I trod firmly beside the Sergeant, who was still real enough for anybody.

We came to a crossroads in the passage where the light was brighter. A cleaner brighter passage with shiny steel walls ran away to each side, disappearing from view only where the distance brought its walls, floor and roof to the one gloomy point. I thought I could hear a sound like hissing steam and another noise like great cogwheels grinding one way, stopping and grinding back again. The Sergeant paused to take a reading from a clock in the wall, then turned sharply to the left and called for me to follow.

I shall not recount the passages we walked or talk of the one with the round doors like portholes or the other place where the Sergeant got a box of matches for himself by putting his hand somewhere into the wall. It is enough to say that we arrived, after walking at least a mile of plate, into a well-lit airy hall which was completely circular and filled with indescribable articles very like machinery but not quite as intricate as the more difficult machines. Large expensive-looking cabinets of these articles were placed tastefully about the floor while the circular wall was one mass of these inventions with little dials and meters placed plentifully here and there. Hundreds of miles of coarse wire were

visible running everywhere except about the floor and there
were thousands of doors like the strong-hinged doors of ovens
and arrangements of knobs and keys that reminded me of
American cash registers.

The Sergeant was reading out figures from one of the many
clocks and turning a small wheel with great care. Suddenly the
silence was split by the sound of loud frenzied hammering from
the far end of the hall where the apparatus seemed thickest and
most complex. The blood ran away at once from my startled
face. I looked at the Sergeant but he still attended patiently to
his clock and wheel, reciting numbers under his breath and
taking no notice. The hammering stopped.

I sat down to think and gather my scattered wits on a smooth
article like an iron bar. It was pleasantly warm and comforting.
Before any thought had time to come to me there was another
burst of hammering, then silence, then a low but violent noise
like passionately-muttered oaths, then silence again and finally
the sound of heavy footsteps approaching from behind the tall
cabinets of machinery.

Feeling a weakness in my spine, I went over quickly and stood
beside the Sergeant. He had taken a long white instrument like
a large thermometer or band conductor's baton out of a hole in
the wall and was examining the calibrations on it with a frown
of great preoccupation. He paid no attention to me or to the
hidden presence that was approaching invisibly. When I heard
the clanging steps rounding the last cabinet, against my will
I looked up wildly. It was Policeman MacCruiskeen. He was
frowning heavily and bearing another large baton or thermometer which was orange-coloured. He made straight for the
Sergeant and showed him this instrument, putting a red finger
on a marking that was on it. They stood there silently examining
each other's instruments. The Sergeant looked somewhat
relieved, I thought, when he had the matter thought out and
marched away to the hidden place that MacCruiskeen had just
come from. Soon we heard the sound of hammering, this time
gentle and rhythmical.

MacCruiskeen put his baton away into the wall in the hole
where the Sergeant's had been and turned to me, giving me
generously the wrinkled cigarette which I had come to regard as
the herald of unthinkable conversation.

'Do you like it?' he inquired.

'It is neat,' I replied.

'You would not believe the convenience of it,' he remarked cryptically.

The Sergeant came back to us drying his red hands on a towel and looking very satisfied with himself. I looked at the two of them sharply. They received my glance and exchanged it privately between them before discarding it.

'Is this eternity?' I asked. 'Why do you call it eternity?'

'Feel my chin,' MacCruiskeen said, smiling enigmatically.

'We call it that,' the Sergeant explained, 'because you don't grow old here. When you leave here you will be the same age as you were coming in and the same stature and latitude. There is an eight-day clock here with a patent balanced action but it never goes.'

'How can you be sure you don't grow old here?'

'Feel my chin,' MacCruiskeen said again.

'It is simple,' the Sergeant said. 'The beard does not grow and if you are fed you do not get hungry and if you are hungry you don't get hungrier. Your pipe will smoke all day and will still be full and a glass of whiskey will still be there no matter how much of it you drink and it does not matter in any case because it will not make you drunker than your own sobriety.'

'Indeed,' I muttered.

'I have been here for a long time this today morning,' Mac-Cruiskeen said, 'and my jaw is still as smooth as a woman's back and the convenience of it takes my breath away, it is a great thing to downface the old razor.'

'How big is all this place?'

'It has no size at all,' the Sergeant explained, 'because there is no difference anywhere in it and we have no conception of the extent of its unchanging coequality.'

MacCruiskeen lit a match for our cigarettes and then threw it carelessly on the plate floor where it lay looking very much important and alone.

'Could you not bring your bicycle and ride through all of it and see it all and draw a chart?' I asked.

The Sergeant smiled at me as if I were a baby.

'The bicycle is easy,' he said.

To my astonishment he went over to one of the bigger ovens,

manipulated some knobs, pulled open the massive metal door and lifted out a brand-new bicycle. It had a three-speed gear and an oil-bath and I could see the vaseline still glistening on the bright parts. He put the front wheel down and spun the back wheel expertly in the air.

'The bicycle is an easy pancake,' he said, 'but it is no use and does not matter. Come and I will demonstrate the *res ipsa*.'

Leaving the bicycle, he led the way through the intricate cabinets and round behind other cabinets and in through a doorway. What I saw made my brain shrink painfully in my head and put a paralysing chill across my heart. It was not so much that this other hall was in every respect an exact replica of the one we had just left. It was more that my burdened eye saw that one of the cabinet doors in the wall was standing open and a brand-new bicycle was leaning against the wall, identically like the other one and leaning even at the same angle.

'If you want to take another walk ahead to reach the same place here without coming back you can walk on till you reach the next doorway and you are welcome. But it will do you no good and even if we stay here behind you it is probable that you will find us there to meet you.'

Here I gave a cry as my eye caught a spent match lying clearly on the floor.

'What do you think of the no-shaving?' MacCruiskeen asked boastfully. 'Surely that is an uninterruptible experiment?'

'It is inescapable and highly intractable,' the Sergeant said.

MacCruiskeen was examining some knobs in a central cabinet. He turned his head and called to me.

'Come over here,' he called, 'till I show you something to tell your friends about.'

Afterwards I saw that this was one of his rare jokes because what he showed me was something that I could tell nobody about, there are no suitable words in the world to tell my meaning. This cabinet had an opening resembling a chute and another large opening resembling a black hole about a yard below the chute. He pressed two red articles like typewriter keys and turned a large knob away from him. At once there was a rumbling noise as if thousands of full biscuit-boxes were falling down a stairs. I felt that these falling things would come out of the chute at any moment. And so they did, appearing for a few seconds in the air and then disappearing down the black hole below. But what can I say about them? In colour they were not white or black and certainly bore no intermediate colour; they were far from dark and anything but bright. But strange to say it was not their unprecedented hue that took most of my attention. They had another quality that made me watch them wild-eyed, dry-throated and with no breathing. I can make no attempt to describe this quality. It took me hours of thought long afterwards to realize why these articles were astonishing. *They lacked an essential property of all known objects.* I cannot call it shape or configuration since shapelessness is not what I refer to at all. I can only say that these objects, not one of which resembled the other, were of no known dimensions. They were not square or rectangular or circular or simply irregularly shaped nor could it be said that their endless variety was due to dimensional dissimilarities. Simply their appearance, if even that word is not inadmissible, was not understood by the eye and was in any event indescribable. That is enough to say.

When MacCruiskeen had unpressed the buttons the Sergeant asked me politely what else I would like to see.

'What else is there?'

'Anything.'

'Anything I mention will be shown to me?'

'Of course.'

The ease with which the Sergeant had produced a bicycle that would cost at least eight pounds ten to buy had set in motion in my head certain trains of thought. My nervousness had been largely reduced to absurdity and nothingness by what I had seen and I now found myself taking an interest in the commercial possibilities of eternity.

'What I would like,' I said slowly, 'is to see you open a door and lift out a solid block of gold weighing half a ton.'

The Sergeant smiled and shrugged his shoulders.

'But that is impossible, it is a very unreasonable requisition,' he said. 'It is vexatious and unconscionable,' he added legally.

My heart sank down at this.

'But you said *anything*.'

'I know, man. But there is a limit and a boundary to everything within the scope of reason's garden.'

'That is disappointing,' I muttered.

MacCruiskeen stirred diffidently.

'Of course,' he said, 'if there would be no objection to me assisting the Sergeant in lifting out the block . . .'

'What! Is that a difficulty?'

'I am not a cart-horse,' the Sergeant said with simple dignity. 'Yet, anyhow,' he added, reminding all of us of his great-grandfather.

'Then we'll all lift it out,' I cried.

And so we did. The knobs were manipulated, the door opened and the block of gold, which was encased in a well-made timber box, was lifted down with all our strength and placed on the floor.

'Gold is a common article and there is not much to see when you look at it,' the Sergeant observed. 'Ask him for something confidential and superior to ordinary pre-eminence. Now a magnifying glass is a better thing because you can look at it and what you see when you look is a third thing altogether.'

Another door was opened by MacCruiskeen and I was handed a magnifying glass, a very ordinary-looking instrument with a bone handle. I looked at my hand through it and saw nothing that was recognizable. Then I looked at several other things but saw nothing that I could clearly see. MacCruiskeen took it back with a smile at my puzzled eye.

'It magnifies to invisibility,' he explained. 'It makes everything so big that there is room in the glass for only the smallest particle of it – not enough of it to make it different from any other thing that is dissimilar.'

My eye moved from his explaining face to the block of gold which my attention had never really left.

'What I would like to see now,' I said carefully, 'is fifty cubes of solid gold each weighing one pound.'

MacCruiskeen went away obsequiously like a trained waiter and got these articles out of the wall without a word, arranging them in a neat structure on the floor. The Sergeant had strolled away idly to examine some clocks and take readings. In the meantime my brain was working coldly and quickly. I ordered a bottle of whiskey, precious stones to the value of £200,000, some bananas, a fountain-pen and writing materials, and finally a serge suit of blue with silk linings. When all these things were on the floor, I remembered other things I had overlooked and ordered underwear, shoes and banknotes, and a box of matches. Mac-Cruiskeen, sweating from his labour with the heavy doors, was complaining of the heat and paused to drink some amber ale. The Sergeant was quietly clicking a little wheel with a tiny ratchet.

'I think that is all,' I said at last.

The Sergeant came forward and gazed at the pile of merchandise.

'Lord, save us,' he said.

'I am going to take these things with me,' I announced.

The Sergeant and MacCruiskeen exchanged their private glance. Then they smiled.

'In that case you will need a big strong bag,' the Sergeant said. He went to another door and got me a hogskin bag worth at least fifty guineas in the open market. I carefully packed away my belongings.

I saw MacCruiskeen crushing out his cigarette on the wall and noticed that it was still the same length as it had been when lit half an hour ago. My own was burning quietly also but was completely unconsumed. I crushed it out also and put it in my pocket.

When about to close the bag I had a thought. I unstooped and turned to the policemen.

'I require just one thing more,' I said. 'I want a small weapon suitable for the pocket which will exterminate any man or any million men who try at any time to take my life.'

Without a word the Sergeant brought me a small black article like a torch.

'There is an influence in that,' he said, 'that will change any man or men into grey powder at once if you point it and press the knob and if you don't like grey powder you can have purple powder or yellow powder or any other shade of powder if you tell me now and confide your favourite colour. Would a velvet-coloured colour please you?'

'Grey will do,' I said briefly.

I put this murderous weapon into the bag, closed it and stood up again.

'I think we might go home now.' I said the words casually and took care not to look at the faces of the policemen. To my surprise they agreed readily and we started off with our resounding steps till we found ourselves again in the endless corridors,

I carrying the heavy bag and the policemen conversing quietly about the readings they had seen. I felt happy and satisfied with my day. I felt changed and regenerated and full of fresh courage.

'How does this thing work?' I inquired pleasantly, seeking to make friendly conversation. The Sergeant looked at me.

'It has helical gears,' he said informatively.

'Did you not see the wires?' MacCruiskeen asked, turning to me in some surprise.

'You would be astonished at the importance of the charcoal,' the Sergeant said. 'The great thing is to keep the beam reading down as low as possible and you are doing very well if the pilot-mark is steady. But if you let the beam rise, where are you with your lever? If you neglect the charcoal feedings you will send the beam rocketing up and there is bound to be a serious explosion.'

'Low pilot, small fall,' MacCruiskeen said. He spoke neatly and wisely as if his remark was a proverb.

'But the secret of it all-in-all,' continued the Sergeant, 'is the daily readings. Attend to your daily readings and your conscience will be as clear as a clean shirt on Sunday morning. I am a great believer in the daily readings.'

'Did I see everything of importance?'

At this the policemen looked at each other in amazement and laughed outright. Their raucous roars careered away from us up and down the corridor and came back again in pale echoes from the distance.

'I suppose you think a smell is a simple thing?' the Sergeant said smiling.

'A smell?'

'A smell is the most complicated phenomenon in the world,' he said, 'and it cannot be unravelled by the human snout or understood properly although dogs have a better way with smells than we have.'

'But dogs are very poor riders on bicycles,' MacCruiskeen said, presenting the other side of the comparison.

'We have a machine down there,' the Sergeant continued, 'that splits up any smell into its sub- and inter-smells the way you can split up a beam of light with a glass instrument. It is very interesting and edifying, you would not believe the dirty smells that are inside the perfume of a lovely lily-of-the mountain.'

'And there is a machine for tastes,' MacCruiskeen put in, 'the taste of a fried chop, although you might not think it, is forty per cent the taste of...'

He grimaced and spat and looked delicately reticent.

'And feels,' the Sergeant said. 'Now there is nothing so smooth as a woman's back or so you might imagine. But if that feel is broken up for you, you would not be pleased with women's backs, I'll promise you that on my solemn oath and parsley. Half of the inside of the smoothness is as rough as a bullock's hips.'

'The next time you come here,' MacCruiskeen promised, 'you will see surprising things.'

This in itself, I thought, was a surprising thing for anyone to say after what I had just seen and after what I was carrying in the bag. He groped in his pocket, found his cigarette, re-lit it and proffered me the match. Hampered with the heavy bag, I was some minutes finding mine but the match still burnt evenly and brightly at its end.

We smoked in silence and went on through the dim passage till we reached the lift again. There were clock-faces or dials beside the open lift which I had not seen before and another pair of doors beside it. I was very tired with my bag of gold and clothes and whiskey and made for the lift to stand on it and put the bag down at last. When nearly on the threshold I was arrested in my step by a call from the Sergeant which rose nearly to the pitch of a woman's scream.

'Don't go in there!'

The colour fled from my face at the urgency of his tone. I turned my head round and stood rooted there with one foot before the other like a man photographed unknowingly in the middle of a walk.

'Why?'

'Because the floor will collapse underneath the bottom of your feet and send you down where nobody went before you.'

'And why?'

'The bag, man.'

'The simple thing is,' MacCruiskeen said calmly, 'that you cannot enter the lift unless you weigh the same weight as you weighed when you weighed into it.'

'If you do,' said the Sergeant, 'it will extirpate you unconditionally and kill the life out of you.'

I put the bag, clinking with its bottle and gold cubes, rather roughly on the floor. It was worth several million pounds. Standing there on the plate floor, I leaned on the plate wall and searched my wits for some reason and understanding and consolation-in-adversity. I understood little except that my plans were vanquished and my visit to eternity unavailing and calamitous. I wiped a hand on my damp brow and stared blankly at the two policemen, who were now smiling and looking knowledgeable and complacent. A large emotion came swelling against my throat and filling my mind with great sorrow and a sadness more remote and desolate than a great strand at evening with the sea far away at its distant turn. Looking down with a bent head at my broken shoes, I saw them swim and dissolve in big tears that came bursting on my eyes. I turned to the wall and gave loud choking sobs and broke down completely and cried loudly like a baby. I do not know how long I was crying. I think I heard the two policemen discussing me in sympathetic undertones as if they were trained doctors in a hospital. Without lifting my head I looked across the floor and saw MacCruiskeen's legs walking away with my bag. Then I heard an oven door being opened and the bag fired roughly in. Here I cried loudly again, turning to the wall of the lift and giving complete rein to my great misery.

At last I was taken gently by the shoulders, weighed and guided into the lift. Then I felt the two large policemen crowding in beside me and got the heavy smell of blue official broadcloth impregnated through and through with their humanity. As the floor of the lift began to resist my feet, I felt a piece of crisp paper rustling against my averted face. Looking up in the poor light I saw that MacCruiskeen was stretching his hand in my direction dumbly and meekly across the chest of the Sergeant who was standing tall and still beside me. In the hand was a small white paper bag. I glanced into it and saw round coloured things the size of florins.

'Creams,' MacCruiskeen said kindly.

He shook the bag encouragingly and started to chew and suck loudly as if there was almost supernatural pleasure to be had from these sweetmeats. Beginning for some reason to sob again, I put my hand into the bag but when I took a sweet, three or four others which had merged with it in the heat of the policeman's pocket came out with it in one sticky mass of plaster. Awkwardly and foolishly I tried to disentangle them but failed completely and then rammed the lot into my mouth and stood there sobbing and sucking and snuffling. I heard the Sergeant sighing heavily and could feel his broad flank receding as he sighed.

'Lord, I love sweets,' he murmured.

'Have one,' MacCruiskeen smiled, rattling his bag.

'What are you saying, man,' the Sergeant cried, turning to view MacCruiskeen's face, 'are you out of your mind, man alive? If I took one of these – not one but half of a corner of the quarter of one of them – I declare to the Hokey that my stomach would blow up like a live landmine and I would be galvanized in my bed for a full fortnight roaring out profanity from terrible stoons of indigestion and heartscalds. Do you want to kill me, man?'

'Sugar barley is a very smooth sweet,' MacCruiskeen said, speaking awkwardly with his bulging mouth. 'They give it to babies and it is a winner for the bowels.'

'If I ate sweets at all,' the Sergeant said, 'I would live on the "Carnival Assorted". Now *there* is a sweet for you. There is great sucking in them, the flavour is very spiritual and one of them is good for half an hour.'

'Did you ever try Liquorice Pennies?' asked MacCruiskeen.

'Not them but the "Fourpenny Coffee-Cream Mixture" have a great charm.'

'Or the Dolly Mixture?'

'No.'

'They say,' MacCruiskeen said, 'that the Dolly Mixture is the best that was ever made and that it will never be surpassed and indeed I could eat them and keep eating till I got sick.'

'That may be,' the Sergeant said, 'but if I had my health I would give you a good run for it with the Carnival Mixture.'

As they wrangled on about sweets and passed to chocolate bars and sticks of rock, the floor was pressing strongly from underneath. Then there was a change in the pressing, two clicks were heard and the Sergeant started to undo the doors, explaining to MacCruiskeen his outlook on Ju-jubes and jelly-sweets and Turkish Delights.

With sloped shoulders and a face that was stiff from my dried tears, I stepped wearily out of the lift into the little stone room and waited till they had checked the clocks. Then I followed them into the thick bushes and kept behind them as they met the attacks of the branches and fought back. I did not care much.

It was not until we emerged, breathless and with bleeding hands, on the green margin of the main road that I realized that a strange thing had happened. It was two or three hours since the Sergeant and I had started on our journey yet the country and the trees and all the voices of every thing around still wore an air of early morning. There was incommunicable earliness in everything, a sense of waking and beginning. Nothing had yet grown or matured and nothing begun had yet finished. A bird singing had not yet turned finally the last twist of tunefulness. A rabbit emerging still had a hidden tail.

The Sergeant stood monumentally in the middle of the hard grey road and picked some small green things delicately from his person. MacCruiskeen stood stooped in knee-high grass looking over his person and shaking himself sharply like a hen. I stood myself looking wearily into the bright sky and wondering over the wonders of the high morning.

When the Sergeant was ready he made a polite sign with his thumb and the two of us set off together in the direction of the barrack. MacCruiskeen was behind but he soon appeared silently in front of us, sitting without a move on the top of his quiet bicycle. He said nothing as he passed us and stirred no breath or limb and he rolled away from us down the gentle hill till a bend received him silently.

As I walked with the Sergeant I did not notice where we were or what we passed by on the road, men, beasts or houses. My brain was like an ivy near where swallows fly. Thoughts were darting around me like a sky that was loud and dark with birds but none came into me or near enough. Forever in my ear was the click of heavy shutting doors, the whine of boughs trailing their loose leaves in a swift springing and the clang of hobnails on metal plates.

When I reached the barrack I paid no attention to anything or anybody but went straight to a bed and lay on it and fell into a full and simple sleep. Compared with this sleep, death is a restive thing, peace is a clamour and darkness a burst of light.

CHAPTER 9

I WAS AWAKENED the following morning by sounds of loud hammering[1] outside the window and found myself immediately recalling – the recollection was an absurd paradox – that I had been in the next world yesterday. Lying there half awake, it is not unnatural that my thoughts should turn to de Selby. Like all the greater thinkers, he has been looked to for guidance on many of the major perplexities of existence. The commentators, it is to be feared, have not succeeded in extracting from the vast store-house of his writings any consistent, cohesive or comprehensive corpus of spiritual belief and praxis. Nevertheless, his ideas of paradise are not without interest. Apart from the contents of the famous de Selby 'Codex',[2] the main references are to be found

[1] Le Clerque (in his almost forgotten *Extensions and Analyses*) has drawn attention to the importance of percussion in the de Selby dialectic and shown that most of the physicist's experiments were extremely noisy. Unfortunately the hammering was always done behind locked doors and no commentator has hazarded even a guess as to what was being hammered and for what purpose. Even when constructing the famous water-box, probably the most delicate and fragile instrument ever made by human hands, de Selby is known to have smashed three heavy coal-hammers and was involved in undignified legal proceedings with his landlord (the notorious Porter) arising from an allegation of strained floor-joists and damage to a ceiling. It is clear that he attached considerable importance to 'hammer-work'. (v. *Golden Hours*, pp. 48–9.) In *The Layman's Atlas* he publishes a rather obscure account of his inquiries into the nature of hammering and boldly attributes the sharp sound of percussion to the bursting of 'atmosphere balls' evidently envisaging the air as being composed of minute balloons, a view scarcely confirmed by later scientific research. In his disquisitions elsewhere on the nature of night and darkness, he refers in passing to the straining of 'air-skins', *al.* 'air-balls' and 'bladders'. His conclusion was that 'hammering is anything but what it appears to be'; such a statement, if not open to explicit refutation, seems unnecessary and unenlightening.

Hatchjaw has put forward the suggestion that loud hammering was a device resorted to by the savant to drown other noises which might give some indication of the real trend of the experiments. Bassett has concurred in this view, with, however, two reservations.

2 The reader will be familiar with the storms which have raged over this most tantalizing of holograph survivals. The 'Codex' (first so-called by Bassett in his monumental *De Selby Compendium*) is a collection of some two thousand sheets of foolscap closely hand-written on both sides. The signal distinction of the manuscript is that not one word of the writing is legible. Attempts made by different commentators to decipher certain passages which look less formidable than others have been characterized by fantastic divergencies, not in the meaning of the passages (of which there is no question) but in the brand of nonsense which is evolved. One passage, described by Bassett as being 'a penetrating treatise on old age' is referred to by Henderson (biographer of Bassett) as 'a not unbeautiful description of lambing operations on an unspecified farm'. Such disagreement, it must be confessed, does little to enhance the reputation of either writer.

Hatchjaw, probably displaying more astuteness than scholastic acumen, again advances his forgery theory and professes amazement that any person of intelligence could be deluded by 'so crude an imposition'. A curious contretemps arose when, challenged by Bassett to substantiate this cavalier pronouncement, Hatchjaw casually mentioned that eleven pages of the 'Codex' were all numbered '88'. Bassett, evidently taken by surprise, performed an independent check and could discover no page at all bearing this number. Subsequent wrangling disclosed the startling fact that both commentators claimed to have in their personal possession the 'only genuine Codex'. Before this dispute could be cleared up, there was a further bombshell, this time from far-off Hamburg. The Norddeutsche Verlag published a book by the shadowy Kraus purporting to be an elaborate exegesis based on an authentic copy of the 'Codex' with a transliteration of what was described as the obscure code in which the document was written. If Kraus can be believed, the portentously-named 'Codex' is simply a collection of extremely puerile maxims on love, life, mathematics and the like, couched in poor ungrammatical English and entirely lacking de Selby's characteristic reconditeness and obscurity. Bassett and many of the other commentators, regarding this extraordinary book as merely another manifestation of the mordant du Garbandier's spleen, pretended never to have heard of it notwithstanding the fact that Bassett is known to have obtained, presumably by questionable means, a proof of the work many months before it appeared. Hatchjaw alone did not ignore the book. Remarking dryly in a newspaper article that Kraus's 'aberration' was due to a foreigner's confusion of the two English words code and codex, declared his intention of publishing 'a brief brochure' which would effectively discredit the German's work and all similar 'trumpery frauds'. The failure of this work to appear is popularly attributed to Kraus's machinations in Hamburg and lengthy sessions on the transcontinental wire. In any event, the wretched Hatchjaw was again arrested, this time at the suit of his own publishers who accused him of the larceny of some of the firm's desk fittings. The case was adjourned and subsequently struck out owing to the failure to appear of certain unnamed witnesses from abroad. Clear as it is that this fantastic in the *Rural Atlas* and in the so-called 'substantive' appendices to the *Country Album*. Briefly he indicates that the happy state is 'not unassociated with water' and that 'water is rarely absent from any wholly satisfactory situation'. He does not give any closer definition of this hydraulic elysium but mentions that he has written more fully on the subject elsewhere.[3] It is not clear, unfortunately, whether the reader is expected to infer that a wet day is more enjoyable than a dry one or that a lengthy course of baths is a reliable method of achieving peace of mind. He praises the equilibrium of water, its circumambiency, equiponderance and equitableness, and declares that water, 'if not abused'[4] can achieve 'absolute superiority'. For the rest, little remains save the

---

charge was without a vestige of foundation, Hatchjaw failed to obtain any redress from the authorities.

It cannot be pretended that the position regarding this 'Codex' is at all satisfactory and it is not likely that time or research will throw any fresh light on a document which cannot be read and of which four copies at least, all equally meaningless, exist in the name of being the genuine original.

An amusing diversion in this affair was unwittingly caused by the mild Le Clerque. Hearing of the 'Codex' some months before Bassett's authoritative 'Compendium' was published, he pretended to have read the 'Codex' and in an article in the *Zuercher Tageblatt* made many vague comments on it, referring to its 'shrewdness', 'compelling if novel arguments', 'fresh viewpoint', etc. Subsequently he repudiated the article and asked Hatchjaw in a private letter to denounce it as a forgery. Hatchjaw's reply is not extant but it is thought that he refused with some warmth to be party to any further hanky-panky in connection with the ill-starred 'Codex'. It is perhaps unnecessary to refer to du Garbandier's contribution to this question. He contented himself with an article in *l'Avenir* in which he professed to have deciphered the 'Codex' and found it to be a repository of obscene conundrums, accounts of amorous adventures and erotic speculation, 'all too lamentable to be repeated even in broad outline'.

3 Thought to be a reference to the 'Codex'.

4 Naturally, no explanation is given of what is meant by 'abusing' water but it is noteworthy that the savant spent several months trying to discover a satisfactory method of 'diluting' water, holding that it was 'too strong' for many of the novel uses to which he desired to put it. Bassett suggests that the de Selby Water Box was invented for this purpose although he cannot explain how the delicate machinery is set in motion. So many fantastic duties have been assigned to this inscrutable mechanism (witness Kraus's absurd sausage theory) that Bassett's speculation must not be allowed the undue weight which his authoritative standing would tend to lend it.

record of his obscure and unwitnessed experiments. The story is one of a long succession of prosecutions for water wastage at the suit of the local authority. At one hearing it was shown that he had used 9,000 gallons in one day and on another occasion almost 80,000 gallons in the course of a week. The word 'used' in this context is the important one. The local officials, having checked the volume of water entering the house daily from the street connection, had sufficient curiosity to watch the outlet sewer and made the astonishing discovery that *none of the vast quantity of water drawn in ever left the house*. The commentators have seized avidly on this statistic but are, as usual, divided in their interpretations. In Bassett's view the water was treated in the patent water-box and diluted to a degree that made it invisible – in the guise of water, at all events – to the untutored watchers at the sewer. Hatchjaw's theory in this regard is more acceptable. He tends to the view that the water was boiled and converted, probably through the water-box, into tiny jets of steam which were projected through an upper window into the night in an endeavour to wash the black 'volcanic' stains from the 'skins' or 'air-bladders' of the atmosphere and thus dissipate the hated and 'insanitary' night. However far-fetched this theory may appear, unexpected colour is lent to it by a previous court case when the physicist was fined forty shillings. On this occasion, some two years before the construction of the water-box, de Selby was charged with playing a fire hose out of one of the upper windows of his house at night, an operation which resulted in several passers-by being drenched to the skin. On another occasion[5] he had to face the curious charge of hoarding

5 Almost all of the numerous petty litigations in which de Selby was involved afford a salutary example of the humiliations which great minds may suffer when forced to have contact with the pedestrian intellects of the unperceiving laity. On one of the water-wastage hearings the Bench permitted itself a fatuous inquiry as to why the defendant did not avail himself of the metered industrial rate 'if bathing is to be persisted in so immoderately'. It was on this occasion that de Selby made the famous retort that 'one does not readily accept the view that paradise is limited by the capacity of a municipal waterworks or human happiness by water-meters manufactured by unemancipated labour in Holland'. It is some consolation to recall that the forcible medical examination which followed was characterized by an enlightenment which redounds to this day to the credit of the medical profession. De Selby's discharge was unconditional and absolute.

water, the police testifying that every vessel in his house, from the bath down to a set of three ornamental egg-cups, was brimming with the liquid. Again a trumped-up charge of attempted suicide was preferred merely because the savant had accidentally half-drowned himself in a quest for some vital statistic of celestial aquatics.

It is clear from contemporary newspapers that his inquiries into water were accompanied by persecutions and legal pin-prickings unparalleled since the days of Galileo. It may be some consolation to the minions responsible to know that their brutish and barbaric machinations succeeded in denying posterity a clear record of the import of these experiments and perhaps a primer of esoteric water science that would banish much of our worldly pain and unhappiness. Virtually all that remains of de Selby's work in this regard is his house where his countless taps[6] are still as he left them, though a newer generation of more delicate mind has had the water turned off at the main.

Water? The word was in my ear as well as in my brain. Rain was beginning to beat on the windows, not a soft or friendly rain but large angry drops which came spluttering with great force upon the glass. The sky was grey and stormy and out of it I heard the harsh shouts of wild geese and ducks labouring across the wind on their coarse pinions. Black quails called sharply from their hidings and a swollen stream was babbling dementedly. Trees, I knew, would be angular and ill-tempered in the rain and boulders would gleam coldly at the eye.

I would have sought sleep again without delay were it not for the loud hammering outside. I arose and went on the cold

6 Hatchjaw (in his invaluable *Conspectus of the de Selby Dialectic*) has described the house as 'the most water-piped edifice in the world'. Even in the living-rooms there were upwards of ten rough farmyard taps, some with zinc troughs and some (as those projecting from the ceiling and from converted gas-brackets near the fireplace) directed at the unprotected floor. Even on the stairs a three-inch main may still be seen nailed along the rail of the balustrade with a tap at intervals of one foot, while under the stairs and in every conceivable hiding-place there were elaborate arrangements of cisterns and storage-tanks. Even the gas pipes were connected up with this water system and would gush strongly at any attempt to provide the light.

Du Garbandier in this connection has permitted himself some coarse and cynical observations bearing upon cattle lairages.

floor to the window. Outside there was a man with sacks on his shoulders hammering at a wooden framework he was erecting in the barrack yard. He was red-faced and strong-armed and limped around his work with enormous stiff strides. His mouth was full of nails which bristled like steel fangs in the shadow of his moustache. He extracted them one by one as I watched and hammered them perfectly into the wet wood. He paused to test a beam with his great strength and accidentally let the hammer fall. He stooped awkwardly and picked it up.

Did you notice anything?

No.

The hammer, man.

It looks an ordinary hammer. What about it?

You must be blind. It fell on his foot.

Yes?

And he didn't bat an eyelid. It might have been a feather for all the sign he gave.

Here I gave a sharp cry of perception and immediately threw up the sash of the window and leaned out into the inhospitable day, hailing the workman excitedly. He looked at me curiously and came over with a friendly frown of interrogation on his face.

'What is your name?' I asked him.

'O'Feersa, the middle brother,' he answered. 'Will you come out here,' he continued, 'and give me a hand with the wet carpentry?'

'Have you a wooden leg?'

For answer he dealt his left thigh a mighty blow with the hammer. It echoed hollowly in the rain. He cupped his hand clownishly at his ear as if listening intently to the noise he had made. Then he smiled.

'I am building a high scaffold here,' he said, 'and it is lame work where the ground is bumpy. I could find use for the assistance of a competent assistant.'

'Do you know Martin Finnucane?'

He raised his hand in a military salute and nodded.

'He is almost a relation,' he said, 'but not completely. He is closely related to my cousin but they never married, never had the time.'

Here I knocked my own leg sharply on the wall.

'Did you hear that?' I asked him.

He gave a start and then shook my hand and looked brotherly and loyal, asking me was it the left or the right?

Scribble a note and send him for assistance. There is no time to lose.

I did so at once, asking Martin Finnucane to come and save me in the nick of time from being strangled to death on the scaffold and telling him he would have to hurry. I did not know whether he could come as he had promised he would but in my present danger anything was worth trying.

I saw Mr O'Feersa going quickly away through the mists and threading his path carefully through the sharp winds which were racing through the fields, his head down, sacks on his shoulders and resolution in his heart.

Then I went back to bed to try to forget my anxiety. I said a prayer that neither of the other brothers was out on the family bicycle because it would be wanted to bring my message quickly to the captain of the one-legged men. Then I felt a hope kindling fitfully within me and I fell asleep again.

WHEN I AWOKE again two thoughts came into my head so closely together that they seemed to be stuck to one another; I could not be sure which came first and it was hard to separate them and examine them singly. One was a happy thought about the weather, the sudden brightness of the day that had been vexed earlier. The other was suggesting to me that it was not the same day at all but a different one and maybe not even the next day after the angry one. I could not decide that question and did not try to. I lay back and took to my habit of gazing out of the window. Whichever day it was, it was a gentle day – mild, magical and innocent with great sailings of white cloud serene and impregnable in the high sky, moving along like kingly swans on quiet water. The sun was in the neighbourhood also, distributing his enchantment unobtrusively, colouring the sides of things that were unalive and livening the hearts of living things. The sky was a light blue without distance, neither near nor far. I could gaze at it, through it and beyond it and see still illimitably clearer and nearer the delicate lie of its nothingness. A bird sang a solo from nearby, a cunning blackbird in a dark hedge giving thanks in his native language. I listened and agreed with him completely.

Then other sounds came to me from the nearby kitchen. The policemen were up and about their incomprehensible tasks. A pair of their great boots would clump across the flags, pause and then clump back. The other pair would clump to another place, stay longer and clump back again with heavier falls as if a great weight were being carried. Then the four boots would clump together solidly far away to the front door and immediately would come the long slash of thrown-water on the road, a great bath of it flung in a lump to fall flat on the dry ground.

I arose and started to put on my clothes. Through the window I could see the scaffold of raw timber rearing itself high into the heavens, not as O'Feersa had left it to make his way methodically through the rain, but perfect and ready for its dark destiny. The sight did not make me cry or even sigh. I thought it was sad, too sad. Through the struts of the structure I could see the good country. There would be a fine view from the top of the scaffold on any day but on this day it would be lengthened out by five miles owing to the clearness of the air. To prevent my tears I began to give special attention to my dressing.

When I was nearly finished the Sergeant knocked very delicately at the door, came in with great courtesy and bade me good morning.

'I notice the other bed has been slept in,' I said for conversation. 'Was it yourself or MacCruiskeen?'

'That would likely be Policeman Fox. MacCruiskeen and I do not do our sleeping here at all, it is too expensive, we would be dead in a week if we played that game.'

'And where do you sleep then?'

'Down below – over there – beyant.'

He gave my eyes the right direction with his brown thumb. It was down the road to where the hidden left turn led to the heaven full of doors and ovens.

'And why?'

'To save our lifetimes, man. Down there you are as young coming out of a sleep as you are going into it and you don't fade when you are inside your sleep, you would not credit the time a suit or a boots will last you and you don't have to take your clothes off either. That's what charms MacCruiskeen – that and the no shaving.' He laughed kindly at the thought of his comrade. 'A comical artist of a man,' he added.

'And Fox? Where does he live?'

'Beyant, I think.' He jerked again to the place that was to the left. 'He is down there beyant somewhere during the daytime but we have never seen him there, he might be in a distinctive portion of it that he found from a separate ceiling in a different house and indeed the unreasonable jumps of the lever-reading would put you in mind that there is unauthorized interference with the works. He is as crazy as bedamned, an incontestable character and a man of ungovernable inexactitudes.'

'Then why does he sleep here?' I was not at all pleased that this ghostly man had been in the same room with me during the night.

'To spend it and spin it out and not have all of it forever unused inside him.'

'All what?'

'His lifetime. He wants to get rid of as much as possible, undertime and overtime, as quickly as he can so that he can die as soon as possible. MacCruiskeen and I are wiser and we are not yet tired of being ourselves, we save it up. I think he has an opinion that there is a turn to the right down the road and likely that is what he is after, he thinks the best way to find it is to die and get all the leftness out of his blood. I do not believe there is a right-hand road and if there is it would surely take a dozen active men to look after the readings alone, night and morning. As you are perfectly aware the right is much more tricky than the left, you would be surprised at all the right pitfalls there are. We are only at the beginning of our knowledge of the right, there is nothing more deceptive to the unwary.'

'I did not know that.'

The Sergeant opened his eyes wide in surprise.

'Did you ever in your life,' he asked, 'mount a bicycle from the right?'

'I did not.'

'And why?'

'I do not know. I never thought about it.'

He laughed at me indulgently.

'It is nearly an insoluble pancake,' he smiled, 'a conundrum of inscrutable potentialities, a snorter.'

He led the way out of the bedroom to the kitchen where he had already arranged my steaming meal of stirabout and milk on the table. He pointed to it pleasantly, made a motion as if lifting a heavily-laden spoon to his mouth and then made succulent spitty sounds with his lips as if they were dealing with the tastiest of all known delicacies. Then he swallowed loudly and put his red hands in ecstasy to his stomach. I sat down and took up the spoon at this encouragement.

'And why is Fox crazy?' I inquired.

'I will tell you that much. In MacCruiskeen's room there is a little box on the mantelpiece. The story is that when Mac-Cruiskeen was away one day that happened to fall on the 23rd of June inquiring about a bicycle, Fox went in and opened the box and looked into it from the strain of his unbearable curiosity. From that day to this . . .'

The Sergeant shook his head and tapped his forehead three times with his finger. Soft as porridge is I nearly choked at the sound his finger made. It was a booming hollow sound, slightly tinny, as if he had tapped an empty watering-can with his nail.

'And what was in the box?'

'That is easily told. A card made of cardboard about the size of a cigarette-card, no better and no thicker.'

'I see,' I said.

I did not see but I was sure that my easy unconcern would sting the Sergeant into an explanation. It came after a time when he had looked at me silently and strangely as I fed solidly at the table.

'It was the colour,' he said.

'The colour?'

'But then maybe it was not that at all,' he mused perplexedly.

I looked at him with a mild inquiry. He frowned thoughtfully and looked up at a corner of the ceiling as if he expected certain words he was searching for to be hanging there in coloured lights. No sooner had I thought of that than I glanced up myself, half expecting to see them there. But they were not.

'The card was not red,' he said at last doubtfully.

'Green?'

'Not green. No.'

'Then what colour?'

'It was not one of the colours a man carries inside his head like nothing he ever looked at with his eyes. It was . . . different. MacCruiskeen says it is not blue either and I believe him, a blue card would never make a man batty because what is blue is natural.'

'I saw colours often on eggs,' I observed, 'colours which have no names. Some birds lay eggs that are shaded in a way too delicate to be noticeable to any instrument but the eye, the tongue could not be troubled to find a noise for anything so nearly not-there. What I would call a green sort of complete white. Now would that be the colour?'

'I am certain it would not,' the Sergeant replied immediately, 'because if birds could lay eggs that would put men out of their wits, you would have no crops at all, nothing but scarecrows crowded in every field like a public meeting and thousands of them in their top hats standing together in knots on the hillsides. It would be a mad world completely, the people would be putting their bicycles upside down on the roads and pedalling them to make enough mechanical movement to frighten the birds out of the whole parish.' He passed a hand in consternation across his brow. 'It would be a very unnatural pancake,' he added.

I thought it was a poor subject for conversation, this new colour. Apparently its newness was new enough to blast a man's brain to imbecility by the surprise of it. That was enough to know and quite sufficient to be required to believe. I thought it was an unlikely story but not for gold or diamonds would I open that box in the bedroom and look into it.

The Sergeant had wrinkles of pleasant recollection at his eyes and mouth.

'Did you ever in your travels meet with Mr Andy Gara?' he asked me.

'No.'

'He is always laughing to himself, even in bed at night he laughs quietly and if he meets you on the road he will go into roars, it is a most enervating spectacle and very bad for nervous people. It all goes back to a certain day when MacCruiskeen and I were making inquiries about a missing bicycle.'

'Yes?'

'It was a bicycle with a criss-cross frame,' the Sergeant explained, 'and I can tell you that it is not every day in the week that one like that is reported, it is a great rarity and indeed it is a privilege to be looking for a bicycle like that.'

'Andy Gara's bicycle?'

'Not Andy's. Andy was a sensible man at the time but a very curious man and when he had us gone he thought he would do a clever thing. He broke his way into the barrack here in open defiance of the law. He spent valuable hours boarding up the windows and making MacCruiskeen's room as dark as night time. Then he got busy with the box. He wanted to know what the inside of it felt like, even if it could not be looked at. When he put his hand in he let out a great laugh, you could swear he was very amused at something.'

'And what did it feel like?'

The Sergeant shrugged himself massively.

'MacCruiskeen says it is not smooth and not rough, not gritty and not velvety. It would be a mistake to think it is a cold feel like steel and another mistake to think it blankety. I thought it might be like the damp bread of an old poultice but no, Mac-Cruiskeen says that would be a third mistake. And not like a bowl-full of dry withered peas, either. A contrary pancake surely, a fingerish atrocity but not without a queer charm all its own.'

'Not hens' piniony under-wing feeling?' I questioned keenly.

The Sergeant shook his head abstractedly.

'But the criss-cross bicycle,' he said, 'it is no wonder it went astray. It was a very confused bicycle and was shared by a man called Barbery with his wife and if you ever laid your eye on big Mrs Barbery I would not require to explain this thing privately to you at all.'

He broke off his utterance in the middle of the last short word of it and stood peering with a wild eye at the table. I had finished eating and had pushed away my empty bowl. Following quickly along the line of his stare, I saw a small piece of folded paper lying on the table where the bowl had been before I moved it. Giving a cry the Sergeant sprang forward with surpassing lightness and snatched the paper up. He took it to the window, opened it out and held it far away from him to allow for some disorder in his eye. His face was puzzled and pale and stared at the paper for many minutes. Then he looked out of the window fixedly, tossing the paper over at me. I picked it up and read the roughly printed message:

'ONE-LEGGÈD MEN ON THEIR WAY TO RESCUE PRISONER. MADE A CALCULATION ON TRACKS AND ESTIMATE NUMBER IS SEVEN. SUBMITTED PLEASE. — FOX.'

My heart began to pound madly inside me. Looking at the Sergeant I saw that he was still gazing wild-eyed into the middle of the day, which was situated at least five miles away, like a man trying to memorize forever the perfection of the lightly clouded sky and the brown and green and boulder-white of the peerless country. Down some lane of it that ran crookedly through the fields I could see inwardly my seven true brothers hurrying to save me in their lame walk, their stout sticks on the move together.

The Sergeant still kept his eye on the end of five miles away but moved slightly in his monumental standing. Then he spoke to me.

'I think,' he said, 'we will go out and have a look at it, it is a great thing to do what is necessary before it becomes essential and unavoidable.'

The sounds he put on these words were startling and too strange. Each word seemed to rest on a tiny cushion and was soft and far away from every other word. When he had stopped speaking there was a warm enchanted silence as if the last note of some music too fascinating almost for comprehension had receded and disappeared long before its absence was truly noticed. He then moved out of the house before me to the yard, I behind him spellbound with no thought of any kind in my head. Soon the two of us had mounted a ladder with staid unhurrying steps and found ourselves high beside the sailing gable of the barrack, the two of us on the lofty scaffold, I the victim and he my hangman. I looked blankly and carefully everywhere, seeing for a time no difference between any different things, inspecting methodically every corner of the same unchanging sameness. Nearby I could hear his voice murmuring again:

'It is a fine day in any case,' he was saying.

His words, now in the air and out of doors, had another warm breathless roundness in them as if his tongue was lined with furry burrs and they came lightly from him like a string of bubbles or like tiny things borne to me on thistledown in very gentle air. I went forward to a wooden railing and rested my weighty hands on it, feeling perfectly the breeze coming chillingly at their fine hairs. An idea came to me that the breezes high above the ground are separate from those which play on the same level as men's faces: here the air was newer and more unnatural, nearer the heavens and less laden with the influences of the earth. Up here I felt that every day would be the same always, serene and chilly, a band of wind isolating the earth of men from the far-from-understandable enormities of the girdling universe. Here on the stormiest autumn Monday there would be no wild leaves to brush on any face, no bees in the gusty wind. I sighed sadly.

'Strange enlightenments are vouchsafed,' I murmured, 'to those who seek the higher places.'

I do not know why I said this strange thing. My own words were also soft and light as if they had no breath to liven them. I heard the Sergeant working behind me with coarse ropes as if he were at the far end of a great hall instead of at my back and then I heard his voice coming back to me softly called across a fathomless valley:

'I heard of a man once,' he said, 'that had himself let up into the sky in a balloon to make observations, a man of great personal charm but a divil for reading books. They played out the rope till he was disappeared completely from all appearances, telescopes or no telescopes, and then they played out another ten miles of rope to make sure of first-class observations. When the time-limit for the observations was over they pulled down the balloon again but lo and behold there was no man in the basket and his dead body was never found afterwards lying dead or alive in any parish ever afterwards.'

Here I heard myself give a hollow laugh, standing there with a high head and my two hands still on the wooden rail.

'But they were clever enough to think of sending up the balloon again a fortnight later and when they brought it down the second time lo and behold the man was sitting in the basket without a feather out of him if any of my information can be believed at all.'

Here I gave some sound again, hearing my own voice as if I was a bystander at a public meeting where I was myself the main speaker. I had heard the Sergeant's words and understood them thoroughly but they were no more significant than the clear sounds that infest the air at all times – the far cry of gulls, the disturbance a breeze will make in its blowing and water falling headlong down a hill. Down into the earth where dead men go I would go soon and maybe come out of it again in some healthy way, free and innocent of all human perplexity. I would perhaps be the chill of an April wind, an essential part of some indomitable river or be personally concerned in the ageless perfection of some rank mountain bearing down upon the mind by occupying forever a position in the blue easy distance. Or perhaps a smaller thing like movement in the grass on an unbearable breathless yellow day, some hidden creature going about its business – I might well be responsible for that or for some important part of it. Or even those unaccountable distinctions that make an evening recognizable from its own morning, the smells and sounds and sights of the perfected and matured essences of the day, these might not be innocent of my meddling and my abiding presence.

'So they asked where he was and what had kept him but he gave them no satisfaction, he only let out a laugh like one that Andy Gara would give and went home and shut himself up in his house and told his mother to say he was not at home and not receiving visitors or doing any entertaining. That made the people very angry and inflamed their passions to a degree that is not recognized by the law. So they held a private meeting that was attended by every member of the general public except the man in question and they decided to get out their shotguns the next day and break into the man's house and give him a severe threatening and tie him up and heat pokers in the fire to make him tell what happened in the sky the time he was up inside it. That is a nice piece of law and order for you, a terrific indictment of democratic self-government, a beautiful commentary on Home Rule.'

Or perhaps I would be an influence that prevails in water, something sea-borne and far away, some certain arrangement of sun, light and water unknown and unbeheld, something far-from-usual. There are in the great world whirls of fluid and vaporous existences obtaining in their own unpassing time, unwatched and uninterpreted, valid only in their essential un-understandable mystery, justified only in their eyeless and mind-less immeasurability, unassailable in their actual abstraction; of the inner quality of such a thing I might well in my own time be the true quintessential pith. I might belong to a lonely shore or be the agony of the sea when it bursts upon it in despair.

'But between that and the next morning there was a stormy night in between, a loud windy night that strained the trees in their deep roots and made the roads streaky with broken branches, a night that played a bad game with root-crops. When the boys reached the home of the balloon-man the next morn-ing, lo and behold the bed was empty and no trace of him was ever found afterwards dead or alive, naked or with an overcoat. And when they got back to where the balloon was, they found the wind had torn it up out of the ground with the rope spinning loosely in the windlass and it invisible to the naked eye in the middle of the clouds. They pulled in eight miles of rope before they got it down but lo and behold the basket was empty again. They all said that the man had gone up in it and stayed up but it is an insoluble conundrum, his name was Quigley and he was by all accounts a Fermanagh man.'

Parts of this conversation came to me from different parts of the compass as the Sergeant moved about at his tasks, now right, now left and now aloft on a ladder to fix the hang-rope on the summit of the scaffold. He seemed to dominate the half of the world that was behind my back with his presence – his movements and his noises – filling it up with himself to the last farthest corner. The other half of the world which lay in front of me was beautifully given a shape of sharpness or roundness that was faultlessly suitable to its nature. But the half behind me was black and evil and composed of nothing at all except the menacing policeman who was patiently and politely arranging the mechanics of my death. His work was now nearly finished and my eyes were faltering as they gazed ahead, making little sense of the distance and taking a smaller pleasure in what was near.

There is not much that I can say.

No.

Except to advise a brave front and a spirit of heroic resignation.

That will not be difficult. I feel too weak to stand up without support.

In a way that is fortunate. One hates a scene. It makes things more difficult for all concerned. A man who takes into consideration the feelings of others even when arranging the manner of his own death shows a nobility of character which compels the admiration of all classes. To quote a well-known poet, 'even the ranks of Tuscany could scarce forbear to cheer'. Besides, unconcern in the face of death is in itself the most impressive gesture of defiance.

I told you I haven't got the strength to make a scene.

Very good. We will say no more about it.

A creaking sound came behind me as if the Sergeant was swinging red-faced in mid-air to test the rope he had just fixed. Then came the clatter of his great hobs as they came again upon the boards of the platform. A rope which would stand his enormous weight would never miraculously give way with mine.

You know, of course, that I will be leaving you soon?

That is the usual arrangement.

I would not like to go without placing on record my pleasure in having been associated with you. It is no lie to say that I have always received the greatest courtesy and consideration at your hands. I can only regret that it is not practicable to offer you some small token of my appreciation.

Thank you. I am very sorry also that we must part after having been so long together. If that watch of mine were found you would be welcome to it if you could find some means of taking it.

But you have no watch.

I forgot that.

Thank you all the same. You have no idea where you are going . . . when all this is over?

No, none.

Nor have I. I do not know, or do not remember, what happens to the like of me in these circumstances. Sometimes I think that perhaps I might become part of . . . the world, if you understand me?

I know.

I mean – the wind, you know. Part of that. Or the spirit of the scenery in some beautiful place like the Lakes of Killarney, the inside meaning of it if you understand me.

I do.

Or perhaps something to do with the sea. 'The light that never was on sea or land, the peasant's hope and the poet's dream.' A big wave in mid-ocean, for instance, it is a very lonely and spiritual thing. Part of that.

I understand you.

Or the smell of a flower, even.

Here from my throat bounded a sharp cry rising to a scream. The Sergeant had come behind me with no noise and fastened his big hand into a hard ring on my arm, started to drag me gently but relentlessly away from where I was to the middle of the platform where I knew there was a trapdoor which could be collapsed with machinery.

Steady now!

My two eyes, dancing madly in my head, raced up and down the country like two hares in a last wild experience of the world I was about to leave for ever. But in their hurry and trepidation they did not fail to notice a movement that was drawing attention to itself in the stillness of everything far far down the road.

'The one-leggèd men!' I shouted.

I know that the Sergeant behind me had also seen that the far part of the road was occupied for his grip, though still unbroken, had stopped pulling at me and I could almost sense his keen stare running out into the day parallel with my own but gradually nearing it till the two converged a quarter of a mile away. We did not seem to breathe or be alive at all as we watched the movement approaching and becoming clearer.

'MacCruiskeen, by the Powers!' the Sergeant said softly.

My lifted heart subsided painfully. Every hangman has an assistant. MacCruiskeen's arrival would make the certainty of my destruction only twice surer.

When he came nearer we could see that he was in a great hurry and that he was travelling on his bicycle. He was lying almost prostrate on top of it with his rear slightly higher than his head to cut a passage through the wind and no eye could travel quickly enough to understand the speed of his flying legs as they thrashed the bicycle onwards in a savage fury. Twenty yards away from the barrack he threw up his head, showing his face for the first time, and saw us standing on the top of the scaffold engaged in watching him with all our attention. He leaped from the bicycle in some complicated leap which was concluded only when the bicycle had been spun round adroitly to form a seat for him with its bar while he stood there, wide-leggèd and diminutive, looking up at us and cupping his hands at his mouth to shout his breathless message upwards:

'The lever – nine point six nine!' he called.

For the first time I had the courage to turn my head to the Sergeant. His face had gone instantly to the colour of ash as if every drop of blood had left it, leaving it with empty pouches and ugly loosenesses and laxities all about it. His lower jaw hung loosely also as if it were a mechanical jaw on a toy man. I could feel the purpose and the life running out of his gripping hand like air out of a burst bladder. He spoke without looking at me.

'Let you stay here till I come back reciprocally,' he said.

For a man of his weight he left me standing there alone with a speed that was astonishing. With one jump he was at the ladder. Coiling his arms and legs around it, he slid to the ground out of view with a hurry that was not different in any way from an ordinary fall. In the next second he was seated on the bar of

MacCruiskeen's bicycle and the two of them were disappearing into the end of a quarter of a mile away.

When they had gone an unearthly weariness came down upon me so suddenly that I almost fell in a heap on the platform. I called together all my strength and made my way inch by inch down the ladder and back into the kitchen of the barrack and collapsed helplessly into a chair that was near the fire. I wondered at the strength of the chair for my body seemed now to be made of lead. My arms and legs were too heavy to move from where they had fallen and my eyelids could not be lifted higher than would admit through them a small glint from the red fire.

For a time I did not sleep, yet I was far from being awake. I did not mark the time that passed or think about any question in my head. I did not feel the ageing of the day or the declining of the fire or even the slow return of my strength. Devils or fairies or even bicycles could have danced before me on the stone floor without perplexing me or altering by one whit my fallen attitude in the chair. I am sure I was nearly dead.

But when I did come to think again I knew that a long time had passed, that the fire was nearly out and that MacCruiskeen had just come into the kitchen with his bicycle and wheeled it hastily into his bedroom, coming out again without it and looking down at me.

'What has happened?' I whispered listlessly.

'We were just in time with the lever,' he replied, 'it took our combined strengths and three pages of calculations and rough-work but we got the reading down in the nick of zero-hour, you would be surprised at the coarseness of the lumps and the weight of the great fall.'

'Where is the Sergeant?'

'He instructed me to ask your kind pardon for his delays. He is lying in ambush with eight deputies that were sworn in as constables on the spot to defend law and order in the public interest. But they cannot do much, they are outnumbered and they are bound to be outflanked into the same bargain.'

'Is it for the one-leggèd men he is waiting?'

'Surely yes. But they took a great rise out of Fox. He is certain to get a severe reprimand from headquarters over the head of it. There is not seven of them but fourteen. They took off their wooden legs before they marched and tied themselves together in pairs so that there were two men for every two legs, it would remind you of Napoleon on the retreat from Russia, it is a masterpiece of military technocratics.'

This news did more to revive me than would a burning drink of finest brandy. I sat up. The light appeared once more in my eyes.

'Then they will win against the Sergeant and his policemen?' I asked eagerly.

MacCruiskeen gave a smile of mystery, took large keys from his pocket and left the kitchen. I could hear him opening the cell where the Sergeant kept his bicycle. He reappeared almost at once carrying a large can with a bung in it such as painters use when they are distempering a house. He had not removed his sly smile in his absence but now wore it more deeply in his face. He took the can into his bedroom and came out again with a large handkerchief in his hand and his smile still in use. Without a word he came behind my chair and bound the handkerchief tightly across my eyes, paying no attention to my movements and my surprise. Out of my darkness I heard his voice:

'I do not think the hoppy men will best the Sergeant,' he said, 'because if they come to where the Sergeant lies in secret ambush with his men before I have time to get back there, the Sergeant will delay them with military manoeuvres and false alarms until I arrive down the road on my bicycle. Even now the Sergeant and his men are all blindfolded like yourself, it is a very queer way for people to be when they are lying in an ambush but it is the only way to be when I am expected at any moment on my bicycle.'

I muttered that I did not understand what he had said.

'I have a private patent in that box in my bedroom,' he explained, 'and I have more of it in that can. I am going to paint my bicycle and ride it down the road in full view of the hoppy lads.'

He had been going away from me in my darkness while saying this and now he was in his bedroom and had shut the door. Soft sounds of work came to me from where he was.

I sat there for half an hour, still weak, bereft of light and feebly wondering for the first time about making my escape. I must have come back sufficiently from death to enter a healthy tiredness again for I did not hear the policeman coming out of the bedroom again and crossing the kitchen with his unbeholdable and brain-destroying bicycle. I must have slept there fitfully in my chair, my own private darkness reigning restfully behind the darkness of the handkerchief.

CHAPTER 11

IT IS AN UNUSUAL experience to waken restfully and slowly, to let the brain climb lazily out of a deep sleep and shake itself and yet have no encounter with the light to guarantee that the sleep is really over. When I awoke I first thought of that, then the scare of blindness came upon me and finally my hand joyously found MacCruiskeen's handkerchief. I tore it off and gazed around. I was still splayed stiffly in my chair. The barrack seemed silent and deserted, the fire was out and the evening sky had the tones of five o'clock. Nests of shadow had already gathered in the corners of the kitchen and in under the table.

Feeling stronger and fresher, I stretched forth my legs and braced my arms with exertions of deep chesty strength. I reflected briefly on the immeasurable boon of sleep, more particularly on my own gift of sleeping opportunely. Several times I had gone asleep when my brain could no longer bear the situations it was faced with. This was the opposite of a weakness which haunted no less a man than de Selby. He, for all his greatness, frequently fell asleep for no apparent reason in the middle of everyday life, often even in the middle of a sentence.[1]

1 Le Fournier, the conservative French commentator (in his *De Selby – Dieu ou Homme?*) has written exhaustively on the non-scientific aspects of de Selby's personality and has noticed several failings and weaknesses difficult to reconcile with his dignity and eminence as a physicist, ballistician, philosopher and psychologist. Though he did not recognize sleep as such, preferring to regard the phenomenon as a series of 'fits' and heart-attacks, his habit of falling asleep in public earned for him the enmity of several scientific brains of the inferior calibre. These sleeps took place when walking in crowded thoroughfares, at meals and on at least one occasion in a public lavatory. (Du Garbandier has given this latter incident malignant publicity in his pseudo-scientific 'redaction' of the police court proceedings to which he added a virulent preface assailing the savant's moral character in terms which, however intemperate, admit of no ambiguity.) It is true that some of these sleeps occurred without warning at meetings of learned societies when the physicist had been asked to state his views on

some abstruse problem but there is no inference, *pace* du Garbandier, that they were 'extremely opportune'.

Another of de Selby's weaknesses was his inability to distinguish between men and women. After the famous occasion when the Countess Schnapper had been presented to him (her *Glauben ueber Ueberalls* is still read) he made flattering references to 'that man', 'that cultured old gentleman', 'crafty old boy' and so on. The age, intellectual attainments and style of dress of the Countess would make this a pardonable error for anybody afflicted with poor sight but it is feared that the same cannot be said of other instances when young shop-girls, waitresses and the like were publicly addressed as 'boys'. In the few references which he ever made to his own mysterious family he called his mother 'a very distinguished gentleman' (*Lux Mundi*, p. 307), 'a man of stern habits' (ibid., p. 308) and 'a man's man' (Kraus: *Briefe*, xvii). Du Garbandier (in his extraordinary *Histoire de Notre Temps*) has seized on this pathetic shortcoming to outstep, not the prudent limits of scientific commentary but all known horizons of human decency. Taking advantage of the laxity of French law in dealing with doubtful or obscene matter, he produced a pamphlet masquerading as a scientific treatise on sexual idiosyncrasy in which de Selby is arraigned by name as the most abandoned of all human monsters.

Henderson and several lesser authorities of the Hatchjaw–Bassett school have taken the appearance of this regrettable document as the proximate cause of Hatchjaw's precipitate departure for Germany. It is now commonly accepted that Hatchjaw was convinced that the name 'du Garbandier' was merely a pseudonym adopted for his own ends by the shadowy Kraus. It will be recalled that Bassett took the opposite view, holding that Kraus was a name used by the mordant Frenchman for spreading his slanders in Germany. It may be observed that neither of these theories is directly supported by the writings of either commentator: du Garbandier is consistently virulent and defamatory while much of Kraus's work, blemished as it is by his inaccurate attainments in scholarship, is not at all unflattering to de Selby. Hatchjaw seems to take account of this discrepancy in his farewell letter to his friend Harold Barge (the last he is known to have written) when he states his conviction that Kraus was making a considerable fortune by publishing tepid refutations of du Garbandier's broadsides. This suggestion is not without colour because, as he points out, Kraus had extremely elaborate books on the market – some containing expensive plates – within an incredibly short time of the appearance of a poisonous volume under the name of du Garbandier. In such circumstances it is not easy to avoid the conclusion that both books were produced in collaboration if not written by the one hand. Certainly it is significant that the balance of the engagements between Kraus and du Garbandier was unfailingly to the disadvantage of de Selby.

Too much credit cannot be given to Hatchjaw for his immediate and heroic decision to go abroad 'to end once and for all a cancerous corruption which has become an intolerable affront to the decent instincts of humanity'. Bassett, in a note delivered at the quay-side at the moment of departure, wished Hatchjaw every success in his undertaking but deplored the fact that he was in the wrong ship, a sly hint that he should direct his steps to Paris rather than to Hamburg. Hatchjaw's friend Harold Barge has left an interesting record of the last interview in the commentator's cabin. 'He seemed nervous and out of sorts, striding up and down the tiny floor of his apartment like a caged animal and consulting his watch at least once every five minutes. His conversation was erratic, fragmentary and unrelated to the subjects I was mentioning myself. His lean sunken face, imbued with unnatural pallor, was livened almost to the point of illumination by eyes which burned in his head with a sickly intensity. The rather old-fashioned clothes he wore were creased and dusty and bore every sign of having been worn and slept in for weeks. Any recent attempts which he had made at shaving or washing were clearly of the most perfunctory character; indeed, I recall looking with mixed feelings at the sealed port-hole. His disreputable appearance, however, did not detract from the nobility of his personality or the peculiar spiritual exaltation conferred on his features by his selfless determination to bring to a successful end the desperate task to which he had set his hand. After we had traversed certain light mathematical topics (not, alas, with any degree of dialectical elegance), a silence fell between us. Both of us, I am sure, had heard the last boat-train (run, as it happened, in two sections on this occasion) draw alongside and felt that the hour of separation could not be long delayed. I was searching in my mind for some inanity of a non-mathematical kind which I could utter to break the tension when he turned to me with a spontaneous and touching gesture of affection, putting a hand which quivered with emotion upon my shoulder. Speaking in a low unsteady voice, he said: "You realize, no doubt, that I am unlikely to return. In destroying the evil things which prevail abroad, I do not exclude my own person from the ambit of the cataclysm which will come and of which I have the components at this moment in my trunk. If I should leave the world the cleaner for my passing and do even a small service to that man whom I love, then I shall measure my joy by the extent to which no trace of either of us will be found after I have faced my adversary. I look to you to take charge of my papers and books and instruments, seeing that they are preserved for those who may come after us." I stammered some reply, taking his proffered hand warmly in my own. Soon I found myself stumbling on the quay again with eyes not innocent of emotion. Ever since that evening I have felt that there is something sacred and precious in my memory of that lone figure in the small shabby cabin, setting out alone and almost unarmed to pit his slender frame against the snake-like denizen of far-off Hamburg. It is a memory I will always carry with me proudly so long as one breath animates this humble temple.'

Barge, it is feared, was actuated more by kindly affection for Hatchjaw than for any concern for historical accuracy when he says that the latter was 'almost unarmed'. Probably no private traveller has ever gone abroad accompanied by a more formidable armoury and nowhere outside a museum has there been assembled a more varied or deadly collection of lethal engines. Apart from explosive chemicals and the unassembled components of several bombs, grenades and landmines. he had four army-pattern revolvers, two rook-rifles, angler's landing gear (!), a small machine-gun, several minor firing-irons and an unusual instrument resembling at once a pistol and a shotgun, evidently made to order by a skilled gunsmith and designed to take elephant ball. Wherever he hoped to corner the shadowy Kraus, it is clear that he intended that the 'cataclysm' should be widespread.

The reader who would seek a full account of the undignified fate which awaited the courageous crusader must have recourse to the page of history. Newspaper readers of the older generation will recall the sensational reports of his arrest for *impersonating himself*, being arraigned at the suit of a man called Olaf (var. Olafsohn) for obtaining credit in the name of a world-famous literary 'Gelehrter'. As was widely remarked at the time, nobody but either Kraus or du Garbandier could have engineered so malignant a destiny. (It is noteworthy that du Garbandier, in a reply to a suggestion of this kind made by the usually inoffensive Le Clerque, savagely denied all knowledge of Hatchjaw's whereabouts on the continent but made the peculiar statement that he had thought for many years that 'a similar imper-sonation' had been imposed on the gullible public at home many years before there was any question of 'a ridiculous adventure' abroad, implying apparently that Hatchjaw was not Hatchjaw at all but either another person of the same name or an impostor who had successfully maintained the pretence, in writing and otherwise, for forty years. Small profit can accrue from pursuing so peculiar a suggestion.) The facts of Hatchjaw's original incarceration are not now questioned by any variety of fates after being released. None of these can be regarded as verified fact and many are too absurd to be other than morbid conjecture. Mainly they are: (1) that he became a convert to the Jewish faith and entered the ministry of that persuasion; (2) that he had resort to petty crime and drug-peddling and spent much of his time in jail; (3) that he was responsible for the notorious 'Munich Letter' incident involving an attempt to use de Selby as the tool of international financial interests; (4) that he returned home in disguise with his reason shattered; and (5) that he was last heard of as a Hamburg brothel-keeper's nark or agent in the lawless dockland fastnesses of that maritime cosmopolis. The definitive work on this strange man's life is, of course, that of Henderson but the following will also repay study: Bassett's *Recollections*, Part vii; *The Man Who Sailed Away: A Memoir* by H. Barge; Le Clerque's Collected Works, Vol. III, pp. 118–287; Peachcroft's *Thoughts in a Library* and the Hamburg chapter in Goddard's *Great Towns*.

I arose and stretched my legs up and down the floor. From my chair by the fire I had noticed idly that the front wheel of a bicycle was protruding into view in the passage leading to the rear of the barrack. It was not until I sat down again on the chair after exercising for a quarter of an hour that I found myself staring at this wheel in some surprise. I could have sworn it had moved out farther in the interval because three-quarters of it was now visible whereas I could not see the hub the last time. Possibly it was an illusion due to an altered position between my two sittings but this was quite unlikely because the chair was small and would not permit of much variation of seat if there was any question of studying comfort. My surprise began to mount to astonishment.

I was on my feet again at once and had reached the passage in four long steps. A cry of amazement – now almost a habit with me – escaped from my lips as I looked around. MacCruiskeen in his haste had left the door of the cell wide open with the ring of keys hanging idly in the lock. In the back of the small cell was a collection of paint-cans, old ledgers, punctured bicycle tubes, tyre repair outfits and a mass of peculiar brass and leather articles not unlike ornamental horse harness but clearly intended for some wholly different office. The front of the cell was where my attention was. Leaning half-way across the lintel was the Sergeant's bicycle. Clearly it could not have been put there by MacCruiskeen because he had returned instantly from the cell with his can of paint and his forgotten keys were proof that he had not gone back there before he rode away. During my absence in my sleep it is unlikely that any intruder would have come in merely to move the bicycle half-way out of where it was. On the other hand I could not help recalling what the Sergeant had told me about his fears for his bicycle and his decision to keep it in solitary confinement. If there is good reason for locking a bicycle in a cell like a dangerous criminal, I reflected, it is fair enough to think that it will try to escape if given the opportunity. I did not quite believe this and I thought it was better to stop thinking about the mystery before I was compelled to believe it because if a man is alone in a house with a bicycle which he thinks is edging its way along a wall he will run away from it in fright; and I was by now so occupied with the thought of my escape that I could not afford to be frightened of anything which could assist me.

The bicycle itself seemed to have some peculiar quality of shape or personality which gave it distinction and importance far beyond that usually possessed by such machines. It was extremely well-kept with a pleasing lustre on its dark-green bars and oil-bath and a clean sparkle on the rustless spokes and rims. Resting before me like a tame domestic pony, it seemed unduly small and low in relation to the Sergeant yet when I measured its height against myself I found it was bigger than any other bicycle that I knew. This was possibly due to the perfect proportion of its parts which combined merely to create a thing of surpassing grace and elegance, transcending all standards of size and reality and existing only in the absolute validity of its own unexceptionable dimensions. Notwithstanding the sturdy cross-bar it seemed ineffably female and fastidious, posing there like a mannequin rather than leaning idly like a loafer against the wall, and resting on its prim flawless tyres with irreproachable precision, two tiny points of clean contact with the level floor. I passed my hand with unintended tenderness – sensuously, indeed – across the saddle. Inexplicably it reminded me of a human face, not by any simple resemblance of shape or feature but by some association of textures, some incomprehensible familiarity at the fingertips. The leather was dark with maturity, hard with a noble hardness and scored with all the sharp lines and finer wrinkles which the years with their tribulations had carved into my own countenance. It was a gentle saddle yet calm and courageous, unembittered by its confinement and bearing no mark upon it save that of honourable suffering and honest duty. I knew that I liked this bicycle more than I had ever liked any other bicycle, better even than I had liked some people with two legs. I liked her unassuming competence, her docility, the simple dignity of her quiet way. She now seemed to rest beneath my friendly eyes like a tame fowl which will crouch submissively, awaiting with out-hunched wings the caressing hand. Her saddle seemed to spread invitingly into the most enchanting of all seats while her two handlebars, floating finely with the wild grace of alighting wings, beckoned to me to lend my mastery for free and joyful journeyings, the lightest of light running in the company of the swift groundwinds to safe havens far away, the whir of the true front wheel in my ear as it spun perfectly beneath my clear eye and the strong fine back wheel with unadmired industry raising gentle dust on the dry roads. How desirable her seat was, how charming the invitation of her slim encircling handle-arms, how unaccountably competent and reassuring her pump resting warmly against her rear thigh!

With a start I realized that I had been communing with this strange companion and – not only that – conspiring with her. Both of us were afraid of the same Sergeant, both were awaiting the punishments he would bring with him on his return, both were thinking that this was the last chance to escape beyond his reach; and both knew that the hope of each lay in the other, that we would not succeed unless we went together, assisting each other with sympathy and quiet love.

The long evening had made its way into the barrack through the windows, creating mysteries everywhere, erasing the seam between one thing and another, lengthening out the floors and either thinning the air or putting some refinement on my ear enabling me to hear for the first time the clicking of a cheap clock from the kitchen.

By now the battle would be over, Martin Finnucane and his one-leggèd men would be stumbling away into the hills with blinded eyes and crazy heads, chattering to each other poor broken words which nobody understood. The Sergeant would now be making his way inexorably through the twilight home-wards, arranging in his head the true story of his day for my amusement before he hanged me. Perhaps MacCruiskeen would remain behind for the present, waiting for the blackest of the night's darkness by some old wall, a wrinkled cigarette in his mouth and his bicycle now draped with six or seven greatcoats. The deputies would also be going back to where they came from, still wondering why they had been blindfolded to prevent them seeing something wonderful – a miraculous victory with no fighting, nothing but a bicycle bell ringing madly and the screams of demented men mixing madly in their darkness.

In the next moment I was fumbling for the barrack latch with the Sergeant's willing bicycle in my care. We had travelled the passage and crossed the kitchen with the grace of ballet dancers, silent, swift and faultless in our movements, united in the acuteness of our conspiracy. In the country which awaited us outside we stood for a moment undecided, looking into the lowering night and inspecting the dull sameness of the gloom.

It was to the left the Sergeant had gone with MacCruiskeen, to that quarter the next world lay and it was leftwards that all my troubles were. I led the bicycle to the middle of the road, turned her wheel resolutely to the right and swung myself into the centre of her saddle as she moved away eagerly under me in her own time.

How can I convey the perfection of my comfort on the bicycle, the completeness of my union with her, the sweet responses she gave me at every particle of her frame? I felt that I had known her for many years and that she had known me and that we understood each other utterly. She moved beneath me with agile sympathy in a swift, airy stride, finding smooth ways among the stony tracks, swaying and bending skilfully to match my changing attitudes, even accommodating her left pedal patiently to the awkward working of my wooden leg. I sighed and settled forward on her handlebars, counting with a happy heart the trees which stood remotely on the dark roadside, each telling me that I was further and further from the Sergeant.

I seemed to cut an unerring course between two sharp shafts of wind which whistled coldly past each ear, fanning my short side hairs. Other winds were moving about in the stillness of the evening, loitering in the trees and moving leaves and grasses to show that the green world was still present in the dark. Water by the roadside, always over-shouted in the roistering day, now performed audibly in its hidings. Flying beetles came against me in their broad loops and circles, whirling blindly against my chest; overhead geese and heavy birds were calling in the middle of a journey. Aloft in the sky I could see the dim tracery of the stars struggling out here and there between the clouds. And all the time she was under me in a flawless racing onwards, touching the road with the lightest touches, surefooted, straight and faultless, each of her metal bars like spear-shafts superbly cast by angels.

A thickening of the right-hand night told me that we were approaching the mass of a large house by the road. When we were abreast of it and nearly past it, I recognized it. It was the house of old Mathers, not more than three miles from where my own house was. My heart bounded joyfully. Soon I would see my old friend Divney. We would stand in the bar drinking yellow whiskey, he smoking and listening and I telling him my strange story. If he found any part of it difficult to believe completely I would show him the Sergeant's bicycle. Then the next day we could both begin again to look for the black cashbox.

Some curiosity (or perhaps it was the sense of safety which comes to a man on his own hillside) made me stop pedalling and pull gently at the queenly brake. I had intended only to look back at the big house but by accident I had slowed the bicycle so much that she shuddered beneath me awkwardly, making a gallant effort to remain in motion. Feeling that I had been inconsiderate I jumped quickly from the saddle to relieve her. Then I took a few paces back along the road, eyeing the outline of the house and the shadows of its trees. The gate was open. It seemed a lonely place with no life or breath in it, a dead man's empty house spreading its desolation far into the surrounding night. Its trees swayed mournfully, gently. I could see the faint glinting of the glass in the big sightless windows and fainter, the sprawl of ivy at the room where the dead man used to sit. I eyed the house up and down, happy that I was near my own people. Suddenly my mind became clouded and confused. I had some memory of seeing the dead man's ghost while in the house searching for the box. It seemed a long time ago now and doubtless was the memory of a bad dream. I had killed Mathers with my spade. He was dead for a long time. My adventures had put a strain upon my mind. I could not now remember clearly what had happened to me during the last few days. I recalled only that I was fleeing from two monstrous policemen and that I was now near my home. I did not just then try to remember anything else.

I had turned away to go when a feeling came upon me that the house had changed the instant my back was turned. This feeling was so strange and chilling that I stood rooted to the road for several seconds with my hands gripping the bars of the bicycle, wondering painfully whether I should turn my head and look or go resolutely forward on my way. I think I had made up my mind to go and had taken a few faltering steps forward when some influence came upon my eyes and dragged them round till they were again resting upon the house. They opened widely in surprise and once more my startled cry jumped out from me. A bright light was burning in a small window in the upper storey.

I stood watching it for a time, fascinated. There was no reason why the house should not be occupied or why a light should not be showing, no reason why the light should frighten me. It seemed to be the ordinary yellow light of an oil-lamp and I had seen many stranger things than that – many stranger lights, also – in recent days. Nevertheless I could not persuade myself that there was anything the least usual in what my eyes were looking at. The light had some quality which was wrong, mysterious, alarming.

I must have stood there for a long time, watching the light and fingering the reassuring bars of the bicycle which would take me away swiftly at any time I chose to go. Gradually I took strength and courage from her and from other things which were lurking in my mind – the nearness of my own house, the nearer nearness of Courahans, Gillespies, Cavanaghs, and the two Murrays, and not further than a shout away the cottage of big Joe Siddery, the giant blacksmith. Perhaps whoever had the light may have found the black box and would yield it willingly to anyone who had suffered so much in search of it as I had. Perhaps it would be wise to knock and see.

I laid the bicycle gently against the gate-pier, took some string from my pocket and tied her loosely to the bars of the ironwork; then I walked nervously along the crunching gravel towards the gloom of the porch. I recalled the great thickness of the walls as my hand searched for the door in the pitch darkness at the rear of it. I found myself well into the hall before I realized that the door was swinging half-open, idly at the mercy of the wind. I felt a chill come upon me in this bleak open house and thought for a moment of returning to the bicycle. But I did not do so. I found the door and grasped the stiff metal knocker, sending three dull rumbling thuds through the house and out around the dark empty garden. No sound or movement answered me as I stood there in the middle of the silence listening to my heart. No feet came hurrying down the stairs, no door above opening with a flood of lamplight. Again I knocked on the hollow door, got no response and again thought of returning to the companionship of my friend who was at the gate. But again I did not do so. I moved farther into the hallway, searched for matches and struck one. The hall was empty with all doors leading from it closed; in a corner of it the wind had huddled a blowing of dead leaves and along the walls was the stain of bitter inblown rain. At the far end I could glimpse the white winding stairway. The match spluttered in my fingers and went out, leaving me again standing in the dark in indecision, again alone with my heart.

At last I summoned all my courage and made up my mind to search the upper storey and finish my business and get back to the bicycle as quickly as possible. I struck another match, held it high above my head and marched noisily to the stairs, mounting them with slow heavy footfalls. I remembered the house well from the night I had spent in it after spending hours searching it for the black box. On the top landing I paused to light another match and gave a loud call to give warning of my approach and awaken anybody who was asleep. The call, when it died away without reply, left me still more desolate and alone. I moved forward quickly and opened the door of the room nearest me, the room where I thought I once slept. The flickering match showed me that it was empty and had been long unoccupied. The bed was stripped of all its clothes, four chairs were locked together, two up-ended, in a corner and a white sheet was draped over a dressing-table. I slammed the door shut and paused to light another match, listening intently for any sign that I was watched. I heard nothing at all. Then I went along the passage throwing open the door of every room to the front of the house. They were all empty, deserted, with no light or sign of light in any of them. Afraid to stand still, I went quickly to all the other rooms, but found them all in the same way and ended by running down the stairs in growing fright and out of the front door. Here I stopped dead in my tracks. The light from the upper window was still streaming out and lying against the dark. The window seemed to be in the centre of the house. Feeling frightened, deluded, cold and bad-tempered I strode back into the hall, up the stairs and looked down the corridor where the doors of all the rooms to the front of the house were. I had left them all wide open on my first visit yet no light now came from any one of them. I walked the passage quickly to make sure that they had not been closed. They were all still open. I stood in the silence for three or four minutes barely breathing and making no sound, thinking that perhaps whatever was at work would make some move and show itself. But nothing happened, nothing at all.

I then walked into the room which seemed most in the centre of the house and made my way over to the window in the dark, guiding myself with my hands outstretched before me. What

I saw from the window startled me painfully. The light was streaming from the window of the room next door on my right-hand side, lying thickly on the misty night air and playing on the dark-green leaves of a tree that stood nearby. I remained watching for a time, leaning weakly on the wall; then I moved backwards, keeping my eyes on the faintly-lighted tree-leaves, walking on my toes and making no sound. Soon I had my back to the rear wall, standing within a yard of the open door and the dim light on the tree still plainly visible to me. Then almost in one bound I was out into the passage and into the next room. I could not have spent more than one quarter of a second in that jump and yet I found the next room dusty and deserted with no life or light in it. Sweat was gathering on my brow, my heart was thumping loudly and the bare wooden floors seemed to tingle still with the echoing noises my feet had made. I moved to the window and looked out. The yellow light was still lying on the air and shining on the same tree-leaves but now it was streaming from the window of the room I had just left. I felt I was standing within three yards of something unspeakably inhuman and diabolical which was using its trick of light to lure me on to something still more horrible.

I stopped thinking, closing up my mind with a snap as if it were a box or a book. I had a plan in my head which seemed almost hopelessly difficult, very nearly beyond the extremity of human effort, desperate. It was simply to walk out of the room, down the stairs and out of the house on to the rough solid gravel, down the short drive and back to the company of my bicycle. Tied down there at the gate she seemed infinitely far away as if now in another world.

Certain that I would be assailed by some influence and prevented from reaching the hall door alive, I put my hands down with fists doubled at my sides, cast my eyes straight at my feet so that they should not look upon any terrible thing appearing in the dark, and walked steadily out of the room and down the black passage. I reached the stairs without mishap, reached the hall and then the door and soon found myself on the gravel feeling very much relieved and surprised. I walked down to the gate and out through it. She was resting where I had left her, leaning demurely against the stone pier; my hand told me that the string was unstrained, just as I had tied it. I passed my hands about her hungrily, knowing that she was still my accomplice in the plot of reaching home unharmed. Something made me turn my head again to the house behind me. The light was still burning peacefully in the same window, for all the world as if there was somebody in the room lying contentedly in bed reading a book. If I had given (or had been able to give) unrestricted rein to either fear or reason I should have turned my back forever on this evil house and rode away there and then upon the bicycle to the friendly home which was waiting for me beyond four bends of the passing road. But there was some other thing interfering with my mind. I could not take my eye from the lighted window and perhaps it was that I could resign myself to going home with no news about the black box so long as something was happening in the house where it was supposed to be. I stood there in the gloom, my hands gripping the handlebars of the bicycle and my great perplexity worrying me. I could not decide what was the best thing for me to do.

It was by accident that an idea came to me. I was shifting my feet as I often did to ease my bad left leg when I noticed that there was a large loose stone on the ground at my feet. I stooped and picked it up. It was about the size of a bicycle-lamp, smooth and round and easily fired. My heart had again become almost audible at the thought of hurling it through the lighted window and thus provoking to open action whoever was hiding in the house. If I stood by with the bicycle I could get away quickly. Having had the idea, I knew that I should have no contentment until the stone was fired; no rest would come to me until the unexplainable light had been explained.

I left the bicycle and went back up the drive with the stone swinging ponderously in my right hand. I paused under the window, looking up at the shaft of light. I could see some large insect flitting in and out of it. I felt my limbs weakening under me and my whole body becoming ill and faint with apprehension. I glanced at the nearby porch half expecting to glimpse some dreadful apparition watching me covertly from the shadows. I saw nothing but the impenetrable patch of deeper gloom. I then swung the stone a few times to and fro at the end of my straight arm and lobbed it strongly high into the air. There was a loud smash of glass, the dull thuds of the stone landing and rolling along the wooden floor and at the same time the tinkle of broken

glass falling down upon the gravel at my feet. Without waiting
at all I turned and fled at top speed down the drive until I had
again reached and made contact with the bicycle.

Nothing happened for a time. Probably it was four or five
seconds but it seemed an interminable delay of years. The whole
upper half of the glass had been carried away, leaving jagged
edges protruding about the sash; the light seemed to stream more
clearly through the gaping hole. Suddenly a shadow appeared,
blotting out the light on the whole left-hand side. The shadow
was so incomplete that I could not recognize any part of it but
I felt certain it was the shadow of a large being or presence who
was standing quite still at the side of the window and gazing
out into the night to see who had thrown the stone. Then it
disappeared, making me realize for the first time what had happened and sending a new and deeper horror down upon me.
The certain feeling that something else was going to happen
made me afraid to make the smallest move lest I should reveal
where I was standing with the bicycle.

The developments I expected were not long in coming. I was
still gazing at the window when I heard soft sounds behind me.
I did not look round. Soon I knew they were the footsteps of a
very heavy person who was walking along the grass margin of
the road to deaden his approach. Thinking he would pass without seeing me in the dark recess of the gateway, I tried to remain
even more still than my original utter immobility. The steps suddenly clattered out on the roadway not six yards away, came up
behind me and then stopped. It is no joke to say that my heart
nearly stopped also. Every part of me that was behind me –
neck, ears, back and head – shrank and quailed painfully before
the presence confronting them, each expecting an onslaught of
indescribable ferocity. Then I heard words.

'This is a brave night!'

I swung round in amazement. Before me, almost blocking out
the night, was an enormous policeman. He looked a policeman
from his great size but I could see the dim sign of his buttons
suspended straight before my face, tracing out the curvature of
his great chest. His face was completely hidden in the dark and
nothing was clear to me except his overbearing policemanship,
his massive rearing of wide strengthy flesh, his domination and
his unimpeachable reality. He dwelt upon my mind so strongly

that I felt many times more submissive than afraid. I eyed him weakly, my hand faltering about the bars of the bicycle. I was going to try to make my tongue give some hollow answer to his salutation when he spoke again, his words coming in thick friendly lumps from his hidden face.

'Will you follow after me till I have a conversation with you privately,' he said, 'if it was nothing else you have no light on your bicycle and I could take your name and address for the half of that.'

Before he had finished speaking he had eased off in the dark like a battleship, swinging his bulk ponderously away the same way as he had come. I found my feet obeying him without question, giving their six steps for every two of his, back along the road past the house. When we were about to pass it he turned sharply into a gap in the hedge and led the way into shrubberies and past the boles of dark forbidding trees, leading me to a mysterious fastness by the gable of the house where branches and tall growings filled the darkness and flanked us closely on both sides, reminding me of my journey to the underground heaven of Sergeant Pluck. In the presence of this man I had stopped wondering or even thinking. I watched the swaying outline of his back in the murk ahead of me and hurried after it as best I could. He said nothing and made no sound save that of the air labouring in his nostrils and the brushing strides of his boots on the grass-tangled ground, soft and rhythmical like a well-wielded scythe laying down a meadow in swaths.

He then turned sharply in towards the house and made for a small window which looked to me unusually low and near the ground. He flashed a torch on it, showing me as I peered from behind his black obstruction four panes of dirty glass set in two sashes. As he put his hand out to it I thought he was going to lift the lower sash up but instead of that he swung the whole window outwards on hidden hinges as if it were a door. Then he stooped his head, put out the light and began putting his immense body in through the tiny opening. I do not know how he accomplished what did not look possible at all. But he accomplished it quickly, giving no sound except a louder blowing from his nose and the groaning for a moment of a boot which had become wedged in some angle. Then he sent the torchlight back at me to show the way, revealing nothing of himself except his feet and the knees of his blue official trousers. When I was in, he leaned back an arm and pulled the window shut and then led the way ahead with his torch.

The dimensions of the place in which I found myself were most unusual. The ceiling seemed extraordinarily high while the floor was so narrow that it would not have been possible for me to pass the policeman ahead if I had desired to do so. He opened a tall door and, walking most awkwardly half-sideways, led the way along a passage still narrower. After passing through another tall door we began to mount an unbelievable square stairs. Each step seemed about a foot in depth, a foot in height and a foot wide. The policeman was walking up them fully sideways like a crab with his face turned still ahead towards the guidance of his torch. We went through another door at the top of the stairs and I found myself in a very surprising apartment. It was slightly wider than the other places and down the middle of it was a table about a foot in width, two yards in length and attached permanently to the floor by two metal legs. There was an oil-lamp on it, an assortment of pens and inks, a number of small boxes and file-covers and a tall jar of official gum. There were no chairs to be seen but all around the walls were niches where a man could sit. On the walls themselves were pinned many posters and notices dealing with bulls and dogs and regulations about sheep-dipping and school-going and breaches of the Fire-arms Act. With the figure of the policeman, who still had his back to me making an entry on some schedule on the far wall, I had no trouble in knowing that I was standing in a tiny police station. I looked around again, taking everything in with aston-ishment. Then I saw that there was a small window set deeply in the left wall and that a cold breeze was blowing in through a gaping hole in the lower pane. I walked over and looked out. The lamplight was shining dimly on the foliage of the same tree and I knew that I was standing, not in Mathers' house, *but inside the walls of it*. I gave again my surprised cry, supported myself at the table and looked weakly at the back of the policeman. He was carefully blotting the figures he had entered on the paper on the wall. Then he turned round and replaced his pen on the table. I staggered quickly to one of the niches and sat down in a state of complete collapse, my eyes glued on his face and my mouth drying up like a raindrop on a hot pavement. I tried to say something several times but at first my tongue would not respond. At last I stammered out the thought that was blazing in my mind:

'I thought you were dead!'

The great fat body in the uniform did not remind me of anybody that I knew *but the face at the top of it belonged to old Mathers*. It was not as I had recalled seeing it last whether in my sleep or otherwise, deathly and unchanging; it was now red and gross as if gallons of hot thick blood had been pumped into it. The cheeks were bulging out like two ruddy globes marked here and there with straggles of purple discolouration. The eyes had been charged with unnatural life and glistened like beads in the lamp-light. When he answered me it was the voice of Mathers.

'That is a nice thing to say,' he said, 'but it is no matter because I thought the same thing about yourself. I do not understand your unexpected corporality after the morning on the scaffold.'

'I escaped,' I stammered.

He gave me long searching glances.

'Are you sure?' he asked.

Was I sure? Suddenly I felt horribly ill as if the spinning of the world in the firmament had come against my stomach for the first time, turning it all to bitter curd. My limbs weakened and hung about me helplessly. Each eye fluttered like a bird's wing in its socket and my head throbbed, swelling out like a bladder at every surge of blood. I heard the policeman speaking at me again from a great distance.

'I am Policeman Fox,' he said, 'and this is my own private police station and I would be glad to have your opinion on it because I have gone to great pains to make it spick and span.'

I felt my brain struggling on bravely, tottering, so to speak, to its knees but unwilling to fall completely. I knew that I would be dead if I lost consciousness for one second. I knew that I could never awaken again or hope to understand afresh the terrible way in which I was if I lost the chain of the bitter day I had had. I knew that he was not Fox but Mathers. I knew Mathers was dead. I knew that I would have to talk to him and pretend that everything was natural and try perhaps to escape for the last time with my life to the bicycle. I would have given everything I had in the world and every cashbox in it to get at that moment one look at the strong face of John Divney.

'It is a nice station,' I muttered, 'but why is it inside the walls of another house?'

'That is a very simple conundrum, I am sure you know the answer of it.'

'I don't.'

'It is a very rudimentary conundrum in any case. It is fixed this way to save the rates because if it was constructed the same as any other barracks it would be rated as a separate hereditament and your astonishment would be flabbergasted if I told you what the rates are in the present year.'

'What?'

'Sixteen and eightpence in the pound with thruppence in the pound for bad yellow water that I would not use and fourpence by your kind leave for technical education. Is it any wonder the country is on its final legs with the farmers crippled and not one in ten with a proper bull-paper? I have eighteen summonses drawn up for nothing else and there will be hell to pay at the next Court. Why had you no light at all, big or small, on your bicycle?'

'My lamp was stolen.'

'Stolen? I thought so. It is the third theft today and four pumps disappeared on Saturday last. Some people would steal the saddle from underneath you if they thought you would not notice it, it is a lucky thing the tyre cannot be taken off without undoing the wheel. Wait till I take a deposition from you. Give me a description of the article and tell me all and do not omit anything because what may seem unimportant to yourself might well give a wonderful clue to the trained investigator.'

I felt sick at heart but the brief conversation had steadied me and I felt sufficiently recovered to take some small interest in the question of getting out of this hideous house. The policeman had opened a thick ledger which looked like the half of a longer book which had been sawn in two to fit the narrow table. He put several questions to me about the lamp and wrote down my replies very laboriously in the book, scratching his pen noisily and breathing heavily through his nose, pausing occasionally in his blowing when some letter of the alphabet gave him special difficulty. I surveyed him carefully as he sat absorbed in his task of writing. It was beyond all doubt the face of old Mathers but now it seemed to have a simple childlike quality as if the wrinkles of a long lifetime, evident enough the first time I looked at him, had been suddenly softened by some benign influence and practically erased. He now looked so innocent and good-natured and so troubled by the writing down of simple words that hope began to flicker once again within me. Surveyed coolly, he did not look a very formidable enemy. Perhaps I was dreaming or in the grip of some horrible hallucination. There was much that I did not understand and possibly could never understand to my dying day – the face of old Mathers whom I thought I had buried in a field on so great and fat a body, the ridiculous police station within the walls of another house, the other two monstrous policemen I had escaped from. But at least I was near my own house and the bicycle was waiting at the gate to take me there. Would this man try to stop me if I said I was going home? Did he know anything about the black box?

He had now carefully blotted his work and passed the book to me for my signature, proffering the pen by the handle with great politeness. He had covered two pages in a large childish hand. I thought it better not to enter into any discussion on the question of my name and hastily made an intricate scrawl at the bottom of the statement, closed the book and handed it back. Then I said as casually as I could:

'I think I will be going now.'

He nodded regretfully.

'I am sorry I cannot offer you anything,' he said, 'because it is a cold night and it would not do you a bit of harm.'

My strength and courage had been flowing back into my body and when I heard these words I felt almost completely strong again. There were many things to be thought about but I would not think of them at all until I was secure in my own house. I would go home as soon as possible and on the way I would not put my eye to right or left. I stood up steadily.

'Before I go,' I said, 'there is one thing I would like to ask you. There was a black cashbox stolen from me and I have been searching for it for several days. Would you by any chance have any information about it?'

The instant I had this said I was sorry I had said it because if it actually was Mathers brought miraculously back to life he might connect me with the robbery and the murder of himself and wreak some terrible vengeance. But the policeman only smiled and put a very knowing expression on his face. He sat down on the edge of the very narrow table and drummed upon it with his nails. Then he looked me in the eye. It was the first time he had done so and I was dazzled as if I had accidentally glanced at the sun.

'Do you like strawberry jam?' he asked.

His stupid question came so unexpectedly that I nodded and gazed at him uncomprehendingly. His smile broadened.

'Well if you had that box here,' he said, 'you could have a bucket of strawberry jam for your tea and if that was not enough you could have a bathful of it to lie in it full-length and if that much did not satisfy you, you could have ten acres of land with strawberry jam spread on it to the height of your two oxters. What do you think of that?'

'I do not know what to think of it,' I muttered. 'I do not understand it.'

'I will put it another way,' he said good-humouredly. 'You could have a house packed full of strawberry jam, every room so full that you could not open the door.'

I could only shake my head. I was becoming uneasy again.

'I would not require all that jam,' I said stupidly.

The policeman sighed as if despairing to convey to me his line of thought. Then his expression grew slightly more serious.

'Tell me this and tell me no more,' he said solemnly. 'When you went with Pluck and MacCruiskeen that time downstairs in the wood, what was your private opinion of what you saw? Was it your opinion that everything there was more than ordinary?'

I started at the mention of the other policemen and felt that I was once more in serious danger. I would have to be extremely careful. I could not see how he knew what had happened to me when I was in the toils of Pluck and MacCruiskeen but I told him that I did not understand the underground paradise and thought that even the smallest thing that happened there was miraculous. Even now when I recalled what I had seen there I wondered once more whether I had been dreaming. The policeman seemed pleased at the wonder I had expressed. He was smiling quietly, more to himself than to me.

'Like everything that is hard to believe and difficult to comprehend,' he said at last, 'it is very simple and a neighbour's child could work it all without being trained. It is a pity you did not think of the strawberry jam while you were there because you could have got a barrel of it free of charge and the quality would be extra and superfine, only the purest fruit-juice used and little or no preservatives.'

'It did not look simple – what I saw.'

'You thought there was magic in it, not to mention monkey-work of no mean order?'

'I did.'

'But it can all be explained, it was very simple and the way it was all worked will astonish you when I tell you.'

Despite my dangerous situation, his words fired me with a keen curiosity. I reflected that this talk of the strange underground region with the doors and wires confirmed that it did exist, that I actually had been there and that my memory of it was not the memory of a dream – unless I was still in the grip of the same nightmare. His offer to explain hundreds of miracles in one simple explanation was very tempting. Even that knowledge might repay me for the uneasiness I felt in his company. The sooner the talking stopped the sooner I could attempt my escape.

'How was it done, then?' I asked.

The Sergeant smiled broadly in amusement at my puzzled face. He made me feel that I was a child asking about something that was self-evident.

'The box,' he said.

'The box? *My* box?'

'Of course. The little box did the trick, I have to laugh at Pluck and MacCruiskeen, you would think they had more sense.'

'Did you find the box?'

'It was found and I entered into complete possession of it in virtue of section 16 of the Act of '87 as extended and amended. I was waiting for you to call for it because I know by my own private and official inquiries that you were the party that was at the loss of it but my impatience gave in with your long delay and I sent it to your house today by express bicycle and you will find it there before you when you travel homewards. You are a lucky man to have it because there is nothing so valuable in the whole world and it works like a charm, you could swear it was a question of clockwork. I weighed it and there is more than four ounces in it, enough to make you a man of private means and anything else you like to fancy.'

'Four ounces of what?'

'Of omnium. Surely you know what was in your own box?'

'Of course,' I stammered, 'but I did not think there was *four* ounces.'

'Four point one two on the Post Office scales. And that is how I worked the fun with Pluck and MacCruiskeen, it would make you smile to think of it, they had to run and work like horses every time I shoved the readings up to danger-point.'

He chuckled softly at the thought of his colleagues having to do hard work and looked across at me to see the effect of this simple revelation. I sank back on the seat flabbergasted but managed to return a ghostly smile to divert suspicion that I had not known what was in the box. If I could believe him he had been sitting in this room presiding at four ounces of this inutterable substance, calmly making ribbons of the natural order, inventing intricate and unheard of machinery to delude the other policemen, interfering drastically with time to make them think they had been leading their magical lives for years, bewildering, horrifying and enchanting the whole countryside. I was stupefied and appalled by the modest claim he had made so cheerfully, I could not quite believe it, yet it was the only way the terrible recollections which filled my brain could be explained. I felt again afraid of the policeman but at the same time a wild excitement gripped me to think that this box and what was in it was at this moment resting on the table of my own kitchen. What would Divney do? Would he be angry at finding no money, take this awful omnium for a piece of dirt and throw it out on the manure heap? Formless speculations crowded in upon me, fantastic fears and hopes, inexpressible fancies, intoxicating foreshadowing of creations, changes, annihilations and god-like interferences. Sitting at home with my box of omnium I could do anything, see anything and know anything with no limit to my powers save that of my own imagination. Perhaps I could use it even to extend my imagination. I could destroy, alter and improve the universe at will. I could get rid of John Divney, not brutally, but by giving him ten million pounds to go away. I could write the most unbelievable commentaries on de Selby ever written and publish them in bindings unheard of for their luxury and durability. Fruits and crops surpassing anything ever known would flower on my farm, in earth made inconceivably fertile by unparalleled artificial manures. A leg of flesh and bone yet stronger than iron would appear magically upon my left thigh. I would improve the weather to a standard day of sunny peace with gentle rain at night washing the world to make it fresher and more enchanting to the eye. I would present every poor labourer in the world with a bicycle made of gold, each machine with a saddle made of something as yet uninvented but softer than the softest softness, and I would arrange that a warm gale would blow behind every man on every journey, even when two were going in opposite directions on the same road. My sow would farrow twice daily and a man would call immediately offering ten million pounds for each of the piglings, only to be outbid by a second man arriving and offering twenty million. The barrels and bottles in my public house would still be full and inexhaustible no matter how much was drawn out of them. I would bring de Selby himself back to life to converse with me at night and advise me in my sublime undertakings. Every Tuesday I would make myself invisible –

'You would not believe the convenience of it,' said the policeman bursting in upon my thoughts, 'it is very handy for taking the muck off your leggings in the winter.'

'Why not use it for preventing the muck getting on your leggings at all?' I asked excitedly. The policeman looked at me in wide-eyed admiration.

'By the Hokey I never thought of that,' he said. 'You are very intellectual and I am certain that I am nothing but a gawm.'

'Why not use it,' I almost shouted, 'to have no muck anywhere at any time?'

He dropped his eyes and looked very disconsolate.

'I am the world's champion gawm,' he murmured.

I could not help smiling at him, not, indeed, without some pity. It was clear that he was not the sort of person to be entrusted with the contents of the black box. His oafish underground invention was the product of a mind which fed upon adventure books of small boys, books in which every extravagance was mechanical and lethal and solely concerned with bringing about somebody's death in the most elaborate way imaginable. I was lucky to have escaped from his preposterous cellars with my life. At the same time I recalled that I had a small account to settle with Policeman MacCruiskeen and Sergeant Pluck. It was not the fault of these gentlemen that I had not been hanged on the scaffold and prevented from ever recovering the black box. My life had been saved by the policeman in front of me, probably by accident, when he decided to rush up an alarming reading on the lever. He deserved some consideration for that. I would probably settle ten million pounds upon him when I had time to consider the matter fully. He looked more a fool than a knave. But MacCruiskeen and Pluck were in a different class. It would probably be possible for me to save time and trouble by adapting the underground machinery to give both of them enough trouble, danger, trepidation, work and inconvenience to make them rue the day they first threatened me. Each of the cabinets could be altered to contain, not bicycles and whiskey and matches, but putrescent offals, insupportable smells, unbehold-able corruptions containing tangles of gleaming slimy vipers each of them deadly and foul of breath, millions of diseased and decayed monsters clawing the inside latches of the ovens to open them and escape, rats with horns walking upside down along the ceiling pipes trailing their leprous tails on the policemen's heads, readings of incalculable perilousness mounting hourly upon the –

'But it is a great convenience for boiling eggs,' the policeman put in again, 'if you like them soft you get them soft and the hard ones are as hard as iron.'

'I think I will go home,' I said steadily, looking at him almost fiercely. I stood up. He only nodded, took out his torch and swung his leg off the table.

'I do not think an egg is nice at all if it is underdone,' he remarked, 'and there is nothing so bad for heartburn and indiges-tion, yesterday was the first time in my life I got my egg right.'

He led the way to the tall narrow door, opened it and passed out before me down the dark stairs, flashing the torch ahead and swinging it politely back to me to show the steps. We made slow progress and remained silent, he sometimes walking sideways and rubbing the more bulging parts of his uniform on the wall. When we reached the window, he opened it and got out into the shrubberies first, holding it up until I had scrambled out beside him. Then he went ahead of me again with his light in long swishing steps through the long grass and undergrowth, saying nothing until we had reached the gap in the hedge and were again standing on the hard roadside. Then he spoke. His voice was strangely diffident, almost apologetic.

'There was something I would like to tell you,' he said, 'and I am half-ashamed to tell you because it is a question of principle and I do not like taking personal liberties because where would the world be if we all did that?'

I felt him looking at me in the dark with his mild inquiry. I was puzzled and a little disquieted. I felt he was going to make some further devastating revelation.

'What is it?' I asked.

'It is about my little barrack . . .' he mumbled.

'Yes?'

'I was ashamed of my life of the shabbiness of it and I took the liberty of having it papered the same time as I was doing the hard-boiled egg. It is now very neat and I hope you are not vexed or at any loss over the head of it.'

I smiled to myself, feeling relieved, and told him that he was very welcome.

'It was a sore temptation,' he continued eagerly to reinforce his case, 'it was not necessary to go to the trouble of taking down the notices off the wall because the wallpaper put itself up behind them while you would be saying nothing.'

'That is all right,' I said. 'Good night and thank you.'

'Goodbye to you,' he said, saluting me with his hand, 'and you can be certain I will find the stolen lamp because they cost one and sixpence and you would want to be made of money to keep buying them.'

I watched him withdrawing through the hedge and going back into the tangle of trees and bushes. Soon his torch was only an intermittent flicker between the trunks and at last he disappeared completely. I was again alone upon the roadway. There was no sound to be heard save the languorous stirring of the trees in the gentle night air. I gave a sigh of relief and began to walk back towards the gate to get my bicycle.

CHAPTER 12

THE NIGHT seemed to have reached its middle point of intensity and the darkness was now much darker than before. My brain was brimming with half-formed ideas of the most far-reaching character but I repressed them firmly and determined to confine myself wholly to finding the bicycle and going home at once.

I reached the embrasure of the gateway and moved about it gingerly, stretching forth my hands into the blackness in search of the reassuring bars of my accomplice. At every move and reach I either found nothing or my hand came upon the granite roughness of the wall. An unpleasant suspicion was dawning on me that the bicycle was gone. I started searching with more speed and agitation and investigated with my hands what I am sure was the whole semi-circle of the gateway. She was not there. I stood for a moment in dismay, trying to remember whether I had untied her the last time I had raced down from the house to find her. It was inconceivable that she had been stolen because even if anybody had passed at that unearthly hour, it would not be possible to see her in the pitch darkness. Then as I stood, something quite astonishing happened to me again. Something slipped gently into my right hand. It was the grip of a handle-bar − *her* handlebar. It seemed to come to me out of the dark like a child stretching out its hand for guidance. I was astonished yet could not be certain afterwards whether the thing actually had entered my hand or whether the hand had been searching about mechanically while I was deep in thought and found the handlebar without the help or interference of anything unusual. At any other time I would have meditated in wonder on this curious incident but I now repressed all thought of it, passed my hands about the rest of the bicycle and found her leaning awkwardly against the wall with the string hanging loosely from her crossbar. She was not leaning against the gate where I had tied her.

My eyes had become adjusted to the gloom and I could now

see clearly the lightish road bounded by the formless obscurities of the ditch on either side. I led the bicycle to the centre, started upon her gently, threw my leg across and settled gently into her saddle. She seemed at once to communicate to me some balm, some very soothing and pleasurable relaxation after the excitements of the tiny police station. I felt once more comfortable in mind and body, happy in the growing lightness of my heart. I knew that nothing in the whole world could tempt me from the saddle on this occasion until I reached my home. Already I had left the big house a far way behind me. A breeze had sprung up from nowhere and pushed tirelessly at my back, making me flit effortlessly through the darkness like a thing on wings. The bicycle ran truly and faultlessly beneath me, every part of her functioning with precision, her gentle saddle-springs giving unexceptionable consideration to my weight on the undulations of the road. I tried as firmly as ever to keep myself free of the wild thought of my four ounces of omnium but nothing I could do could restrain the profusion of half-thought extravagances which came spilling forth across my mind like a horde of swallows – extravagances of eating, drinking, inventing, destroying, changing, improving, awarding, punishing and even loving. I knew only that some of these undefined wisps of thought were celestial, some horrible, some pleasant and benign; all of them were momentous. My feet pressed down with ecstasy on the willing female pedals.

Courahan's house, a dull silent murk of gloom, passed away behind me on the right-hand side and my eyes narrowed excitedly to try to penetrate to my own house two hundred yards further on. It formed itself gradually exactly in the point I knew it stood and I nearly roared and cheered and yelled out wild greetings at the first glimpse of these four simple walls. Even at Courahan's – I admitted it to myself now – I could not quite convince myself beyond all doubt that I would ever again see the house where I was born, but now I was dismounting from the bicycle outside it. The perils and wonders of the last few days seemed magnificent and epic now that I had survived them. I felt enormous, important and full of power. I felt happy and fulfilled.

The shop and the whole front of the house was in darkness. I wheeled the bicycle smartly up to it, laid it against the door and walked round to the side. A light was shining from the kitchen

window. Smiling to myself at the thought of John Divney, I tiptoed up and looked in.

There was nothing altogether unnatural in what I saw but
I encountered another of those chilling shocks which I thought
I had left behind me forever. A woman was standing at the table
with some article of clothing neglected in her hands. She was
facing up the kitchen towards the fireplace where the lamp was
and she was talking quickly to somebody at the fire. The fireplace
could not be seen from where I stood. The woman was Pegeen
Meers whom Divney had once talked of marrying. Her appearance amazed me far more than her presence in my own kitchen.
She seemed to have grown old, very fat and very grey. Looking at
her sideways I could see that she was with child. She was talking
rapidly, even angrily, I thought. I was certain she was talking to
John Divney and that he was seated with his back to her at the
fire. I did not stop to think on this queer situation but walked
past the window, lifted the latch of the door, opened the door
quickly and stood there looking in. In the one glance I saw two
people at the fire, a young lad I had never seen before and my
old friend John Divney. He was sitting with his back half-towards
me and I was greatly startled by his appearance. He had grown
enormously fat and his brown hair was gone, leaving him quite
bald. His strong face had collapsed to jowls of hanging fat. I could
discern a happy glimmer from the side of his fire-lit eye; an open
bottle of whiskey was standing on the floor beside his chair. He
turned lazily towards the open door, half-rose and gave a scream
which pierced me and pierced the house and careered up to
reverberate appallingly in the vault of the heavens. His eyes were
transfixed and motionless as they stared at me, his loose face
shrunk and seemed to crumble to a limp pallid rag of flesh. His
jaws clicked a few times like a machine and then he fell forward
on his face with another horrible shriek which subsided to
heartrending moans.

I was very frightened and stood pale and helpless in the doorway. The boy had jumped forward and tried to lift Divney up;
Pegeen Meers had given a frightened cry and rushed forward
also. They pulled Divney round upon his back. His face was
twisted in a revolting grimace of fear. His eyes again looked in
my direction upside down and backwards and he gave another
piercing scream and frothed foully at the mouth. I took a few

steps forward to assist in getting him up from the floor but he made a demented convulsive movement and choked out the four words 'Keep away, keep away,' in such a tone of fright and horror that I halted in my tracks, appalled at his appearance. The woman pushed the pale-faced boy distractedly and said:

'Run and get the doctor for your father, Tommy! Hurry, hurry!'

The boy mumbled something and ran out of the open door without giving me a glance. Divney was still lying there, his face hidden in his hands, moaning and gibbering in broken undertones; the woman was on her knees trying to lift his head and comfort him. She was now crying and muttered that she knew something would happen if he did not stop his drinking. I went a little bit forward and said:

'Could I be of any help?'

She took no notice of me at all, did not even glance at me. But my words had a stange effect on Divney. He gave a whining scream which was muffled by his hands; then it died down to choking sobs and he locked his face in his hands so firmly that I could see the nails biting into the loose white flesh beside his ears. I was becoming more and more alarmed. The scene was eerie and disturbing. I took another step forward.

'If you will allow me,' I said loudly to the woman Meers, 'I will lift him and get him into bed. There is nothing wrong with him except that he has taken too much whiskey.'

Again the woman took no notice whatever but Divney was siezed by a convulsion terrible to behold. He half-crawled and rolled himself with grotesque movements of his limbs until he was a crumpled heap on the far side of the fireplace, spilling the bottle of whiskey on his way and sending it clattering noisily across the floor. He moaned and made cries of agony which chilled me to the bone. The woman followed him on her knees, crying pitifully and trying to mumble soothing words to him. He sobbed convulsively where he lay and began to cry and mutter things disjointedly like a man raving at the door of death. It was about me. He told me to keep away. He said I was not there. He said I was dead. He said that what he had put under the boards in the big house was not the black box but a mine, a bomb. It had gone up when I touched it. He had watched the bursting of it from where I had left him. The house was blown to bits. I was dead. He screamed to me to keep away. I was dead for sixteen years.

'He is dying,' the woman cried.

I do not know whether I was surprised at what he said, or even whether I believed him. My mind became quite empty, light, and felt as if it were very white in colour. I stood exactly where I was for a long time without moving or thinking. I thought after a time that the house was strange and I became uncertain about the two figures on the floor. Both were moaning and wailing and crying.

'He is dying, he is dying,' the woman cried again.

A cold biting wind was sweeping in through the open door behind me and staggering the light of the oil-lamp fitfully. I thought it was time to go away. I turned with stiffer steps and walked out through the door and round to the front of the house to get my bicycle. It was gone. I walked out upon the road again, turning leftwards. The night had passed away and the dawn had come with a bitter searing wind. The sky was livid and burdened with ill omen. Black angry clouds were piling in the west, bulging and glutted, ready to vomit down their corruption and drown the dreary world in it. I felt sad, empty, and without a thought. The trees by the road were rank and stunted and moved their stark leafless branches very dismally in the wind. The grasses at hand were coarse and foul. Waterlogged bog and healthless marsh stretched endlessly to left and right. The pallor of the sky was terrible to look upon.

My feet carried my nerveless body unbidden onwards for mile upon mile of rough cheerless road. My mind was completely void. I did not recall who I was, where I was or what my business was upon earth. I was alone and desolate yet not concerned about myself at all. The eyes in my head were open but they saw nothing because my brain was void.

Suddenly I found myself noticing my own existence and taking account of my surroundings. There was a bend in the road and when I came round it an extraordinary spectacle was presented to me. About a hundred yards away was a house which astonished me. It looked as if it were painted like an advertisement on a board on the roadside and, indeed, very poorly painted. It looked completely false and unconvincing. It did not seem to have any depth or breadth and looked as if it would not deceive a child. That was not in itself sufficient to surprise me because I had seen pictures and notices by the roadside before. What bewildered me was the sure knowledge, deeply rooted in my mind, that this was the house I was searching for and that there were people inside it. I had never seen with my eyes ever in my life before anything so unnatural and appalling and my gaze faltered about the thing uncomprehendingly as if at least one of the customary dimensions were missing, leaving no meaning in the remainder. The appearance of the house was the greatest surprise I had encountered ever, and I felt afraid of it.

I kept on walking but walked more slowly. As I approached, the house seemed to change its appearance. At first, it did nothing to reconcile itself with the shape of an ordinary house but it became uncertain in outline like a thing glimpsed under ruffled water. Then it became clear again and I saw that it began to have some back to it, some small space for rooms behind the frontage. I gathered this from the fact that I seemed to see the front and the back simultaneously from my position approaching what should have been the side. As there was no side that I could see I thought that the house must be triangular with its apex pointing towards me but when I was only fifteen yards away I saw a small window facing me and I knew from that that there must be *some* side to it. Then I found myself almost in the shadow of the structure, dry-throated and timorous from wonder and anxiety. It seemed ordinary enough at close quarters except that it was very white and still. It was momentous and frightening; the whole morning and the whole world seemed to have no purpose at all save to frame it and give it some magnitude and position so that I could find it with my simple senses and pretend to myself that I understood it. A constabulary crest above the door told me that it was a police station. I had never seen a police station like it.

I stopped in my tracks, I heard distant footsteps on the road behind me, heavy footsteps hurrying after me. I did not look round but remained standing motionless ten yards from the police station, waiting for the hurrying steps. They grew louder and louder and heavier and heavier. At last he came abreast of me. It was John Divney. We did not look at each other or say a single word. I fell into step beside him and both of us marched into the police station. We saw, standing with his back to us, an enormous policeman. His back appearance was unusual. He was standing behind a little counter in a neat whitewashed day-room; his mouth was open and he was looking into a mirror which hung upon the wall.

'It's my teeth,' we heard him say abstractedly and half-aloud. 'Nearly every sickness is from the teeth.'

His face, when he turned, surprised us. It was enormously fat, red and widespread, sitting squarely on the neck of his tunic with a clumsy weightiness that reminded me of a sack of flour. The lower half of it was hidden by a violent red moustache which shot out from his skin far into the air like the antennae of some unusual animal. His cheeks were red and chubby and his eyes were nearly invisible, hidden from above by the obstruction of his tufted brows and from below by the fat foldings of his skin. He came over ponderously to the inside of the counter and Divney and I advanced meekly from the door until we were face to face.

'Is it about a bicycle?' he asked.

PUBLISHER'S NOTE

ON ST VALENTINE'S DAY, 1940, the author wrote to William Saroyan about this novel, as follows:

'I've just finished another book. The only thing good about it is the plot and I've been wondering whether I could make a crazy . . . play out of it. When you get to the end of this book you realize that my hero or main character (he's a heel and a killer) has been dead throughout the book and that all the queer ghastly things which have been happening to him are happening in a sort of hell which he earned for the killing. Towards the end of the book (before you know he's dead) he manages to get back to his own house where he used to live with another man who helped in the original murder. Although he's been away three days, this other fellow is twenty years older and dies of fright when he sees the other lad standing in the door. Then the two of them walk back along the road to the hell place and start thro' all the same terrible adventures again, the first fellow being surprised and frightened at everything just as he was the first time and as if he'd never been through it before. It is made clear that this sort of thing goes on for ever – and there you are. It is supposed to be very funny but I don't know about that either . . . I think the idea of a man being dead all the time is pretty new. When you are writing about the world of the dead – and the damned – where none of the rules and laws (not even the law of gravity) holds good, there is any amount of scope for back-chat and funny cracks.'

14 February, 1940

B. O'N.

Elsewhere, the author wrote:

'Joe had been explaining things in the meantime. He said it was again the beginning of the unfinished, the re-discovery of the familiar, the re-experience of the already suffered, the fresh-forgetting of the unremembered. Hell goes round and round. In shape it is circular and by nature it is interminable, repetitive and very nearly unbearable.'

THE POOR MOUTH

(AN BÉAL BOCHT)

A BAD STORY ABOUT THE HARD LIFE

Edited by Myles na Gopaleen (Flann O'Brien)
Translated by Patrick C. Power

'if a stone be cast, there is no
foreknowledge of where it may land'

PREFACE TO THE FIRST EDITION

I BELIEVE THAT this is the first book ever published on the subject of Corkadoragha. It is timely and opportune, I think. Of great advantage both to the language itself and to those studying it is that a little report on the people who inhabit that remote Gaeltacht should be available after their times and also that some little account of the learned smooth Gaelic which they used should be obtainable.

This document is exactly as I received it from the author's hand except that much of the original matter has been omitted due to pressure of space and to the fact that improper subjects were included in it. Still, material will be available ten-fold if there is demand from the public for the present volume.

It is understandable that anything mentioned here concerns only Corkadoragha and it is not to be understood that any reference is intended to the Gaeltacht areas in general; Corkadoragha is a distinctive place and the people who live there are without compare.

It is a cause of jubilation that the author, Bonaparte O'Coonassa, is still alive today, safe in jail and free from the miseries of life.

The Editor
The Day of Want, 1941

FOREWORD

IT IS SAD to relate that neither praise nor commendation is deserved by Gaelic folk – those of them who are moneyed gentle-folk or great bucks (in their own estimation) – because they have allowed a fascicle such as *The Poor Mouth* to remain out of print for many years; without young or old having an opportunity to see it, nor having any chance of milking wisdom, shrewdness and strength from the deeds of the unusual community that lives west in Corkadoragha – the seed of the strong and the choicest of paupers.

They live there to this day, but they are not increasing in numbers and the sweet Gaelic dialect, which is oftener in their mouths than a scrap of food, is not developing but rather declining like rust. Apart from this fact, emigration is thinning out the remote areas, the young folk are setting their faces towards Siberia in the hope of better weather and relief from the cold and tempest which is natural to them.

I recommend that this book be in every habitation and mansion where love for our country's traditions lives at this hour when, as Standish Hayes O'Grady says 'the day is drawing to a close and the sweet wee maternal tongue has almost ebbed'.

The Editor
The Day of Doom, 1964

CHAPTER 1

Why I speak ♣ my birth ♣ my mother and the
Old-Grey-Fellow ♣ our house ♣ the glen where I was born ♣
the hardships of the Gaels in former times

I AM NOTING down the matters which are in this document
because the next life is approaching me swiftly – far from us be
the evil thing and may the bad spirit not regard me as a brother!
– and also because our likes will never be there again. It is right
and fitting that some testimony of the diversions[1] and adventures[2]
of our times should be provided for those who succeed us
because our types will never be there again nor any other life in
Ireland comparable to ours who exists no longer.

O'Coonassa is my surname in Gaelic, my first name is Bonaparte and Ireland is my little native land. I cannot truly remember
either the day I was born or the first six months I spent here in
the world. Doubtless, however, I was alive at that time although
I have no memory of it, because I should not exist now if I were
not there then and to the human being, as well as to every other
living creature, sense comes gradually.

The night before I was born, it happened that my father and
Martin O'Bannassa were sitting on top of the hen-house, gazing
at the sky to judge the weather and also chatting honestly and
quietly about the difficulties of life.

– Well, now, Martin, said my father, the wind is from the
north and there's a forbidding look about the White Bens; before
the morning there'll be rain and we'll get a dirty tempestuous
night of it that will knock a shake out of us even if we're in the
very bed. And look here! Martin, isn't it the bad sign that the
ducks are in the nettles? Horror and misfortune will come on
the world tonight; the evil thing and sea-cat will be a-foot in the
darkness and, if 'tis true for me, no good destiny is ever in store
for either of us again.

– Well, indeed, Michelangelo, said Martin O'Bannassa, 'tis no
little thing you've said there now and if you're right, you've told
nary a lie but the truth itself.

I was born in the middle of the night in the end of the house.[3]
My father never expected me because he was a quiet fellow and

did not understand very accurately the ways of life. My little bald skull so astounded him that he almost departed from this life the moment I entered it and, indeed, it was a misfortune and harmful thing for him that he did not, because after that night he never had anything but misery and was destroyed and rent by the world and bereft of his health as long as he lived. The people said that my mother was not expecting me either and it is a fact that the whisper went around that I was not born of my mother at all but of another woman. All that, nevertheless, is only the neighbours' talk and cannot be checked now because the neighbours are all dead and their likes will not be there again. I never laid eyes on my father until I was grown up but that is another story and I shall mention it at another time in this document.

I was born in the West of Ireland on that awful winter's night – may we all be healthy and safe! – in the place called Corkadoragha and in the townland named Lisnabrawshkeen. I was very young at the time I was born and had not aged even a single day; for half a year I did not perceive anything about me and did not know one person from the other. Wisdom and understanding, nevertheless, come steadily, solidly and stealthily into the mind of every human being and I spent that year on the broad of my back, my eyes darting here and there at my environment. I noticed my mother in the house before me, a decent, hefty, big-boned woman; a silent, cross, big-breasted woman. She seldom spoke to me and often struck me when I screamed in the end of the house. The beating was of little use in stopping the tumult because the second tumult was worse than the first one and, if I received a further beating, the third tumult was worse than the second one. However, my mother was sensible, level-headed and well-fed; her like will not be there again. She spent her life cleaning out the house, sweeping cow-dung and pig-dung from in front of the door, churning butter and milking cows, weaving and carding wool and working the spinning-wheel, praying, cursing and setting big fires to boil a houseful of potatoes to stave off the day of famine.

There was another person in the house in front of me – an old crooked, stooped fellow with a stick, half of whose face and all of whose chest were invisible because there was a wild, wool-grey beard blocking the view. The hairless part of his face was brown, tough and wrinkled like leather and two sharp shrewd

eyes looked out from it at the world with a needle's sharpness.
I never heard him called anything but the Old-Grey-Fellow. He
lived in our house and very often my mother and he were not of
the same mind and, bedad, it was an incredible thing the amount
of potatoes he consumed, the volume of speech which issued
from him and what little work he performed around the house.
At first in my youth I thought he was my father. I remember
sitting in his company one night, both of us gazing peacefully
into the great red mass of the fire where my mother had placed
a pot of potatoes as big as a barrel a-boiling for the pigs – she
herself was quiet in the end of the house. It happened that the
heat of the fire was roasting me but I was not able to walk at that
time and had no means of escape from the heat on my own. The
Old-Grey-Fellow cocked an eye at me and announced:
   – 'Tis hot, son!
   – There's an awful lot of heat in that fire truly, I replied, but
look, sir, you called me son for the first time. It may be that
you're my father and that I'm your child, God bless and save us
and far from us be the evil thing!
   – 'Tisn't true for you, Bonaparte, said he, for I'm your
grandfather. Your father is far from home at the present but his
name and surname in his present habitation are Michelangelo
O'Coonassa.
   – And where is he?
   – He's in the jug! said the Old-Grey-Fellow.
   At that time I was only about in the tenth month of my life
but when I had the opportunity I looked into the jug. There was
nothing in it but sour milk and it was a long time until I understood the Old-Grey-Fellow's remark, but that is another story
and I shall mention it in another place in this document.
   There is another day of my youth which is clear in my memory
and eminently describable. I was sitting on the floor of the house,
still unable to walk or even stand and watching my mother
sweeping the house and settling the hearth neatly with the tongs.
The Old-Grey-Fellow came in from the field and stood looking
at her until she had finished the work.
   – Woman, said he, it is a harmful, untimely work that you're
at there and you may be sure that neither good nor fine instruction will come of it for the fellow who's there on his backside
on the floor of our house.

— Any word and nearly every sound out of you are sweet to me, said she, but truly I don't understand what you're saying.

— Well, said the Old-Fellow, when I was a raw youngster growing up, I was (as is clear to any reader of the good Gaelic books) a child among the ashes.[4] You have thrown all the ashes of the house back into the fire or swept them out in the yard and not a bit left for the poor child on the floor — he pointed a finger towards me — to let him into. It's an unnatural and unregulated training and rearing he'll have without any experience of the ashes. Therefore, woman, it's disgraceful for you not to leave the hob full of dirt and ashes just as the fire leaves it.

— Very well, said my mother, 'tis true for you although you seldom talk a bit of sense and I'll be glad to put back all I swept from the hob.

And she did so. She took a bucket full of muck, mud and ashes and hen's droppings from the roadside and spread it around the hearth gladly in front of me. When everything was arranged, I moved over near the fire and for five hours I became a child in the ashes — a raw youngster rising up according to the old Gaelic tradition. Later at midnight I was taken and put into bed but the foul stench of the fireplace stayed with me for a week; it was a stale, putrid smell and I do not think that the like will ever be there again.

We lived in a small, lime-white, unhealthy house, situated in a corner of the glen on the right-hand side as you go eastwards along the road. Doubtless, neither my father nor any of his people before him built the house and placed it there; it is not known whether it was god, demon or person who first raised the half-rotten, rough walls. If there were a hundred corners in all that glen, there was a small lime-white cabin nestling in each one and no one knows who built any of them either. It has always been the destiny of the true Gaels (if the books be credible) to live in a small, lime-white house in the corner of the glen as you go eastwards along the road and that must be the explanation[5] that when I reached this life there was no good habitation for me but the reverse in all truth. As well as the poverty of the house in itself, it clung to a lump of rock on the perilous shoulder of the glen (although there was a fine site available lower down) and if you went out the door without due care as to where you stepped, you could be in mortal danger immediately because of the steep gradient.

Our house was undivided, wisps of rushes above us on the roof and rushes also as bedding in the end of the house. At sundown rushes were spread over the whole floor and the household lay to rest on them. Yonder a bed with pigs upon it; here a bed with people; a bed there with an aged slim cow stretched out asleep on her flank and a gale of breath issuing from her capable of raising a tempest in the centre of the house; hens and chickens asleep in the shelter of her belly; another bed near the fire with me on it.

Yes! people were in bad circumstances when I was young and he who had stock and cattle possessed little room at night in his own house. Alas! It was always thus. I often heard the Old-Grey-Fellow speak of the hardship and misery of life in former times.

– There was a time, said he, when I had two cows, a cart-horse, a race-horse, sheep, pigs and other lesser animals.[6] The house was narrow and, upon me soul, 'twas a tight troublesome situation we were in when the night came. My grandfather slept with the cows and I myself slept with the horse, Charlie, a quiet, gentle animal. The sheep used often start fighting and many times I went without a wink of sleep from the bleating and the roaring they used have. One night my grandfather was hurt and wounded but we didn't know whether 'twas the sheep or the cows that were the cause of it or whether my grandmother herself started the quarrel. But another night a gentleman arrived, a school-inspector that went astray in the bog-mist and happened to come on the mouth of the glen. Looking for help and lodging he was, maybe, and when he saw what was to be seen in the low light of the fire, he let a long roar of amazement out of him and stood there on the threshold staring in. Says he: Isn't it a shameful, improper and very bad thing for ye to be stretched out with the brute beasts, all of ye stuck together in the one bed? And isn't it a shameful, bad and improper state that ye're in here tonight? 'Tis true for you, I replied to the gentleman, but sure we can't help the bad state you've mentioned. The weather is bitter and everyone of us must be inside from it, whether he has two legs or four under him. If that's the way it is, says the gentleman, wouldn't it be easy for you to put up a little hut at the side of the yard and it a bit out from the house? Sure and 'twould be easy,

says I. I was full of wonder at all he said because I never thought
of the like nor of any other plan that would be handy to improve
the bad state we were in – all of us stuck together in the end of
the house. The next day I gathered the neighbours and explained
exactly to them the gentleman's advice. They praised that advice
and within a week we had put up a fine hut adjacent to my
house. But alas! things are not what they seem to be! When I,
my grandmother and two of my brothers had spent two nights
in the hut, we were so cold and drenched wet that it is a wonder
we did not die straight away and we couldn't get any relief until
we went back to the house and were comfortable again among
the cattle. We've been that way ever since, just like every poor
bit of a Gael in this side of the country.

The Old-Grey-Fellow often provided accounts such as this of
the old times and from him I received much of the sense and
wisdom which is now mine. However, concerning the house
where I was born, there was a fine view from it. It had two
windows with a door between them. Looking out from the
right-hand window, there below was the bare hungry countryside of the Rosses and Gweedore; Bloody Foreland yonder and
Tory Island far away out, swimming like a great ship where the
sky dips into the sea. Looking out of the door, you could see the
West of County Galway with a good portion of the rocks of
Connemara, Aranmore in the ocean out from you with the small
bright houses of Kilronan, clear and visible, if your eyesight were
good and the Summer had come. From the window on the left
you could see the Great Blasket, bare and forbidding as a horrible
other-worldly eel, lying languidly on the wave-tops; over yonder
was Dingle with its houses close together. It has always been said
that there is no view from any house in Ireland comparable to
this and it must be admitted that this statement is true. I have
never heard it said that there was any house as well situated as
this on the face of the earth. And so this house was delightful
and I do not think that its like will ever be there again.[7] At any
rate, I was born there and truly this cannot be stated concerning
any other house, whether that fact be praise or blame!

CHAPTER 2

A bad smell in our house ♣ the pigs ♣ the coming of Ambrose
♣ the hard life ♣ my mother in danger of death ♣ Martin's plan
♣ we are saved and are safe ♣ the death of Ambrose

IN MY YOUTH we always had a bad smell in our house. Sometimes it was so bad that I asked my mother to send me to school,
even though I could not walk correctly. Passers-by neither
stopped nor even walked when in the vicinity of our house but
raced past the door and never ceased until they were half a mile
from the bad smell. There was another house two hundred yards
down the road from us and one day when our smell was
extremely bad the folks there cleared out, went to America and
never returned. It was stated that they told people in that place
that Ireland was a fine country but that the air was too strong
there. Alas! there was never any air in our house.

A member of our household was guilty of this stench.
Ambrose was his name. The Old-Fellow was very attached
to him. Ambrose was Sarah's son. Sarah was a sow which we
possessed and when progeny was bestowed on her, it was
bestowed plentifully. In spite of her numerous breasts, there was
none for Ambrose when the piglets were sucking their nourishment from her. Ambrose was shy and when hunger struck the
piglets (it strikes their likes suddenly and all at the same moment)
he was left at the end without a breast. When the Old-Fellow
realized that this little piglet was becoming feeble and losing his
vigour, he brought him into the house, settled a bed of rushes
for him by the fireside and fed him from time to time with cow's
milk out of an old bottle. Ambrose recovered without delay,
grew strongly and became fine and fat. But alas! God has permitted every creature to possess its own smell and the pig's inherited
aroma is not pleasant. When Ambrose was little, he had a little
smell. When his size increased, his smell grew accordingly. When
he was big, the smell was likewise big. At first, the situation was
not too bad for us throughout the day, because we left all the
windows open, the door unshut and great gales of wind swept
through the house. But when darkness fell and Sarah came in
with the piglets to sleep, that indeed was the situation which

defies both oral and written description. Often in the middle of the night it seemed to us that we could never see the morning alive. My mother and the Old-Fellow often arose and went outside to walk ten miles in the rain trying to escape from the stench. After about a month of Ambrose in our house, the horse, Charlie, refused to come in at night and was found every morning drenched and wet (there was never a night without a downpour upon us). But he was, nevertheless, in good humour despite all he had suffered from the inclemency of the weather. Indeed, it was I who bore the hardship without a doubt because I could not walk nor find any means of self-locomotion.

Matters continued thus for a little while. Ambrose was swelling rapidly and the Old-Grey-Fellow said that shortly he would be strong enough to be out in the air with the other pigs. He was the Old-Fellow's pet and that is why my mother could not drive out the unfragrant pig from the house by cudgelling, although her health was failing due to the putrid stench.

We noticed suddenly that Ambrose, all in one night it seemed, had increased to a fearful size. He was as tall as his mother but much wider. His belly reached the ground and his flanks were so swollen that they would frighten you. One day the Old-Grey-Fellow was putting down a large pot of potatoes for the pig's dinner when he noticed that all was neither good nor natural.

– Upon me soul! said he, this one here is about to burst!

When we scrutinized Ambrose sharply, it was evident that the poor creature was almost completely cylindrical. I do not know whether it was due to over-eating or whether dropsy or some other fell disease struck him. I have not, however, narrated all. The smell was now almost insufferable for us and my mother fainted in the end of the house, her health having failed due to this new stench.

– If this pig is not put out of the house at once, said she feebly from the bed in the end of the house, I'll set these rushes on fire and then an end will be put to the hard life in this house of ours and even if we finish up later in hell, I've never heard there are pigs there anyway!

The Old-Fellow was puffing at the pipe strenuously in an attempt to fill the house with smoke as a defence against the stench. He replied to her:

– Woman! said he, the poor creature is sick and I'm slow to

push him out and he without his health. 'Tis true that this stench is beyond all but don't you see that the pig himself is making no complaint, although he has a snout on him just like yourself there.

– He's dumb from the stench, said I.

– If that's the way it is, said my mother to the Old-Fellow, I'll put the rushes in flames!

The two of them continued nagging at one another for a long while but at last the Old-Fellow agreed to eject Ambrose. He went forward coaxing the pig to the door with whistling, nonsensical talk and pet-words but the beast stayed as he was, unmoved. It must have been that the pig's senses were deadened by the smell and that they failed to hear all the Old-Fellow had to say. At any rate, the Old-Fellow took a cudgel and drove the pig to the door – lifting him, beating him and pushing him with the weapon. When he reached the door it appeared to us that he was too fat to go out between the jambs. He was released and he returned to his fireside bed where he fell asleep.

– Upon me soul! said the Old-Grey-Fellow, but the creature is too well-fed and the doorway is too narrow although there is room in it for the horse himself.

– If that's the way it is, said my mother from the bed, then 'tis that way and it is hard to get away from what's in store for us.

Her voice was weak and low and I was certain that she was now willing to bow to fate, to the rottenness of the pig, and to face heaven. But suddenly a smothering fire arose in the end of the house – my mother burning the place. Back went the Old-Fellow in one leap, threw a couple of old sacks on the smoke and beat them with a big stick until the fire was quenched. He then beat my mother and gave her beneficial advice while doing so.

God bless us and save us! there was never as hard a life as that which Ambrose gave us for a fortnight after this. There is no describing the smell in our house. The pig was doubtlessly ill and vapour arose from him reminiscent of a corpse unburied for a month. The house was rotten and putrid from top to bottom as a result of him. During that time my mother was in the end of the house unable to stand or speak. At the end of the fortnight, she bade us adieu and goodbye quietly and feebly and set her face towards eternity. The Old-Fellow was in the bed, smoking his pipe energetically during the night as a shield against the stench.

He leapt up and dragged my mother out to the roadside, thus saving her from death that night although both of them were drenched to the skin. The following day the beds were put out by the road and the Old-Fellow said that there we would remain henceforth because, said he, it is better to be without house than life and even if we are drowned in the rain at night, that death itself is better than the other one within.

Martin O'Bannassa was going along the road that day and when he saw the unfragrant beds outside beneath the sky and our deserted house, he stopped and struck up a conversation with the Old-Fellow.

— 'Tis true that I don't understand life and the reason that the beds are outside, but look at the house on fire!

The Old-Fellow gazed at the house and shook his head.

— That's no fire, said he, but a rotten pig in our house. That's not smoke that's drifting from the house, as you think, Martin, but pig-steam.

— That steam is not pleasing to me, said Martin.

— There's no health in it! retorted the Old-Fellow.

Martin pondered the question for a while.

— It must be the way, said he, that this pig of yours is a pet and that you wouldn't want to cut his throat and bury him?

— 'Tis true indeed for you, Martin, said he.

— If that's the way, said Martin, I'll give ye help!

He went up on the roof of the house and put scraws of grass on the chimney-opening. He then closed the door and blocked the windows with mud and rags to keep air from going in or coming out.

— Now, said he, we must be quiet for an hour.

— Upon me soul, said the Old-Grey-Fellow, I don't understand this work but it's a wonderful world that's there today and if you're pleased with what you've done, I won't go against you.

At the end of that hour, Martin O'Bannassa opened the door and we all went in except my mother who was still weak and feeble on the damp rushes. Ambrose was stretched, cold and dead, on the hearth-stone. He had died of his own stench and a black cloud of smoke almost smothered us. The Old-Fellow was very sad but gave heartfelt thanks to Martin and ceased puffing his pipe for the first time in three months. Ambrose was buried in an honourable and becoming manner and we were all once more very well in that house. My mother recovered fast from her ill-health and was once more energetic, boiling large pots of potatoes for the other pigs.

Ambrose was an odd pig and I do not think that his like will be there again. Good luck to him if he be alive in another world today!

CHAPTER 3

I go to school ♣ 'Jams O'Donnell' ♣ the two-pound grant ♣
pigs again in our house ♣ the Old-Grey-Fellow's plan ♣
one of our pigs missing ♣ the shanachee and the gramophone

I WAS SEVEN years old when I was sent to school. I was tough,
small and thin, wearing grey-wool breeches[1] but otherwise
unclothed above and below. Many other children besides me
were going to school that morning with the stain of the ashes still
on the breeches of many of them. Some of them were crawling
along the road, unable to walk. Many were from Dingle, some
from Gweedore, another group floated in from Aran. All of us
were strong and hearty on our first school day. A sod of turf was
under the armpit of each one of us. Hearty and strong were we!

The master was named Osborne O'Loonassa. He was dark,
spare and tall and unhealthy with a sharp, sour look on his face
where the bones were protruding through the yellow skin. A
ferocity of anger stood on his forehead as permanent as his hair
and he cared not a whit for anyone.

We all gathered into the schoolhouse, a small unlovely hut
where the rain ran down the walls and everything was soft and
damp. We all sat on benches, without a word or a sound for fear
of the master. He cast his venomous eyes over the room and they
alighted on me where they stopped. By jove! I did not find his
look pleasant while these two eyes were sifting me. After a while
he directed a long yellow finger at me and said:

– Phwat is yer nam?

I did not understand what he said nor any other type of speech
which is practised in foreign parts because I had only Gaelic as a
mode of expression and as a protection against the difficulties of
life. I could only stare at him, dumb with fear. I then saw a great
fit of rage come over him and gradually increase exactly like a
rain-cloud. I looked around timidly at the other boys. I heard a
whisper at my back:

– Your name he wants!

My heart leaped with joy at this assistance and I was grateful
to him who prompted me. I looked politely at the master and
replied to him:

– Bonaparte, son of Michelangelo, son of Peter, son of Owen, son of Thomas's Sarah, grand-daughter of John's Mary, grand-daughter of James, son of Dermot . . .[2]

Before I had uttered or half-uttered my name, a rabid bark issued from the master and he beckoned to me with his finger. By the time I had reached him, he had an oar in his grasp. Anger had come over him in a flood-tide at this stage and he had a businesslike grip of the oar in his two hands. He drew it over his shoulder and brought it down hard upon me with a swish of air, dealing me a destructive blow on the skull. I fainted from that blow but before I became totally unconscious I heard him scream:

– Yer nam, said he, is Jams O'Donnell![3]

Jams O'Donnell? These two words were singing in my ears when feeling returned to me. I found that I was lying on my side on the floor, my breeches, hair and all my person saturated with the streams of blood which flowed from the split caused by the oar in my skull. When my eyes were in operation again, there was another youngster on his feet being asked his name. It was apparent that this child lacked shrewdness completely and had not drawn good beneficial lessons for himself from the beating which I had received because he replied to the master, giving his common name as I had. The master again brandished the oar which was in his grasp and did not cease until he was shedding blood plentifully, the youngster being left unconscious and stretched out on the floor, a bloodied bundle. And during the beating the master screamed once more:

– Yer nam is Jams O'Donnell!

He continued in this manner until every creature in the school had been struck down by him and all had been named *Jams O'Donnell*. No young skull in the countryside that day remained unsplit. Of course, there were many unable to walk by the afternoon and were transported home by relatives. It was a pitiable thing for those who had to swim back to Aran that evening and were without a bite of food or a sup of milk since morning.

When I myself reached home, my mother was there boiling potatoes for the pigs and I asked her for a couple for lunch. I received them and ate them with only a little pinch of salt. The bad situation in the school was bothering me all this time and I decided to question my mother.

— Woman, said I, I've heard that every fellow in this place is called *Jams O'Donnell*. If that's the way it is, it's a wonderful world we have and isn't O'Donnell the wonderful man and the number of children he has?

— 'Tis true for you, said she.

— If 'tis true itself, said I, I've no understanding of that same truth.

— If that's the way, said she, don't you understand that it's Gaels that live in this side of the country and that they can't escape from fate? It was always said and written that every Gaelic youngster is hit on his first school day because he doesn't understand English and the foreign form of his name and that no one has any respect for him because he's Gaelic to the marrow. There's no other business going on in school that day but punishment and revenge and the same fooling about *Jams O'Donnell*. Alas! I don't think that there'll ever be any good settlement for the Gaels but only hardship for them always. The Old-Grey-Fellow was also hit one day of his life and called *Jams O'Donnell* as well.

— Woman, said I, what you say is amazing and I don't think I'll ever go back to that school but it's now the end of my learning!

— You're shrewd, said she, in your early youth.

I had no other connection with education from that day onwards and therefore my Gaelic skull has not been split since. But seven years afterwards (when I was seven years older), it came to pass that wonderful things happened in our neighbourhood, things connected with the question of learning and, for this reason, I must present some little account of them here.

The Old-Fellow was one day in Dingle buying tobacco and tasting spirits, when he heard news which amazed him. He did not believe it because he never trusted the people of that town. The next day he was selling herrings in the Rosses and had the same news from them there; he then half-accepted the story but did not altogether swallow it. The third day he was in Galway city and the story was there likewise. At last he believed it believingly and when he returned, drenched and wet (the downpour comes heavily on us unfailingly each night), he informed my mother of the matter (and me also who was eavesdropping in the end of the house!).

— Upon me soul, said he, I hear that the English Government is going to do great work for the good of the paupers here in this

place, safe and saved may everyone be in this house! It is fixed to
pay the likes of us two pounds a skull for every child of ours that
speaks English instead of this thieving Gaelic. Trying to separate
us from the Gaelic they are, praise be to them sempiternally!
I don't think there'll ever be good conditions for the Gaels while
having small houses in the corner of the glen, going about in
the dirty ashes, constantly fishing in the constant storm, telling
stories at night about the hardships and hard times of the Gaels
in sweet words of Gaelic is natural to them.

– Woe is me! exclaimed my mother, and I with only the one
son; this dying example here that's on his backside over on the
floor there.

– If that's the way, said the Old-Fellow, you'll have more
children or else you're without resource!

During the following week, a staunch black gloom came over
the Old-Grey-Fellow, a portent that his mind was filled with
difficult complicated thoughts while he endeavoured to solve the
question of the want of children. One day, while in Cahirciveen,
he heard that the new scheme was under way; that the good
foreign money had been received already in many houses in that
district and that an inspector was going about through the countryside counting the children and testing the quality of English
they had. He also heard that this inspector was an aged crippled
man without good sight and that he lacked enthusiasm for his
work as well. The Old-Fellow pondered all that he heard and
when he returned at night (drenched and wet), he informed us
that there is no cow unmilkable, no hound unraceable and, also,
no money which cannot be stolen.

– Upon me soul, said he, we'll have the full of the house before
morning and everyone of them earning two pounds for us.

– It's a wonderful world, said my mother, but I'm not expecting anything of that kind and neither did I hear that a house
could be filled in one night.

– Don't forget, said he, that Sarah is here.

– Sarah, indeed! said my startled mother.

Amazement leaped up and down through me when I heard
the mention of the sow's name.

– The same lady exactly, said he. She has a great crowd of a
family at present and they have vigorous voices, even though
their dialect is unintelligible to us. How do we know but that

their conversation isn't in English. Of course, youngsters and piglets have the same habits and take notice that there's a close likeness between their skins.

– You're reflective, replied my mother, but they must have suits of clothes made for them before the inspector comes to look at them.

– They must indeed, said the Old-Grey-Fellow.

– It's a wonderful world these days, said I from the back-bed at the end of the house.

– Upon me soul, but 'tis wonderful, said the Old-Fellow, but in spite of the payment of this English money for the good of our likes, I don't think there'll ever be good conditions for the Gaels.

The following day we had these particular residents within, each one wearing a grey-wool clothing while squealing, rooting, grunting and snoring in the rushes in the back of the house. A blind man would know of their presence from the stench there. Whatever the condition of the Gaels was at that time, our own condition was not at all good while these fellows were our constant company.

We kept a good vigil for the inspector's arrival. We were obliged to wait quite a while for him but, as the Old-Fellow said, whatever is coming will come. The inspector approached us on a rainy day when there was bad light everywhere and a heavy twilight in the end of our house where the pigs were. Whoever said that the inspector was old and feeble, told the truth. He was English and had little health, the poor fellow! He was thin, stooped and sour-faced. He cared not a whit for the Gaels – no wonder! – and never had any desire to go into the cabins where they lived. When he came to us, he stopped at the threshold and peered short-sightedly into the house. He was startled when he noticed the smell we had but did not depart because he had much experience of the habitations of the true Gaels. The Old-Grey-Fellow stood respectfully and politely near the door in front of the gentleman, I beside him and my mother was in the back of the house caring and petting the piglets. Occasionally, a piglet jumped into the centre of the floor and without delay returned to the twilight. One might have thought that he was a strong male youngster, crawling through the house because of the breeches which he wore. A murmur of talk arose all this time from my mother and the piglets; it was difficult to understand because of the noise of wind and rain outside. The gentleman looked sharply about him, deriving but little pleasure from the stench. At last he spoke:

– How many?

– Twalf, sor![4] said the Old-Grey-Fellow courteously.

– Twalf?

The other man threw another quick glance at the back of the house while he considered and attempted to find some explanation for the speech he heard.

– All spik Inglish?

– All spik, sor, said the Old-Fellow.

Then the gentleman noticed me standing behind the Old-Grey-Fellow and he spoke gruffly to me:

– Phwat is yer nam? said he.

– Jams O'Donnell, sor!

It was apparent that neither I nor my like appealed to this elegant stranger but this answer delighted him because he could now declare that he questioned the young folk and was answered in sweet English; the last of his labours was completed and he might now escape freely from the stench. He departed amid the rain-showers without word or blessing for us. The Old-Grey-Fellow was well satisfied with what we had accomplished and I had a fine meal of potatoes as a reward from him. The pigs were driven out and we were all quiet and happy for the day. Some days afterwards the Old-Grey-Fellow received a yellow letter and there was a big currency note within it. That is another story and I shall narrate it at another time in this volume.

When the inspector had gone and the pigs' odour cleared from the house, it appeared to us that the end of that work was done and the termination of that course reached by us. But, alas! things are not what they seem and if a stone be cast, there is no fore-knowledge of where it may land. On the following day, when we counted the pigs while divesting them of their breeches, it appeared that we were missing one. Great was the lamentation of the Old-Grey-Fellow when he noticed that both pig and suit of clothes had been snatched privily from him in the quiet of the night. It is true that he often stole a neighbour's pig and he often stated that he never slaughtered one of his own but sold them all, although we always had half-sides of bacon in our house.

Night and day there was constant thieving in progress in the parish — paupers impoverishing each other — but no one stole a pig except the Old-Fellow. Of course, it was not joy which flooded his heart when he found another person playing his own tune.

— Upon me soul, said he to me, I'm afraid they're not all just and honest around here. I wouldn't mind about the young little pig but there was a fine bit of stuff in that breeches.

— Everyone to his own opinion, my good man, said I, but I don't think that anyone took that pig or the breeches either.

— Do you think, said he, that fear would keep them from doing the stealing?

— No, I replied, but the stench would.

— I don't know, son, said he, but that you're truly in the right. I don't know but that the pig is off rambling?

— It's an unfragrant rambling if 'tis true for you, my good man, said I.

That night the Old-Fellow stole a pig from Martin O'Bannassa and killed it quietly in the end of the house. It happened that the conversation had reminded him that our bacon was in short supply. No further discussion concerning the lost pig took place then.

A new month called March was born; remained with us for a month and then departed. At the end of that time we heard a loud snorting one night in the height of the rain. The Old-Fellow thought that yet another pig was being snatched from him by force and went out. When he returned, his companion consisted of none other than our missing pig, drenched and wet, the fine breeches about him in saturated rags. The creature seemed by his appearance to have trudged quite an area of the earth that night. My mother arose willingly when the Old-Fellow stated that it was necessary to prepare a large pot of potatoes for the one who had after all returned. The awakening of the household did not agree too well with Charlie and, having lain awake, looking furious during the talking and confusion, he suddenly arose and charged out into the rain. The poor creature never favoured socializing much. God bless him!

The return in darkness of the pig was amazing but still more amazing was the news which he imparted to us when he had partaken of the potatoes, having been stripped of the breeches by the Old–Grey–Fellow. The Old–Fellow found a pipe with a good jot of tobacco in one pocket. In another he found a shilling and a small bottle of spirits.

– Upon me soul, said he, if 'tis hardship that's always in store for the Gaels, it's not that way with this creature. Look, said he, directing his attention to the pig, where did you get these articles, sir?

The pig threw a sharp glance out of his two little eyes at the Old-Fellow but did not reply.

– Leave the breeches on him, said my mother. How do we know but that he'll be coming to us every week and wonderful precious things in his pockets – pearls, necklaces, snuff and maybe a money-note – wherever in Ireland he can get them. Isn't it a marvellous world today altogether?

– How do we know, said the Old-Grey-Fellow in reply to her, that he will ever again return but live where he can get these good things and we'd be for ever without the fine suit of clothes that he has?

– True for you, indeed, alas! said my mother.

The pig was now stark naked and was put with the others.

A full month went by before we received an explanation of the complicated matter of that night. The Old-Fellow heard a whisper in Galway, half a word in Gweedore and a phrase in Dunquin. He synthesized them all and one afternoon, when the day was done and the nocturnal downpour was mightily upon us, he told the following interesting story.

There was a gentleman from Dublin travelling through the country who was extremely interested in Gaelic. The gentleman understood that in Corkadoragha there were people alive who were unrivalled in any other region and also that their likes would never be there again. He had an instrument called a gramophone[5] and this instrument was capable of memorizing all it heard if anyone narrated stories or old lore to it; it could also spew out all it had heard whenever one desired it. It was a wonderful instrument and frightened many people in the area and struck others dumb; it is doubtful whether its like will ever be there again. Since folks thought that it was unlucky, the gentleman had a difficult task collecting the folklore tales from them.

For that reason, he did not attempt to collect the folklore of our ancients and our ancestors except under cover of darkness when both he and the instrument were hidden in the end of a cabin and both of them listening intently. It was evident that he was a wealthy person because he spent much money on spirits every night to remove the shyness and disablement from the old people's tongues. He had that reputation throughout the countryside and whenever it became known that he was visiting in Jimmy's or Jimmy Tim Pat's[6] house, every old fellow who lived within a radius of five miles hastened there to seek tongue-loosening from this fiery liquid medicine; it must be mentioned that many of the youths accompanied them.

On the night of which we speak, the gentleman was in the house of Maximilian O'Penisa quietly resting in the darkness and with the hearing-machine by him. There were at least a hundred old fellows gathered in around him, sitting, dumb and invisible, in the shadow of the walls and passing around the gentleman's bottles of spirits from one to the other. Sometimes a little spell of weak whispering was audible but generally no sound except the roar of the water falling outside from the gloomy skies, just as if those on high were emptying buckets of that vile wetness on the world. If the spirits loosened the men's tongues, it did not result in talk but rather in rolling and tasting on their lips the bright drops of spirits. Time went by in that manner and it was rather late in the night. As a result of both the heavy silence inside and the hum of the rain outside, the gentleman was becoming a little disheartened. He had not collected one of the gems of our ancients that night and had lost spirits to the value of five pounds without result.

Suddenly he noticed a commotion at the doorway. Then, by the weak light of the fire, he saw the door being pushed in (it was never equipped with a bolt) and in came a poor old man, drenched and wet, drunk to the full of his skin and creeping instead of walking upright because of the drunkenness. The creature was lost without delay in the darkness of the house but wherever he lay on the floor, the gentleman's heart leaped when he heard a great flow of talk issuing from that place. It really was rapid, complicated, stern speech – one might have thought that the old fellow was swearing drunkenly – but the gentleman did not tarry to understand it. He leaped up and set the machine near the one who was spewing out Gaelic. It appeared that the gentleman thought the Gaelic extremely difficult and he was overjoyed that the machine was absorbing it; he understood that good Gaelic is difficult but that the best Gaelic of all is well-nigh unintelligible. After about an hour the stream of talk ceased. The gentleman was pleased with the night's business. As a token of his gratitude he put a white pipe, a jot of tobacco and a little bottle of spirits in the old fellow's pocket who was now in an inebriated slumber where he had fallen. Then the gentleman departed homewards in the rain with the machine, leaving them his blessing quietly but no one responded to it because drunkenness had come in a flood-tide now through the skull of everyone of them who was present.

It was said later in the area that the gentleman was highly praised for the lore which he had stored away in the hearing-machine that night. He journeyed to Berlin, a city of Germany in Europe, and narrated all that the machine had heard in the presence of the most learned ones of the Continent. These learned ones said that they never heard any fragment of Gaelic which was so good, so poetic and so obscure as it and that they were sure there was no fear for Gaelic while the like was audible in Ireland. They bestowed fondly a fine academic degree on the gentleman and, something more interesting still, they appointed a small committee of their own members to make a detailed study of the language of the machine to determine whether any sense might be made of it.

I do not know whether it was Gaelic or English or a strange irregular dialect which was in the old speech which the gentleman collected from among us here in Corkadoragha but it is certain that whatever word was uttered that night, came from our rambling pig.

CHAPTER 4

The comings and goings of the Gaeligores ♣ the Gaelic college ♣ a Gaelic feis in our countryside ♣ the gentlemen from Dublin ♣ sorrow follows the jollity

ONE AFTERNOON I was reclining on the rushes in the end of the house considering the ill-luck and evil that had befallen the Gaels (and would always abide with them) when the Old-Grey-Fellow came in the door. He appeared terrified, a severe fit of trembling throughout his body and limbs, his tongue between his teeth dry and languid and bereft of vigour. I forget whether he sat or fell but he alighted on the floor near me with a terrible thump which set the house dancing. Then he began to wipe away the large beads of sweat which were on his face.

– Welcome, my good man! said I gently, and also may health and longevity be yours! I've just been thinking of the pitiable situation of the Gaels at present and also that they're not all in the same state; I perceive that yourself are in a worse situation than any Gael since the commencement of the reign of Gaelicism. It appears that you're bereft of vigour?

– I am, said he.

– You're worried?

– I am.

– And is it the way, said I, that new hardships and new calamities are in store for the Gaels and a new overthrow is destined for the little green country which is the native land of both of us?

The Old-Grey-Fellow heaved a sigh and a sad withdrawn appearance spread over his face, leading me to understand that he was meditating on eternity itself. He did not reply to me but his lips were dry and his voice weak and feeble.

– Little son, said he, I don't think that the coming night's rain will drench anyone because the end of the world will arrive before that very night. The signs are there in plenty through the firmament. Today I saw the first ray of sunshine ever to come to Corkadoragha, an unworldly shining a hundred times more venomous than the fire and it glaring down from the skies upon me and coming with a needle's sharpness at my eyes. I also saw a breeze going across the grass of a field and returning when it reached the other side. I heard a crow screeching in the field with a pig's voice, a blackbird bellowing and a bull whistling. I must say that these frightening things don't predict good news. Bad and all as they were, I heard another thing that put a hell of fright in my heart . . .

– All that you say is wonderful, loving fellow, said I honestly, and a little account of that other sign would be nice.

The Old-Fellow was silent for a while and when he withdrew from that taciturnity, he did not produce speech but a hoarse whispering into my ear.

– I was coming home today from Ventry, said he, and I noticed a strange, elegant, well-dressed gentleman coming towards me along the road. Since I'm a well-mannered Gael, into the ditch with me so as to leave all the road to the gentleman and not have me there before him, putrifying the public road. But alas! there's no explaining the world's wonders! When he came as far as me and I standing there humbly in the dung and filth of the bottom of the ditch, what would you say but didn't he stop and, looking fondly at me, *didn't he speak to me!*

Amazed and terrified, I exhaled all the air in my lungs. I was then dumb with terror for a little while.

– But . . . said the Old-Fellow, laying a trembling hand upon my person, dumb also but making the utmost endeavour to regain his power of speech, but . . . wait! *He spoke to me in Gaelic!*

When I had heard all this, I became suspicious. I thought that the Old-Fellow was romancing or raving in a drunken delirium . . . There are things beyond the bounds of credibility.

– If 'tis true for you, said I, we'll never live another night and without a doubt, the end of the world is here today.

It is, however, mysterious and bewildering how the human being comes free from every peril. That night arrived both safely and punctually and in spite of all, we were safe. Another thing: as the days went by, it was evident that the Old-Fellow spoke the truth about the gentleman who addressed him in Gaelic. Oftentimes now there were gentlemen to be seen about the roads, some young and others aged, addressing the poor Gaels in awkward unintelligible Gaelic and delaying them on their way to the field. The gentlemen had fluent English from birth but they never practised this noble tongue in the presence of the Gaels lest, it seemed, the Gaels might pick up an odd word of it as a protection against the difficulties of life. That is how the group, called the Gaeligores nowadays, came to Corkadoragha for the first time. They rambled about the countryside with little black notebooks for a long time before the people noticed that they were not *peelers* but gentle-folk endeavouring to learn the Gaelic of our ancestors and ancients. As each year went by, these folk became more numerous. Before long the place was dotted with them. With the passage of time, the advent of spring was no longer judged by the flight of the first swallow but by the first Gaeligore seen on the roads. They brought happiness and money and high revelry with them when they came; pleasant and funny were these creatures, God bless them! and I think that their likes will not be there again!

When they had been coming to us for about ten years or thereabouts, we noticed that their number among us was diminishing and that those who remained faithful to us were lodging in Galway and in Rannafast while making day-trips to Corkadoragha. Of course, they carried away much of our good Gaelic when they departed from us each night but they left few pennies as recompense to the paupers who waited for them and had kept the Gaelic tongue alive for such as them a thousand years. People found this difficult to understand; it had always been said that accuracy of Gaelic (as well as holiness of spirit) grew in proportion to one's lack of worldly goods and since we had the choicest poverty and calamity, we did not understand why the scholars were interested in any half-awkward, perverse Gaelic which was audible in other parts. The Old-Grey-Fellow discussed this matter with a noble Gaeligore whom he met.

– Why and wherefore, said he, are the learners leaving us? Is it the way that they've left so much money with us in the last ten years that they have relieved the hunger of the countryside and that for this reason, our Gaelic has declined?

– I don't think that Father Peter[1] has the word *decline* in any of his works, said the Gaeligore courteously.

The Old-Grey-Fellow did not reply to this sentence but he probably made a little speech quietly for his own ear.

– 'He struck out by the doorway' – do you use that sentence? said the Gaeligore.

– Forget it, boy! said the Old-Fellow and left him with the question still unsolved in his skull.

In spite of it all, he succeeded in solving that difficulty. It was explained to him – no one knows by whom, but it was someone with little Gaelic who was there – it was explained what was upside-down and amiss and back-to-front with Corkadoragha as a centre of learning. It appeared that:

1. The tempest of the countryside was too tempestuous.
2. The putridity of the countryside was too putrid.
3. The poverty of the countryside was too poor.
4. The Gaelicism of the countryside was too Gaelic.
5. The tradition of the countryside was too traditional.

When the Old-Fellow realized that matters were thus, he pondered the matter in his mind for a week. He saw that the learners were in danger of death from the constant vomiting and spite of the sky; that they could not take shelter in the people's dwellings because of the stench and smell of the pigs. By the end of the week, it seemed to him that everything would be satisfactory if we had a college as there was in the Rosses and Connemara. He pondered this intensely for another week and at the end of that time all was clear and definite in his own mind; we should have a big Gaelic feis in Corkadoragha to collect the money for the college. That very night he visited some respectable people in Letterkenny to arrange the managements and details of the feis; before morning he was about the same business in the Great Blasket and, meanwhile, he had sent important letters to Dublin, using the post-mistress as an amanuensis. Of course, there was no one in Ireland as eager in the Gaelic cause as the Old-Grey-Fellow was that night; that the college was built finally on the Old-Fellow's land was no wonder; land which was extremely high-priced when it was bought from him! The feis itself was held in his own field and he received two days' rent for the little plot where the platform stood. If pennies are falling, he often said, see to it that they fall into your own pocket; you won't sin by covetousness if you have all the money in your own possession.

Yes! we shall never forget the feis of Corkadoragha and the revelry that was ours during it. The night beforehand a large gang of men worked diligently in the midst of the rain erecting a platform at the gable-end of our house while the Old-Fellow stood on the door-step, dry from the rain, directing the work by instruction and good counsel. None of these fellows ever had good health again after the downpour and storm of that night, while one of those who did not survive was buried before that platform was dismantled on which he had laid down his life for the cause of the Gaelic language. May he be safe today on the platform of heaven for ever. Amen.

At this time, I was about fifteen years of age, an unhealthy, dejected, broken-toothed youth, growing with a rapidity which left me weak and without good health. I think I never remember before or since so many strangers and gentlemen coming together in one place in Ireland. Crowds came from Dublin and Galway city, all with respectable, well-made clothes on them; an occasional fellow without any breeches on him but wearing a lady's underskirt instead. It was stated that such as he wore Gaelic costume and, if this was correct, what a peculiar change came in your appearance as a result of a few Gaelic words in your head! There were men present wearing a simple unornamented dress – these, I thought, had little Gaelic; others had such nobility, style and elegance in their feminine attire that it was evident that their Gaelic was fluent. I felt quite ashamed that there was not even one true Gael among us in Corkadoragha. They had yet another distinction which we did not have since we lost true Gaelicism – they all lacked names and surnames but received honorary titles, self-granted, which took their style from the sky and the air, the farm and the storm field and fowl. There was a bulky, fat, slow-moving man whose face was grey and flabby and appeared suspended between deaths from two mortal diseases; he took unto himself the title of *The Gaelic Daisy*. Another poor fellow whose size and energy were that of the mouse, called himself *The Sturdy Bull*. As well as these, the following gentlemen were also present as I remember:

> Connacht Cat
> The Little Brown Hen
> The Bold Horse
> The Gaudy Crow
> The Running Knight
> Roseen of the Hill
> Goll Mac Morna

Popeye the Sailor
The Humble Bishop
The Sweet Blackbird
Mary's Spinning-wheel
The Sod of Turf
Baboro
My Friend Drumroosk[2]
The Oar
The Other Beetle
The Skylark
The Robin Redbreast
The Bout of Dancing
The Bandy Ulsterman
The Slim Fox
The Sea-cat
The Branchy Tree
The West Wind
The Temperate Munsterman
William the Sailor
The White Egg
Eight Men
Tim the Blacksmith
The Purple Cock
The Little Stack of Barley
The Dative Case
Silver
The Speckled Fellow
The Headache
The Lively Boy
The Gluttonous Rabbit
The High Hat
John of the Glen
Yours respectfully
The Little Sweet Kiss

The morning of the feis was cold and stormy without halt or
respite from the nocturnal downpour. We had all arisen at
cockcrow and had partaken of potatoes before daybreak. During
the night the Gaelic paupers had been assembling in Corkadoragha from every quarter of the Gaeltacht and, upon my soul,

ragged and hungry was the group we saw before us when we arose. They had potatoes and turnips in their pockets and consumed them greedily in the feis-field; as beverage afterwards they had the rainwater. It was high morning before the gentle-folk arrived because the bad roads had delayed their motor-cars. When the first motor came in view, many paupers were terrified by it; they ran from it with sharp screams and hid among the rocks but issued forth again boldly when they saw there was no harm whatever in those new-fangled machines. The Old-Grey-Fellow welcomed the noble Gaels from Dublin and offered them a drink of buttermilk as a mark of respect and as a nourishing potion after their journey. They withdrew then to arrange the details of the function and to elect feis-officers. When they had done, the assembly was informed that the Gaelic Daisy had been elected President of the Feis, the Eager Cat as Vice-President, the Dative Case as Auditor, the West Wind as Secretary and the Old-Grey-Fellow as Treasurer. After another bout of discussion and conversation, the President and the other great bucks climbed up on the platform in the presence of the populace and then the Grand Feis of Corkadoragha commenced. The President placed a yellow watch on the table before him, stuck his thumbs into the armpits of his waistcoat and delivered this truly Gaelic oration:

– Gaels! he said, it delights my Gaelic heart to be here today speaking Gaelic with you at this Gaelic feis in the centre of the Gaeltacht. May I state that I am a Gael. I'm Gaelic from the crown of my head to the soles of my feet – Gaelic front and back, above and below. Likewise, you are all truly Gaelic. We are all Gaelic Gaels of Gaelic lineage. He who is Gaelic, will be Gaelic evermore. I myself have spoken not a word except Gaelic since the day I was born – just like you – and every sentence I've ever uttered has been on the subject of Gaelic. If we're truly Gaelic, we must constantly discuss the question of the Gaelic revival and the question of Gaelicism. There is no use in having Gaelic, if we converse in it on non-Gaelic topics. He who speaks Gaelic but fails to discuss the language question is not truly Gaelic in his heart; such conduct is of no benefit to Gaelicism because he only jeers at Gaelic and reviles the Gaels. There is nothing in this life so nice and so Gaelic as truly true Gaelic Gaels who speak in true Gaelic Gaelic about the truly Gaelic language. I hereby declare this feis to be Gaelically open! Up the Gaels! Long live the Gaelic tongue!

When this noble Gael sat down on his Gaelic backside, a great tumult and hand-clapping arose throughout the assembly. Many of the native Gaels were becoming feeble from standing because their legs were debilitated from lack of nourishment, but they made no complaint. Then the Eager Cat stepped forward, a tall, broad, self-confident man whose face was dark blue from the frequent shaving of his abundant facial hair. He delivered himself of another finer oration:

– Gaels! said he, I bid you heartily welcome here to this feis today and I wish good health, long life, success and prosperity to each and every one of you until the crack of doom and while Gaels are alive in Ireland. Gaelic is our native language and we must, therefore, be in earnest about Gaelic. I don't think the Government is in earnest about Gaelic. I don't think they're Gaelic at heart. They jeer at Gaelic and revile the Gaels. We must all be strongly in favour of Gaelic. Likewise, I don't think the university is in earnest about Gaelic. The commercial and industrial classes are not in favour of Gaelic. I often wonder whether *anyone* is in earnest about Gaelic. No liberty without unity! Long live our Gaelic tongue!

– No liberty without royalty![3] said the Old-Grey-Fellow in my ear. He always had great respect for the King of England.

– It appears, said I, that this Gaelic gentleman is fully in earnest about Gaelic?

– Apparently he's too well nourished in the upper part of his head, said the Old-Grey-Fellow.

Not only one fine oration followed this one but eight. Many Gaels collapsed from hunger and from the strain of listening while one fellow died most Gaelically in the midst of the assembly. Yes! we had a great day of oratory in Corkadoragha that day!

When the last word had been said from the platform about Gaelic, the revelry and tumult of the feis began. The President presented a silver medal as prize for him who was most in earnest about Gaelic. Five competitors, who sat together on a wall, were entered for that competition. Early in the day they commenced speaking Gaelic with all their might and without interruption in the stream of talking, while they discoursed only about Gaelic.

I never heard such rapid, sturdy, strong Gaelic as this flood-tide
which poured down upon us from the wall. For three hours or
thereabouts, the speech was sweet and the words recognisable,
one from the other. By afternoon the sweetness and the sense
had almost completely departed from it and all that was audible
were nonsensical chatterings and rough inarticulate grunts. At
fall of darkness one man collapsed on the ground, another fell
asleep (but not silent!) and a third fellow was borne home,
stricken by brain-fever which carried him off to the other life
before morning. That left two of them bleating feebly by the wall
with the nocturnal rains pouring down on them destructively.
Midnight had come before the competition really ended. One
of the men halted suddenly the sound that was ramblingly issuing
from him and the other one was presented with the silver medal
by the President and also with a fine oration. As to the other one
who lost in the contest, he has never spoken since that night and
he will never certainly speak again. All the Gaelic which he had
in his head, said the Old-Grey-Fellow, he has spoken it tonight!
As to the rogue who won the medal, he set his house on fire
while he himself was within exactly one year after the feis-day
and neither he nor his house have been seen after that conflagration. Wherever their habitation be today, in Ireland or on high,
safe may be the five men who competed for the medal that day!

Eight more died on that same day from excess of dancing and
scarcity of food. The Dublin gentlemen said that no Gaelic dance
was as Gaelic as the Long Dance, that it was Gaelic according to
its length and truly Gaelic whenever it was truly long. Whatever
the length of time needed for the longest Long Dance, it is
certain that it was trivial in comparison with the task we had
in Corkadoragha on that day. The dance continued until the
dancers drove their lives out through the soles of their feet and
eight died during the course of the feis. Due to both the fatigue
caused by the revels and the truly Gaelic famine that was ours
always, they could not be succoured when they fell on the rocky
dancing floor and, upon my soul, short was their tarrying on
this particular area because they wended their way to eternity
without more ado.

Even though death snatched many fine people from us, the
events of the feis went on sturdily and steadily, we were ashamed
to be considered not strongly in favour of Gaelic while the

President's eye was upon us. As far east and west as the eye might rove, there were men and women, young and old, dancing, hopping and twisting distressingly in a manner which recalled to one a windy afternoon at sea.

A peculiar little incident took place at the coming of twilight when the people had spent the whole day dancing and no one had a scrap of skin under his feet. The President graciously permitted a five-minute break and all dropped down gratefully on the damp ground. After the break, the Eight-Hand Reel was announced and I noticed the gentleman entitled Eight Men swallowing fiercely from a bottle which he had in his pocket. When the Eight-Hand Reel was announced, he threw away the bottle and went on alone to the dancing place. Others followed him to step it out in his company but he threatened them angrily, shouted that the house was full and made a violent foray with his boot on anyone who came near him. Before long, he was really frenzied and was not quietened until a terrible blow was struck on the back of his head by a large stone. I never yet saw anyone so bold, uppish and unmanageable as he was before he was struck or so peaceable and quiet after the casting of the stone by the Old-Grey-Fellow. Doubtless, a few words often lead a man astray.

As to myself, I never ceased until I reached the magic bottle, thrown aside by Eight Men. There was a fine nip still in it and by the time I had this in my stomach, a remarkable change had come over the world. The air was sweet, the appearance of the countryside had improved and there was pleasure of heart in the very rain. I sat down on the fence and sang a Gaelic song at the top of my voice, accompanying the tune with the jingle of the empty bottle on the stones. When I had finished the song and looked over my shoulder, I saw none other than Eight Men stretched out in the muck with blood dripping profusely from the hole made by the stone. If he was really alive, then it was evident that life was not very vigorous within him and I was of the opinion that he was in danger of imminent dissolution. 'If he is departing from us,' said I to myself, 'he won't be able to take to the place beyond any other bottle he has to drink.' I leaped over the fence, bent down and ran my fingers inquisitively over the gentleman. Before long I discovered another little bottle of the ardent water and may I say that I neither made stay or delay until I was in a secluded place while my throat was being scorched by that oil of the sun. Of course, I did not have any training in toping at that time, not even knowledge of what I was about. If the bare truth be told, I did not prosper very well. My senses went astray, evidently. Misadventure fell on my misfortune, a further misadventure fell on that misadventure and before long the misadventures were falling thickly on the first misfortune and on myself. Then a shower of misfortunes fell on the misadventures, heavy misadventures fell on the misfortunes after that and finally one great brown misadventure came upon everything, quenching the light and stopping the course of life.[4] I did not feel anything for a long while; I did not see anything, neither did I hear a sound. Unknown to me, the earth was revolving on its course through the firmament. It was a week before I felt that a stir of life was still within me and a fortnight before I was completely certain that I was alive. A half-year went by before I had recovered fully from the ill-health which that night's business had bestowed on me, God give us all grace! I did not notice the second day of the feis.

Yes! I think that I shall never forget the Gaelic feis which we had in Corkadoragha. During the course of the feis many died whose likes will not be there again and, had the feis continued a week longer, no one would be alive now in Corkadoragha in all truth. Apart from the malady which I contracted from the bottle and the amazing weird things which I saw, there is one other matter that fixes the day of the feis firmly in my memory: from that day forward the Old-Grey-Fellow was in possession of a yellow watch!

CHAPTER 5

Hunting in the Rosses ♣ the beauty and wonders of that
countryside ♣ Ferdinand O'Roonassa the shanachee ♣
my nocturnal walk ♣ I'm hunted by the evil thing ♣
I'm safe from peril

ONCE UPON a time when the potatoes were becoming scarce in
our house and we were worried by the shadow of famine, the
Old-Grey-Fellow announced that it was timely for us to go
hunting if we desired to keep our souls within our bodies instead
of permitting them to fly out into the firmament like the little
melodious birds.

– 'Tis no good for the people to be living in the shadow of
one another if all that's left of them is shadows.[1] I never did hear
that anyone's shadow was effective as a shelter against the hunger.

I certainly derived but little pleasure of heart from this conversation. At this time I was almost twenty years old and one of
the laziest and most indolent persons living in Ireland. I had no
experience of work and neither had I found any desire for it ever
since the day I was born. I had never been out in the field. I was of
the opinion that hunting entailed particular hardship: perpetual
moving in the heart of the hills, perpetual watchfulness while
stretched out in the damp grass, perpetual hiding, perpetual
fatigue; I would have been satisfied without any hunting while
I lived.

– Where in Ireland, do you think, sir, said I, is the best hunting
to be found?

– Oh little teeny weeny son, said he, it's in the Rosses in
Donegal that the best hunting is to be found and every other
thing in that place is excellent also.

The melancholy almost lifted from me when I heard that we
were going towards the Rosses. I never was in that part of the
country but I had heard so much from the Old-Fellow concerning it that I had desired for a long time to go there; if I had had
the choice, I am not certain whether I should have preferred to
journey to heaven or to the Rosses. You might have thought
from the Old-Fellow's conversation that your bargain would be
better if you went to the Rosses. It is hardly necessary to state
that the same gentleman had been reared in the Rosses.

According to what I had heard, he was the best man in the Rosses during his youth. There was no one in the countryside comparable to him where jumping, ransacking, fishing, love-making, drinking, thieving, fighting, ham-stringing, cattle-running, swearing, gambling, night-walking, hunting, dancing, boasting and stick-fighting were concerned.

He alone killed Martyn in Gweedore in 1889 when the afore-said person attempted to take Father MacFadden a prisoner to Derry; he alone assassinated Lord Leitrim near Cratlough in 1875; he alone first inscribed his name in Gaelic on any cart and was prosecuted on that historic occasion; he alone founded the Land League, the Fenians and the Gaelic League. Yes! he had had a busy broad life and it had been of great benefit to Ireland. Were it not that he was born when he was and led the life he had, conversational subjects would be scarce among us today in this country.

— Will we be looking for rabbits? said I most politely.

— We won't! said he, or if you wish: We wull na!

— Crabs or lobsters?

— Naw!

— Wild pigs?

— They're not pigs and they're not wild! said he.

— If that's the way, sir, said I, come along and I won't put any more questions on you for the present because you're not too talkative.

We left my mother snoozing in the rushes behind us and we moved off in the direction of the Rosses.

On the road we met a man from the Rosses named Jams O'Donnell and we saluted him kindly. He stopped in front of us, recited the Lay of Victories, walked three steps of mercy with us, took a tongs from his pocket and threw it after us. In addition to that, he had the appearance of one who had a five-noggin bottle in his pocket as well and had a pledge of hand and word with a maiden in Glendown. He lived in a corner of the glen on your right-hand side as you go eastward along the road. It was evident that he was Ultonian according to the formula in the good books. He was an old-timer and rebellious.

— Are you very well? said the Old-Fellow.

— I'm only middling, said Jams, and I've no Gaelic, only Ulster Gaelic.[2]

– Were you ever at the feis at Corkadoragha, sir? said the
Old-Grey-Fellow.

– I was na! said he, but I was carousing in Scotland.

– I thought, said I, that I saw you with the crowd of fellows
that were gathered at the gate of the feis-field.

– I was na with thon crowd that were at the gate, Captain!
said he.

– Did you ever read *Séadna*?[3] said the Old-Fellow sincerely.

We continued conversing lightly and courteously together
for a long while, discussing the affairs of the day and talking of
the hard times. I gathered quite an amount of information
about the Rosses from the other two during the conversation
and also about the bad circumstances of the people there; all
were barefoot and without means. Some were always in difficulty, others carousing in Scotland. In each cabin there was:
(i) one man at least, called the 'Gambler', a rakish individual,
who spent much of his life carousing in Scotland, playing cards
and billiards, smoking tobacco and drinking spirits in taverns;
(ii) a worn, old man who spent the time in the chimney-corner
bed and who arose at the time of night-visiting to shove his
two hooves into the ashes, clear his throat, redden his pipe and
tell stories about the bad times; (iii) a comely lassie called Nuala
or Babby or Mabel or Rosie for whom men came at the dead
of every night with a five-noggin bottle and one of them seeking to espouse her. One knows not why but that is how it was.
He who thinks that I speak untruly, let him read the good
books, or the *guid buiks*.

At last we reached the Rosses and when we did, we had walked
quite a portion of the earth's crust. Of course, it is a happy
countryside even if it is hungry. For the first time since birth,
I saw a countryside which was not drenched by the flowing of the
rain. In every direction, the variegated colours of the firmament
pleased the eye. A soft sweet breeze followed at our heels and
helped us while we walked. High up in the skies there was a
yellow lamp known as the sun, shedding heat and light down
upon us. Far away there were tall blue stacks of mountains standing east and west and watching us. A nimble stream accompanied
the main road; it was hidden in the bottom of the ditch but we
knew of its presence because of the soft murmuring it bestowed
on our ears. At both sides was a brown-black bog, speckled with

rocks. I had no fault to find with the Rosses nor with any one of them. One Ross was as delightful as the other.

With regard to hunting, the Old-Grey-Fellow had commenced this before I noticed that the appearance of the countryside suggested that it was huntable or that the Old-Fellow was on the trail. He leaped suddenly over the fence. I followed him. Before us in a little field stood a strong stone-built house. In the twinkling of an eye the Old-Fellow had opened a window and had disappeared out of sight into the building. I stood for a moment pondering the wonders of life and then, as I was about to follow him through the window, he came out as precipitately.

– There was always good hunting in that house, said he to me. He opened his hand and what might one imagine was there but five shillings in silver, a fine elegant lady's necklace and a small golden ring. He placed these objects in some inside pocket with satisfaction and hurried me away with him onwards.

– 'Tis the schoolmaster, O'Beenassa, that owns that house, said he, and it's seldom I went off empty from it.

– If that's the way, sir, said I honestly, isn't it the unusual world that's there today and isn't the kind of hunting we're doing now very irregular?

– If that's the way, said the shrewd creature, 'tis time!

Having reached another slate-roofed house, the Old-Fellow entered it and returned after a time with a full fist of red money that he found in a cup on the dresser; in another house he stole a silver spoon; in yet another house he took such a quantity of food that it replaced our lost energy after the perambulations and difficulties of the day.

– Is it the way, said I finally, that there's no one alive in this countryside or is it that they're all cleared out from us to America? Whatever way things are in this part of the world, all the houses are empty and everyone away from home.

– 'Tis clear, wee little son, said the Old-Fellow, that you haven't read the good books. 'Tis now the evening and according to literary fate, there's a storm down on the sea-shore, the fishermen are in difficulties on the water, the people are gathered on the strand, the women are crying and one poor mother is screaming: Who'll save my Mickey? That's the way the Gaels always had it with the coming of night in the Rosses.

– It's unbelievable, said I, the world that's there today.

And sure enough, having hunted and thieved from house to house, we came at last to a high hill from which we had a view of the edge of the ocean westwards where the big white-foamed waves were coming ashore. On the summit of the hill the weather was mild but it was evident from the angry appearance of the sea that the people below were in a storm of wind, and that the situation of the fisherman who was at sea could be unpleasant. I could not see the women on the strand weeping because of the distance between us but, doubtless, they were there.

We sat on a rock, I and the Old-Grey-Fellow, until we had rested. The pockets and clothes of the Old-Fellow were crammed as a result of his thieving, not to mention the valuable articles he had beneath his armpit and in his hand. He certainly had had an excellent bag that day and our visit was hardly of benefit to the people of the Rosses. The Old-Fellow requested me to carry some of the loot for him.

– We'll go now, said he, to the cabin of my friend, Ferdinand O'Roonassa, in Killeagh where I'll put down the night and you can move off home after having spuds and new milk for yourself. I'll get a little cart from Ferdinand and I'll be home tomorrow with all I've taken today, thanks to the hunting.

– Very well, sir, said I.

We went. Ferdinand lived in a little house in the corner of the glen as you journey westwards along the road. We received a great Gaelic welcome there. Ferdinand was an old worn man and only his daughter, Mabel, lived with him (a small, well-made, comely girl) and an old woman (it is unknown whether she was his wife or his mother) who was dying for twenty years in the bed in the chimney-corner and who was still on this side of the Great Contest. She had a son named Mickey (his nickname was the *Gambler*) but he was carousing yonder in Scotland.

The Old-Fellow's goods were concealed – it was evident that everyone had experience in this line of business – and then we all sat down to potatoes. When dietary business had been terminated, the Old-Grey-Fellow remarked to Ferdinand that I was a young person, lacking much knowledge of the world and that I never heard a real shanachee recounting real folklore in the old Gaelic manner.

– Therefore, Ferdinand, said he, you should tell us a story, please.

– Sure, I'd tell ye a story gladly, said Ferdinand, only that it isn't proper for a shanachee to talk in a house at night-visiting without settling himself down comfortably by the fire and putting his two hooves into the ashes; but I'm far off from the fire where I'm sitting and the pains won't let me get up and push my chair to the hob. 'Twas that misfortunate pair, the Sea-cat and the Peerkus, that gave me the same pains, death-tying to the two of them!

– Don't mind it, said the Old-Grey-Fellow, I'll pull up your chair and yourself as well.

No sooner was that said than it was done. The shanachee, O'Roonassa, was placed at the warm side of the fire and we all congregated about, heating ourselves, although the evening was not at all cold. I looked curiously at the shanachee. He settled his body luxuriantly in the chair, fixed his backside carefully beneath him, shoved his two hooves into the ashes, reddened his pipe and, when he was at his ease, he cleared his windpipe and began to spew discourse upon us.

– I did na know and I a little child in the ashes, said he, and our Pats or Mickileen or curly Nora of Big Nelly of young Peter did na know either, why he was called the Captain. However, the signs were on him that he spent a good bit of his life on the sea. It looked as if he liked his own company the best because he lived in a little lime-white house in the corner of the glen on the right-hand side as you go the road eastwards and begor, 'twas seldom the people of the place laid an eye on him. There was a far-off lonesome look about him and 'tis often I heard it said that there was some big shameful mark on his life. 'Twas said that he spent a good bit of his life carousing in Scotland, that he drank more than water and buttermilk when he was young and that 'twasn't the good thing he always did and he boozed, because he was a cross prickly fellow who never tried to tame the flood-tides of anger that come over everyone sometimes. Apart from that, he was a pleasant polite fellow to anyone who took to him, or that's what I heard. Many's the story and the tale of a story they had about him. They said he was a priest in Scotland, that he went a few steps out of the way and was put out of the Church. Other people said that he killed a man in a pub when he was young and came to the Rosses when on the run. Everyone had his own story.

Well, the Night of the Big Wind came. A heavy sea arose and, as usual, the fishermen were in difficulties in the mouth of the harbour, trying to come ashore. The wives and the women were standing, watching in torment the poor men on the shelf of rock, their boat broken in the water, and terrible breakers without number threatening them every minute with drowning, running in from the western dark of night and throwing great hanks of seaweed on the black brow of the rocks. Every great murderous wave drenched the watchers on the strand; they were wet to the marrow from the foam of the sea. A mother's shout arose above the scream of the wind: Oh! oh! who will save my Paddy?

Neither I nor Pats nor Mickileen nor young Peter's big Nelly's curly Nora expected the answer she got to this. There was a movement behind the people and forward came the Captain with a jump. He threw off his coat and was in the sea before sense could be talked to him. Ochone! said the people, another good man lost!

Well, there were struggle and effort and bad work and life and death that night in the sea; but to make a hard story easy, the Captain succeeded in reaching the rock, tying the two that were out there to the rope he had around him and, God save us all! the three of them were pulled safely ashore. It seems that the Captain damaged himself that night because he was found dead the next day.

'Twas in the wake-house I heard the full story.

When he was young and carousing in Scotland, the Captain killed a brother of one of the men on the rock and the sister of the other. He spent twenty years in jail yonder before he returned to settle down alone in the little house in the corner of the glen. Whatever sin was on his soul was cleaned off that night when he did the bold deed on the rock and made up fully for everything before he died. 'Tis amazing how fate drives us in this life from the bad act to the good one and back again. Doubtless, it was the Sea-cat that drove the Captain to the killing of the first two and another power put it in his power to bring the other two safe from the sentence of death. There are many things that we don't understand and will never understand.

The shanachee had come to the end and the Old-Fellow and myself thanked him liberally for this fine story which he had related.

Darkness was falling over the world by this time and I considered it time for me to set my foot on the long road ahead of me to Corkadoragha. As I was about to bid farewell, a polite and truly Gaelic knock came to the door and two men, whom I did not know, entered. Little was said before I understood that one of them had pledge of word and hand with curly-headed Mabel who was now slumbering in the end of the house and that they had a five-noggin bottle to complete the bargain and wish it success. I fondly bade farewell to Ferdinand and the Old-Grey-Fellow and went out under the nocturnal skies.

It was now dark in the Rosses but, I thought, the appearance of the world was somehow changed. I was outside for a while before I understood what was unusual around me. The ground was dry and no downpour came upon me. It was evident that the Rosses and Corkadoragha were dissimilar because no night came in the latter without showers of rain out of the skies pouring upon us. The night here was eerie and unnatural but, doubtless it had its own charm.

The Old-Fellow had already described the route to Corkadoragha to me and I set off vigorously. The stars lighted me, the ground beneath my feet was level and the cold condiment of the nocturnal wind sharpened my appetite for potatoes. We would have a high life for three months as a result of the thieving performed by my friend that day. I struck up a little whistling tune as I walked. I had a five-mile walk along by the sea, then inland towards the east, led by the whims of the by-roads. The crooning of the ocean remained in my ears for an hour with the salt smell of the seaweed swarming into my nose; nevertheless, I was travelling through maritime fields out of sight of the ocean. As I was about to part company with the sea, the path led me to a cliff-top and I stood for a while to look. There was a large sandy strand below; white where the quiet wavelets were coming calmly ashore; rough and troubled near me at the foot of the cliff; filled with broken rocks which were hirsute with the herbs of the sea and bright with little water-pools which shone in the twilight and were awaiting patiently the full of the tide. Everything was so calm and peaceful that I sat down to enjoy the occasion where I was and to allow the fatigue to escape from my bones.

I should not say that I did not snooze a little but suddenly there was a great explosion in the midst of the stillness and I was again fully awake and on my guard, of course. Whatever demon or person was about, I thought that it was two hundred yards or thereabouts on my left-hand side and within the rugged area in the shade of the cliff and concealed where no eye could see it. I never heard such a peculiar, unrecognizable sound. On one hand, it was firm like one stone falling upon the other; on the other, it resembled a fat cow falling into a water-filled bog-hole. I remained motionless, listening, with my heart full of terror. There was now no sound there except what came softly from the water on the beach below. There was, however, another thing which I felt. The air was now putrid with an ancient smell of putridity which set the skin of my nose humming and dancing. Fear and melancholy and disgust came over me. The noise and that smell were connected! A strong desire came upon me to be at home safe and in the end of the house resting among the pigs. Loneliness came on me; I was alone in that place and the unknown evil thing had encountered me.

I do not know whether I was inquisitive or bold at that moment but a strong desire possessed me to investigate what was ahead and to ascertain whether there was any earthly explanation for the sound and smell which I had perceived. I arose and went west, east and then north, making no halt until I was standing below on the sand of the beach. The soft damp sand was beneath my feet. I walked carefully towards the location of the sound. The evil smell was now really strong and worsening with each footstep I took on my way. In spite of it, I advanced, praying that my courage should not fail me. A cloud had covered the stars and, for a while, the appearance of the land by the sea was not easily visible. Suddenly my eye comprehended one shadow which was blacker than the others which were at the foot of the cliff and the evil smell now assailed me in such a manner as to upset my stomach. I halted there to collect my wits and to grasp my courage. Before I had the opportunity, nevertheless, to do either of these two things, the black object moved from where it was. Despite the great terror which captured me at that moment, my eyes observed every detail clearly before them. A large quadruped had arisen and was now standing in the midst of the rocks, spewing showers of putrid stench around it. At first I thought that an exceedingly bulky seal stood before me but later the four feet denied this. Then, the dull sheen in the sky increased slightly and I saw that a great strong hairy object was in my company that night, grey-haired and with prickly red eyes, staring at me angrily. The darkness had now become rotten with its breath, causing my health to forsake me at full speed. Suddenly there came from the evil thing a trembling and a snorting and I noticed that it was determined to attack me and, perhaps, to eat me. No word of Gaelic which I have ever heard can describe the terror which took hold of me. A fit of trembling oppressed my limbs from the crown of my head to the soles of my feet; my heart missed every other beat and the perspiration poured thickly from me. I thought at that stage that my career on the green soil of Ireland would be short. I never had such an unhealthy position as I had that night by the great ocean. The bitter lean fear, the small smooth cowardly fear, came suddenly upon me. Within me arose a storm of blood, a well of sweat and excessive fuss of mind. Another bark issued from the grey object yonder. At the same time a ghostly movement came in my feet, an unearthly movement which carried my body swiftly and with the lightness of wind over the rough land where I was. The evil thing was pursuing me. Coughing and a rotten stench were behind me, chasing and moving me over the Paradise of Ireland.

By the time I had once more regained perception and my comprehension of life, I had travelled a long distance. No longer did I have the great sea of seaweed and sand under my eyes and the evil spirit was no longer at my heels. I was safe from that nameless demon. I was neither injured nor eaten but, weary though I was, I did not desist from vehement flight until I was safe at home in Corkadoragha.

The following day the Old-Grey-Fellow returned to us with his hunting-bag. We welcomed him tenderly and we all sat down to potatoes. When everybody within the house, both porcine and human, was replenished with potatoes, I took the Old-Fellow aside and whispered in his ear. I stated that my health was not too good after the events of the preceding night.

– Is it boozing you were at, oh young little son, he said, or was it night-hunting?

– In truth, no sir! I replied, but a great thing on legs was chasing me. I don't know any word of Gaelic for it but it was not to my good, without a doubt. I don't know how I managed to escape from it but I'm here today and it's a great victory for

me. 'Twould be a shameful thing if I was lost from this life and
I in the flower of my youth because my likes will not be there
again.

— Were you in Donegal at that time, my soul? said he.

— I was.

A ruminative cloud gathered over the face of the Old-Grey-
Fellow.

— Could you put down on paper, said he, the shape and
appearance of this savage thing for me?

The memory of the previous night was so firmly fixed in my
mind that I made little delay in drawing an image of the creature
when I had procured paper. It was thus:

The Old-Fellow looked closely at the picture* and a shadow
crept over his visage.

— If that's how it is, son, said he fearfully, it's good news that
you're alive today and in your health among us. What you met
last night was the Sea-cat! The Sea-cat!!

The blood drained from my face when I heard that evil name
being mentioned by the Old-Fellow.

— It seems, said he, that he was after coming out of the sea to
carry out some mischievous work in the Rosses because he had
often been in that area in the past, attacking the paupers and
scattering death and ill-luck liberally among them. His name is
always in the people's mouths there.

---

* The good reader will kindly notice the close resemblance between the
Sea-cat, as delineated by O'Coonassa, and the pleasant little land which is
our own. Many things in life are unintelligible to us but it is not without
importance that the Sea-cat and Ireland bear the same shape and that both
have all the same bad destiny, hard times and ill-luck attending on them
which have come upon us.

— The Sea-cat...? said I. My feet were not too staunch beneath me while I stood there.

— The same cat.

— Is it the way, said I weakly, that no one else saw the Sea-cat before this?

— 'Tis my idea that they did, said he slowly, but no account of it was got from them. They did not live!

There was a little cessation of conversation between us.

— I'll go to the rushes, said I, and let you take to the pipe!

CHAPTER 6

I become a man ♣ marriage-fever ♣ I and the Old-Grey-Fellow
in the Rosses ♣ I marry ♣ death and misfortune

WHEN I HAD become a man (but was neither healthy nor virile)
I thought one day that it was otherwise with me than it was with
those in Corkadoragha who were my contemporaries and had
grown up in my company. They were married and had numerous
children. Doubtless, some of these were going to school at this
time and being christened Jams O'Donnell by the master. I had
no wife and it seemed to me that no one had a whit of respect
for me as a result. At that stage I did not know the basic facts of
life or anything else. I thought that babies fell out of the skies
and that those who desired them needed only to have good luck
and a fine spacious field. Nevertheless, I had a small suspicion
that things were not thus. There were folks – old crippled persons
– with large farms of land who were childless, while other people
who lacked land enough to support a hen but who had a house
filled with little folks. I considered it a reasonable thing to lay
this question before the Old-Grey-Fellow.

– Why and wherefore, sir, said I to him one day, am I not
married?

– Whoever is patient, said he, is satisfied.

We said no more at that time but I pondered the matter for a
month at my ease while stretched in the rushes at the end of the
house. I noticed that men married women and women married
men always. Although I often heard Martin O'Bannassa describe
me as a poor creature when he was in my mother's company, I was
of the opinion that many a woman would accept me willingly.

One day, when I was on the road, I met a lady from Upper
Corkadoragha. She saluted me quietly and I addressed to her
some few words.

– Lady, said I, I'm grown to man's age and you see I've got
no family. Is there any chance, oh sprightly honest lady, that
you'd marry me?

I received neither blessing nor kind reply but away she went
along the road with all her might, swearing aloud. By the time

that the nocturnal waters were descending, a tall robust black-haired man came to my mother inquiring about me. He held a blackthorn stick in his grasp and had a frown of great anger on him. My mother sensed that his plans did not include good deeds and sweet words where I was concerned and she said that I was absent from home and she expected me to return. It happened that I was at this moment in the position normal for me, i.e. resting in the rushes at the end of the house. The black-haired man departed from us but he uttered many foul words and unblessed epithets when he did so. His visit put terror into my heart because I realized that his visit had some connection with the lady whom I had met on the road.

After pondering the matter for another year, I approached the Old-Fellow once more.

– Honest fellow! said I, I'm two years waiting now without a wife and I don't think I'll ever do any good without one. I'm afraid the neighbours are mocking me. Do you think is there any help for the fix I'm in or will I be all alone until the day of my death and everlasting burial?

– Boy! said the Old-Fellow, 'twould be necessary for you to know some girl.

– If that's the way, I replied, where do you think the best girls are to be got?

– In the Rosses, without a doubt!

The Sea-cat entered my mind and I became a little worried. However, there is little use denying the truth and I trusted the Old-Fellow.

– If 'tis that way, said I in a bold voice, I'll go to the Rosses tomorrow to get a woman.

The Old-Fellow was dissatisfied with this kind of thing and endeavoured for a while to coax me from the marriage-fever that had come upon me but, of course, I had no desire to break the resolution which was fixed for a year in my mind. He yielded finally and informed my mother of the news.

– Wisha! said she, the poor creature!

– If he manages to get a woman out of the Rosses, said the Old-Grey-Fellow, how do we know but that she'll have a dowry? Wouldn't the likes of that be a great help to us at present in this house when the spuds are nearly finished and the last drop reached in the end of the bottle with us?

– I wouldn't say that you haven't the truth of it! said my mother.

They decided at last to yield completely to me. The Old-Fellow said that he was acquainted with a man in Gweedore who had a nice curly-headed daughter who was, as yet, unmarried although the young men from the two sandbanks were all about her, frenzied with eagerness to marry. Her father was named Jams O'Donnell and Mabel was the maiden's name. I said that I would be satisfied to accept her. The following day the Old-Fellow put a five-noggin bottle in his pocket and both of us set out in the direction of Gweedore. In the middle of the afternoon we reached that townland after a good walk while the daylight was still in the heavens. Suddenly the Old-Fellow halted and sat down by the roadside.

– Are we yet near the habitation and enduring home of the gentleman, Jams O'Donnell? asked I softly and quietly, querying the Old-Fellow.

– We are! said he. There is his house over yonder.

– Fair enough, said I. Come on till we settle the deal and get our evening spuds. There's a sharp hunger on my hunger.

– Little son! said the Old-Fellow sorrowfully, I'm afraid that you don't understand the world. 'Tis said in the good books that describe the affairs of the Gaelic paupers that it's in the middle of the night that two men come visiting if they have a five-noggin bottle and are looking for a woman. Therefore we must sit here until the middle of the night comes.

– But 'twill be wet tonight. The skies above are full.

– Never mind! There's no use for us trying to escape from fate, oh bosom friend!

We did not succeed in escaping that night either from fate or the rain. We were drenched into the skin and to the bones. When we reached Jams O'Donnell's floor finally, we were completely saturated, water running from us freely, wetting both Jams and his house as well as every thing and living creature present. We quenched the fire and it had to be rekindled nine times.

Mabel was in bed (or had gone to her bed) but there is no necessity for me to describe the stupid conversation carried on by the Old-Fellow and Jams when they were discussing the question of the match. All the talk is available in the books which I have mentioned previously. When we left Jams at the bright dawn of day, the girl was betrothed to me and the Old-Fellow was drunk. We reached Corkadoragha at the midhour of day and were well satisfied with the night's business.

I need hardly remark that there were revelry and high frolics in this townland when my wedding-day came. The neighbours arrived to congratulate me. The Old-Fellow had, by this time, drunk the dowry-money which he had procured and there was not a good drop in the house to offer to the neighbours. When they realized that matters were thus, gloom and ill-humour took hold of them. Threatening whispers were heard from the men occasionally and the women set themselves to devouring all our potatoes and drinking all our butter-milk so as to inflict a three-months' scarcity upon us. A species of terror came upon the Old-Fellow when he saw how matters stood with the company. He whispered privily in my ear.

– Fellow! said he, if this gang doesn't get spirits and tobacco from us, I'm afraid one of our pigs will be stolen from us this night.

– All the pigs and my wife will be stolen as well, sir, I replied.

Mabel was in the end of the house at this juncture with my mother on top of her. The poor girl was trying to escape back to her father's house and my mother endeavouring to make her see reason and informing her that it is compulsory to submit to Gaelic fate. There was great weeping and tumult that night in our house.

It was Martin O'Bannassa himself who rescued us. When everything was truly in a bad state, he walked in carrying a small barrel of true water under his armpit. He quietly presented me with the barrel and congratulated me courteously on my marriage. When the company inside realized that the door of hospitality was finally opened, they wished to be merry and good-humoured and commenced to drink, dance and make music with all their might. After some time, they made a racket which shook the walls of the house, dismaying and terrorizing the pigs. The woman in the end of the house was given a full cup of that fiery water – despite the fact that she had no stomach for it – and before long she ceased her struggling and fell into a drunken slumber in the rushes. According as the men drank their fill, they lost the inherited good manners and good habits they had. By the time midnight had come, blood was being spilled liberally and there were a few men in the company without a stitch of clothing about them. At three in the morning, two men died after a bout of fighting which arose in the end of the house – poor Gaelic paupers without guile who had no experience of the lightning-water in Martin's barrel. As for the Old-Fellow, he almost faced eternity together with the other two. He was not in the fight and no blow was struck on him but during the dancing he sat in a place near the barrel. I considered that it was a good thing that my wife lost her senses and was not aware of the conduct of that wedding-feast. There was no sweet sound there and any hand which was raised did not accomplish a good deed.

Yes! when I had been married a month or so, contention and angry speech arose between my wife and my mother. The situation worsened daily and at last the Old-Fellow advised us to clear out of the house altogether and to settle down in another place because, said he, it has always been thus with every newly-wed couple. It was neither right nor proper, said he, that two women should live under the same roof. It was clear to me that the trouble between them was annoying him and disturbing his night's sleep. We adapted for our habitation the old hut which had been formerly built for the animals. When that was accomplished, and we had installed the beds of rushes, I and my wife left the other house together with two pigs and a few small household effects to begin life in the new domicile. Mabel was skilled in potato-boiling and we lived together peacefully for a year, both of us companionable in the end of the house. Often the Old-Grey-Fellow came in to converse with us in the afternoon.

Yes! life is extraordinary. One time when I returned from Galway in the black of night, what do you think I noticed but that we had acquired a new piglet in the end of the house. My wife was sleeping while the tiny little bright-skinned thing was squealing in the centre of the house. I took it carefully and allowed it to drop from my hand with amazement when I realized precisely what I had. It had a small bald head, a face as large as a duck-egg and legs like my own. I had a baby-child. Need I say that the sudden raising of my heart was both joyous and indescribable? We had a young male child! I felt importance and superiority filling my heart and substance coming in my body!

I left the kitten gently down alongside his mother and rushed out to the Old-Fellow, holding the bottle of spirits which I had kept hidden for a year. We drank a glass and yet another glass together in the darkness and then we drank the health of the young son. After some time, when some of the neighbours heard the shouting and the inebriated commotion that we caused, they knew that true water was available for nothing and they arose from their rushy beds and congregated in to keep us company. We had a great night until morning. We decided to name the young man Leonardo O'Coonassa.

Alas! happiness is not lasting and neither is joy for any Gaelic pauper because he does not escape for long the scourging of fate. One day, while playing on the sward in front of the door with Leonardo when he was a year and a day old, I noticed some indisposition come suddenly upon him and that he was not far from eternity. His little face was grey and a destructive cough attacked his throat. I grew terrified when I could not calm the creature. I left him down on the grass and ran in to find my wife. What do you think but that I found her stretched out, cold in death on the rushes, her mouth wide open while the pigs snorted around her. When I reached Leonardo again in the place I had left him, he was also lifeless. He had returned whence he had come.

Here then, reader, is some evidence for you of the life of the Gaelic paupers in Corkadoragha and an account of the fate which awaits them from their first day. After great merriment comes sorrow and good weather never remains for ever.

CHAPTER 7

Sitric the beggar ♣ famine and ill-luck ♣ seeking seals at the Rock ♣ a night of storm ♣ one man who did not return ♣ lodgings among the seals

THERE WAS a man in this townland at one time and he was named Sitric O'Sanassa. He had the best hunting, a generous heart and every other good quality which earn praise and respect at all times. But alas! there was another report abroad concerning him which was neither good nor fortunate. He possessed the very best poverty, hunger and distress also. He was generous and open-handed and he never possessed the smallest object which he did not share with the neighbours; nevertheless, I can never remember him during my time possessing the least thing, even the quantity of little potatoes needful to keep body and soul joined together. In Corkadoragha, where every human being was sunk in poverty, we always regarded him as a recipient of alms and compassion. The gentlemen from Dublin who came in motors to inspect the paupers praised him for his Gaelic poverty and stated that they never saw anyone who appeared so truly Gaelic. One of the gentlemen broke a little bottle of water which Sitric had, because, said he, it spoiled the effect. There was no one in Ireland comparable to O'Sanassa in the excellence of his poverty; the amount of famine which was delineated in his person. He had neither pig nor cup nor any household goods. In the depths of winter I often saw him on the hillside fighting and competing with a stray dog, both contending for a narrow hard bone and the same snorting and angry barking issuing from them both. He had no cabin either, nor any acquaintance with shelter or kitchen heat. He had excavated a hole with his two hands in the middle of the countryside and over its mouth he had placed old sacks and branches of trees as well as any useful object that might provide shelter against the water which came down on the countryside every night. Strangers passing by thought that he was a badger in the earth when they perceived the heavy breathing which came from the recesses of the hole as well as the wild appearance of the habitation in general.

One day when I, the Old-Grey-Fellow and Martin O'Bannassa were sitting together on the brow of a hillock discussing the hard life and debating the poor lot which was now (and would always be) Ireland's, our conversation turned to our own folks at home and the potato scarcity and especially to Sitric O'Sanassa.

— I don't think, sirs, said Martin, that Sitric has got a spud for two days.

— Upon me soul, said the Old-Fellow, but you're truly right, and there's no health to be got from the rough grass that covers this hill.

— I saw the poor fellow yesterday, said I, and he outside drinking the rainwater.

— 'Tis a tasty drop if 'tisn't nourishing, said the Old-Fellow. If the Gaels could get food out of the sky's rain, I don't think there would be a thin belly in all this area.

— If 'tis my opinion the nice company wants, said Martin, I'd say that the same poor harmless man is not far off from eternity. Whoever is without a spud for long is unhealthy.

— Oh people of the sweet words, said I earnestly, unless my eyes are astray, Sitric is now coming out of his cave.

Down on the level land Sitric was standing and gazing about him, a tall spear of a man who was so thin with hunger that one's eye might fail to notice him if he were standing laterally towards one. He appeared both gay and foolish, lacking any proper control over his feet because of the inebriation caused to him by the morning air. Having stood for a while, he collapsed in a weakness on the bog.

— There's not much standing, said the Old-Grey-Fellow, in anyone who's long without a spud.

— 'Tis the truth you've told there, friend, said Martin, and that truth is true.

— For fear, oh respectable great ones, said I, that he is going from us at the present moment and taking a step in the way of all truth, I judge that it would be a good thing for us to speak with him at least, if only to prosper him on his course.

They agreed with me and down we went until we were in the same place as the infirm one. He stirred when he perceived the footsteps about him and saluted us in a low voice but courteously and kindly. Frankly, he was in a low state at this time. His breath was escaping feebly from him and, as to the red blood within him, there was no evidence of its presence to be seen on any part of his skin.

– Is it long since you ate a bite of food, Sitric, oh friend of friends? inquired Martin genially.

– I didn't taste a spud for a week, replied Sitric to him, and it's a month since I tasted a bit of fish. All that's laid before me at mealtime is hunger itself and I don't even get salt with that. I ate a scrap of turf last night and I wouldn't say that this black feeding agreed too well with my belly, God save us all! I was empty last night but now, anyway, my belly is full of pains. Isn't it slowly, friends, that death comes to him who desires it?

– Woe to him who eats the bog! said the Old-Fellow. There is no health in the turf but, of course, how do we know but that we'll have the bogs and hills yet for food, God save the hearers!

Sitric moved out of the position he was in and rolled over on his back on the ground with his bloodshot eyes staring at us.

– Worthy people, said he, would ye carry me to the seaside and throw me into the sea? There's not the weight of a rabbit in me and 'twould be a small deed for well-fed sound men to throw me over a cliff.

– There's no fear for you, my soul! said Martin sadly, because there'll be a spud of mine for you while we've pigs at home and a pot boiling for them. You there, said he to me, over with you and get a big spud from the pigs' pot in my own wee cabin.

I set off with a will and did not halt until I had procured the biggest potato in the pot and had brought it back to the place of famine. The man on the ground devoured the potato greedily and when he had swallowed the meal, I noticed that he had recovered remarkably from his ill-health. He sat up.

– That was the tasty eating and I'm full up of thanks, said he, but you see I'm not so pleased to be begging from ye or to be leaving the pigs short. I'll be for ever without a house and the sooner I'm thrown into the sea, the sooner ye'll all be easy. I want to be under the water and never come up again . . .

– I never heard, said the Old-Fellow, that anyone was ever at ease who went off to sea without a boat under him!

– . . . Bad as the salt-sea is, replied Sitric, 'twould be easy on the fellow who lives in this dirty hole and the downpour on top of his head every night and with nothing in front of him but constant muck, the wet and raw famine . . .

– Don't forget, said I, that you're a Gael and that it isn't happiness that's in store for you!

– . . . and the distress and the hardship and ill-luck . . . said Sitric.

– 'Tisn't natural to have the showers down on top of us always, said the Old-Fellow, without a spot of sunlight between them an odd time.

– . . . and the rotten badgers and the Sea-cat and the brown sea-mice that come on top of my head every night . . . said Sitric.

– How do we know, said Martin, but that the sun will reach Corkadoragha yet?

– . . . and for ever to the devil's end is misery, trouble and exhaustion; weather, frost, snow, thunder and lightning; the spite of the earth down every night out of the skies . . .

– O'Sanassa will have another day![1] said I, like a false prophet.

– . . . and the fleas! said Sitric.

It was apparent that he was ill-humoured, badly situated, in bad shape and in a bad way. I had never heard him swearing nor complaining previously. This type of thing was not correct nor Gaelic and we made an attempt to quieten him and cheer him up, lest he might go into the ocean unknown to us later. Martin O'Bannassa uttered the timely word.

– I was in Dingle yesterday, said he, and I was talking to a man from the Great Blasket. He said that seals were plentiful on Irish Mickelaun and that the islanders were intending to kill a few head of them. The oil is valuable and the meat tastes nice.

– There's danger in that work, friend! said I.

I did not relish very much any proposition to confront and, perhaps, handle these fellows. It occurred to me that one might quite easily garner death or injury while tackling this business.

– I thought, said Martin, that 'twould be a good thing for us to bring off a couple of them from the Rock to Corkadoragha. If we had oil, the darkness wouldn't be so heavy.

– I'd rather, said I, to be alive in the darkness than dead in much light.

I noticed the Old-Fellow frown, a sign that within his skull great labour was in progress. Finally he spoke:

– Look here, Sitric, said he, if you had a whole seal for yourself and he salted in your house, there would be no danger of famine for you in three months and you wouldn't be looking for begged spuds. I'd say we should *all* go into the sea, kill the seals in the holes and bring them home with us.

– There's sense in that saying, sweet fellow, said Sitric, but I couldn't fight the smallest seal that was ever on a sea-rock because I can't stand on my feet at the present.

– Don't mind that, son, said Martin, I'll send you a boy tonight with two more spuds and tomorrow we'll all set out on the waves when you'll have strength and vigour in you.

The matter was left thus. Despite the fact that the Old-Fellow said that we were *all* going on the waves, I lcft the bed very early on the following morning and, when I had consumed a moiety of potato, I faced for the hill. I had never been at sea and had no appetite for that kind of business and it appeared that, as long as I knew what would benefit me, I would never go to slay seals in that region under the sea which is their natural habitat. I considered that the best health on that day was obtainable on the hillsides. I had a couple of cold potatoes as sustenance and spent the whole day quietly sitting on my backside underneath the rain, pretending to be hunting. When it was light, I noticed the Old-Grey-Fellow, Martin O'Bannassa and Sitric O'Sanassa meeting and departing seawards with pikes, ropes, knives and other useful objects on their shoulders.

During the day, showers of rain came upon me and I was soaked and exhausted, of course, when I reached the house at nightfall. I went eagerly to the potatoes and when I had swallowed them, inquired about those who were abroad. My mother listened to the gale which assailed the house and when she relaxed, I noticed that she was worried.

– I don't think, said she, that this group will return safely tonight because they were never before at sea. Woe to whoever drew the journey on them!

– The rowing and swimming that's to be found on the hill, said I, is far nicer!

I brought in the pigs and we all went to the rush-beds. At this time the rain was pelting roughly on the house; great voices of thunder were shouting in the heights of the heavens; flashes of lightning which one might not see east or west were cleaving the darkness; dashes of the very brine were bursting over the window-glass although ten miles of road separated the house from the edge of the sea-shore. On a night such as this, of course, the ones who were out would not be worried about seals but rather endeavouring to learn the sailor's skill in one single effort with the object of reaching land safely. I also remembered that I would be the head of the house if it happened that the Old-Fellow failed to return from his sea-journey.

After all, things are not what they appear to be, in Corka-doragha at any rate. By the time that daylight had arrived and tranquillity had returned to the weather, the Old-Fellow and Martin O'Bannassa came in the door, both extremely exhausted and wet to the marrow; yet they called loudly for potatoes. Great welcomes were given to them and the table was prepared for food.

– Where's the third man that was with ye on the journey? said I. Is Mister O'Sanassa here in the company of the blessed yonder?

– He's alive and in excellent health, said Martin, but he is still under the sea.

– Wisha, said I, that's good but I pledge you, word and hand, sir, that I don't understand your talk.

When they had become belly-swollen with abundance of potatoes, the two sailors explained the night's business to me and it was an amazing business without a word of a lie. It appears that the three borrowed a canoe in Dunquin and they went away to the Rock. By the time they had arrived at the seals' home, they noticed a large hole in the flank of a rock and tested it with an oar. The hole led under sea-level and there was a strong surge of water around it. None of the three in the canoe had any great desire to dive into this mysterious region and they remained as they were for a long while, their verbal exceeding their venatic labours. Finally the older pair blew such a gale of advice and speech into the ears of O'Sanassa that he agreed to bind a rope around his waist and jump down in one bound into the depths of the hole. He went and was given plenty of rope. The sea was becoming choppy by this time and the sky looked bad. O'Sanassa had promised to return to the surface when he had the opportunity to report on the lower regions to the pair who were dry. There was no account of him, nevertheless, and in the course of time, the tune of the wind did not show any improvement. They decided to draw in the rope and to pull the fellow below safely

out of the water by force. They heaved mightily on the rope but
did not succeed; it remained fast against the opening of the hole.
While they were consulting together after ceasing to pull, what
should you imagine but that they felt a stir in the rope; the one
below informing them that he was not in eternity! By this time
the wind and the rain were locked together, the canoe was at
one stage high in the sky and at another at the bottom of the
great sea and ocean. The Old-Fellow resolved to head eastwards
towards land and leave the one below where he was, considering
how long he had spoken about the lower regions! Martin, however, opposed this plan. It seemed to him that he would never
see ground or land again because of the volume of sea-water and
wind that were around him, above him and beneath him. He
decided it might be shrewd to move down to where O'Sanassa
was still alive. He donned the appearance of courage, bade adieu
to the Old-Fellow and leaped into the sea. The Old-Fellow was
alone for a long time, awaiting news from the pair below, probably, and both loneliness and fear came upon him. The tempest
became more boisterous, neither the sky nor the sea nor the
sandy wind distinguishable one from the other. It is not known
whether the Old-Fellow headed down into the seals' hole or was
blown out of the boat but, at all events, he moved down to the
lower reaches of the sea. His head was injured and, unfortunately,
his bones also on the spikes of rock when he entered the sea;
there was a strong pull in the hole and he was swallowed without
delay. When he had regained command of his senses again, he
was stretched on a ledge of rock which stood clear and dry of the
water, with daylight shining down upon him from a crevice high
up and away from where he was. It happened that there was a
bend in the cave; initially it went under the water and then
curved upwards through the crag. Apparently there was a large
spacious room there, a fine shore here and a trough of water
yonder where all was serene after the tempest outside. When the
Old-Fellow's eyes had been accustomed to the dim light of this
place, he noticed O'Sanassa and O'Bannassa together, sitting by
a dead seal, chewing the tasteless meat. He went towards them
and greeted them.

– Where did ye get the black fellow? said he to Martin.

– There's a houseful of them in the bottom of the hole, both
large and small, said Martin. Be seated at the table, mister!

That is how they were accommodated for the night. They rigged a lamp for oil which was squeezed out of the seal's liver and spent the time conversing about the hard life and the minimal nourishment which Gaels would ever have. By the time that morning had come, the Old-Fellow stated that it was unnatural for him to lack a potato for so long a period and that he had decided, therefore, to face up into the water and set out for home. Martin praised this speech but would you believe that Sitric stretched out a hand to them, bidding them farewell and a prosperous voyage.

– Upon me soul! said the Old-Fellow to Martin in amazement, and the devil sweep you!

Mr O'Sanassa then expounded his own view of the situation. Where he was, he had freedom from the inclement weather, the famine and the abuse of the world. Seals would constitute his company as well as his food. Sky-water dripped from the roof of the cave which would serve both as condiment and as wine against thirst. It did not appear that he would desert such a well-built comfortable abode after all he had experienced of the misery of Corkadoragha. That was definite, he declared.

– Everyone to his own counsel! said Martin, but I've no wish to live under the sea any longer.

They left him there and there he has been ever since then. At times since then he has been seen at high tide, wild and hirsute as a seal, vigorously providing fish with the community with whom he lodged. I often have heard the neighbours say that Mr O'Sanassa was a skilful fisherman because he had, by this time, grown into a tasty fish and that a whole winter's oil was within him. I do not think, of course, that anyone has had the courage to chase him. To this day he is buried alive and is satisfied, safe from hunger and rain over on the Rock.

CHAPTER 8

The hard times ♣ the time of the Deluge in Corkadoragha ♣
Maeldoon O'Poenassa ♣ Hunger-stack ♣ I'm far from home
♣ misery and hardship ♣ I'm in the throes of death ♣
journey's end ♣ streams of whiskey ♣ back home

IN ONE WAY or another, life was passing us by and we were suffering misery, sometimes having a potato and at other times having
nothing in our mouths but sweet words of Gaelic. As far as the
weather in itself was concerned, things were becoming worse. It
seemed to us that the rainfall was becoming more offensive with
each succeeding year and an occasional pauper was drowned on
the very mainland from the volume of water and celestial emesis
which poured down upon us; a non-swimmer was none too
secure in bed in these times. Great rivers flowed by the doorway
and, if it be true that the potatoes were all swept from our fields,
it is also a fact that fish were often available by the wayside as a
nocturnal exchange. Those who reached their beds safely on
dry land, by the morning found themselves submerged. At night
people often perceived canoes from the Blaskets going by and
the boatmen considered it a poor night's fishing which did not
yield to them a pig or a piglet from Corkadoragha in their nets.
It has been said that O'Sanassa swam over from the Rock one
night to gaze again at his native countryside; but who knows
whether the visitor was but a common seal. It need hardly be
said that the local people became peevish at that time; hunger
and misfortune assailed them and they were not dry for three
months. Many of them set out for eternity gladly and those who
remained in Corkadoragha lived on little goods and great
littleness there. One day I put the matter to the Old-Fellow and
I entered into conversation with him.

– Do you think, oh gentle person, said I, that we'll ever again
be dry?

– I really don't know, oh mild one, said he, but if this rain
goes on like this, 'tis my idea that the fingers and toes of the
Gaelic paupers will be closed and have webs on them like the
ducks from now on to give them a chance of moving through
the water. This is no life for a human being, son!

– Are you certain that the Gaels are people? said I.

– They've that reputation anyway, little noble, said he, but no confirmation of it has ever been received. We're not horses nor hens; seals nor ghosts; and, in spite of all that, it's unbelievable that we're humans – but all that is only an opinion.

– Do you think, oh sublime ancient, said I, that there will ever be good conditions for the Gaels or will we have nothing for ever but hardship, famine, nocturnal rain and Sea-cattishness?

– We'll have it all, said he, and day-rain with it.

– If we do, I replied, it's my opinion that 'tis well for O'Sanassa over on the Rock. He won't be badly off while fish are in the sea for food and he'll have a sleeping-hole in the Rock on the day of storm.

– You may be sure that the seals have their own troubles, said the Old-Fellow. They're the worried unhappy fellows.

– Is it the way, said I, that the great bursts of rain were just as heavy before this as they are now in these times?

The Old-Grey-Fellow displayed a brown-toothed laugh, a sign that my question had but little sense in it.

– You may as well know, young quiet one, said he, that this rain is only a summer shower to the fellow who knows about the times that were there long ago. In my grandfather's time there were people that never felt dry ground or a healthy place for sleeping from birth till death and who never tasted anything but fish and sky-water. 'Twas fish we used have in the field that time. Whoever couldn't swim well, went off to heaven.

– Is that the way it was?

– But in that time I heard my father praising the good weather and saying it was fine and that there was nothing wrong with it compared with the sky-crucifying that people got and he a young fellow. The people that time thought that the time of the Deluge was after coming again.

– Did anyone live after the great waters of that time? said I.

– Only an occasional person lived. But the weather was so contrary ages before that again, that it is said that everyone in the countryside was drowned except a man named Maeldoon O'Poenassa.[1] The man was intelligent and shrewd enough to put together the first boat in this part of the country and to rig it, a job that benefited him. He went off, alive and safe, on the high tide and took all kinds of things left behind by the people who had said goodbye to this life – fine spuds, torn alive from the ground by the flood, small household effects, little drops of spirits and valuable pieces of gold that were put aside for ages. By the time that he escaped from Corkadoragha, he was rich and thoroughly satisfied with himself without a doubt, I promise you.

– And where did he go in the boat, darling fellow? said I, greatly interested in his talk. My friend pointed his wrinkled finger to the White Bens which were away from us north-eastwards.

– The middle one of these is called Hunger-stack, said he, because O'Poenassa succeeded in reaching the top of that peak. In these times it was like an island of the sea to a boatman and 'tis said that he was the only man who got to the top of the mountain; it was too steep and the way up was troublesome for a fellow depending on his feet.

– Did he ever come down?

– Never truly! The way that's too steep going up is the same coming down and whoever would go footing the path down from the top would be undertaking self-destruction and 'twould be eternity he'd reach instead of the level land. He landed from the boat on the peak and himself and the boat are there since – if the sign of their remains is to be noticed there now.

– It appears, therefore, blessed man, said I with great beneficent thoughts oozing from me at that time, that there are precious non-contemptible articles on the top of Hunger-stack until this day – golden pennies and every other thing which O'Poenassa snatched away with him on the day of the squall?

– They're there, said he, if what we have in Corkadoragha of storytelling-gems and next-door-folklore from our ancestors and ancients is true and believable.

– 'Tis sweet hearing what you've told, old man of the liberality, said I, and my thankfulness is thankful to you.

By the time that I had reached the rushes that night, I did not get a wink nor an ounce of sleep due to the multitude of thoughts which assailed me and lured me on the subject of Hunger-stack. With the keen mind's eye I saw the summit of the mountain, the ribs of the boat and the man's bones clearly and, near them in that lonely place, all the plundered fortune which O'Poenassa took away with him in the time of the Deluge. I thought that this was a great shame – paupers suffering from famine here and means of salvation yonder and no means of acquiring it at hand. I should say that at this point of time I formed the resolution of going to the summit of that mountain one day of my life whether I was dead or alive, big or small, belly-cheered or in the depths of hunger. I was of the opinion that one might be better off seeking death searching for the good life on Hunger-stack than suffering hard times for ever in Corkadoragha. It were better for a man to die on the mountain from celestial water than to live at home famished in the centre of the plain. I considered the matter for myself during the night and, in that half-bright time when the day was breaking in upon the blackness of night, I had decided everything in my mind. I would go to Hunger-stack one day. I would go to seek the money and if I returned home safely after all the difficulty, I would be henceforward exceedingly rich, bellyful, frequently inebriated.

Lest there be nothing on the summit but nourishment for myself, I decided to keep the resolution in my own mind firmly and strongly and neither to share it with the neighbours nor inform the Old-Fellow of it. I began then to observe the course of the bad weather, taking note of the ways of the tempest and the customs of the winds to discover whether there was any part of day or year more suitable than another for travelling to Hunger-stack. For a year, that is how things were and at the end of that time, I noticed that my labours were all in vain. In Corkadoragha the height of the wind and the strength of the rain were always similar, night and day without fail, in summer as in winter. It was a silly business to wait for the day of fine weather and, finally, I decided that it was time for me to set out on my course.

The shoulder of the mountain was so steep and my health so precarious that my little wretched back was capable of carrying only a light and slender load. I collected secretly what few things that were necessary – a bottle of water, a knife, a bag for the gold and a measure of potatoes.

I remember well the morning I started on my journey. The water was bursting out of the sky in such profusion that it terri-fied me and injured the crown of my head. At first I had not resolved to journey to the mountain that day but I considered that the country-folk were about to be drowned and that it appeared I would be safe if I succeeded even in climbing a few

steps up the flank of the hill. Were it not for the heavy precipita-
tion of that morning, it is to be feared that I would never have
had the courage to forsake the little house where I was born and
face the mountain of destiny; my ominous unknown objective.

It was dark. When I pulled my body out of the damp rushes,
I grasped my travelling bundle which I had concealed in a hollow
in the wall and I quietly moved out. The rain and the wild
appearance of the infernal twilight struck fear and terror into my
heart. I discovered the place where I judged the main road to be
and I shuffled along, walking and half-walking, falling and half-
falling, towards the mountain. A stream of water, which reached
my knees, was coming strongly against me and certainly my
movement at that time was not very good but consisted of constant stumbling and half-limping, at one time stretched in the
watery muck, occasionally lifted from the earth by the spite of
the wind and wrapped up in the rainy gale, unable to control my
person. Doubtless, that morning I possessed Gaelic misery.

After all the difficulty, I was clearly advancing a little, because
I felt the ground rising beneath me and causing me more hardship. Salty showers of perspiration bubbled down over my eyes
to add to my other miseries and I thought my feet were bathed
more by blood than water. But I was now set on my course and
had no wish to yield to anything but death alone.

When I was fairly far up on the ridge of the hill, I noticed a
flood of rivers of water bearing down upon me together with
trees, large stones and small farms of land; to this day I am amazed
how I failed to acquire a mortal fracture of the skull from this
diabolical onrush. At times home-sickness came over me but
nevertheless courage did not entirely fail me. With all my might
I pressed onwards although I was often pressed backwards by a
lump of the mountain hitting the crown of my head. I assure you
that I spent that night-till-day working with my two feet and that
labour was strenuous and sudorific.

When the puny semi-illumination which passes for day
among us in Corkadoragha arrived, what an amazing sight was
revealed to me! I found myself almost on the summit of the
mountain, my colour alternating between red and blue because
of the bloodshed and the nocturnal buffetings, while my body
was stripped of the last scrap of cloth. The crown of my head
almost touched the black-bellied fierce clouds and a great

deluge of rain issued from them; a deluge so heavy that my hair was being plucked rapidly from me. In spite of every effort and stout endeavour on my part, I was drinking the very rain and became dangerously belly-swollen, something which did not improve my control of walking. Beneath me I noticed naught but mist and morning vapours. Above, I saw the mountain occasionally, while around me was nothing but rocks, filth and the continual moist gale. I moved on. It was an amazing place and very amazing also was the weather. I think its like will not be there again.

Without a doubt I was a long while on the summit before I noticed the exact lie of the land. On the summit was a little flat plain, pools of water behind and yonder, yellow fretful rivers flowing between them and filling my ears with an unearthly mysterious humming. In places there were villages of leaning white rocks or a mesh of bottomless dark-mouthed holes where rapid waters were falling incessantly. Certainly the area did not have a normal appearance and, although Corkadoragha was bad, I should have praised it gladly at that hour.

I proceeded to visit and examine minutely the place by walking, falling and swimming in an endeavour to discover whether there was any trace of the boat or any account of Maeldoon O'Poenassa. Hunger was tickling my intestines and an indescribable fatigue filling my limbs with unhealthy drowsiness. However, since I knew that I was nigh to eternity and that I had little opportunity to better my lot, I continued sliding forwards and backwards erratically with my eye seeking eagerly for some human habitation while my throat sought to avoid swallowing an excessive quantity of rain. It was thus for a long while.

I do not know whether I allowed a large part of the day to slip by in sleep or in semi-consciousness, but if it were thus, it amazes me now that I ever awoke again. Be that as it may, it was apparent to me that the twilight of the night was coming on the day of morning and that the cold and strength of the tempest were increasing. By this time I had lost all my blood and was on the point of bowing to fate, lying willingly in the mud and setting my face towards heaven when I noticed a little light shining weakly far away from me, half-lost in the mist and the sheets of rain. A little start of joy stirred in my heart. Strength returned to my body and I set off cripple-footed but energetically towards the light, if it were really such. This, I thought, was all that lay between me and the mouth of perpetual eternity.

It really was a light that was issuing from a cave which ran between two rocks. The cave-mouth was narrow and slender but, of course, I was as thin as an oar from the misery, the hardship and the loss of blood of the previous day. I was inside and safe from the gale without delay; before me was the light and I approached it. I had had no experience of creeping in a stone cave but nevertheless my movement was nimble as I went towards the location of that flame within.

When I had reached the spot, I believed that I was not overly satisfied with the situation of the place, the company present or the business in hand. Within there was a cell or small room with space for four or five men; bare and rocky it was with water dripping from the walls. Great flames of fire arose from the stony floor and, in the background, a well of fresh water bubbled up animatedly, forming a stream which flowed towards me in the cave. However what almost took the sight from my eyes was an old person, half-sitting, half-lying by the flames and away from me, a species of chair beneath him and his appearance suggested that he was dead. A few unrecognizable rags were wrapped around him, the skin of his hand and face was like wrinkled brown leather and he had an appearance totally unnatural about him. His two eyes were closed, his black-toothed mouth was open and his head inclined feebly to one side. A fit of trembling seized me, stemming from both cold and fear. I had finally met Maeldoon O'Poenassa!

I recalled suddenly the resolution which led me to this place and, God save the hearers! no sooner did I remember the golden pennies than I held them in my grasp! They were scattered near at hand, here and there about the floor, thousands of them, together with golden rings, gems, pearls and heavy yellow chains. The leather satchel from which they had come was there and it was really fortunate that this was so because I was stark naked at this time and both packless and pocketless. My hands automatically collected the pennies and before long the bag held as much gold as I was capable of carrying. While engaged in this activity, I felt my heart recover and play a little musical tune.

I had no desire whatever to look towards the dead man and

when the gold was collected, I proceeded to creep back through the cave. I had reached the opening with the terrifying voices of wind and rain assaulting my ears, when a luckless thought struck me with a thud.

If Maeldoon O'Poenassa were dead, who had lighted the fire and who tended it?

I do not know whether a fit of frenzy took hold of me at this time or whether I died temporarily from fear but what I did was to return back to the fellow who was within. I found him there exactly as I had left him. I moved timidly towards him, proceeding across the watery floor on feet, belly and hands. Suddenly one of my hands slipped and my head fell, causing my face to strike destructively against the ground. It appears that I tasted the yellow water which flowed from the fountain near the fire and when I did so, I was terribly startled. I took a drop of it in the palm of my hand and swallowed it appreciatively. What do you say it was? *Whiskey!* It was yellow and sharp but it really had the correct taste. In front of me a stream of whiskey was coming from the rock and flowing away, unbought and undrunk. Amazement surged up in my head until it injured me. I went to the well on my knees, to the place where the yellow water was bursting up, and consumed enough to set every bone a-tremble. I looked sharply at the fire while I was near it and it was evident that here was another small fountain of the same spirits but this one, however, was alight and the flames rose and fell accordingly as the stuff was issuing forth.

At any rate, that is how matters stood. If Maeldoon O'Poenassa were dead, it was apparent that he had lived for ages on the nourishment of whiskey from the first well and was protected against cold by the second, quietly spending his life, free from all want, as Sitric O'Sanassa had long ago among the seals.

I looked at him. No stir was made by him, even that of breathing. Fear did not permit me to go to him where he was but I made some rude noises from my position and cast a light stone which hit the bridge of his nose. He did not stir.

– He has nothing to say, said I, half to myself and half aloud.

My heart faltered once more. I heard a sound coming from the corpse which resembled someone speaking from behind a heavy cloak, a sound that was hoarse and drowned and inhuman which took my bodily vigour from me for a little while.

– And what narrative might give thee pleasure?[2]

I remained dumb without the opportunity of answering the question. Then I saw the dead person – if he were dead or only soaked with spirits–weariness – endeavouring to settle himself on his stony seat, to shove his hooves in the direction of the fire and to clear his throat for storytelling. The puny voicelet issued from him once more and I almost died with terror:

– It is unknown wherefore the yellow-haired, small, unenergetic man was named the Captain – he whose place and habitation and steadfast home was a little lime-white house in the corner of the valley. He was wont to spend the year from Hallowe'en until May Day carousing in Scotland and from May Day until Hallowe'en carousing in Ireland. At one time . . .[3]

On hearing these ghostly words, I do not know whether I was seized by a flood–tide of sickness or terror or of disgust, but finally I laid hold on my courage and, when I became aware once more of the great movement of the universe, I was outside beneath the sharp lashes of the rain with the bag of gold on my thin bare back and slipping downhill towards the plain, aided by stream and slope. For a while I felt I was in the limitless skies, at another time submerged, for yet another while broken and bruised against the rocks with sharp and heavy objects falling thickly upon, splitting my head and my body at yet another time. Doubtless, the way downhill was frightful and misfortunate when I was returning from the mountain but early in the journey I received some blow from a pinnacle of rock which deprived me of any command I had over my senses and down I went as a wisp without feeling or reason, carried by wind and water.

When I regained consciousness, it was morning and I was stretched on my back in the soft and most filthy filth which is nowhere else to be found except in Corkadoragha. All my skin was ripped and torn like an old suit of clothes but the bag of gold was still secure in my grasp despite the buffeting suffered by my hands during the journey. I was still a mile from the little house which was home and sleeping quarters for me.

If I was fatigued and exhausted, I was satisfied. I spent half an hour endeavouring to stand on my feet. When I succeeded finally, I buried the gold and set off for home limping. I had the money! I was in possession and had won! I endeavoured to strike up a little tune but no sound issued from me. My throat was punctured and, truly, neither my tongue nor my mouth were in good condition.

When I came to the doorway without a stitch of clothes, the Old-Grey-Fellow was there and tending his pipe, pondering at his ease the hard times. I greeted him quietly. He gazed at me for a while, sharply and silently.

– Upon me soul! said I, I'm ravenous for spuds after crawling in the sea-water for the good of my health.

The Old-Fellow removed the pipe from his beak.

– There's no understanding the world that's there today at all, said he, and especially in Corkadoragha. A pig rambled off on us a little while ago and when he returned, he had a worthwhile suit of clothes on him. You went off from us fully-dressed and you're back again as stark-naked as you were the day you were born!

At this stage I was guiding the potatoes from mouth to stomach and he received no reply from me.

CHAPTER 9

Discontented about my wealth ♣ to town in search of boots ♣
my night-walk ♣ the Sea-cat in Corkadoragha ♣ a peeler in
our house ♣ misery and ill-luck ♣ I meet a relative ♣
conclusion of my story

HE WHO IS threatened throughout his life with misery and is
short of potatoes, does not understand easily what happiness
is nor the management and correct handling of wealth either.
After my journey to Hunger-stack, I lived again for a year in the
old Gaelic manner – wet and hungry by day and by night and
unhealthy, having nothing in the future but rain, famine and
ill-luck. The bag of gold was safely in the ground and I had not
yet taken it to the surface. I spent many nights in the rushes at
the end of the house scourging my mind, trying to decide what
I should do with the money or what fine and uncommon article
I might buy with it. It was a hard, impossible task. I thought first
of buying foodstuffs but since I had tasted nothing except fish
and potatoes, it was unlikely that the variety of foods consumed
by the gentle-folk of Dublin would agree with me even if I had
the opportunity of buying them or even knew their names!
I then bethought me of liquor but I remembered that few people
took to drink in Corkadoragha who were not wafted on death's
way after the first bout. I considered buying a hat as a shelter
against the rain but decided that no hat existed which would
last five minutes undamaged and unrotted by the edge of the
weather. The same held good for clothing. The Old-Grey-
Fellow possessed a golden watch since the day of the feis but
I never understood the utility of that small machine or what
point on earth there was to it. I desired neither cup nor household furniture nor pig-platter. I was sunk in poverty, half-dead
from hunger and hardship; yet I failed to think of any pleasant
useful object that I needed. Certainly, it seemed to me, the rich
ones had worry and fret of mind!

I arose one morning when the rain was splashing out of the
skies. I was feeble for a time about the house, without interest in
anything and not paying any attention to any one thing more
than the other. Suddenly I noticed that the floor of the house
was red – black-red in places and brown-red elsewhere. I was

amazed at this and accosted my mother while she was engaged in pig-feeding activities by the fireside.

— Is it the way, good woman, said I, that the end of the world and the termination of the universe is with us at long last and that there are red showers down on top of us in the dead of the night?

— No and it's not that way, ugly little treasure! said she, but the Old-Grey-Fellow is spouting blood here all the morning.

— I believe that it was out of his nose that this fountain of blood was belching? said I.

— No and it's not that way, little kisser! said she, but deadly unhealable wounds that he has got in his two feet. He had a competition here this morning with Martin O'Bannassa to see who'd lift a big piece of a rock. Poor Martin was beaten, God save the hearers! because he couldn't move the rock. The Old-Fellow was lucky as he always is. He managed to lift the rock as high as his waist and he won whatever stake that they had between them.

— He was always strong! said I.

— But then, because of the amount of the weight, the stone fell from his hands and fell misfortunately on his two feet so that they burst and every bone and bonelet in them was broken, I fear. The ugly fellow was going around the house, shouting for a long time after this work but whatever means of movement he had, it wasn't his feet.

— I never thought, said I, that the Old-Fellow had that much blood.

— If he had, said she, he doesn't have it now!

It happened that this set me meditating on the money that I possessed. If the Old-Fellow had been wearing boots, I thought, less damage might have been done when the stone landed on his hooves. Who knew but that my own feet might be injured and damaged in like manner? What better article might I buy but a pair of boots?

The following day I set out for the place where I had the bag of gold underground. I fell in with Martin O'Bannassa along the road and questioned him about mercantile matters, although I had no experience of them.

— A question for you, Martin, friend, said I. Do you know any words for boots?

– I do indeed, said he. I remember one day being in Derry and eavesdropping in that city. A man went into a shop there and bought boots. I heard clearly the words he spoke to the shop-keeper – *bootsur*. Without a doubt, that is the English for boots – *bootsur*.

– I give you thanks, Martin, said I, and another thanks on top of that one.

I set out. The bag of gold was safe where I had left it. I took out twenty golden pennies and replaced the bag again in the ground. When that task was completed, I went off sturdily for whatever city I might meet as I walked towards the west – Galway or Caherciveen or some other place such as these. There were many houses and shops and people there; business noisily proceeding on every side. I searched the town until I found a boot-shop and I went in cheerfully. A genial portly man was in charge of the shop and when he laid eyes on me, put a hand in his pocket and offered me a red penny.

– Away now, islandman! said he without bitterness in his voice nevertheless.

I received the penny gratefully, put it in my pocket and took out one of my own golden coins.

– And now, said I courteously, *bootsur!*

– *Boots?*

– *Bootsur!*

I do not know whether the fellow was either amazed or did not understand my English, but he stood for a long while gazing at me. He then moved back and fetched many pairs of boots. He gave me my choice. I took the most elegant pair; he took the golden penny and both of us returned our several thanks. I bundled the boots into an old sack which I had and set out on the road home.

Yes! I experienced both fear and shame with regard to the boots. Since the day of the great feis, there were neither boots nor any trace of them to be noticed in Corkadoragha. These elegant bright objects were matters for fun and mockery to the people. I feared that I might become a butt for ridicule in front of the neighbours if I could not educate them previously about the elegance and cultivation connected with boots. I decided to hide the boots and ponder the question at my ease.

After a month I was becoming discontented about these same

boots. I possessed them and yet did not. They were in the ground and I did not profit by them when I bought them. I never had them on my feet and lacked even a minute's experience of wearing them. If I did not acquire some practice with boots secretly and some knowledge of the skill of boot-movement in general, I should never have sufficient boldness to appear in them before the public.

One night (the most nocturnal night I ever knew because of the quantity of rain and the blackness of the black-darkness) I arose from the rushes on the quiet and journeyed out through the countryside noiselessly. I went to the boot-grave and dug them up to the surface with my hands. They were slippery, wet, soft and pliable so that my feet fitted into them without too much difficulty. I tied the laces and went through the countryside, the venomous wind tearing me and the squalls of rain belting the crown of my head abominably. I surmise that I travelled ten miles by the time I reburied the boots. They pleased me greatly in spite of the foot-squeezing, tormenting and foot-hurt I received from them. I was very exhausted when I reached the rushes before daybreak.

It was the time for morning-potatoes when I awoke and hardly on my feet when I noticed that something in life was awry. The Old-Grey-Fellow was away from home (which never happened at potato-time) and the neighbours were standing in small groups, conversing together fearfully and in undertones. Everything looked eerie and the very rain appeared uncommon. My mother was worried and silent.

— Is it the way, loving maiden, said I softly, that the Gaelic misery is at an end now and that the paupers are waiting for the final explosion of the great earth?

— The story is worse than that, I think, said she.

I failed to draw another word from her because of the worried displeasure which had come over her. I moved out. I noticed Martin O'Bannassa out in the field, looking fearfully at the ground. I moved over until I stood with him and bestowed my blessing most courteously upon him.

— What bad news has come to the village, said I, or is it some new defeat that is in store for the Gaels?

He did not reply for a little while and when he spoke, the hoarseness of terror was in his voice. He placed his lips to my ears.

— Last night, said he, the evil thing was in Corkadoragha.

– The evil thing?

– The Sea-cat! Look!

He pointed his finger towards the ground.

– Look at that spoor, said he, and that spoor! Both of them crossing the country!

I released a small startled sound from me.

– It wasn't cows nor horses nor pigs nor any earthly type that left them, said he quickly, but the Sea-cat from Donegal. May we all be safe! It's a misfortunate, catastrophic, unutterable thing the bad plight and the ill-luck that will come upon us after this day. Of course, 'twould be better for a fellow to jump into the sea and reach eternity. Bad as that place is, the lot that will be ours in Corkadoragha from now on will be infernally insufferable.

I agreed sorrowfully with him and departed. Without a doubt, Martin and the neighbours were referring to my boot-marks. I feared to inform them of the truth because they would have jeered me or set out to slay me.

This wonder lasted for two days, everyone expecting that the heavens would collapse or that the ground crack and the people would be swept away to some lower region. I was relaxed during all this time, free of fear and enjoying the special information which I carried in my heart. Many persons congratulated me on my courage.

On the morning of the third day, I noticed when I arose that we had company in our house. A big tall stranger was standing outside the door, conversing with the Old-Fellow. He wore good navy-blue clothes, bright buttons and huge big boots. I heard him speak in bitter English while the Old-Fellow endeavoured to appease him in Gaelic and broken English. When the stranger observed me at the end of the house, he ceased speaking and leaped through the rushes until he reached me. He was a rough burly fellow and he set my heart trembling with fear. He took a firm grip of my arm.

– Phwat is yer nam? said he.

I nearly swallowed my tongue through sheer fright. When speech returned, I replied to him:

– Jams O'Donnell.

He then let loose a stream of English which overwhelmed me like the nocturnal water. I did not understand a single word. The Old-Fellow approached and spoke to me.

— It was the Sea-cat and no doubt about it, said he, and the first misfortune has arrived. What we have here is a peeler and 'tis yourself that he's looking for.

When I heard this talk a great nervous trembling came upon me. The peeler released another stream of English.

— He's saying, said the Old-Fellow, that some scoundrel murdered a gentleman in Galway lately and that he stole a lot of gold pieces from him. He says that the peelers have evidence that you were buying things with gold a while ago and he says that you're to lay out all you have in your pocket on the table.

The peeler emitted an angry bark. If I failed to understand the words, the roughness of his voice was intelligible indeed. I placed the contents of my pockets on the table, even the nineteen pieces of gold. He glanced at them and then at me. When he had satisfied his eyes, he vomited out other shouts in English and took a firmer hold on me.

— He's saying, said the Old-Fellow, that 'twould be a good thing if you'd go with him.

After hearing this statement, I fear that I lost my senses and that my command over life and limb and person was minimal. I could not distinguish night from bright day nor rain from drought at that moment in the end of the house. Darkness gathered around me and distraction. For a while I recognized nothing around apart from the hold which the peeler had upon me and that we were proceeding together along the road, far away from Corkadoragha, where I had spent my life and where my friends and my kinsfolk had lived since bygone days.

I half-remember being in a big city full of gentle-folk wearing boots; they were speaking sincerely together, going by and climbing into coaches; no rain fell and the weather was not cold. I have a faint memory of being in a noble palace; being a while with a great crowd of peelers who spoke to me and to one another in English; being yet another while in prison. I never understood a single item of all that happened around me nor one word of the conversation nor my interrogation.[1] I remember slightly being in a large ornate hall with others before a gentleman who wore a white wig. Many other elegant people were there, some speaking and others listening. This business continued for three days and I was greatly interested in everything that I saw. When all this was completed, I believe I was imprisoned again.

One morning I was awakened early and ordered to prepare at once to move. This order left me between worry and joy. I was safe and dry and free from hunger while locked up but, nevertheless, I desired to be back once more with my people in Corkadoragha. But to my amazement, it was not towards the town that the peelers took me but towards some place they call a *station*. We were there for a time while I gazed with interest at the great coaches going by pushing big black objects ahead of them which were sniffing and coughing and emitting suffocating smoke. I noticed another pauper who had a Gaelic appearance about him coming into the station with two peelers while he conversed with them in English.

I paid no attention to him until I felt after a while that he was alongside me and addressing me.

– It's clear, said he in Gaelic, that you're in no good situation at present.

– I like this place well enough, said I.

Do you understand, said he, what you have got from the gentlemen and big bucks of this town?

– I understand nothing, said I.

– You've got twenty-nine years in jail, friend, and you're being brought to that other prison now.

It was a little while before I understood the meaning of this talk. Then I collapsed in a faint on the ground and I should be there still in the same shameful state were it not that a bucket of water was thrown over me.

When I was set on my feet again, I felt light in the head and half-conscious. I observed that certain coaches had come into the station and that people, both gentle-folk and paupers, were coming out of them. I laid my eyes on one man and, without any volition on my part, my gaze remained on him. It was apparent to me that there was something familiar about him. I had never seen him before but he was not a stranger in appearance. He was an old man, bent and broken and as thin as a stem of grass. He wore dirty rags, was barefooted and his two eyes were burning in his withered skull. They stared at me.

We approached timidly and slowly towards one another, filled with fear and welcome. I noticed that he was trembling, his lips were shaking and lightning shot from his eyes. I spoke to him quietly in English.

— Phwat is yer nam?

He spoke voice-brokenly and aimlessly.

— Jams O'Donnell! said he.

Wonder and joy swept over me as flashes of lightning out of the celestial sky. I lost my voice and I nearly lost my senses again.

My father! my own father!! my own little father!!! my kinsman, my progenitor, my friend!!!! We devoured one another with our eyes eagerly and I offered him my hand.

— The name and surname that's on me, said I, is also Jams O'Donnell. You're my father and it's clear that you've come out of the jug.

— My son! said he. My little son!! my little sonny!!!

He took hold of my hand and ate and swallowed me with his eyes. Whatever flood-tide of joy had come over him at that time, I noticed that the ugly fellow had little health; certainly, he had not benefited from the bout of joy which he derived from me at that hour in the station; he had become as white as snow and saliva dripped from the edges of his lips.

— I'm told, said I, that I've earned twenty-nine years in the same jug.

I wished that we had had conversation and that the eerie staring, which was confusing us both, should cease. I saw a softness creep into his eyes and quiet settle over his limbs. He beckoned with his finger.

— Twenty-nine years I've done in the jug, said he, and it's surely an unlovely place.

— Tell my mother, said I, that I'll be back . . .

A strong hand suddenly grasped the back of my rags, rudely sweeping me away. A peeler was assaulting me. I was sent into a running bound by a destructive shove in the small of the back.

— *Kum along blashketman!* said the peeler.

I was cast into a coach and we set out on our journey without delay. Corkadoragha was behind me — perhaps for ever — and I was on my way to the faraway jail. I fell on the floor and wept a headful of tears.

Yes! that was the first time that I laid eyes on my father and that he laid eyes on me; one wee moment at the station and then – separation for ever. Certainly, I suffered Gaelic hardship throughout my life – distress, need, ill-treatment, adversity, calamity, foul play, misery, famine and ill-luck.

I do not think that my like will ever be there again!

TRANSLATOR'S PREFACE

THIS CELEBRATED satirical work, *An Béal Bocht*, first published in 1941, is here translated for the first time under the title of *The Poor Mouth*. In Gaelic and in Anglo-Irish dialect, 'putting on the poor mouth' means making a pretence of being poor or in bad circumstances in order to gain advantage for oneself from creditors or prospective creditors. It may also mean simply 'grumbling' according to the lexicographer Dr Patrick Dinneen, a scholar who received scant respect from Myles na Gopaleen.

The author, Brian O'Nolan, who writes under his *nom de plume*, Myles na Gopaleen, was an accomplished Gaelic scholar and handles Gaelic in this work in a masterly but also in a rather idiosyncratic manner which makes translation at times a rather exacting task.

The third edition, which contains many interpolations and emendations, is the text translated here. Wherever this particular edition presented difficulties or ambiguities, the earlier editions have been consulted. In this text the author included some humorous 'translations' of single words which he added to the ends of the pages as footnotes. They occur only in the first chapter of the third edition and have been included here in notes at the back of the book.

In *The Poor Mouth* Myles comments mercilessly on Irish life and not only on the Gaeltacht. Words such as 'hard times', 'poverty', 'drunkenness', 'spirits' and 'potatoes' recur in the text with almost monotonous regularity. The atmosphere reeks of the rain and the downpour and with relentless insistence he speaks of people who are 'facing for eternity' and the like. The key-words in this work are surely 'downpour', 'eternity' and 'potatoes' set against a background of squalor and poverty.

The principal difficulty attending the translation of this work has been due to Myles's parodying the style of certain Gaelic authors such as Máire (Séamas Ó Grianna) from the Rosses in County Donegal and Tomás Ó Criomhthainn from the Great

Blasket Island in County Kerry. This daunting task must always face the translator who wishes to reproduce in another language the subtle nuances and flavour of the original.

For too long *An Béal Bocht* has been inaccessible to those who were ignorant of Gaelic or whose knowledge of the old language of Ireland was inadequate for a proper understanding of Myles's satirical work. It is time that this book, which should have acted as a cauterization of the wounds inflicted on Gaelic Ireland by its official friends, might do its work in the second official language of Ireland. That it may do so, is the translator's wish and hope.

Patrick C. Power M.A., Ph.D.

NOTES

(D. ... *An Béal Bocht*, Dolmen Press, Dublin, 1964)

Chapter 1

1 *diversions:* Appears in D. as *divarsions* which is explained in a footnote as *scléip* (fun, revelry).

2 *adventures:* In D. appears as *advintures*; explained in footnote as *eachtraí* (adventures).

3 ... *the end of the house:* This phrase appears again and again in the text; *tóin an tí* in Gaelic (lit. the backside of the house!)

4 ... *a child among the ashes:* Translation of a cliché used continually by Máire (Séamas Ó Grianna) in his novels (ina thachrán ar fud a' ghríosaigh).

5 *explanation:* Myles uses *axplinayshin* in D. and in a footnote explains: *cúis, bun an scéil* (cause, basis of the story).

6 *animals:* Myles used *béastana* which he explains in a footnote as *beithidhigh*, cf. *Béarla 'bastes'* (beasts, cf. English 'bastes'!).

7 ... *its like will ever be there again:* This translation of the celebrated phrase used by Tomás Ó Criomhthainn in his *An t-Oileánach* (Dublin, 1927) is one of the ever-recurring sayings used by Myles in *An Béal Bocht*. Ó Criomhthainn's statement is ... mar ná beidh ár leithéidí arís ann (because our likes will not be there again).

Chapter 3

1 *grey-wool breeches:* In Gaelic '*brístí de ghlas na gcaorach*', this phrase occurs in books written by writers such as Máire. The wool is undyed. The Gaelic writers generally refer only to the breeches as if the child wore nothing else!

2 *Bonaparte . . . :* In Gaelic this occurs as '*Bonapáirt Mícheálangaló Pheadair Eoghain Shorcha Thomáis Mháire Sheáin Shéamais Dhiarmada . . .*' This is more euphonious than the translation but Gaelic here has the advantage because of the possibility of using genitive cases for each word after the first one.

3 *Jams O'Donnell:* In Máire's novel, *Mo Dhá Róisín*, the author speaks of a pupil hearing himself called by his official name *James Gallagher* on his first schoolday. He had never heard it before! Myles seems to use the name as a generic term for the Gaeltacht man as seen by those outside his boggy rainy ghetto.

4 *sor:* In D. this spelling appears for *sir*. The Gaelic pun is untranslatable – *sor* means *louse* in English!

5 *gramophone:* In D. the word is *gramofón* and in early editions *gramafón* which contain a footnote (omitted in D.) which states: *fónagram*.

6 *Jimmy Tim Pat:* This, of course, should be *Jimmy, son of Tim, son of Pat* but it is left as in Gaelic because this form of nomenclature is quite common in parts of the Limerick, Cork and Kerry countryside still. It is limited, however, to three names unlike the jocular ancestral invocation referred to in note 2 above.

Chapter 4

1 *Father Peter:* This is Father Peter O'Leary (an t-Athair Peadar Ó Laoghaire) the Cork priest whose insistence on the use of ordinary everyday speech in Gaelic literature was such an influential factor in the development of modern writing in the language.

2 *My Friend Drumroosk:* In the original this is: *Mo Chara Droma Rúisc* which may mean either *My Carrick-on-Shannon* or *My Friend D.* as above. The pun is untranslatable.

3 *No liberty without royalty:* This appears as *Ní saoirse go Seoirse* – *No liberty without George*. To retain the alliterative and syllabic correspondence in translation as in Gaelic, *royalty* has been used.

4 *misfortunes . . . misfortunes:* The original Gaelic expression *Thit and lug ar an lag orm* means *I became extremely dismayed* while literally it is: *The lug fell on the lag on me!* To retain sense and style, *misfortune* and *misadventure* have been used.

Chapter 5

1 *shadows . . . :* This is commentary on the Gaelic expression *Ar scáth a chéile a mhaireann na daoine* (People live in one another's shadows), meaning *People depend upon one another*.

2 Throughout this chapter in Gaelic snatches of Ulster dialect

are used. Except in a few cases, this has not been represented in translation.

3 *Séadna:* This is the title of a famous book by Fr Peter O'Leary (published 1904) which has been the most influential work of his and a book of major importance in modern Gaelic literature.

Chapter 7

1 In Gaelic the saying 'Beidh lá eile ag an bPaorach!' (Power will have another day) is supposed to have been first used by Edmund Power of Dungarvan in the autumn of 1798 as he stood on the gallows, a position which negatived the hope expressed in the saying! In *An Béal Bocht* parodies the expression in 'O'Sanassa will have another day'. By the way, the original saying was often on the lips of Mr Eamon De Valera.

Chapter 8

1 *Maeldoon O'Poenassa:* Note that *Immram Maíle Dúin* (The Voyage of Maeldoon), an ancient Gaelic story of the eighth or ninth century, provided Myles with the name of the gentleman in this chapter who sailed through the Deluge to Hunger-stack.

2 and 3 These portions of the chapter are written in the form of Gaelic used during the period A.D. 1000–1250.

Chapter 9

1 The assertion by O'Coonassa that he understood nothing of his trial and, later on, of his sentence is reminiscent of very many injustices inflicted on Gaelic speakers in Ireland during the years of British rule. Especially notorious was the hanging of the Joyces in Dublin in the last century after a trial which they never understood and for a crime which they did not commit.

THE HARD LIFE
AN EXEGESIS OF SQUALOR

All the persons in this book are real and none is fictitious even in part

*Tout le trouble du monde vient
de ce qu'on ne sait pas rester seul dans sa chambre*

PASCAL

I honourably present to Graham Greene
whose own forms of gloom I admire, this misterpiece

CHAPTER 1

IT IS NOT that I half knew my mother. I knew half of her: the lower half – her lap, legs, feet, her hands and wrists as she bent forward. Very dimly I seem to remember her voice. At the time, of course, I was very young. Then one day she did not seem to be there any more. So far as I knew she had gone away without a word, no good-bye or good night. A while afterwards I asked my brother, five years my senior, where the mammy was.

– She is gone to a better land, he said.

– Will she be back?

– I don't think so.

– Mean to say we'll never see her again?

– I do think we will. She is staying with the old man.

At the time I found all this very vague and unsatisfying. I had never met my father at all but in due time I was to see and study a faded brown photograph – a stern upright figure wearing great moustaches and attired in a uniform with a large peaked cap. I could never make out what the uniform stood for. He might have been a field-marshal or an admiral, or just an orderly officer in the fire brigade; indeed, he might have been a postman.

My memory is a bit mixed about what exactly happened after the mammy went away but a streel of a girl with long lank fair hair arrived to look after myself and the brother. She did not talk very much and seemed to be in a permanent bad temper. We knew her as Miss Annie. At least that is what she ordered us to call her. She spent a lot of time washing and cooking, specializing in boxty and kalecannon and eternally making mince balls covered with a greasy paste. I got to hate those things.

– If we're ever sent to jail, the brother said one night in bed, we'll be well used to it before we go in. Did you ever see the like of the dinner we're getting? I would say that woman Annie is a bit batty.

– If you mean the mince balls, I said, I think they're all right – if we didn't see so many of them, so often.

– I'm certain they're very bad for us.

– Well, that paste stuff is too thick.

– How well the mammy thought nothing of a bit of ham boiled with cabbage once a week. Remember that?

– I don't. I hadn't any teeth at that time. What's ham?

– Ham? Great stuff, man. It's a class of a red meat that comes from the county Limerick.

That's merely my recollection of the silly sort of conversation we had. Probably it is all wrong.

How long this situation – a sort of interregum, lacuna or hiatus – lasted I cannot say, but I do remember that when myself and the brother noticed that Miss Annie was washing more savagely, mangling and ironing almost with ferocity, and *packing*, we knew something was afoot. And we were not mistaken.

One morning after breakfast (stirabout and tea with bread and jam) a cab arrived and out of it came a very strange elderly lady on a stick. I saw her first through the window. Her hair peeping from under her hat was grey, her face very red, and she walked slowly as if her sight was bad. Miss Annie let her in, first telling us that here was Mrs Crotty and to be good. She stood in silence for a moment in the kitchen, staring rather blankly about her.

– These are the two rascals, Mrs Crotty, Miss Annie said.

– And very well they're looking, God bless them, Mrs Crotty said in a high voice. Do they do everything they're told?

– Oh, I suppose they do, but sometimes it's a job to make them take their milk.

– Well, faith now, Mrs Crotty said in a shocked tone, did you ever hear of such nonsense? When I was their age I could never get *enough* milk. Never. I could drink jugs of it. Buttermilk too. Nothing in the wide world is better for the stomach or the nerves. Night and day I am telling Mr Collopy that but you might as well be talking to *that table*!

Here she struck the table with her stick. Miss Annie looked startled that her trivial mention of milk should induce such emphasis. She took off her apron.

– We'll see, she said ominously. Is the cabby outside? I have all the stuff ready in there.

– Yes, Mr Hanafin is out there. Just call him in. Are these young gentlemen washed?

– As far as possible. What the pair of them need is a good bath. You know the way the water is here.

– The Lord save us, Mrs Crotty said grimacing, is there anything under heaven's sky more terrible than dirt. But sure we'll see after all that in good time, please God. Well now!

Miss Annie went out and came back with Mr Hanafin the cabby. He had a ruby face, maybe from all the porter he drank, and was correctly dressed – hard hat and a caped surcoat of dark green.

– The top of the morning to you all, he said genially. I was just saying, Mrs Crotty, that Miss Annie is looking very well.

– Is that so? Well, she had a bit of a handful here but then Mr Collopy is another handful and maybe a little rest from him was as good to her as a fortnight in Skerries.

– Ah now she has great colour, Mr Hanafin replied pleasantly. Is them two young archdukes to be me passengers?

– Yes, Miss Annie said, they are the main cargo. See you don't spill them out.

– Be the dad, Mr Hanafin said smiling, Marius will be delighted. We'll get a right trot this morning.

– Who is Marius, the brother asked.

– The mare, man.

Afterwards the brother told me he thought this was a strange name for a mare. Maria would have been better. He was a very wide-awake character even then. I think I used some coarse word here about the animal outside. He told me I should not speak like that.

– Why?

– Teresa would not like it.

– Who is Teresa?

– Our sister.

– Our *sister*? WHAT?

Mrs Crotty told Miss Annie to show Mr Hanafin where the baggage was, and she led him into the back room off the kitchen. There was a lot of noisy fumbling and pulling. The bulk of the baggage could only be explained by having blankets and pillows and other bedclothes tied up, for the wardrobe of the brother and myself was not . . . well . . . extensive. Perhaps there were curtains there, too.

At last Mr Hanafin had everything packed away on the roof

of the cab. It was summer and the brother and I travelled as we stood. Miss Annie carefully locked the house and she and Mrs Crotty stowed themselves fastidiously in the back seat of the cab, ourselves sitting facing them. The journey was enjoyable, great houses sliding past, trams clanging in the middle of the road, large thickly-made horses hauling heavy drays, and our own Marius making delightful music with her hooves. As I was later to know, our destination was Warrington Place, a rather junior continuation of lordly Herbert Place along the canal on the south side of the great city of Dublin.

Reckoning backwards, I find I was about five years old. The year was 1890, and my young bones told me that a great change was coming in my life. Little did I know just then how big the change. I was about to meet Mr Collopy.

CHAPTER 2

THERE IS SOMETHING misleading but not dishonest in this portrait of Mr Collopy. It cannot be truly my impression of him when I first saw him but rather a synthesis of all the thoughts and experiences I had of him over the years, a long look backwards. But I do remember clearly enough that my first glimpse of him was, so to speak, his absence: Mrs Crotty, having knocked imperiously on the door, immediately began rooting in her handbag for the key. It was plain she did not expect the door to be opened.

– There is a clap of rain coming, she remarked to Miss Annie.

– Seemingly, Miss Annie said.

Mrs Crotty opened the door and led us in single file into the front kitchen, semi-basement, Mr Hanafin bringing up the rear with some bags.

He was sitting there at the range in a crooked, collapsed sort of cane armchair, small reddish eyes looking up at us over the rims of steel spectacles, the head bent forward for closer scrutiny. Over an ample crown, long grey hair was plastered in a tattered way. The whole mouth region was concealed by a great untidy dark brush of a moustache, discoloured at the edges, and a fading chin was joined to a stringy neck which disappeared into a white celluloid collar with no tie. Nondescript clothes contained a meagre frame of low stature and the feet wore large boots with the laces undone.

– Heavenly fathers, he said in a flat voice, but you are very early. Morning, Hanafin.

– Morra, Mr Collopy, Mr Hanafin said.

– Annie here had everything infastatiously in order, Mrs Crotty said, thanks be to God.

– I wonder now, Miss Annie said.

– Troth, Mr Collopy, Mr Hanafin beamed, but I never seen you looking better. You have a right bit of colour up whatever you are doing with yourself at all.

The brother and myself looked at Mr Collopy's slack grey face and then looked at each other.

– Well, the dear knows, Mr Collopy said, I don't think hard work ever hurt anybody. Put that stuff in the back room for the present, Hanafin. Well now, Mrs Crotty, are these the two pishrogues out of the storm? They are not getting any thinner from the good dinners you have been putting into them, Annie, and that's a fact.

– Seemingly, Miss Annie said.

– Pray introduce me if you please, Mrs Crotty.

We went forward and had our names recited. Without rising, Mr Collopy made good an undone button at the neck of the brother's jersey and then shook hands with us solemnly. From his waistcoat he extracted two pennies and presented one to each of us.

– I cross your hands with earthly goods, he said, and at the same time I put my blessing on your souls.

– Thanks for the earthly goods, the brother said.

– Manus and Finbarr are fine names, fine Irish names, Mr Collopy said. In the Latin Manus means big. Remember that. Ecce Sacerdos Manus comes into the Missal, and that Manus is such an uplifting name. Ah but Finbarr is the real Irish for he was a saint from the County Cork. Far and wide he spread the Gospel thousands of years ago for all the thanks he got, for I believe he died of starvation at the heel of the hunt on some island on the river Lee, down fornenst Queenstown.

– I always heard that St Finbarr was a Protestant, Mrs Crotty snapped. Dug with the other foot. God knows what put it into the head of anybody to put a name the like of that on the poor *bookul*.

– Nonsense, Mrs Crotty. His heart was to Ireland and his soul to the Bishop of Rome. What is sticking out of that bag, Hanafin? Are they brooms or shovels or what?

Mr Hanafin had reappeared with a new load of baggage and followed Mr Collopy's gaze to one item.

– Faith now, Mr Collopy, he replied, and damn the shovels. They are hurling sticks. Best of Irish ash and from the County Kilkenny, I'll go bail.

– I am delighted to hear it. From the winding banks of Nore, ah? Many a good puck I had myself in the quondam days of my nonage. I could draw on a ball in those days and clatter in a goal from midfield, man.

– Well it's no wonder you are never done talking about the rheumatism in your knuckles, Mrs Crotty said bleakly.

– That will do you, Mrs Crotty. It was a fine manly game and I am not ashamed of any wounds I may still carry. In those days you were damn nothing if you weren't a hurler. Cardinal Logue is a hurler and a native Irish speaker, revered by Pope and man. Were *you* a hurler, Hanafin?

– In my part of the country – Tinahely – we went in for the football.

– Michael Cusack's Gaelic code, I hope?

– Oh, certainly, Mr Collopy.

– That's good. The native games for the native people. By dad and I see young thullabawns of fellows got out in baggy drawers playing this new golf out beyond on the Bull Island. For pity's sake sure that isn't a game at all.

– Oh you'll always find the fashionable jackeen in Dublin and that's a certainty, Mr Hanafin said. They'd wear nightshirts if they seen the British military playing polo in nightshirts above in the park. Damn the bit of shame they have.

– And then you have all this talk about Home Rule, Mr Collopy asserted. Well how are you! We're as fit for Home Rule here as the blue men in Africa if we are to judge by those Bull Island looderamawns.

– Sit over here at the table, Mrs Crotty said. Is that tea drawn, Annie?

– Seemingly, Miss Annie said.

We all sat down and Mr Hanafin departed, leaving a shower of blessings on us.

It is seemly for me to explain here, I feel, the nature and standing of the persons present. Mr Collopy was my mother's half-brother and was therefore my own half-uncle. He had married twice, Miss Annie being his daughter by his first marriage. Mrs Crotty was his second wife but she was never called Mrs Collopy, why I cannot say. She may have deliberately retained the name of her first husband in loving memory of him or the habit may have grown up through the absence of mind. Moreover, she always called her second husband by the formal style of Mr Collopy as he also called her Mrs Crotty, at least in the presence of other parties; I cannot speak for what usage obtained in private. An ill-disposed person might suspect that they were not married at all and that Mrs Crotty was a kept-woman or resident prostitute. But that is quite unthinkable, if only because of Mr Collopy's close interest in the Church and in matters of doctrine and dogma, and also his long friendship with the German priest from Leeson Street, Father Kurt Fahrt, S.J., who was a frequent caller.

It is seemly, as I have said, to give that explanation but I cannot pretend to have illuminated the situation or made it more reasonable.

CHAPTER 3

THE YEARS PASSED slowly in this household where the atmosphere could be described as a dead one. The brother, five years older than myself, was first to be sent to school, being marched off early one morning by Mr Collopy to see the Superior of the Christian Brothers' school at Westland Row. A person might think the occasion was one merely of formal introduction and enrolment, but when Mr Collopy returned, he was alone.

– By God's will, he explained, Manus's foot has been placed today on the first rung of the ladder of learning and achievement, and on yonder pinnacle beckons the lone star.

– The unfortunate boy had no lunch, Mrs Crotty said in a shrill voice.

– You might consider, Mrs Crotty, that the Lord would provide, even as He does for the birds of the air. I gave the bosthoon a tuppence. Brother Cruppy told me that the boys can get a right bag of broken biscuits for a penny in a barber's shop there up the lane.

– And what about milk?

– Are you out of your wits, woman? You know the gorawars you have to get him to drink his milk in this kitchen. He thinks milk is poison, the same way *you* think a drop of malt is poison. That reminds me – I think I deserve a smahan. Where's my crock?

The brother, who had become more secretive as time went on, did not confide much in me about his new station except that 'school was a bugger'. Sooner than I thought, my own turn was to come. One evening Mr Collopy asked me where the morning paper was. I handed him the nearest I could find. He handed it back to me.

– This morning's I told you.

– I think that's this morning's.

– You *think*? Can you not read, boy?

– Well . . . no.

– Well, may the sweet Almighty God look down on us with

compassion! Do you realize that at your age Mose Art had written four symphonies and any God's amount of lovely songs? Pagan Neeny had given a recital on the fiddle before the King of Prussia and John the Baptist was stranded in the desert with damn the thing to eat only locusts and wild honey. Have you no shame man?

– Well, I'm young yet.

– Is that a fact now? You are like the rest of them, you are counting from the wrong end. How do you know you are not within three months of the end of your life?

– Oh my God!

– Hah?

– But –

– You may put your buts back in your pocket. I will tell you what you'll do. You'll get up tomorrow morning at the stroke of eight o'clock and you will give yourself a good wash for yourself.

That night the brother said in bed, not without glee, that somehow he thought I would soon be master of Latin and Shakespeare and that Brother Cruppy would shower heavenly bread on me with his class in Christian Doctrine and give me some idea of what the early Christians went through in the arena by thrashing the life out of me. Unhappy was the eye I closed that night. But the brother was only partly right. To my surprise, Mr Collopy next morning led me at a smart pace up the bank of the canal, penetrated to Synge Street and rang the bell at the residential part of the Christian Brothers' establishment there. When a slatternly young man in black answered, Mr Collopy said he wanted to see the Superior, Brother Gaskett. We were shown into a gaunt little room which had on the wall a steel engraving of the head of Brother Rice, founder of the Order, a few chairs and a table – nothing more.

– They say piety has a smell, Mr Collopy mused, half to himself. It's a perverse notion. What they mean is only the absence of the smell of women.

He looked at me.

– Did you know that no living woman is allowed into this holy house. That is as it should be. Even if a Brother has to see his own mother, he has to meet her in secret below at the Imperial Hotel. What do you think of that?

– I think it is very hard, I said. Couldn't she call to see him here and have another Brother present, like they do in jails when there is a warder present on visiting day?

— Well, that's the queer comparison, I'll warrant. Indeed, this house may be a jail of a kind but the chains are of purest eighteen-carat finest gold which the holy brothers like to kiss on their bended knees.

The door opened silently and an elderly stout man with a sad face glided in. He smiled primly and gave us an odd handshake, keeping his elbow bent and holding the extended hand against his breast.

— Isn't that the lovely morning, Mr Collopy, he said hoarsely.

— It is, thank God, Brother Gaskett, Mr Collopy replied as we all sat down. Need I tell you why I brought this young ruffian along?

— Well, it wasn't to teach him how to play cards.

— You are right there, Brother. His name is Finbarr.

— Well now, look at that! That is a beautiful name, one that is honoured by the Church. I presume you would like us to try to extend Finbarr's knowledge?

— That is a nice way of putting it, Brother Gaskett. I think they will have to be very big extensions because damn the thing he knows but low songs from the pantomimes, come-all-ye's by Cathal McGarvey, and his prayers. I suppose you'll take him in, Brother?

— Of course I will. Certainly, I will teach him everything from the three Rs to Euclid and Aristophanes and the tongue of the Gael. We will give him a thorough grounding in the Faith and, with God's help, if one day he should feel like joining the Order, there will always be a place for him in this humble establishment. After he has been trained, of course.

The tail-end of that speech certainly startled me, even to tempting me to put in some sort of caveat. I did not like it even as a joke, nor the greasy Brother making it.

— I . . . I think that could wait a bit, Brother Gaskett, I stammered.

He laughed mirthlessly.

— Ah but of course, Finbarr. One thing at a time.

Then he and Mr Collopy indulged in some muttered consultation jaw to jaw, and the latter got up to leave. I also rose but he made a gesture.

– We'll stay where we are now, he said. Brother Gaskett thinks you might start right away. Always better to take the bull by the horns.

Though not quite unexpected, this rather shocked me.

– But, I said in a loud voice, I have no lunch . . . no broken biscuits.

– Never mind, Brother Gaskett said, we will give you a half-day to begin with.

That is how I entered the sinister portals of Synge Street School. Soon I was to get to know the instrument known as 'the leather'. It is not, as one would imagine, a strap of the kind used on bags. It is a number of such straps sewn together to form a thing of great thickness that is nearly as rigid as a club but just sufficiently flexible to prevent the breaking of the bones of the hand. Blows of it, particularly if directed (as often they deliber-ately were) to the top of the thumb or wrist, conferred imme-diate paralysis followed by agony as the blood tried to get back to the afflicted part. Later I was to learn from the brother a certain routine of prophylaxis he had devised but it worked only partly.

Neither of us found out what Mr Collopy's reason was for sending us to different schools. The brother thought it was to prevent us 'cogging', or copying each other's home exercises, of which we were given an immense programme to get through every night. This was scarcely correct, for an elaborate system for 'cogging' already existed in each school itself, for those who arrived early in the morning. My own feeling was that the move was prompted by Mr Collopy's innate craftiness and the general principle of *divide et impera*.

CHAPTER 4

AND STILL the years kept rolling on, and uneventfully enough, thank God. I was now about eleven, the brother sixteen and convinced he was a fully grown man.

One day in spring about half-three I was trudging wearily home from school at Synge Street. I was on the remote, or canal side of the roadway near home. I happened to glance up at the house when about fifty yards away and, turned to cold stone, stopped dead in my tracks. My heart thumped wildly against my ribs and my eyes fell to the ground. I blessed myself. Timidly I looked up again. Yes!

To the left of the house entrance and perhaps fifteen yards from it a tallish tree stood in the front garden. Head and shoulders above the tree but not quite near it was the brother. I stared at the apparition in the manner fascinated animals are reputed to stare at deadly snakes about to strike. He began waving his arms in a sickening way, and the next prospect I had of him was his back. He was returning towards the house *and he was walking on air!* Now thoroughly scared, I thought of Another who had walked on water. I again looked away helplessly, and after a little time painfully stumbled into the house. I must have looked very pale but went in and said nothing.

Mr Collopy was not in his usual chair at the range. Annie – we had now learned to drop the 'Miss' – placed potatoes and a big plate of stew before me. I thought it would be well to affect a casual manner.

– Where's Mr Collopy? I asked.

She nodded towards the back room.

– He's inside, she said. I don't know what father's at. He's in there with a tape taking measurements. I'm afraid poor Mrs Crotty's getting worse. She had Dr Blennerhassett again this morning. God look down on us all!

Mrs Crotty was certainly sick. She had taken to the bed two months before and insisted that the door between her bedroom and the kitchen should be always left slightly ajar so that her cries, often faint, could be heard either by Mr Collopy or Annie. Neither myself nor the brother ever entered the room but all the same I had accidentally seen her on several occasions. This was when she was coming down the stairs leaning on Mr Collopy and clutching the banister with one frail hand, her robe or night-dress of fantastic shape and colour and a frightening pallor on her spent face.

    — I'm afraid she *is* pretty sick, I said.

    — Seemingly.

I finished with a cup of tea, then casually left the kitchen and went upstairs, my heart again making its excitement known. I entered the bedroom.

The brother, his back to me, was bending over a table examining some small metal objects. He looked up and nodded abstractedly.

    — Do you mind, I said nervously, do you mind answering a question?

    — What question? I have got a great bit of gear here.

    — Listen to the question. When I was coming in a while back, did I see you walking on the air?

He turned again to stare at me and then laughed loudly.

    — Well, by damn, he chuckled, I suppose you did, in a manner of speaking.

    — What do you mean?

    — Your question is interesting. Did it look well?

    — If you want to know, it looked unnatural and if you are taking advantage of a power not of God, if you are dealing in godless things of darkness, I would strongly advise you to see Father Fahrt, because these things will lead to no good.

Here he sniggered.

    — Have a look out of the window, he said.

I went and did so very gingerly. Between the sill and a stout branch near the top of the tree stretched a very taut wire, which I now saw came in at the base of the closed window and was anchored with some tightening device to the leg of the bed, which was in against the wall.

    — My God Almighty! I exclaimed.

    — Isn't it good?

    — A bloody wire-walker, by cripes!

– I got the stuff from Jem out of the Queen's. There's nothing at all to it. If I rigged the wire across this room tomorrow and only a foot from the floor, you'd walk it yourself with very little practice. What's the difference? What's the difference if you're an inch or a mile up? The only trouble is what they call psychological. It's a new word but I know what it means. The balancing part of it is child's play, and the trick is to put all idea of height out of your mind. It *looks* dangerous, of course, but there's money in that sort of danger. Safe danger.

– What happens if you fall and break your neck?

– Did you ever hear of Blondin? He died in his bed at the age of seventy-three, and fifty years ago he walked on a wire across Niagara Falls, one hundred and sixty feet above the roaring water. And several times – carrying a man on his back, stopping to fry eggs, a great man altogether. And didn't he appear once in Belfast?

– I think you are going off your head.

– I'm going to make money, for I have . . . certain schemes, certain very important schemes. Look what I have here. A printing machine. I got it from one of the lads at Westland Row, who stole it from his uncle. It's simple to operate, though it's old.

But I could not detach my mind from that wire.

– So you're to be the Blondin of Dublin?

– Well, why not?

– Niagara is too far away, of course. I suppose you'll sling a wire over the Liffey?

He started, threw down some metal thing, and turned to me wide-eyed.

– Well, sweet God, he said, you have certainly said something. *You have certainly said something.* Sling a wire over the Liffey? The Masked Daredevil from Mount Street! There's a fortune there – *a fortune!* Lord save us, why didn't I think of it?

– I was only joking, for goodness' sake.

– *Joking?* I hope you'll keep on joking like that. I'll see Father Fahrt about this.

– To bless you before you risk your life?

– Balls! I'll need an organizer, a manager. Father Fahrt knows a lot of those young teachers and I'll get him to put me on to one of them. They're a sporty crowd. Do you remember Frank Corkey, N.T.? He was in this house once, a spoilt Jesuit. That man would blow up the walls of Jerusalem for two quid. He'd be the very man.

– And get sacked from his school for helping a young madman to kill himself?

– I'll get him. You wait and see.

That ended that day's surprising disputation. I was secretly amused at the idea of the brother getting on to Father Fahrt about organizing a walk across the Liffey on a tight-wire, with Mr Collopy sprawled in his cane armchair a few feet away listening to the appeal. I had heard of earthquakes and the devastation attending them. Here surely would be a terrible upheaval.

But once more I reckoned without the brother. Without saying a word he slipped off one day up to 35, Lower Lesson Street and saw Father Fahrt privately. He said so when he returned that evening, looking slightly daunted.

– The holy friar, he said, won't hear of it. Asked did I think I was a cornerboy or had I no respect for my family. Public pranks is what he called walking the high wire. Threatened to tell ould Collopy if I didn't put the idea out of my head. Asked me to promise. I promised, of course. But I'll find Corkey on my own and we'll make a damn fine day of it, believe you me. Had I no respect for my family, ah? What family?

– No Jesuit likes being mistaken for a Barnum, I pointed out.

Rather bitterly he said: You'll hear more about this.

I felt sure I would.

CHAPTER 5

IT HAD BECOME evident to me that one of the brother's schemes was in operation, for a considerable stream of letters addressed to him began to arrive at the house, and he had become more secretive than ever. I refused to give him the satisfaction of asking him what he had been up to. I will tell all about that later but just now I wish to give an account of the sort of evening we had in our kitchen, not once but very many times, and the type of talk that went on. As usual, the subject under discussion was never named.

The brother and myself were at the table, struggling through that wretched homework, cursing Wordsworth and Euclid and Christian Doctrine and all similar scourges of youth. Mr Collopy was slumped in his cane armchair, the steel-rimmed glasses far down his nose. In an easy chair opposite was Father Kurt Fahrt who was a very tall man, thin, ascetic, grey-haired, blue about the jaws with a neck so slender that there would be room, so to speak, for two of them inside his priestly collar. On the edge of the range, handy to the reach of those philosophers, was a glass. On the floor beside Mr Collopy's chair was what was known as 'the crock'. It was in fact a squat earthenware container, having an ear on each side, in which the Kilbeggan Distillery marketed its wares. The Irish words for whiskey – *Uisge Beatha* – were burnt into its face. This vessel was, of course, opaque and therefore mysterious; one could not tell how empty or full it was, nor how much Mr Collopy had been drinking. The door of Mrs Crotty's bedroom was, as usual, very slightly ajar.

– What the devil ails you, Father, Mr Collopy asked almost irritably.

– Oh it's nothing much, Collopy, Father Fahrt said.

– But heavens above, this scrabbling and scratching –

– Forgive me. I have a touch of psoriasis about the back and chest.

– The sore *what*?

— Psoriasis. A little skin ailment.

— Lord save us, I thought you said you had sore eyes. Is there any question of scabs or that class of thing?

— Oh not at all. I am taking treatment. An ointment containing stuff known as chrysarobin.

— Well, this sore-whatever-it-is causes itching?

Father Fahrt laughed softly.

— Sometimes it feels more like etching, he smiled.

— The man for that is sulphur. Sulphur is one of the great sovereign remedies of the world. Bedamn but a friend of mine uses a lot of sulphur even in his garden.

Here Father Fahrt unconsciously scratched himself.

— Let us forget about such trivial things, he said, and thank God it is not something serious. So you're getting worked up again about your plan?

— It's a shame, Father, Mr Collopy said warmly. It's a bloody shame and that's what it is.

— Well, Collopy, what are we for in this world? We are here to suffer. We must sanctify ourselves. That's what suffering is for.

— Do you know, Father, Mr Collopy said testily, I am getting a bit sick in my intesteens at all this talk of yours about suffering. You seem to be very fond of suffering when other people do it. What would you do if you had the same situation in your own house?

— In my own house I would do what my Superior instructs me to do. My Order is really an army. We are under orders.

— Give me your glass, Your Holiness.

— Not much now, Collopy.

There was a small silence here that seemed portentous, though I did not raise my head to look.

— Father, said Mr Collopy at last, you would go off your bloody head if you had the same situation in your own house. You would make a show of yourself. You would tell Father Superior to go to hell, lep out the front door and bugger off down to Stephen's Green. Oh, I'm up to ye saints. Well up to ye. Do you not think that women have enough suffering, as you call it, bringing babbies into the world? And why do they do that? Is it because they're mad to sanctify themselves? Well faith no! It's because the husband is one great torch ablaze with the fires of lust!

– Collopy, please, Father Fahrt said in mild remonstrance. That attitude is quite wrong. Procreation is the *right* of a married man. Indeed it is his duty for the greater glory of God. It is a duty enjoined by the sacrament of marriage.

– Oh is that so, Mr Collopy said loudly, is that so indeed. To bring unfortunate new bosthoons into this vale of tears for more of this suffering of yours, ah? Another woman maybe. Sweet Lord!

– Now, now, Collopy.

– Tell me this, Father. Would you say it's *natural* for a woman to have children?

– Provided she is married in a union blessed by the Church – yes. Most natural and most desirable. It is a holy thing to raise children to the greater glory of God. Your catechism will tell you that. The celibate and priestly state is the holiest of all but the station of the married man is not ignoble. And of course the modest married woman is the handmaid of the Lord.

– Very good, Mr Collopy said warmly. Then tell me this. Is the other business natural?

– Certainly. Our bodies are sacred temples. It is a function.

– Very well. What name have you for the dirty ignoramuses who more or less ban that function?

– It is, ah, thoughtlessness, Father Fahrt said in his mildest voice. Perhaps if a strong hint were dropped . . .

– *If a hint were dropped*, Mr Collopy exploded. *If a hint were dropped!* Well the dear knows I think you are trying to destroy my temper, Father, and put me out of my wits and make an unfortunate shaughraun out of me. If a hint were dropped, my hat and parsley! Right well you know that I have the trotters wore off me going up the stairs of that filthy Corporation begging them, telling them, ordering them to do something. I have shown you copies of the letters I have sent to that booby the Lord Mayor. That's one man that knows all about chains, anyhow. What result have I got? Nothing at all but abuse from cornerboys and jacks in office.

– Has it ever entered your head, Collopy, that perhaps you are not the most tactful of men?

– Tact, is it? Is that the latest? Give me your glass.

Another pause for decantation and recollection.

– What I would like to do, Mr Collopy said sententiously, is write and publish a long storybook about your theories in favour of suffering. Damn the thing you know about suffering yourself. Only people of no experience have theories. Of course you are only spewing out what you were taught in the holy schools. 'By the sweat of thy brow shalt thou mourn.' Oh the grand old Catholic Church has always had great praise for sufferers.

– That phrase you quoted was inaccurate, Collopy.

– Well, am I supposed to be a deacon or a Bible scholar or what? You won't find Quakers or swaddlers coming out with any of this guff about suffering. They treat their employees right, they have proper accommodation for them, they know how to make plenty of money honestly and they are as holy – every man-jack of them – as any blooming Jesuit or the Pope of Rome himself.

– Let us leave the Holy Father out of this dispute, whatever about humble members of my Society, Father Fahrt said piously.

Suddenly he scratched himself earnestly.

– Did I hear you right when you said 'humble', Father? An humble Jesuit would be like a dog without a tail or a woman without a knickers on her. Did you ever hear tell of the Spanish Inquisition?

– I did of course, Father Fahrt said unperturbed. The faith was in danger in Spain. If a bad wind will blow out your candle, you will protect your candle with the shade of your hand. Or perhaps some sort of cardboard shield.

– Cardboard shield? Mr Collopy echoed scornfully. Well, damn the cardboard shields the Dominicans used in Spain, those blood-stained bowsies.

– My own Order, Father Fahrt said modestly, was under the thumb of the Suprema in Madrid and yet I make no complaint.

– Well, isn't that very good of you, Father? Your own Order was kicked about by those barbarian hooligans in the cowls and *you* make no complaint, sitting there with a glass of malt in your hand. Faith but you're the modest, dacent man, God bless you.

– I merely meant, Collopy, that in a scheme to eradicate serious evil, sometimes we must all suffer.

– And what's wrong with that, Father? Isn't suffering grand?

– It is not pleasant but it is salutary.

– You have a smart answer for everything. 'Do you believe in

the true faith?' 'No.' 'Very well. Eight hundred lashes.' If that's
the Catholic Church for you, is it any wonder there was a
Reformation? Three cheers for Martin Luther!

Father Fahrt was shocked.

– Collopy, please remember that you belong to the true fold
yourself. That talk is scandalous.

– True fold? Do I? And doesn't the Lord Mayor and the other
gougers in the City Hall? And look at the way they're behaving
– *killing* unfortunate women?

– Never mind that subject.

– Till the day I die I'll mind that subject, Mr Collopy retorted
excitedly. Eight hundred lashes for telling the truth according to
your conscience? What am I talking about – the holy friars in
Spain propagated the true faith by driving red hot nails into the
backs of unfortunate Jewmen.

– Nonsense.

– And scalding their testicles with boiling water.

– You exaggerate, Collopy.

– And ramming barbed wire or something of the kind up
where-you-know. And all *A.M.D.G.*, to use your own motto,
Father.

– For heaven's sake Collopy have sense, Father Fahrt said
calmly and sadly. I do not know where you have read those lurid
and silly things.

– Father Fahrt, Mr Collopy said earnestly, you don't like the
Reformation. Maybe I'm not too fond of it myself, either. But
it was our own crowd, those ruffians in Spain and all, who provoked it. They called decent men heretics and the remedy was
to put a match to them. To say nothing of a lot of crooked Popes
with their armies and their papal states, putting duchesses and
nuns up the pole and having all Italy littered with their bastards,
and up to nothing but backstairs work and corruption at the
courts of God knows how many decent foreign kings. Isn't that
a fact?

– It is not a fact, Collopy. The Reformation was a doctrinal
revolt, inspired I have no doubt by Satan. It had nothing to do
with human temporal weaknesses in the Papacy or elsewhere.

– Well now, do you tell me, Mr Collopy sneered.

– Yes, I do. I hate no man, not even Luther. Indeed, by his
translation of the Bible, he can take credit for having in effect

invented my own language, *die schöne deutsche Sprache*. But he was possessed by the Devil. He was a heretic. Heresiarch would be a better word. And when he died in 1545 –

– Excuse me, Father Fahrt.

I was profoundly startled to hear the brother interjecting. He had been undisguisedly following this heated colloquy but it seemed to me unthinkable and provocative that he should intervene. Clearly Mr Collopy and Father Fahrt were equally surprised as they swung round their necks to look at him.

– Yes, my lad? Father Fahrt said.

– Luther did not die in 1545, said the brother. It was 1546.

– Well, well, now, maybe you are right, Father Fahrt said good-humouredly. Maybe you are right. Alas, my old head was never very good for figures. Well, Collopy, I see you have a theologian in the family.

– An historian, the brother said.

– And I'll correct that correction, Mr Collopy said acidly. A bloody young gurrier that won't apply himself with application to his studies, that's what we have. Give me that glass of yours, Father.

There was another intermission while the brother with great elaboration of manner reapplied himself to his studies. After taking a long draught from his new drink, Mr Collopy sank farther back in his shapeless chair and sighed very deeply.

– I'm afraid, Father Fahrt, he said at last, we are only wasting time and just annoying each other with these arguments. These things have been argued out years ago. You'd imagine we here were like Our Lord disputing with the doctors in the temple. The real question is this: What action can we take? *What can be done?*

– Well, that's certainly a more reasonable approach, Collopy. Much more reasonable. And much more practical.

– *Quod faciamemus*, ah?

– Have you thought about a public meeting at all?

– By the jappers I have, many a time, Mr Collopy said with some sadness. I gave it my best considerations. It would be no good. And do you know why? Only men go to public meetings. No lady would be found dead at a public meeting. You know that? You would find only prostitutes hanging around. And men? What good are *they*? Sure they don't give a goddam if women were dying like flies in the street. They have only two uses for women, Father – either go to bed with them or else thrash the life out of them. I was half thinking of trying to enlist the support of this new Gaelic League but I'm afraid they're nothing only a crowd of thooleramawns. They wouldn't understand this crisis in our national life. They would think I was a dirty old man and send for the D.M.P.

– Um.

Father Fahrt frowned speculatively.

– What about making a move at Dublin Castle? They could certainly put pressure on the Corporation.

– And get myself locked up? I am not a damned fool.

– Ah! With politics I am not familiar.

– I'm buggered if I can see what's political about this but those ruffians in the Castle will arrest an Irishman and charge him with treason if his trousers are a bit baggy or he forgot to shave. But here's an approach that came into my head . . .

– What is that, Collopy?

– Why not have the whole scandalous situation denounced from the pulpit?

– Oh . . . dear.

Father Fahrt gave a low, melodious, sardonic laugh.

– The Church's first concern, Collopy, is with faith and morals. Their application to everyday life is pretty wide but I fear your particular problem is far, far outside the pale. We couldn't possibly raise such a matter in a church. It might even give scandal. If I were to start forth on the subject in University Church, I think I know what Father Superior would say, not to mention his Grace the Archbishop.

– But, look here –

– No, no, now, Collopy. *Ecclesia locuta, causa finita est.*

– Ah well, that's the way, I suppose, Mr Collopy said with tired resignation. The Church keeps very far from the people in their daily troubles and travail, but by gob it wasn't like that when we had the Penal Laws, with Paddy Whack keeping a look-out for the soldiery from the top of the ditch on a Sunday morning and the poor pishrogues of peasants below in their rags answering the Hail Mary in Irish. 'Tis too grand you are getting, Father, yourself and your Church.

– I'm afraid there is such a thing as Canon Law, Collopy.

– We have too much law in this country. I even thought of getting in touch with the Freemasons.

– I hope not. It is sinful to have any truck with those people. They despise the Holy Spirit.

– I doubt if they despise women as much as the damned Lord Mayor and his Corporation do.

– There is one remedy I am sure you haven't tried, Collopy. Here Father Fahrt urgently scratched again.

– I'm sure there is. Probably thousands. What's the one remedy?

– Prayer.

– The what was that?

– *Prayer.*

– Prayer? I see. You'd never know, we might try that yet. You can move mountains with prayer, I believe, but I'm not trying to move mountains. I'm trying to put a bomb under that Lord Mayor. But there is one very farfetched idea I've had and damned if I know would it work. I'd want influence . . . a word in high places . . . great tact and plawmaus . . . perhaps a word of support from his Grace. Indeed it might be a complete and final solution to the whole terrible crux. If it came off I would go on a pilgrimage to Lough Derg in thanksgiving.

– It must be a miracle you're looking for if you'd go that far, Collopy, Father Fahrt said smiling. And what is this idea of yours?

– Trams, Father. *Trams.* I don't know how many distinct routes we have here in the city, but say the total is eight. One tram for each route in each direction would suffice, or sixteen trams in all. Old trams repaired and redecorated would do.

– Are you serious, Collopy? Trams?

– Yes, trams. They would have to be distinctive, painted black all over, preferably, and only one sign up front and rear – just the one word WOMEN. Understand? It would be as much as a man's life was worth to try to get into one of them.

– Well, well. At least this idea is novel. Would there be a charge?

– Very likely there would be a penny fare at the beginning. To look for a free service at the start, that would be idealism. But once we have the cars running, we could start an agitation for the wiping out of the penny fare in the interest of humanity.

– I see.

– I would like you to think this thing over, Father. Let us say that a lady and gentleman are walking down the street and have a mind to go for a stroll in the Phoenix Park. Fair enough. But first one thing has to be attended to. They wait at a tram stop. Lo and behold, along comes the Black Tram. The lady steps on board and away she goes on her own. And the whole beauty of the plan is this: *she can get an ordinary tram back* to rejoin her waiting friend. Do you twig?

– Yes, I think I understand.

– Ah, Father, you don't know how dear to my heart this struggle is and the peace that will come down on top of my head when it is happily ended for ever. Decent people should look after women – isn't that right? The weaker sex. Didn't God make them the same as he made you and me, Father?

– He surely did.

– Then why don't we give them fair play? Mean to say, you or I can walk into a pub –

– I *beg* your pardon, Collopy. I certainly can not walk into a public house. You never saw a priest in a public house in your life.

– Well, *I* can walk into a pub and indeed I often do.

– Well, well, Collopy, you are full of ideas but I must be moving. I didn't realize the hour.

– Good enough, but you will call again. Think about what I've said. Can I offer you a final glasheen for the road?

– No thanks indeed, Collopy. Good night now lads, and mind the Greek article haw–hee–taw.

In unison:

– Good night, Father Fahrt.

He went out with dignity, Mr Collopy his escort.

CHAPTER 6

IT HAD BEEN a dull autumn day and in the early evening I decided that the weather would make it worth while looking for roach in the canal. My rod was crude enough but I had hooks of a special size which I had put away in a drawer in the bedroom. I got out the rod and went up for a hook. To my surprise the drawer was littered with sixpenny postal orders and also envelopes addressed to the brother describing him as 'Director, General Georama Gymnasium'. I decided to leave this strange stuff alone, took a hook and went off up along the canal. Perhaps my bait was wrong but I caught nothing and was back home in about an hour. The brother was in the bedroom when I returned, busy writing at the smaller table.

– I was out looking for roach, I remarked, and had to get a hook in that drawer. I see it's full of sixpenny postal orders.

– Not full, he said genially. There are only twenty-eight. But keep that under your hat.

– Twenty-eight is fourteen bob.

– Yes, but I expect a good few more.

– What's all this about General Georama Gymnasium?

– Well, it's my name for the moment, he said.

– What's Georama?

– If you don't know what a simple English word means, the Brothers in Synge Street can't be making much of a hand of you. A georama is a globe representing the earth. Something like what they have in schools. The sound of it goes well with general and gymnasium. That's why I took it. Join the GGG.

– And where did all those postal orders come from?

– From the other side. I put a small ad. in one of the papers. I want to teach people to walk the high wire.

– Is that what the General Georama Gymnasium is for, for heaven's sake?

– Yes. And it's one of the cheapest courses in the world. A

great number of people want to walk the high wire and show off. Some of them may be merely mercenary and anxious to make an easy, quick fortune with some great circus.

– And are you teaching them this by post?

– Well, yes.

– What's going to happen if one of them falls and gets killed?

– A verdict of death by misadventure, I suppose. But it's most unlikely because I don't think any of them will dare to get up on the wire any distance from the ground. If they're young their parents will stop them. If they're old, rheumatism, nerves and decayed muscles will make it impossible.

– Do you mean you're going to have a correspondence course with those people?

– No. They get a copy of my four-page book of instructions. Price sixpence only. It's for nothing. A packet of fags and a box of matches would cost you nearly that, and no fag would give you the thrill of thinking about the high wire.

– This looks to me like a swindle.

– Rubbish. I'm only a bookseller. The valuable instructions and explanations are given by Professor Latimer Dodds. And he has included warnings of the danger as well.

– Who is Professor Latimer Dodds?

– A retired trapeze and high wire artist.

– I never heard of him.

– Here, take a look at the course yourself. I'm posting off copies just now to my clients.

I took the crudely-printed folder he handed me and put it in my pocket, saying that I would look over it later and make sure that Mr Collopy didn't see it. I didn't want the brother to appraise my reactions to his handiwork, for already I had a desire to laugh. Downstairs, Mr Collopy was out and Annie was in the bedroom colloguing with Mrs Crotty. I lit the gas and there and then had a sort of free lesson on how to walk the high wire. The front page or cover read 'THE HIGH WIRE – Nature Held at Bay – Spine-chilling Spectacle Splenetizes Sporting Spectators – By Professor H. Q. Latimer Dodds'.

Lower down was the title of the Gymnasium and our own address. There was no mention of the brother by name but a note said 'Consultations with the Director by appointment only'. I was horrified to think of strangers calling and asking Mr

Collopy to be good enough to make an appointment for them with the Director of the Gymnasium.

The top of the left inside page had a Foreword which I think I may quote:

It were folly to asseverate that periastral peripatesis on the *aes ductile*, or wire, is destitute of profound peril not only to sundry *membra*, or limbs, but to the back and veriest life itself. Wherefore is the reader most graciously implored to abstain from *le risque majeur* by first submitting himself to the most perspicacious scrutiny by highly-qualified physician or surgeon for, in addition to anatomical verifications, evidence of Ménière's Disease, caused by haemorrhage into the equilibristic labyrinth of the ears, causing serious nystagmus and insecurity of gait. If giddiness is suspected to derive from gastric disorder, resort should be had to bromide of potassium, acetanilide, bromural or chloral. The aural labyrinth consists of a number of membranous chambers and tubes immersed in fluid residing in the cavity of the inner ear, in mammals joined to the cochlea. The membranous section of the labyrinth consists of two small bags, the saccule and the utricle, and three semi-circular canals which open into it. The nerves which supply the labyrinth end with a number of cells attired in hair-like projections which, when grouped, form the two otolith organs in the saccule and utricle and the three *cristae* of the semi-circular canals. In the otolith organs the hair-like protruberances are embedded in a gelatinous mess containing calcium carbonate. The purpose of this grandiose apparatus, so far as *homo sapiens* is concerned, is the achievement of remaining in an upright posture, one most desirable in the case of a performer on the high wire who is aloft and far from the ground.

I found that conscientiously reading that sort of material required considerable concentration. I do not know what it means and I have no doubt whatever that the brother's 'clients' will not know either.

The actual instructions as to wire-walking were straightforward enough. Perhaps it was the brother's own experience (for he was undoubtedly Professor Latimer Dodds) which made him advise a bedroom as the scene of opening practices. The wire was to be slung about a foot from the floor between two beds very heavily weighted 'with bags of cement, stone, metal safes or other ponderous objects'. When the neophyte wire-walker was ready to begin practice, the massive bedsteads were to be dragged apart by 'friends', so that the necessary tension of the wire would be established and maintained. 'If it happens that the weight on a bed turns out to be insufficient to support the weight of the performer on the wire, the friends should sit or lie on the bed.' Afterwards practice was transferred to 'the orchard' where two stout adjacent fruit trees were to be the anchors of the wire, the elevation of which was to be gradually increased. The necessity for daily practice was emphasized and (barring accidents) a good result was promised in three months. A certain dietetic regimen was prescribed, with total prohibition of alcohol and tobacco, and it was added that even if the student proved absolutely hopeless in all attempts at wire-walking, he would in any event feel immensely improved in health and spirits at the end of that three months.

I hastily put the treatise in my pocket as I heard the steps of Mr Collopy coming in the side-door. He hung his coat up on the back of the door and sat down at the range.

– A man didn't call about the sewers? he asked.

– The sewers? I don't think so.

– Ah well, please God he'll be here tomorrow. He's going to lay a new connection in the yard, never mind why. He is a decent man by the name of Corless, a great handball player in his day. Where's that brother of yours?

– Upstairs.

– Upstairs, faith! What is he doing upstairs? Is he in bed?

– No. I think he's writing.

– Writing? Well, well. Island of Saints and Scholars. Upstairs writing and burning the gas. Tell him to come down here if he wants to write.

Annie came out of the back room.

– Mrs Crotty would like to see you, Father.

– Oh, certainly.

I went upstairs to warn the brother. He nodded grimly and stuffed a great wad of stamped envelopes, ready for the post, under his coat. Then he put out the gas.

CHAPTER 7

MANY MONTHS had passed and the situation in our kitchen was as many a time before: myself and the brother were at the table weaving the web of scholarship while Mr Collopy and Father Fahrt were resting themselves at the range with the crock, tumblers and a jug of water between them.

The plumber Corless had long ago come and gone, ripping up the back yard and carrying out various mysterious works, not only there but in Mrs Crotty's bedroom. Sundry lengths of timber had been delivered for Mr Collopy himself and, since these things went on mostly while the brother and I were at school, we were told by Annie that the hammering and constructional bedlam to be heard from the sick woman's room were 'very sore on the nerves'. It was a point of apathy, or tact, or safety-first with the brother and myself to ask no questions as to what was afoot or evince any curiosity. 'They might only be making a coffin,' the brother said to me, 'and of course that's a very religious business. People can be very sensitive there. We are better minding our own business.'

On this evening Mr Collopy had given an incoherent little cry.

– A pipe, Collopy. Just a pipe.

– And when did this start?

– It is a fortnight now.

– Well...I see no objection if it suits you, though I think it's a bad habit and a dirty habit. Creates starch in the stomach, I believe.

– Like many a thing, Father Fahrt said urbanely, it is harmless in moderation. Please God I will not become an addict...

Here he peremptorily scratched himself about the back.

– Haven't I one cross to bear as it is? But the doctor I saw recently thought my mind was a bit inclined to wander, a very bad thing in our Order. Father Superior voiced the view that I was doing too much work, perhaps. I would not take a drug, so the doctor said tobacco in moderation was a valuable sedative.

He smokes himself of course. This pipe was a penance for the first week. But now it is good. Now I can think.

– I'll keep my eye on you and by dad I might follow suit myself starch and all. I needn't tell you I also have my worries . . . my confusions. My work is inclined to get out of hand.

– You will win, Collopy, for your persistence is heroic. The man whose aim is to smooth out the path of the human race cannot easily fail.

– Well, I hope that's true. Give me your glass.

Here new drinks were decanted with sacramental piety and precision.

– It's a queer thing, Father Fahrt mused, that men in my position have again and again to attack the same problem, solve it, and yet find that the solution is never any easier to reach. Next week I have to give a retreat at Kinnegad. After that, other retreats at Kilbeggan and Tullamore.

– Hah! Kilbeggan? That's where my little crock here came from, refilled a hundred times since. And emptied a hundred times too, by gob.

– I like to settle on a central theme for a retreat. Often it is not simple to think of a good one. No hell fire preaching by our men, of course.

Mr Collopy nodded, reflectively. When eventually he spoke there was impatience in his voice.

– You Jesuits, Father, are always searching for nice little out-of-the-way points, some theological rigmarole. Most of you fellows think you are Aquinas. For God's sake haven't you got the Ten Commandments? What we call the Decalogue?

– Ah, Saint Thomas! Yes, in his *Summa* he has many interesting things to say about the same Decalogue. So had Duns Scotus and Nicolaus de Lyra. Of course it is the true deposit.

– Mean to say, why don't the people of this country obey the Ten Commandments given in charge of Moses? 'Honour thy father and thy mother.' The young people of today think the daddy is a tramp and the mammy a poor skivvy. Isn't that right?

Here the brother coughed.

– Oh no, Father Fahrt said.

He also coughed here but I think the pipe was responsible.

– It is just that young people are a bit thoughtless. I would say you were as bad as the rest, Collopy, when you were a young fellow.

– Yes, Father. I could trust you to say that. I suppose you also think I coveted my neighbour's wife?

– No, Collopy, not while you were a young fellow.

– *What?* You mean when I grew up to man's estate –

– No, no, Collopy, it is my jest.

– Faith then and I don't think the Commandments are the right thing for God's anointed to be funny about. I never put my hand near a married woman and there are two of them on my committee, very valuable, earnest souls.

– What nonsense! I know that.

– You want to scarify the divils in the town of Kinnegad? There are pubs in that place. What about our other old friend 'Thou shalt not steal'?

– A much neglected ordinance.

– Well if the pishrogues of publicans there are anything like the Dublin ones, they are hill and dale robbers. They water the whiskey and then give you short measure. They give you a beef sandwich with no beef in it, only scraws hacked off last Sunday's roast by the mammy upstairs with her dirty hands. Some of those people don't wash themselves for weeks on end and that's a fact. Do you know why some of those ladies often miss Mass? They'd have to wash themselves. And darn their damned stockings.

– As usual I think you exaggerate, Collopy.

– And false witness, is it? There's people in this town that can't open their jaws without spilling out a flood of lies and slanders. To biting a nice ripe apple they would prefer back-biting any day.

– Yes, the tongue can be reckless.

– And adultery? The Lord save us! Don't talk to me about adultery.

– I know, Collopy, that you are devoted to women and their wants. But I am afraid that they are not *all* angels. Sometimes one meets the temptress. You mentioned biting a ripe apple. Do not forget the Garden of Eden.

– Baah! Adam was a damn fool, a looderamawn if you like. Afraid of nobody, not even the Almighty. A sort of poor man's Lucifer. Why didn't he tell that strap of a wife he had to go to hell?

– Excuse me, Father Fahrt.

That heart of mine, faultless registrar, gave a little jump of dismay. It was the brother, again interrupting his betters. They turned and stared at him, Mr Collopy frowning darkly.

– Yes, Manus?

– The wife of Adam in the Garden of Eden was Eve. She brought forth two sons, Cain and Abel. Cain killed Abel but afterwards in Eden he had a son named Henoch. Who was Cain's wife?

– Well, Father Fahrt said, there has been disputation on that point already.

– Even if Eve had a daughter not mentioned, she would be Cain's sister. If she hadn't, then Cain must have married his own mother. Either way it seems to be a bad case of incest.

– What sort of derogatory backchat is that you are giving out of you about the Holy Bible? Mr Collopy bellowed.

– I'm only asking, the brother said doggedly.

– Well, may God in his mercy help us. The father and the mother of a good thrashing is what *you* badly need.

– Now, now, Father Fahrt said smoothly, that question has been examined by the Fathers. What we nowadays know by the term incest was not sinful in the case of our first parents, since it was inevitable if the human race was to survive. We will discuss it another time, Manus, you and I.

– That's right, Father, Mr Collopy said loudly. Encourage him. Give your blessing to the badness that's in him. By damn but I'll have a word with Brother Cruppy in Westland Row. I'll tell him –

He broke off here and we all sat still. It came again, a faint cry from Mrs Crotty's room.

– *Is Father Fahrt there?*

Mr Collopy got up and hurried in, closing the door tight.

– Ah, please God there is nothing wrong, Father Fahrt said softly.

We sat in silence, looking at each other. After some minutes Mr Collopy reappeared.

– She would like to see you, Father, he said in a strange low voice.

– Of course, the priest said rising.

He gently went into where I knew only a candle served. Mr Collopy slumped back into his chair, preoccupied, quite unaware of ourselves at the table. Mechanically he sipped his drink, staring at the gleam of the fire through the bars of the range. The brother nudged me and rolled his eyes.

– Ah dear O, Mr Collopy murmured sadly.

He poured another drink into his glass, nor did he forget Father Fahrt.

– We know not the day . . . nor the hour. All things come to him who waits. It's the very divil.

Again he slumped into silence, and for what seemed a long, long time there was no sound at all except that of the alarm clock above the range, which we began to hear for the first time. In the end Father Fahrt came quietly from the room and sat down.

– I am very pleased, Collopy, he said.

Mr Collopy looked at him anxiously.

– Was it, he asked, was it . . . ?

– She is at peace. Her little harmless account is clear. Here we see God's grace working. She is at peace. She was smiling when I left her. The poor thing is very ill.

– You . . . did the needful?

– Surely. A sweet, spiritual safeguard is not another name for death. Often it means a miraculous recovery. I know of many cases.

The brother spoke.

– Should I go for Dr Blennerhassett?

– No, no, Mr Collopy said. He is due to call tonight anyway.

– Let us not be presumptuous, Collopy, Father Fahrt said gently. We do not know God's ways. She may be on her feet again in two weeks. We should pray.

But in four days Mrs Crotty was dead.

CHAPTER 8

ABOUT THE time of Mrs Crotty's death, the brother's 'business' had grown to a surprising size. He had got a box – fitly enough, a soap-box – from Davies the grocers, and went down to the hall every morning very early to collect the little avalanche of letters awaiting him there before they should come to the notice of Mr Collopy. Still using our home address, he had become, in addition to Professor Latimer Dodds, The Excelsior Turf Bureau operated, I suspect, on the old system of dividing clients into groups equal to the number of runners in a given race, and sending a different horse with any chance to each group. No matter which horse won, a group of clients would have backed it, and one of the brother's rules of business was that a winning client should send him the odds to five shillings. He was by now smoking openly in the house and several times I saw him coming out of or going into a public house, usually with a rather down-at-heel character. He had money to spend.

He also operated the Zenith School of Journalism, which claimed to be able to explain how to make a fortune with the pen in twelve 'clear, analytical, precise and unparagoned lessons'. As well he was trying to flood Britain with a treatise on cage-birds, published by the Simplex Nature Press, which also issued a Guide to Gardening, both works obviously composed of material looted from books in the National Library. He had put away his little press and now had printing done by an impoverished back-lane man with some small semblance of machinery. He once asked me to get stamps for him, giving me two pounds; this gives some idea of the volume of his correspondence.

He seemed in a bad temper the evening the remains of Mrs Crotty were brought to the church at Haddington Road; he did not come home afterwards but walked off without a word, possibly to visit a public house. Next morning dawned dark, forbidding and very wet, suitable enough, I thought, for a funeral. I thought of Wordsworth and his wretched 'Pathetic

Fallacy'. The brother, still in a bad temper, went down as usual to collect his mail.

– To hell with this house and this existence, he said when he came back. Now we will have to trail out to Deansgrange in this dirty downpour.

– Mrs Crotty wasn't the worst, I said. Surely you don't begrudge her a funeral? You'll need one yourself some day.

– She was all right, he conceded. It's her damned husband I'm getting very tired of ...

Mr Hanafin called with his cab for myself, the brother, Mr Collopy and Annie. The hearse and two other cabs were waiting at the church, the cabs accommodating mysterious other mourners who hurried to Mr Collopy and Annie with whispers and earnest handshakes. Myself and the brother were ignored. As the Mass was about to begin, a third cab arrived with three elderly ladies and a tall, emaciated gentleman in severe black. These, I gathered later, were members of the committee assisting Mr Collopy in his work, whatever that was.

The hearse elected to take the route along Merrion Road by the sea, where a sort of hurricane was in progress. The cabs following stumbled on the exposed terrain. Mr Collopy, showing some signs of genuine grief, spoke little.

– Poor Mrs Crotty was very fond of the sea, he said at last.

– Seemingly she was, Annie remarked. She told me once that when she was a girl, nothing could keep her out of the sea at Clontarf. She could swim and all.

– Yes, a most versatile woman, Mr Collopy said. And a saint.

A burial on a wet day, with the rain lashing down on the mourners, is a matter simply of squalor. The murmured Latin at the graveside seemed to make the weather worse. The brother, keeping well to the back of the assembly, was quietly cursing in an undertone. I was surprised and indeed a bit shocked to see him surreptitiously taking a flat half-pint bottle from his hip pocket and, with grimaces, swallowing deep draughts from it. Surely this was unseemly at the burial of the dead? I think Father Fahrt noticed it.

When all was over and the sodden turgid clay in on top of the deceased, we made for the gate. Mr Collopy was walking with a breathless stout man who had come on foot. When it was made known to us that this poor man had no conveyance, the brother gallantly offered his seat in the cab; this was gratefully accepted. The brother said he could borrow a bicycle near by but I was certain his plan was to borrow more than a bicycle, for there was a pub at Kill Avenue, which was also near by.

On the way home Mr Collopy was a bit more animated, no doubt relieved that a painful stage in the ordeal was over, and introduced us to the stranger as Mr Rafferty.

– I will not say, Rafferty, he said, that what-you-know was the sole reason for the woman's demise. Not the *sole* reason, mind you. But by Christ it had plenty to do with it.

– Don't you know it had, Mr Rafferty said. Can't you be bloody sure it had. Lord save us, you'd wonder is this a Christian country at all.

– It's a country of crawthumpers.

– I had an idea the other night, Mr Collopy. In two years there will be a Corporation election. I believe you own your own house and you would be eligible for membership. Why not go forward as a candidate? You could put down a motion at the City Hall and shame all that bastards. The Town Clerk could be ordered to instruct the City Engineer or Surveyor or whatever he is called to dot the town with what we need.

– I thought of that, Mr Collopy replied. But two years, you said? Only the Almighty knows how many unfortunate women would be brought to an early grave in that time. Ah, man alive, the worry and trouble of it all might even bring myself there.

– Now don't be letting silly thoughts like that come into your head. Ireland needs you and you know that.

Mr Rafferty, politely refusing an invitation to come all the way with us, was dropped off at Ballsbridge. When we reached the house, we took off our dripping coats, Mr Collopy poked up the fire in the range, quickly had the crock on view, and sank into his chair.

– Annie, he said, get me three glasses.

When these were produced, he poured three generous measures of whiskey into each and added a little water.

– On a morning like this, he said ceremoniously, and on a sad occasion like this, I think everyone here is entitled to a good stiff drink if we're not going to get our death of cold. I disapprove of anybody taking strong drink before the age of forty-five but in God's name let us take it as medicine. It is better than all those pills and drugs and falthalals those ruffians in the chemist shops will give you, first-class poison for the liver and kidneys.

We drank to that: for me it was my first taste of whiskey but I was surprised to find that Annie treated the occasion quite casually, as if she was used to liquor. I found it made me drowsy, and I decided to go to bed for a few hours. I did so and slept soundly. I got up about five and was not long back in the kitchen when the brother came in. Mr Collopy had evidently spent the entire interval with the crock and did not notice the brother much or the unseemly fact that he was drunk. There is no other word for it: drunk. He sat down heavily and looked at Mr Collopy.

– On a day like this, Mr Collopy, he said, I think I might have a drop of that tonic you have there.

– For once I think you are right, Mr Collopy replied, and if you will get another glass we will see what can be done.

The glass was got and generously furnished. I was offered nothing and the drinking went on in silence. Annie began to lay the table for tea.

– I don't think, Mr Collopy said at last, there there will be any need for you boys to go to school tomorrow and maybe the day after. Mourning, you know. The Brothers will understand.

The brother put his glass down on the range with a clinking thud.

– Is that so, Mr Collopy, he said in a testy voice. Well now is that so? Let me tell you this. I am not going back to that damned school tomorrow, the day after or any day.

Mr Collopy started up in astonishment.

– What was that? he asked.

– I've left school – from today. I've had my bellyful of the ignorant guff that is poured out by those maggots of Christian Brothers. They're illiterate farmers' sons. They probably got their learning at some dirty hedge school.

– Will you for pity's sake have some respect for the cloth of those saintly servants of God, Mr Collopy said sharply.

– They're not servants of God, they are slaves to their own sadistic passions, they are humbugs and impostors and a disgrace to their cloth. They are ruining the young people of this country and taking pride in their abominable handiwork.

– Have you no shame?

– I have more shame than those buggers have. Anyhow, I'm finished with school for good. I want to earn my living.

– Well now, is that so? Doing what? Driving a tram or a bread-cart, or maybe sweeping up after the horses on the roads?

– I said I wanted to earn my living. What am I talking about – I *am* earning my living. I am a publisher, an international tutor. Look at that!

Here he had rummaged in his inside pocket and pulled out a spectacular wad of notes.

– Look at that, he cried. There's about sixty-five pounds in that bundle and upstairs I have twenty-eight pounds in postal orders not yet cashed. You have your pension and no work to do, and no desire to do any.

– That will do you, Mr Collopy retorted with rising temper, that is quite enough. You say I have no work to do. Where you got that information I cannot say. But let me tell you this, you and your brother. I have been engaged on one of the most arduous and patriotic projects ever attempted by any man in this town. You will hear all about it when I'm gone. You have a damned cheek to say I do no work. What, with my health in the state it's in?

– Don't ask me that. I've left school and that's all.

The subject seemed to become inert and was dropped. It had been a tiring day, physically and emotionally, and both Mr Collopy and the brother were the worse for drink. Later, in bed, the brother asked me whether I intended to continue going to the Brothers in Synge Street.

– I might as well for the present, I replied, until I can find some job to fit into.

– Please yourself, he said, but I don't think this place is suitable for me. An Irish address is no damned use. The British dislike and distrust it. They think all the able and honest people live in London. I am giving that matter some thought.

CHAPTER 9

DURING THE year that followed Mrs Crotty's death, the atmosphere of the house changed somewhat. Annie joined some sort of a little club, probably composed mostly of women who met every afternoon to play cards or discuss household matters. She seemed to be – heavens! – coming out of her shell. Mr Collopy returned to his mysterious work with renewed determination, not infrequently having meetings of his committee in our kitchen after warning everybody that this deliberative chamber was out of bounds for that evening. From an upper window I occasionally saw the arrival of his counsellors. Two elderly ladies and the tall, gaunt man of the funeral came, also Mr Rafferty with a young lady who looked to me, in the distance at least, to be pretty.

The brother went from strength to strength and eventually reached the stage of prosperity that is marked by borrowing money for industrial expansion. From little bits of information and from inference, I understood that he had borrowed £400 short-term with interest at twenty per cent. A quick turn-over, no matter how small the profit, was the brother's business axiom. He happened to read of the discovery in an old English manor house of 1,500 two-volume sets of a survey in translation of Miguel de Cervantes Saavaedra, his work and times. The volumes are very elegant, bound in leather and handsomely illustrated; the first contained an account of the life of Cervantes, the second extracts from his major works. These volumes were printed and published in Paris in 1813, with a consignment apparently shipped to England, stored and forgotten. A London bookseller bought the lot for a small sum and to him the brother wrote offering 3s. 6d. cash per set for the whole consignment. At the time I thought the transaction foolhardy, for surely the London man could be presumed to have had a clear idea of the market. But once again the brother seemed to know what he was about. Using the name of the Simplex Nature Press, he put advertisements into English newspapers recklessly praising the work as to content and format, and also making the public an astonishingly generous offer, viz., any person buying Volume I for 6s. 6d. would also get Volume II for absolutely nothing. The offer, which was of limited duration, could not be repeated. No fewer than 2,500 acceptances reached him, quite a few from colleges, and he was many times later to adopt this system of enticement, offering something for nothing. The deal showed a clear profit of about £121. It also indirectly affected myself, for when wooden packing cases began to arrive full of those memorials of Cervantes, he politely suggested that I should take my bed and other gear to another room which was empty, as the original room was now his 'office' as well as his bedroom. I had no objection to this move, and agreed. Unfortunately the first four packing cases arrived when both myself and the brother were out, and Mr Collopy had to sign for them. I was the first to arrive home to find them piled in the kitchen. Mr Collopy was frowning from his chair.

– In God's name, he said loudly, what is that bucko up to?

– I don't know. I think there are books in those cases.

– *Books?* Well now! What sort of books is he peddling? Are they dirty books?

– Oh I don't think so. They might be Bibles.

– Faith and that would take me to the fair altogether. You heard what he said about the pious and godly Christian Brothers some months ago. Now by the jappers he is all for being a missionary to the niggers in Black Africa or maybe the Injuns. Well, there's no doubt about it, we rare up strange characters in this country. I don't think he knows anything about the Word of God. I'm not sure that he knows even his prayers.

– My mention of the Bible was only a guess, I protested.

Mr Collopy had risen and was at the press in search of his crock and glass. Fortified with them, he sat down again.

– We'll see what's in them all in good time, he announced sternly, and if those books are dirty books, lascivious peregrinations on the fringes of filthy indecency, cloacal spewings in the face of Providence, with pictures of prostitutes in their pelts, then out of this house they will go and their owner along with them. You can tell him that if you see him first. And I would get Father Fahrt to exorcise all fiendish contaminations in this kitchen and bless the whole establishment. Do you hear me?

    – Yes, I hear.

    – Where is he now?

    – I don't know. He is a very busy man. Perhaps he is at confession.

    – The what was that?

    – He might be seeing the clergy on some abstruse theological point.

    – Well, *I'll* abstruse *him* if he is up to any tricks because this is a God-fearing house.

I sat down to attack my loathsome homework with the idea of being free at eight o'clock so that I could meet a few of the lads for a game of cards. Mr Collopy sat down quietly sipping his whiskey and gazing at the glare of the fire.

It was about eleven when I got home that night, to find no trace of Mr Collopy nor the piled boxes. Next morning I learnt that Mr Collopy had gone to bed early and the brother, arriving home about ten, went out again to summon Mr Hanafin to assist him in getting the boxes up to his office. No doubt the reward was a handsome tip, though a soiled glass in the sink suggested that further recompense from the crock had been sought by either Mr Hanafin or the brother himself. I warned the latter, before I set off for school, of Mr Collopy's dire suspicions about the books and the threats to fire him out of the house. Was Cervantes an immoral writer?

    – No, the brother said grimly, but I won't be long here in any case. I think I know how to fix the oul divil. Have a look at these books.

They were thick octavo volumes of real beauty in an old-fashioned way, and there were many clear pictures of the wood-cut kind. If only as an adornment to bookshelves, they were surely good value for six and sixpence.

Later in the day the brother cunningly inscribed a dedication to Mr Collopy in each volume and ceremoniously presented them in the kitchen.

    – At first, he told me, he was mollified, then he was delighted and said I had very true taste. Cervantes, he said, was the Aubrey de Vere of Spain. His *Don Quixote* was an immortal masterpiece of the classics, clearly inspired by Almighty God. He told me not to fail to send a copy to Father Fahrt. I had to laugh. There's a *pair* of humbugs in it. Can you give me a hand to do some packing? I have bought a load of brown paper.

I had to, of course.

It was a peculiarity of the brother never to stop in his tracks or rest on his oars. In a matter of days he was back at work in his private mine, the National Library.

After some weeks he asked my opinion of three manuscripts he had compiled for issue as small books by the Simplex Nature Press. The first was the 'Odes and Epodes of Horace done into English Prose by Dr Calvin Knottersley, D.Litt. (Oxon)'; the second was 'Clinical Notes on Pott's Fracture, by Ernest George Maude, M.D., F.R.C.S.'; and the third was 'Swimming and Diving. A Manly and Noble Art, by Lew Paterson'. It was clear that these compositions were other people's work rehashed but I offered no comment other than a warning of the folly of making Dr Maude a Fellow of the Royal College of Surgeons. A register of such Fellows was in existence, and somebody was bound to check.

– How do you know there isn't a Fellow named Maude? the brother asked.

– So much the worse if there is, I answered.

But I noticed later that the doctor had lost that honour.

IT WAS A vile night as we sat in the kitchen, Mr Collopy and I. He was slumped at the range in his battered armchair, reading the paper. I was at the table, indolently toying with school exercises, sometimes pausing to reflect on the possibilities of getting a job. I was really sick of the waste of time known as study, a futile messing about with things which did not concern me, and I rather envied the brother's free, almost gay, life. I could sense his growing maturity and his determination to make money, a lot of it, as quickly as possible without undue worry as to the methods used. This night he was out, possibly conferring on some new deal in a public house. Annie was also out.

There was a knock and I admitted Father Fahrt. Mr Collopy greeted him without rising.

— Evening, Father. And isn't it a caution!

— Ah yes, Collopy, but we had a good summer, thank God. You and I don't go out much, anyway.

— I think we deserve a smahan, Father, to keep the winter out of us.

As Father Fahrt produced his pipe, now a treasured solace, Mr Collopy dragged himself up, went to the press and took down the crock, two glasses, and fetched a jug of water.

— Now, he said.

Drinks were poured and delicately savoured.

— I will tell you a funny one, Father, Mr Collopy said. A damn funny one. I will give you a laugh. We had a committee meeting last Wednesday. Mrs Flaherty was there. She told us all about her dear friend, Emmeline Pankhurst. Now there is a bold rossie for you if you like, but she's absolutely perfectly right. She'll yet do down that scoundrel, Lloyd George. I admire her.

— She has courage, Father Fahrt agreed.

— But wait till you hear. When we got down to our own business, discussing ways and means and ekcetera, out comes the bold Mrs Flaherty with *her* plan. Put a bomb under the City Hall!

– Lord save us!

– Blow all that bastards up. Slaughter them. Blast them limb from limb. If they refuse to do their duty to the ratepayers and to humanity. They do not deserve to live. If they were in ancient Rome they would be crucified.

– But Collopy, I thought you were averse to violence?

– That may be, Father. That may well be. But Mrs Flaherty isn't. She would do all those crooked corporators in in double quick time. What she calls for is *action*.

– Well, Collopy, I trust you explained the true attitude to her – your own attitude. Agitation, persistent exposure of the true facts, reprimand of the negligence of the Corporation, and the rousing of public opinion. Whatever Mrs Flaherty could do on those lines, now that she is at large, there is little she could do if she were locked up in prison.

– She wouldn't be the first in this country, Father, who went to prison for an ideal. It's a habit with some people here.

– For public agitation you must be in the middle of the public. They must see you.

– How would the Church look on Mrs Flaherty's scheme?

– I have no doubt it would merit strong condemnation and censure. Such a thing would be highly sinful. I think it could be classed as murder. It is not lawful to kill to ameliorate public misrule or negligence. Assassination is never justified. One must put one's trust in elections and the vote, not in shedding human blood.

– I fear, Father Fahrt, that that is the gospel of chicks and goslings. My forebears were brave, strong-arm fellows. And what about the early Christian martyrs. They thought nothing of shedding their own blood in defence of a principle. Give me your glass.

– There is no comparison, of course. Thanks.

– Now listen here, Father. Listen carefully. This is the first part of November. In the year 1605 in England, King James the First was persecuting the Catholics, throwing them into prison and plundering their property. It was diabolical, worse than in Elizabeth's time. The R.C.s were treated like dogs, and their priests like pigs. It would put you in mind of the Roman emperors, except that a thullabawn like Nero could at least boast that he was providing public entertainment. Well, what happened?

– James was a very despicable monarch, Father Fahrt said slowly.

– I will tell you what happened. A man named Robert Catesby thinks to himself that we've had as much of this sort of carry-on as we're going to take. And he thought of the same plan as Mrs Flaherty. He planned to blow up the parliament house and annihilate the whole bloody lot of the bosthoons, His Majesty included. I know the thanks you'd get if you told *him* to busy himself with elections and votes. He'd slap your face and give you a knee in the belly. Remember, remember the Fifth of November.

– They lived in another age, of course, Father Fahrt answered.

– Right and wrong don't change with the times and you know that very well, Father. Catesby got Guy Fawkes on his side, a brave man that was fighting in Flanders. And Grant and Keyes and the two Winters, and God's amount of sound men, Romans all. Fawkes was the kingpin and the head bottlewasher of the whole outfit. He managed to get a ton and a half of gunpowder stuffed into a cellar under the House of Lords. But there were two other men lending a good hand all the time and saying God bless the work. I mean Greenway and Garnet. Know who *they* were, Father?

– I think I do.

– Of course you do. They were *Jesuits*. Hah?

– My dear man, Jesuits also can make mistakes. They can err in judgement. They are human.

– Faith then they didn't err in judgement when Guy Fawkes was found out. They scooted like greased lightning and Father Greenway and another priest managed to get to a healthier country. Father Garnet was not so alive to himself. He got caught and for his pains he got a length of hempen rope for himself on the gallows high.

– A martyr for the Faith, of course, Father Fahrt said evenly.

– And Fawkes. They gave him tortures you wouldn't see outside hell itself to make him give the names of the others. Be damn but he wouldn't. But when he heard that Catesby and a crowd of his segocias had been chased, caught and killed, he broke down and made some class of a confession. But do you know what? When this rigmarole was put before him for signa-ture, believe it or not but he couldn't sign it. The torture had him banjaxed altogether. His hands were all broken be the thumbscrews. What's your opinion of that?

– The torture Fawkes so heroically endured, Father Fahrt said, was admittedly appalling and terrifying, the worst torture that the head of man could think of. It was called *per gradus ad ima*. He was subjected to it by direct order of the King. He was very brave.

– I needn't tell you he and several others got the high jump. But Lord save us, poor Fawkes couldn't climb up the ladder to the gallows, he was so badly bet and broken up in the torture. He had to be carried up. And he was hanged outside the building he tried to blow up for the greater glory of God.

– I suppose that's true enough, Father Fahrt said meekly.

– For the greater glory of God. How's this you put Latin on that?

– *Ad majorem Dei gloriam.* It is our own Society's watchword.

– Quite right. *A.M.D.G.* Many a time I've heard it. But if blowing up councillors is bad and sinful as you said, how do you account for two Jesuits, maybe three, being guilty of that particular transaction, waging war on the civil power? Isn't Mrs Flaherty in the same boat as Mr Fawkes?

– I have pointed out, Collopy, that events and opinions vary drastically from one era to another. People are influenced by quite different things in dissimilar ages. It is difficult, even impossible, for the people of today to assess the stresses and atmosphere of Fawkes's day. Cicero was a wise and honest man and yet he kept slaves. The Greeks were the most sophisticated and civilized people of antiquity, but morally a great many of them were lepers. With them sins of the flesh was a nefarious preoccupation. But that does not invalidate the wisdom and beauty of the things many of them left behind them. Art, poetry, literature, architecture, philosophy and political systems, these were formulated and developed in the midst of debauchery. I have – ah-ha – sometimes thought that a degraded social climate is essential to inspire great men to achievement in the arts.

Mr Collopy put down his glass and spoke somewhat sternly, wagging a finger.

– Now look at here, Father Fahrt, he said, I'm going to say something I've said in other ways before. Bedamn but I don't know that I can trust you men at all. Ye are for ever trimming and adjudicating yourselves to the new winds that do blow. In case of doubt, send for a Jesuit. For your one doubt he will give you twenty new ones and his talk is always full of 'ifs' and 'buts', rawmaish and pseudo-theology. The word I have heard used for that sort of thing is *casuistry*. Isn't that right? Casuistry.

– There is such a word but it's not true in this case.

– Oh now you can always trust a Jesuit to make mischief and complicate simple things.

– That word Jesuit. Our founder Ignatius was a Spaniard and had a different name for the Order, but it was called Societas Jesu by command of the Holy Father Paul III. Originally the title Jesuit was one of hatred and contempt. What was intended as an insult we accepted as a compliment.

– I suppose that's what I mean – you are for ever double-thinking and double-talking. You slither everywhere like quicksilver. There's no pinning a Jesuit down. Then we're told it is a mendicant order. Sure there isn't a better-got collection of men on the face of the earth, churches and palaces all over the world. I know a thing or two. I've read books. I'll tell you something about 35 Lower Leeson Street, the poor cave you hid in yourself.

– What?

– The emaciated friars in that place have red wine with their dinners. That's more than Saint Peter himself had. But Saint Peter got himself into a sort of a diversion with a cock. The holy fathers below in Clongowes Wood know all about cocks, too. They have them roasted and they eat them at dinner. And they are great men for scoffing claret.

– Such talk is most unworthy. We eat and drink according to our means. The suggestion that we are, well . . . sybarites and gluttons is nonsense. And offensive nonsense, Collopy. I do not like such talk.

– Well, is that so? Mr Collopy said testily. Is criticizing the Jesuits a new sin? Would you give somebody five rosaries in the confessional for that? Faith then, if criticizing the Jesuits is a fall from grace, let us say a Hail Mary for the repose of the soul of Pope Paul IV, for he told Ignatius Loyola that there were a lot of things wrong with the Order that would have to be put right. Did you know that? And did Ignatius bend the knee in front of the Holy Father? Not on your life. Give me your damn glass.

– Thanks. I do not say that Ignatius was without fault. Neither was Peter. But Ignatius was canonized in 1622 by Pope Gregory XV, only sixty-six years after his death. He is now in Paradise.

– You know he died without the last rites?

– I do. He was called suddenly. He was weak of body but his labours in this world were prodigious, and nobody can take from him credit for the great deed of founding the Order, which is now and ever has been the intellectual vanguard of the Catholic Church.

– I wouldn't say the story is quite so simple as that, Father Fahrt. By Dad, the same Order caused a lot of bad bloody ructions at one time.

– The Fathers are all over the world, they speak and write in all languages, they have built a wonderful apparatus for the propagation of the faith.

– Some people at one time thought they were trying to banjax and bewilder the One, Holy and Apostolic. Oh and there are good people who are alive today and think the Church had a very narrow escape from the boyos of yesteryear.

– I know it is useless asking who those important people are.

– In the days of my youth I met a Jesuit in Belfast and he said the Jesuits were the cause of the Franco-Prussian War and the Boer War, for ever meddling in politics, and keeping a sharp eye out for Number One – money.

– Do you tell me so? A Jesuit?

– Yes, a Jesuit. He was a married man, of course.

– Some dreadful apostate, you mean?

– He was a most religious man, and told me he hoped his daughter would become a nun.

– You must have been talking to the ghost of Martin Luther.

– I think the Jesuits are jealous of Luther. He also tried to destroy the Catholic Church. I often think he made a better attempt than you people did.

– Dear me, Collopy, you are very irresponsible. If you talked like that among strangers, you would be in grave danger of giving scandal, of leading others on to sin. You should be more circumspect.

– I am as fond of my altar and my home, Father Fahrt, as the next. But I revere truth. I *love* truth.

– Well, that is good news.

– I think you are fond of truth, too, provided it is the truth you like, the truth that suits your book.

– Nonsense. Truth is truth.

– There is a phrase in Irish – I'm sorry that through no fault of mine I am largely unacquainted with the old tongue. But the phrase says this: 'The truth does be bitter.' I think you know how right that is.

– *Magna est veritas et prevalebit.*

– You never said a truer word, Father.

– Aren't we the stupid and presumptuous pair to be talking in this loose way about the Order of men such as Ignatius and Francis Xavier?

– Hold on a moment now.

– Xavier was the evangelist of Japan. Jesuit evangelists preached the Gospel, often in face of persecution and martyrdom, to the Indians of North America, to the natives of the Philippines and the countries of South America, even to the English when the Catholic Church was proscribed there. They went everywhere. Nothing stopped them.

– Hold on a moment now, Father. Whisht now for a minute and listen to me. It is true that the Jesuits were everywhere and had a finger in every pie. They were cute hawks. They were far too powerful, not only in the Church itself but in the world. They made all sorts of kings and queens and captains take to themselves a Jesuit chaplain. Can you imagine Parnell with a Jesuit chaplain?

– Parnell was not a Catholic, and I don't believe he was a real Irishman. It is an English name.

– Those devout priests infested the courts of Europe and had the same courts in their pockets. They were sacerdotal politicians and that's what they were. Those ignorant and drunken princes and emperors were no match for them. Sure they'd excommunicate you as soon as they'd look at you.

– Nonsense. A priest has no power of excommunication.

– Maybe so. But hadn't they the bishop in their pockets as well. The bishop had to do as they ordered him.

– You're annoying me, Collopy. Here, play with this glass.

– Certainly. But there were two very great men in France, Pascal and Voltaire. That pair had no time for the Jesuits at all, and neither had the Jansenist crowd. Am I right?

– Yes, reasonably so.

– The Jesuits had rows with the Sorbonne, with the Franciscans and the Dominicans on questions of doctrine. A lot of pious and intelligent men thought the Jesuits were heretics or schismatics. Faith now and there was no smoke without fire – hellfire, maybe. Onwards from 1760 or so, they were given their marching orders in Portugal, France and parts of Italy itself. Messengers and runners and wrenboys were dispatched wholesale by several states in Europe to Rome to try to bully the Pope into suppressing the Order. And fair enough, they weren't wasting their time. The Pope of that fine day was Clemens XIV. Lo and behold, in 1773 he issued a Bull suppressing the Order because it could no longer carry out the work for which it was founded.

– Yes, Father Fahrt said, *Dominus ac Redemptor Noster.*

– Excuse me, I said.

It was brazenly cheeky on my part to try to emulate the brother as interlocutor. But my labours at school on Schuster's Church History were not to be denied.

– Yes? Mr Collopy said rather grumpily.

– *Dominus ac Redemptor Noster* was not a Bull. It was a Brief. There is a difference.

– The boy is perfectly right, Father Fahrt said.

Mr Collopy did not like the pedantic intrusion.

– Call the thing what you like, he said crankily, the fact remains that the Holy Father suppressed the Society. That was a matter of faith and morals and in doing that the Pope was infallible.

– Collopy, Father Fahrt said sharply, that merely proves again that you do not know what you are talking about. It was not till 1870, when Pius IX was pontiff, that the Vatican Council proclaimed the dogma of papal infallibility. You are almost one hundred years out. Furthermore, the suppression of a religious order has nothing to do with faith and morals in the universal church.

– You are being technical as usual, Father, Mr Collopy said in a bantering tone. Hand over your glass like a good man.

– Thanks. Not much now.

– One of the bitterest objections to the machinations of the Jesuits was this. Some of the priests mixed up their missionary work with trading and money-making and speculation. A French Jesuit named Father La Valette was up to his ears in buying and selling. Mendicant order my foot.

— These were isolated cases.

— They were not. The Order was some class of an East India Company. It was heavenly imperialism but with plenty of money in the bank.

— Well, well. Speaking for myself I have nothing at all in the bank but I have my tramfare in my pocket, thank God.

— And where do you get that tobacco you are smoking?

— From the Society's vast plantations in Panama, Father Fahrt said heavily. That suppression was a very serious blow and was the result of secret scheming by our agnostic enemies. Our missions in India, China and throughout Latin America collapsed. It was a victory for the Jansenists. It was a very sad episode.

— Fair enough, Mr Collopy replied, but th'oul Jesuits weren't bet yet. Trust them! They soon started their counter-scheming. Oh trust Wily Willie, S.J.!

— It was their duty before God to try to salvage the Order. In Belgium some ex-Jesuits formed a new society named the 'Fathers of the Faith'. Catherine of Russia would not allow that Brief to take effect, and the Jesuits tried to carry on in that country. After a time the two communities merged. You can take it, Collopy, that my Order was on the way back from then.

— By damn but you are not telling me anything I don't know, Mr Collopy said warmly. You couldn't keep that crowd down. Too cute.

— Is that what you think? Very good. This is a fresh drink. I am going to drink to the health, spiritual and physical, of my Society.

— I'll drink with you, Mr Collopy said, but with mental reservations.

They had the toast between them in a preoccupied way.

— And let us devoutly remember, Father Fahrt said after a long pause, the great Bull *Sollicitudo Omnium Ecclesiarum*, promulgated on August the 7th, 1814, by Pope Pius VII after he returned from France. You know what that meant, Collopy?

— Well, I suppose your crowd got your way as usual.

— That Bull restored the Society throughout the whole world. And we were welcomed back in the countries which before had driven us out. Ah, the ways of the Almighty are surely a mystery.

– So are the ways of the Jesuits, Mr Collopy said. Did any money change hands? Or was he one of the Popes who made a fortune selling scapulars and indulgences?

– Collopy, I think I have misjudged you. You are not serious. You are merely trying to annoy me. You don't believe in what you say at all. As they say in Ireland, you are only trying to gig me. You ought to be ashamed of yourself. At the back of it all, you are a pious Godfearing man, may the Lord be good to you.

– I never make jokes about religious matters, Mr Collopy said solemnly. If you want to praise me or compliment me, just give a thought to the important work I have been devoting my life to. The work that will not stop until this old heart stops.

– Well, what we have been discussing is a sort of a headline for you. Cherish in your heart a recollection of the tenacity of the Jesuit Fathers. If your aim is praise-worthy, you will achieve it by undeviating faith in it and by never ceasing to invoke the blessing of God on it. Don't you agree?

– What else have I been doing for years? By the jappers, it's a slow achievement I'm making of it. The divil himself is in the hearts of that Corporation ownshucks.

– They are just thoughtless, misguided.

– They are just a gang of ignorant, pot-bellied, sacrilegious, money-scooping robbers, very likely runners from the bogs, hop-off-my-thumbs from God-forsaken places like Carlow or the County Leitrim. The sons of pig-dealers and tinkers. In heaven's name what would people the like of that know about the duties of a city councillor? I wouldn't say they had a boot on their foot till they were eighteen.

– But shouldn't their clerks advise them? Surely *they're* Dublin men?

– That gurriers wouldn't think of advising a man to take off his clothes before he took a bath. Are you fooling me, Father?

– Indeed and I'm not.

Heavy steps were heard on the gravel outside and the handle of the door was turned.

It was the brother. One glance was enough for me. His face was flushed and he lurched slightly. In his hand was a small cigar, a bit the worse for the heavy rain outside.

– Good evening all, he said pleasantly enough. Good evening, Father Fahrt.

He sat down in the centre and spread his wet legs towards the range.

– I see we have got to cigars, Mr Collopy said.

His mood was genial enough, thanks to the crock and his sword-play with Father Fahrt.

– Yes, we *have* got to cigars, the brother replied jauntily, just as Father Fahrt has progressed to the pipe. Degeneracy is contagious.

– And what important mission were we on tonight? Mr Collopy asked.

– Well, since you ask me, it *was* important. Important for this house, and indeed this city, too. I have very bad news for you, Mr Collopy. For all, in fact. This day week –

– What rodomondario is this you are giving us?

– This day week, I am leaving you. I am going to London to make my fortune.

– Well now! Is that a fact? Well the dear knows.

– London, my lad? Father Fahrt said. Well, well. It's a great place and there is opportunity there, but the English look for hard work. From the Irish, anyhow. I must give you a letter to some of our men over there. You have heard of Farm Street? But sometimes work is not so easy to get. You are not thinking of the coalmining, are you?

Here the brother laughed, as if in genuine amusement.

– No, Father, he said, unless you mean buying a mine and putting enormous royalties into the bank.

– Well, what are you going to do? Mr Collopy asked sharply.

– Well, what I've done so far is to take the lease of two rooms or offices in Tooley Street.

– And in God's name where is that?

– It is fairly central and very near the Thames. And there are several railway stations within easy distance. I mean, suppose the police were after me?

– The what? *The police?*

Mr Collopy was not sure he had heard aright. The brother laughed again.

– Yes, the police. They'd hardly think of watching *all* the stations. Even if they did, there is a very good chance that I could escape by water. After I get settled down, I will have my private barge moored in the river. They will never suspect a move like that. We important men must think of everything.

– I think you are going off your head and it's not the first time I thought that. What about money for your passage and your lodgings beyond? If you expect me –

– Mr Collopy, you mustn't embarrass me with such talk.

– So far as I remember, Father Fahrt interposed, our people still run a shelter. Lay brothers are in charge and I believe the cost per night is next to nothing. I could give you a letter, of course.

– Have you got money? Mr Collopy demanded.

– I have, or I will have during the week.

– Is it honest money? If there is any damned nonsense about swindling anybody or robbing shops or besting unfortunate simple people, I can tell you plump and plain that you will not have to go as far as London to make contact with the police. I would not think twice of calling them in myself for if there is one thing that is abominable it is dishonesty. It is one of the worst inventions of Satan. I don't want any curse brought on this house. You have heard of Mayor Lynch of Galway? Mark that. Mark that well.

– You are uncharitable, Collopy, Father Fahrt said. Why assume bad things? Why meet the devil halfway?

– I live in this house, Mr Collopy said irritably, and I have experience.

– For all we know, this enterprising young man may yet bring great honour to this house.

– Yes indeed.

Mr Collopy's tone had taken on a bitter edge.

– I myself may also bring great honour to this house by achieving the great aim of my life. Then they'll put a plaque on the wall outside and you will have women from all over the world coming on pilgrimages to see my humble house. By that time, of course, I'll be above in Deans's Grange having a good rest for myself.

The brother yawned artificially.

– Gentlemen, he said, I'm tired and I want to get a night's sleep. We can talk more about my plans tomorrow.

He rose and stumbled out towards the stairs. We who remained looked at each other, mutely.

WHEN I GOT to bed later the brother was asleep, no doubt in the anaesthesia of whiskey. In the morning I asked him whether he was serious about the project in Tooley Street.

– Course I'm serious, he answered.

– And what are you going to do there?

– I am going to open the London University Academy. I'll teach *everything* by correspondence, solve all problems, answer all questions. I might start a magazine first, and then a newspaper, but first I'll have to build up slowly. I'll teach the British how to learn French or cure chilblains. I'll be a limited company, of course. Already I have a solicitor working on the papers. My branch office will be the British Museum. If you like, I'll give you a job later on.

I suppose that was generous but for some reason the offer did not immediately attract me. Dryly I said:

– I'd want to get to know those railway stations you mentioned last night in case I had to skip. In a hurry.

– Don't talk rubbish. My operations are always within the law. But the British won't be nervous because if the bobbies were after me and managed to close the roads and railways and the river, haven't they the Tower of London to stuff me into? It's just across the river from Tooley Street.

– Well, many a good Irishman spent a time there.

– True.

– And lost his life.

– Well, I'll prepare and circulate a series entitled How to Escape from the Tower of London. Three guineas for the complete course, with daggers, revolvers and rope-ladders supplied to students at very little over cost.

– Aw, shut up, I said.

When I got back from Synge Street that evening, everybody was out but a note from Annie said that my dinner was in the oven. Immediately afterwards I attacked my damned homework, for I had planned to spend the evening at a small poker school in the home of my school friend, Jack Mulloy. Did card games attract me much? I don't know but Jack's sister, Penelope, who served mugs of tea and bits of cake at 'half-time', certainly did. She was what was known as a good hoult, with auburn hair, blue eyes and a very nice smile. And to be honest, I think she was fond of myself. I remember being puzzled to think that she and Annie belonged to the same sex. Annie was a horrible, limp, lank streel of a creature. But she had a good heart and worked hard. Mr Collopy was fussy about his meals and though he dressed rather like an upper-class tramp, he had a horror of laundries and mass-washing. To participate in that, he held, was a certain way to get syphilis and painful skin diseases. Annie had to wash his shirts and other things, though he personally looked after his celluloid collar, which he washed with hot water every second day. She also had to compound various medicines for him, all of which contained sulphur, though I never heard what afflictions those potions were intended to remedy or prevent. In the last eighteen months or so, she was asked to undertake another duty to which she agreed willingly enough. The brother had given up the early-rising of his schooldays but would often hand Annie some money for 'what-you-know' from his bedside. He was in need of a cure, and the poor girl would slip out and bring him back a glass of whiskey.

Mr Collopy came in about five o'clock, followed shortly afterwards by Annie. He seemed in a bad temper. Without a word he collapsed into his armchair and began reading the paper. The brother came in about six, loaded with books and small parcels. He naturally perceived the chill and said nothing. The tea turned out to be a very silent, almost menacing, meal. I kept thinking of Penelope. Tea with *her* would be a very different affair, an ambrosial banquet of unheard-of delicacy, and afterwards sweet colloquy by the fire, though perhaps with an undertone of melancholy. Was it easy, I wondered, or was it quite impossible to write really good and touching poetry. Something to reach the heart, to tell of love? Very likely it was quite impossible for the like of myself to attempt anything of the kind, though the brother could be trusted to explain the art and simplify it in six easy lessons by correspondence. Of course I never raised the

matter with him, for he would only make me angry. Penelope?
I meditated on the name. I remembered that Penelope was the
wife of Ulysses and no matter how many libertines assailed her
while her good man was away at the wars, she was ever faithful
to him. She would consider yielding to their low and improper
solicitations, she said, as soon as she had her knitting finished.
Every night she would unravel whatever bit of it she had done
during the day, so that the task was never accomplished. Just what
was that as an attitude? Deep and pure love, of course. With
more than a little touch of cunning, perhaps. Did my own lovely
Penelope have both those qualities. Well, I would see her later
on that night.

When the tea things had been cleared away, Mr Collopy
resumed reading his paper but after a time, he suddenly sat up
and glared at the brother, who was dozing opposite him at the
range.

— I want a word with you, mister-me-friend, he said abruptly.
The brother sat up.

— Well? he said. I'm here.

— Do you know a certain party by the name of Sergeant
Driscoll of the D.M.P.?

— I don't know any policemen. I keep far away from them.
They're a dangerous gang, promoted at a speed that is proportionate to the number of people they manage to get into trouble.
And they have one way of getting the most respectable people
into very bad trouble.

— Well, is that a fact? And what is the one way?

— Perjury. They'd swear a hole in an iron bucket. They are all
the sons of gobhawks from down the country.

— I mentioned Sergeant Driscoll of the D.M.P. —

— The wilds of Kerry, I'll go bail. The banatee up at six in the
morning to get ready thirteen breakfasts out of a load of spuds,
maybe a few leaves of kale, injun meal, salt and buttermilk.
Breakfast for Herself, Himself, the eight babies and the three
pigs, all out of the one pot. That's the sort of cods we have looking after law and order in Dublin.

— I mentioned Sergeant Driscoll of the D.M.P. He was here
this morning. God help me, being interviewed by the police has
been *my* cross, and at my time of life.

— Well, it is a good rule never to make any statement. Don't give him the satisfaction. Say that you first must see your solicitor, no matter what he is accusing you of.

– Accusing *me* of? It had nothing to do with me. It was *you* he was looking for. He was making inquiries. There may yet be deleterious ructions, you can take my word for that.

– What, *me*? And what have *I* done?

– A young lad fell into the river at Islandbridge, hurt his head and was nearly drowned. He had to be brought to hospital. Sergeant Driscoll and his men questioned this lad and the other young hooligans with him. And *your* name was mentioned.

– I know nothing about any young lads at Islandbridge.

– Then how did they get your name? They even knew this address, and the Sergeant said they had a little book with this address here on the cover.

– Did you see the book?

– No.

– This is the work of some pultogue that doesn't like me, one that has it in for me over some imaginary grievance. A trouble-maker. This town is full of them. I'm damn glad I'm clearing out. Give me a blood-thirsty and depraved Saxon any day.

– I've never known you not to have an answer. You are the right stainless man.

– I refuse to be worried about what brats from the slums say or think, or at country rozzers either.

– Those youngsters, Sergeant Driscoll said, were experiment-ing with a frightfully dangerous contraption, a sort of death machine. They had fixed a wire across the Liffey, made fast to lamp-posts or trees on either side. And this young bosthoon gets his feet into a pair of special slippers or something of the kind. What do you think of that?

– Nothing much, except it reminds me of a circus.

– Yes, or The Dance of Death at the Empire Theatre at Christmas. Lord look down on us but I never heard of such recklessness and sinful extravaganza. It is the parents I pity, the suffering parents that brought them up by wearing their fingers to the bone and going without nourishing food in their old age to give the young poguemahones an education. A touch of the strap, night and morning, is what those boyos badly need.

– And how did one of them get into the water?

– How do you think? He gets out walking on this wire until

he's half-way, then he flies into a panic, gets dizzy, falls down
into the deep water, hitting his head off a floating baulk of timber.
And of course not one of those thooleramawns could swim. It
was the mercy of God that a bailiff was within earshot. He heard
the screaming and the commotion and hurried up. But an un-
employed man was there first. Between the pair of them they
got this half-drowned young character out of the river and held
him upside-down to drain the water out of him.

   — And the pinkeens, the brother interposed.

   — It was a direct act of Providence that those men were there.
The high-wire genius had to be lurried into hospital, Jervis
Street, and there is no need to try to be funny about it. You could
be facing murther today, or manslaughter.

   — I've told you I had nothing to do with it. I know nothing.
I am unaware of the facts.

   — I suppose you'd swear that.

   — I would.

   — And you have the brazen cheek to sit there and accuse the
long-suffering D.M.P. of being addicted to perjury.

   — And so they are.

   — Faith then, and if I was on the jury I would know who to
believe about that Islandbridge affair.

   — If I was charged with engineering that foolish prank, I
would stop at nothing to unmask the low miscreant who has
been trying to put stains on my character.

   — Yes, I know right well what you mean. One lie would lead
to another till you got so bogged down in mendacity and appalling perjury that the Master of the Rolls or the Recorder or
whoever it would be would call a halt to the proceedings and
send the papers to the Attorney-General. And faith then your
fat would be in the fire. You could get five years for perjury and
trying to pervert the course of justice. And the same Islandbridge
case would be waiting for you when you came out.

   — I don't give a goddam about any of those people.

   — Do you tell me? Well, *I* do. This is my house.

   — You know I'm leaving it very soon.

   — And Sergeant Driscoll said you were to call at College Street
for an interview.

   — I'll call at no College Street. Sergeant Driscoll can go to hell.

   — Stop using bad, depraved language in this house or you may leave it sooner than you think. You are very much mistaken if you think I am content to be hounded and pestered by policemen over your low and contemptible schemes to delude simple young people –

– Oh, rubbish!

– And rob them, rob them of money they never earned but filched from the purses of their long-suffering parents and guardians.

– I told you I don't know any simple young people at Island-bridge. And any young people I do know, they're not simple.

– You have one of the lowest and most lying tongues in all Ireland and that's a sure fact. You are nothing but a despicable young tramp. May God forgive me if I have been in any way to blame for the way I brought you up.

– Why don't you blame those crows, the holy Christian Brothers? God's Disjointed.

– I have warned you several times to stop desecrating my kitchen with your cowardly blackguarding of a dedicated band of high-minded Christian teachers.

– I hear Brother Cruppy is going to throw off the collar and get married.

– Upon my word, Mr Collopy said shrilly, you are not too old to have a stick taken to. Remember that. A good thrashing would work wonders.

He was clearly very angry. The brother shrugged and said nothing but it was lucky just then that there was a knock at the outer door. It was Mr Rafferty, who at first demurred at my invitation to come in.

– I was only passing, he said. I just wanted to see Mr Collopy for a moment or two.

But he did come in. I was happy to see that the hostilities within had suddenly subsided. Mr Collopy offered his hand without rising.

– Take a chair, Rafferty, take a chair. It's a bit hash this evening.

– Yes indeed, Mr Collopy. Very hash.

– Will you join me in a smahan?

– Now, Mr Collopy, you should know me by now. Weekends only. It's a rule and a cast-iron one. I promised the missus.

– All right, keep the promise. To thine old self be true. Thine

own self, I mean. I'll treat myself in God's name because I am
not feeling too good in my health. Not too good at all.

He rose to go to the press.

— You know what I called for, of course?

— Indeed and I do. And I have it here.

Having arranged a glass with the crock on the range, he pulled
from the back of the press a long brown paper parcel, which he
laid carefully on the table. Then he poured out his drink and sat
down.

— The name they have for it, Rafferty, is worth remembering.

He turned to my surprise to myself.

— You there, he said. What's the Greek for water?

— *Hydor*, I said. High door.

— And measuring anything, how did the Greeks get at that?

— *Metron*. Met her on. A measure.

— There now Rafferty, didn't I tell you, what? That articles
on the table is a clinical hydrometer. As we agreed, you are to
bring it to Mrs Flaherty. Tell her to take careful readings day and
night for a fortnight from next Saturday at noon. And keep the
most meticulous records.

— Oh, I understand how important that is, Mr Collopy. And
I'll make Mrs Flaherty understand.

— In these modern times, you are damn nothing unless you
can produce statistics. Columns and columns of figures, readings
and percentages. Suppose they set up a Royal Commission on
this thing. Where would we be if we couldn't produce our
certified statistics? What would we look like in the witness chair?

— We would not be very impressive and that's a sure thing,
Rafferty said.

— We'd look like bloody gawms. We'd make a holy show of
ourselves before the world and people would ask each other who
let us out. Isn't that right?

— Too right indeed.

— And when Mrs Flaherty has given us her readings, we will
give the next fortnight to Mrs Clohessy.

— Very good idea, Mr Collopy.

— And I predict one thing. When we have got all the readings
and compared them, bedamn but you'll find very little difference
in them, only slight variations. We might establish a great new
scientific fact. Who knows?

– Do you tell me that, Mr Collopy?

– I do, and that is the way the history of the whole world has been changed in the past. Patient men are looking for a particular thing, the answer to a profound difficulty. And what by the jappers happens? By accident they solve an entirely different problem. And I don't care how many problems are solved with the aid of the clinical hydrometer so long as what we ourselves are so worried about is put right.

– Hear, hear, Mr Collopy. I'll go off now, and straight to Mrs Flaherty's.

– And God be with you, Rafferty. See you at our usual committee on Friday night.

– Right. Good night.

Just after he left, I went out myself. For I had a tryst with the Sors: and with Penelope.

CHAPTER 12

THE OLD KITCHEN seemed the same but the brother had gone, and with him those stormy little scenes with Mr Collopy. I am sorry I cannot present an interesting record of the events and words of his actual departure. He had stressed with Annie the great importance of an early knock so as to make sure he would catch the morning mail boat from Kingstown to Holyhead. Annie did her duty but she found nobody in the brother's bed nor any sign of his packed belongings. He had stolen away some time in the night, perhaps finishing his last Irish sleep in somebody else's house or, perhaps again, marking his departure with a valedictory carousal with his cronies. I felt offended that I should have been included in his boycott for I felt I had something of the status of a fellow-conspirator, apart from being his brother, but his mysterious exit infuriated Mr Collopy. I never knew quite why, but I suspected that he had planned a magnanimous farewell, a prayer of God Speed and perhaps the present of one of his prize cut-throat razors. Mr Collopy was ever fond of an occasion, and with encouragement, alike from the company and his crock, he could attain great heights of eloquence. The showman in him had been slighted and he was very offended. He casually asked me whether the brother could be expected back on a visit for Christmas but I truthfully replied at the time that I had no idea. Annie seemed to take no notice whatsoever of this change in our house, even though it meant less work for her.

About three weeks after the brother's flight, I received a letter from him. It was in a costly long envelope, in the top left-hand corner of which were intertwined the letters L.U.A. (I was amused afterwards to notice in an Irish dictionary that *lua* means 'a kick'.) The notepaper inside was very thick and expensive, indeed it was noisy to unfold. The heading, in black, shining crusted letters was LONDON UNIVERSITY ACADEMY, 120 Tooley Street, London, S.W.2. Down along the left margin was a list of

the matters in which the Academy offered tuition – Boxing,
Foreign Languages, Botany, Poultry Farming, Journalism, Fret-
work, Archaeology, Swimming, Elocution, Dietetics, Treatment
of High Blood Pressure, Ju–Jutsu, Political Science, Hypnotism,
Astronomy, Medicine in the Home, Woodwork, Acrobatics and
Wire-Walking, Public Speaking, Music, Care of the Teeth,
Egyptology, Slimming, Psychiatry, Oil Prospecting, Railway
Engineering, A Cure for Cancer, Treatment of Baldness, La
Grande Cuisine, Bridge and Card Games, Field Athletics, Pre-
vention and Treatment of Boils, Laundry Management, Chess,
The Vegetable Garden, Sheep Farming, Etching and Drypoint,
Sausage Manufacture in the Home, The Ancient Classics, Thau-
maturgy Explained, and several other subjects the nature of
which I did not understand properly from their names. What
corpus of study was alluded to, for instance, in The Three Balls?
Or Panpendarism? Or The Cultivation of Sours?

Here was the letter:

'Sorry I could not write before now but I was terribly busy not
only settling in at Tooley Street and organizing the office but
also meeting people and making contacts. I suppose everybody
got a bit of a shock when they found the bird had flown that
morning but I could not face a formal farewell with Collopy
puling and puking in the background with tears of whiskey
rolling down his cheeks and gaunt Father Fahrt giving me his
blessings in lordly Latin and maybe Annie quietly crying into her
prashkeen. You know how I dislike that sort of thing. It makes
me nervous. I'm sorry all the same that I had to be a bit secretive
with yourself but the plans I have been working on made it essential that Collopy would know nothing because he has a wonderful gift for making trouble and poking his nose in where it will
deluge everything with a dirty sneeze. Did you know that he has
a brother in the police at Henley, not far from here? If he knew
my exact address – which in no circumstances should you reveal
to the bugger – I am sure I would have the other fellow peering
around here, and for all I know he may be worse than Collopy
himself. Needless to say I did not use any of the addresses the
Rev. Fahrt gave me, for Jesuits can be a far closer police force
than the men in blue. When I get things more advanced you
must come over and give me a hand because I know this industry

I'm entering on is only in its infancy, that there's bags of money in it if the business is properly run, and plenty to go round for everybody. It's a better life here, too. The pubs are better, food is good and cheap, and the streets aren't crawling with touchers like Dublin. Information and help can be got on any subject or person under the sun for a quid, and often for only a few drinks.

'Do not pay too much attention to the list of subjects in the margin. I don't see why we shouldn't deal with them and plenty more as well, e.g. Religious Vocations, but I am not yet publicly using this notepaper. You could regard the list in the margin as a manifesto, a statement of what we intend to do. We really aim at the mass-production of knowledge, human accomplishment and civilization. We plan the world of the future, a world of sophisticated and genial people, all well-to-do, impatient with snivellers, sneaks and politicians on the make; not really a Utopia but a society in which all *unnecessary* wrongs, failures, and mis-behaviours are removed. The simplest way to attack this problem is to strike at the cause, which is ignorance and non-education, or miseducation. Every day you meet people going around with two heads. They are completely puzzled by life, they understand practically nothing and are certain of only one thing – that they are going to die. I am not going to go so far as to contradict them in that but I believe I can suggest to them a few good ways of filling up the interval. A week ago I met a nice class of a negro, apparently a seaman, in a pub in Tower Bridge Road. He was a gloomy character at first but in three meetings I taught him to play chess. Now he is delighted with himself and thinks he is a witch-doctor. I also had a night's drinking with one of the thou-sands of ladies who flood the streets here. She wanted me to go with her but no fear. By her accent I knew she was Irish; so she was, Castleconnell on the Shannon. Same old story about a job as a maid, a tyrannical mistress and a young pup of a son that started pulling her about when she was making the beds. She came to the conclusion that if that sort of thing was the custom of the country, she might as well get paid for it. There is some logic in her argument but it is painfully clear that she knows next to nothing about business. I talked to her about her mother and the green hills of Erin and in no time I had her sniffling, though maybe it was the gin. Those girls are very fond of that stuff. But don't get the impression that I'm a preacher saving souls every night by infesting the pubs. It's only an odd night I do that, and when I'm on my own. I'm far too busy for that sort of gallivanting. The total staff in the office just now is four – a typist, a clerk and One Other. The One Other is my partner, who has put a decent share of spondulics into the venture. With his money and my brains, I do not see what there is to stop us. Better still, he has a well-to-do mother who lives in a grand house in Hampstead. He does not live with her or in fact get on with her too well, apparently because she made him spend two years at Oxford when he was younger. He says he was horrified by that place. He signs his name M. B. Barnes. When I looked for his Christian name – and you can't have a partner in a new resounding enterprise without using his Christian name, even when reprimanding or insulting him – I found that his full name was Milton Byron Barnes. Maybe this got him jeered at by the Oxford ignoramuses and made him sour for life. He is a gloomy type but knows what work is; and he knows how to talk to people. He is not a poet, of course, but is convinced that his father, long dead, thought he was a poet and that he owed it to the masters of the past to commemorate their genius by saddling his unfortunate son with their names. At the moment we are nursing a slight difference between us. He feels one of the fields we must cover is advertising, newspaper and magazine and otherwise. He is convinced that this is the coming thing and keeps quoting High o'er the fence leaps Sunny Jim, FORCE is the food that raises him. He is right that there is big money to be made there but we have not got the capital to wade in – yet. I keep telling him more satisfaction and happiness can be achieved by teaching 10,000 Englishmen to play billiards properly at four guineas for four lessons than by grappling and grovelling in this underground of publicity but his answer is that he does not want to make anybody happy and certainly doesn't want to be happy himself, he just wants to make a lot of money. I find that mentality a bit cynical, but I'm sure I'll bring him round to my own sound views in good time. We had dinner with his old lady twice and I found her quite good and intelligent. I feel it will not be long until she becomes a patron of our Academy and help it along at important stages with infusions of the red blood of LSD. You know, that is why rich people were made and why we should never envy or insult them. They are people brought into the world armed with the weapons for helping others. Contrast them with Collopy, who spends all his time obstructing and annoying others, poking about to find bad things in order to make them worse, interfering, bickering, and fomenting ill will and fights among friends. More than once I have thought of getting together a course entitled Your Own Business and the Minding of It. I would put Collopy down for free tuition. I'm in digs with another man, an elderly bachelor who owns a tobacco shop and spends his spare time reading Greek. How do I like such company? Very well, for I don't have to buy cigarettes, and the landlady is so old that she occasionally forgets to ask for the rent.

'Keep anything I've said in this note or any other I send under your hat, and don't give anybody in Dublin the firm's address. I'll write soon again. Pass on to me any news that arises. Slip the enclosed pound note with my compliments to Annie. The best of luck.'

I sighed and put the letter in my pocket. There was not much in it really.

IN THE MONTHS that followed the weather was particularly vile: it was a season of downpours and high wind, and the temperature at night was such as to compel me to heap two overcoats on top of my bed. But Mr Collopy ignored the nightly tempest. He left the house frequently about eight and people told me that he was a familiar figure, sheltering under a sodden umbrella, on the fringe of the small crowds attending street-corner meetings in Foster Place or the corner of Abbey Street. He was not in any way concerned with the purpose or message of those meetings. He was there to heckle, and solely from the angle of his own mysterious preoccupation. His main demand was that first things should come first. If the meeting advocated a strike in protest against low wages on the railways, he would counter by roaring that the inertia of the Corporation was more scandalous and a far more urgent matter for the country.

One night he came home very thoroughly drenched, and instead of going straight to bed, he sat at the range taking solace from his crock.

– For heaven's sake go to bed, Father, Annie said. You are drownded. Go to bed and I will make you punch.

– Ah no, he said brightly. In such situations my early training as a hurler will stand to me.

Sure enough, he had a roaring cold the following morning and did stay in bed for a few days by command of Annie, who did not lack his own martinet quality. Gradually the cold ebbed but when he was about the house again his movements were very awkward and he complained loudly of pains in his bones. Luckily he was saved the excruciation of trying to go upstairs, for he had himself built a lavatory in the bedroom in Mrs Crotty's time. But his plight was genuine enough, and I suggested that on my way to school I should drop in a note summoning Dr Blennerhassett.

– I am afraid, he said, that that good man is day tros. He means well but damn the thing he knows about medicine.

– But he might know something about those pains of yours.

– Oh, all right.

Dr Blennerhassett did call and said Mr Collopy had severe rheumatism. He prescribed a medicament which Annie got from the chemist – red pills in a round white box labelled 'The Tablets'. He also said, I believe, that the patient's intake of sugar should be drastically reduced, that alcohol should not in any circumstances be consumed, that an endeavour should be made to take mild exercise, and to have hot baths as often as possible. Whether or not Mr Collopy met those four conditions or any of them, he grew steadily worse as the weeks went by. He took to using a stick but I actually had to assist him in the short distance between his armchair and his bed. He was a cripple, and a very irascible one.

I had arranged one night to attend a session of Jack Mulloy's poker school, but a crafty idea had crept into my head. A late start for 8.30 p.m. had been fixed, apparently because Jack had to go somewhere or do something first. I deliberately put my watch an hour fast, and hopefully knocked on the door in nearby Mespil Road at what was really half seven. A pause, and the door was opened by Penelope.

– My, you're early, she said in that charming husky voice.

I gracefully stepped into the hall and said it was nearly half eight. I showed her my watch.

– Your watch is crazy, she said, but come in to the fire. Will you have a cup of coffee?

– I will, Penelope, if you will have one with me.

– I won't be a moment.

Wasn't that a delightful little ruse of mine? So far as I could see, we were alone in the house. Silly ideas came into my head, ideas that need not be mentioned here. I was the veriest tyro in such situations. Into my head came the names of certain voluptuaries and libertines of long ago, and then I began to wonder how the brother would handle matters were he in my place. She came with a pot of coffee, biscuits, and two delightful little cups. In the light her belted dress was trim, modest, a little bit mysterious; or perhaps I mean enchanting.

– Well now, Finbarr, she said, tell me all the news and leave nothing out.

– There's no news.

– I don't believe that. You are hiding something.

– Honestly, Penelope.

– How is Annie?

– Annie's in good order. She never changes. In fact she never changes even her clothes. But poor Mr Collopy is crucified with rheumatism. He is a complete wreck, helpless and very angry with himself. He kept going out to get drowned in the rain every night a few months ago, and this is the price of him.

– Ah, the poor man.

– And what about poor me? I have to act the male nurse while I'm in the house.

– Well, everybody needs help some time or other. You might grow to be a helpless old man yourself. How would you like that?

– I wouldn't fancy it. Probably I'd stick my head in the gas oven.

– But if you had very bad rheumatism you couldn't do that. You wouldn't be able to stoop or bend.

– Couldn't I get you to call and help me to get my head in?

– Ah no, Finbarr, that would not be a nice thing. But I would call all right.

– To do what?

– To nurse you.

– Heavens, that would be very nice.

She laughed. I must have allowed true feeling to well up in that remark. I certainly meant what I said, but did not like to appear too brash.

– Do you mean to say, I smiled, that I would have to have a painful and loathsome disease before you would call to see me?

– Oh, not at all, Finbarr, she said. But I'd be afraid of Mr Collopy. He once called me 'an unmannerly schoolgirl', all because I told him in the street that his shoelaces were undone.

– His bootlaces, you mean, I corrected. To hell with Mr Collopy.

– Now, now, now.

– Well, he gets on my nerves.

– You spend too much time in that kitchen. You don't go out enough. Do you ever go to a dance?

– No. I don't know the first thing about dancing.

– That's a pity. I must teach you.

– That would be grand.

– But first we'd have to get the loan of a gramophone somewhere.

– I think I might manage that.

Our conversation, as may be seen, was trivial and pointless enough, and the rest of it was that kind.

Finally I got a bit bolder and took her hand in my own. She did not withdraw it.

– What would you do, I asked, if I were to kiss your hand?

– Well, well! I would scream the house down probably.

– But why?

– That's the why.

Uproar ensued all right, but it was in the hall. Jack Mulloy with two other butties had come in and were jabbering loudly as they hung up their coats. Alas, I had to disengage my excited mind and turn my thought to cards.

Curiously, I won fifteen shillings that night and was reasonably cheerful over the whole evening's proceedings, not excluding the little interlude with Penelope, as I made my way home. The route I took was by Wilton Place, a triangular shaded nook not much used by traffic. I knew from other experiences that it was haunted by prostitutes of the very lowest cadres, and also by their scruffy clients. A small loutish group of five or six people were giggling in the shadows as I approached but became discreetly silent as I passed. But when I had gone only two yards or so, I heard one solitary word in a voice I swore I knew:

– *Seemingly.*

I paused involuntarily, deeply shocked, but I soon walked on. I had, in fact, been thinking of Penelope, and that one word threw my mind into a whirl. What was the meaning of this thing sex, what was the nature of sexual attraction? Was it all bad and dangerous? What was Annie doing late at night, standing in a dark place with young blackguards? Was I any better myself in my conduct, whispering sly things into the ear of lovely and innocent Penelope? Had I, in fact, at the bottom of my heart dirty intentions, some dark deed postponed only because the opportunity had not yet presented itself.

As I had expected, the kitchen was empty, for I had assisted Mr Collopy to bed before going out earlier. I did not want to be there when Annie came. I got notepaper and an envelope, went upstairs and got into bed.

I lay there with the light on for a long time, reflecting. Then I wrote a confidential and detailed letter to the brother about, first, the very low and painful condition of Mr Collopy; and second, the devastating incident concerning Annie. I paused before signing my name and for a wild few minutes considered writing a little about myself and Penelope. But reason, thank God, prevailed. I said nothing but signed and sealed the letter.

CHAPTER 14

A REPLY WAS not long coming, taking the form of a parcel and a letter. I opened the letter first, and here it is:

'Many thanks for your rather alarming communication.

'From what you say it is clear to me that Collopy is suffering from rheumatoid arthritis, very likely of the peri-articular type. If you can persuade him to let you have a look, you will find that the joints are swollen and of fusiform shape and I think you will find that he is afflicted at the hands and feet, knees, ankles and wrists. Probably his temperature is elevated, and total rest in bed is most desirable. The focus of infection for rheumatoid arthritis is usually bad teeth and the presence in the gums of pyorrhoea alveolaris, so that he should order Hanafin's cab and call on a dentist. But happily we have invented here in the Academy a certain cure for the disorder, provided the treatment is sedulously followed. I am sending you under separate cover a bottle of our patent Gravid Water. It will be your own job to make sure that he takes a t/spoonful of it three times a day after meals. See to the first dose before you leave the house in the morning, inquire about the daytime dose when you get back from school, and similarly ensure the evening dose. It would be well to tell Annie of the importance of this treatment and the need for regularity . . .'

At this stage I opened the parcel and under many wrappings uncovered a large bottle which bore a rather gaudy label. Here was its message:

THE GRAVID WATER
The miraculous specific for
the complete cure within one
month of the abominable
scourage known as Rheumatoid
Arthritis.

Dose – one t-spoonful three
times daily after meals.
Prepared at
LONDON ACADEMY LABORATORIES

Well, this might be worth trying, I thought, but immediately soaked the bottle in water and removed the label, for I knew that nothing would induce Mr Collopy to touch the contents if he knew or suspected that they had originated with the brother. I then resumed reading the letter:

'I was certainly shocked to hear that Annie has been consorting with cornerboys up the canal. These are dirty merchants and if she continues, disease will be inevitable. I am sure that neither you nor I could attempt any estimate of how cunning and cute she is or how totally ignorant and innocent. Does she know the Facts of Life? Apart from venereal disease, does she know of the danger of pregnancy? I don't think the arrival of an illegitimate on the doorstep would alleviate Collopy's rheumatoid condition.

'You did not say in your letter that you suspected that she had some infection but if she has, diagnosis without examination at this distance is rather difficult. I think we may rule out Granuloma Inguinale. It takes the form of very red, beefy ulceration. A clear symptom is ever-increasing debility and marked physical wasting, often ending in extreme cachexia and death. It is mostly met with in tropical countries, and almost confined to negroes. We may discount it.

'For similar reasons of rarity, we may discard the possibility of Lymphogranuloma Venereum. This is a disease of the lymph glands and lymph nodes, and one finds a hot, painful group of swollen buboes in the inguinal area. There will be headaches, fever and pains in the joints. The causitive agent is a virus. Here again, however, Lymphogranuloma Venereum is a near-monopoly of the negro.

'The greatest likelihood is that Annie, if infected, labours under the sway of H.M. Gonococcus. In women the symptoms are so mild at the beginning as to be unnoticed but it is a serious and painful invasion. There is usually fever following infection of the pelvic organs. Complications to guard against include

endocarditis, meningitis and skin decay. Gonococcal endocarditis can be fatal.

'There remains, of course, the Main Act. This disease is caused
by a virus known as *spirochaeta pallida* or *treponema pallidum*. We
can have skin rash, lesions of the mouth, enlargement of lymph
glands, loss of scalp hair, inflammation of the eyes, jaundice from
liver damage, convulsions, deafness, meningitis and sometimes
coma. The Last Act, the most serious, in most cases takes a
cardiovascular form where the main lesion is seated in the
thoracic aorta directly near the heart. The extensible tissue is
ruined, the aorta swells and a saccular dilatation or an aneurysm
may take shape. Sudden death is quite common. Other results
are G.P.I. (paresis), locomotor ataxia, and wholesale contamina-
tion of the body and its several organs. My London Academy
Laboratories markets a three-in-one remedy "Love's Lullaby"
but as this specific involves fits and head-staggers in persons
who have in fact not been infected at all, it would be unwise to
prescribe for Annie on the blind.

'I would advise that at this stage you would keep her under
very minute observation and see if you can detect any symptoms
and then get in touch with me again. You might perhaps devise
some prophylactic scheming such as remarking apropos of
nothing that conditions on the canal bank are nothing short of a
scandal with men and women going about there poxed up to
the eyes, drunk on methylated spirits, flooding the walks with
contaminated puke and making it unsafe for Christians even to
take a walk in that area. You could add that you are writing
to the D.M.P. urging the arrest at sight of any characters found
loitering there. We all know that probably Annie is a cute and
cunning handful but very likely she is not proof against a good
fright. On the other hand you might consider telling Mr
Collopy what you know, for it would be easier for a father to
talk straight to his own daughter on this very serious subject, on
the off-chance that Annie is innocent and quite uninstructed;
in fact it would be his duty to do so. If you see fit to adopt that
course, it would be natural to bring Father Fahrt into the picture,
for the matter has a self-evident spiritual content. If being on
the scene you would feel embarrassed to thus take the initiative,
I could write from here to Mr Collopy or Father Fahrt or both,
telling of the information I have received (not disclosing the

source) and asking that steps should be taken for prevention and/or cure.

'However, I must say that I doubt whether Annie is in trouble at all and the best plan might be to keep wideawake so far as yourself is concerned, report to me if there are any symptoms or other development, and take no action for the present.'

Well, that was a long and rather turgid letter but I found myself in agreement with the last paragraph. In fact I put the whole subject out of my head and merely dedicated myself to Mr Collopy's rheumatism.

CHAPTER 15

I DULY PRODUCED the bottle of Gravid Water to Mr Collopy, saying it was a miracle cure for rheumatism which I had got from a chemist friend. I also produced a tablespoon and told him he was to take a spoonful without fail three times a day after meals. And I added that I would keep reminding him.

– Oh well now, I don't know, he said. Are there salts in it?

– No, I don't think so.

– Is there anything in the line of bromide or saltpetre?

– No. I believe the stuff in the fluid is mostly vitamins. I would say it is mainly a blood tonic.

– Ah-Ah? The blood is all, of course. It's like the mainspring on a watch. If a man lets his blood run down, he'll find himself with all classes of boils and rashes. And scabs.

– And rheumatism, I added.

– And who is this chemist when he is at home?

– He's . . . he's a chap I know named Donnelly. He works in Hayes, Conyngham and Robinson. He is a qualified man, of course.

– Oh very well. I'll take a chance. Amn't I nearly crippled? What have I to lose?

– Nothing at all.

There and then he took his first tablespoonful and after a week of the treatment said he felt much better. I was glad of this and emphasized the necessity of persevering in the treatment. From time to time I wrote to the brother for a fresh bottle.

After six weeks I began to notice something strange in the patient's attempts at movement. His walk became most laborious and slow and the floor creaked under him. One night in bed I heard with a start a distant rending crash coming from his bedroom off the kitchen. I hurried down to find him breathless and tangled in the wreckage of his bed. It seems that the wire mattress, rusted and rotted by Mrs Crotty's nocturnal diuresis (or bed-wetting) had collapsed under Mr Collopy's weight.

– Well, the dear knows, he said shrilly, isn't this the nice state of affairs? Help me out of this.

I did so, and it was very difficult.

– What happened? I asked.

– Faith and can't you see? The whole shooting-gallery collapsed under me.

– The fire is still going in the kitchen. Put on your overcoat and rest there. I'll take this away and get another bed.

– Very well. That catastrophe has me rightly shaken. I think a dram or two from the crock is called for.

Not in a very good temper, I took down the whole bed and put the pieces against the wall in the passage outside. Then I dismantled the brother's bed and reerected it in Mr Collopy's room.

– Your bed awaits, sir, I told him.

– Faith now and that was quick work, he said. I will go in directly I finish this nightcap. You may go back to your own bed.

On the following day, Sunday, I went in next door and borrowed their weighing scales. When I managed to get Mr Collopy to stand on the little platform, the needle showed his weight to be 29 stone! I was flabbergasted. I checked the machine by weighing myself and found it was quite accurate. The amazing thing was that Mr Collopy was still the same size and shape as of old. I could attribute his extraordinary weight only to the brother's Gravid Water, so I wrote to him urgently explaining what had happened. And the letter I got back was surprising enough in itself. Here it is:

'It is not only in Warrington Place that amazing things are happening; they are happening here as well. A week ago the mother of Milton Byron Barnes, my partner, died. In her will, which came to light yesterday, she left him her house and about £20,000 in cash and she left £5,000 TO ME! What do you think of that? It looks like the blessing of God on my Academy.

'I was indeed sorry about what you tell me of Mr Collopy. The cause of it is too obvious – excessive dosage. On the label of the bottle the term "t-spoonful" meant "tea-spoonful", not "tablespoonful". The Gravid Water, properly administered was calculated to bring about a gradual and controlled increase in weight and thus to cause a redevelopment of the rheumatoid joints by reason of the superior weight and the increased work they would have to do.

'Unfortunately the alarming overweight you report is an irreversible result of the Gravid Water; there is no antidote. In this situation we must put our trust in God. In humble thanks for my own legacy and to help poor Mr Collopy, I have made up my mind to bring him and Father Fahrt on a pilgrimage to Rome. The present Pontiff, Pius X, or Giuseppe Sarto, is a very noble and holy man, and I do not think it is in the least presumptuous to expect a miracle and have Mr Collopy restored to his proper weight. Apart from that, the trip will be physically invigorating, for I intend to proceed by sea from London to the port of Ostia in the Mediterranean, only about sixty miles from the Eternal City. Please advise both pilgrims accordingly and tell them to see immediately about passports and packing clothes.

'You should have ingestion of the Gravid Water discontinued and need not disclose the spiritual aim of the pilgrimage to Mr Collopy. I will write again in a week or so.'

CHAPTER 16

THE VELOCITY and efficiency of the brother's methods were not long being made manifest. Before Mr Collopy had time to bestir himself about the passport, he received out of the blue for completion documents of application for a passport. This was, of course, the brother's doing. Father Fahrt heard nothing; he must already have a passport, else how could he be in Ireland? A few days afterwards I myself received a registered package containing visa application forms to be completed immediately by Mr Collopy and Father Fahrt and returned to the brother in London. Enclosed also was quite a sum in cash. He wrote:

'See that the visa documents enclosed are signed and returned to me here within forty-eight hours. If Collopy has not yet got his passport fixed up, will you yourself do any running around on his behalf that is necessary and if need be get a photographer *to call to the house*. We leave Tilbury on the *Moravia* in nine days and we don't want things messed up by petty delays or for the sake of saving a few pounds. Tell Father Fahrt that he need have no worry about ecclesiastical permission to travel, as I have had an approach made to the Provincial of the English Jesuits and you may be sure a letter has already gone to the Leeson Street house.

'I have already bought three first-class tickets to the port of Ostia, near Rome. N.B. The Cardinal Archbishop of Ostia is ex officio the Dean of the Sacred College and since our objective is a private audience with the Holy Father, he could be very useful if we could contact him en route. Father Fahrt may have a line on him.

'Dress clothes are essential where an audience is concerned but tell Collopy not to trouble about that. I will have him fixed up with a monkey suit either here in London or when we get to Rome.

'I have booked two adjoining rooms on the first floor of the Hotel Élite et des Étrangers, a big place near the station, and where there is a lift. Father Fahrt will have to look after himself, as these lads are not allowed to stay in hotels. Probably he will stay in the Jesuit house here, or in some convent.

'I enclose one hundred and twenty pounds in notes, being forty pounds each for Collopy and Father Fahrt in respect of the Dublin–London journey, twenty pounds for yourself to meet embarkation expenses, and twenty for Annie to keep her quiet. Tell her to keep away from that canal bank while her dear father is on an important spiritual mission abroad.

'Your plan must be to get Hanafin to drive the party to West-land Row to get the very first boat train to Kingstown on the evening of the seventh. Do not hesitate to tip porters or others heavily to assist Collopy in these difficult moving operations, and if necessary carry him. Arm yourself with a half-pint towards the journey to the boat but tell Father Fahrt to restrain Collopy from any heavy drinking on board, for he probably knows next to nothing about sailing and if he is going to get sick, drink will make the performance all the more atrocious.

'I will meet the party at Euston, with all necessary transport and assistance, early on the morning of the eighth.

'Please attend to all these matters without fail and send me a telegram if there is any hold-up.'

And so, indeed, it came to pass.

I had privately advised Mr Collopy to buy two new suits, a heavy one for travel and a light one to meet the Roman weather. He absolutely refused to buy a new overcoat, disinterring an intact but quaint garment in which he said he was married to his first wife. (I had never heard of anyone having been married in an overcoat.) Father Fahrt, being of continental origin, understood everything perfectly and did not need advice on any matter. He did not disguise his emotion at the prospect of meeting the Holy Father in person and referred to this, not as a possibility but as something which had already been arranged. For all I knew, he had invoked the mysterious apparatus of his Order, from which even the Pope was not immune.

On the late evening of the seventh the two travellers, looking very spruce, were at their accustomed station in the kitchen,

savouring refreshment from the crock and looking very pleased.
For once Annie showed a slight strain of excitement.

– Could I make you hang sangwiches for the journey? she
asked.

– God Almighty, woman, Mr Collopy said in genuine astonishment, do you think we are going to the zoo? Or Leopards-
town races?

– Well, you might be hungry.

– Yes, Mr Collopy said rather heavily, that could happen. But
there is one well-known remedy for hunger. Know what that is?
A damn good dinner. Sirloin, roast potatoes, asparagus, Savoy
cabbage and any God's amount of celery sauce. With, beforehand, of course, a plate of hot mushroom soup served with
French rolls. With a bottle of claret, the château class, beside
each plate. Am I right, Father Fahrt?

– Collopy, I don't find that meal very homogeneous.

– Maybe so. But is it nourishing?

– Well, it would scarcely kill you.

– Damn sure it never killed me when the mother was alive.
Lord save us – there was a woman that could bake a farl of wheaten
bread! Put a slobber of honey on that and you had a banquet, man.

– The only creatures who eat sensibly, Father Fahrt said, are
the animals. Nearly all humans over-eat and kill themselves
with food.

– Except in the slums, of course, Mr Collopy corrected.

– Ah yes, Father Fahrt said sadly. The curse there is cheap
drink and worse – methylated spirits. God pity them.

– In a way they have more than we have, they have constitu-
tions of cast iron.

– Yes, but acid is the enemy of iron. I believe some of those
poor people buy a lot of hair oil. Not for their heads, of course.
They drink it.

– Yes. That reminds me, Father. Hand me your glass. This
isn't hair oil I have here.

While he busied himself with the libations, there was a knock.
I hurried to the door and admitted Mr Hanafin.

– Well, Fathers above, he beamed as he saw the pair at the
range.

– Evening, Hanafin, Mr Collopy said. Sit down there for a
minute. Annie, get a glass for Mr Hanafin.

— So we're off tonight to cross the briny ocean?

— Yes, Mr Hanafin, Father Fahrt said. We have important business to attend to on the mainland.

— Yes, Mr Hanafin, I added, and you have just four minutes to finish that drink. I am in charge of this timetable. We all leave for Westland Row station in four minutes.

My voice was peremptory, stern.

— I must say, gentlemen, Mr Hanafin said, that I never seen ye looking better. Ye are very spruce. I never seen you, Mr Collopy, with a better colour up.

— That is my blood pressure, Mr Collopy replied facetiously.

I was strict with my four-minute time-limit. When it was up we embarked on the task of getting Mr Collopy into his ancient tight overcoat. That completed, Mr Hanafin and I half-assisted, half-dragged him out to the cab and succeeded, Father Fahrt assisting from the far door, in hoisting him into the cab's back. The springs wheezed as he collapsed backwards on to the seat. Soon after the aged Marius broke into a leisurely trot and in fifteen minutes we pulled up outside Westland Row station. There is a long flight of steps from street level to the platform.

— Everybody wait here till I come back, I said.

I climbed the stairs and approached a porter standing beside the almost empty boat train.

— Listen here, I said, there's a very heavy man below in a cab that wouldn't be able for those stairs on his own. If you get another man to come down with you and give us a hand, there's a ten bob each for you in it.

His eyes gleamed, he bawled for Mick, and soon the three of us descended. Getting Mr Collopy out of the cab was more a matter of strategy than strength but soon he was standing breathless and shaky on the pathway.

— Now, Mr Collopy, I said, those stairs are the devil. There are four of us here and we are going to carry you up.

— Well, faith now, Mr Collopy said mildly. I am told they used to carry the Roman Emperors about the Forum in Rome, dressed up in purest cloth of gold.

I posted a porter at each shoulder to grip him by the armpits while Mr Hanafin and I took charge of a leg apiece, rather as if they were the shafts of a cart. Clearly the porters were deeply shocked at the weight they had to deal with at the rear but we assailed the stairs, trying to keep the passenger as horizontal as possible, and found the passage easy enough. Father Fahrt hurried ahead and opened the door of an empty first-class carriage, and Mr Collopy was adroitly put standing on the floor. He was very pleased and beamed about him as if he himself had just performed some astonishing feat. Mr Hanafin hurried down to get the luggage, while I bought the tickets.

It was nearly three-quarters of an hour before the train moved and half an hour before anybody else entered our compartment. I produced a small glass and to his astonishment, handed it to Mr Collopy. Then I produced a flat half-pint bottle from my hip pocket.

– I have already put a little water into this stuff, I said, so you can have a drink of it with safety.

– Well, merciful martyrs in heaven, Father Fahrt, Mr Collopy said gleefully, did you ever hear the like of it? Drinking whiskey in a first-class carriage and us on a pilgrimage to kneel at the feet of the Holy Father!

– Please do not take much, Father Fahrt said seriously. It is not good to do this in public.

When the train pulled up alongside the mailboat at Kingstown, I repeated my stratagem with the two porters. We got Mr Collopy comfortably seated, at his own request, in the dining saloon. I felt tired and told him and Father Fahrt that I must be off.

– God bless you for your help, my boy, Father Fahrt said.

– When you get back, Mr Collopy said, tell Annie that there are two pairs of dirty socks at the bottom of my bed. They want to be washed and darned.

– Right.

– And if Rafferty calls about hydrometer readings, tell him to keep the machine in circulation. Make a note of this. Next on the list is Mrs Hayes of Sandymount. Next, Mrs Fitzherbert of Harold's Cross. He knows those people. I'll be home by then.

– Very good. Good-bye now, and good luck.

And so they sailed away. How did they fare? That peculiar story was revealed in dispatches I received from the brother, and which I now present.

CHAPTER 17

ABOUT THREE weeks after the departure of the travellers I received the following letter from the brother:

Well, here we are in Rome at the Hotel Élite et des Étrangers. Spring comes earlier here and it is already very warm.

Our voyage to Ostia on the *Moravia* was without much incident and for me quite enjoyable. I haven't been so drunk for years, though an Englishman I chummed up with went a bit further. He fell and broke his leg. Collopy, who never showed any sign of sickness, drank plenty too but spent most of his time in bed. (Thank God we had decent beds and not those frightful bunks.) First, the job of trying to dress him on a tilting floor was at least an hour's for Father Fahrt, a steward and myself. Once dressed, he found movement on shipboard almost impossible. I had to give another steward not tips but a massive salary to lend a special hand but gangways and steps were nearly insuperable. I used to bring people down to the bedroom to drink and talk with him. He was not in the least depressed by his situation, and the sea air certainly had a good effect. Father Fahrt rather let us down. He soon found there were four members of his own Order on board and was huddled with them for most of every day. He came down to Collopy only in the evening, and for some reason has refused all drinks. He is in very good shape and temper, though, and is now staying in a Jesuit house here. He comes faithfully to the hotel every morning at eleven.

Collopy is much easier to handle and dress on terra firma – indeed, he could dress himself if he was using the tramp's rags he wears in Dublin – and we usually spend the first part of the day till lunch time sitting in the sun and talking. Irish whiskey is impossible to get, of course, and Collopy is drinking absinthe. I am drinking so much brandy myself that I sometimes get afraid of heart failure. In the afternoons we usually hire a wagonette and go for a slow tour of sights such as the Colosseum and the

Forum; we have been twice to the piazza of St Peter's. At night, I see Collopy put to bed and just disappear until the small hours. I find the Eternal City is full of brothels but I keep clear of them. There are some damn fine night clubs, most of them, I am told, illegal.

And now for the inside trickery. I knew we could rely on Father Fahrt to start secret schemings without even being asked. Yesterday morning he brought along a Monsignor Cahill, a remarkable character and a Corkman. He is a sort of Vatican civil servant and attends on the Holy Father personally. He is not only an interpreter who has expert knowledge of at least eight languages (he says) but he is also a stenographer whose job it is to take down all remarks and observations made by the Holy Father in the course of an audience. He translates the supplications of pilgrims orally but takes down only the replies. He is a most friendly man, is always genuinely delighted to see anybody from Ireland, and knows exactly what to do with a good glass of wine. He took a great fancy to Collopy who, to my own great surprise, has a detailed knowledge of Cork city.

He promised to do everything possible to arrange a private audience but Father Fahrt has a far bigger card in his pack. He knows, or has made it his business to get to know, a certain Cardinal Baldini. This man is what they call a domestic prelate, and works every day in the papal suite. He has, of course, enormous power and can fix anything. Father Fahrt is very cagey and has promised Collopy nothing solid beyond saying that the Pontiff is very busy and one must be patient. Personally I have no doubt at all that this audience will come off. I believe in it sufficiently to have bought Collopy a monkey suit. Cardinal Baldini is a Franciscan and lives at the Franciscan monastery at the Via Merulana, where there is also the fine church of Santo Antonio di Padua. (My Italian is improving fast.) That is all for now. Will write again in a few days. M.

P.S. Keep your eye on Annie. I hope there is no canal nonsense going on.

CHAPTER 18

THE NEXT letter I received was a short one, a week afterwards. Here is what he wrote:

Well, the expected happened. Father Fahrt came as usual this morning and after some small talk, casually told Collopy and myself to have our monkey suits on that evening at six because we were all going to pay a call on Cardinal Baldini at his monastery. It was a most dramatic revelation. Obviously Father Fahrt had been working quietly and silently behind the scenes, in the Jesuit fashion. I knew the private audience had been fixed but said nothing.

Having first fixed myself up, I took the precaution of beginning the job of getting Collopy into his dress clothes at five and it was a wise move, for it took nearly an hour. He looked very funny in the end.

We drove with Father Fahrt to the Via Merulana. The Monastery was a simple, austere place but apparently very big. The reception room was comfortable enough but full of holy pictures. Cardinal Baldini when he came in was a short, stout man, very jovial in manner. We kissed his ring as he greeted us in perfect English. We sat down at our ease.

'And how are all my friends in Dublin?' he asked Collopy.

'Faith and they are in very good form, Your Eminence. I did not know you were there.'

'I paid a visit in 1896. And I spent ten years in England.'

'Well, well.'

Then Father Fahrt started yapping out of him about the charm of foreign travel, how it broadens the mind and shows the Catholic how universal the universal church is.

'I was never one to roam,' Collopy said. 'Somehow a man must stay where his work is.'

'True indeed,' Cardinal Baldini said, 'but our vineyard is indeed commodious. And every year that passes it gets bigger.

Look at the work that is yet to be done in Africa, in China, even in Japan.'

'I realize how immense the job is,' Collopy replied, 'because I have been doing missionary work of my own. Not the religious kind, of course.'

Here Father Fahrt began talking about the central point of all religion – the Vatican and the Holy Father.

Finally, the Cardinal turned to Collopy and said:

'Mr Collopy, I believe yourself and your little party would like to have a private audience with the Holy Father?'

'Your Eminence, it would be indeed a great honour.'

'Well, I have arranged it. The afternoon of the day after tomorrow at four o'clock.'

'We are all most grateful to you, Eminence,' Father Fahrt said.

That was about all. We drove back to the hotel very pleased with ourselves. I went straight to the American bar there to cele-brate. The audience will be over by the time you get this. I will write immediately and give you an account of it. – M.

CHAPTER 19

I MUST LET the next extraordinary letter speak for itsef. It put the heart across me.

Several days have passed since that audience and it is only now that I am able, with Monsignor Cahill's help, to send you this letter. Please keep it safely as I have no copy.

There was a frightful, appalling row.

As a matter of fact the Pope told us all to go to hell. He threatened to silence Father Fahrt.

The papal palaces are to the right of the basilica as you approach it and just past the entrance, Father Fahrt led us to a small office run by the Swiss Guards. It was a private rendezvous for in five minutes Cardinal Baldini appeared, welcomed us and gave each of us a thick guide or catalogue. As there was plenty of time to spare, he led us through this enormous and dazzling place talking all the time, showing us the loggia of Gregory XIII, a wonderful gallery; the Throne Room; the Sala Rotunda, a round hall full of statues; the Raphael salon, with many of the great man's paintings; part of the Vatican Museum; the Sistine Chapel and many other places I cannot remember, nor can I remember much from the Cardinal's stream of talk except that the Vatican has a parish priest (not the Pope). The splendour of it all was stupendous. God forgive me, I thought it was a bit vulgar in places and that all the gilt and gold was sometimes a bit overdone.

'The late Leo,' Cardinal Baldini said, 'was at home with kings and princes and rejoiced in art and the higher learning. Of course his *Rerum Novarum* was a great thing for the labouring classes. But the man you are going to meet is the Pope of the Poor and the humble. In any way he can help them, he always does.'

'Is that a fact?' Collopy said.

I thought of the miracle we were hoping for concerning his weight. But he had yet been told nothing of that.

We came to a door and entered a beautiful room. This was the ante-room to the Pope's study. The Cardinal bade us wait and passed through another door. The place was delightfully peaceful. After some minutes the other door opened and the Cardinal beckoned to us. We allowed Collopy, slowly progressing on his stick, to lead the way, myself in the middle and Father Fahrt last.

The Holy Father was seated behind a desk, with Monsignor Cahill sitting some distance to his right. Pius X was smallish, rather thin and looked fairly old. He smiled thinly at us, rose and came round to meet us. We knelt and kissed the Fisherman's Ring and heard his voice raised in Latin as he imparted what I suppose was the apostolic benediction.

He then went back to his seat behind the desk while the pilgrims and the Cardinal advanced to chairs facing it. I chose a chair far to the side, for I did not want to make any remarks or have any questions addressed to me. I noticed that Monsignor Cahill had paper and a pencil ready.

The Pope said something in Italian to Mr Collopy and Monsignor Cahill instantly translated, also rapidly translating his reply back into Italian.

THE POPE – How do things fare in your country, beloved Ireland?

COLLOPY – Only middling, Your Holiness. The British are still there.

THE POPE – And is the country not prosperous?

COLLOPY – I do not think so, Your Holiness, for there is much unemployment in Dublin.

THE POPE – Ah, that grieves our heart.

FATHER FAHRT (in Italian) – Some of the Irish tend to be a bit indolent, Sanctissime Pater, but their faith is perhaps the strongest in Christendom. I am a German and have seen nothing like it in Germany. It is inspiring.

THE POPE – Ireland was ever dear to our heart. She is a blessed country. Her missionaries are everywhere.

(After a little more desultory conversation Mr Collopy said something in a low voice which I did not catch. Monsignor Cahill instantly translated. The Pope seemed startled. Mr Collopy then made a much longer mumbled speech which was also quickly translated. I am indebted to Monsignor Cahill for a transcription of the Pope's remarks, which were in Latin and Italian, and the translation is also largely his.)

COLLOPY spoke.
THE POPE
Che cosa sta dicendo questo poveretto?
What is this poor child trying to say?
MONSIGNOR CAHILL spoke.
THE POPE
E tocco? Nonnunquam urbis nostrae visitentium capitibus affert vaporem. Dei praesidium hujus infantis amantissimi invocare velimus.

Is this child in his senses? Sometimes the heat of our city brings vapour into the heads. We invoke God's protection for a beloved child.

COLLOPY spoke again.
MONSIGNOR CAHILL spoke.
THE POPE
Ho paura che abbiate fatto un errore, Eminenza, nel potar qui questo pio uomo. Mi sembra che sia un po' tocco. Forse gli manca una rotella. He sbagliato indirizzo? Non siamo medici che curano il corpo.

Dear Cardinal, I fear you have made a mistake in bringing this pious man to see us. I fear the Lord has laid a finger on him. We would not say that his head is working properly. Can it be that he is in the wrong place? We are not a doctor for the body.

FATHER FAHRT spoke.
THE POPE
Ma questo è semplicemente mostruoso. Neque hoc nostrum officium cum concilii urbani officio est confundendum.

But this is monstrous. Nor should our office be confused with that of a city council.
CARDINAL BALDINI spoke.
THE POPE
Nobis presentibus istud dici indignum est. Num consilium istud inusitatum rationis legibus continetur? Nunquam nos ejusmodi quicquam audivimus.

It is a derogation of our presence. Does such an unheard-of suggestion lie within reason? We have never heard of such a thing before.

COLLOPY mumbled something.
MONSIGNOR CAHILL spoke.

THE POPE

Graviter commovemur ista tam mira observatione ut de tanta re sententiam dicamus. Intra hos parietes dici dedecet. Hic enim est locus sacer.

We are deeply troubled by such a strange supplication for our intervention on such a question. It is improper that such a matter should be mentioned within these walls. This is a sacred place.

CARDINAL BALDINI spoke in Italian.

THE POPE

Non possiamo accettare scuse e pretesti. Il Reverendo Fahrt ha sbagliato. Ci da grande dolore.

We cannot accept pretexts and excuses. Father Fahrt has lapsed. He fills us with sorrow.

FATHER FAHRT spoke in Italian.

THE POPE

Non possiamo accettare ciò. Sembra ci sia un rilassamento nella disciplina nella Società di Gesù in Irlanda. Se il Padre Provinciale non agisce, dovremo noi stessi far tacere il Reverendo Fahrt.

We do not accept that at all. There seems to be a weakness of discipline in the Sociey of Jesus in Ireland. If Father Provincial in Ireland does not move, we will silence Father Fahrt ourselves.

COLLOPY mumbled something.

MONSIGNOR CAHILL spoke.

CARDINAL BALDINI spoke in Italian.

THE POPE

È inutile parlarne. Quest' uomo soffre di allucinazionie di ossessioni, e è stato condotto su questa via del Reverendo Fahrt. Come abbiamo già detto, tutto questo ci rattrista profondamente, Cardinale.

It is no good. This man is suffering from serious delusions and obsessions and he is being encouraged in this disorder by Father Fahrt. As we have said, it brings sorrow to our heart, Cardinal.

CARDINAL BALDINI spoke.

THE POPE

Homo miserrimus in valetudinario a medico curandus est.

This poor man needs attention in hospital.

CARDINAL BALDINI spoke again.
THE POPE

Bona mulier fons gratiae. Attamen ipsae in parvularum rerum suarum occupationibus verrentur. Nos de tantulis rebus consulere non decet.

A good woman is a fountain of grace. But it is themselves whom they should busy about their private little affairs. It is not seemly to consult us on such matters.

CARDINAL BALDINI spoke yet again.
THE POPE

Forsitan poena leviora ille Reverendus Fahrt adduci possit ut et sui sit memor et quae sacerdotis sint partes intellegere.

Perhaps a milder penance will bring Father Fahrt to recollect himself and have true regard to his holy duties.

The Pope then rose and the members of the audience also rose.
THE POPE

Nobis nunc abeundum esse videtur. Illud modo ex liberis meis quaero ut de üs cogiteat quae exposui.

I think we should now retire. I ask my children to meditate upon the thoughts we have voiced.

The Holy Father then made the Sign of the Cross, and disappeared through a door behind him.

We silently filed out through the ante-room, Cardinal Baldini walking ahead with Father Fahrt, the two of them talking together quietly. At the time I had no idea, of course, what the subject of the audience had been or what had been said in Latin or Italian by the Pope. It was only when I interviewed Monsignor Cahill the following day that I got the information I have set down here. I asked him what the *subject* of Mr Collopy's representations were. He said he had given his word of honour that he would not disclose this to anybody.

My progress at Mr Collopy's side in the Vatican corridors was slow and tedious. No miracle had cured his fabulous weight. I suppose there was still time.

CHAPTER 20

I WAS LYING in bed one morning, having already decided I would not go to school that day and thinking that perhaps I would never go back to it. The brother's last extraordinary letter about the Holy Father and Father Fahrt had contained a cheque for twenty-five pounds. I had already trained Annie to bring me some breakfast in bed and was lying there at my ease, smoking and thinking. I could hear men shouting at horses on the tow-path, hauling a barge. It was amazing how quickly life changed. The brother's legacy of £5,000 was a miracle in itself, and another miracle was his feat in founding a new sort of university in London. Then you had the three of them inside the Vatican arguing with the Holy Father himself. It would not surprise me if the brother turned out to be appointed Governor of Rome or even came home in the purple of a cardinal, for I knew that in the old days it was common for Popes to appoint mere children to be cardinals. I thought I would join the brother in London. Even if his business did not suit me, there would be plenty of other jobs to be had there. Suddenly Annie came into the room and handed me an orange envelope. It was a cablegram.

COLLOPY DEAD AND FUNERAL IS
TOMORROW HERE IN ROME AM WRITING

I nearly fell out of the bed. Annie stood staring at me.

– Seemingly they are on their way home? she asked.

– Em, yes, I stammered. They will probably take the short route home direct to London. The brother's business, you know.

– Isn't it well for them, she said, to be globe-trotting and gallivanting?

– It can be very tiring.

– Ah yes, but look at the money they have. Isn't it well for them?

She went away and I lay there, quite desolated – I who had

been reflecting on the amazing suddenness with which life changed. I had lied automatically to Annie and only now realized that the dead man was her father. I lit another cigarette and realized that I had no idea what I should do. What *could* I do?

After a time I got up and hung disconsolately about the house for a time. Annie had gone out, presumably to buy food. I was completely in a quandary about breaking the bad news to her. How would she take it? That question was quite beyond me. I thought a couple of good bottles of stout would do me no harm. I was about to pull on my overcoat when I paused, pulled out the cable again and stared at it. Then I did what I suppose was something cowardly. I put the thing on the kitchen table and walked quickly out of the house. I crossed over the canal at Baggot Street Bridge and was soon sitting in a pub looking at a bottle of stout.

I was not yet really in the habit of heavy drinking but this time I was there for many, many hours trying desperately to think clearly. I had not much success. When I did leave it was nearly three o'clock and I had six stouts under my arm when I staggered home.

There was nobody there. The cablegram was gone and in its place a note saying THERE IS SOMETHING IN THE OVEN. I found a chop and some other things and began to eat. Annie had friends of her own and probably had gone to one of them. It was just as well. I felt enormously heavy and sleepy. Carefully gathering my stouts, a glass and a corkscrew, I went up to bed and soon fell headlong into a deep, sodden sleep. It was early morning when I awoke. I pulled a stout and lit a cigarette. Gradually, the affairs of the preceding day came back to me.

When Annie arrived with breakfast (for which I had little taste) her eyes were very red. She had been crying a lot but she was collected and calm.

– I am very sorry, Annie, I said.

– Why did they not bring him home to bury him here with my mother?

– I do not know. I am waiting for a letter.

– How well they wouldn't think even of me.

– I am sure they did the best they could in the circumstances.

– Seemingly.

The next three or four days were very grim. There was almost

total silence in the house. Neither of us could think of anything
to say. I went out a bit and drank some stout but not much. In
the end a letter did arrive from the brother. This is what he had
to say:

'My cablegram must have been a great shock to you, to say
nothing of Annie. Let me tell you what happened.

'After the Vatican rumpus, Father Fahrt and Collopy, but
particularly Collopy, were very depressed. I was busy thinking
about getting back to London and my business. Father Fahrt
thought that some distraction and uplift were called for and
booked two seats for a violin recital in a small hall near the hotel.
He foolishly booked the most expensive seats without making
sure they were not in an upstairs gallery. They were, and
approached by a narrow wooden stairs. This concert was in the
afternoon. Halfway up the first flight of stairs there was a small
landing. Collopy painfully led the way up with his stick and the
aid of the banister, Father Fahrt keeping behind to save him if
he overbalanced and fell backwards. When Collopy got to this
landing and stepped on to the middle of it, there was a rending,
splintering crash, the whole floor collapsed and with a terrible
shriek, Collopy disappeared through the gaping hole. There was
a sickening thud and more noise of breakage as he hit bottom.
Poor Father Fahrt was distracted, rushed down, alerted the door-
man, got the manager and other people and had a message sent
to me at the hotel.

'When I arrived the scene was grotesque. There was apparently no access to the space under the stairs and two carpenters
using hatches, saws and chisels were carefully breaking down the
woodwork in the hallway below the landing. About a dozen
lighted candles were in readiness on one of the steps, casting a
ghastly light on the very shaken Father Fahrt, two gendarmes,
a man with a bag who was evidently a doctor and a whole mob
of sundry characters, many of them no doubt onlookers who
had no business there.

'The carpenters eventually broke through and pulled away
several boards as ambulance men arrived with a stretcher. The
doctor and Father Fahrt pushed their way to the aperture.
Apparently Collopy was lying on his back covered with broken
timbers and plastering, one leg doubled under him and blood

pouring from one of his ears. He was semi-conscious and groaning pitifully. The doctor gave him some massive injection and then Father Fahrt knelt beside him, and hoarse, faltering whispers told us he was hearing a confession. Then, under the shattered stairway of this cheap Roman hall, Father Fahrt administered the Last Rites to Collopy.

'Getting the unfortunate man on the stretcher after the doctor had given him another knock-out injection was an enormous job for the ambulance men, who had to call for assistance from two bystanders. Nobody could understand his prodigious weight. (N.B. – I have changed the label on the Gravid Water bottle to guard strictly against overdosage.) It was fully twenty minutes before Collopy, now quite unconscious, could be got from under the stairs, and four men were manning the stretcher. He was driven off to hospital.

'Father Fahrt and I walked glumly back to the hotel. He told me he was sure the fall would kill Collopy. After an hour or so he got a telephone call from the hospital. A doctor told him that Collopy was dead on admission, from multiple injuries. He, the doctor, would like to see us urgently and would call to the hotel about six.

'When he arrived, he and Father Fahrt had a long conversation in Italian one word of which, I need hardly say, I did not understand.

'When he had gone, Father Fahrt told me the facts. Collopy had a fractured skull, a broken arm and leg and severe rupture of the whole stomach region. Even if none of those injuries was individually fatal, no man of Collopy's age could survive the shock of such an accident. But what had completely puzzled the doctor and his colleagues was the instantaneous onset of decomposition in the body and its extraordinarily rapid development. The hospital has got in touch with the city health authorities, who feared some strange foreign disease and had ordered that the body be buried the next morning. The hospital had arranged for undertakers to attend, at our expense, the following morning at 10 a.m. and a grave had been booked at the cemetery of Campo Verano.

'I was interested in that mention of premature and rapid decomposition of the body. I am not sure but I would say that here was the Gravid Water again. I said nothing, of course.

'We were early enough at the hospital. Collopy had already been coffined, and a hearse with horses, and a solitary cab, were waiting. I saw the Director and gave him a cheque to cover everything. Then we started out for the church of San Lorenzo Fuori le Mura, near the cemetery, where Father Fahrt said Requiem Mass. The burial afterwards was indeed a simple affair, for myself and the good priest were the only mourners, and it was he who said the prayers at the graveside.

'We drove back in the cab to the hotel in silence. Father Fahrt had told me that Collopy had made a will and that it was in possession of a Dublin firm of solicitors named Sproule, Higgins and Fogarty. I will have to see those people. In the cab I made up my mind to go home immediately to Dublin, then to London, giving Father Fahrt some money and letting him fend for himself. You will see me almost as soon as you get this letter.'

Well, that was the brother's last communiqué from the Continent. And I did see him, two days later.

CHAPTER 21

THE BROTHER walked in unannounced about three-thirty in the afternoon. Thank God Annie was out. He threw his coat and hat on the kitchen table, nodded affably and sat down opposite me at the range in Mr Collopy's ramshackle old chair.

– Well, he said briskly, and how are we?

He was very well dressed but I concluded he was half drunk.

– We are fair to middling, I said, but that business in Rome has my nerves shattered. You seem to be bearing up pretty well yourself?

– Oh, one has to take these things, he said, making a pouting gesture with his mouth. Nobody will mourn much for us when we go for the long jump and don't fool yourself that they will.

– I liked the poor old man. He wasn't the worst.

– All right. His death wasn't the happiest he could get. In fact it was ridiculous. But look at it this way. In what better place could a man die than in Rome, the Eternal City, by the side of Saint Peter?

– Yes, I said wryly. There was timber concerned in both cases. Saint Peter was crucified.

– Ah, true enough. I have often wondered how exactly crucifixions were carried out in practice. Did they crucify a man horizontally with the cross lying on the ground and then hoist him upright?

– I don't know but I suppose so.

– Well by Gob they would have a job hoisting Collopy up. I am sure that man weighed at least thirty-five stone at the end and sure he wasn't anything like the size of you or myself.

– Have you no compunction about your Gravid Water?

– Not at all. I think his metabolism went astray. But anybody who takes patent medicines runs a calculated risk.

– Was Mr Collopy the first the Gravid Water was tried on?

– I would have to look that up. Look, get two glasses and a sup of water. I've a little drop here before we go out.

He produced a half-pint bottle which was one-third full. I got the glasses, he divided the whiskey and there we were, our glasses on the range and sitting vis-à-vis, for all the world as if we were Mr Collopy and Father Fahrt. I asked him how Father Fahrt was.

– He is still in Rome, of course. He is in a very morbid state but tries hard at this business of pious resignation. I think he has forgotten about the Pope's threats. I'm sure they were all bluff, anyway. And how's our friend Annie?

– She seems resigned, too. I told her what you said about the necessity for hasty burial. She seemed to accept it. Of course, I said nothing about the Gravid Water.

– Just as well. Here's luck!

– G'luck!

– I rang up those solicitors Sproule, Higgins and Fogarty and made an appointment for half four this evening. We'd better get out now and have a drink first.

– All right.

We took a tram to Merrion Square and went into a pub in Lincoln Place.

– Two balls of malt, the brother ordered.

– No, I interposed. Mine is a bottle of stout.

He looked at me incredulously and then reluctantly ordered a stout.

– In our game, he said, it doesn't do to be seen drinking stout or anything of that kind. People would take you for a cabman.

– I might be that yet.

– Oh, there is one thing I forgot to tell you. On the night before the funeral I got in touch with one of those monumental sculpture fellows and ordered a simple headstone to be ready not later than the following night. I paid handsomely for it and the job was done. It was erected the following morning and I have paid for kerbing to be carried out as soon as the grave settles.

– You certainly think of everything, I said in some admiration.

– Why wouldn't I think of that? I might never be in Rome again.

– Still . . .

– I believe you are a bit of a literary man.

– Do you mean the prize I got for my piece about Cardinal Newman?

— Well, that and other things. You have heard of Keats, of course?

— Of course. *Ode to a Grecian Urn. Ode to Autumn.*

— Exactly. Do you know where he died?

— I don't. In his bed, I suppose?

— Like Collopy, he died in Rome and he is buried there. I saw his grave. Mick, give us a ball of malt and a bottle of stout. It is beautiful and very well kept.

— That is very interesting.

— He wrote his own epitaph. He had a poor opinion of his standing as a poet and wrote a sort of a jeer at himself on his tombstone. Of course it may have been all cod, just looking for praise.

— What's this the phrase was?

— He wrote: *Here lies one whose name is writ on water.* Very poetical, ah?

— Yes, I remember it now.

— Wait till I show you. Drink up that, for goodness' sake! I took a photograph of Collopy's grave just before I left. Wait till you see now.

He rummaged in his inside pocket and produced his wallet and fished a photograph out of it. He handed it to me proudly. It showed a large plain mortuary slab bearing this inscription:

X

COLLOPY

of Dublin

1848–1910

Here lies one whose name
is writ in water

R.I.P.

— Isn't it good, he chuckled. 'In water' instead of 'on water'?

— Where's his Christian name? I asked.

— Bedammit but I didn't know it. Neither did Father Fahrt.

— Well where did you get the year of his birth?

— Well, that was more or less a guess. The hospital people said he was a man of about seventy-two, and that's what the doctor has on the death certificate which I have in my pocket. So I just subtracted. What do you think of the stone?

— My turn to buy a drink. What will you have?

THE HARD LIFE 603

– Ball of malt.

I ordered another drink.

– I think the stone looks very well, I said, and you showed great foresight in providing it. I think you should stake out Annie on a trip to her father's grave.

– A very good idea, he said. Excellent.

– We had better finish up here and keep that appointment.

We were slightly late arriving at the office of Sproule, Higgins and Fogarty. A bleak male clerk took our names and went into a room marked MR SPROULE. He then beckoned us in. Mr Sproule was an ancient wrinkled thing like his own parchments, remarkably like a character out of Dickens. He rose to a stooped standing and shook hands with us, waving us to chairs.

– Ah, he said, wasn't it sad about poor Mr Collopy?

– You got my letter from Rome, Mr Sproule? the brother said.

– I did indeed. We have a correspondent of our own in Rome, too, the only firm in Dublin with one. We have a lot of work with the Orders.

– Yes, the brother said. We would like to have some idea of what's in the will. Here, by the way, is the death certificate.

– That will be very useful indeed. Thank you. Now I have the will here. I'm sure you don't want to be troubled with all the legalistic rigmarole we lawyers must insist on.

– No, Mr Sproule, I said impatiently.

– Well, we don't know the exact value of the estate because it consists mostly of investments. But I will summarize the testator's wishes. First, there are capital bequests. The house at Warrington Place he leaves to his daughter Annie, with a thousand pounds in cash. To each of his two half-nephews – and that is you gentlemen – he leaves five hundred pounds in cash provided each is in residence with him in his house at the date of his death.

– Great Lord, the brother cried, that lets me out! I haven't been living there for months.

– That is most unfortunate, Mr Sproule said.

– And me that's after burying him in Rome and raising a headstone to his memory, all out of my own pocket!

He looked to each of us incredulously.

– That can't be helped, I said severely. What else is there, Mr Sproule?

– After all that has been done, Mr Sproule went on, we have
to set up the Collopy Trust. The Trust will pay the daughter Annie
three hundred pounds a year for life. The Trust will erect and
maintain three establishments which the testator calls rest rooms.
There will be a rest room at Irishtown, Sandymount, at Harold's
Cross and at Phibsborough. Each will bear the word PEACE very
prominently on the door and each will be under the patronage
of a saint – Saint Patrick, Saint Jerome and Saint Ignatius. Each
of these establishments will bear a plaque reading, for instance,
'THE COLLOPY TRUST – Rest Room of Saint Jerome'. You will
note that they are very well dispersed, geographically.

– Yes indeed, I said. Who is going to design those buildings?

– My dear sir, Mr Collopy thought of everything. That
has already been done. Architect's approved plans are lodged
with me.

– Well is that the lot? the brother asked.

– Substantially, yes. There are a few small bequests and a sum
for Masses in favour of Rev. Kurt Fahrt, S.J. Of course, nothing
can be paid until the will is admitted to probate. But I take it that
will be automatic.

– Very good, I said. My brother lives in London but I am still
here. At the old address.

– Excellent. I can write to you.

We turned to go. Abruptly the brother turned at the door.

– Mr Sproule, he said, may I ask you a question?

– A question? Certainly.

– What was Mr Collopy's Christian name?

– What?

Mr Sproule was clearly startled.

– Ferdinand, of course.

– Thanks.

When we found ourselves again in the street, I found that the
brother was not as downcast as I thought he might be.

– Ferdinand? Fancy! What I need badly at this moment he
said, is a drink. I am five hundred pounds poorer since I went
into that office.

– Well, let us have a drink to celebrate that I'm better off.

– Right. I want to keep near the Kingstown tram, for I'm
going to jump the boat tonight. I left my bags in London on the
way here. This place will do.

He led the way into a public house in Suffolk Street and to my surprise agreed to drink half-ones instead of balls of malt, in view of the long night's travelling he had to face. He was in a reminiscent, nostalgic mood, and talked of many things in our past lives.

– Have you made up your mind, he asked eventually, what you're going to do with yourself?

– No, I said, except that I have decided to pack up school.

– Good man.

– As regards making a living, I suppose that five hundred pounds will give me at least another two years to think about it if I need all that time.

– Would you not join me at the university in London.

– Well, I'll consider that. But I have a terrible feeling that sooner or later the police will take a hand in that foundation.

– Nonsense!

– I don't know. I feel the ice is pretty thin, smart and all as you are.

– I haven't put a foot wrong yet. Have you ever thought about getting into this new motor business? It's now a very big thing on the other side.

– No, I never thought much about that. I would need capital. Besides, I know nothing whatever about machines. For all the good those damned Brothers have been to me, I know nothing about anything.

– Well, I was the same. The only way to learn anything is to teach yourself.

– I suppose so.

– Tell me this, the brother said rather broodily, how is Annie and how do you get on with her?

– Annie is all right, I said. She is recovering from that terrible affair in Rome. I think she feels grateful to yourself for what you did, though she doesn't talk about it. Do you know what? It would be a nice thing if you gave her a present of a hundred pounds to keep the house and everything going until the will is fixed up.

– Yes, that is a good idea. I'll post a cheque from London and write her a nice letter.

– Thanks.

– Tell me: does she look after you all right?

— Perfectly.

— Grub, laundry, socks and all that?

— Of course. I live like a lord. Breakfast in bed if you please.

— That's good. Lord, look at the time! I'll have to look slippy if I'm to get that boat. Yes, I'm very pleased that Annie is turning out like that. She is a good-hearted girl.

— But what are you talking about, I said rather puzzled. Hasn't she been looking after a whole houseful all her life? Poor Mrs Crotty in her day never did a hand's turn. She was nearly always sick and, God rest the dead, but Mr Collopy was a handful in himself, always asking whether there was starch in his food, no matter what you gave him. He even suspected the water in the tap.

— Ah yes. All the same, he paid his debt. I was delighted at the generous way he is treating her in the will.

— So am I.

— Yes indeed. Look, we will have two last drinks for the road. Paddy, two glasses of malt!

— Right, sir.

He brought those deep yellow drinks and placed them before us.

— You know, the brother said, a substantial house and three hundred pounds a year for life is no joke. By God it is no joke.

He carefully put some water in his whiskey.

— Annie is an industrious, well-built quiet girl. There are not so many of them knocking about. And you don't see many of that decent type across in London. Over there they are nearly all prostitutes.

— Perhaps you don't meet the right people.

— Oh I meet enough, don't you worry. Decent people are rare everywhere.

I grunted.

— And decent people who are well got are the rarest of all.

— Occasionally decent people get a right dose of Gravid Water.

He ignored this and picked up his drink.

— In my opinion, he said solemnly, half your own battle was won if you decided to settle down. Tell me this much: have you ever had a wish for Annie?

— WHAT ...?

He raised the glass of whiskey to his lips and drained it all away in one monstrous gulp. He then slapped me on the shoulder.

– Think about it!

The slam of the door told me he was gone. In a daze I lifted my own glass and without knowing what I was doing did exactly what the brother did, drained the glass in one vast swallow. Then I walked quickly but did not run to the lavatory. There, everything inside me came up in a tidal surge of vomit.

THE DALKEY ARCHIVE

*I dedicate these pages
to my Guardian Angel,
impressing upon him
that I'm only fooling
and warning him
to see to it that
there is no misunderstanding
when I go home.*

CHAPTER 1

DALKEY IS A little town maybe twelve miles south of Dublin, on the shore. It is an unlikely town, huddled, quiet, pretending to be asleep. Its streets are narrow, not quite self-evident as streets and with meetings which seem accidental. Small shops look closed but are open. Dalkey looks like an humble settlement which must, a traveller feels, be next door to some place of the first importance and distinction. And it is – vestibule of a heavenly conspection.

Behold it. Ascend a shaded, dull, lane-like way, *per iter*, as it were, *tenebricosum*, and see it burst upon you as if a curtain had been miraculously whisked away. Yes, the Vico Road.

Good Lord!

The road itself curves gently upward and over a low wall to the left by the footpath enchantment is spread – rocky grassland falling fast away to reach a toy-like railway far below, with beyond it the immeasurable immanent sea, quietly moving slowly in the immense expanse of Killiney Bay. High in the sky which joins it at a seam far from precise, a caravan of light cloud labours silently to the east.

And to the right? Monstrous arrogance: a mighty shoulder of granite climbing ever away, its overcoat of furze and bracken embedded with stern ranks of pine, spruce, fir and horse-chestnut, with further on fine clusters of slim, meticulous euca-lyptus – the whole a dazzle of mildly moving leaves, a farrago of light, colour, haze and copious air, a wonder that is quite vert, verdant, vertical, verticillate, vertiginous, in the shade of branches even vespertine. Heavens, has something escaped from the lexicon of Sergeant Fottrell?

But why this name Vico Road? Is there to be recalled in this magnificence a certain philosopher's pattern of man's lot on earth – thesis, antithesis, synthesis, chaos? Hardly. And is this to be compared with the Bay of Naples? That is not to be thought of, for in Naples there must be heat and hardness belabouring desiccated Italians – no soft Irish skies, no little breezes that feel almost coloured.

At a great distance ahead and up, one could see a remote little obelisk surmounting some steps where one can sit and contemplate all this scene: the sea, the peninsula of Howth across the bay and distantly, to the right, the dim outline of the Wicklow mountains, blue or grey. Was the monument erected to honour the Creator of all this splendour? No. Perhaps in remembrance of a fine Irish person He once made – Johannes Scotus Erigena, perhaps, or possibly Parnell? No indeed: Queen Victoria.

Mary was nudging Michael Shaughnessy. She loitered enticingly about the fringes of his mind; the deep brown eyes, the light hair, the gentleness yet the poise. She was really a nuisance yet never far away. He frowned and closed his fist, but intermittent muttering immediately behind him betokened that Hackett was there.

– How is she getting on, he asked, drawing level, that pious Mary of yours?

It was by no means the first time that this handsome lout had shown his ability to divine thought, a nasty gift.

– Mind your own business, Shaughnessy said sourly. I never ask about the lady you call Asterisk Agnes.

– If you want to know, she's very well, thank you.

They walked in, loosely clutching their damp bathing things.

In the low seaward wall there was a tiny gap which gave access to a rough downhill path towards the railway far below; there a footbridge led to a bathing place called White Rock. At this gap a man was standing, supporting himself somewhat with a hand on the wall. As Shaughnessy drew near he saw the man was spare, tall, clean-shaven, with sparse fairish hair combed sideways across an oversize head.

– This poor bugger's hurt, Hackett remarked.

The man's face was placid and urbane but contorted in a slight grimace. He was wearing sandals and his right foot in the region of the big toe was covered with fresh blood. They stopped.

– Are you hurt, sir? Hackett asked.

The man politely examined each of them in turn.

– I suppose I am, he replied. There are notices down there about the dangers of the sea. Usually there is far more danger on land. I bashed my right toes on a sharp little dagger of granite I didn't see on that damned path.

– Perhaps we could help, Shaughnessy said. We'd be happy to assist you down to the Colza Hotel in Dalkey. We could get you a chemist there or maybe a doctor.

The man smiled slightly.

– That's good of you, he replied, but I'm my own doctor. Perhaps though you could give me a hand to get home?

– Well, certainly, Shaughnessy said.

– Do you live far, sir? Hackett asked.

– Just up there, the man said, pointing to the towering trees. It's a stiff climb with a cut foot.

Shaughnessy had no idea that there was any house in the fastness pointed to, but almost opposite there was a tiny gate discernible in the rough railing bounding the road.

– So long as you're sure there *is* a house there, Hackett said brightly, we will be honoured to be of valuable succour.

– The merit of the house is that hardly anybody except the postman knows it's there, the other replied agreeably.

They crossed the road, the two escorts lightly assisting at each elbow. Inside the gate a narrow but smooth enough pathway fastidiously picked its way upward through treetrunks and shrubs.

– Might as well introduce myself, the invalid said. My name's De Selby.

Shaughnessy gave his, adding that everybody called him Mick. He noticed that Hackett styled himself just Mr Hackett: it seemed an attitude of polite neutrality, perhaps condescension.

– This part of the country, De Selby remarked, is surprisingly full of tinkers, gawms and gobshites. Are you gentlemen skilled in the Irish language?

The non-sequitur rather took Shaughnessy aback, but not Hackett.

– I know a great lot about it, sir. A beautiful tongue.

– Well, the word *mór* means big. In front of my house – we're near it now – there is a lawn surprisingly large considering the terrain. I thought I would combine *mór* and lawn as a name for the house. A hybrid, of course, but what matter? I found a looderamawn in Dalkey village by the name of Teague McGetti-gan. He's the local cabman, handyman, and observer of the weather; there is absolutely nothing he can't do. I asked him to paint the name on the gate, and told him the words. Now wait till you see the result.

The house could now be glimpsed, a low villa of timber and brick. As they drew nearer De Selby's lawn looked big enough but regrettably it was a sloping expanse of coarse, scruffy grass embroidered with flat weeds. And in black letters on the wooden gate was the title: LAWNMOWER. Shaughnessy and Hackett sniggered as De Selby sighed elaborately.

– Well the dear knows I always felt that Teague was our domestic Leonardo, Hackett chuckled. I'm well acquainted with the poor bastard.

They sidled gently inward. De Selby's foot was now dirty as well as bloody.

CHAPTER 2

OUR MUTILATED friend seems a decent sort of segotia, Hackett remarked from his armchair. De Selby had excused himself while he attended to 'the medication of my pedal pollex', and the visitors gazed about his living room with curiosity. It was oblong in shape, spacious, with a low ceiling. Varnished panelling to the height of about eighteen inches ran right round the walls, which otherwise bore faded greenish paper. There were no pictures. Two heavy mahogany bookcases, very full, stood in embrasures to each side of the fireplace, with a large press at the blank end of the room. There were many chairs, a small table in the centre and by the far wall a biggish table bearing sundry scientific instruments and tools, including a microscope. What looked like a powerful lamp hovered over this and to the left was an upright piano by Liehr, with music on the rest. It was clearly a bachelor's apartment but clean and orderly. Was he perhaps a musician, a medical man, a theopneust, a geodetic chemist . . . a savant?

– He's snug here anyway, Mick Shaughnessy said, and very well hidden away.

– He's the sort of man, Hackett replied, that could be up to any game at all in this sort of secret HQ. He might be a dangerous character.

Soon De Selby reappeared, beaming, and took his place in the centre, standing with his back to the empty fireplace.

– A superficial vascular lesion, he remarked pleasantly, now cleansed, disinfected, anointed, and with a dressing you see which is impenetrable even by water.

– You mean, you intend to continue swimming? Hackett asked.

– Certainly.

– Bravo! Good man.

– Oh not at all – it's part of my business. By the way, would it be rude to enquire what is the business of you gentlemen?

– I'm a lowly civil servant, Mick replied. I detest the job, its low atmosphere and the scruff who are my companions in the office.

– I'm worse off, Hackett said in mock sorrow. I work for the father, who's a jeweller but a man that's very careful with the keys. No opportunity of giving myself an increase in pay. I suppose you could call me a jeweller too, or perhaps a sub-jeweller. Or a paste jeweller.

– Very interesting work, for I know a little about it. Do you cut stones?

– Sometimes.

– Yes. Well I'm a theologist and a physicist, sciences which embrace many others such as eschatology and astrognosy. The peace of this part of the world makes true thinking possible. I think my researches are nearly at an end. But let me entertain you for a moment.

He sat down at the piano and after some slow phrases, erupted into what Mick with inward wit, would dub a headlong chromatic dysentery which was 'brilliant' in the bad sense of being inchoate and, to his ear at least, incoherent. A shattering chord brought the disorder to a close.

– Well, he said, rising, what did you think of that?

Hackett looked wise.

– I think I detected Liszt in one of his less guarded moments, he said.

– No, De Selby answered. The basis of that was the canon at the start of César Franck's well-known sonata for violin and piano. The rest was all improvisation. By me.

– You're a splendid player, Mick ventured archly.

– It's only for amusement but a piano can be a very useful instrument. Wait till I show you something.

He returned to the instrument, lifted half of the hinged top and took out a bottle of yellowish liquid, which he placed on the table. Then opening a door in the nether part of a bookcase, he took out three handsome stem glasses and a decanter of what looked like water.

– This is the best whiskey to be had in Ireland, faultlessly made and perfectly matured. I know you will not refuse a taiscaun.

– Nothing would make me happier, Hackett said. I notice that there's no label on the bottle.

– Thank you, Mick said, accepting a generous glass from De

Selby. He did not like whiskey much, or any intoxicant, for that matter. But manners came first. Hackett followed his example.

– The water's there, De Selby gestured. Don't steal another man's wife and never water his whiskey. No label on the bottle? True. I made that whiskey myself.

Hackett had taken a tentative sip.

– I hope you know that whiskey doesn't mature in a bottle. Though I must say that this tastes good.

Mick and De Selby took a reasonable gulp together.

– My dear fellow, De Selby replied, I know all about sherry casks, temperature, subterranean repositories and all that extravaganza. But such considerations do not arise here. This whiskey was made last week.

Hackett leaned forward in his chair, startled.

– What was that? he cried. A week old? Then it can't be whiskey at all. Good God, are you trying to give us heart failure or dissolve our kidneys?

De Selby's air was one of banter.

– You can see, Mr Hackett, that I am also drinking this excellent potion myself. And I did not say it was a week old. I said it was made last week.

– Well, this is Saturday. We needn't argue about a day or two.

– Mr De Selby, Mick interposed mildly, it is clear enough that you are making some distinction in what you said, that there is some nicety of terminology in your words. I can't quite follow you.

De Selby here took a drink which may be described as profound and then suddenly an expression of apocalyptic solemnity came over all his mild face.

– Gentlemen, he said, in an empty voice, I have mastered time. Time has been called an event, a repository, a continuum, an ingredient of the universe. I can suspend time, negative its apparent course.

Mick thought it funny in retrospect that Hackett here glanced at his watch, perhaps involuntarily.

– Time is still passing with me, he croaked.

– The passage of time, De Selby continued, is calculated with reference to the movements of the heavenly bodies. These are fallacious as determinants of the nature of time. Time has been studied and pronounced upon by many apparently sober men –

Newton, Spinoza, Bergson, even Descartes. The postulates of the Relativity nonsense of Einstein are mendacious, not to say bogus. He tried to say that time and space had no real existence separately but were to be apprehended only in unison. Such pursuits as astronomy and geodesy have simply befuddled man. You understand?

As it was at Mick he looked the latter firmly shook his head but thought well to take another stern sup of whiskey. Hackett was frowning. De Selby sat down by the table.

– Consideration of time, he said, from intellectual, philosophic or even mathematical criteria is fatuity, and the preoccupation of slovens. In such unseemly brawls some priestly fop is bound to induce a sort of cerebral catalepsy by bringing forward terms such as infinity and eternity.

Mick thought it seemly to say something, however foolish.

– If time is illusory as you seem to suggest, Mr De Selby, how is it that when a child is born, with time he grows to be a boy, then a man, next an old man and finally a spent and helpless cripple?

De Selby's slight smile showed a return of the benign mood.

– There you have another error in formulating thought. You confound time with organic evolution. Take your child who has grown to be a man of twenty-one. His total life-span is to be seventy years. He has a horse whose life-span is to be twenty. He goes for a ride on his horse. Do these two creatures subsist simultaneously in dissimilar conditions of time? Is the velocity of time for the horse three and a half times that for the man?

Hackett was now alert.

– Come here, he said. That greedy fellow the pike is reputed to grow to be up to two hundred years of age. How is our time-ratio if he is caught and killed by a young fellow of fifteen?

– Work it out for yourself, De Selby replied pleasantly. Divergences, incompatibilities, irreconcilables are everywhere. Poor Descartes! He tried to reduce all goings-on in the natural world to a code of mechanics, kinetic but not dynamic. All motion of objects was circular, he denied a vacuum was possible and affirmed that weight existed irrespective of gravity. *Cogito ergo sum*? He might as well have written *inepsias scripsi ergo sum* and prove the same point, as *he* thought.

– That man's work, Mick interjected, may have been mistaken in some conclusions but was guided by his absolute belief in Almighty God.

– True indeed. I personally don't discount the existence of a supreme *supra mundum* power but I sometimes doubted if it is benign. Where are we with this mess of Cartesian methodology and Biblical myth-making? Eve, the snake and the apple. Good Lord!

– Give us another drink if you please, Hackett said. Whiskey is not incompatible with theology, particularly magic whiskey that is ancient and also a week old.

– Most certainly, said De Selby, rising and ministering most generously to the three glasses. He sighed as he sat down again.

– You men, he said, should read all the works of Descartes, having first thoroughly learnt Latin. He is an excellent example of blind faith corrupting the intellect. He knew Galileo, of course, accepted the latter's support of the Copernican theory that the earth moves round the sun and had in fact been busy on a treatise affirming this. But when he heard that the Inquisition had condemned Galileo as a heretic, he hastily put away his manuscript. In our modern slang he was yellow. And his death was perfectly ridiculous. To ensure a crust for himself, he agreed to call on Queen Christina of Sweden three times a week at five in the morning to teach her philosophy. Five in the morning in that climate! It killed him, of course. Know what age he was?

Hackett had just lit a cigarette without offering one to anybody.

– I feel Descartes' head was a little bit loose, he remarked ponderously, not so much for his profusion of erroneous ideas but for the folly of a man of eighty-two thus getting up at such an unearthly hour and him near the North Pole.

– He was fifty-four, De Selby said evenly.

– Well by damn, Mick blurted, he was a remarkable man however crazy his scientific beliefs.

– There's a French term I heard which might describe him, Hackett said. *Idiot-savant.*

De Selby produced a solitary cigarette of his own and lit it. How had he inferred that Mick did not smoke?

– At worst, he said in a tone one might call oracular, Descartes

was a solipsist. Another weakness of his was a liking for the
Jesuits. He was very properly derided for regarding space as
a plenum. It is a coincidence, of course, but I have made the
parallel but undoubted discovery that *time* is a plenum.

– What does that mean? Hackett asked.

– One might describe a plenum as a phenomenon or existence
full of itself but inert. Obviously space does not satisfy such a
condition. But time is a plenum, immobile, immutable, ineluctable, irrevocable, a condition of absolute stasis. Time does not
pass. Change and movement may occur within time.

Mick pondered this. Comment seemed pointless. There
seemed no little straw to clutch at; nothing to question.

– Mr De Selby, he ventured at last, it would seem impertinent
of the like of me to offer criticism or even opinions on what
I apprehend as purely abstract propositions. I'm afraid I harbour
the traditional idea and experience of time. For instance, if you
permit me to drink enough of this whiskey, by which I mean
too much, I'm certain to undergo unmistakable temporal punishment. My stomach, liver and nervous system will be wrecked
in the morning.

– To say nothing of the dry gawks, Hackett added.

De Selby laughed civilly.

– That would be a change to which time, of its nature, is quite
irrelevant.

– Possibly, Hackett replied, but that academic observation will
in no way mitigate the reality of the pain.

– A tincture, De Selby said, again rising with the bottle and
once more adding generously to the three glasses. You must
excuse me for a moment or two.

Needless to say, Hackett and Mick looked at each other in
some wonder when he had left the room.

– This malt seems to be superb, Hackett observed, but would
he have dope or something in it?

– Why should there be? He's drinking plenty of it himself.

– Maybe he's gone away to give himself a dose of some
antidote. Or an emetic.

Mick shook his head genuinely.

– He's a strange bird, he said, but I don't think he's off his
head, or a public danger.

– You're certain he's not derogatory?

– Yes. Call him eccentric.

Hackett rose and gave himself a hasty extra shot from the bottle, which in turn Mick repelled with a gesture. He lit another cigarette.

– Well, he said, I suppose we should not overstay our welcome. Perhaps we should go. What do you say?

Mick nodded. The experience had been curious and not to be regretted; and it could perhaps lead to other interesting things or even people. How commonplace, he reflected, were all the people he did know.

When De Selby returned he carried a tray with plates, knives, a dish of butter and an ornate basket full of what seemed golden bread.

– Sit in to the table, lads – pull over your chairs, he said. This is merely what the Church calls a collation. These delightful wheaten farls were made by me, like the whiskey, but you must not think I'm like an ancient Roman emperor living in daily fear of being poisoned. I'm alone here, and it's a long painful pilgrimage to the shops.

With a murmur of thanks the visitors started this modest and pleasant meal. De Selby himself took little and seemed preoccupied.

– Call me a theologian or a physicist as you will, he said at last rather earnestly, but I am serious and truthful. My discoveries concerning the nature of time were in fact quite accidental. The objective of my research was altogether different. My aim was utterly unconnected with the essence of time.

– Indeed? Hackett said rather coarsely as he coarsely munched. And what was the main aim?

– To destroy the whole world.

They stared at him. Hackett made a slight noise but De Selby's face was set, impassive, grim.

– Well, well, Mick stammered.

– It merits destruction. Its history and prehistory, even its present, is a foul record of pestilence, famine, war, devastation and misery so terrible and multifarious that its depth and horror are unknown to any one man. Rottenness is universally endemic, disease is paramount. The human race is finally debauched and aborted.

– Mr De Selby, Hackett said with a want of gravity, would it be rude to ask just how you will destroy the world? You did not make it.

– Even you, Mr Hackett, have destroyed things you did not make. I do not care a farthing about who made the world or what the grand intention was, laudable or horrible. The creation is loathsome and abominable, and total extinction could not be worse.

Mick could see that Hackett's attitude was provoking brusqueness whereas what was needed was elucidation. Even marginal exposition by De Selby would throw light on the important question – was he a true scientist or just demented?

– I can't see, sir, Mick ventured modestly, how this world could be destroyed short of arranging a celestial collision between it and some other great heavenly body. How a man could interfere with the movements of the stars – I find that an insoluble puzzle, sir.

De Selby's taut expression relaxed somewhat.

– Since our repast is finished, have another drink, he said, pushing forward the bottle. When I mentioned destroying the whole world, I was not referring to the physical planet but to every manner and manifestation of life on it. When my task is accomplished – and I feel that will be soon – nothing living, not even a blade of grass, a flea – will exist on this globe. Nor shall I exist myself, of course.

– And what about us? Hackett asked.

– You must participate in the destiny of all mankind, which is extermination.

– Guesswork is futile, Mr De Selby, Mick murmured, but could this plan of yours involve liquefying all the ice at the Poles and elsewhere and thus drowning everything, in the manner of the Flood in the Bible?

– No. The story of that Flood is just silly. We are told it was caused by a deluge of forty days and forty nights. All this water must have existed on earth before the rain started, for more can not come down than was taken up. Commonsense tells me that this is childish nonsense.

– That is merely a feeble rational quibble, Hackett cut in. He liked to show that he was alert.

– What then, sir, Mick asked in painful humility, is the secret, the supreme crucial secret?

De Selby gave a sort of grimace.

– It would be impossible for me, he explained, to give you gentlemen, who have no scientific training, even a glimpse into my studies and achievements in pneumatic chemistry. My work has taken up the best part of a life-time and, though assistance and co-operation were generously offered by men abroad, they could not master my fundamental postulate: namely, the annihilation of the atmosphere.

– You mean, abolish air? Hackett asked blankly.

– Only its biogenic and substantive ingredient, replied De Selby, which, of course, is oxygen.

– Thus, Mick interposed, if you extract all oxygen from the atmosphere or destroy it, all life will cease?

– Crudely put, perhaps, the scientist agreed, now again genial, but you may grasp the idea. There are certain possible complications but they need not trouble us now.

Hackett had quietly helped himself to another drink and showed active interest.

– I think I see it, he intoned. Exit automatically the oxygen and we have to carry on with what remains, which happens to be poison. Isn't it murder though?

De Selby paid no attention.

– The atmosphere of the earth, meaning what in practice we breathe as distinct from rarefied atmosphere at great heights, is composed of roughly 78 per cent nitrogen, 21 oxygen, tiny quantities of argon and carbon dioxide, and microscopic quantities of other gases such as helium and ozone. Our preoccupation is with nitrogen, atomic weight 14.008, atomic number 7.

– Is there a smell off nitrogen? Hackett enquired.

– No. After extreme study and experiment I have produced a chemical compound which totally eliminates oxygen from any given atmosphere. A minute quantity of this hard substance, small enough to be invisible to the naked eye, would thus convert the interior of the greatest hall on earth into a dead world provided, of course, the hall were properly sealed. Let me show you.

He quietly knelt at one of the lower presses and opened the door to reveal a small safe of conventional aspect. This he opened with a key, revealing a circular container of dull metal of a size that would contain perhaps four gallons of liquid. Inscribed on its face were the letters DMP.

– Good Lord, Hackett cried, the DMP! The good old DMP! The grandfather was a member of that bunch.

De Selby turned his head, smiling bleakly.

– Yes – the DMP – the Dublin Metropolitan Police. My own father was a member. They are long-since abolished, of course.

– Well what's the idea of putting that on your jar of chemicals?

De Selby had closed the safe and press door and gone back to his seat.

– Just a whim of mine, no more, he replied. The letters are in no sense a formula or even a mnemonic. But that container has in it the most priceless substance on earth.

– Mr De Selby, Mick said, rather frightened by these flamboyant proceedings, granted that your safe is a good one, is it not foolish to leave such dangerous stuff here for some burglar to knock it off?

– Me, for instance? Hackett interposed.

– No, gentlemen, there is no danger at all. Nobody would know what the substance was, its properties or how activated.

– But don't *we* know? Hackett insisted.

– You know next to nothing, De Selby replied easily, but I intend to enlighten you even more.

– I assure you, Mick thought well to say, that any information entrusted to us will be treated in strict confidence.

– Oh, don't bother about that, De Selby said politely, it's not information I'll supply but experience. A discovery I have made – and quite unexpectedly – is that a deoxygenated atmosphere cancels the apparently serial nature of time and confronts us with true time and simultaneously with all the things and creatures which time has ever contained or will contain, provided we evoke them. Do you follow? Let us be serious about this. The situation is momentous and scarcely of this world as we know it.

He stared at each of his two new friends in turn very gravely.

– I feel, he announced, that you are entitled to some personal explanation concerning myself. It would be quite wrong to regard me as a christophobe.

– Me too, Hackett chirped impudently.

– The early books of the Bible I accepted as myth, but durable myth contrived genuinely for man's guidance. I also accepted as

fact the story of the awesome encounter between God and the
rebel Lucifer. But I was undecided for many years as to the outcome of that encounter. I had little to corroborate the revelation
that God had triumphed and banished Lucifer to hell forever.
For if – I repeat *if* – the decision had gone the other way and
God had been vanquished, who but Lucifer would be certain to
put about the other and opposite story?

– But why should he? Mick asked incredulously.

– The better to snare and damn mankind, De Selby answered.

– Well now, Hackett remarked, that secret would take some
keeping.

– However, De Selby continued, perplexed, I was quite mistaken in that speculation. I've since found that things are as set
forth in the Bible, at least to the extent that heaven is intact.

Hackett gave a low whistle, perhaps in derision.

– How could you be sure? he asked. You have not been
temporarily out of this world, have you, Mr De Selby?

– Not exactly. But I have had a long talk with John the Baptist.
A most understanding man, do you know, you'd swear he was a
Jesuit.

– Good heavens! Mick cried, while Hackett hastily put his
glass on the table with a click.

– Ah yes, most understanding. Perfect manners, of course, and
a courteous appreciation of my own personal limitations. A very
interesting man the same Baptist.

– Where did this happen? Hackett asked.

– Here in Dalkey, De Selby explained. Under the sea.

There was a small but absolute silence.

– While time stood still? Hackett persisted.

– I'll bring both of you people to the same spot tomorrow.
That is, if you wish it and provided you can swim, and for a short
distance under water.

– We are both excellent swimmers, Hackett said cheerfully,
except I'm by far the better of the pair.

– We'd be delighted, Mick interrupted with a sickly smile, on
the understanding that we'll get safely back.

– There is no danger whatever. Down at the headquarters of
the Vico Swimming Club there is a peculiar chamber hidden in
the rocks at the water's edge. At low tide there is cavernous access
from the water to this chamber. As the tide rises this hole is

blocked and air sealed off in the chamber. The water provides a total seal.

— This could be a chamber of horrors, Hackett suggested.

— I have some masks of my own design, equipped with compressed air, normal air, and having an automatic feed-valve. The masks and tank are quite light, of aluminium.

— I think I grasp the idea, Mick said in a frown of concentration. We go under the water wearing these breathing gadgets, make our way through this rocky opening to the chamber, and there meet John the Baptist?

De Selby chuckled softly.

— Not necessarily and not quite. We get to the empty chamber as you say and I then release a minute quantity of DMP. We are then subsisting in timeless nitrogen but still able to breathe from the tanks on our backs.

— Does our physical weight change? Hackett asked.

— Yes, somewhat.

— And what happens then?

— We shall see what happens after you have met me at this swimming pool at eight o'clock tomorrow morning. Are you going back by the Colza Hotel?

— Certainly.

— Well have a message sent to Teague McGettigan to call for me with his damned cab at 7.30. Those mask affairs are bothersome to horse about with.

Thus the appointment was made, De Selby affable as he led his visitors to his door and said goodbye.

CHAPTER 3

HACKETT WAS frowning a bit and taciturn as the two strolled down the Vico Road towards Dalkey. Mick felt preoccupied, his ideas in some disarray. Some light seemed to have been drained from the sunny evening.

– We don't often have this sort of diversion, Hackett, he remarked.

– It certainly isn't every day we're offered miraculous whiskey, Hackett answered gloomily, and told at the same time we're under sentence of death. Shouldn't other people be warned? Our personal squaws, for instance?

– That would be what used to be called spreading despondency and disaffection, Mick warned pompously. What good would it do?

– They could go to confession, couldn't they?

– So could you. But the people would only laugh at us. So far as you are concerned, they'd say you were drunk.

– That week-old gargle was marvellous stuff, he muttered reflectively after a pause. I feel all right but I'm still not certain that there wasn't some sort of drug in it. Slow-acting hypnotic stuff, or something worse that goes straight to the brain. We might yet go berserk by the time we reach the Colza. Maybe we'll be arrested by Sergeant Fottrell.

– Divil a fear of it.

– I certainly wouldn't like to swear the truth of today in court.

– We have an appointment early tomorrow morning, Mick reminded him. I suggest we say nothing to anybody about today's business.

– Do you intend to keep tomorrow's date?

– I certainly do. But I'll have to use the bike to get here from Booterstown at that hour.

They walked on, silent in thought.

It is not easy to give an account of the Colza Hotel, its owner Mrs Laverty, or its peculiar air. It had been formerly, though not in any recent time, an ordinary public house labelled 'Constantine Kerr, Licensed Vintner' and it was said that Mrs Laverty, a widow, had remodelled the bar, erased the obnoxious public house title and called the premises the Colza Hotel.

Why this strange name?

Mrs Laverty was a most religious woman and once had a talk with a neighbour about the red lamp suspended in the church before the high altar. When told it was sustained with colza oil, she piously assumed that this was a holy oil used for miraculous purposes by Saint Colza, VM,* and decided to put her house under this banner.

Here is the layout of the bar in the days when Hackett and Shaughnessy were customers:

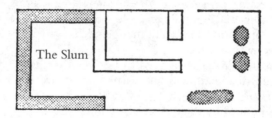

The area known as 'The Slum' was spacious with soft leather seating by the wall and other seats and small tables about the floor. Nobody took the hotel designation seriously, though Mrs Laverty stoutly held that there were 'many good beds' upstairs. A courageous stranger who demanded a meal would be given rashers and eggs in a desultory back kitchen. About the time now dealt with Mrs Laverty had been long saving towards a pilgrimage to Lourdes. Was she deaf? Nobody was sure. The doubt had arisen some years ago when Hackett openly addressed her as Mrs Lavatory, of which she never took any notice. Hard of hearing, perhaps, she may also have thought that Hackett had never been taught to speak properly.

When Hackett and Shaughnessy walked in after the De Selby visit, the 'Slum' or habitat of cronies was occupied by Dr Crewett, a very old and wizened and wise medical man who had seen much service in the RAMC but disdained to flaunt a

* Virgin Martyr.

military title. A strange young man was sitting near him and Mrs Laverty was seated behind the bar, knitting.

– Hello to all and thank God to be back in civilization, Hackett called. Mrs L, give me two glass skillets of your patent Irish malt, please.

She smiled perfunctorily in her large homely face and moved to obey. She did not like Hackett much.

– Where were ye? Dr Crewett asked.

– Walking, Mick said.

– You gents have been taking the intoxicating air, he observed. Your complexions do ye great credit.

– It has been a good day, doctor, Mick added civilly.

– We have been inhaling oxygen, theology and astral physics, Hackett said, accepting two glasses from Mrs Laverty.

– Ah, physics? I see, the young stranger said politely. He was slim, black-haired, callow, wore thick glasses and looked about nineteen.

– The Greek word *kinesis* should not be ignored, Hackett said learnedly but with an air of jeer.

– Hackett, Mick interjected in warning, I think it's better for us to mind our own business.

– It happens that I'm doing medicine at Trinity, the stranger added. I'm out here looking for digs.

– Why come out to this wilderness, Hackett asked, and have yourself trailing in and out of town every day?

– This is a new friend of ours, Dr Crewett explained. May I introduce Mr Nemo Crabbe?

Nods were exchanged and Hackett raised his glass in salute.

– If you mean take rooms in Trinity, Crabbe replied, no, thanks. They are vile, ramshackle quarters, and a resident student there is expected to empty his own charley.

– In my days in Egypt we hadn't even got such a thing. But there was limitless sand and wastes of scrub.

– Besides, Crabbe added, I like the sea.

– Well, fair enough, Hackett growled, why not stay right here. This is a hotel.

Mrs Laverty raised her head, displeased.

– I have already told the gentleman, Mr Hackett, she said sharply, that we're full up.

– Yes, but of what?

Dr Crewett, a peace-maker, intervened.

– Mrs Laverty, I think I'll buy a glawsheen all round if you would be so kind.

She nodded, mollified a bit, and rose.

– Damned physics and chemistry are for me a scourge, Crabbe confided to all. It's my father who insists on this medicine nonsense. I have no interest at all in it, and Dr Crewett agrees with my attitude.

– Certainly, the medico nodded.

– He believes that doctors of today are merely messenger boys for the drug firms.

– Lord, drugs, Hackett muttered.

– And very dangerous and untested drugs many of them are, Dr Crewett added.

– Nobody can take away Dr Glauber's great triumph, Hackett remarked, grasping his new drink. I've often wondered that since *glauben* means 'to think', whether *Glauber* means thinker? Remember the pensive attitude of the seated one.

– It doesn't, Mick said brusquely, for he had briefly studied German.

– Actually, poetry is my real interest, Crabbe said. I suppose I have something in common with Shelley and Byron. The sea, I mean, and poetry. The sea is a poem in itself.

– It has metre, too, Hackett's voice sneered. Nothing finer than a good breeze and a 12-metre boat out there in the bay.

Mrs Laverty's gentle voice was heard from her averted face.

– I'm very fond of poetry. That thing the Hound of Heaven is grand. As a girl I knew bits of it by heart.

– Some people think it's doggerel.

– I suppose, Crabbe ventured, that all you good friends think my Christian name is odd. Nemo.

– It *is* odd, Mick agreed in what was meant to be a kindly tone. And if I may say so, your father must be an odd man.

– It was my mother, I believe.

– You could always change it, Crabbe, Dr Crewett suggested. In common law a man can call himself and be known by any name he likes.

– That reminds me of the poor man whose surname was Piss, Hackett recounted. He didn't like it and changed it by deed-poll to Vomit.

– I implore you not to be facetious, the unsmiling Crabbe replied. The funny thing is that I like the name Nemo. Try thinking of it backwards.

– Well, you have something there, Hackett granted.

– Poetic, what?

There was a short silence which Dr Crewett broke.

– That makes you think, he said thoughtfully. Wouldn't it be awful to have the Arab surname Esra?

– Let us have another round, Sussim L, Mick said facetiously, before I go home to beautiful Booterstown.

She smiled. She was fond of him in her own way. But had she heard his hasty transliteration? Hackett was scribbling a note.

– Mrs L, he said loudly, could you see that Teague McGettigan gets this tonight? It's about an urgent appointment with another man for tomorrow morning.

– I will, Mr Hackett.

They left soon afterwards, going homewards by tram. Hackett got off at Monkstown, not far away, where he lived.

Mick felt well enough, and wondered about the morrow. After all, De Selby had done nothing more than talk. Much of it was astonishing talk but he had promised actual business at an hour not so long after dawn. Assuming he turned up with his gear, was there risk? Would the unreliable Hackett be there?

He sighed. Time, even if there was no such thing, would tell.

CHAPTER 4

MILD AIR with the sea in a stage whisper behind it was in Mick's face as his bicycle turned into the lane-like approach to the Vico Road and its rocky swimming hole. It was a fine morning, calm, full of late summer.

Teague McGettigan's cab was at the entrance, the horse's head submerged in a breakfast nose-bag. Mick went down the steps and saluted the company with a hail of his arm. De Selby was gazing in disfavour at a pullover he had just taken off. Hackett was slumped seated, fully dressed and smoking a cigarette, while McGettigan in his dirty raincoat was fastidiously attending to his pipe. De Selby nodded. Hackett muttered 'More luck' and McGettigan spat.

— Boys-a-dear, McGettigan said in a low voice from his old thin unshaven face, ye'll get the right drenching today. Ye'll be soaked to the pelt.

— Considering that we're soon to dive into that water, Hackett replied, I won't dispute your prophecy, Teague.

— I don't mean that. Look at that bloody sky.

— Cloudless, Mick remarked.

— For Christ's sake look down there by Wickla.

In that quarter there was what looked like sea-haze, with the merest hint of the great mountain behind. With his hands Mick made a gesture of nonchalance.

— We might be down under the water for half an hour, I believe, Hackett said, or at least that's Mr De Selby's story. We have an appointment with mermaids or something.

— Get into your togs, Hackett, De Selby said impatiently. And you, too, Mick.

— Ye'll pay more attention to me, Teague muttered, when ye come up to find ye'r superfine clothes demolished be the lashin rain.

— Can't you keep them in your cursed droshky? De Selby barked. His temper was clearly a bit uncertain.

All got ready. Teague sat philosophically on a ledge, smoking and having the air of an indulgent elder watching children at play. Maybe his attitude was justified. When the three were ready for the water De Selby beckoned them to private consultation. The gear was spread out on a flattish rock.

– Now listen carefully, he said. This apparatus I am going to fit on both of you allows you to breathe, under water or out of it. The valve is automatic and needs no adjustment, nor is that possible. The air is compressed and will last half an hour by conventional effluxion of time.

– Thank God, sir, that your theories about time are not involved in the air supply, Hackett remarked.

– The apparatus also allows you to hear. My own is somewhat different. It enables me to do all that but speak and be heard as well. Follow?

– That seems clear enough, Mick agreed.

– When I clip the masks in place your air supply is *on*, he said emphatically. Under water or on land you can breathe.

– Fair enough, Hackett said politely.

– And listen to this, De Selby continued, I will go first, leading the way, over there to the left, to this cave opening, now submerged. It is only a matter of yards and not deep down. The tide is now nearly full. Follow close behind me. When we get to the rock apartment, take a seat as best you can, do nothing, and wait. At first it will be dark but you won't be cold. I will then annihilate the terrestrial atmosphere and the time illusion by activating a particle of DMP. Now is all that clear? I don't want any attempt at technical guff or questions at this time.

Hackett and Mick mutely agreed that things were clear.

– Down there you are likely to meet a personality who is from heaven, who is all-wise, speaks all languages and dialects and knows, or can know, everything. I have never had a companion on such a trip before, and I do hope events will not be complicated.

Mick had suddenly become very excited.

– Excuse the question, he blurted, but will this be John the Baptist again?

– No. At least I hope not. I can request but cannot command.

– Could it be . . . anybody? Hackett asked.

– Only the dead.

– Good heavens!

— Yet that is not wholly correct. Those who were never on earth could appear.

This little talk was eerie. It was as if a hangman were courteously conversing with his victim, on the scaffold high.

— Do you mean angels, Mr De Selby? Mick enquired.

— Deistic beings, he said gruffly. Here, stand still till I fix this.

He had picked up a breathing mask, with its straps and tank affair at the back.

— I'll go after you, Mick muttered, with Hackett at the rear.

In a surprisingly short time they were all fully dressed for a visit under the sea to the next world, or perhaps the former world. Through his goggles Mick could see Teague McGettigan studying an early Sunday paper, apparently at a rear racing page. He was at peace, with no interest whatever in supernatural doings. He was perhaps to be envied. Hackett was standing impassive, an Apollo space-man. De Selby was making final adjustments to his straps and with a gesture had led the way to the lower board.

Going head-down into cold water in the early morning is a shock to the most practised. But in Mick's case the fog of doubt and near-delusion in the head, added to by the very low hiss of his air supply, made it a brief but baffling experience. There was ample light as he followed De Selby's kicking heels and a marked watery disturbance behind told him that Hackett was not far away. If he was cursing, nobody heard.

Entry to the 'apartment' was efficient enough for beginners. If not adroit. De Selby readily found the opening and then, one by one, the others made their way upwards, half-clambering, half-swimming. They left the water quite palpably and Mick found himself crouching in an empty space on a rough floor strewn with rocks and some shells. Everything was dark and a distant sussurus must have been from the sea which had just been left. The company was under the water and presumably in an atmosphere that could be breathed, though only for a short time. *Time*? Yes, the word might be repeated.

De Selby beckoned Mick on with a tug at the arm, and he did the same for Hackett behind. Then they stopped. Mick crouched and finally squatted on a roundish rock; De Selby was to his left and the three had come to some sort of resting posture. Hackett gave Mick a nudge, though the latter did not know if it meant commiseration, encouragement or derision.

From his movements it was evident even in the gloom that De Selby was busy at some technical operation. Mick could not see what he was doing but no doubt he was detonating (or whatever is the word) a minuscule charge of DMP.

Though wet, he did not feel cold, but he was apprehensive, puzzled, curious. Hackett was near but quite still.

A faint light seemed to come, a remote glow. It gradually grew to define the dimension of the dim apartment, making it appear unexpectedly large and strangely dry.

Then Mick saw a figure, a spectre, far away from him. It looked seated and slightly luminescent. Gradually it got rather clearer in definition but remained unutterably distant, and what he had taken for a very long chin in profile was almost certainly a beard. A gown of some dark material clothed the apparition. It is strange to say that the manifestation did not frighten him but he was flabbergasted when he heard De Selby's familiar tones almost booming out beside him.

– I must thank you for coming. I have two students with me.

The voice that came back was low, from far away but perfectly clear. The Dublin accent was unmistakable. The extraordinary utterance can here be distinguished only typographically.

– *Ah not at all, man.*

– You're feeling well, as usual, I suppose?

– *Nothing to complain of, thank God. How are you feeling yourself, or how do you think you're feeling?*

– Tolerably, but age is creeping in.

– *Ha-ha. That makes me laugh.*

– Why?

– *Your sort of time is merely a confusing index of decomposition. Do you remember what you didn't know was your youth?*

– I do. But it's *your* youth I wanted to talk about. The nature of your life in youth compared with that of your hagiarchic senility must have been a thunderous contrast, the ascent to piety sudden and even distressing. Was it?

– *You are hinting at anoxic anoxæmia? Perhaps.*

– You admit you were a debauched and abandoned young man?

– *For a pagan I wasn't the worst. Besides, maybe it was the Irish in me.*

– The Irish in you?

— *Yes. My father's name was Patrick. And he was a proper gobshite.*

— Do you admit that the age or colour of women didn't matter to you where the transaction in question was coition?

— *I'm not admitting anything. Please remember my eyesight was very poor.*

— Were all your rutting ceremonials heterosexual?

— *Heterononsense! There is no evidence against me beyond what I wrote myself. Too vague. Be on your guard against that class of fooling. Nothing in black and white.*

— My vocation is enquiry and action, not literature.

— *You're sadly inexperienced. You cannot conceive the age I lived in, its customs, or judge of that African sun.*

— The heat, hah? I've read a lot about the Eskimoes. The poor bastards are perished throughout their lives, covered with chilblains and icicles but when they catch a seal — ah, good luck to them! They make warm clothes out of the hide, perform gluttonly feats with the meat and then bring the oil home to the igloo where they light lamps and stoves. Then the fun begins. Nanook of the North is certainly partial to his nookie.

— *I reprobate concupiscence, whether fortuitous or contrived.*

— You do *now*, you post-gnostic! You must have a red face to recall your earlier nasty gymnastiness, considering you're now a Father of the Church.

— *Rubbish. I invented obscene feats out of bravado, lest I be thought innocent or cowardly. I walked the streets of Babylon with low companions, sweating from the fires of lust. When I was in Carthage I carried about with me a cauldron of unrealized debauchery. God in his majesty was tempting me. But Book Two of my Confessions is all shocking exaggeration. I lived within my rough time. And I kept the faith, unlike a lot more of my people in Algeria who are now Arab nincompoops and slaves of Islam.*

— Look at all the time you squandered in the maw of your sexual fantasies which otherwise could have been devoted to Scriptural studies. Lolling loathsome libertine!

— *I was weak at the time but I find your condescension offensive. You talk of the Fathers. How about that ante-Nicene thooleramawn, Origen of Alexandria? What did he do when he found that lusting after women distracted him from his sacred scrivenery? I'll tell you. He stood up, hurried out to the kitchen, grabbed a carving knife and — pwitch! — in one swipe deprived himself of his personality! Ah?*

– Yes. Let us call it heroic impetuosity.

– *How could Origen be the Father of Anything and he with no knackers on him? Answer me that one.*

– We must assume that his spiritual testicles remained intact. Do you know him?

– *I can't say I ever met him in our place.*

– But, dammit is he there? Don't you know everything?

– *I do not. I can, but the first wisdom is sometimes not to know. I suppose I could ask the Polyarch.*

– Who on earth is the Polyarch?

– *He's not on earth, and again I don't know. I think he's Christ's Vicar in Heaven.*

– Are there any other strange denizens?

– *Far too many if you ask me. Look at that gobhawk they call Francis Xavier. Hobnobbing and womanizing in the slums of Paris with Calvin and Ignatius Loyola in warrens full of rats, vermin, sycophants, and syphilis. Xavier was a great travelling man, messing about in Ethiopia and Japan, consorting with Buddhist monkeys and planning to convert China single-handed. And Loyola? You talk about me but a lot of that chap's early saintliness was next to bedliness. He made himself the field-marshal of a holy army of mendicants but maybe merchandizers would be more like it. Didn't Pope Clement XIV suppress the Order for its addiction to commerce, and for political wirepulling? Jesuits are the wili-est, cutest and most mendacious ruffians who ever lay in wait for simple Christians. The Inquisition was on the track of Ignatius. Did you know that? Pity they didn't get him. But one party who wouldn't hear of the Pope's Brief of Suppression was the Empress of Rooshia. Look at that now!*

– Interesting that your father's name was Patrick. Is he a saint?

– *That reminds me. You have a Professor Binchy in your university outfit in Dublin and that poor man has been writing and preaching since he was a boy that the story about Saint Patrick is all wrong and that there were really two Saint Patricks. Binchy has his hash and parsley.*

– Why?

– *Two Saint Patricks? We have four of the buggers in our place and they'd make you sick with their shamrocks and shenanigans and bullshit.*

– Who else? What about Saint Peter?

– *Oh he's safe and sound all right. A bit of a slob to tell you the truth. He often encorpifies himself.*

– What was that?

– *Encorpifies himself. Takes on a body, as I've done now for your convenience. How could the like of you make anything out of an infinity of gases? Peter's just out to show off the keys, bluster about and make himself a bloody nuisance. Oh there have been a few complaints to the Polyarch about him.*

– Answer me this question. The Redeemer said 'Thou art Peter and upon this rock I shall found my Church'. Is there any justification for the jeer that He founded his Church upon a pun, since Petros means 'rock'?

– *Not easy to say. The name Petros does not occur in classical, mythological or biblical Greek apart from your man the apostle and his successor and later namesakes – except for a freedman of Berenice (mother of Herod Agrippa) mentioned in Josephus,* Jewish Antiquities 18, 6, 3, *in a passage relating to the later years of Tiberius's reign, that is, the thirties* A.D. *Petro occurs as a Roman surname in Suetonius's* Vespasiae 1, *and Petra as a woman's name in Tacitus,* Annals 11, 4.

– And you don't care a lot about him?

– *The lads in our place, when he barges around encorpified and flashing the keys, can't resist taking a rise out of him and pursue him with the cackles of a rooster, cock-adoodle-doo.*

– I see. Who else? Is Judas with you?

– *That's another conundrum for the Polyarch. Peter stopped me one time and tried to feed me a cock-and-bull story about Judas coming to the Gate. You get my joke? Cock–and–bull story?*

– Very funny. Is your mother Monica there?

– *Wait now! Don't try and get a dig at me that way. Don't blame me. She was here before me.*

– To lower the temperature of your steaming stewpot of lust and depravity, you married or took as concubine a decent poor young African girl, and the little boy you had by her you named Adeodatus. But even yet nobody knows your wife's name.

– *That secret is safe with me still.*

– Why should you give such a name to your son while you were yourself still a debauched pagan, not even baptized?

– *Put that day's work down to the mammy – Monica.*

– Later, you put your little wife away and she shambled off to the wilderness, probably back into slavery, but swearing to remain faithful to you forever. Does the shame of that come back to you?

— *Never mind what comes back to me, I done what the mammy said, and everybody — you too — has to do what the mammy says.*

— And straightaway, as you relate in Book Six of your Confessions, you took another wife, simultaneously committing bigamy and adultery. And you kicked her out after your *Tolle Lege* conjuring tricks in the garden when you ate a handful of stolen pears. Eve herself wasn't accused in respect of more than one apple. In all this disgraceful behaviour do we see Monica at work again?

— *Certainly. God also.*

— Does Monica know that you're being so unprecedentedly candid with me?

— *Know? She's probably here unencorpified.*

— You betrayed and destroyed two decent women, implicated God in giving a jeering name to a bastard, and you blame all this outrage on your mother. Would it be seemly to call you a callous humbug?

— *It would not. Call me a holy humbug.*

— Who else is in your kingdom? Is Judas?

— *Paul is in our place, often encorpified and always attended by his physician Luke, putting poultices on his patient's sore neck. When Paul shows too much consate in himself, the great blatherskite with his epistles in bad Greek, the chronic two-timer, I sometimes roar after him 'You're not on the road to Damascus now!' Puts him in his place. All the same that* Tolle Lege *incident was no conjuring trick. It was a miracle. The first book I picked up was by Paul and the lines that struck my eyes were these: 'Not in rioting or drunkenness, nor in chambering or wantonness, nor in strife or envying: but put ye on the Lord Jesus Christ and make not provision for the flesh in the lust thereof.' But do you know, I think the greatest dog's breakfast of the lot is St Vianney.*

— I never heard of him.

— *'Course you have. Jean-Baptiste. You'd know him better as the curé of Ars.*

— Oh yes. A French holy man.

— *A holy fright, you mean. Takes a notion when he's young to be a priest, as ignorant as the back of a cab, couldn't make head nor tail of Latin or sums, dodges the column when Napoleon is looking for French lads to be slaughtered in Rooshia, and at the heel of the hunt spends sixteen to eighteen hours a day in the confessional — hearing, not telling — and takes to performing miracles, getting money from nowhere and taking on hand to tell the future. Don't be talking. A diabolical wizard of a man.*

– Your household abounds in oddities.

– *He performs his miracles still in our place. Gives life to bogus corpses and thinks nothing of raising from the dead a dummy mummy.*

– I repeat a question I've already asked: is Judas a member of your household?

– *I don't think the Polyarch would like me to say much about Judas.*

– He particularly interests me. The Gospel extols love and justice. Peter denied his Master out of pride, vanity and perhaps fear. Judas did something similar but from a comprehensible motive. But Peter's home and dried. Is Judas?

– *Judas, being dead, is eternal.*

– But where is he?

– *The dead do not have whereness. They have condition.*

– Did Judas earn paradise?

– *Pulchritudo tam antiqua et tam nova sero amavit.*

– You are shifty and you prevaricate. Say yes or no to this question: did you suffer from hæmorrhoids?

– *Yes. That is one reason that I encorpify myself with reluctance.*

– Did Judas have any physical affliction?

– *You have not read my works. I did not build the City of God. At most I have been an humble urban district councillor, never the Town Clerk. Whether Judas is dead in the Lord is a question notice of which would require to be given to the Polyarch.*

– De Quincey held that Judas enacted his betrayal to provoke his Master into proclaiming his divinity by deed. What do you think of that?

– *De Quincey also consumed narcotics.*

– Nearly everything you have taught or written lacks the precision of Descartes.

– *Descartes was a recitalist, or formulist, of what he took, often mistakenly, to be true knowledge. He himself established nothing new, nor even a system of pursuing knowledge that was novel. You are fond of quoting his* Cogito Ergo Sum. *Read my works. He stole that. See my dialogue with Evodius in* De Libero Arbitrio, *or the Question of Free Choice. Descartes spent far too much time in bed subject to the persistent hallucination that he was thinking. You are not free from a similar disorder.*

– I have read all the philosophy of the Fathers, before and after Nicaea: Chrysostom, Ambrose, Athanasius.

– If you have read Athanasius you have not understood him. The result of your studies might be termed a corpus of patristic paddeology.

– Thank you.

– You are welcome.

– The prime things – existence, time, the godhead, death, paradise and the satanic pit, these are abstractions. Your pronouncements on them are meaningless, and within itself the meaninglessness does not cohere.

– Discourse must be in words, and it is possible to give a name to that which is not understood nor cognoscible by human reason. It is our duty to strive towards God by thought and word. But it is our final duty to believe, to have and to nourish faith.

– I perceive some of your pronouncements to be heretical and evil. Of sin, you said it was necessary for the perfection of the universe and to make good shine all the more brightly in contrast. You said God is not the cause of our doing evil but that free will is the cause. From God's omniscience and foreknowledge He knows that men will sin. How then could free will exist?

– God has not foreknowledge. He is, and has knowledge.

– Man's acts are all subject to predestination and he cannot therefore have free will. God created Judas. Saw to it that he was reared, educated, and should prosper in trade. He also ordained that Judas should betray His Divine Son. How then could Judas have guilt?

– God, in knowing the outcome of free will, did not thereby attenuate or extirpate free will.

– That light-and-shade gentleman you once admired so much, Mani, held that Cain and Abel were not the sons of Adam and Eve but the sons of Eve and Satan. However that may be, the sin in the garden of Eden was committed in an unimaginably remote age, eons of centuries ago, according to the mundane system of computing time. According to the same system the doctrine of the Incarnation and the Redemption is now not even two thousand years old. Are all the millions and millions of uncountable people born between the Creation and the Redemption to be accounted lost, dying in original sin though themselves personally guiltless, and to be considered condemned to hell?

– If you would know God, you must know time. God is time. God

is the substance of eternity. God is not distinct from what we regard as years. God has no past, no future, no presence in the sense of man's fugitive tenure. The interval you mention between the Creation and the Redemption was ineffably unexistent.

– That is the sort of disputation that I dub 'flannel' but granted that the soul of man is immortal, the geometry of a soul must be circular and, like God, it cannot have had a beginning. Do you agree with that?

– *In piety it could thus be argued.*

– Then our souls existed before joining our bodies?

– *That could be said.*

– Well, where were they?

– *None but the Polyarch would say that.*

– Are we to assume there is in existence somewhere a boundless reservoir of souls not yet encorpified?

– *Time does not enter into an act of divine creation. God can create something which has the quality of having always existed.*

– Is there any point in my questioning you on your one-time devotion to the works of Plotinus and Porphyry?

– *No. But far preferable to the Manichæan dualism of light and darkness, good and evil, was Plotinus's dualism of mind and matter. In his doctrine of emanation Plotinus was only slightly misled. Plotinus was a good man.*

– About 372, when you were eighteen, you adopted Manichæanism and did not discard the strange creed until ten years later. What do you think now of that jumble of Babylonian cosmology, Buddhism and ghostly theories about light and darkness, the Elect and the Hearers, the commands to abstain from fleshmeat, manual labour and intercourse with women? Or Mani's own claim that he was himself the Paraclete?

– *Why ask me now when you can read the treatise against this heresy which I wrote in 394? So far as Mani himself is concerned, my attitude maybe be likened to that of the King of Persia in 376. He had Mani skinned alive and then crucified.*

– We must be going very soon.

– *Yes. Your air is nearly gone.*

– There is one more question on a matter that has always baffled me and on which nothing written about you by yourself or others gives any illumination. *Are you a Nigger?*

– *I am a Roman.*

– I suspect your Roman name is an affectation or a disguise. You are of Berber stock, born in Numidia. Those people were non-white. You are far more aligned with Carthage than Rome, and there are Punic corruptions even in your Latin.

– *Civis Romanus sum.*

– The people of your homeland today are called Arabs. Arabs are not white.

– *Berbers were blond white people, with lovely blue eyes.*

– All true Africans, notwithstanding the racial stew in that continent, are to some extent niggers. They are descendants of Noah's son Ham.

– *You must not overlook the African sun. I was a man that was very easily sunburnt.*

– What does it feel like to be in heaven for all eternity?

– *For all eternity? Do you then think there are fractional or temporary eternities?*

– If I ask it, will you appear to me here tomorrow?

– *I have no tomorrow. I am. I have only nowness.*

– Then we shall wait. Thanks and goodbye.

– *Goodbye. Mind the rocks. Go with God.*

With clambering, Hackett in the lead, they soon found the water and made their way back to this world.

THE MORNING was still there, bland as they had left it. Teague McGettigan was slumped in charge of his pipe and newspaper and gave them only a glance when, having discarded their masks, they proceeded without thought to brisk towelling.

— Well, De Selby called to Mick, what did you think of that?

Mentally, Mick felt numb, confused; and almost surprised by ordinary day.

— That was . . . an astonishing apparition, he stammered. And I heard every word. A very shrewd and argumentative man whoever he was.

De Selby froze in his half-naked stance, his mouth falling a bit open in dismay.

— Great crucified Lord, he cried, don't tell me you didn't recognize Augustine?

Mick stared back, still benumbed.

— I thought it was Santa Claus, Hackett remarked. Yet his voice lacked the usual intonation of jeer.

— I suppose, De Selby mused, beginning to dress, that I do you two some injustice. I should have warned you. A first encounter with a man from heaven can be unnerving.

— Several of the references were familiar enough, Mick said, but I couldn't quite pinpoint the personality. My goodness, the Bishop of Hippo!

— Yes. When you think of it, he did not part with much information.

— If I may say so, Hackett interposed, he didn't seem too happy in heaven. Where was the glorious resurrection we've all been promised? That character underground wouldn't get a job handing out toys in a store at Christmas. He seemed depressed.

— I must say that the antics of his companions seemed strange, Mick agreed. I mean, according to his account of them.

De Selby stopped reflectively combing his sparse hair.

— One must reserve judgement on all such manifestations,

he said. I am proceeding all the time on a theory. We should remember that that might not have been the genuine Augustine at all.

– But who, then?

The wise master stared out to sea.

– It could be even Beelzebub himself, he murmured softly.

Hackett sat down abruptly, working at his tie.

– Have any of you gentlemen got a match? Teague McGettigan asked, painfully standing up. Hackett handed him a box.

– The way I see it, Teague continued, there will come an almighty clump of rain and wind out of Wickla about twelve o'clock. Them mountains down there has us all destroyed.

– I'm not afraid of a shower, Hackett remarked coldly. At least you know what it is. There are worse things.

– Peaks of rock prod up into the clouds like fingers, Teague explained, until the clouds is bursted and the wind carries the wather down here on top of us. Poor buggers on a walking tour around Shankill would get soaked, hang-sangwiches in sodden flitters and maybe not the price of a pint between them to take shelter in Byrnes.

Their dressing, by reason of their rough rig, was finished. De Selby and Hackett were smoking, and the time was half nine. Then De Selby energetically rubbed his hands.

– Gentlemen, he said with some briskness, I presume that like me you have had no breakfast before this early swim. May I therefore invite you to have breakfast with me at Lawnmower. Mr McGettigan can drive us up to the gate.

– I'm afraid I can't go, Hackett said.

– Well, it's not that my horse Jimmy couldn't pull you up, Teague said, spitting.

– Come now, De Selby said, we all need inner fortification after an arduous morning. I have peerless Limerick rashers and there will be no shortage of that apéritif.

Whether or not Hackett had another engagement Mick did not know but he immediately shared his instinct to get away, if only, indeed, to think, or try not to think. De Selby had not been deficient in the least in manners or honourable conduct but his continuing company seemed to confer uneasiness – perhaps vague, unformed fear.

– Mr De Selby, Mick said warmly, it is indeed kind of you to invite Hackett and me up for a meal but it happens that I did in fact have breakfast. I think we'd better part here.

— We'll meet soon again, Hackett remarked, to talk over this morning's goings-on.

De Selby shrugged and beckoned McGettigan to help him with his gear.

— As you will, gentlemen, he said politely enough. I certainly could do with a bite and perhaps I will have the pleasure of Teague's company. I thought the weather, the elements, all the forces of the heavens made a breakfast-tide lecture seemly.

— Good luck to your honour but there's nourishment in that bottle you have, Teague said brightly, taking away his pipe to say it loudly.

They separated like that and Hackett and Mick went on their brief stroll into Dalkey, Mick wheeling the bicycle with some distaste.

— Have you somewhere to go? he asked.

— No I haven't. What did you make of that performance?

— I don't know what to say. You heard the conversation, and I presume both of us heard the same thing.

— Do you believe . . . it all happened?

— I suppose I have to.

— I need a drink.

They fell silent. Thinking about the séance (if that ill-used word will serve) was futile though disturbing and yet it was impossible to shut such thoughts out of the head. Somehow Mick saw little benefit in any discussion with Hackett. Hackett's mind was twisted in a knot identical with his own. They were as two tramps who had met in a trackless desert, each hopelessly asking the other the way.

— Well, Hackett said moodily at last, I haven't thrown overboard my suspicions of yesterday about drugs, and even hypnotism I wouldn't quite discount. But we have no means of checking whether or not all that stuff this morning was hallucination.

— Couldn't we ask somebody? Get advice?

— Who? For a start, who would believe a word of the story?

— That's true.

— Incidentally, those underwater breathing masks were genuine. I've worn gadgets like that before but they weren't as smart as De Selby's.

– How do we know there wasn't a mixture of some brain-curdling gas in the air-tank?

– That's true by God.

– I quite forgot I was wearing the thing.

They had paused undecided at a corner in the lonely little town. Mick said that he thought he'd better go home and get some breakfast. Hackett thought it was too early to think of food. Well Mick had to get rid of his damned bike. Couldn't he leave it at the comic little police station in charge of Sergeant Fottrell? But what was the point of that? Wouldn't he have the labour of collecting it another time? Hackett said that there had been no necessity to have used it at all in the first place, as there was such a thing as an early tram to accommodate eccentric people. Mick said no, not on Sunday, not from Booterstown.

– I know Mrs L would let me in, Hackett observed pettishly, except I know the big sow is still in bed snoring.

– Yes, it's been a funny morning, Mick replied sympathetically. Here you are, frustrated from joining the company of a widow who keeps a boozer, yet it is not half an hour since you parted company with Saint Augustine.

– Yes.

Hackett laughed bitterly. Mick had in fact business of his own later in the day, he remembered, as on nearly every Sunday. At three-thirty he would meet Mary at Ballsbridge and very likely they would go off to loaf amorously and chatter in Herbert Park. The arrangement was threatening to take on the tedium of routine things. When eventually they were married, if they were at all, wouldn't the sameness of life be worse?

– I'm going to rest my mind, he announced, and rest it in Herbert Park later today, avec ma femme, ma bonne amie.

– My own Asterisk lady abstains on Sundays, Hackett said listlessly, lighting a cigarette.

But suddenly he came to life.

– Consternation was caused this morning, he cried, by the setting off of a small charge of DMP. Here comes the DMP in person!

True enough. Wheeling a bicycle, Sergeant Fottrell was coming towards them from a side road. His approach was slow and grave. Here one beheld the majesty of the law – inevitable, procedural, sure.

It is not easy to outline his personal portrait. He was tall, lean, melancholy, clean-shaven, red in the face and of indeterminate age. Nobody, it was said, had ever seen him in uniform, yet he was far from being a plain-clothes man; his constabularity was unmistakable. Summer and winter he wore a light tweed overcoat of a brown colour; a trace of collar and tie could be discerned about the neck but in his nether person the trousers were clearly of police blue, and the large boots also surely of police issue. Dr Crewett claimed to have seen the sergeant once with his overcoat off when assisting with a broken-down car and no inner jacket of any kind was disclosed, only shirt. The sergeant was friendly, so to speak, to his friends. He drank whiskey freely when the opportunity offered but it did not seem to affect him at all. Hackett held that this was because the sergeant's normal sober manner was identical with the intoxicated manner of other people. But what the sergeant believed, what he said and how he said it was known throughout all south County Dublin.

Now he had stopped and saluted at his cloth cap.

– That's the great morning, lads, he said, gratuitously.

There was agreement that it was. The sergeant seemed to be maturing the air and the early street.

– I see you have been to the water, he remarked genially, for far-from-simple cavortings in the brine?

– Sergeant, Hackett said, you have no idea how far from simple.

– I recede portentously from the sea, the sergeant beamed, except for a fastidious little wade for the good of my spawgs. For the truth is that I'm destroyed with the corns. Our work is walking work if you understand my portent.

– True enough, Sergeant, Mick agreed, I have often seen you with that bicycle but never up on it.

– It is emergency machinery for feats of captaincy. But there are dangers of a mental nature inherent in the bicycle and that story I will relate to you coherently upon another day.

– Yes.

Hackett was meditating on something.

– Funny thing, he said, I left a little bottle behind me in the Colza last night by accident. Perigastric thiosulphate, you know. My damned stomach is full of ructions and eructations.

– Well by damn, the sergeant sighed sympathetically, that is an infertile bitching. I cry for any creature, man or woman, who is troublous in the stomach enpitments. Mrs Laverty would be in her bed now or mayhap awash in her private bath internally.

– Brandy is good for a sick stomach, Mick ventured with studied tactlessness.

– Brandy? Baugh! Hackett grimaced.

– Not brandy but Brannigan, the sergeant cried, striking his crossbar. Brannigan the chemist, and he's an early-Mass man. He would now be shovelling gleefully at his stirabout, and supinely dietetic. Come down along here now.

Glumly Mick followed Hackett's downcast back as the sergeant led the way down the street to a corner shop and smartly knocked on the residential door. The small meek Mr Brannigan had scarcely opened it when they were all crowded in the hallway. Mick felt annoyed at this improvised and silly tactic. What would passers-by think of two bicycles outside at such an hour, with the sergeant's the most recognizable in the whole country? Hackett might be forced to swallow a dose of salts rather than disavow his lie about digestion trouble, and good enough for him.

– I have a man here, Mr Brannigan, avic, the sergeant announced cheerfully, that has a raging confusion in his craw, a stainless citizen and a martyr. Let us make our way sedulously to the shop.

Mr Brannigan with vague noises had produced keys and opened a door in the narrow hall; then they were all in the shop, with its gaudy goods and showcases. Under the high ceiling Mr Brannigan looked tiny (or perhaps his nearness to the sergeant was the real reason), the face quite round, round glasses in it and an air of being pleased.

– Which of the gentlemen, Sergeant, he asked quietly, is out of humour with himself?

The sergeant clapped a hand officially on Hackett's shoulder.

– Mr Hackett is the patient inexorably, he said.

– Ah. Where is the seat of the trouble, Mr Hackett?

The patient made a clutching motion at his stomach.

– Here, he muttered, where nearly everybody's damn trouble lies.

– Ah-ha. Have you been taking anything in particular for it?

– I have. But I can't tell you what. Something from a prescription I haven't got on me.

– Well well now. I would recommend a mix of acetic anhydride with carbonic acid. In solution. Excellent stuff in the right proportions. I won't be a minute getting it.

– No, no, Hackett said in genuine remonstrance. I daren't take drugs I'm not used to. Very nice of you and the Sergeant, Mr Brannigan, but I can wait.

– But we've any amount of proprietary things here, Mr Hackett. Even temporary relief, you know . . .

But the sergeant had been examining a large bottle he had taken down from a low shelf by the counter.

– By the pipers, he cried happily, here is the elixir of youth innocuously in its mundane perfection!

He handed the bottle to Hackett and reached up for another which he put in Mick's hand. The label was,

HURLEY'S TONIC WINE

A glass three times a day or as required assures lasting benefit to the kidneys, stomach and nervous system. As recommended by doctors, nurses and geriatric institutions.

– Mind you, that's not a bad sedative for the inner man, Mr Brannigan said seriously. Many ladies in the town are very partial to it.

– Sir Thomas O'Brannigan, the sergeant intoned grandly, I will buy a bottle of it myself – put it down to me – and when you have emplaced delicate stem glasses we will all have a sup of it superbly, for the dear knows how sick we could all be in the heel of the day.

Mr Brannigan smiled and nodded. Hackett hastily examined their faces in the uncertain light.

– I suppose it would pull us together a bit, he conceded. I'll have a bottle too.

That Sunday morning had been surely one of manicoloured travail. After acerb disputation between De Selby and Saint Augustine, here they were for at least an hour in that closed pharmacy drinking Hurley's Tonic Wine and listening to Sergeant Fottrell's *pensées* on happiness, health, the wonders of foreign travel, law and order, and bicycles. The tonic was, as one suspected it would be, a cheap red wine heavily fortified. Its social purpose was clear enough. It enabled prim ladies, who would be shocked at the idea of entering a public house, to drink liquor that was by no means feeble, in the defensible interest of promoting health.

Mick had also bought a bottle and they were in the midst of a fourth bottle which Mr Brannigan had gallantly put up 'on the house' when Mick felt that sheer shame required that the little party should end. Hackett agreed that he felt much better but not so Mick; even genuine wine does not help much, and he felt a little bit queasy. The sergeant was quite unmoved, and undeterred in loquacity. When they were back in the street Mick turned to him.

– Sergeant, the day is getting older and more people are now about. Would you mind if I left this bike in your station till tomorrow? I think for me a tram home would be the business.

– Benignly certain, he replied, courteously. Tell Policeman Pluck that I ordained the custody unceremoniously.

He then departed about his public business with many blessings commending his friends to God.

– Do you know, Hackett mentioned as they moved off, all that Augustinian chat is gradually bringing half-forgotten things bubbling up in my head. Didn't he have a ferocious go at Pelagius?

– The heretic? Yes.

– What do you mean heretic?

– That's what he was. Some synod condemned and excommunicated him.

– I thought only the Pope could pronounce on heresy.

– No. He appealed to the Pope without result.

– I see. Other bad eggs were the Manichees and the Donatists. I know that. I don't mind about them at all. But if my memory isn't all bunched, I believe Pelagius was a grand man and a sound theologian.

– You don't know much on the subject. Don't pretend.

– He believed Adam's lapse (and personally I wouldn't take the slightest notice of such fooling) harmed only himself. The guilt was his alone and this yarn about everybody being born in original sin is all bloody bull.

– Oh, as you will.

– Who, believing in God, could also believe that the whole

human race was prostrate in ruin before Christ came, the day before yesterday?

— Augustine, for one, I think.

— New-born infants are innocent and if they die before baptism, they have a right to heaven. Baptism is only a rite, a sort of myth.

— According to De Selby, John the Baptist was no myth. He met the man. He probably regards him as a personal friend.

— Are *you* baptized?

— I suppose so.

— Suppose so? Is a hazy opinion enough if your soul depends on it?

— For heaven's sake shut up. Haven't we had enough for today and yesterday?

— An awkward question, what?

— At this rate I'll probably meet Martin Luther on top of the tram.

Hackett contemptuously lit a cigarette and stopped.

— I'll leave you here, go for a walk, get a paper, sit down and read a lot of boring muck, and wait for a chance to slip into the Colza. But remember this: *I'm a Pelagian.*

Policeman Pluck was young, raw-boned, mottled of complexion and wore an expression of friendly stupidity. He had a bicycle upside-down on the floor of the day-room attending to a hernia at the front rim, grating white powder on to a protruding intestine. His salute for Mick was an inane smile in which his scrupulously correct uniform seemed to concur, though all visible teeth seemed to be bad and discoloured.

— Morning, Mr Pluck. I met the sergeant and he told me I could leave this other machine here for a day or two. I'll get a tram.

— Well he did, did he? grinned Policeman Pluck. Ah, the dacent lovable man!

— Is that all right?

— You are welcome, sir, and lave it be the wall there. But the sergeant's tune will change when he comes up with that cabman Teague.

— What has Teague done?

Policeman Pluck blanched slightly at the recollection of horror.

— Yesterday he met a missionary father, a Redempiorist, at the

station and druv him up to the parochial house. Well, Teague
and his jinnet wasn't five minits in the PP's holy grounds but
before they left it they had the whole place in a pukey mess of a
welter of dung.

    — Ah, unfortunate, that.

    Enough to dress two drills of new spring spuds.

    — Still, Teague was hardly to blame.

    — Do you expect the sergeant to have the jinnet in the dock
for sacrilege? Or for a sin against the Holy Ghost? I'll tell you
wan thing, boy.

    — What's that?

    — You'll have a scarifying mission, an iron mission, there will
be rosaries on the bended knees for further orders, starting
tomorra. There'll be hell to pay. But thank God it's the weemen's
week first.

    — Thank God, Mr Pluck, Mick called back at the door, I'm
not even a parishioner.

    Why should he take account of hellfire sermons anyway?
Had he not been, in a kind of a way, in heaven?

CHAPTER 6

MARY WAS not a simple girl, not an easy subject to write about nor Mick the one to write. He thought women in general were hopeless as a theme for discussion or discourse, and surely for one man the one special – *la femme particulière*, if that sharpens the meaning – must look dim, meaningless and empty to others if he should talk genuinely about her or think aloud. The mutual compulsion is a mystery, not just a foible or biogenesis, and this sort of mystery, even if comprehensible to the two concerned, is at least absolutely private.

Mary was no sweetie-pie nor was she pretty but (to Mick's eyes) she was good-looking and dignified. Brown-eyed, her personality was russet and usually she was quiet and recollected. He was, he thought, very fond of her and did not by any means regard her as merely a member of her sex, or anything so commonplace and trivial. She was a true obsession with him (he suspected) and kept coming into his head on all sorts of irrelevant occasions without, so to speak, knocking. Hackett's relations with the peculiar girl he mixed around with seemed perfunctory, like having a taste for marmalade at breakfast or meditatively paring fingernails in public-house silences.

Mick was absolutely sure in mind about few things but he thought he could sincerely say that Mary was an unusual girl. She was educated, with a year in France, and understood music. She had wit, could be lively, and it took little to induce for a while gaiety of word and mood. Her people, whom he did not know, had money. She was tasteful and fastidious in dress . . . and why not? She worked in what was called a fashion house, with a top job which Mick knew paid well and involved consorting only with people of standing. Her job was one thing they had never talked about. That her earnings were a secret was something he was deeply thankful for because he knew that they could scarcely be less than his own. A disclosure, even accidental, would be his humiliation though he knew all this situation was very silly. Yet work at the fol-the-lols of couture did nothing to impair Mary's maturity of mind. She read a lot, talked politics often and once even mentioned her half-intentions of writing a book. Mick did not ask on what subject, for somehow he found the idea distasteful. Without swallowing whole all the warnings one could readily hear and read about the spiritual dangers of intellectual arrogance and literary freebooting, there *was* menace in the overpoise that high education and a rich way of living could confer on a young girl. Unknowingly, she could exceed her own strength. Did she find his own company a stabilizing pull? Mick had to doubt that, for the truth was that he was not too steady himself. Confession once a month was all very well but he was drinking too much. He would give up drink. Also, he would make Mary more of his own quiet kind, and down to earth.

Yet what was the real position about him and her? Uncertain. He was going to marry her, that was intended. And that was one other subject never mentioned outright in all the long three years of their togetherness. His rotten job, poor pay and worse prospects were always there, physical and repulsive manifestations, like erysipelas. But what other course was open to him? To her, even? In some unthinkable extremity he might perhaps turn to a sad celibacy, yet if somebody else were to come and carry her away, he was sure he would take leave of his senses. He would do some frightful thing, quite stupid but unavoidable.

They were in Herbert Park.

Lolling on a sloping bank of short grass near the lake where ducks and toy boats were moving in a mild uproar of children, their talk had been desultory. He was not anxious to present for inspection his new spiritual status – yet, he asked himself, was she not entitled to know?

– I didn't see you at Mass this morning, she remarked. Was this an opening for him? She was smoking but there was nothing rank, in the Hackett sense, about the fumes. She was a lady, and entitled to a cigarette. Sophistication, call it.

– No. I went off very early for a swim at Dalkey.

– With Hackett?

– Yes.

– Well that's something new. Swimming is all right but getting up at dawn for it, surely that's a rather British attitude? But Hackett up early on Sunday is something startling.

— Stranger things happen.

— How does he like the water when he's absolutely sober?

— We were meeting another man at the Vico. We wanted to be on our own to do some underwater exploration.

— Who was the other man — anybody I know?

— Hardly. We'd only met him ourselves the day before.

— Marine biology with some Trinity College chap — would that be it?

— No, no, a very queer hawk to tell you the truth, Mary, though we did also meet a lad from Trinity.

— Well, well. That makes four.

— Now don't confuse things. The Trinity poet fellow wasn't with us at all this morning.

— But this queer fellow. How queer was he?

Mick gazed about the gentle trees, the shrubs, the flowers, the motley people with prams and noise. It was all normal, and even attractive. De Selby and his associates was another matter.

— I don't mean queer in any bad sense. He was a strange man. He had unusual notions about the world, the universe, time . . . a physicist, really.

— Yes?

— His ideas quite transcended this earth — this damn earth we're lying on now.

— Is that so? That Dalkey is a place I'll have to find out more about. But about transcending this earth . . . the simplest priest does that every Sunday.

— Not quite in De Selby's way. That's his name — De Selby.

— De Selby? Sounds foreign. Probably a spy.

— Oh De Selby's no foreigner. Not a bit of him. If the way he talks is any sign he's a native of our beloved Ireland. And he doesn't like Ireland, or like anywhere else in this world.

— Don't tell me he's another angry patriot?

— Certainly not.

— What exactly are you driving at, Mick?

— It's hard to convey it, my sweet dote. Hard to believe it, too.

She sat up and looked at him as he sprawled there, his hand shading his face. Her curiosity was awakened but that was not what Mick wanted; not yet, anyhow. A proper talk might help a lot when his own mind was clearer and possibly his experience wider.

– What's going on, Mick? Tell me. Tell me your damned story if you have one.

He sat up to show at least that this wasn't fooling. Here was more of the messing in which he was so expert in accidentally involving himself.

– Mary, let me put this in a few separate sentences. They all tot up to a pretty strange state of affairs. It could even mean some danger.

– Well, *what*? Her voice was sharp.

– This man De Selby keeps unusual company when he's on his own, he said in a low, even voice that seemed to belie the message. One of his butties is Saint John the Baptist.

– Mick! God forgive you!

– I'm serious.

– What sort of talk is that? This is Sunday, not that that makes any difference.

– He's also met many other holy characters such as Tertullian, I think. And maybe Athanasius.

She was tense and frowning now.

– And don't leave out Hackett. You told me already Hackett was there.

He looked her steadily in her brown eyes.

– Quite true. And with him both of us met Saint Augustine.

There was a small silence here. Even the noise around about seemed muted. Mary lit a cigarette.

– Mick, she asked seriously, what's the purpose of all this bosh? Am I supposed to laugh?

– No indeed.

– Where did you meet Saint Augustine?

– Under the sea at Vico.

– *Under the sea?*

– Yes. The three of us.

– And what happened?

– There was a long and complicated talk between De Selby and Saint Augustine.

– How could people talk under the sea, apart from the fact that one of them has been dead for centuries?

– We were in a cave.

– This is absolute lunacy, Mick. You know that.

– Hackett and I couldn't do any talking but we were there, we could listen, and did.

Another silence. Absolute lunacy is what his talk sounded to Mick himself, but what choice had he if this matter was to be dragged up at all? Suddenly he felt glad Hackett had been there, otherwise he might join Mary in her inference that he had been the victim of delusions. And another thing, both of them had been dead sober.

– Was a feed of whiskey the foundation of this rigmarole?

– We had no drink whatsoever, any of us. And I'll tell you another thing about De Selby...

– Not that he had two heads?

– No. He is going to destroy the world.

– Good Lord! How?

– He claims he has the means. I don't pretend to understand it exactly, and can't explain it. It's a very abstruse, technical matter. He has invented a sort of miraculous substance. De Selby can pollute and destroy the whole atmosphere, the air we breathe.

That account of their chat is not accurate, but it was substantially the way the queer experience was mentioned. And they did not stop there. Mary went on asking other questions, and expressing incredulity or mild ridicule. His attitude was a quiet one, polite, obdurate. He hinted a little at his personal blamelessness, his innocence, even his simplicity. The events had not been of his contriving. But all the same he took care to make it plain that he was not apologizing. He was himself and he had his little rights.

In the end Mary seemed to accept, not what he had so baldly related but the fact that something very unusual had really happened and, though evidently he was confused, he was not telling outlandish lies. That was something; a mysterious something, but something.

After a time they got up and strolled out towards Lansdowne Road. Of course the wide streets they walked were unnecessarily common, the people ordinary if not colourless, and for himself he was depressed. Why not? Mary was silent when not talking superficially.

It was near six when they stopped at a tree.

Mary said that she had two tickets for a certain musical event that night. Her tone was indolent. She did not feel very like going. Did he? He said no.

– This night please God I'll go to bed early, Mary. And sleep long and deeply without dreams.

– You're tired?

– Between this world and the next I'm worn out. But it's probably this dead heat.

– Yes, and the complications about De Selby. I'll think over what you told me and try to be serious. I have a sort of an idea. I'll tell you about it when I'm sure. We must have a talk together with Hackett. Give me a ring, as usual. And . . . listen, Mick.

– Yes, Mary?

– Have a few bottles of stout for your supper if you have any at home.

– Well . . . thanks for the suggestion. Yes, Mary.

Believe it or not, light or no light, they kissed as privately as possible under that tree.

And homeward bound, he dallied for a time at Crowe's. The evening congregation there was cheerful, the malt benevolent and bronze. Mary was a superb lady. Soon he felt more bright-minded. And he reaffirmed his vow to cut his whiskey-drinking right out. If it had to be something for the immediate future, there was nothing wrong with stout.

CHAPTER 7

SURPRISINGLY, WHAT followed for Mick was a rest – short enough, only eight or nine days, but his mixed-up mind simmered down a good bit when the De Selby encounters were reconsidered in the quiet of a more rested head. Nothing whatever had happened, he reminded himself, but talk. True, there seemed to have been a breach of the natural order in that apparition of Augustine in the grotesque chamber under the wave but several explanations might be forthcoming, including that of a temporary psychic malaise, a phantasm such as would arise from taking mescalin or morphine. Hackett's suspicion that De Selby had administered a very slow-acting drug to them was by no means out of the question, though he regretted that instead of that ridiculous wine-bibbing session in the chemist's shop, the two of them had not instantly sat down and compared their experience in detail and verified that their recollections of the De Selby–Augustine duologue were identical. Then Hackett was, of course, unreliable and impetuous while Mick personally had no scientific training in evaluating a strange occurrence in retrospect, though he would now know better how to receive any development it might be God's will to permit. Meanwhile he was in no hurry to revisit Dalkey, though his bicycle still rested there.

The telephone rang in the room he shared with three others in Dublin Castle, and he was beckoned to the instrument. That would be Mary. They had a bargain that such calls should be brief, for his own lack of privacy was total. It is hard to say why he hated others to hear his meaningless responses.

– I'm off to London tomorrow in the interest of furthering the holy cause of my firm, she said.

– For how long?

– About a week.

What she said next startled him a bit. She had had a talk with her mother, but no names mentioned; she had merely said that somebody she knew was troubled and perplexed, and she wondered what could be done. The mother had very strongly advised that this person should go and see Father Cobble at Milltown Park. He was a most kind and understanding man, and ever willing to counsel the wanderer.

– He's one of the Jesuit Fathers there, of course, Mary added. But do nothing till I get back. I may give Father Cobble a ring this evening to see how he's fixed. Meantime, keep away from that hotel in Dalkey. And Mick, mind yourself.

Well damn it, he thought – was this to be a development, an unexpected divagation, a new horizon? Back to his mind came Augustine's slighting references to St Ignatius and his Order. What irony was here, he timidly consulting a Jesuit about De Selby!

He chuckled to himself (a good sign, perhaps) as he returned to his arid papers. Time would tell.

But four days later the telephone rang again. Who could this be? He grunted acquiescence when a deep male voice mentioned his full name.

– Ah! My name is Cobble, Father George Cobble. A dear friend has mentioned your name to me. I rang to say that I would be most happy to see you at any time.

– That is very good of you but –

– Not at all, my dear boy. When any little shadow falls on one, as it may on any of us, that little shadow is better shared.

– Oh, I understand.

– When the little shadow is spread over a wider surface, it grows less opaque, and with God's grace it might disappear completely.

– Father, I had arranged to go away for about a week. A little holiday break, if you understand me.

– Well now. That is good and cheerful news. I believe you live in Dalkey.

– No, no. Booterstown.

– Ah yes. I see. You will be back tomorrow week, I am sure. That will be the first day of September. Would you have a cup of tea with me, say at six that evening, at the Royal Marine, Dunleary?

– That is most kind of you. You see, it is another person I wanted to talk about.

– Excellent. That then is our appointment.

– Very good, Father. Six o'clock on the first.

That is how this Father Cobble shuffled gently into Mick's life and affairs, unasked by him. His story about a short holiday was, of course, an improvisation but not, let it be said, anything of panic. He wanted no sudden confrontation with this Jesuit Father for a number of reasons, and straightway felt mildly angry that Mary had committed him this way, showing small feeling for his intellectual integrity. First he would have to tell Hackett and see what he had to say, assuming it would be possible to get him to take the prospect seriously. Secondly, he was anxious to have the facts, and all of them, from Mary about Father Cobble. What sort of a man was he, what age, of what ecclesiastical status and exactly what sort of 'problems' did he advise on? The last point was the most important, he felt. The well-meaning but meddling and obtuse clergyman was often more than a mere nuisance. In questioning and praying to isolate and analyse a visitor's problem (if the latter in fact had a problem) he could grow to be a considerable new problem himself. And Mick reminded himself that while he observed reasonably well the rules of the Church, he had never found himself much in rapport in the human scene with any priest. In the confessional he had often found their queries naïve, stupid, occasionally impertinent; and the feeling that they meant well and were doing their best was merely an additional exasperation. He was complete enough in himself, he thought: educated, tolerant, contemptuous of open vice or licentious language but ever careful to show charity to those who in weakness had strayed. If he had a weakness all his own, it was thoughtless indulgence in alcohol; this dulled moral insight, unbalanced the judgement and – heavens! – could lead the mind to sinful reveries of the carnal kind. With God's help alcohol would soon be put in its place, but not in any sudden silly peremptory gesture. A modulation – adult, urbane, unhurried – was called for.

His mother? It might be thought odd that his poor mother, with whom he lived alone, so little occupied his thoughts. She was simple and devout in the manner of Mrs Laverty but much older. She was indeed an old woman and to talk to her even in the mildest and most superficial way about the like of De Selby was unthinkable; the very idea itself was almost funny. If she understood a word, she would charitably conclude that he had 'a sup taken', for, having loved his father and accepted that he had died from drink, she well knew he was no stranger to the taverns. Yet, it is strange and sad to live so close to one so dear and yet have no real point of contact outside banal and trivial smalltalk, no access to exchanges of the mind. Did he not notice the state nearly all his shirts were getting into? How often must he be reminded to buy at least four pairs of socks? Ah, but it was a sweet dead-end.

He went to a play at the Gaiety. Halfway through he knew he was wasting his time. And the following evening he took a tram to Dalkey. Hackett had no telephone at home or at business and this was the only way of chancing a meeting with him or leaving a message. The light of the Colza looked brighter, though no doubt the candlepower was the same as ever. Even as he pushed the door he could hear Hackett's voice beyond the inner partition. Hackett was elevated in voice and manner when he found him in the 'Slum' with Sergeant Fottrell, though each was separately seated. Behind the bar was Larry, an oldish small grey character who never had much to say, nominally the cellarman but charged with countless chores, from cleaning latrines and grates to watering the plants in pots all over the house upstairs. Hackett nodded to his old friend Mick.

– God bless you and isn't it the sublime and fabulous evening, thanks be to the Lord and His Holy Mother, the sergeant said smiling.

– Good night to you, Sergeant. I must apologize for not yet having called for the bike.

– 'Tis no harm at all, boy. I have it imprisoned in a cell without a chance of parole, and I ordered Policeman Pluck to subject it to fastidious oiling about the hubs and levers.

Mick said thanks and asked Larry for a pint.

– I was just telling the Sergeant, said Hackett loudly, about Judas Iscariot. Now *there* was a decent man that was taken in and made a gobshite out of. The unfortunate poor whore was like a man going round with his head in a sack, and maybe drunk.

– He answered for what he did, the same as we all will have to, Mick replied. He found Hackett irked him.

– Now listen here. Don't give me any of that sort of talk at all. I've looked into this whole thing in Marsh's Library. Judas was an intellectual type. He knew what he was doing. Furthermore, he was swindled. He got the worst deal of the lot in the whole shooting match.

– We are not sure what deal he got in the end. Remember De Selby's effort to find out.

– O'Scariot was a man of deciduous character inferentially, Sergeant Fottrell announced.

– We know at least what he did. He got thirty pieces of silver. What sort of pay is that?

– We are not sure of the value of that payment in terms of today.

– Answer the question, man, Hackett pursued hotly. What relationship could that payment bear to the value of what he sold?

– He was a businessman and should himself be a proper judge of value.

– He was shamelessly swindled by those crooks the Pharisees.

Mick was briefly silent, drinking his porter, hoping that Hackett would cool down. He was breaking their agreement, in the presence of the sergeant, to hold their peace. Mick thought to pull the talk to another trend.

– They say he bought a field with the money, he ventured.

– Ah now, interposed the sergeant, I have often thought that that divil of a man was at heart a country Irishman, consecutively because of his eerie love of the sod.

– Hardly, Mick muttered.

– His soft yearning for good parturitional land phlegmatically, with its full deposits of milk and honeysuckle.

– As I said before, Hackett barked savagely, Peter was a worse louser and lackey, perpetrated his low perfidity *after* Judas had betrayed his Master, and got nothing but thanks for his day's work. Yes sir! The Case of the Missing Witness. Judas may have had a good and honourable intention, as De Quincey held. Peter's conduct was mean and cowardly, his first concern being his own skin. Yes, that's one thing I'm going to work for.

– What?

– Rehabilitating Judas Iscariot.

– He was the class of a man, the sergeant put in, that you would meet exactly in a place like Swanlinbar, or in Cushendun of a fair day.

– How will you do that?

– Agitate to have the record amended. All the obloquy heaped on him is based on nothing but inference. I hope to have part of the Bible rewritten.

– The Holy Father would have a say in that.

– To hell with the Holy Father. I will work to secure that the Bible contains the Gospel according to Saint Judas.

– Saint Judas, pray for us, the sergeant recited solemnly, then drank solemnly.

Hackett glared at him, then turned on Mick.

– Who better than Judas could tell the inner truth and declare what his intentions were – his plan?

– The historicity of the existing Gospels, he explained, is not seriously disputed anywhere. It is equally accepted that Judas left no record. You ask who but Judas could tell the inner truth? Perhaps. But he didn't. He told nothing.

Hackett's features were arranged in a deep sneer.

– For a learned and enlightened man, you are surely a buck ignoramus. The Roman Church's Bible has a great lot of material named Apocrypha. There have been apocryphal Gospels according to Peter, Thomas, Barnabas, John, Judas Iscariot and many others. My task would be to retrieve, clarify and establish the Iscariot Gospel.

– Suppose you did find an historically plausible testament and then found Judas saying something you didn't expect at all, something dead contrary to your argument?

– Don't be more of a poor bastard than you can help.

Mick poured the rest of the pint down the inside of his neck and replaced the tumbler on the counter with finality.

– My decision, he announced, is to buy a glawsheen of whiskey for you two gentlemen and another pint for myself. Larry, please do the needful in the cause of peace.

– Isn't that most timely and herbaceous? the sergeant remarked genially. Hackett frowned but seemed a bit mollified, perhaps thinking that his talk had been too emphatic and should not be pursued. Mick hoped he could get through to his real mission.

– I want to tell you about something, he said as Larry hurried about his task. Somebody I mentioned De Selby to has accidentally taken a slightly embarrassing step without my knowledge.

Hackett stared at him glumly.

— I think I know who the somebody is, he growled. What has she done?

— Well, it was her mother. She arranged for a Jesuit to see me.

— A what? A *Jesuit*?

— Yes. But apparently this Father Cobble from Milltown knows nothing yet except that somebody's in trouble. And personally I know nothing of Father Cobble and haven't yet been able to find out. The meeting has been provisionally arranged for this day week at the Royal Marine.

— Well sweet God, why start messing about with those nosey interfering gobhawks?

— It wasn't *my* idea, I told you. But what do you think of my meeting him, giving him a very brief account, a rough outline, of De Selby and then inviting him to come up the Vico with me to visit him?

Hackett grimaced, laughed mirthlessly, and savoured his new drink.

— Be clear at the outset, he said, that I won't be present. That would be too much. De Selby might push out the boat and arrange a high-class dinner party to welcome this priest. Chief guests John the Baptist, Jerome, the Little Flower, Saint Thomas à Kempis, Matt Talbot, the four Saint Patricks, and Saint Joan.

— But what do you think? Be serious.

— If your idea is to simplify the descent of Augustine, I think you would be going the right way about complicating it. The matter might be referred to Rome, and then where were we? We might be excommunicated.

This attitude was roughly what Mick had expected. But his mind was already made up. Hackett would have been no addition to the little tea-party, anyway.

— I don't agree, he replied, because Jesuits are intelligent and trained men, whatever else they may be. But even complication would be preferable to permanent mystery with no bottom to it. You don't deny that both of us are very puzzled about that early Sunday swim of ours. Those men are bound to have some experience of diabolism, if that is what is in question here. We can't let a matter like this just rest and forget about it.

— I can.

— Yes. You have a mind and courage much superior to what I have. Both of us heard De Selby's threat to destroy all mankind, and both of us were witnesses of his possession of a unique instrument of destruction. To sit and do nothing would be, well . . . inhuman.

— We were not witness of his possession of a unique weapon of destruction. He certainly has an impressive gadget, or chemical, or drug. He destroyed nothing.

— He destroyed the atmosphere and annihilated time as we understand it — exactly as he predicted he would.

— You magnify what are mere impressions and you give yourself a status of grandeur. You know what happened to one Redeemer of humanity. Do you want to be another?

— I'm determined to do something, and the Father Cobble suggestion is as good as any, though it's not my own.

— As you please.

— Lawrence of Arabian sands, chanted Sergeant Fottrell, be at my back insidiously and replenish the beakers of the company continentally.

— Thanks, Sergeant, Hackett said casually.

— And furthermore, Mick continued, after this drink I am going to see De Selby, and ask him will he receive the reverend Father.

And he did, alone.

MICK WAS startled at the promptness with which the door was opened after a knock, as if De Selby had been waiting behind it after having been warned of an approaching visitor by supernatural telephone. There he stood, smiling primly and bidding welcome. He led the way, not into the room of the previous visit but to a smaller apartment at the back which, for its shelves and cases of bottles and jars, electrical apparatus, crucibles, scales, measuring vessels and all the conventional paraphernalia of scientific experiment, one must call a laboratory. There were however at the empty fireplace a few comfortable chairs and a small chess table. He took Mick's hat and from somewhere behind him produced a bottle and two glasses.

— You'll forgive me saying it, Michael, he remarked as he sat down, but I'm glad your companion is not with you. I found him rather superficial.

This rather dismayed Mick, for De Selby's manners hitherto had been pretty faultless. But he showed no sign.

— Ah well he's a bit hasty and thoughtless sometimes, he replied. Glad I caught you at home. May I ask whether you have had any further, em . . . spiritual experiences since, sub aqua or otherwise?

De Selby had risen and carefully poured out two drinks.

— Oh yes. More wide-ranging but not so illuminating. Old Testament characters tend to be simple, ignorant and superstitious compared with those Christian sophists, heresiarchs and mendacious early Fathers.

— Indeed? Whom did you speak to, if I may ask?

— Two of the boyos, separately. Jonas was one of them, or Jonah as the Protestants call him. Why do those untutored blatherskites insist so much on being trivially different?

— Jonas? The man who was swallowed by a whale?

— The proper answer to that is yes and no, though you are on the right track. I personally don't believe it was a whale. In old times the shark was an immense creature, up to ninety feet in length.

– Does it matter much whether it was a whale or a shark?

– It does to me in my office as theologian. The references in the Bible, in Testaments Old and New, are consistently to 'a great fish'. The whale as such is never mentioned, and in any event the whale is not a fish. Scientists hold, with ample documentation in support, that the whale was formerly a land animal, its organs now modified for sea-living. It is a mammal, suckles its young, is warm-blooded and must come to the surface for breath, like man himself. It is most unlikely that there were any whales in the sea in the time of Jonas.

– You surprise me, Mr De Selby. The belief that it was a whale is pretty universal.

– That may be, but the creature has been the subject of much casuistry, no doubt stimulated by the Jesuits. Its flesh is quite edible, like the dolphin's. Roman Catholics are forbidden, as we know, to eat fleshmeat on Fridays. But on those days they have not hesitated to eat whale, on the specious ground that it is a fish. It is not a fish even in its mode of propulsion, which is by its tail. A whale's great tail is horizontal whereas the tail of absolutely every real fish is vertical.

– Well, well. You seem to be well versed also in what I will call natural piscine philosophy.

– Oh, now now. Another point is that the shark is piscivorous, whereas the whale subsists almost exclusively on plankton, which one might describe as minute marine vegetables.

This discourse did in fact impress Mick, maybe because his personal Bible studies had been as minute as plankton. Apparently little was outside the range of De Selby's reading or meditation.

– Tell me, Mick ventured, had Jonas himself any idea about the true identity of his . . . host?

Here De Selby swallowed a long slow trickle of his peerless *hausgemacht*, and paused before replying.

– To tell you the truth, Michael, I found Jonas to be a bit of a ballocks.

– *What?* Not only the word itself but the sinister fervour of its pronunciation was like a slap in the face to Mick – and earnest, perhaps, of an innocence he did not know he had.

– And the Lord was also of the same opinion.

– But Jonas was a prophet, wasn't he?

– He was a prophet who disgraced himself. He disobeyed God's orders because, muryaa, he knew better. That's why he was heaved into the sea.

– How did he disobey?

– He was commanded by the Lord to go and preach in the great and evil city of Nineveh. But he knew better than the Lord, knew that the people would repent and reform, that going there was a waste of time, and instead took ship to go elsewhere. A frightful storm arose, the Lord's punishment for Jonas, and the crew, knowing their lives were all in danger because of him, threw him into the sea. The storm immediately died down but meanwhile for Jonas Mr Shark arrived.

– Well, that's what I asked. Did Jonas give any evidence to justify your choice of a shark?

– The Bible merely says that he spent three days and nights in the *belly* of the creature. Not clear how anybody could distinguish night from day in the darkness.

– Perhaps hunger would be a guide?

– If 'belly' means 'stomach', there's a big difference between the belly of a shark and that of a whale. A whale's stomach is like a house or a flat – it has several compartments. You could have a dining-room there, a bedroom, a kitchen, perhaps a library.

– But you talked to Jonas. Did he make any remark himself about the inside of the monster that gobbled him?

– Not at all. He talked bull, like a cheap politician or a first-year Jesuit novice.

– That was disappointing.

– Well, he was eventually vomited up on dry land. We can't expect the victims of miracles to explain the miracles. Besides, several of those old-time prophets were mouthpieces in the pejorative American meaning.

They drank in silence, pondering this strange occurrence, the dark mystery infixed in it, unresolved even by a consultation between De Selby and Jonas himself; very strange indeed. But who was De Selby's second colloquist, Mick wondered, as another generous drink was poured for him. Saint Teresa of Avila?

– Who was the subject of your second interview, Mr De Selby?

– Ah yes. Francis of Assisi, of course, founder of the Franciscans. A strange man. Like Ignatius of Loyola, his early life was profligate and deplorable, and again like him, he saw the truth in the course of a dangerous illness. But Francis was a genuine saint, and a poet, too.

– Funny thing, Mick responded, I recently met another poet myself – in the Colza Hotel, of all places. A chap by the name of Nemo Crabbe. He is doing medicine against his will at Trinity but refuses to live in the College because every student has to empty his own charley.

De Selby blinked a little in surprise.

– Dear me, he said mildly, do they not have servants there, or houseboys?

– Apparently not. Was your interview with Saint Francis important?

De Selby paused in recollection.

– Of only middling importance. He was very honest and did little more than verify what is now received knowledge about him. I told him his canonization only two years after his death was hasty and presumptuous. He bluntly told me to make that complaint to Gregory the Ninth.

– Is it true that he preached to the birds, and all that kind of thing?

– Possibly not literally but as a man he was most gentle and kind to all kind creatures, seeing nothing but God's handiwork all about him. He could perhaps be faulted for a streak of pantheism.

– Yes. I do not know much about him except that he and the birds appear so often on calendars at Christmas.

– Oh he was the genuine article and not a trick-of-the-loop merchant like Augustine. He totally lacked arrogance. And he did receive the Stigmata of the Crucified after a fast of forty days on a mountain. But the poor fellow was very shy about that . . .

De Selby chuckled genially.

– He seemed to blush at the mention of it as if I was complimenting a schoolboy on winning the hundred yards dash.

They paused in their talk from these two sacred conferences to a general survey of De Selby's ghastly plan for world catastrophe. Mick asked him did he not find the known world of the common man, lit up and shot through with the magic of the preternatural world to which he had access, far too absorbing and wonderful an organized creation to be destroyed summarily and utterly? He grew stern at the mention of such themes. No, this globe only was in question and the destruction he planned was a prescribed doom, terrible but ineluctable, and a duty before God so far as he personally was concerned. The whole world was corrupt, human society an insufferable abomination. God had founded his own true Church but contemplated benevolently the cults of even capricious dæmons provided they were intrinsically good. Christianity is God's religion but Judaism, Buddhism, Hinduism and Islam are tolerable manifestations of God; the Old and New Testaments, the Veda, Koran and Avesta are all sacred documents but in fact every one of those organized religions were in decomposition and atrophy. The Almighty had led De Selby to the DMP substance so that the Supreme Truth could be protected finally and irrevocably from all the Churches of today.

— In fact, Mick asked, is this a second divine plan for the salvation of mankind?

— You could call it that.

— Salvation by way of complete destruction?

— There is no other way. All will be called home and judged.

Mick did not feel like pursuing such colloquy. Though somewhat shielded by the gentle fumes of his host's whiskey, his mind felt sickeningly clouded by the modest claim of De Selby — for it was nothing less — that he was in fact a new Messiah. Mick thought: what blasphemous drollery! Yet . . . DMP did exist. He knew that, so did Hackett. Oh, hells bells!

He remembered the errand that brought him and suddenly he was not shy or hesitant at all in mentioning Father Cobble; in fact he was relieved in recalling the good priest, and gladly enough he accepted another drink — but a small one.

— Mr De Selby, he said, please do not think I wish to heap you with vulgar flattery but I honestly do find your remarks on comparative religions, theocracy and the final imponderables of physical death and eternity fascinating.

— Eschatology has always attracted the minds of men who use reason.

— Well, talking of Churches, there's an old friend of mine, Father Cobble . . .

— Father Cobble? What a name! I know a Father Stone, a Cistercian.

THE DALKEY ARCHIVE 673

— Easy, Mr De Selby. Father Cobble's a Jesuit.

— Ah — *ignatius elenchi*! What fine friends you have, Michael.

— Actually he is a most intelligent man. He could give you an argument, I'll bet. He knows all about philosophy and Church history.

— I don't doubt that, for the Jesuits are well set-up chaps in their own business — or think they are.

— Would you be annoyed if I brought him along for an evening on the first of next month? He's excellent company — that I'll guarantee.

De Selby laughed genuinely and deeply, and topped up the drinks with a little water.

— Of course bring him up, he smiled. Cultured company is one thing I conspicuously lack in this house, though privacy, alas, is essential most of the time for my work. You understand that, I know. But that does not mean that I have to live in solitary confinement. But tell me one thing, Michael.

— Certainly. What is that?

— Is the reverence partial to a glass of good whiskey or does he go for the red wine?

A nice question, about a man he'd never even met.

— I . . . I'm not sure. Our meetings have always been on neutral ground.

— Never mind. There's plenty of wine here, though not home-made.

Thus was the bargain arranged. But it was at least an hour later when Mick shook hands with De Selby at his door. His talk had suddenly veered into native politics and here at last was terrain where he was uncertain and sometimes lost, but where Mick was the very experienced guide.

CHAPTER 9

THE OLD COLOURED houses of irregular size along the narrow quays of the Liffey seem to lean outward as if to study themselves in the water; but on his pleasant walk there this time, Mick's eye was not dwelling pleasurably on them. He was thinking, though not in gloom. There had come to him an idea that seemed bright, masterly, bold even. True, it would not dissipate the underwater ghost of Augustine nor extinguish the neuro-psychotic aberrations of De Selby but he became convinced it would enable him *to do something* to prevent, perhaps perma-nently but certainly for the present, the carrying out of any genuine plan to visit the human race with havoc. He was pleased. He resolved to go to a quiet place where alcoholic drinks were to be had and then, please God, not have one but try something healthy, refreshing, harmless. Plain thinking – planning – was called for.

And Father Cobble? Yes, Mick would keep that arrangement to bring him on a visit to De Selby. The visit might well be valuable and, also, he was glad that Hackett had reneged. He felt Hackett's presence might have been a complication, even an obstacle, and this was also true of the steps he would have to take later to give effect to his new idea.

His steps led him to the Metropole in Dublin's main street. It was not called a cinema, restaurant, dance hall or drinking den, though it contained all of these delights. Drinking was done in a quiet, softly-lighted lounge downstairs where tables were sequestered by tall fixed screens of dark wood. It was a favourite resort of parish priests from the country and, though service was by waitresses, lady customers were excluded.

He sat down and ordered a small Vichy water. When another order had been served in the division next to him he was sharply startled by the unseen customer's thanks, unmistakable in content if not in tone.

– In gratitude for that bottle, me dear colleen, I will make a novena for the implenishment of your soul irreciprocally to Saint Martin of Tours himself.

No help for it: Mick picked up his drink and moved in. Happily, Sergeant Fottrell was alone. In old-fashioned courtesy he stood up and put out a hand.

– Well, the Lord forbid but you must be following me detectively?

Mick laughed.

– No indeed. I wanted a quiet drink and thought nobody would know me down here.

– Ah, but the divil minds his own children.

Curiously, this unscheduled collision with the sergeant did not seem to erode Mick's half-formed desire to be by himself. In fact he was glad to see the sergeant. He apologized once more for having failed to retrieve his bicycle from the station in Dalkey. The sergeant took his long upper lip from his glass of barley wine with a wince of total absolution.

– Where the bicycle is, he said gravely, is a far safer place than the high highroad itself, intuitively.

– Oh, I just thought it might be in the way.

– It is under lock and key in cell number two and you are far better in your health to be divorced from it. Tell me this item: how did you find Policeman Pluck?

– I had met him before, of course. A very pleasant man.

– What was he doing perceptively?

– He was busy mending a puncture.

– Ah-ha!

The sergeant sniggered, took another sup from his drink and frowned slightly in thought.

– That will be the third puncture in seven days, he said, in what seemed to be a tone of satisfaction.

– That looks a pretty awful record, Mick replied. Is it sheer bad luck or is it the bad roads?

– 'Tis the Council must take the credit for the little back roads, the worst in Ireland. But Policeman Pluck got his punctures at half one on Monday, two o'clock on Wednesday, and half six on Sunday.

– How on earth do you know that? Does he keep a diary of them?

– He does not. I know the dates and times protruberantly

because it was my good self who carried out the punctures with my penknife.

– Good heavens, why?

– For Policeman Pluck's good luck. But sitting here I have been considering meditatively those talking pictures upstairs. They are a quaint achievious science certainly.

– They are a great advance on silent films.

– You know how they are worked?

– Oh yes. The photo-electric cell.

– Yes then. Why if you can turn light into sound you cannot turn sound into light?

– You mean invent a *phono*-electric cell?

– Of a particular certainty, but for sure that invention would be a hard pancake. I do often contemplate what sort of a light the noble American Constitution would make, given out by President Roosevelt.

– A very interesting speculation.

– Or a speech by Arthur Griffith?

– Yes indeed.

– Charles Stewart Parnell held the dear belief that all Ireland's woes and tears were the true result of being so fond of green. Wrap the green flag round me, boys. If you put that grand man's speeches through the cell (and many a month he spent in a cell himself) wouldn't it be the hemochromic thing if the solution was a bright green light?

Mick laughed at this, and at the whole wonderful idea. There had been, he seemed to remember, an organ that 'played' light on a screen, enchanting patterns of mixes and colour. But that was not what the sergeant had conceived.

– Yes. And that would be the colour of Caruso's voice, or John McCormack singing *Down by the Sally Gardens*? But tell me, Sergeant. Why did you persistently puncture Policeman Pluck's tyres?

The sergeant beckoned the waitress, ordered a barley wine for himself and a small bottle of 'that' for his friend. Then he leaned forward confidentially.

– Did you ever discover or hear tell of mollycules? he asked.

– I did of course.

– Would it surprise or collapse you to know that the Molly-cule Theory is at work in the parish of Dalkey?

– Well . . . yes and no.

– It is doing terrible destruction, he continued, the half of the people is suffering from it, it is worse than the smallpox.

– Could it not be taken in hand by the Dispensary Doctor or the National Teachers, or do you think it is a matter for the head of the family?

– The lock, stock and barrel of it all, he replied almost fiercely, is the County Council.

– It seems a complicated thing all right.

The sergeant drank delicately, deep in thought.

– Michael Gilhaney, a man I know, he said finally, is an example of a man that is nearly banjaxed from the operation of the Mollycule Theory. Would it astonish you ominously to hear that he is in danger of being a bicycle?

Mick shook his head in polite incomprehension.

– He is nearly sixty years of age by plain computation, the sergeant said, and if he is itself, he has spent no less than thirty-five years riding his bicycle over the rocky roadsteads and up and down the pertimious hills and into the deep ditches when the road goes astray in the strain of the winter. He is always going to a particular destination or other on his bicycle at every hour of the day or coming back from there at every other hour. If it wasn't that his bicycle was stolen every Monday he would be sure to be more than halfway now.

– Halfway to where?

– Halfway to being a bloody bicycle himself.

Had Sergeant Fottrell for once betrayed himself into drunken rambling? His fancies were usually amusing but not so good when they were meaningless. When Mick said something of the kind the sergeant stared at him impatiently.

– Did you ever study the Mollycule Theory when you were a lad? he asked. Mick said no, not in any detail.

– That is a very serious defalcation and an abstruse exacerbation, he said severely, but I'll tell you the size of it. Everything is composed of small mollycules of itself and they are flying around in concentric circles and arcs and segments and innumerable various other routes too numerous to mention collectively, never standing still or resting but spinning away and darting hither and thither and back again, all the time on the go. Do you follow me intelligently? Mollycules?

– I think I do.

– They are as lively as twenty punky leprechauns doing a jig on the top of a flat tombstone. Now take a sheep. What is a sheep only millions of little bits of sheepness whirling around doing intricate convulsions inside the baste. What else is it but that?

– That would be bound to make the sheep dizzy, Mick observed, especially if the whirling was going on inside the head as well.

The sergeant gave him a look which no doubt he himself would describe as one of non-possum and noli-me-tangere.

– That's a most foolhardy remark, he said sharply, because the nerve-strings and the sheep's head itself are whirling into the same bargain and you can cancel out one whirl against the other and there you are – like simplifying a division sum when you have fives above and below the bar.

– To say the truth I did not think of that.

– Mollycules is a very intricate theorem and can be worked out with algebra but you would want to take it by degrees with rulers and cosines and familiar other instruments and then at the wind-up not believe what you had proved at all. If that happened you would have to go back over it till you got a place where you could believe your own facts and figures as exactly delineated from Hall and Knight's Algebra and then go on again from that particular place till you had the whole pancake properly believed and not have bits of it half-believed or a doubt in your head hurting you like when you lose the stud of your shirt in the middle of the bed.

– Very true, Mick decided to say.

– If you hit a rock hard enough and often enough with an iron hammer, some mollycules of the rock will go into the hammer and contrariwise likewise.

– That is well known, he agreed.

– The gross and net result of it is that people who spend most of their natural lives riding iron bicycles over the rocky road-steads of the parish get their personalities mixed up with the personalities of their bicycles as a result of the interchanging of the mollycules of each of them, and you would be surprised at the number of people in country parts who are nearly half people and half bicycles.

Mick made a little gasp of astonishment that made a sound like the air coming from a bad puncture.

– Good Lord, I suppose you're right.

– And you would be unutterably flibbergasted if you knew the number of stout bicycles that partake serenely of humanity.

Here the sergeant produced his pipe, a thing he did very rarely in public, and in silence commenced the laborious business of filling and ramming it from his battered tin of very dark tobacco. Mick began to muse and think of country places he had known in his younger days. He thought of one place he had been fond of.

Brown bogs and black bogs were neatly arranged on each side of the road with rectangular boxes carved out of them here and there, each with a filling of yellow-brown brown-yellow water. Far away near the sky tiny people were stooped at their turf-work, cutting out precisely-shaped sods with their patent spades and building them into a tall memorial the height of a horse and cart. Sounds came from them, delivered to his ears without charge by the west wind, sounds of laughing and whistling and bits of verses from the old bog-songs. Nearer, a house stood attended by three trees and surrounded by the happiness of a coterie of fowls, all of them picking and rooting and disputating loudly in the unrelenting manufacture of their eggs. The house was quiet in itself and silent but a canopy of lazy smoke had been erected over the chimney to indicate that people were within engaged on tasks. Ahead of him went the road, running swiftly across the flat land and pausing slightly to climb slowly up a hill that was waiting for it in a place where there was tall grass, grey boulders and rank stunted trees. The whole overhead was occupied by the sky, translucent, impenetrable, ineffable and incomparable, with a fine island of cloud anchored in the calm two yards to the right of Mr Jarvis's outhouse.

The scene was real and incontrovertible but at variance with the talk of the sergeant. Was it not monstrous to allege that the little people winning turf far away were partly bicycles? He took a sideways view of him. He had now compacted his turf-like tobacco and produced a box of matches.

– Are you sure about the humanity of bicycles? Mick enquired of him. Does it not go against the doctrine of original sin? Or is the Molecule Theory as dangerous as you say?

The sergeant was drawing fiercely at the pipe as his match spluttered.

— It is between twice and three times as dangerous as it might be, he replied gloomily. Early in the morning I often think it is four times and, for goodness' sake, if you lived here for a few days and gave full and free rein to your observation and inspection, you would know how certain the sureness of the certainty is.

— Policeman Pluck did not look like a bicycle, Mick said. He had no back wheel on him and hadn't so much as a bell on his right thumb.

The sergeant looked at him with some commiseration.

— You cannot expect him to grow handlebars out of his neck but I have seen him attempt things more acutely indescribable than that. Did you ever notice the queer behaviour of bicycles in the country, or the more-man-bicycles?

— I did not.

— It's an indigenous catastrophe. When a man lets things go too far, you will not see much because he spends a lot of time leaning with one elbow on walls or standing propped up by one foot at the path. Such a man is a futile phenomenon of great charm and intensity and a very dangerous article.

— Dangerous to other people, you mean?

— Dangerous to himself and everybody. I once knew a man named Doyle. He was thirty-one per cent.

— Well, that's not too serious.

The sergeant was puffing industriously, his pipe now in fine order.

— Maybe. You can thank me. There were three Doyle brothers in the house and they were too contemptuously poor to have a bicycle apiece. Some people never know how fortunate they are when they are poorer than each other. But bedamn but one of the brothers won a prize of ten pounds in *John Bull*. When I got precise wind of this tiding I knew I would have to take quick steps unless there was to be two new bicycles in the family, because you will understand that I can steal only a limited number of bicycles in a month. Luckily I knew the postman well and I gave him a talking-to to divert the cheque to myself. The postman! Ah, great, sweet, brown stirabout!

Recollection of this public servant seemed to move the

sergeant to sad sardonic chuckles, with intricate gesturings of his red hands.

— The postman? Mick asked.

— Seventy-two per cent, he said quietly.

— Great Lord!

— A round of twenty-nine miles on the bicycle every single day for forty years, hail, rain or snowballs. There was very little hope of getting his number down below fifty again. I got him to cash the cheque in a private sub-office and we split the money in the public interest paternalistically.

Funny thing, Mick did not feel that the sergeant had been dishonest; he had been sentimental, rather, and the state of the postman meant that no moral issue was involved.

He asked the sergeant how the bicycle, for its part, would behave from day to day in a situation like this.

— The behaviour of a bicycle with a very high content of *homo sapiens*, he explained, is very cunning and entirely remarkable. You never see them moving by themselves but you meet them in the least accountable places unexpectedly. Did you ever see a bicycle leaning against the dresser in a warm kitchen when it is pouring outside?

— I did.

— Not very far from the fire?

— Yes.

— Near enough to the family to hear the conversation?

— I suppose so.

— Not a thousand miles from where they keep the eatables?

— I did not notice that. Good Lord, you do not mean to say that these bicycles *eat food*?

— They were never seen doing it, nobody ever caught them with a mouthful of seedy cake. All I know is that food disappears.

— What!

— It is not the first time I have noticed crumbs at the front wheels of some of those gentlemen.

Rather feebly Mick gestured to the waitress and ordered another drink. The sergeant was in deadly earnest, no doubt about that. And this was the man Mick had decided to call in to help him in resolving the great St Augustine enigma. He felt strangely depressed.

– Nobody takes any notice, the sergeant said softly. Tom thinks that Pat is responsible for missing grubsteaks, and Pat thinks that Tom is instrumental. Very few of the people guess what is going on in such a fearsomely infractional house. There are other things, too . . . but it's better not to talk of them.

– Oh come now, Sergeant. What sort of other things?

– Well, a man riding a lady's bicycle. It's the height of sulphurous immorality, the PP would be within his rights in forbidding such a low character to put as much as his nose inside the church.

– Yes . . . such conduct is unseemly.

– God help the nation that weakens on such matters. You would have bicycles demanding votes, and they would look for seats on the County Council to make the roads far worse than they are for their own ulterior motivation. But against that and on the other hand, a good bicycle is a great companion, a friend, there is great charm about it.

– All the same, I doubt if I'll ever again get up on that bicycle of mine you have in the station out in Dalkey.

The sergeant shook his head genially.

– Ah now, a little of it is a good thing, it makes you hardy and puts iron into you. But shure walking too far too often too quickly isn't safe at all either. The cracking of your feet on the road makes a certain amount of road come up into you. When a man dies they say he returns to clay funereally but too much walking fills you up with clay far sooner (or buries bits of you along the road) and brings your death halfway to meet you. It is not easy to know fastidiously what is the best way to move yourself from one place to another.

There was a little silence. Mick thought of mentioning how intact one could remain by restricting oneself to air travel but decided not to; the sergeant would surely object on the ground of cost. Mick noticed his face had become clouded and that he was staring into the bowl of his pipe.

– I will tell you a secret confidentially, he said in a low voice. My own grandfather was eighty-three when we buried him. For five years before his death he was a horse.

– *A horse?*

– A horse in everything but extraneous externalities, because he had spent years of his life – far too many for safety, be the pipers – in the saddle. Usually he was lazy and quiet but now and again he would go for a smart gallop, clearing the hedges in great style. Did you ever see a man on two legs galloping?

– I did not.

– Well, I am given to understand it is a great sight. He always said he won the Grand National when he was a lot younger and used to annoy the life out of his family with stories about the intricate jumps and the insoluble tallness of them.

– And the grandfather got himself into this condition by too much horse-riding?

– That was the size of it. His old horse Dan was in the contrary way of thinking and gave so much trouble, coming into the house at night, interfering with young girls during the day and committing indictable offences, that they had to shoot him. The polis of the time was not sympathetic exiguously. They said they would have to arrest the horse and have him up at the next Petty Sessions unless he was done away with. So the family shot him but if you ask me it was my grandfather they shot and it is the horse that is buried in Cloncoonla churchyard.

The sergeant fell to musing on his complicated ancestry but had the presence of mind to beckon the waitress with his pipe and order a repeat dose of the quiet medicine.

– In a way, Mick observed, your grandfather's case was not so bad. I mean, a horse is at least a creature, a living thing, man's companion on earth and indeed he is accounted everywhere a noble animal. Now, if it was a pig . . .

The sergeant turned and beamed on him, and gave a long contented puff at his pipe.

– You say that from a good heart, and it is subsidiary and solemn of you. The Irish people have great graw for the horse. When Tipperary Tim died, the cabhorse that won the Grand National and the only one of the whole field left standing, be the holy God you'd swear it was a beloved Archbishop that had gone to his eternal reward. Strong men was seen crying.

– Yes, and think of Orby, the great horse that won the National for Boss Croker. To this day he lies there at Sandyford.

– Ah yes. And then there was Master McGrath, the dog that was faster than the wind. A statue of him stands at a crossroads down in Tipp, where the mother comes from.

Both of them pleasurably savoured their kinship with the

higher animals, though personally Mick drew the line at becoming one of them by a process of prolonged carnal intercussion.

– Well, Sergeant, I am delighted that we are quite agreed on
one thing at least. Human metamorphosis vis-à-vis an iron
bicycle is quite another matter. And there is more to it than the
monstrous exchange of tissue for metal.

– And what would that be? the sergeant asked curiously.

– All decent Irishmen should have a proper national outlook.
Practically any bike you have in Ireland was made in either
Birmingham or Coventry.

– I see the point intimately. Yes. There is also an element of
treason entailed. Quite right.

It seemed that this point had never occurred to him and a
frown gathered about him as he inwardly considered it, puffing
stolidly and compacting the tobacco in his bowl with a well-
charred finger.

– Oh, now, he said at last, faith and the bicycle is no hilarity
of itself as a gigantic social problem. In me younger days it led to
a hanging.

– Is that so?

– It did bedad. I was stationed in Borrisokane at the time and
there was a very famous man there be the name of McDadd.
McDadd held the national record for the hundred miles on the
solid tyre. I need not tell you with exactitude what the solid tyre
did for him. We had to hang the bicycle.

– Hang the bicycle?

– McDadd had a first-class grudge against another man named
MacDonaghy but he did not go near MacDonaghy. He knew
how things stood there, and he gave MacDonaghy's bicycle a
ferocious thrashing with a crowbar. After that McDadd and Mac-
Donaghy had a fast fist fight and MacDonaghy – a dark man with
glasses – did not live to know who the winner was.

– Well, wouldn't that be a case of manslaughter?

– Not with the sergeant we had in them days. He held it
was murder most foul and a bad case of criminality into the
same bargain. We couldn't find McDadd for a long time or
make sure where the most of him was. We had to arrest his
bicycle as well as himself and we minutely watched the two of
them under secret observation for a week to see where the
majority of McDadd was and whether the bicycle was mostly

in McDadd's backside *pari passu* and vice versa if you understand my meaning.

– I think I do, but I can also see the possibility of a charge of conspiracy.

– Maybe so, maybe not. The sergeant gave his ruling at the end of the week. His position was painful in the extremity of pain because he was a close friend of McDadd after office hours. He condemned the bicycle and it was the bicycle that was hanged.

It seemed to Mick a very summary form of justice, and apparently the sentence had been imposed and carried out without the formality of court proceedings.

– I think that perhaps there was a miscarriage of the carriage-way there, he commented.

– They were rough days, the sergeant replied, smoking thoughtfully. But there was a great wake afterwards, and the bicycle was buried in the same grave as MacDonaghy. Did you ever see a bicycle-shaped coffin?

– No.

– It is a very inconvoluted item of wood-working, you would want to be a master class carpenter to make a good job of the handlebars, to say nothing of the pedals and the backstep.

– I don't doubt that.

– Ah yes. The days of racing on the solid tyre were sad days for Ireland.

The sergeant fell silent again. One could almost hear the gentle wash of the tide of memory in his head.

– There were tragedic cases, too, of another kind entirely. I remember an old man. He was harmless enough but he had the people driven loopy by the queer way he moved and walked. He'd go up a little gentle hill at a speed of maybe half a mile an hour but at other times he would run so fast that you'd swear he was doing up to fifteen emm pee aitch. And that's a fact by damn.

– Did anybody find out what was wrong with him?

– One very intelligent, perspicuous and infractious man did. It was meself. Do you know what was wrong with the poor bugger?

– No. What?

– He was suffering severely from Sturmey Archer. He was the

first in the country to fit the three-speed gear at the turn of the century.

– Yes, I think I can see the various possible complications. For instance, I think racing bikes have forks with special springing in them. Yes. It's all very interesting. But now, I promised to be home early and I'm going to buy a final drink.

Mick beckoned the waitress.

– I want to ask you about something, he added.

As the drinks were coming he bethought himself, as they say in the old books. He had enjoyed the sergeant's peroration and his abstruse subject. It would be fitting, perhaps, to call him the poor man's De Selby. But the latter was still his preoccupation – perhaps he should say his night-and-day obsession. Yet he had a plan now, one that was at once ingenious and daring. He thought it would be only wise and judicious to have the sergeant participate unwittingly in it, for if he were to find certain things out afterwards of his own motion, his undoubted gift for the maladroit could in the end wreck the scheme. Mick had already in his mind assigned a part – again an unwitting one – to Hackett. The date and timing of the operation depended now on one thing only: finding out how De Selby proposed to circulate his deadly DMP substance simultaneously all over the world so as to obviate the condition of insulation, the sort of seal that had obtained in the case of the submarine cavern at Dalkey.

He was not clear how he could do this in a reasonably short time, and prolonged twisting and turning of his own brain yielded no guess about how this mighty task could be accomplished. Even a world Power with tens of thousands of aeroplanes would be daunted by such an undertaking and, supernatural as De Selby's contacts seemed to be, it was doubtful indeed if flights of angels could be invoked. In fact there was no proof that the Almighty approved of De Selby at all. God might be on Mick's side.

– Sergeant Fottrell, he said seriously, I suppose you know Mr De Selby of the Vico Road?

A gentle frown gathered on the face.

– An exemplary and august personality, he replied, but a whit contumacious.

That was promising: respect leavened with suspicion.

– Exactly. I know him rather well myself but he has me

worried. In that house of his in the woods he has been carrying out experiments. He is a scientist, of course.

– Ah yes. Piercing insentiently the dim secrets of the holy world.

– Now I am not saying that he is breaking the law. But I do know that he is endangering the community. He does not know, and probably could not be persuaded, that his experiments might get out of control and visit us all with an epidemic of appalling disease, with goodness knows how many people dying like flies and passing on the pestilence to other people as they do so; not only here in Dublin and Dalkey but possibly in England and other parts of the world.

The sergeant had rekindled his pipe.

– That is a most unfavourable and incontinent tiding, he said. That is worse than the question of the bicycles.

– I'm glad you look at it in that way. You are a man, Sergeant, who is bigger than his job, otherwise you would not have stolen bicycles to curtail the deadly cycling of afflicted parties and indeed deliberately puncturing Policeman Pluck's machine.

This speech obviously pleased the sergeant, as Mick intended it would.

– There are times, he said, when I must take my superior officer to be the Man Above. It is my plain duty to guard members of the human race, sometimes from themselves. Not everybody understands the far from scrutable periculums of the intricate world.

– I quite agree. Now I happen to know that Mr De Selby had been artificially incubating the bacteria which cause typhoid fever in humans. Typhoid is a very serious and dangerous disease, even worse than typhus.

– An insatiable importunity.

– Yes.

– An indiscriminate exacerbation much to be inveighed against meticulously.

– Mr De Selby has tens of millions of those microbes in a metal container like a little keg. He has it in his house, locked in a safe.

– A safe, faith?

– Yes. In the interest of humanity I plan to carry off this container of dangerous bugs away from the scientist's house – steal it if you will – and put it in some safe place where it will do no harm.

– Ah! Well now! Steal it? Yes indeed. I would consider that not contumelious or derogatory.

– Then I can rely, Sergeant, on your co-operation?

He was now relaxed, apparently relieved that the project was no more than to take away something which was, while dangerous, of no monetary value.

– Not only my co-operation but my active condonement of the *res ipsa*. But locked in a safe? I do not know the skills of poking a safe's lock.

– Nor do I. And blowing it up or using force would be very dangerous. But that sort of hazard does not arise at all. The safe looks massive and strong but it is old-fashioned. Look at this!

From a small inside pocket of his jacket Mick extracted a key and held it up.

– I've told you, Sergeant, that our friend is careless, he said, and perhaps I should have said criminally careless and quite reckless. This is the key of the safe. I picked it up from the floor of his sitting-room on a recent visit.

– Well great cripes, the sergeant cried blankly.

– Our task is really simple enough, Mick continued. First we must see to it that on a given evening Mr De Selby is not at home. I think I can arrange that without much trouble. When he is out, there will be nobody else there. And our intrusion will be brief.

– Succinctly so, by dad.

– When we've got the container we will hide it in the shrubbery, near the little gate at the Vico Road. We will then go home. The following morning early I will collect it in a taxi. Then leave the rest to me. The only little snag is how to get into the house.

– That would not be a fastidious worry, the sergeant replied pleasantly, for if he is as careless as you say, I could deal deftly with a window, without wincing.

– But not break one, I hope. We don't want to alarm or alert him.

– No then. I have a good pen-knife.

– Ah, that is the business, Sergeant. We can take it that everything is agreed then?

– Except the date of the accomplishment.

– Yes. I'll let you know that in good time.

Mick rose, and in good conspirator's fashion, put out his hand. The sergeant grasped it.

– To the grand defence and preservation of the race of Adam, he intoned solemnly.

CHAPTER 10

FOR MICK a short time of inactivity and rest was to follow, and he was glad of it. He now had a plan to meet this DMP menace and felt that hasty or impetuous moves would do nothing but harm. It was his own plan, with himself as the only real performer, the other two – Hackett and Sergeant Fottrell – being unsuspecting associates. He thought it was wise to avoid meeting either for the time being, for top secrecy was essential; questions by either – particularly the inquisitive Hackett – could lead only to embarrassing evasions.

Mary had not returned and possibly would not before his meeting with Father Cobble, to be followed by a call the same evening on De Selby. That was the next move in the natural sequence, and nothing could be done to accelerate it. What could a week matter in this sombre situation? It seemed to be in character to be leisurely himself in the diabolical scheme he had outlined. Mick's curiosity about how he aimed to distribute his lethal chemical simultaneously all over the world had much abated, for if his own simple plan worked, the interest of the question was academic.

Thus for some days his life was quiet, almost decorous. He thought a bit about his growing, if secret, importance in the world he walked, his quiet command of the issues in a confrontation that was quite fabulous. And what little weapon fortified the iron calm of his nerves? The answer to that, he was sure, was Vichy water.

His attendance at his small job was perhaps more perfunctory than usual; in the evening he usually went for a swim at nearby Blackrock, had a few minerals afterwards, then home and early to bed. He kept feeling, not without pride, that he was taking the correct, easy-going, civilized course of De Selby himself in face of portentous possibility and unheard-of katabolism.

However, one day at lunch-time he made a small, subordinate

move. It was within the plan but he went about it with what may be called casual care. His general lack of domestic responsibility, his easy day-to-day spending of everything he earned and his rather improvident attitude to existence were all possible reasons why he never had a bank account and was quite inexperienced in the rubric of writing cheques. Now he gathered together small sums he had put aside at home, sold some books and a pocket watch he never used and did not need and found he had £25, and a little over. He went to the head office of the Bank of Ireland at College Green in the centre of Dublin and, after seeing some important official, opened a current account with a lodgment of £21, and received his first cheque-book. Very silly, of course, but he could not suppress a small surge of elation. Yet there had been no question of bolstering up his personal dignity: there had been another, a solid reason.

The first day of September was a Saturday. On the preceding evening some uneasiness came upon him. It would be necessary to see Hackett soon to instruct him in his role. Since Mick would be in Dalkey on Saturday evening anyway, there seemed to be no objection to making a trip to the Colza on Friday on chance of meeting him and spying out the land generally. It was not unlikely but he might get some tidings of De Selby also.

He pondered the matter, then told himself to stop being punctilious and self-conscious about trivialities, and took a tram to Dalkey about nine in the evening.

The Colza Hotel was quiet and indeed from the outside looked deserted but in the Slum department of the bar he found Dr Crewett and young Nemo Crabbe conversing civilly, with Mrs Laverty behind the counter, knitting. He saluted everybody, ordered a Vichy water and sat down.

– Well, gentlemen, he asked, has there been any sign of my friend Hackett?

Dr Crewett nodded.

– Yes, he said. The gentleman was in earlier with that precocious lady of his. I think he is teaching her to swim.

– We didn't like to ask outright, Crabbe said, because that friend of yours has an uncertain temper, particularly when taking refreshments. He might think we were spying.

Dr Crewett gave a smile which was perhaps more a leer.

– You must remember, Mick, that in teaching a lady to swim,

you must first pick out a quiet, inconspicuous part of the shore, and then you must help her to take all her clothes off.

Crabbe guffawed at this.

– She hadn't a whole damn lot to take off, he chuckled.

– Ah it doesn't matter, Mick said easily. I just wanted to mention something to him – nothing important. Any other news, good or bad?

– Nothing much, the doctor said.

– It's a slack time, Mick remarked.

– Wasn't there something about the PP? Crabbe interposed.

– There was vague talk about the PP being annoyed about something and ordering Sergeant Fottrell to call on him. Probably tales of inadequate bathing costumes down at White Rock, sunbathing or some other nonsense of the kind. Some prurient busybody trying to make trouble.

– I don't think it was that, doctor, Mick said.

– This is a terrible country for sexual obsession, Crabbe remarked. I give you five cities – Tyre, Sidon, Gomorrah, Sodom and Dublin.

– No. I heard that Teague McGettigan's nag misbehaved himself, in the opinion of his reverence, all around the grounds of the parochial house.

Dr Crewett laughed.

– Mrs Laverty, he called, give us two more drinks here and a Vichy water for my poor friend. Dear me, that's good. 'The Role of the Horse in History'. Paul Revere's Ride; the Charge of the Light Brigade; the Wooden Horse of Troy; and the Catharsis of Teague's Cabhorse.

– I saw the animal only once, Crabbe said, and I'm surprised that he had the energy for such a performance.

They attended to their new drinks.

– Yes, Crabbe added, there's another item of news, very trivial. I got digs, not here but in Dunleary. A woman by the name of Muldowney. A clean enough place. I have hardly anything to eat there except breakfast. Mrs Muldowney hates drink, denounces it strongly and constantly, and takes any God's amount of it.

– On the QT, of course, Mick agreed, thinking of Hurley's Tonic Wine.

The conversation had become desultory, tending to lapse. There was simply nothing to talk about.

– It's a pity, Mick ventured at last, that most of us haven't the money to go and live abroad. Our sort of people seem to flourish in an alien clime. One reason may be that this country's too damp.

– It's too full of humbugs and hypocrites, Crabbe said.

– We like to think, Dr Crewett said, that the Irish are the main people who built the modern United States. I think it's true that they and the Italians, both sterling Roman Catholic races, are answerable for the enduring system of crime and vice in America.

Under the skin Dr Crewett was a true misanthrope.

– It was more of the European mainland I was thinking, Mick explained, and, of course, Britain. Shaw would have rotted if he'd stayed here. And look at Stanford, John Field, Tom Moore, Hugh Lane and even Balfe. Consider the wonderful international reputation won by the late James Joyce, most of his life a poor refugee, a miserable fugitive of a teacher in schools all over Europe.

Dr Crewett abruptly put down his glass.

– What do you mean 'the late James Joyce'? Are you serious?

– Serious?

– Yes.

– Of course I'm serious.

– I thought everybody knew that Joyce's death – all those reports in foreign newspapers in the confusion of war – was all my eye.

– You mean that Joyce is still alive?

– Certainly I do.

– Then why didn't he contradict the reports? Such unfounded reports could be actionable.

– Because he put the story out himself.

Mick paused here. The doctor was speaking seriously and, in any event, downright levity was foreign to his cynical nature.

– I find that very hard to believe, Mick said finally.

– Anything of Joyce's that I've read, Crabbe observed, I thought very fine and poetic. His *Portrait of the Artist*, for instance. He's a man I would certainly like to meet. Dr Crewett, if he's still alive, where is he?

Dr Crewett made a vague, head-shaking gesture.

– I never heard the full story, he said. There was some scandal,

I believe. I don't know whether it was military, marital or moral. He was ordered out of France by the Germans, that much is certain, and it is obvious he couldn't go anywhere eastward. He may initially have made his way to Spain, or got to England with the help of the French Resistance. Anyhow, he was in England and using another name six months after his alleged death.

– But granted that, it is a considerable time ago now. How do you know he's still alive?

– I know a man who was speaking to him a matter of months ago. News of his genuine death could not nowadays be distorted or suppressed.

This made Mick quite excited and, in response, Dr Crewett added:

– But what does it matter? It's his own business and, anyway, he has stopped writing.

– Yes, but where is he?

– Could he be in the United States? Crabbe asked. He would certainly be well treated there, probably be given a chair at one of the universities.

– No, he's not, the doctor replied. I don't think it's any secret that he's still alive, but . . . well . . . his actual whereabouts is a confidential matter. I believe a well-known public man is entitled to privacy if he elects to have it, and particularly if there is some good reason for electing to have it.

This rather affected sort of talk made Mick impatient. Very likely it was intended to tease. If Joyce had left the European mainland and was not in America, he must be in Britain, Ireland or the Isle of Man. The continents of Asia and Africa would be unthinkable habitations for such a man. And the Isle of Man was too small for anybody seeking concealment and anonymity. It seemed clear enough that Dr Crewett knew the location of the hide-out and was possibly engendering self-importance by being difficult about the thing. It was a 'confidential matter' then? That was just tomfoolery as far as the doctor was concerned. His courtly considerations, everybody knew, had never deterred him from butting into the private affairs of other people. Mick thought a direct assault was the proper course.

– Now, Dr Crewett, he said as sternly as he could, I don't think it is reasonable to withhold *any* information about Joyce from the

like of me. You know that I greatly esteem the man and that
I would be solicitous in any way I could for his well-being. If in
fact I knew where he was living – or hiding, if you like – I would
absolutely respect his desire to remain unknown and concealed.
I would be the last in the world to make such information public
property.

The doctor betrayed a slight grimace which he quickly concealed with a gulp from his glass.

– My dear man, he said, you know very well there's no question of my not trusting you. I merely meant that any information
I was given was given as being under the rose, strictly confidential. You understand? Ah, we'll talk about it again.

– Very good, Mick said shortly. As you please.

He was sure he knew what the doctor meant: he preferred to
say nothing in the presence of Nemo Crabbe, still comparatively
a stranger to all of them.

– Crabbe, Mick said brightly, have you managed to become
a little more reconciled to the toilsome process of becoming a
medical doctor?

Crabbe pulled his mouth into a scowl.

– Not a bit of it, he replied. So far as I can see, we students of
today are laboriously studying to obtain a certificate that we're
out of date. Revolutionary advances in diagnosis, treatment and
pharmacology take place every few months nowadays. A new
wonder-drug makes dozens of familiar medicaments obsolete
overnight. Look at penicillin and the antibiotics generally.

Yes, that was an intelligent enough point, Mick thought.
Would it be appropriate here to expatiate on Sergeant Fottrell's
bicyclosis? Hardly.

– When Fleming accidentally produced what he called penicillin in 1928, Dr Crewett observed, he did not invent something or discover anything new. When I was a young fellow in
the County Carlow I often saw farm labourers treating boils
on the back of their necks by anchoring putrescent cow-dung to
the infected place, usually with a dirty scarf. This dung quietly
wiped out the staphylococci.

Mick seemed to have some vague recollection of that kind
himself.

– Well, Fleming got the Nobel prize, he said. For what?

– What he did was a sheer accident in the lab, the doctor

rejoined, but he deserved great credit for accurately observing what he saw, and scientifically recording it.

– But the introduction of penicillin, Mick protested, was a veritable upheaval in the treatment of a great many diseases.

– I've got a good few shots of that stuff in my time, Crabbe said.

– Fleming's secondary achievement, Dr Crewett said, was to synthesize the fungoid process by devising artificial cultures. But the intrinsic secret of penicillin was known to folk medicine for centuries, possibly for thousands of years.

– Yes, I feel that's true.

– That's why it's foolish for men in western Europe to be supercilious about witch-doctors, their brews and decoctions, eye of newt and toe of frog, and so on. Those savages knew nothing of chemistry or pathology but they were capable of carrying on uncomprehended but sound medicinal traditions. The birds and the brute creation have similar instinctive remedies for their own sicknesses.

– Let us have another drop, Mrs Laverty, Crabbe called, and then I must be off about my business.

Mrs Laverty came out from her fortress and arranged the glasses, remarking that it was very close and that she thought there was thunder in the air, judging by her corns, which were at her.

– Leaving aside the stupidities of academic training in medicine, Crabbe said coarsely, who the hell wants to be a GP?

– It's a way of life, Dr Crewett said. Even a very bad doctor can earn a living.

– Earn a living, yes, Crabbe returned, but heavens, what a life!

– Better than working in the salt mines.

Crabbe drank with a little tinge of savagery.

– If and when I qualify, he rasped, I'm sure I'll make a damn fool of myself in some unusual way, perhaps like Schweitzer or Livingstone.

– Well then you'll be famous, Dr Crewett replied sardonically, and admired all over the world.

– Aw, go to hell.

Pseudo-technical dialogues of this kind did not interest Mick very much, and he scarcely heard the rest of it. After Crabbe had departed, he turned afresh on Dr Crewett.

– I'm reasonably sure that Joyce is somewhere in this country, for it is inconceivable that he would live in England, and Dublin, congenial as even the changed town of today might be, would be too dangerous for a famous man whose plight was that he must not be recognized. Where is he?

The doctor smiled craftily.

– I told you the information I have is confidential, he declared, which means that if I impart it to you, you must receive it in confidence and in no circumstances pass it on to anybody else.

This was more morbid humbug, Mick concluded, but there was no harm on his part in a naïve play of reciprocation.

– I accept that but subject to one condition. As a piece of information I will keep it to myself. But I would feel entitled to use it merely to make contact with Joyce himself and, on doing that, it is possible he might release me from the obligation of keeping his whereabouts quiet. I might be able to show that his fears, whatever they are, are illusory.

– Oh, I could scarcely question that except that if you did run Joyce to earth, he'd be pretty certain to ask you how you knew where to look for him. I certainly wouldn't like my own name to be mentioned.

– Do you know him?

– No, I don't.

– Then the point is immaterial, though in any case I wouldn't dream of mentioning your name.

Dr Crewett's little passing frown seemed to say that he was not pleased that his existence should thus be summarily discarded.

– Tell me, he said. What do you want to see Joyce about? Why do you want to meet him?

Quite a question, that: gratuitous, impertinent, stupid.

– Anybody's reasons for wishing to know the man should be obvious enough, Mick said coldly. In my own case, the first reason is curiosity. I believe the picture of himself he has conveyed in his writings is fallacious. I believe he must be a far better man or a far worse. I think I have read all his works, though I admit I did not properly persevere with his play-writing. I consider his poetry meretricious and mannered. But I have an admiration for all his other work, for his dexterity and resource in handling language, for his precision, for his subtlety in conveying the image of Dublin and her people, for his accuracy in setting down speech authentically, and for his enormous humour.

As a spontaneous appraisal of literary work, this unpremedi-
tated pronouncement was not bad at all, Mick thought. But after
all, was he not a well-read man for his age and upbringing, and
fearless enough in facing books in which might lurk danger to
morals? He was.

Dr Crewett put down his glass.

– Well by the damn, he said, you are certainly fond of your
Joyce. I never suspected you of such enthusiasms.

Mick allowed goodwill to return to his face.

– You might remember that this Colza is not exactly a literary
salon. Such matters do not properly arise here as a subject of
converse.

– True, I suppose. True.

– I've read some of the stupid books written *about* Joyce and
his work, mostly by Americans. A real book about Joyce, springing from many long talks with him, could clear up misunder-
standings and mistakes, and eliminate a lot of stupidity.

– Lord, don't tell me that you are also an author and exegetist
in your own right?

– No, I don't claim to be that at all but if I could gather
together the material, a friend of mine would be well able to
turn it into a fine, fresh book. I happen to know somebody who
can write very well. Stylishly.

– Well . . . that's an idea.

– My point is that such a development could take place without disclosing to the public Joyce's present abode.

– I quite see that, but perhaps Joyce wouldn't be so convinced
of the prudence of such a publication, with its implication that
the master is not dead at all.

Mick finished his drink abruptly.

– I think we've had enough of this skirmishing, Dr Crewett.
Where is James Joyce living at the present time?

– In Skerries.

It would be a mere shadow of the truth to say that this disclosure deeply startled the enquirer, though it is not easy exactly
to say why. Joyce had to be *somewhere*. Skerries is a small, pretty
watering-place twenty miles north of Dublin with an ample,
sandy strand very safe for youngsters, a spot for deep-sea swimmers on a rocky headland, and round the corner a neat little
harbour. Perhaps Mick's surprise that Joyce should be living in

such a place grew from the fact that he himself knew it, and liked it well. When a schoolboy he had spent ten days there, and had many times since made a daily trip to revisit the scene. In fact it was there that he had first learned to swim, and it was there he first met Hackett. Was it now an ominous sort of place, a social hazard? Perhaps.

It was surprising, too, that Joyce should go to ground so near Dublin city, in fact in the County Dublin.

Yet what was so funny? Perhaps Skerries was a sagacious choice. As a resort it had its season – a long season, for it is in an area famous for its very light rainfall. The natives were quite accustomed to having strangers and visitors in their midst, and even retired people who remain on in town out of season. Most householders who had the accommodation took guests. Yes, perhaps here again one had silence, exile and cunning.

– Well, that is very interesting, doctor, Mick said briskly, and certainly unexpected. Have we any other information?

– I don't know his address, if that's what you mean.

– That wouldn't bother me. I'd ferret that out on the spot. Are there any other particulars? For instance, is he using his own name in any situation where he must produce *some* name?

– No. I know absolutely nothing more but wouldn't be surprised to know he's using his own name.

– Ah, well well. Does he drink, for instance, and if so, where? Or would he have a morning cup of coffee in some pretty little shop?

Dr Crewett smiled bleakly.

– No information. I think I've told you everything I know – and that's very little – but I imagine his life would be rather that of a recluse.

Mick pondered his little clues and they seemed to make up quite a workable pattern, considering that only a little seaside town he knew well was the territory.

– Well, thanks very much, doctor, for all the secrets you've given me, and so generously.

– In confidence, mind, he said, wagging his finger waggishly.

It was not long until Mick was making his way to a homeward tram. He was preoccupied. It was strange how fast somewhat grisly spices were accumulating on his platter. First, the central menace of De Selby, and his own plan to foil him. Then the baffling Saint Augustine episode. Next, the accidental Father Cobble complication, to be enacted on the morrow. And now this Joyce phantasm, a man back from beyond the grave, armed only with the plea that he had never gone there, yet hiding under a name unknown in a little town.

Surely it was enough to baffle any man, if not frighten him? Yet Mick was on the edge of congratulating himself that he was the phlegmatic type, one who was not without his own cunning, a gift for scheming, and a certain rough courage.

As the tram lurched on its way, he became certain of one thing. He would go to Skerries, for a matter of days if necessary, search every nook and cranny of it, and find Joyce if he was there. He would strip him of all his secrets, his dreams, boasts and regrets, and present them on a tray to that unpredictable, domineering, able, fascinating girl Mary. Would she thank him, though – or tell him off for meddling in the affairs of strangers? Hardly . . . not surely in the case of a man like Joyce. She had herself advanced no mean distance in the Republic of Letters, knew a lot more about French literature than he did. She was inquisitive concerning the nature of genius, personally creative and therefore receptive. No. The true story of Joyce would be ideal material for the exercise of her rich mind. She would produce her own unprecedented book.

CHAPTER 11

AT THE TIME of these events, the Royal Marine Hotel in Dun-leary was a big hulk of faded splendour, with hints of red plush and gilt of bygone good times. Yet there was comfort there still, good food, and the peculiar solace which sometimes can be got from cross-channel accents.

Mick arrived twenty minutes too early, sat in the lounge and fortified himself with a precautionary glass of the French water. His intention was to represent to Father Cobble that De Selby was an eccentric man, though of exceptional intellectual powers, and that he seemed spiritually very confused; and that perhaps he would be the better for a straightforward talk on the immutab-ility of the Christian ideal, the immortality of the soul, and the respect which was due to the Church. He aimed also to steer a theme, such as the propagation throughout the world of Christ's message, round to the nature of the secret scheme which De Selby was harbouring for dissemination simultaneously every-where of his ghastly DMP. He saw it would be worse than futile to inform Father Cobble about the unearthly problem which confronted him in his effort to shield mankind from an un-paralleled sort of threat.

Father Cobble came punctually. He had the look which his deep booming voice had told Mick he would have – a thin, dark, very small man of sixty or so, with a lined but pleasant, well-meaning face. He was very well-dressed. As he paused in the large lounge gazing enquiringly about him, Mick rose, went to his side, touched his arm and put his hand out.

– Father Cobble, I think?

– Ah!

He shook hands affably.

– Well, well. You are Michael, of course. Excellent. Capital.

– Perhaps we might sit over there, Father, Mick said, leading the way to his little table. The priest smiled and sat down, neatly stowing his hat and furled umbrella at a nearby stand.

– And isn't it the heavy evening, he said agreeably. I can't say I enjoy this sort of heat. I've spent many years in Rome; the thermometer's higher, there, of course, but somehow it's a different sort of heat.

– Everybody says the exhausting thing here is the humidity of the atmosphere, Father, but I've never quite understood what that means.

Father Cobble was looking brightly about him.

– I think we may take it that the strong sunlight of summer extracts vapours from our sodden landscape, he remarked, but I imagine that situation is beyond human redress. Of course in some big cities, particularly in America, the problem is met indoors by air conditioning. Our own house in Cleveland has this arrangement and, believe me, it makes an enormous differ-ence. Well now! What about a nice cup of tea and perhaps some sugartops?

– *Sugartops?*

– Yes, yes. You know, those little circular cakes with icing on top, white or pink. I'm serious.

What a horrible suggestion! Was this sybaritism as understood by the Jesuits? Mick gave what was intended to sound like a gentle little laugh.

– Father, I couldn't possibly.

– Ah, perhaps tea then with freshly-cut ham sandwiches?

– You see, Father, I usually do not have a proper lunch in the middle of the day. This means that I am a ravening wolf when I get home in the evening, and then I plough into a great dinner. It is not an hour since I laid down my knife and fork.

Father Cobble chuckled and surprisingly produced a packet of cigarettes.

– Let me confess the truth, he said. I am in the same boat. Do have a cigarette. We also dine in the evening. I'm afraid our House has brought some exotic customs here.

– No harm. The Irish Church is very insular. He pointed to his glass, not yet quite empty. If I might make a suggestion, Father, I think both of us deserve a drop of decent drink. A curiosity is that whiskey is an antidote to heat. When empire-builders have to live in hot foreign climates abroad, they con-sume great quantities of whiskey. At the moment I happen to be ignoring whiskey for a secret little reason of my own but I insist that you have a glass of Kilbeggan.

– Well now, perhaps that is an idea, Michael.

Mick ignored his detestable familiarity, beckoned a waiter and ordered the two drinks. Father Cobble was now smoking, relaxed, and gazing with interest about him.

– Well now. You have a friend who is in trouble?

– Not exactly in trouble, Father. At least I think he would be astonished if anybody told him he was, and offered sympathy. It is only that some of his attitudes and ways of thinking have struck me as eccentric, not to say unbalanced.

– Yes. Would I be right in saying that strong drink is involved here?

This reading amused Mick a little. What could be simpler than alcoholism, a spirituous rather than a spiritual disorder? He would be very happy indeed if that was all the trouble with De Selby.

– Oh not at all, Father. He is by no means a strict TT any more than you or I, but I would define the origin of his trouble as an overweening intellectual arrogance.

– Ah. The old sin of pride.

– His name is De Selby and he is a sort of a scientist.

– A foreigner caught up with some pagan dialectic?

– He is not a foreigner. He speaks exactly like a Dublin man, and the word 'pagan' would not occur to me in connexion with him. In fact he believes in God and claims to have verified the divine existence by experiment. I think you could say he lacks the faith because he is in no need of it. He *knows*.

He could sense Father Cobble turning his head slightly and staring.

– What an extraordinary man, he said. Yes. We priests in the line of duty do come across a great number of very strange people. One must be careful. If drink be not in question, how can you be sure there is no narcosis of some other kind?

– One cannot be certain of anything like that, of course, Mick replied, but he is absolutely rational, occasionally even brilliant, in his talk. You can judge for yourself shortly.

– Indeed yes. May I ask – this is mere polite curiosity – why you thought I could be of help?

– To be honest, I didn't. That was somebody else's idea. But I'm sure a man of your attainments, Father, could not fail to do good in any situation. And you will be relieved to hear that De Selby is invariably polite, urbane and civilized. I suspect, indeed, that he enjoys argument. And he is an authority on the Bible.

He could see that Father Cobble's attitude and appetite were being whetted. He was glad of this, because theological conversational infighting between him and De Selby might put the latter off his guard so far as he, Mick, was concerned and he thus might somehow leak his scheme for the simultaneous worldwide deployment of DMP. But this, he had to remind himself, lacked the importance it initially had, for if his own plan were successfully put into operation and in time, De Selby with all his works and pomps would be a nullity, at least for the time being.

Father Cobble had very smartly finished his glass of malt, summoned a waiter and ordered similar drinks, which he paid for with a ten shilling note. Mick was a bit surprised. The internal mechanics of the Jesuit Order (or Society, as they called themselves) was to him a mystery. It was one of the mendicant orders but he thought this term had a technical meaning. How could mendicants live in the grandiose palaces and colleges which the Jesuits customarily inhabit? The answer seemed to be that every Jesuit Father – and postulant for that matter – is personally a mendicant inasmuch as he is forbidden to have any means or goods whatsoever. If his duties call for him to make a journey, across the town or across the world, he has to go to some superior or bursar and ask for his fare. It appeared that the Order was very wealthy, its members utterly indigent. He had heard that the Fathers lived and ate well in their princely abodes. Good luck to them!

On the short tram journey to Dalkey they went upstairs, for Father Cobble was still engaged very earnestly with a cigarette. Mick was wondering whether smoking was forbidden *intra muros* and was the priest, in a sort of a way, mitching? But he did not like to ask. Indeed, as a non-smoker himself, it was none of his business. The subject of their conversation was, curiously, swimming. Father thought it was an excellent exercise, taught discipline and self-reliance, and one never knew when this skill would come in useful, even to the point of saving life. No, he could not swim himself. It had been his life-long regret that his student days had been spent in inland establishments without even a decent river at hand. The country was backward insofar as providing swimming-baths for schools and colleges was concerned. Certain tasks and habits should be inculcated in early youth, the formative time of life. A priest friend of his, a keen swimmer, had told him of an amusing experience at the Forty Foot at Sandycove. His reverence was in the water when a very fat man arrived, undressed very quickly, accidentally bashed a toe on a sharp dagger of rock on his way to the water, fell and severely gashed his elbow. He sat there, cursing and bellowing forth the most lurid language, but his face quickly changed colour when the man in the water emerged to towel himself and then don the clothes of a priest, collar and all. Father Cobble laughed softly at his own story. Clearly he was a man of the world. Had the two glasses of whiskey slackened the grip of austerity which, Mick reflected, is not natural or permanent with any man.

Their walk up the Vico Road was pleasant and tranquil, and the seaward prospect as enchanting as ever in the softness of the evening. But finally there they were, a little after eight, standing outside De Selby's door.

He opened it himself, playing out immediately his undeniable charm, relieved his visitors of hats and umbrella and led the way into the room in which Hackett and Mick had first conferred with him. De Selby was clearly in good spirits and Mick hoped vaguely that this was not occasioned by a new break-through in the diabolical laboratory.

– I may tell you, Father Cobble, he said, and you, Michael, that I've done something which may seem rude but not so intended. I have ordered Teague McGettigan to call with his cab at ten o'clock to drive you to the tram. Do you know, it can be cold these nights when the sun goes down.

They expostulated cheerfully about this arrangement, of course, but it pleased Father Cobble, who discerned it to be a friendly gesture. Then the talk began, only to be interrupted temporarily while De Selby produced his home-made whiskey, this time in a large decanter – glasses and water. It seemed that he had correctly divined Father Cobble's taste in this thing. Mick instinctively knew that this was no time to start a dialogue about Vichy water, something new in his relations with De

Selby. Duty bade him silently acquiesce in whiskey, even if it choked him.

Talk was rather desultory, partly due to De Selby's politeness as host, partly because Father Cobble, an Englishman, was also polite and academic and seemed to lack polemical ardour or to have real appetite for argument. Mick felt he had to start something or somehow attend to the management of this meeting, if the occasion was not to be inarticulate futility. He patiently waited for the lull which would enable him to cast his fly.

– Father Cobble, our host Mr De Selby has perfected a chemical organism – I do not understand exactly what it is – which, he considers, would be of inexpressible benefit to communities of men throughout the world. If I understand the situation aright, his problem is to make this substance available universally at the same time, as an atmospheric change in one place could cause havoc in another unless a comparable change could have been synchronistically arranged for the other . . .

– Dear me, Father Cobble murmured.

– Please continue, De Selby said benignly. It is always valuable to hear another person define what he is pleased to call one's problems.

Mick blushed faintly but was unshaken in his aim to induce De Selby to say something to Father Cobble about DMP.

– Well, he continued, this idea of mine is probably outlandish but I thought there might be some parallel between the propagation of the faith and the worldwide dissemination of this substance.

– Good gracious now, Father Cobble said, evidently stimulated, setting down his glass. That is certainly an interesting query, outlandish or not. It is rather as if a large manufacturer of tobacco were to include in his packet a slip telling the smoker which were the best matches to use.

De Selby had lit a cigarette, not having offered one to the priest: this seemed a personal quirk of his.

– There is really no problem, Father, he said.

– But this is interesting. In the present state of the world, missionary work has taken on a totally new character. This globe of ours has shrunk pathetically. Modern achievements in radio and television, tape recording and all the magic of the cinema have so radically improved communication – *communication*, I repeat

– that the old-fashioned preacher going into the wilds is now almost obsolete. Beside the pulpit we may now place the microphone. I mean, Mr De Selby, that these organs of communication are equally open to yourself.

This was not the way Mick wanted the subject to be handled.

– Gentlemen, he said, I've already said that my suggestion was outlandish. I don't think really that there is any parallel because, while the Church is disseminating an idea, a faith, Mr De Selby's task is disseminating a thing, a commodity. There is a big difference. An idea could be infectious, sweeping pell-mell over an entire community. But not so a thing.

– What exactly is this substance or commodity? Father Cobble asked, puzzled.

– I believe it changes the air, Mick replied.

– Let us say it is an atmospheric rejuvenator, De Selby said, perhaps not unlike, in its effects, the apparatus they have in big cinemas for changing the air every two minutes.

– Would it be suitable for use in large churches?

– Well, I hadn't thought of that.

It was clear that Father Cobble's interest was not casual. It may be that he had had training as a physicist and was accustomed to speculation about the purely mechanistical lot of man on this earth. He said that if it was shown beyond all doubt that 'this invention' was good and of true benefit to the human race, the Church would certainly not oppose it. But whether the great ecclesiastical organizations could be properly called in to encourage its adoption and use – that was another question. The Church was ever watchful where strictly lay matters were sought to be obtruded within its sacred jurisdiction. He recollected that when it was first proposed that concrete should be used in the construction of churches, there was quite a to-do, and the matter had to be referred to Rome. Missionaries brought not only the faith to unenlightened peoples but also most of the boons of modern hygiene – clean drinking water, baths, lavatories, insecticides and all manner of medicaments to counter the depredations of mice, monkeys, rats, beetles and cockroaches. *Mens sana in corpore sano* was indeed a very wise adage. The air in many parts of the pagan world – particularly in Africa – was far from satisfactory or salubrious. The climate was the root of the trouble. In parts of Africa the air was fetid, and charged with

a deplorable stench. Did Mr De Selby think his preparation
could retrieve such a situation?

De Selby replied that he hesitated to go so far. In reality his
little atmospheric preoccupation was still at the stage of experiment. His main interest in the air we breathe was its gaseous
constitution. Was its nitrogenous content ideal, for instance?

It was plain enough to Mick that the wily old sage was lying,
if one allows that there was any real meaning in his talk at all. He
had no intention of divulging the truth about DMP.

Father Cobble said it was most advisable that so important and
useful an intervention in the physical world should be brought
to adjudication as soon as possible; men gifted with large ideas
of that kind had a duty before God to develop them.

De Selby said that he was under certain difficulties. This was
not a matter that could be investigated by a vast pharmaceutical
laboratory. It entailed research, so far as he was concerned, and
several departments of this new science were inchoate and
obscure. Probably no physicist would be qualified to join him in
his studies. This was not to say he was held up by mere shortage
of staff. Far from it. His experiments were almost at an end.
He was now at the stage of checking and verifying various
conclusions which had emerged from his work over many years.
It had been hard endeavour but the end-product, so to speak,
was in sight.

He then courteously shared out more drink.

His own Society, Father Cobble pointed out, was not
properly ranked among the missionary orders. Theirs was the
task of disciplining the Church's roster for intellectual duty. It
was a heavy burden but they were willing indeed to assume it
and he thought he could proudly say that they were making
a job of it! Two ideas occurred to him. There were several
renowned Jesuit universities in the world and it was more than
possible that the department of physics in one of them could
be of valuable assistance to Mr De Selby. Some of the most
distinguished men in that sphere were members of the Society.
The second idea concerned a brother of his own. His brother
had sound scientific training and had always had that valuable
stimulus – curiosity. True, he was at present head of a small
boot polish factory at Leeds, but it might be remembered that
he was a BSc of Glasgow University. Father Cobble thought

this scientist would be happy to come over for a chat with Mr De Selby.

The latter was grateful for the offer but, really, such a visit would be an imposition on the decent man. Research, properly so-called, was at an end. Nothing remained but the tying of loose ends.

Mick, in a final return to the attack, pointed out to De Selby that the question he had originally raised was not the intrinsic merit of the product or its impact on mankind but its simultaneous dispersal throughout the world.

De Selby laughed.

– Faith now but you seem obsessed with difficulties, even when they're not there. What's wrong with the Post Office?

– The *Post Office*?

– Certainly. If I wanted to send letters out to arrive simultaneously in London and New York, nothing is necessary beyond a brief glance at postal times. If I had a thousand packages to despatch so that all would arrive on the same day at different points throughout the globe, I believe a good postman would draw up a schedule of posting times and stamp charges in his spare time for a few guineas.

So that was the plan! Why had it not occurred to Mick, to Hackett, to everybody? Why had they been so obtuse?

It would be a waste of time to enquire to whom the packages would be addressed. It didn't matter: they would be opened anyway – *if* they were ever posted.

Evidently Father Cobble's curiosity had waned somewhat, as his humour grew rosier with De Selby's cheerful distillate.

– The Post Office, he said, is nearly as universal as the Church. I have often thought of that. You walk along a poor, deserted lane. Behold, you see a little letter-box, a postbox, built into the wall. It is perhaps 10,000 miles from Hong Kong but if you push a letter into it, addressed to Hong Kong, it will miraculously go.

– I agree, Father, Mick said. It's marvellous.

De Selby withdrew to return with a basket of assorted biscuits and to take a fresh, determined grip of the decanter. And that is how the evening went. Shortly after ten a shambling bout of knocking told them that Teague McGettigan had arrived, and Father Cobble and Mick were intoxicated and tired enough to be grateful for this small mercy. De Selby they left, cheerful but unperturbed.

How did Mick feel going homeward with his reverence? Not vexed, not stultified: his own word would be *intact*. He had learnt something, but his plan of campaign was unaffected. Father Cobble was a nonentity. The evening had been pleasant enough but if anybody came out of the encounter with a sad lack of any credit, it was poor Mary.

CHAPTER 12

THE FLOOR of that apartment in Mick's head which he liked
to call the spare room was becoming a bit littered and untidy.
Several tides seemed to be running simultaneously on the same
shore, if that metaphor serves better. Matters had altered somewhat and he felt that he should now set out, in due order, the
problems as they had grown and hardened in his mind, think
out in what sequence they should be tackled and the results
reconciled. Beforehand let it be agreed that the Father Cobble
episode, silly and pointless as it was in the event, had cleared
away worry about De Selby's plan for disseminating his poison.
Use of the Post Office was true anti-climax, considering the
grandeur of the threat, but it removed the question completely
from the list of things to be done by Mick, and was also salutary
in reminding him that a mind portentous in ingenuity had
withal its pathetic simplicities. Here then is the list, as he mentally drew it up, of the imponderable tasks which seemed to
confront him.

1. De Selby's cask had to be stolen as soon as possible, with
the co-operation of Sergeant Fottrell.

2. To the end of (1) he would make a bogus appointment
with De Selby at the Colza Hotel and, by pre-arrangement with
Hackett, have him detained there while he, Mick, and the
sergeant rifled his house.

3. To the end of (2) he would have to fix on a date, with a
time about 9 p.m., and in the meantime see Hackett, taking care
to remember to keep Sergeant Fottrell informed.

4. He would have to devise, at a longer remove, a method of
ensuring that De Selby would not resume manufacture or pro-
duction of his deadly DMP, for an interim solution of the awful
menace was no solution at all. At the same time his Christian
conscience forbade the simple killing of De Selby.

5. Investigation of the James Joyce situation at Skerries was
an urgent necessity to the greater honour and promotion to

celebrity of his virgin Mary, but did he love Mary so fully and deeply as he had been persuading himself he did? Did she secretly despise him?

6. Assuming he met Joyce and won his confidence, could the contretemps at (4) be resolved by bringing together De Selby and Joyce and inducing both to devote their considerable brains in consultation to some recondite, involuted and incomprehensible literary project, ending in publication of a book which would be commonly ignored and thus be no menace to universal sanity? Would Joyce take to De Selby, and vice versa? Does a madman reciprocally accept a dissimilar madness? Could the conjunction of the two conceivably bring forth something more awful even than DMP? (All those were surely very harassing puzzles.)

7. Was he losing sight of the increase and significance of his own personal majesty? Well, it seemed that he had been, probably out of the force of habit of his lowly way of life theretofore. Nobody, possibly not even Mary, seemed to think that he mattered very much. But his present situation was that he was on the point of rescuing everybody from obliteration, somewhat as it was claimed that Jesus had redeemed all mankind. Was he not himself a god-figure of some sort?

8. Did not the Saint Augustine apparition mean that all was not well in heaven? Had there been some sublime slip-up? If he now carried out successfully his plan to rescue all God's creatures, was there not a sort of concomitant obligation on him to try at least to save the Almighty as well as his terrestrial brood from all his corrupt Churches – Catholic, Greek, Mohammedan, Buddhist, Hindu and the innumerable manifestations of the witch doctorate?

9. Was it his long-term duty to overturn the whole Jesuit Order, with all its clowns of the like of Father Cobble, or persuade the Holy Father to overturn it once again – or was it his duty to overturn the Holy Father himself?

Those were the sort of questions, or speculations, which filled Mick's mind for some days and nights. They made his head feel like a hive full of bees and he had to remind himself that his own reason must be kept on tight rein. He finally decided that the De Selby DMP transaction was paramount, as most of the others largely depended on it. Depending on a chance encounter with

Hackett in Dalkey was awkward and time-wasting and the first step was to make an appointment with him (which he forthwith did by postcard) to meet at 6 p.m. after work two evenings later in the bar of Westland Row railway station in Dublin city. Such a location may seem odd and conspiratorial but nothing of that kind was intended: it was a quiet, free-and-easy place, little known to passing citizens, and perhaps his choice of it was prompted by so simple a thing as that it gave both of them a convenient way of getting home afterwards by rail. That at least was the sort of triviality that seemed to keep obtruding on his grandiose affairs.

He kept that appointment and Hackett arrived, as usual, late. And he was not in his pleasantest mood. He followed a rather coarse greeting with a complaint.

– If you want to see me about something, that's fair enough, but on a hot dry evening like this when what I want is a pint, why must you fix on a place where they don't serve pints?

Mick decided to be unresponsive and precise, since his business was important.

– All we have to do, he replied, is walk down the stairs to the street and into any nearby pub. Alternatively we can stay here and you can have a whiskey as a consolation, or even a large coffee. I'm drinking Vichy water for a change, for the good of my guts, and it's not everywhere you get it. They have it here.

– What's wrong with the Colza?

– It's too far away.

– All right. Get me a whiskey.

They sat down at the back and Mick tried to explain his needs concisely. He wanted to raid De Selby's house to get something and he would invent some colourable pretext for meeting him at the Colza Hotel. He would not be there but it would be Hackett's job to hold De Selby there in conversation and if possible ply him with drinks. The question was – which evening?

– What do you want to rob the poor bastard of? That barrel of chemicals he has?

– Perhaps. What does it matter to you?

– Well, Mick, if *you* don't trust De Selby, maybe I don't trust *you*. What are you going to do with the stuff?

– Nothing. That is to say, I intend to leave it in an absolutely safe place, where nobody can get at it and indeed where nobody will know what it is.

Hackett nodded thoughtfully.

– The position seems to be, he said, that De Selby can destroy the world with it. Your proposition is that De Selby's power should be transferred to yourself.

– That is not true, Mick answered very firmly. I do not possess the secret of the stuff's detonation. Only De Selby himself knows that.

– That may be only a half-truth. He may have the formula written down and you might be able to lift that from his desk as well as make off with the barrel.

– Well, by the damn! Is that likely with a man like De Selby?

– It's at least possible.

– My sole purpose is to get this dangerous stuff out of the way for good.

Here Hackett called for another drink.

– Suppose you get only the cask. That's three-quarters of the battle, isn't it? In a situation so critical, what is to prevent you kidnapping De Selby and torturing him until he yields his secrets?

Mick gave a laugh that was genuine enough.

– Hackett, he replied, you're getting fanciful and macabre. It's only in books and on films that things are done that way.

Hackett attended to his glass reflectively.

– Well, he announced finally, I don't give a damn about this thing. If you know what you're doing, it's all right with me. I'm not at all sure what De Selby is really up to, and I don't give a damn if that house of his in the trees is a knocking-shop. Provided De Selby turns up at the Colza I'll keep him there all right and as regards drink, I'll do my best to make him ply *me* with it. You needn't be afraid he'll walk in on you when you've broken into his house. As a matter of fact I'll slip him a Mickey Finn if necessary.

– No, no, that shouldn't be necessary. In fact it would be very undesirable, as we don't want to startle or alarm him.

– Well, I'll bring a dose along just in case.

Here again Mick wanted to be exact.

– My own operation, he explained, won't take long at all. De Selby will naturally find out in due course that his stuff is gone, but what can he do? What would be the point of reporting the theft to the police? I mean, what could he report as having been taken?

– Hurry up and buy another round. He could report the theft of his metal cask. He could say, if he liked, that it was full of gold sovereigns or something else very valuable of the kind.

Mick shook his head.

– Details of a theft must be genuine and particularized, he replied, but what you say reminds me of a possible snag. I don't know the weight of that container. Perhaps it may be too heavy to carry and that my attempt may have to be abandoned for the time being. If things turn out that way, it's all the more reason why you should treat De Selby gently at the Colza. I will leave no marks of forcible entry at his house and he need have no suspicions aroused. That will make way for a second attempt if need be.

He raised his voice.

– Miss, please bring us two drinks of the same.

Hackett seemed satisfied enough.

– Well, all right, he said. But what date? I'm a bit tied up just now. I'm in that inter-pub snooker tournament again. This night week would be the earliest I'd be certain of.

This was a bit late, Mick thought, but argument with Hackett was usually of no avail. The reason he had given to cover a whole week was obviously not genuine. He must have some private gambit of his own on hand. Still, that date would have to serve, for Mick had to make a dud appointment with De Selby in the meantime. Yes. And it occurred to him that within that week it might be possible to pay at least an exploratory visit to Skerries. If he could realize the Joyce contact, he could perhaps arrange the preliminaries of his admittedly rather fanciful nexus between Joyce and De Selby not only for their current good but for the good of all mankind. There seemed to be a prospect that his own activities might knot up together. Life is better simple, he reflected. He accepted Hackett's night, which happened to be a Friday. He told him he would make the appointment at the Colza with De Selby for 8.30 p.m., and that his short visit to the house would begin not later than nine. He said nothing about Sergeant Fottrell.

As they went down the stairs to the street (as he might have known they would instead of getting a train) Hackett asked him whether he would like to join him in a visit to Mulligan's, wherever that was. No, he hadn't a snooker match there in his tournament but he had planned a few games for practice. A great difficulty in this kind of thing, he explained, was the variation in quality of tables and other gear as between pub and pub. Some of the houses didn't seem to know that the cues should be straight, and tipped.

Mick declined the invitation. Though he understood billiards and snooker, he did not play and had always found both games boring as a spectacle – the more skilfully played, the more boring. When they parted he made for the General Post Office and sent this message to Sergeant Fottrell on a letter-card:

> Will call next Friday evening at 8.45 to have a stroll and talk about the bicycle race.

Enigmatic, maybe, but unmistakable to the redoubtable sergeant. He then walked out and sank into one of the public seats at the Nelson Pillar. Two new little questions had come into his head for leisurely adjudication.

Assuming everything went as planned at the Vico Road, he should be free about half nine. Should he then go into the Colza Hotel, with or without the sergeant, and apologize to De Selby for being late for his appointment with him there – yet to be made? He met this query by lazily putting off the decision until the night in question.

Number two – should he in fact use one or even two of the intervening days to visit Skerries? The answer here was quite clear – yes – and it exhilarated him. It was a new direction, a development in his tortuous affairs. There was a sort of challenge there: challenges were to be met, not frowningly put away to be considered another time.

He got up and walked slowly back to Westland Row station. He could get a train home there, of course, but his main purpose was to look up the timetables of the other line, the Great Northern Railway, which served Skerries.

Well, things seemed to be moving at last, he murmured to himself as he got into his home-bound train and the train, as if in agreement, moved out.

HE EXAMINED IT idly as it lay on his knee. It looked spent, he thought – perhaps a bit wrinkled for its age and showing signs of wear. Yet it had seen very little real wear. Was it, like a man's face, a reflex of the travail and struggles of the mind? That was possible. He was looking at the back of his right hand as the train rushed through the bright countryside, Dublin's market garden, provenance of new potatoes, peas, beans, strawberries, tomatoes and even mushrooms. It was God's own little pantry, plenteous kingdom of black earth and small rain, always urgent in a flourish of growth and ripening, or generous harvesting. It seemed much more alive than his hand, but maybe there was some melancholy in his mood. There often was, he felt, and reason for it.

The town of Skerries has been referred to on another page but it is not easy to convey the air and style of the place. It was a pleasant, small resort with great variety of sea and shore, broad streets in which lurked a surprising number of thatched houses. The long curved harbour with its border of dwellings, shops and pubs was diminutive and pretty except at low tide when the ebb had left a mess in the basin, mostly of rock, weed and slime. High above, near the railway station, an old windmill kept watch on the quiet people.

He left the train and walked the familiar road downhill. He passed the junction with Church Street, a quiet living quarter, and went on to Strand Street, which is the fine, broad, main thoroughfare of the town. There were plenty of people about – the holiday-makers, resident or visiting, easily to be distinguished. But he kept his own mind in restraint. His mission was investigation, and it seemed that pubs and tea-shops were places to be looked at, though neither fitted in with his mind's picture of James Joyce's nature and habits.

He first tried a tea-shop. What was on offer varied between ice cream, tepid tea and fish-and-chips. He found such surroundings dismal indeed, noticed nobody in the least resembling Joyce and could not believe that the latter's austere and fastidious mind could tolerate such confrontations after the sophisticated *auberges* of Paris or Zürich. The conversation?

– Will you for God's sake stop scratching yourself and drink your lemonade?

– I wonder where that poor bastard Charlie got to after last night's argument?

Then a pub: he soon saw that in general they were the old-fashioned kind, still to be found in small Irish towns – dark, with wooden partitions abutting from the counter at intervals, havens of secrecy and segregation. Of all of them that he visited, carefully restricting his drink to small pale sherries in the interest of vigilance, it is fair to say that they were rather dirty, and nearly always the man behind the bar – whether the boss himself or a curate – was in his shirt-sleeves, and the shirt itself was rarely of the best.

The prospect was discouraging. It was possible, he supposed, that Joyce temporarily took refuge somewhere else to escape the descent of witless holiday crowds during the summer. The exile, refugee or runaway has no roots, even in his own country.

One house looked a bit secluded and reserved, and he entered. Yes, it was dark, with a few small knots of men gathered about their dark drinks. The man of the house was a squat, round-faced jovial person of sixty-five, attired to counter-height in a stained pullover. Mick saluted as gaily as he could and asked for a small sherry. This was presented affably enough.

– You look to me like another Dublin man, me good sir, he beamed. The crowd that thinks they keep Skerries alive.

– Well, I'm from that direction, Mick admitted civilly.

– Begob then and good luck to what they have in their trousers pockets. Know what they keep there?

– A few bob, I suppose.

– They keep their hands there.

– Is trade bad, then?

– Ah, not at all, I wouldn't say that. But it's our own crowd and a wild crowd that comes here from Balbriggan and Rush that keeps this old town on its feet. All that holiday scruff isn't worth a damn, when they get two bottles down or maybe three, they think they're gone to the limit of deeboocherie. And bottles of what, though?

— Well, stout, I suppose. Not whiskey, surely?

— Phwaugh! Bottles of Dootch lagger. I have to lay it in specially in the summer. And do you know what it is? It's piss, that's what it is. Horse's piss.

— How do you know what horse's piss tastes like? Mick asked, pleased with the question.

— How . . . how do I know? I had a few pints of it meself in Dublin a few years ago. You'd smell the Clydesdale off of it.

Mick drank politely, and smiled. The natural garrulity of publicans could be a real help in his quest.

— Ah well, he said, every man to his own poison, I suppose. Matter of fact, I ran down here only for a day or two. I heard a rumour that there's an uncle of mine living about here somewhere, calls himself Captain Joyce, I believe. Lost touch with him a good few years ago. A slightly built man with glasses, elderly.

The publican seemed to shake his head.

— Joyce? No, I don't think so. There's so many people coming and going here, you know. Does he take e'r a smahan of Jameson or Tullamore?

— I'm not sure. I know he was abroad. Perhaps he'd be more inclined to have a drop of wine, or maybe a liqueur.

— *Wine?*

The very word seemed to be startling.

— Ah no, not at all, not here. I never had that class of person on the premises, though there's one old army gentleman here that drinks port till the stuff comes out in his socks. But his name is Stewart.

— Oh, it doesn't matter. I suppose I'll ask a few other people but it's really only curiosity. My real purpose is to get some of that salty fresh air you have down here.

— Well, no shortage of that, and no charge for it.

Mick finished his drink and went out. Where else to go? The next nearest pub, of course.

The result there was negative. The shop was low-roofed, gloomy, and the uncommunicative man behind the counter seemed to have the grey bloom of disease on his face. Mick had another small sherry.

— How's the season going this year? he enquired of a nondescript bystander.

— Good few here, the latter replied, and one of them's meself.

That much was already proclaimed by open-necked shirt and his short drink, which was not whiskey: probably brandy.

– Well, Mick said, it's a good place for a quiet rest.

– Could be but not when you have to bring the whole bloody family along. The kids, the wife *and* the wife's sister.

No use, this. Saying 'Anything's better than being on your own', Mick went out. This seemed a very hole-and-corner procedure. It was now half-five, too early in the evening for the public houses to show their full strength. The air was sultry, with little sun. He remembered the contents of the small parcel he had brought, just in case: pyjamas, a towel and bathing togs. He went for a stroll right around the harbour, disdaining the pubs there, got to the headland and walked on till he found a seat near the swimming place known as the Captain's, available at all levels of tidewater. He rested there, digesting his frugal drink and lazily viewing the great semi-circular white-yellow strand below, with groups of people resting with children, dressing or undressing or trying to read. It was a scene of disengagement and repose, the common belief being that an interval of this sort of thing at least once a year was very good for one. Yet he always recoiled from formal summer holidays in a place like Skerries. With the money available, he felt the civilized thing would be a few weeks earlier in the year in the Rhineland, Paris, perhaps Rome and the Mediterranean.

Time, a diluted sort of time, drifted past him, and perhaps he dozed. When he bestirred himself, he went down to the Captain's, stripped and dived in. The incoming tide was fresh and cool, very pleasant. He felt quite reconditioned when he afterwards made his way to the hotel dining-room and asked the waitress to bring him two lightly-boiled fresh eggs. What he might now call habit made him inspect everybody in this cheerful apartment but no – of Joyce there was no sign at all. A good few well-got-up people were eating there, some of them trippers, and a group of loud-voiced men whom he dismissed as harmless drunks. He remained on for a while, reading an evening paper and on his way out paused in the hall to ask the young lady whether she could give him a bed for the night.

– For one night?

– Yes, but I'm not yet certain I'll need it. I won't know for another few hours or so.

– I'll do my best but it would be safer to book now.

He said he would take a chance and probably look in again later. He had in fact two days' leave to have the chance to follow up any Joyce clue. He had got into the habit of thinking ahead.

Up to then his total calls had numbered five, none of them worth a return. But plenty of public houses remained to be checked over. The feeling of fullness after a meal weakened his earlier resolve about mild sherry but he sternly reasserted the regimen. He was engaged on work, and important work. There must be no slipping.

It was after seven when he entered a rather poky establishment on the periphery of the harbour. One drink and the use of eye and ear told him there was nothing there. There was a big enough assembly, mostly of strangers, but they were loud and rowdy, and well on the high-road to a late night. No quiet, sardonic novelist loitered there. Yet was there any unhurried nook deemed seemly for a writer's presence? Or was Joyce a recluse tucked away in a chimney corner, avoiding all occasions of public concourse, fearing and despising the people and keeping to himself? Mick's own plans apart, he hoped not. A delicate reason could easily become unsettled by such an attitude, he felt: men have their own whims but the hurly-burly of human society cannot be annulled or excommunicated without grave danger to the one who tries to do that. Those whose long-time abodes have been monasteries or even jails are seen afterwards, by those who happen to encounter them, to be maimed in mind and heart, often irrevocably. At least that was his impression but honesty made him concede that he had probably never met an individual who had that sort of past.

Two further calls were blank. One of them looked a bit promising at first, for in a quietish pub in the direction of the station he found himself drinking in the company of one who, judging from his dress, language and demeanour, was a Protestant clergyman. Mick was not skilled in discerning the various shades of the Reformed spectrum, and any personal enquiry on the point would be unmannerly. It was clear enough, however, that he was definitely not Joyce. He was courtly (and, be it added, quite sober) and invited Mick to have a drink with him before the latter had a chance to order his own. He was saying as the sherry arrived:

– It'll kill this young State if they're not careful.

– What – whiskey?

– Income tax. I'm convinced it's an immoral form of taxation.

– Does that mean that paying income tax is sinful?

– Well, no. In conscience one is entitled to choose the lesser of two evils. But heavy income tax ruins enterprise and initiative, and ultimately begets despondency and national decay.

– It is widely accepted, Mick reminded him, that this country has for centuries been subjected to vicious over-taxation and exploitation, both by the British Government and a cabal of corrupt and pitiless ruffians called absentee landlords. The Famine was one result of that régime.

– Ah there were bad times in the past.

– And I don't offend your reverence, I hope, by bringing to mind the horror of the tithes, when a beggared peasantry were compelled to support a Church in which they had no belief and for which they had no use.

– Quite, quite. And at a time when their own priests were hunted and persecuted.

– Yes, indeed.

– But . . . *but*, I repeat, the remedy for all such old, indefensible evils is not this outrageous income tax. Not only is it bad of itself but it is quite unsuitable for this country's economy.

Such was their theme as Mick ordered his own two drinks in turn. He found the talk arid and useless.

When he withdrew he walked a good distance to the other end of town – almost to the outskirts, indeed, in the direction of Rush. Public houses can usually be trusted not to disguise themselves but he had almost passed one when only the rasping sound of a cork-puller alerted him. The low roof was thatched and inside, in the slow light of trimmed oil lamps peaceable men were drinking, mostly pints of porter. Conversation was casual and low-pitched and somehow Mick felt that many of the customers were retired fishermen. He asked the resident authority, a neat youngish man, for his little amber drink, and was surprised to hear him say 'It's a brave evenin',' indicating an origin in the far north.

Mick felt tired but still watchful. The lamplight was soft, agreeable, restful as gaslight, but suddenly he thought he heard a voice say something in a tone that made him start. Beyond a partition on the customers' side he saw another man serving within the counter further up the shop. He was oldish, thin, slightly stooped, and he wore glasses. Thick grey hair was brushed back from the forehead. Mick's heart began to thunder. Sweet God, *had he found James Joyce?*

He finished his drink, carefully and in recollection, and then went seeking the lavatory, always to be found in the rear of a house facing the street. On his return he paused at the back part of the shop. The elderly man came forward insecurely, blinking behind his thick glasses.

– A small pale sherry, please.

– Certainly.

He was neat and quiet in his movements as he went about fetching drink. Would he talk readily, Mick wondered. Well, the job was to find out.

– Fairly large crowd in town, he said pleasantly. But whether it's really large or not I'm not so sure, as I'm a rare visitor, I'm sorry to say.

The reply was in the Dublin intonation, quite unmixed, and friendly as if in a true gentleness of nature.

– Ah, I think the town is doing all right this year. Of course we're at the quiet end here, and thank God for that.

– You are a native, I suppose?

– No, no. No indeed.

Mick toyed with his glass, showing nonchalance.

– My own little trip to Skerries, he remarked, isn't really for the purpose of holiday. I came here looking for somebody who's in the town, I believe.

– A relative?

– No. A man I admire very much, a writer.

– Ah. I see?

– My good sir, I will not be so presumptuous as to ask you your name. Instead, I will tell you what it is.

The weak eyes seemed to grope behind their glass walls.

– Tell me . . . my name?

– Yes. Your name is James Joyce.

It was as if a stone had been dropped from a height into a still pool. The body stiffened. He put a hand about his face nervously.

– Quiet, please! Quiet! I am not known by that name here. I insist that you respect my affairs.

The voice was low but urgent.

– Of course I will, Mr Joyce. I shall mention no name again. But it is a really deep pleasure to meet a man of your attainments face to face. Your name stands high in the world. You are a most remarkable writer, an innovator, Dublin's incomparable archivist.

– Ah now, don't be talking like that.

– But I mean it.

– I have had a hurried sort of life. Hither and thither you understand. The last war was a very unfortunate affair for everybody. Neither things nor people will ever be the same. The Hitler reign was an abominable thing. Ah yes, people suffered.

He was speaking freely now in a muted voice and there was a hint, perhaps, of relief.

– I think we all felt its impact, Mick said, even here in Ireland, far from the scene of it. I think at least one more sherry would do me good.

– Of course.

– And will you honour me by having a drink with me?

– No indeed, thank you. I take an occasional drink but not here, of course.

He served from the bottle.

– Your references to my work are kindly, he said, but I may mention that my real work has hardly appeared at all yet. Also, I've had things imputed to me which – ah – I've had nothing to do with.

– Is that so?

– The interruptions in Europe set me back a lot. I lost valuable papers.

– Those are serious drawbacks.

– The dear knows they are.

– Have you a new book in the process of... incubation? Are you writing something new?

He gave a short, brief smile.

– Writing is not quite the word. Assembly, perhaps, is better – or accretion. The task I have set myself could probably be properly termed the translation into language of raw spiritual concepts. I stress here *translation* as distinct from *exposition*. It is a question of conveying one thing in terms of another thing which is... em... quite incongruous.

– Well, I'm sure that is difficult. Yet you have never faltered in conveying subtle or abstract things.

– Faith and that is very complimentary. But I have published little.

Mick decided to change direction.

– You are the second great pioneer I have had the good fortune to know.

– Well well now. And who is my nabs when he is at home?

– His name is De Selby. He is not a literary man so far as I know and it is not easy at all to define his sphere or spheres. He is a mathematical physicist, a chemist, an authority on dynamics and has achieved some astonishing conclusions in the time–space speculation. In fact he seems to have succeeded in interfering with the passing or flow of time. I'm sorry if I appear a bit incoherent but he seems to be able to make time go backwards. And he is also a theologian.

Joyce was showing, by intentness, his interest.

– This De Selby, he said. Where does he live?

– Near Dalkey, if you know where that is.

– Ah, Dalkey? Yes. Interesting little place. I know it well.

– He lives alone, in a very quiet house among the trees on the Vico Road. For all his intellect he is a courteous and hospitable man. Nothing of the mad scientist, you know.

Joyce, his curiosity now well kindled, was thinking.

– That is interesting, yes. Does he also teach or is he a university person?

– No, I don't think so. I don't think he has any job, in the usual sense. He never mentions money but that's possibly because he's plenty of it.

Joyce stared downward, reflecting.

– Wealthy, gifted, free to follow his fancy? It is well for him.

Mick liked this sympathetic thought.

– I had always thought of yourself, he said earnestly, as belonging to that sort of company. Your work seems to lack a sense of hurry – ungainly explosions, artificial tension and that sort of thing. You are not artificial. You understand me?

– Oh no, my position is not quite that. Scientific endeavour is, of course, good. Our family was preoccupied with politics, God help them, and with a little bit of music sometimes.

– Yes, but all these things are things of the mind. De Selby's scientific investigations don't preclude an interest in more abstract matters. Indeed, I am certain he would be delighted to meet yourself . . .

Joyce gave a low chuckle.

— Meet myself? Goodness now! He might not thank you for that suggestion.

— But seriously —

— You see, my work is very personal in the sense that much of the material is in my head. I'm afraid it could not be shared, and that nobody could help me. But of course it is always a pleasure to meet a person of quality.

— I understand. Has your new book got a name yet?

— No. I'm rather at sea as to *language*. I have a firm grip of my thoughts, my argument . . . but communicating the ideas clearly in English is my difficulty. You see, there has been considerable variation as between English on the one hand, and Hebrew and Greek as vehicles of epistemology.

— I know, of course, that you're interested in languages as such . . .

— My thoughts are new, you understand, and I'm afraid . . .

— What's the trouble?

— They tend to be ineffable.

— Dear me. But we talk in abstractions. I would like to get down to something hard and real for a moment and talk about *Finnegans Wake*.

Joyce started slightly.

— Good Lord! Do you know it? It was a well-known song in my young days.

— No, I meant the book.

— I did not know it was printed. Ah, once upon a time I was very fond of singing myself. The Irish airs, the ballads and the old come-all-ye's. When my heart was young, you might say.

— But surely you have heard of a book of that name — *Finnegans Wake*?

— You must remember, please, that I have been out of this country for a long time. If somebody has made an opera out of the old tunes, I am delighted. I wish him well. Tom Moore has always attracted me. 'Oft in the Stilly' is a beautiful song.

— Sentimental, yes.

— That is the usual thing to say, alas. That which touches one is dismissed as sentimental. The genuine old traditional airs, I like them very much too.

Was his mind wandering? Mick's watch told him that closing-time was near. He decided to stay the night in Skerries if necessary.

– Tell me this much, sir, he said. Would you mind if I told De Selby of our conversation without saying where you are, and suggest that you go to Dalkey for a meeting with him, or meet him here or somewhere else you think suitable?

Joyce paused in thought, nervously rubbing the counter with a finger. Possibly things were moving too fast. He frowned slightly.

– I would like to meet the man if you assure me he is discreet, he replied slowly, but I would not like to have him come here.

– I understand.

– He seems a curious man. It is perhaps just possible that he might be able to help me get what I have in mind down on paper, because the invention and involution this work calls for strains a single apparatus of reason. It is the sort of morass of problem and innovation on which the beam of a fresh mind might conceivably throw some light.

– You will not find De Selby's mind infertile or fixed in any mould.

– I am sure of that.

– Could you suggest a date and time of meeting him say at Dalkey?

– That's premature, I'm afraid. I must first have another talk with yourself.

– All right. I can stay here in the hotel tonight and see you bright and early tomorrow morning.

– No. I won't be here at all tomorrow. It's my day off. But before seeing your friend I want to have a long talk with yourself because there are certain things which have to be explained at the outset. I am a man who is much misunderstood. I will say maligned, traduced, libelled and slandered. From what I've heard, certain ignorant men in America have made a laugh of me. Even my poor father wasn't safe. A fellow named Gorman wrote that 'he always wore a monocle in one eye'. Fancy!

– I heard of that sort of thing myself.

– It is intolerable.

– I should not worry about such people.

– Ah, easy to say. Even here, where my identity is quite unknown, I'm regarded as a humbug, a holy Mary Ann, just because
I go to daily Mass. If there's one thing scarce in Catholic Ireland,
it is Christian charity.

Mick bowed his head in sympathy.

– I must agree with you, he said. We are a very mixed people.
But . . . if I'm to get a train back to Dublin tonight, I must leave
now, since I've quite a walk to the station. A further meeting
tomorrow is out of the question. Very well. What other day do
you suggest?

– I think we will have to wait a little bit and meet somewhere
other than here. Tuesday morning next week would suit me.

– Yes. That hotel in the town seems a reasonable clean place.
I suppose they have a bar. Would that suit?

Joyce was silent for a moment, stooped.

– Well, yes . . . I suggest the back room at noon.

– Very good. And I have your permission to tell De Selby
that I've met you and mention the possibility of some literary
collaboration?

– Well, I suppose so.

– Sir, goodbye until Tuesday, and very many thanks.

– God bless you.

CHAPTER 14

MICK'S LATE-NIGHT return from Skerries faced him with an empty day on the morrow, though he left the house as if going to the office as usual. Instinct bade him keep away from Dalkey, where important work was to face him on the approaching Friday. What was he to do with himself on this spare-day?

First he made his way to St Stephen's Green and sought a seat there – easy enough so early in the morning. The Green is a railed-in square pleasure ground near the city centre, an extravagance of flower beds and fountains. A pretty lake, spanned at the centre by a bridge and having little islands, was the home of water fowl, many exotic and matching the flowers in hue and life. And the Green was constantly travelled by a great number of people since it offered a short cut diagonally between Earlsfort Terrace, where University College stood, and the top of Grafton Street – the portal of busy central Dublin. Curiously, this haven of hubbub (for that is what it sometimes seemed) was a good place for reflection and planning, as if all its burbling life was an anæsthesia, perhaps in the manner of finding loneliness in crowds.

He leaned back, closed his eyes, and meditated on what seemed to be his portion of things to be done. There were several things but, if big, they were not really complicated or unmanageable. He rather admired his own adroit manipulation of matters which, in certain regards, transcended this world. He would put a stop to the diabolical plans of De Selby, for instance, but by means of what was no less than comic-opera subterfuge. Again, Mick had been the one to be in a position to demonstrate that James Joyce, a writer and artist of genius, was not dead as commonly supposed but alive and reasonably well in the country of his birth. True, his card had been marked in this regard by the loquacious and bibulous Dr Crewett but Mick doubted if the latter himself believed the information he had given; at all events he had made no attempt to verify it. Perhaps sheer laziness was

the explanation, and Mick was pleased to reflect that sloth
was not a sin that could be laid at his own door.

No indeed, for if anybody was active and alert it was Mick.
Apart from having had a physical confrontation with Joyce, he
had discovered that his mind was unbalanced. He did not realize
that he had finished and published *Finnegans Wake*, for it was too
ridiculous to suppose that some sort of a draft, yet to be worked
upon, had got into print accidentally without his knowledge.
Publishers, Mick knew, were not given to irresponsible tomfoolery, particularly where an important established name was
concerned. Yet Joyce betrayed no eccentricity of manner or
speech in that pub in Skerries, and went about that job in which
Mick so unexpectedly found him with composure and efficiency.
Was De Selby off his rocker as well and, if so, how would two
exquisitely cultivated but distracted minds behave on impact
with each other? Would they coalesce in some quiet and fruitful
way, or clash in murderous disarray? Was Mick getting a bit
misdirected in the head himself in planning to bring those two
men together? Well, hardly. De Selby had given him no overt
signs of insanity but on the contrary had given him proof, in that
meeting with St Augustine, that his powers and contacts were at
least preternatural. Mick could not possibly run any risk about
the reality of the DMP threat. He had, bluntly, an obligation to
the human race, one that could not be gainsaid by an extremity
of cowardice or casuistry.

But Mick's imagination would not be quiet. Would Joyce and
De Selby combine their staggeringly complicated and diverse
minds to produce a monstrous earthquake of a new book, something claiming to supplant the Bible? De Selby could easily
produce the incredible materials, perhaps with the help of
angels, while Joyce could supply the unearthly skill of the
master-writer. The answer here seemed to be that De Selby had
no interest in literature or neo-theology, or in doing anything
to improve or embellish this world or its people: his aim was to
destroy both, with himself and Joyce included in this prodigious
annihilation.

Supposing Mick's introduction of Joyce to De Selby coin-
cided with the latter's discovery that his cask was missing, what
would happen then? Would he blame Joyce and murder him?
That would be most unfortunate, to say the least of it, and it

probably would be impossible for Mick to disavow (at least to himself) his personal share in this bloodshed. Yes, his affairs were ringed with risk: the situation could not be otherwise. And it was too late to go back in the case of De Selby, though in theory Mick could leave Joyce where he was and forget forever the little town of Skerries. Even that was not certain as a possibility, for he had betrayed to Joyce the name of De Selby and his dwelling at Dalkey, and Joyce could well appear on the scene, of his own motion. That would be a detestable development, for it would mean that matters were getting outside Mick's personal control. It seemed clear that he must keep his second appointment with Joyce in Skerries; the movements of a man whose brain was disorganized were unpredictable but it was possible he could be managed by contrived, perhaps unscrupulous, persuasion. But was that man Joyce at all? Could one reputedly so contemptuous of God be now so unusually pious, so meticulous in his observance of his duties as a member of the Church? How could such an attitude, admittedly a later one, be reconciled with the intricate and bombastic scatology of *Ulysses* and, even in an interval of aberration, so base a character as Molly Bloom?

Ah, Molly Bloom! Should he use this free and easy day to contact Mary, perhaps ring her at her Boutique or whatever she called it? He found himself frowning. A sort of numbness crept over him. He had been thinking loosely and emotionally rather than exactly. He sternly told himself to behave rationally and to see to it that when decisions were made, they were sound as well as irrevocable.

The elderly man in Skerries *was* Joyce, with certain departments of his mind upset by experience amid the horror of Nazi Europe. He had not disclaimed literary work but, in his strange job as barman – probably very temporary – he could be forgiven for not dwelling on his past preoccupations. What of his exemplary life as a son of the Church? This was a question that touched on the psychological, the psychotic, perhaps the theological. In such country Mick felt hardly qualified to make judgement: indeed, who could overlook the famous quandary of Saint Paul?

If in fact after a second interview with Joyce an arrangement was made for him to meet De Selby, Mick would have by that time the way made ready. Two elderly men, of giant intellectual potential, who had run wild somewhat in their minds might, in coming together, find a community of endeavour and un-suspected common loyalties. Both certainly knew what whiskey was. Mick wondered whether in the absence of his deadly con-tainer De Selby could continue to produce perfectly mature whiskey which was only seven days old? Could one look forward to the founding of the firm of De Selby, Joyce & Co., distillers, maltsters and warehousemen, to market those high-grade spirits all over the world and make a fortune? Mick smiled at this, again chiding his mind for erupting into fancy.

Then Mary. Well, why should he meet her or even ring her up on this free day of his? He had long thought, or taken it for granted, that he was deeply, hopelessly in love with Mary. Was he? Infatuation is a weakness one readily attributes to other people but his mounting honesty with himself made him stare this awkward question straight. First, Mary was indefatigable in probing and catechizing him, even in matters which were strictly his own business. She was very careful to underline her inde-pendence of him as male escort and was quite unrestrained in expressing her own ideas on art, manners, customs, even politics and the rest of the human equipage. Her *own* ideas? How home-made in fact were they? No doubt glossy magazines abounded in her little palace of fashion, and the art of learning to talk smart was no new one. Probably she could manage brief quotes from Mallarmé or Voltaire when the feat seemed opportune. A reasonable case could be made for establishing that in fact she despised him. What was she, really, but a gilded trollop, probably with plenty of other gents who were devout associates. Or slaves, marionettes?

In recent times his unprecedented contacts with persons (or beings) quite out of the ordinary had tended to direct all his cerebral attention outward, never inwards at his own self. This was an unjustified lapse, plain neglect. He could not hope to counter adequately the moves of others if the nature of himself and his own strength were not in every particular known to him – familiar to him, even. Every man must know how to deploy his forces, all his forces. De Selby was a case in point. Hackett and Mick himself had assumed he had been lying about DMP and his power of suspending time, but he had proved he was not. It was a fact that he had powers not commonly understood, that he was infinitely crafty, and that he was as ready to lie as anybody on minor matters. He was also skilled in saying absolutely nothing about mundane simple matters in a way which would arouse the curiosity of the most stolid – e.g. where did he get his money? He had to eat and drink, buy apparatus and chemicals, even pay the poor rate. Where did he get the common coin to meet such unavoidable if prosaic obligations? If he were living on a fortune already made – well, made of what? Was he a bankrobber from the USA, quietly thriving on an immense haul, possibly after he had gunned down his associates rather than share with them? If De Selby was an enigma, his peculiar aura was that of an evil enigma.

But Mick noted that his own function and standing had risen remarkably. He was *supervising* men of indeterminate calibre, of sanity that was more than suspect. Clearly enough this task had been assigned to him by Almighty God, and this gave him somewhat the status of priest. He was certainly as much a priest as Father Cobble, whom both De Selby and himself had dismissed as stupid. True, Mick lacked regular ecclesiastical faculties but that was a matter that could be attended to with time. A blessed plant must be conceded an interval of ungainliness, awkward and coarse striving, before an enchanting bloom exuding salvational odour could be expected to burst upon the world. He did think – though afterwards he could not be sure – that it was during this morning in St Stephen's Green that it first dawned on him that he should join the Church's ministry and labour as best he might in the old vineyard.

He got up and walked abstractedly about winding pathways. His mood was a formless one of renunciation. What about his mother? That grand lady was old, decayed enough so far as health went. And she had a younger sister, also a widow but comfortably off, in Drogheda. No, separation from his old mother would be no obstacle and the knowledge that he was becoming a priest would shine over her closing years, like a blessed candle.

One other thing. He was spending far too much of his free money on drink. He was by no means a soak or debauché, that was certain. The curse about pubs was that they were so ubiquitous and accessible. If one had something to discuss with another person in Dublin, whether the subject was trivial or critical, inevitably the appointment was made for a public house. The thing was a social malaise, a neurotic flaw in community development, a situation in which the unreliable quality of the climate was perhaps a big factor. There were tea-rooms, of course, coffee-palaces, even lounges in some hotels where a gracious glass of sherry would be forthcoming. Somehow they were each an unsuitable milieu for colloquy between men – and by no means because the pint of porter was not to be had. To say there is a time and a place for everything is trite, but the truth of the sentiment is not to be denied for all that; one could play the accordion while having a bath but probably nobody has ever tried to do that. He abruptly sat down on a seat quite elsewhere in the Green but the beautiful, featureless scene looked the same: people hurrying, birds flying, scurrying and shrieking and a solitary peacock mooching in the shadows at some low shrub. Was there not a futility about what was nice and orderly?

His association with Mary, now that he contemplated it soberly, had been really very superficial and small; perhaps banal would be the juster word. Certainly it had not been sinful and there was nothing at all in it of the sort of conduct he associated with the name of Hackett. He would put an end to the thing with no loss to himself but not too abruptly and certainly with no parade of bad manners. It is really easy to let allegiances, no longer held, lapse.

He kicked idly away a little stone at his foot. Let's see now – which order? Happily, any doubt here was only in detail. To join the ordinary secular clergy was unthinkable, for it would entail spending many years in Maynooth College, an institution founded by the British Government to prevent aspiring Irish clerics from getting their training and education in such centres as Paris and Louvain. He would emerge therefrom as a CC or 'Catholic Curate' and possibly be assigned to some such parish as Swanlinbar. He said it with sorrow, and God forgive him for saying it at all, but the great majority of CCs he had met were ignorant men, possibly schooled in the mechanics of ordinary theology but quite unacquainted with the arts, not familiar with the great classical writers in Latin and Greek, immersed in a swamp of tastelessness. Still, he supposed they could be discerned as the foot-soldiers of the Christian army, not to be examined individually too minutely.

Obviously he was an enclosed order man. Which order? Hard to say. His feeling, not yet properly formed, seemed to tend in

the direction of the more severe and monastic orders, though –
here one may smile forbearingly – he did not in fact know how
many such orders there were and how their rule differed in
severity. One thing he was fairly sure of: the Order of Saint John
of God entailed a vow of silence for life. Somehow in the genial
rowdiness of the Green this seemed a petty enough liability to
embrace. What was wrong with a bit of peace for a change? The
Cistercians were good men, too, he believed, and the Carthu-
sians. He felt vaguely that the term 'enclosed order' was a bit
misleading and perhaps misunderstood. It did not mean complete monastic seclusion, pitilessly frugal diet, being awakened
from plank beds in the middle of the night to say the office,
and being attired during working hours in the roughest and least
elegant of robes. There were, of course, true monks of that heroic
stamp but he took leave to question whether such a regimen was
not sinfully wasteful. *Laborare est orare*, yes, but the contrary was
hardly true. Look at the Holy Ghost Fathers. They were an
enclosed order as far as he knew but they taught school, the
Fathers were eligible for bishoprics in the common outside
Church, and they engaged also, he thought, in foreign mission.
He realized sadly that he was terribly ignorant of the structure,
organization and government of the universal Church. Remote
indeed was his prospect of ever becoming Pope.

In all this formless contemplation his eyes were open, thrown
towards the ground but sightless. Yet vision came back when two
blackish objects, not too clean, came towards him. They were a
pair of shoes, occupied. His eyes lifted to the round, beaming
face of a character whom he knew as Jack Downes. The face was
pleasant and seemed to say that it had been formed somewhere
down the country where abided comely cows, lazy fertile sows,
and homely hens of the pristine egg. He was perhaps twenty-
two, a medical student and, the Dublin phrase, 'a hard chaw'.
This phrase was undeserved, for it suggests that one is forever
loitering about, playing cards, drinking, interfering with girls
and doing absolutely anything except opening a book or attending a lecture. Mick knew that Downes had already impeccably
traversed three years of the medical course. His equal readiness
to ingest the secrets of physic and pints of plain porter puzzled
many people, not excluding Hackett, who sometimes mentioned Downes Syndrome, being 'that degree of stupidity which

can produce information irrelevant to the question asked but imparted with such elaboration and *appoggiatura* that the querist rarely risks saying the answer is wrong'. That was unfair, too, but Mick's opinion had long been that university studies were a barren activity. Dublin's two university colleges were choked with the sons of dishonest country publicans.

– Well, by the damn, Downes growled jovially, what are you doing hiding here, you long-faced sleeveen?

– Morra, Jack. I'm just taking a rest and minding my own business.

– For God's sake? It's nearly twelve. You're about three hours out of bed, and you're resting yourself? Why the hell aren't you earning your living or at least in some chapel saying a Hail Mary for the Holy Souls? I suppose you still call yourself an Irishman. A gobdaw is what I'd call you, Michael.

– Oh, cut it out, Mick said rather testily. It's a bit early in the morning for your big, broad, ignorant Paddy Whack stuff, and I don't want irreligious guff from you at any time.

– Ah-ha? Something's biting you.

He then made the last gesture of succour that was looked for. He sat down.

– Never mind, he said in a tone meant to be gentle, just take it easy and you'll find what you think are troubles will just evaporate. Do you understand Planck's quantum theory?

– I don't.

– Right. No points then in talking about ERGS. Do you know where Chatham Street is?

– Of course I do.

– That's better. That street is quite near and in it is an excellent house called Neary's. If you will arise, rely on my strong arm, I will lead you to it, and there buy you a pint. To tell you the truth, I need one myself.

– Well, that's a good reason for going there.

There was a trace of real dismay in Mick's voice when he looked at Downes. This invitation was athwart the preceding reverie.

– Jack, isn't it a bit early in the day to start that game? By half-one we'd be putting smahans of malt into ourselves.

– Not a bit of it. No fear at all of that. Anyway, I want to talk to you. We'd be overheard if we talked in a place like this.

– When's your next exam?

– November. Plenty of time.

– Wouldn't you be better occupied getting a theory or two into your head than getting porter into your belly?

– That's hard to say. Let's get going.

He stood up in a way that was jaunty yet a bit peremptory. What could Mick do? He was now in a neutral humour. He stood up too and they strolled out of the Green to Grafton Street and were soon in Neary's, an unhurried, secluded refuge. Jack Downes ordered two pints without the formality of asking what Mick's choice was, and he demolished nearly half of his own when it arrived, in one great swallow. He put his feet up on a nearby chair.

– Tell me, Mick, avic, he said solicitously, just what sort of trouble are you in?

Mick gave a little chuckle.

– Trouble? You are the one who first mentioned it. I'm not in any trouble that I know of.

– Good Lord! You looked so desolate sitting there in the Green, like a bereaved scarecrow.

– Well, I have one little item of trouble, but easily susceptible of remedy, I think. Constipation.

– Oh, hell, Downes said disdainfully, sure everybody has that. It's like Original Sin. But look at me. *I'm* in real trouble.

– What's wrong?

– Plenty. I have to be at Kingsbridge Station this evening shortly after six to meet a train. Th'oul fella's coming up to visit me.

– Well isn't that all right? I know that you get on well with your father and I know he's not backward in coming forward with a grant-in-aid on such visits. And your College record is clear.

Downes grunted.

– Look, he said, there has been a bloody complication. Last time he was here, he produced his gold watch, priceless family heirloom, and said there was something wrong with it. We went together to a certain watchmaker, and this genius quickly found out what the trouble was. He quoted a price, which the oul fella paid. I was to collect the watch in a week and keep it safe and sound.

– And did you?

— Yes and no. I collected it all right and it was going and in first class order. Soon I did a very stupid thing.

— Don't tell me you lost it?

— No. I pawned it.

Mick was slowly managing his unwanted pint as he heard those words. Weren't people truly very foolish, himself included?

— Where did you pawn it? he finally asked.

— In Meredith's of Cuffe Street.

That was the accepted pawnshop for university students. Mick pondered the situation. He did not think it a grave one.

— How much did you get on it?

— Two pounds ten. That's all I asked.

— Where's the pawn ticket?

— I have it here.

After a search he produced what looked like the genuine ticket.

— My terrible trouble, Downes said dismally, is that I'm dead broke. Broke to the wide. First thing the daddy will look for is the watch. With no watch, he'll kick up buggery and melia murder. He could make a holy show of me in the station.

— I met him briefly only once. He's not as bad as all that.

— He could be worse when it's a question of that watch. I can't even think up any kind of a story.

Mick emitted a brief laugh.

— If you look at this situation squarely, he intoned, you'll find it's really very simple. Your College affairs are in order and I know your landlady is paid direct, in advance. Your good father will give you an *ex gratia* gift of ten pounds for your good luck. All you have to do is borrow the money to redeem the watch, with your borrowed money outstanding only for a matter of hours. Simple!

— Borrow? But where? I'd need three quid.

— Surely you have a few friends? Ah-ha now, you needn't look at me. Our glasses are empty and it's my turn to buy a drink. And I'm going to have a Vichy water this time.

He gestured at a curate and gave the order, at the same time taking out in his hand all the money in his right trousers pocket — three half crowns and smaller coins. He held forward this sample.

— On my word of honour, Jack, he said seriously, that's absolutely all the money I have on me.

Downes gave the collection a troubled glance.

– I know, he said. A year ago I borrowed twenty-five bob offa the landlady to buy a present for my young sister on the occasion of her Confirmation. I couldn't go there again, of course, though I paid the money back. I have an idea that she got to know I haven't any sister.

As the drinks arrived he fell silent and glum, while Mick began to settle the little matter in his mind. Jack Downes was a decent fellow when all was said, and worth helping. There seemed one obvious course to take, though it involved slight risk to his own financial equilibrium. Jack's salvation was in his pocket: the cheque-book, as yet unused.

In all his muddling supernatural and scientific diversions, Mick reminded himself, he must not lose sight of that true manifestation of humanity's nobility – *compassion*. Beside it any other virtue was shallow and poor. Love and pity were other names for it, or in Latin *caritas*, charity. Even the brute creation was not entirely without it. And if he risked the loss of £3, was it not a cheap way of easing a distressed mind, preventing family rupture and perpetuating conditions that were happy and leading to permanent achievement in another man's life?

Yes, his duty was plain enough. Yet a little caution was called for. There could be no question of writing out a cheque there and then and handing it over. There was an impetuous element in the character of Jack Downes. Any operation Mick started he would have to supervise to the end. He spoke at last.

– Jack, he said, it's quite true that what I showed you is all the money I have. Indeed, I could do with a quid myself in view of certain small expenses I foresee in a day or two. It happens that I have a tiny hidden horde of savings – *tiny*, I repeat, but there to be called upon in an emergency . . .

Downes had been looking at him blankly, and then gave a sort of smile.

– You mean –

– I mean that I have a cheque-book. I will now make out a cheque payable to Bearer and we will walk down to the Bank of Ireland. You will then go into the bank and cash the cheque, writing your name on the back. I will wait outside. When you come out, you will hand me the money, and then we can see what can be done about that watch.

Very pleasing was the effect this simple, generous speech had on Downes. His face became slightly illuminated, and his person exuded geniality.

– Mick, you are a strange sort of an angel in need of a shave, a heavenly witch-doctor.

Mick wrote the cheque, and of this tale there is little more to tell. As Downes disappeared into the bank, Mick wondered whether there would be any question about what was his first cheque ever. Well, there wasn't. Very soon, four clean banknotes were in his hand.

– Next stop, Jack, is Meredith's. We'll walk.

Within half an hour they paused to part. Jack had a venerable half-hunter watch in his pocket as well as some change out of £3. He was loud on the subject of repayment but Mick cut him short and told him to be sure and meet the father that evening. When free, he hurried into an underground restaurant and had strong black coffee and buns. Was it not the sort of repast, he reflected, which behoved the good Samaritan? A newspaper which he bought he found unreadable. He felt confused but happy, and resolutely thrust all thoughts of Mary, De Selby and even Joyce out of his head. Things must be taken in turn, and quietly. What now? He walked into a cinema without bothering to see what was advertised. It was half-price before 5 p.m.

When he got home at the usual time, he felt hungry.

– You look tired, his mother remarked. Another hard day?

– Ah yes, mother, he said, slumping into a chair. Some of those people from down the country can be very troublesome.

CHAPTER 15

MICK WAS punctual enough when at 8.40 p.m. he pushed open the door of the police station in Dalkey on that Friday night. At last action was to take the place of dialogue and dissertation. He returned the salutation of Policeman Pluck who, seated in the dayroom, had contorted his red features into that pucker which was intended for a smile.

– Ah but that's the fine evening, he chuckled, if a man had the time off to mosey up to Larkin's for a couple of cruiskeens of porter, or maybe a talk with that grand dark lump of a girl from Longford that the PP keeps hidden in his kitchen, be the holy powers!

Mick nodded pleasantly.

– Yes, Mr Pluck, but some people have other things to think of. The sergeant and myself are thinking about getting the people around interested in bicycle-racing. A fine healthy sport.

– They will have to take an engineering course in punctures for themselves, he muttered. The Big Wig is inside there at the back.

– Thanks.

Sergeant Fottrell was indeed in what he called his office, kneeling at his bicycle making some adjustment. His bicycle-clips were on.

– Gracious greeting, he said, glancing up.

– Are you ready for the winding trail, Sergeant?

– We are ready and awake, he replied, but in the dire emergency I have had to borrow Policeman Pluck's pump.

– What? Surely you are not going to bring the bicycle with you?

The sergeant stood up and looked at Mick searchingly.

– We are on a rarefied secret business tonight, he said in a confidential tone, and we want nobody to be showering obnoxious attentions on us contemptuously. For me to go out on the roads or streets of this parish without my bicycle would be worse than going out without my trousers on me.

– Well, I know, but . . .

– I have never appeared in public without my bicycle, though that is not to say that I was ever so vexed a fool as to get up on it.

Mick realized that here was no question of etiquette but of discipline tender as steel. Clearly his own role was to be adroit, diplomatic. The thing was to get De Selby's container and hide it overnight as unnoticeably as possible. Argument or contention was unthinkable.

– Of course, Sergeant. I quite realize that a bicycle wheeled by one's side is a form of disguise. I quite approve. But one thought has just crossed my mind.

– Ah, a micro-wave? And what is that?

– I've just remembered that you have *my* bicycle locked up in one of the cells. Would it be a proper thing for me to wheel mine?

The sergeant frowned. The point was apparently a knotty one in cycle liturgy. Mick bit his lip.

– Well, no, the sergeant said slowly. You are in pure divine essence a personality who *rides* a bicycle when he has any inter-course with it at all. But I am of a disfamiliar persuasion. I have never been on top of a bicycle in my life and never will be, world without end.

– Very well, Mick agreed. Let us get going. Let us keep to our timetable.

And they did set out – but by the back door, without the cognisance of Policeman Pluck.

Dusk had long since gathered and they made scarcely any notable spectacle in the little streets of Dalkey, ill-lit by uneven gas-lamps and almost void save for the muted noises and flood of light from an occasional public house, giving notice that life was still intact. Soon they were at the beginning of the gentle climb of the Vico Road. They had long passed the Colza Hotel without mention of it or an acknowledgement by either of them that it was there. Sergeant Fottrell's comportment was casual, secretive, silent. Mick would be happier if the sergeant were more at his ease and he began to talk to him conversationally in a low voice.

– Both of us, Sergeant, he said, are doing something useful and, I suppose, morally meritorious in depriving that man De Selby of the reservoir of deadly germs he is hoarding.

– It is ourselves we are honouring by our patrician prodigality, the sergeant replied in what appeared to be concurrence. Mick grunted genially.

— Well, I want to tell you of a special personal sacrifice of my own. As you know, I am a civil servant.

— Splendour and strong arm, vessel of the State, the sergeant chanted.

— Ah, well, we do our best. A civil servant has so-many days' leave a year. I have just three weeks. He may apply for it all in one bash, or take it in dribs and drabs.

— Or concisely in drabs and dribs, the sergeant suggested. The gentle clicking whisper of his bicycle was ever a shadow over their words.

— But remember, Mick continued, a day is a day and a day's leave is a day's leave. On Saturday work ends at one o'clock and most of us think of that day as a half day. So it is, I suppose. But there is no such thing as a half day's leave. Do you understand?

— I follow you meticulously.

— When we get this article of De Selby's and hide it near the road, it must be collected early tomorrow morning. To leave it there over the weekend would be a risk too appalling to contemplate for one half minute.

The sergeant made an assenting sort of groan.

— Nor a tenth of that. If the laden weight of this diabolical miracle of science was indicatively reasonable maybe we could bring it away on the crossbar of my bicycle and hide it under the bed in the station

This suggestion, the climax of irresponsibility, horrified Mick.

— For heaven's sake, Sergeant, not on your life. That would leave humanity still open to the perils incubated by De Selby. Over the weekend Policeman Pluck might discover it when you were out and try to burst it open, thinking it was a cask of cider.

The sergeant chuckled sardonically.

— Father Cummins, the curate, is away in the County Tipperary visiting his sick mother. We could leave the thing by exiguous stealth inside his confession box in the church. No man subject to his senses would think of looking there for anything.

On the Vico Road they were nearing the tiny gap in the railings which gave access to De Selby's dwelling. Mick caused a halt by deterring the sergeant's bicycle. This was for emphasis.

— Sergeant Fottrell, he said in a hidden earnest voice, I have arranged this operation down to the smallest detail. We dare not depart from the plan. We will get De Selby's thing down to these railings, if necessary by rolling it, and hide it inside for the night. Early tomorrow morning a taxi will stop very near my own house and the driver will wait. When I join him, we will drive here, collect the thing and bring it to where it will be absolutely safe forever. Now isn't that simple?

They moved on, as the sergeant was not inclined to argue the point. He seemed to regard himself, very properly, as a professional adviser on house-breaking, undertaken in the public interest. And when they did reach the gap in the railings he was miraculously deft and fast in extinguishing his bicycle in the shrubs and foliage.

In a quite silent ascent through the trees, Mick carefully guided him by the sleeve. The house was completely in darkness, without the whisper of life from it. Its outline, with some detail, was quite perceptible as it stood in its strange clearing. The hall door was visible but offered no enticement to the sergeant who, now taking Mick by the sleeve, hugged the shadow of the trees and deviously led the way to the back.

Two smallish windows, each with two sashes of equal size, invited them. Their circuit of the house showed it to be surprisingly small and shallow in relation to its frontage.

The sergeant chose a window and produced a slim pocket-knife. He then tried to peer at the region of the catch, began handling the sides of the sash and to Mick's bewilderment, suddenly slid up the bottom one, without benefit of knife, to leave an aperture of about two feet by a foot and a half. Into this he inserted his big head and called softly:

– Is there anybody there? Is there anybody there?

No answer came from the gloom. He withdrew his head and used it to give Mick a gigantic nod. Then in through the aperture he inserted his large right leg and with swift very complicated contortions had the whole of himself inside. As Mick laboriously followed, he reflected that their foolhardy break-in was by no means in the pattern or pace of the underworld as set forth in books. Indeed, so far as he knew, neither of them was armed (if it is agreed not to take account of that knife in the sergeant's pocket). The sergeant carefully and quietly closed the window.

Mick produced a small torch of brilliant but very narrow beam and surveyed the apartment with its eye. They seemed to be in a clean neat sort of kitchen. There was a roughish, scrubbed table, cupboards, shelves with packets and tins on them, a refrigerator, a small electric cooker and a few chairs. These were the quarters of a careful person.

The closed door opened inward readily to Mick's hand and he called softly without result the sergeant's query of 'Is there anybody there?' It was simple to head towards the front of the house, traversing a short passage and arriving in the hall. He guided the sergeant into the sitting-room which the torch soon revealed to be empty. There were some newspapers on the floor and a rug hung from the side of an armchair. On the mantelpiece was a pot and a small cup showing signs of dribble. He went straight to the press with the key between his fingers. The dull metal cask was there, just as he had last seen it. He gestured to the sergeant and silently handed him the torch. The cask tilted readily enough from side to side but he found it difficult, in his kneeling position, to lift it. He pulled at it, sliding it outward. There was a drop of an inch from the bottom of the press to the floor, and it fell outwards towards him on its side, on the thinly carpeted floor. Its construction, beautifully exact, was such that it rested on its median circumference, both extremities being clear of the floor. He rolled it some distance from the press, which he then relocked. He stood up, took the torch from the sergeant, and motioned him to lift the cask and put it on the table. This the sergeant quickly and easily did.

It was clear enough now that a slight relaxation of caution was permissible.

– Is it heavy? Mick whispered.

– Not at all, came a piercing whisper which might be heard in Dalkey, just about the weight of a month-old sheep by the holy hokey.

Why didn't he say a month-old lamb? Mick tried lifting the cask himself. He was surprised, for it belied its massive appearance. He thought it about the weight of a medium-sized typewriter.

– We'll carry it turn about, he whispered, with myself always in front on that difficult track through the trees. We'll go out through the hall door. We must go carefully and slowly. You carry first. I'll open and close the door.

– Inferentially, the sergeant commented, laying strong arms about the prize.

Slow and meticulous was the descent to those railings by the roadside, momentous as the burden was, rapid its stowing away in the undergrowth. Though not a single tiny thing went wrong, Mick's heart kept thumping throughout the journey, and even afterwards, when he and the sergeant with his retrieved bicycle were casually walking down the Vico Road.

– Do you know, the sergeant said in a low confidential voice, do you know something? Do you know what is going to happen at six o'clock tomorrow morning?

– No – what? Mick asked, suddenly a bit scared. What very obvious thing had he overlooked?

– At six or thereabouts, the sergeant intoned, that west wind will bring on its cruel lip a whirlwind of downpours and contumelious cloudbursts to frighten out of their wits the poor farmers and gardeners who have still crops in the ground, slobbers of water fearful to behold.

This prophecy amused Mick a bit. Ever a forward-looking man, the sergeant clearly regarded their own night's work as something done and finished with, a book closed, a meal eaten, a thing never to be mentioned again or even thought of. Mick's involute, hand-knitted, littered mind found such a compact, simple state of affairs indigestible but he was grateful that the sergeant saw things that way, for unconsciously his attitude was an accommodation of Mick's own strange preoccupation.

He played back the ball of weather-talk and was rewarded with short accounts of catastrophes in the far past arising from nature's inexcusable waywardness, the Irish potato-famine of the black eighteen-forties having been due to nothing else but weeks of the blackest frost in the history of mankind! They had reached the station and Mick was holding out a hand in thanks and good-bye when the sergeant guided him inwards by the shoulder.

– A skillet of tea would do the both of us good, he said in a tone intended to be that of wheedle, and pay no attention to Policeman Pluck's snotty snivelling about punctures.

Snivelling he pronounced snyvelling.

CHAPTER 16

WHEN MICK left the police station that night he was surprised to note that it was only slightly after ten o'clock. Against his judgement he decided to visit the Colza and offer his apology in person to De Selby. Readymade lies kept flocking into his head. His appointment that night had been for the purpose of fixing up an appointment with the eminent writer James Joyce. However, while in town he was passing by when a motor car knocked down and injured a cyclist. The police had insisted on his going along to the station and making a written statement as a witness. The police were hopelessly slow and incompetent. They had wrecked his evening on foot of an occurrence he had absolutely nothing to do with, and he could only apologize. He was extremely sorry.

The Colza Hotel could remain open to visitors until eleven but either elasticity of conscience or unreliability of time-pieces on the part of Mrs Laverty made closing time always uncertain. Sergeant Fottrell, the scourge of many a Dalkey publican, paid absolutely no attention to this house beyond occasionally drinking there. Anybody who got drunk there never coupled the offence with the other unthinkable offence of being disorderly.

It was ten-thirteen when Mick got there to find Hackett, a bit dim-eyed, in the bar, with Mrs L knitting behind the counter. Somehow he felt this whole night was tuned in a low key. He bade a general goodnight and sat at the counter. Mrs Laverty set about the surprising request for a bottle of Vichy water.

– Well, you have a great gift for being nearly in time, Hackett said somewhat unsteadily. Reminds me of your mother's disclosure to me that you were an eight-month baby. Your man departed only fifteen minutes ago.

Mick was not sure but perhaps he was relieved at this.

– Thanks, Hackett, he replied. I'm grateful for your co-operation. Actually it wouldn't have mattered in the least whether I'd met him.

– Did your own scheme work out according to plan?

– I think so, yes.

– And where have you put the property of the person of the first part?

– Ah, never mind. It doesn't matter. Somewhere very safe. We may worry about it no more.

Hackett resumed attending to his drink, frowning a little. He was moody, his temper uncertain. He motioned Mick to join him in a back seat in the Slum, and Mick obeyed.

– It's a pity you missed De Selby, Hackett said, because he wanted to meet you for his own reasons. He only hinted to me what they were. He said he knew you had certain suspicions about his intentions with that chemical he used in the Saint Augustine episode. He does not blame you but wanted you to know that he had completely changed his mind. He now admits that he had been under a bad influence, pretty well subject to an exterior power. But by a miracle – or a series of them – his mind was cleared. He wanted you to be informed of that, and to stop worrying. 'Within a few days,' he said, 'I will make a most un-ambiguous retraction of my error. I will make an end of all my experiments and return as a peaceable citizen to Buenos Aires, where my good patient wife is waiting for me. I have plenty of money, honestly earned'...

Mick stared at him.

– That is astonishing talk, he said, and mystifying rather than enlightening. Can anybody believe a word De Selby says or even understand it?

Hackett gestured to Mrs Laverty for a repeat medicament.

– The only direct contact I have had in any of this business, he said, is that of having been with you and De Selby in that meeting with Saint Augustine. But I have never been certain that it was not an hallucination, as I've told you before. De Selby would be the last to deny that he is an accomplished witch-doctor. Very likely we were drugged. There is no limit to the drugs which induce fantasy.

– Hackett, we've discussed this before. No drug could induce an identical fantasy in two separate individuals. All branches of science – chemical, medical, psychological, neuropathic – are all agreed on that.

Hackett grumpily paid for the beaker Mrs Laverty had brought.

– Well listen here, he said, I wish to God I had never met that clown De Selby, and I told him so. I made it clear that I didn't like him and didn't want his Christmas pudding. But that was after he had revealed to me that he has a cell in his house sealed as tight as the sea ever sealed the underwater chamber at the Vico Swimming Club. Apparently he has been going into his domestic eternity wearing his breathing mask practically every day and conversing with the dead. It still seems to be exclusively with the heavenly dead, which seems odd in view of his other claim that he derives his powers from the Devil. What do you say?

– I don't know what to say. I haven't yet heard what his latest disclosures are.

Hackett nodded.

– I can only summarize what he said. One thing I forgot to tell you. He was properly plastered when he came here, and you said my job was to ply him with drink. My real job was to stop him nursing himself into a slumber of insensibility. Mrs L was getting very upset and when he left a quarter of an hour ago, it was in the care of Teague McGettigan. I had to send for the cab. The man was stotious.

Mick shook his head. This was indeed an unhappy, unforeseen diversion. He found it hard to assess its significance: possibly nil, for drunken ranting by a person of De Selby's standing could be macabre and frightening without really meaning anything or calling for serious notice. Still . . .

– No doubt he broke a rule, as we all do now and again, he remarked, and started a rash sampling of that special whiskey of his. Whom did he say he was seeing in that celestial laboratory of his?

Hackett began rummaging in his pocket.

– I tried to scribble down some names, he replied, but one man he seemed to be seeing practically every day was Augustine, as if he was a sort of chaplain in the house.

– Who else?

Hackett was frowning at a ragged piece of paper.

– I'm not sure about some of these names – my attempts were phonetic, mostly. Athenagoras, Ignatius of Antioch, Cyprian, John of Damascus . . .

– Goodness! He does not exclude the Greek Fathers?

– John Chrysostom, Theodore of Mopsuestia, Gregory of Nazianzus...

– Hackett, I confess that my own grasp of patrology is limited but what on earth would De Selby gain by dialogue with Fathers so diverse in origin and even in doctrine? But this time he seems to confine himself to the Fathers proper. I do know that the last of the reputed Fathers was Gregory the Great, who died somewhere around 600.

Hackett laughed. Alcohol had also left its inflexion on his mind and voice.

– We have often read, he said, that such-and-such a Royal Commission has power to send for persons and papers. Well, De Selby has power to send for parsons and papists. His summonses aren't always addressed to individuals to attend for a private collogue. Know whom he had down one morning?

– Who?

– A whole detachment – if that's the word – from the Council of Trent, including, he said, certain cardinals who tried to wreck the unhappy Council through the Pope's scheme to get the Council to denounce the Protestants as heretics.

Mick was aghast at such an excess.

– We must remember the man was drunk when he gave out such extreme language to you, Hackett, he said.

Hackett nodded.

– And you could say that I wasn't too sober listening to him. He was sometimes confused, and not very clear in his words. I could nearly swear he said he offered Saint Augustine a drink, one morning when it was cold.

This was all threatening to put Mick's own carefully formulated plans into disorder – perhaps wreck them. De Selby was no longer the cool scientist who could be met at an agreed level, steel meeting steel. It seemed that on this night he had behaved like a garrulous, dangerous drunk.

– Did he ask for me?

Hackett first pointed to his empty glass and then stared moistly at his friend.

– Did he ask for you? he repeated. Wasn't he here to meet you on foot of an appointment made by yourself?

– I know, but when I failed to show up did he suggest any other arrangement? For instance, did he say I might call on him?

– No. He was very vague. One of the reasons why he was so disappointed that tonight's meeting fell through was that there seemed to be no possibility of an alternative meeting.

– The man was blithero.

– No, not so much that. He hinted at an impending great change, his own departure, the dropping of all the enterprise he has had going on in that house of his. Well . . . I don't know but he seemed to have something pretty big planned.

Mick sighed. If Hackett's report were to be taken seriously, the situation had become deplorably fluid and formless. Yet for all that, Mick reckoned he was still one jump ahead. If one were to trust the alchemy of barleycorn, De Selby was possibly by now being helped out of his clothes by Teague McGettigan preparatory to collapsing into bed, clutched in the airless womb of liquor. It would probably be high noon on another day before his senses returned to him, and then only to a comatose wreck. A good forty-eight hours would pass before he was fit for doing or deciding anything. But Mick himself would be at work early next morning.

– Well, Hackett, he said, I'm going to buy a final drink and then depart. Tomorrow morning I have to bring to a conclusion what I did today. Afterwards, I might try to contact De Selby over the weekend.

He did summon a glass of whiskey, a glass of Vichy, and managed to give a laugh.

– Cheer up, Hackett, he beamed, don't let collision with an odd and exceptional man like De Selby depress you or extinguish your natural ebullience. You're not good company when you have a load on your mind. There's no need for any load. Forget all about it.

Hackett smiled a little.

– You must excuse me, he replied, but I always feel a bit frustrated when thrown into the company of a man already full of booze. Seems like fighting with one arm tied behind you.

They clinked glasses and Mick found himself saying something which surprised him almost as much as Hackett.

– Hackett, he said, I have been much more mixed up in this supernatural play-acting than you have. One way or another it is going to end soon. But I've learnt something – something deep and valuable. First, that there *is* another world, though my glimpses of it have been uncertain and distorted. Second, that I have an immortal soul, which I have been doing nothing to safeguard. Third, that the life I have been living is futile and, indeed, laughable.

Hackett chuckled.

– That is certainly a mouthful.

– The same goes for you, though it is true that you have not been so destitute of purpose as I have been. After all, you have set your heart on winning that snooker tournament.

– Is snooker then sinful?

– No, only meaningless. I'm going to throw up my rotten little job as soon as possible and join the Church.

Perhaps it was the earnest tone and serious manner, but Hackett did sit up.

– You're . . . you're blathering out of you, Mick, surely? At *your* age?

– I'm in earnest. This thought has been running at the bottom of my head all along, no matter how busy I was on other matters – running like a tireless, invisible electric motor. God's grace never left me.

– Well, I'll be damned. Do you mean to tell me that if I happened to meet you in a few years, I'll have to lift my hat to you? You know perfectly well that I hardly ever wear a hat.

Mick smiled benignly. Serious as he was, he did not want this occasion to become ponderous or pompous and therefore verging on the ridiculous. An ill-timed laugh can wreck an important thing.

– I can relieve your mind on that, Hackett, he said brightly. You are most unlikely to meet me after I have graduated among the Lord's anointed. In fact it will be impossible.

– Why? Are you going to be a foreign missions man, preaching the Gospel to the niggers in Zanzibar or some such place?

– No. This is one thing I will not half-do. I'm old enough to know my own mind. I intend to join one of the enclosed orders – and the toughest of the lot, if they will have me.

– And who are they when they're at home?

– The reformed Order of Cistercians, commonly known as the Trappists . . .

A queer clucking sound came from Hackett, and this developed into a bombastic laugh.

– Hell, hell, he sniggered, I'll buy a final drink on that. Have a whiskey this time. Two, Mrs L, he called. As she moved to obey, Mrs Laverty said:

– It's getting on the time, Mr Hackett.

Hackett was momentarily silent, thoughtful, and paid exactly for the goods. He turned to Mick confidentially as by gesture he proposed his health.

– It is curious how an occasion arises for a toast, and arises inevitably, even if one has despaired of it ever arising. Silly words like fate, or predestination, are used for this process.

– Maybe Providence would be a better word.

– Nearly ten years ago, I composed a very clever poem. I locked it in my mind, determined not to parade it until an occasion arose when it would be miraculously apposite. Do you follow me?

– I think I do.

– I was not concerned whether I amassed an undeserved reputation for extemporization. That didn't bother me at all. I just wanted to clinch the issue, put my trump on somebody else's ace. Get me?

– Sounds to me like vanity.

– Wait! This is the occasion. You say you are going to join the Trappists? Right. It is for that announcement that my poem was written so long ago. Here surely is Destiny nakedly at work! But what a pity we haven't an enormous audience.

– Recite your composition, please, Mick ordered.

The other did so, in a solemn voice, and Mick certainly laughed at the end of it. A little bawdy perhaps, but not dirty.

> There was a young monk of La Trappe
> Who contracted a dose of the clap,
> He said Dominus Vobiscum,
> Oh why can't my piss come –
> There's something gone wrong with my . . . tap.

Yes, funny. But Mick's mood was thoughtful as he made his way home that night. He had been wholly serious in what he had said to Hackett. His days as a layman were numbered.

CHAPTER 17

EARLY THE next morning Mick was up and about, the rather shadowed mood of the preceding night dissipated and a feeling of satisfaction in his heart, with no clear reason why. He felt his rather messed up mind was clearing, the road ahead plainer.

He put on his good clothes and the breakfast he quickly made was simple – simple as the little job ahead of him that morning. Slipping quietly out at the appointed time, he found the taxi-cab where it should be and the driver Charlie, whom he knew from occasional other jaunts, reading a newspaper. Here was the rich man's Teague McGettigan.

– That's the grand mornin', thank God, Charlie said.

– It is, indeed, Mick replied, getting in beside him, and I wish I was going off down to Arklow for a day's sea-fishing. I'm sure you wouldn't be in the way on a trip like that, Charlie?

– I'm a divil for ling, sir. Matteradamn what I'm after – pollock, mackerel, black sole or even cod – I always get ling. I'm like a trout-fisher that always catches eels and gets his tackle ruined. Vico Road, sir?

– Vico Road, yes. I'll tell you where.

It was nine and not really early in the morning but the trip through Monkstown, Dunleary and Dalkey was as if through habitations still asleep. There was little movement or traffic except for an occasional battered tram-car.

There was not a soul to be seen on the Vico Road. Mick had Charlie drive a fair bit past the target, then go back and stop twelve yards beyond the gap in the railings.

– Just wait here, Charlie, he instructed, and leave the nearside back door open. I have to collect an awkward class of an article from a friend. I won't be long.

– Right, sir.

Mick could see almost at a glance that the cask was where he had left it but he went upward among the trees and sat down on a shoulder of rock. He thought a little artificial delay was called for.

When he did go back he had little trouble in manhandling the cask and achieving the roadside, carrying it before him, but on reaching the car he had to dump it heavily to the ground.

– This damn thing is heavy, Charlie, he said, recalling the driver from his newspaper. Could you lift it into the back?

– Certainly, sir.

He did so expertly.

– That's one of them new electric mines, I'll go bail, he said, as both got back into their seats. I seen many like that took out of the sea in the first world war.

– Nothing of the kind, I believe, Mick replied airily, though the man who owns it is in the electrical line. He wants it put away for safety in the Bank of Ireland, out of harm's way, and that's our next stop. He's an inventor.

– Ah yes, Charlie said. That class of man can make millions when the rest of us is scratchin' for coppers.

Later, as Mick entered the Bank of Ireland preceded by Charlie carrying the cask, he felt he was in effect entering the Cistercian Order of Trappists. Perhaps there is a certain monastic quality in banks, a sacred symbolism in money, silver and gold.

– Just leave it on the floor by the side-table there, Charlie, he said, and I think this will pay you for all your trouble.

A friendly cashier readily recognized Mick. Could he see somebody behind the scenes for a moment about a private matter. Not the manager, of course, but some . . . authorized officer? Certainly.

Mr Heffernan, when Mick was shown into his surprisingly modern office, was elderly, affable and seemed almost on the point of producing a decanter. When seated and having declined a cigarette, Mick came to the point in what he thought was a brisk manner.

– Mr Heffernan, I am a new customer and a small one. I wanted to enquire about one of the bank's services, of which I've heard. I mean the safe deposit system.

– Yes?

– Is it true that you accept for safe-keeping objects without knowing what they are?

– Yes. Every major bank does.

– But suppose something – a box, say – was in reality an infernal machine? A time-bomb, for instance?

– Well, as Irish institutions go, we're fairly venerable. The
Bank of Ireland is still here, eccentric or murderous depositors
notwithstanding.

– But . . . one must get rid of the old idea that a time-bomb is
necessarily something that ticks. Modern methods, Mr Heffernan, could make a simple thing that looks like an onion, say, to
have the explosive power of 10,000 tons of TNT.

– Well, from the beginning of the world banking has been a
business which entailed risk. That is all I can say. Of course there
are certain limitations on our facilities. The physical size of a
deposit, for instance, has to conform to certain limits and it must
not be a nuisance as, for example, having a bad smell. If you had
become fond of a certain old railway engine and bought it, I'm
afraid we could not accept it as a deposit. But anything within
reason.

– Well, Mr Heffernan, you surprise and relieve me.

They had a messenger bring the cask in. It contained certain
small objects produced by an immediate relative in connexion
with electronic research; he was a physician in private practice with limited resources for safe storage. The objects were of
trifling size *as objects*, and the weight was mostly that of the cask
itself. The thing was guaranteed to emit no harmful radiation.

To Mick himself his piece sounded lame but to Mr Heffernan
it was quite satisfactory. After the signing of some papers, the
bank had taken over De Selby's treasure and its temporary
custodian was once more in the street. And not long after that
he was contemplating a glass of cool Vichy water. Wonderful
how business people who knew their business could so smoothly
do business.

He felt not idle but disoccupied. What would he do with himself until Tuesday, when he had his second meeting with James
Joyce at Skerries?

To consider that further and more fully he had a second drink,
though he genuinely disagreed with even harmless drinking so
early in the day, when it could scarcely be said that the morning
had been properly aired. But the cares on him were heavy, and
somehow he seemed to be taking on the character of a Cabinet
Minister. What did he mean Cabinet Minister? Prime Minister
was the more precise term. Policy in several major regards was
in his sole charge; he was making – and had made – critical

decisions. His resolve to retire from the world personally for the rest of his life was perhaps the most important bit only in so far as it concerned himself and his immortal soul; his recent transaction with the Bank of Ireland concerned the human race, in existence and to come. What of De Selby? To kill him would be gravely sinful but a middle and less brutal course came to mind, one which no doubt betrayed his academic mould of thought. He would spend the vacant weekend committing precisely and temperately to paper the facts concerning De Selby, his chemical work and diabolical scheme, and the action which had been taken, right up to that morning. *And that document he would hand over to the abbot of the Trappist house he joined*, thus passing to an older and wiser head the decision on De Selby's personal future and the fate of the ghastly paraphernalia which no doubt littered the workroom of 'Lawnmower'.

One other thing: the matter of letting Mary know that he had, so to speak, no use for her washing. A letter would be unthinkable and cowardly, and anyway it was desirable to emphasize that it was an austere, enclosed order – not another woman – that had induced him to change his mind so drastically. On Monday or Tuesday he would ask her to meet him in the evening at the Colza Hotel. That spot was pleasantly remote for a heady showdown, if there was to be one, and it was always possible that Hackett might be there.

By then his second investigation of Joyce would be over and perhaps a decision arrived at as to what, if anything, to do about that strange man. To attend to him, and to Mary and Hackett as well, was a grandiose programme for one evening.

CHAPTER 18

DURING HIS train journey to Skerries on Tuesday evening his mood was peaceable: resigned might be a fairer word. *Quisque faber fortunae suae*, the tag says – everybody makes his own mess. Still, he did not think this outlook applicable. He was conscious of a pervasive ambiguity: sometimes he seemed to be dictating events with deific authority, at other times he saw himself the plaything of implacable forces. On this particular trip he felt he must await an exposition of Joyce by himself, and take him at his face value. Joyce had already whetted curiosity by disclosing that he was still working on a book, unnamed, content unhinted at. He could be an impostor, or a unique case of physical resemblance. Yet his appearance was authentic, and clearly he had lived on the European continent. Really, he could not be classed as one of Mick's problems but rather an interesting distraction for one now practised in interfering in the affairs of others. Very properly, Mick had not given his own private or business address, and it could not be said that he knew anything embarrassing.

The hotel was a simple establishment, with no bar, but an old man, nondescript in manner and dress to the point of giving no sign whether he was the boots or the proprietor, guided Mick down a hallway to 'the drawing-room where gents takes a drink'. It was an ill-lit room, small, linoleum on the floor, a few small tables with chairs here and there, and in the grate a flickering fire. Mick was alone and agreed with his host that it was a poor evening for that time of the year, and then ordered a small sherry.

– I'm expecting a friend, he added.

But Joyce was punctual. He came in noiselessly, very soberly attired, quiet, calm, a small black hat surmounting his small ascetic features, in his hand a stout walking stick. He sat down after a slight bow.

– I took the liberty of ordering something on the way in, he said, smiling slightly, because we in the trade like to save each other's feet. I hope you are A1?

Mick laughed easily.

– Excellent, he said. That walk from the station is a tonic in itself. Here's your drink, and I'm paying for it.

Joyce did not reply, having commenced preparing to light a small black cigar.

– I am a little bit flustered, he said finally. You seem to have many connections in this country. I envy you. I know a few people – but friends? Ah!

– Perhaps you are by nature the more solitary type of man, Mick suggested. Maybe company in general doesn't agree with you. Personally, I find interesting people very scarce, and bores to be met everywhere.

He seemed to nod in the gloom.

– One of the great drawbacks of Ireland, he said, is that there are too many Irish here. You understand me? I know it is natural and to be expected, like having wild animals in the zoo. But it's unnerving for one who has been away in the mishmash that is Europe today.

Here he had led Mick to the scene of his enquiry, so to speak. Mick's voice was low, soothing:

– Mr Joyce, I have great respect for you and it would be an honour to be of service to you. I am a bit confused by your eminence as an author and your presence in this part of the world. Would you give me a little information about yourself – in strict confidence, of course.

Joyce nodded as if without guile.

– I will, of course. There is nothing much to tell you. The past is simple enough. The future is what I find remote and difficult.

– I see. Were you expelled from Switzerland by the Hitler people?

– No, France. My wife and family were part of a mass of people fleeing before that terror. My passport was British. I knew I would be arrested, probably murdered.

– What happened to your family?

– I can't say. We got separated.

– Are they dead?

– I know very little except that my son is safe. It was all chaos, bedlam. Trains broke down, lines were damaged. It was improvisation everywhere. A lift in a lorry, perhaps, or stumbling across fields, or holding up for a day or two in a barn. There were soldiers and guerillas and cut-throats roaming the land on all sides. By the Lord God it was not funny. Fortunately the real country folk were recognizable – brave, simple people. Fortunately I could speak French properly.

– And what exactly was your destination?

He paused.

– Well, first, he explained, I wanted to get away from contact with those Germans. My second idea was to get to America. America hadn't entered the war at the time. But any sort of major movement was very difficult. There were spies, saboteurs and thugs of every description high and low. The simplest questions of even food and drink were difficult.

– Yes, war is calamitous.

– I wouldn't dignify that French shambles with the word war. And the black market? Heavens!

– What happened?

– I got to London first. The atmosphere of nerves there was terrible. I didn't feel safe. Mick nodded.

– I remember they hanged your namesake – the broadcaster Joyce.

– Yes. I thought I'd be better off here. I managed to sneak across in a small freighter. Thank God I can still pass for an Irishman.

– What about your family?

– I'm having confidential enquiries made through a friend, and I know my son is safe. Of course I can't risk making enquiries direct.

The conversation was fair enough but not much to Mick's purpose. Was this James Joyce, the Dublin writer of international name? Or was it somebody masquerading, possibly genuinely deranged through suffering? The old, nagging doubt was still there.

– Mr Joyce, tell me about the writing of *Ulysses*.

He turned with a start.

– I have heard more than enough about that dirty book, that collection of smut, but do not be heard saying that I had anything to do with it. Faith now, you must be careful about that. As a matter of fact, I have put my name only to one little book in which I was concerned.

– And what was that?

– Ah, it's a long time ago. Oliver Gogarty and I, when we were in touch, worked together on some short stories. Simple stories: Dublin characterizations you might call them. Yes, they did have some little merit, I think. The world was settled then . . .

– Did you find that sort of association with Gogarty easy?

Joyce chuckled softly.

– The man had talent, he said, but of a widely spread out kind. He was primarily a talker and, up to a point, his talk improved with drink. He was a drunkard, but not habitually. He was too clever for that.

– Well, you were friends?

– Yes, you could say that, I suppose. But Gogarty could have a scurrilous and blasphemous tongue and that didn't suit me, I needn't tell you.

– Was this collaboration genuinely fifty-fifty?

– No. I did the real work, tried to get back into the soul of the people. Gogarty was all for window-dressing, smart stuff, almost Castle cavorting – things not in character. Oh, we had several quarrels, I can tell you.

– What did you call the book?

– We called it *Dubliners*. At the last moment Gogarty wouldn't let his name go on the title page. Said it would ruin his name as a doctor. It didn't matter, because no publisher could be found for years.

– Very interesting. But what else have you written, mainly?

Joyce quietly attended to the ash of his cigar.

– So far as print is concerned, mostly pamphlets for the Catholic Truth Society of Ireland. I am sure you know what I mean – those little tracts that can be had from a stand inside the door of any church; on marriage, the sacrament of penance, humility, the dangers of alcohol.

Mick stared.

– You surprise me.

– Now and again, of course, I attempted something more ambitious. In 1926 I had a biographical piece on Saint Cyril, Apostle of the Slavs, published in *Studies*, the Irish Jesuit quarterly. Under an assumed name, of course.

– Yes. But *Ulysses*?

There was a low sound of impatience in the gloom.

– I don't want to talk about that exploit. I took the idea to be a sort of practical joke but didn't know enough about it to suspect it might seriously injure my name. It began with an American lady in Paris by the name of Sylvia Beach. I know it's a horrible phrase, I detest it, but the truth is that she fell in love with me. Fancy that!

He smiled bleakly.

– She had a bookshop which I often visited in connexion with a plan to translate and decontaminate great French literature so that it could be an inspiration to the Irish, besotted with Dickens, Cardinal Newman, Walter Scott and Kickham. My eye had a broad range – Pascal and Descartes, Rimbaud, de Musset, Verlaine, Balzac, even that holy Franciscan, Benedictine and medical man, Rabelais . . . !

– Interesting. But *Ulysses*?

– Curious thing about Baudelaire and Mallarmé – both were obsessed with Edgar Allan Poe.

– How did Miss Beach express her love for you?

– Ah-ha! Who is Sylvia? She swore to me that she'd make me famous. She didn't at the beginning say how, and anyhow I took it all patiently as childish talk. But her plot was to have this thing named *Ulysses* concocted, secretly circulated and have the authorship ascribed to me. Of course at first I didn't take the mad scheme seriously.

– But how did the thing progress?

– I was shown bits of it in typescript. Artificial and laborious stuff, I thought. I just couldn't take much interest in it, even as a joke by amateurs. I was immersed in those days in what was intrinsically good behind the bad in Scaliger, Voltaire, Montaigne, and even that queer man Villon. But how well-attuned they were, I thought, to the educated Irish mind. Ah, yes. Of course it wasn't Sylvia Beach who showed me those extracts.

– Who was it?

– Various low, dirty-minded ruffians who had been paid to put this material together. Muck-rakers, obscene poets, carnal pimps, sodomous sycophants, pedlars of the coloured lusts of fallen humanity. Please don't ask me for names.

Mick pondered it all, in wonder.

– Mr Joyce, how did you live in all those years?

– Teaching languages, mostly English, and giving grinds.

I used to hang around the Sorbonne. Meals were easy enough to scrounge there, anyway.

– Did the Catholic Truth Society pay you for those booklets you wrote?

– Not at all. Why should they?

– Tell me more about *Ulysses*.

– I paid very little attention to it until one day I was given a piece from it about some woman in bed thinking the dirtiest thoughts that ever came into the human head. Pornography and filth and literary vomit, enough to make even a blackguard of a Dublin cabman blush. I blessed myself and put the thing in the fire.

– Well was the complete *Ulysses*, do you think, ever published?

– I certainly hope not.

Mick paused for a few seconds and pressed the bell for service. What would he say? Frankness in return seemed called for.

– Mr Joyce, he said solemnly, I can tell you that you have been out of touch with things for a long time. The book *Ulysses* was published in Paris in 1922, with your name on the title page. And it was considered a great book.

– God forgive you. Are you fooling me? I am getting on in years. Remember that.

Mick patted his sleeve, and signalled to a server to bring more drinks.

– It was roughly received originally but it has since been published everywhere, including America. Dozens – literally dozens – of distinguished American critics have written treatises on it. Books have even been written about yourself and your methods. And all the copyright money on *Ulysses* must have accrued to your credit. The difficulty of the various publishers is simply that they don't know where you are.

– May the angels of God defend us!

– You're a strange man, Mr Joyce. Bowsies who write trash and are as proud as punch of it are ten a penny. You have your name on a great book, you are ashamed of your life, and ask God's pardon. Well, well, well. I am going out for a moment to relieve myself. I feel that's about the perfect thing to do.

– How dare you impute smutty writings to me?

Mick got up a bit brusquely and went out for the purpose stated, but was disturbed. His bluff, if that was the right name for it, had hardly succeeded. Joyce was serious in his denial, and apparently had never seen the book *Ulysses*. What new line should now be taken?

When he returned and sat down Joyce quickly spoke in a low and serious tone.

– Look here, I hope you don't mind if we change the subject, he said. I spoke of the importance for me of the future. I mean that. I want you to help me.

– I've already said it would be a pleasure.

– Well, you have heard of Late Vocations. I may not be worthy but I want to join the Jesuits.

– *What?* Well . . . !

The shock in Mick's voice was of a rasping kind. Into his mind came that other book, *Portrait of the Artist*. Here had been renunciation of family, faith, even birthland, and that promise of silence, exile and cunning. What did there seem to be here? The garrulous, the repatriate, the ingenuous? Yet was not even a man of genius entitled to change his mind? And what matter if that mind showed signs of unbalance, and memory evidence of decay? The ambition to join the Church's most intellectual of Orders was certainly an enormous surprise, perhaps not to be taken absolutely seriously. Still, he had custody of his immortal soul and who was he, Mick, himself on the brink of the holy prison of the Trappists, to question his wish to take part in the religious life? He might not be taken, of course, by reason of the scandalous literary works attributed to him, or even by reason of age, but that decision was one for Father Provincial of the Society of Jesus, not for Mick.

– My French Plan, if I may call it that, Joyce continued, I could defer until I had the seclusion of the Order. Curious, I have many notes on the *good* and *decorous* things written by those three scoundrels who otherwise dealt in blood – Marat, Robespierre and Danton. Strange . . . like lilies sprouting on a heap of ordure.

Mick drank thoughtfully, arranging his thoughts into wise words.

– Mr Joyce, he said, I believe it takes fourteen years to make a Jesuit Father. That's a long time. You could become a medical doctor in far less than that.

– If God spares me, I would be a postulant even if it took me twenty years. Of what account are those trumpery years in this vale of tears? Do you know any Jesuits personally?

– I do. I know at least one, a Father Cobble, in Leeson Street. He's an Englishman but quite intelligent.

– Ah, excellent. Will you introduce me?

– I will of course. Naturally, that is about all I could do. I mean, Church matters are for the Church to decide. If I were to try to sort of . . . interfere or use pressure, I would be very soon told to mind my own business.

– I quite understand that. All I ask for is a quiet talk with a Jesuit Father after I've been sponsored by some responsible, respectable person like yourself. Leave the rest to him, me and God.

His tone seemed pleased, and in the gloom he gave the impression of smiling.

– Well, I'm glad our little talk is going the right way, Mick said.

– Yes, he murmured. I've just been thinking in recent days of my schooldays at Clongowes Wood College. Of course it's very silly but suppose I were to become a Jesuit as planned, is it not at least possible – *possible*, I repeat – that I would in my old age be appointed Rector of Clongowes? Could it not happen?

– Of course it could.

Joyce's fingers were at his glass of Martini, playing absently. His mind was at grips with another matter.

– I must be candid here, and careful. You might say that I have more than one good motive for wishing to become a Jesuit Father. I wish to reform, first the Society, and then through the Society the Church. Error has crept in . . . corrupt beliefs . . . certain shameless superstitions . . . rash presumptions which have no sanction within the word of the Scriptures.

Mick frowned, considering this.

– Questions of dogma, you mean? These can be involved matters.

– Straightforward attention to the word of God, Joyce rejoined, will confound all Satanic quibble. Do you know the Hebrew language?

– I'm afraid I do not.

– Ah, too few people do. The word *ruach* is most important. It means a breath or a blowing. *Spiritus* we call it in Latin. The

Greek word is *pneuma*. You see the train of meaning we have here? All these words mean life. Life, and breath of life. God's breath in man.

– Do these words mean the same thing?

– No. The Hebrew *ruach* denoted only the Divine Being, anterior to man. Later it came to mean the inflammation, so to speak, of created man by the breath of God.

– I find that not very clear.

– Well . . . one needs experience in trying to grasp celestial concepts through earthly words. This word *ruach* latterly means, not the immanent energy of God but His transcendent energy in imparting the divine content to men.

– You mean that man is part-God?

– Even the ancient pre-Christian Greeks used *pneuma* to denote the limitless and all-powerful personality of God, and man's bodily senses are due to the immanence of that *pneuma*. God wills that man have a transfusion of His *pneuma*.

– Well . . . I don't suppose anybody would question that. What you call *pneuma* is what distinguishes man from the brute?

– As you will, but it is wrong to say that man's possession, charismatically, of *ruach* or *pneuma* makes him part-God. God is of two Persons, the Father and the Son. They subsist in hypostasis. That is quite clear from mention of both Divine Persons in the New Testament. What I particularly call your attention to is the Holy Spirit – the Holy Ghost, to use the more common title.

– And what about the Holy Spirit?

– The Holy Spirit was the invention of the more reckless of the early Fathers. We have here a confusion of thought and language. Those poor ignorant men associated *pneuma* with what they called the working of the Holy Spirit, whereas it is merely an exudation of God the Father. It is an activity of the existing God, and it is a woeful and shameful error to identify in it a hypostatic Third Person. Abominable nonsense!

Mick picked up his glass and gazed into it in dismay.

– Then you don't believe in the Holy Ghost, Mr Joyce?

– There is not a word about the Holy Ghost or the Trinity in the New Testament.

– I am not . . . much experienced in Biblical studies.

Joyce's low grunt was not ill-natured.

– Of course you're not, because you were reared a Catholic. Neither are the Catholic clergy. Those ancient disputants, rhetoricians, theologizers who are collectively called the Early Fathers were buggers for getting ideas into their heads and then assuming that God directly inspired those ideas. In trying to wind up the Arian controversy, the Council of Alexandria in 362, having asserted the equality in nature of the Son with the Father, went on to announce the transfer of a third hypostasis to the Holy Spirit. Without saying boo, or debating the matter at all! Holy poky but wouldn't you think they'd have a little sense?

– I always understood that God was of three Divine Persons.

– Well you didn't get up early enough in the morning, my lad. The Holy Ghost was not officially invented until the Council of Constantinople in 381.

Mick fingered his jaws.

– Goodness, he said. I wonder what the Holy Ghost Fathers would think of that?

Joyce noisily rapped his glass and murmured to the server who appeared and took them away. Then he drew expansively at his cigar.

– One thing you *do* know, he asked – the Nicene Creed?

– Sure everybody knows that.

– Yes. The Father and the Son were meticulously defined at the Council of Nicaea, and the Holy Spirit hardly mentioned. Augustine was a severe burden on the early Church, and Tertullian split it wide open. He insisted that the Holy Spirit was derived from the Father *and* the son – *quoque*, you know. The Eastern Church would have nothing to do with such a doctrinal aberration. Schism!

Joyce paid for two new drinks then sat down. His voice had been lively, as if joyous in disputation. Mick's own mind had been awakened sharply by mention of Augustine, and he struggled to get into words a rather remote idea which was forming. He sampled his sherry.

– That word *pneuma*, Mr Joyce . . . ?

– Yes?

– Well, you remember my friend De Selby, whom I mentioned to you?

– I do indeed. Dalkey.

– I told you he was a physicist . . . a theologian also.

– Yes. Fascinating mixture but not incongruous, mind you.

– You will probably laugh in my face if I told you to believe that I met Saint Augustine in the company of De Selby.

Joyce's cigar glowed dimly.

– Faith, now – *laugh*? Certainly not. There are conditions . . . opiates . . . gases – many ways of confuting weak human reason.

– Thank you, Mr Joyce. I'll talk about the Augustine affair another time, but the circumstance of this encounter involved the operation of a formula whereby De Selby claims to be able to stop the flow of time, or reverse it.

– Well, it is a big claim.

– It is. But the phrase he used to describe his work was 'pneumatic chemistry'. You see? That word *pneuma* again.

– Indeed yes. Life, breath, eternity, recall of the past. I must think about this man De Selby.

– I'm glad you are so serious and reasonable. *Pneuma* in its divine aspect seems to have been concerned somehow in the manifestation of Saint Augustine.

– One must not be astonished at a thing merely because it looks impossible.

Mick's thought was occupied with another encounter disclosing a situation which, if not impossible, was certainly unlikely.

– Mr Joyce, he said, I have another unusual experience which seems to have involved this *pneuma* also.

– Oh, I don't wonder. It's a big subject. We call it pneumatology.

– Yes. I know a Sergeant Fottrell, also of Dalkey. He has an involved theory about the danger of riding bicycles, even if they are fitted with pneumatic tyres.

– Ah, bicycles? I never had any love for those machines. The old Dublin cab was my father's first choice for getting around.

– Well, the sergeant thinks that, *pneuma* in the tyres or not, the rider gets a severe jolting and that there is an exchange or interfusion of bicycle atoms and human atoms.

Joyce quietly drank.

– Well . . . I would not reject the possibility outright. The *pneuma* there might be preserving life, in the sense of preserving the physical integrity of the rider. Half an hour in a laboratory is a thing that would help us here. The interchange of cells of human tissue with elements of metal would seem a surprising occurrence but of course that is merely a rational objection.

– All right. In any case the sergeant had no doubt of it. He personally knew men whose *jobs* entailed much cycling every day and he regarded some of them as more bicycle than man.

Joyce chuckled dimly.

– There we have a choice. Psychical research or cycle research. I prefer the psychical. Ah, indeed . . . my own little troubles are more complicated than the sergeant's. I have to get into the Jesuits, you might say, to clear the Holy Ghost out of the Godhead and out of the Catholic Church.

There was a silence. Mick's business seemed almost at an end. It had been a short evening, yet Joyce's disclosures about himself, past and present, had not been inconsiderable. Joyce moved in his chair.

– Tell me, he said, how soon could I see Father Cobble?

– How soon? Well, as soon as you like, I suppose. These men are usually accessible enough at any time.

– What about tomorrow?

– Goodness!

– You see, I have three days off from work just now – from work as a curate. Could we strike the iron while it's hot?

Mick pondered this urge for action. All he could think about it was – why not?

– Well, I have an appointment at Dalkey tomorrow night. But provided I could meet you somewhere in town about half-six or so, I suppose we could go along and meet Father Cobble. I could telephone him during the day and make the appointment.

– Excellent. Excellent.

– What time would you say for a meeting? The place I suggest is outside St Vincent's Hospital, on the Green. But at what time?

– Yes. I know the hospital. Would seven in the evening suit?

Mick agreed with this: it would fit neatly into his schedule. They fell silent, finishing their drinks. Was there anything else of a semi-private nature to be asked, Mick wondered, for there would be very little opportunity for confidence the following day. Yes, there was: one thing.

– Mr Joyce, he said, I know the subject displeases you but I must return briefly to that work *Ulysses*. Do you mind?

– No, no, but it's just a boring, dirty subject.

– I take it you have no literary agent?

– What would I have the like of that for?

– Well, I mean –

– Do you think the Catholic Truth Society are commercial publishers, on the make?

– Never mind. Would you appoint me your literary agent?

– Call yourself that by all means if it pleases you, I can't imagine why.

– Well, it's like this. Notwithstanding your ignorance, there may be money lying to your credit from the sales of *Ulysses* in the accounts of publishers. There may be several thousands of pounds there. There is no reason why you should not claim money which is your due – no reason that I should not claim it on your behalf.

– You would probably be offended if I were to say that you suffer from an obsession, from an excited imagination.

Mick laughed lightly to put him at ease.

– You ought to know, he said, that a person who seems to get a bit light-headed should be humoured.

– Well, yes . . . flighty children should be treated that way. It saves trouble. But you're no child, even if the bottle is no stranger to you.

Both of them relaxed.

– There can be no harm in me, as your agent, making enquiries. Now can there?

– There certainly would appear to be no breach of the moral law involved, and that's a sure fire. The only thing you must never reveal is my address – particularly not to any of those lascivious pornographic blackguards.

Mick drank audibly.

– Perhaps you may have something else to say, he said mildly, if it turns out that there is a sum of £8000 due on foot of *Ulysses*.

Joyce's voice, when it came, was low and strained.

– What would *I* do with £8000? he demanded – a man who is tomorrow taking the first step to join the Jesuit Order?

– As I think I reminded you before, they call it Society, not Order. And I can tell you this. If they take you, they take you as you are, poor or rich. The founder Loyola was a nobleman, remember that. And another thing . . .

– What?

– If sundry scheming ruffians in Paris or elsewhere imputed to you matter you did not write and sought to besmear your good name, would it not look like Divine Providence if their base handiwork were to turn out to do you immense corporal good?

Joyce smoked testily.

– But I tell you I don't want or need money.

– Maybe you do. The Jesuits have a wide choice. It may be that they are not particularly fond of paupers.

The silence which followed possibly meant that Joyce was acknowledging a quite new idea. He spoke at last.

– All right. If £8000 was in fact earned by that horrible book you mentioned, and can be lawfully got, every penny of it will go to the Jesuits except five pounds, which I will devote to the Holy Souls.

They parted soon after, Mick strolling towards the station, well enough at ease.

He doubted whether the Jesuits would accept a man of his age, other questions apart. Perhaps some other Order would take him as a Brother. Any Order, he hastily warned himself, except the Trappists. He must never mention that community in Joyce's presence.

COMING IN through the Green towards the hospital, Mick's eye penetrated the tracery of shrubs and iron railings. Yes, Joyce was standing there, and Mick paused to appraise him soberly in the wan evening sunlight before he knew he was observed. He was by now no stranger, yet in his solitary standing there he was still a bit surprising. He looked a mature man, at ease, iron-grey hair showing from a small hat, symbol of life's slow ebb-tide: also experience, wisdom and – who knows? – adversity. He was neat in person, clean, and had a walking stick. A dandy? No. The carriage of his head in the fuss of traffic and passing people gave notice that his eyesight was uncertain. If a stranger were to try to classify Joyce socially, he would probably put him down as a scholarly type – a mathematician, perhaps, or a tired senior civil servant; certainly not a writer, still less a great writer gone (as was supposed) queer in the head. Mick did not doubt, incidentally, that he had in fact written those pamphlets for the Catholic Truth Society, for mimicry and mockery were usually among the skills of the intellectually gifted; indeed, it was generally true that precision in playing a role ordained by morbid cerebral hypostasis is characteristic of most persons troubled in the mind. Who has not met and admired with pity the authentic attitude, speech and mannerisms of a Napoleon, a Shelley, even a Michelangelo?

Yet the same Joyce must have been somehow connected with the writing of *Ulysses* and *Finnegans Wake*, certainly far more than the probably hallucinatory attributions of authorship by Sylvia Beach. There was a possibility that both books were the monumental labours of several uniquely gifted minds, but a central, unifying mind seemed inescapable. It was not the false imputations of authorship which drove Joyce askew but rather the lonely exertion of keeping pace with a contrived reputation was what finally put the delicate poise of his head out of balance. Yet of Joyce one cheerful thing could be said – there was no harm in him. He was not even a nuisance, and certainly no danger to himself or others. His desire to become a Catholic priest (and alas, in one of the more discerning Orders) was, of course, fanciful; but it would be a great charity if the Jesuits took him. In their several houses about Dublin and throughout Ireland (to go no further) there was surely some nook, some neat little sinecure where he might come to peace. Again there came to mind that slogan of theirs – *ad majorem Dei gloriam*. It was their duty to help one, now fallen, whom they had once undertaken to educate. Joyce's confusion about *Finnegans Wake* was absolute and it was desirable, Mick reflected, that his pattern of thought should be steered completely away from books and writing. He must try to do that and also stress the impossibility (one thing which apparently Joyce himself had recognized) of the name James Joyce in conversations with the clergy. The name most commonplace throughout all Dublin and Wicklow was Byrne, pronounced Burn. He was a retired teacher named James Byrne, with experience on the continent. And was this not a bright thought coming to Mick just then in the Green? He had already mentioned that name to Father Cobble on the telephone.

He crossed the street and had to touch Joyce's arm before he turned in recognition.

– Ah, he said, good evening. That was a nice dry day.

– It was, Mick replied, and I hope we will have a successful twilight, if you know what I mean. We have a little time in hand before meeting Father Cobble.

Joyce smiled bleakly.

– I hope Father Cobble won't be a severe sort of holy man, he ventured.

– No, Mick replied. I told you he is an Englishman, and the only danger is that he may be stupid.

He took Joyce by the arm and guided him round the corner into Leeson Street.

– I want to mark your card, he said, on a few simple matters. We could talk across in the Green but a brief session in here in Grogan's might be better.

They were entering a public house when Joyce's tentative manner showed his surprise.

– Look, he said, there is nothing better I'd like than a small drink but to go for an interview concerning God's work with alcohol on the breath – surely that would be rash?

Mick pushed him to a seat in the snug and pressed a bell.

– First, he replied, Father Cobble himself, like most Jesuits, is not a bit puzzled about what to do when he finds a glass of malt in his hand. Secondly, we are going to have a few gins, not whiskey. Gin does not smell, or so they say. But it helps the tongue and the imagination. For myself, I am joining you in a drink against my will because I intend to give it up entirely, probably from today.

He ordered two glasses, with tonic water.

Joyce acquiesced in silence but gave the impression that he had never heard of gin. Perhaps Geneva would have been a better name.

– Now listen, Mick said briskly, your name from now on is James Byrne. *Your name is James Byrne.* Have you got that? Can you remember that name?

Joyce nodded.

– Byrne is a collateral name on my mother's side. Of course I can remember it. James Byrne.

He drank deeply, deceived by the tonic water, and nodded firmly.

– Yes, my name is James Byrne.

He drank again, still nodding, pressed the bell and ordered another round. Mick was slightly nervous.

– Do not take this harmless dram too fast, he counselled. Furthermore, you are a retired teacher, with some experience in France.

– Exactly. I could meet any cross-questioning you like on that point.

He seemed calm, confident, even happy. He was more responsive than usual and Mick honestly felt that he would impress a very neutral person like Father Cobble. Would there be any question about his birth certificate? Possibly, but the matter could be shelved temporarily.

They were respectable enough when they knocked on the large, discreet door of the big house at 35, Lower Leeson Street. An unkempt and ill-spoken youth opened it and showed them off the hall into a waiting-room which was (Mick thought) tawdry, gloomy and indeed a bit dirty. Saintliness and cleanliness were not always kin, he reflected, but there was no reason why that boy, who had now departed in search of Father Cobble, had not washed himself that day and cleaned himself up.

– I discern the authentic note of austerity here, Joyce remarked pleasantly.

– Yes, Mick concurred. Not far removed from the desert of ancient times. I can console you by telling you that the Fathers eat very well here and have red wine with dinner.

Joyce smiled knowingly.

– But I suppose it is not compulsory. In my own days in France I avoided table wines. It is a stupid French delusion that safe drinking-water is impossible to get.

The door had opened silently and there before them stood Father Cobble. Mick felt he had just dined, and was in good humour.

– Well, he said, advancing with both hands outstretched, welcome to our humble house.

There was some perfunctory handshaking, and the priest sat down.

– Father Cobble, Mick said, this is my friend James Byrne. He spent many years teaching abroad but he has now, so to speak, returned to the fold.

– Ah, Mr Byrne, it is a pleasure.

– My job here, Father, Mick added, is just to make this introduction and then be off with myself. James just wants to have a little chat with you.

– Of course. We people here are servants and not a bit ashamed to give ourselves that title. We give advice only for the asking . . . He paused and chuckled. Sometimes even without the asking.

– You are very kind, Father, Joyce said. You make me feel at home. You put me at my ease.

There was a pause as if all were waiting for one of them to say something which would at least hint at the purpose of the visit. Finally Father Cobble expertly opened a doorway.

– If it is a spiritual matter you are troubled about, Mr Byrne, he said, I will of course see you alone.

– I am departing anyway, Mick said hastily.

– Do you mean Confession? Joyce asked nervously. Lord no, it's not that. Thank God, I'm in no need of that at all. But it is true that my problem is, well, spiritual.

Father Cobble nodded encouragingly.

– You see, Father, Mick ventured, Mr Byrne wants to enter your house. He knocks at the door.

Here Joyce nodded eagerly.

– Oh well . . . I see, Father Cobble said, clearly a bit puzzled.

– He is by no means as old as he looks, Mick added helpfully.

Father Cobble studied his delicate hands.

– Well, the position is roughly this, he explained. Leaving aside ecclesiastical work proper, the community here is responsible for all its own intellectual work such as literary matters, teaching, and the Society's internal administrative tasks, national and international. We are self-sufficient, almost – if I dare say so – almost on the lines of the primitive Church. To look after our simple temporal needs, we take in boys from institutions, boys usually a bit defective mentally but likely to benefit and improve in surroundings like these. And, gentlemen, I make my own bed.

Joyce gestured slightly, momentarily incoherent.

– Father, he said faintly, it is not that I am destitute or anything like that. I have quite a reasonable job in the catering business. It's just that I'm spiritually . . . at sea. I want to serve the Almighty deliberately and directly. I want to come into one of the Society's houses and . . . well, work there.

– I see, Father Cobble said kindly. Yes. But within our rules it is not very easy to fit in a man like you, Mr Byrne. I will have a word with Father Baldwin of Rathfarnham Castle, our other house, and I'll possibly also talk to Milltown Park. We are rather crude people, Mr Byrne. Frankly, we don't go in for horticulture.

Joyce and Mick glanced at each other.

– Thank God we're never far away from a community of good nuns who gladly supply beautiful flowers for the altar.

– In fact, Father, Mick interposed, that sort of thing was not in Mr Byrne's mind at all.

– Well, take Rathfarnham Castle, the good priest continued. There is always a fair amount of weeding and that sort of thing to be done but I know the Rector encourages the Fathers to lend a hand there, for fresh air is as good for the clergy as it is for their flocks. But real gardening is a different cup of tea. Are you an experienced gardener, Mr Byrne?

Mick noticed Joyce coloured slightly under his natural pallor.

– Indeed and I am not, he said loudly.

– I know they have a full-time gardener there, though nowadays he's getting a bit old. But have you other manual qualifications or skills, Mr Byrne? French polishing, carpentry, book-binding...?

– No, Joyce said curtly.

– The care of brasswork?

– No.

Father Cobble smiled tolerantly.

– Well now, Mr Byrne, he said, in the words of a soldier, we're not beaten yet. I'll be perfectly honest and tell you that there's one thing which has plagued the Society in all its houses in this country...

– Not competition from the Christian Brothers? Mick asked, grinning.

– Ah no. Something much nearer home. I mean the Fathers' underclothes.

– Dear goodness, Joyce said.

– We need not theorize, Father Cobble continued in his mild manner, as to why the Almighty distributed certain skills and crafts as between the sexes. The plain fact is that knitting and sewing and needlework are uniquely the accomplishments of women. The Fathers' underclothes are perpetually in a state of near-collapse, yet our rules prohibit the employment of women here, even in the most menial tasks. That, gentlemen, is a glimpse of the enclosed religious life. Just now my own semmet would make you laugh. Full of holes.

Joyce seemed at sea, embarrassed.

– But Father, surely the nuns could help – even, I mean, as an act of charity?

– No, no, Mr Byrne, our rules do not permit any association of that kind in the domestic sphere. Beautiful flowers for the altar – ah, certainly.

– But, Father, Mick interposed, couldn't, say, old boys from the Jesuit colleges help in a thing like that? Bring stuff home, I mean. After all, they have wives and daughters.

– And mothers and sisters, Joyce added.

Father Cobble smiled remotely.

– The Society of Jesus, gentlemen, has also its dignity.

All paused at this solemnity.

– But good heavens, Father, you must have some way of working –

– If we only knew, Father Cobble observed, why sweat is so corrosive, we would be perhaps getting somewhere. Upon my word my semmet is *rotted*.

Mick's face clouded in some despair.

– But what *do* you do?

– Well, nearly all the Fathers know how to darn socks. Father d'Arbois, a Frenchman here, makes heroic attempts with the underclothes, and one of our houseboys is also quite promising. But thank God there is one bright spot. Father Rector is most generous about renewals. He is very particular about the health of the Fathers. I suspect he has the leg of a floorwalker in Todd Burns.

Joyce, who had been most perplexed, now broke into an easy smile.

– Father Cobble, he said, that household problem may seem formidable but it would not deter myself in the slightest.

– Really, Mr Byrne?

The priest stared at him thoughtfully, and looked towards Mick.

– Do you know, Mr Byrne, he said, I think – forbid that I am being presumptuous – I think you have put an idea into my head. Our sad little situation here obtains equally in our other houses. Not in our Colleges in the country, of course – Clongowes, Mungret, Galway. A matron and staff are provided there but think of our Manresa house at Dollymount, Loyola at Donnybrook, Rathfarnham Castle, Milltown Park. Do you follow me, Mr Byrne? The Fathers' underclothes are in flitters in all those establishments.

Mick stirred uneasily.

– Mr Byrne, Father, he said, is not connected with any of the laundry families or anything like that.

Father Cobble smiled patiently.

– Heaven forbid, he said pleasantly. It is only that I have the embryo of an idea that I think I will put plump and plain before Father Rector.

– And what might that be? Mick asked.

– Quite simple. Just this: that Mr Byrne, having been nominally recruited to our houseboy staff, should be in charge of the maintenance and repair of the Fathers' underclothes in all the Dublin residential establishments.

– Good Lord! Mick gasped.

– To do what he can himself, patiently learning a difficult craft, and to farm out garments to girls of unfortunate class housed by the good nuns at Donnybrook and Merrion, as God and reason may guide him. Gentlemen . . .

Father Cobble beamed serenely on the visitors.

– Gentlemen, what do you say?

Mick stared ahead of him, stunned, and Joyce seemed unnaturally still in his chair, as if dead. Then his voice was heard, aghast, far off:

– The what was that? Me . . . darn . . . Jesuits' . . . semmets?

Father Cobble looked questioningly from one to the other, himself now slightly puzzled. He had just faced up rather neatly, he thought, to a problem which to them had looked intractable enough. Mick thought furiously in this situation of paralysis. He suddenly stood up.

– Father Cobble, he said seriously, I have to go now, and I'll let myself out. Mr Byrne will explain fully in my absence the sort of work he wishes to embark on. In a word, he wishes to start studies with the object of being ordained a priest . . . and indeed a Jesuit priest.

Father Cobble had also staggered to his feet.

– What was that? *What?* May the Blessed Mother look down on us!

Joyce remained seated, immobile.

– What in heaven's name do you mean? Father Cobble demanded.

Mick fingered his hat and put it on his head.

– Exactly what I said, Father. Goodbye now, take care of yourself, and of Mr Byrne. Goodbye, James. I'll see you later.

It was an inexpressible relief to find himself again in the street, though feelings were confused and there was a stale sense of guilt. Had he cynically made a fool of Joyce? Not deliberately, certainly, but it might have been more prudent to have ignored Dr Crewett's disclosure that Joyce was alive and in Ireland. The latter's mental turmoil had possibly been exacerbated rather than eased. Who could be sure? At all events he was now in hands trained to help, and to give succour in its many forms: he was no longer pitifully helpless, in mid-air. And heretofore ranked as 'problem' in Mick's mind, the tag could now be changed to 'disposed of', if not solved.

What remained? A visit to the Colza Hotel in Dalkey straight away to have it out with Mary, and finally slam closed that draughty door.

As he walked towards a tram, his steps were slow and his face preoccupied.

CHAPTER 20

THE THOUGHTS in Mick's head seemed to lurch about in the manner of the big tram which was carrying him to Dalkey but those thoughts lacked the familiarity and predestination of the old tramcar.

His outlook was a bit ragged in setting about what should be the careful, conclusive foray in his life. The two preceding episodes had been rough but not unsatisfactory: he had allayed the De Selby menace, possibly forever, and he had brought James Joyce spiritually to a place where more than likely some shadow of the solace he sought would be forthcoming. Even if it was found that he was indeed a head-case, the Fathers would look after him.

Why should he now be vaguely apprehensive about the rest of the night's business? It concerned, for a change, largely himself and his future. He would simply tell Mary firmly, even crudely, that he had no further time for her, and that that was that finally. Memories, or recollections of tenderness long past, was just sentimentality, silly schoolboy inadequacy, like having a dirty nose. He was a grown man, and should behave like one. Why, though, hadn't he ascertained whether the Cistercians had a home in Dublin? It was a stupid omission, for it put him in the position that night of being ready to go but not knowing where to turn. And what about his mother? If he quit his job and entered a monastery, how would she live? That had been decided: with her younger sister who, if far from opulent, had a healthy daughter and ran a boarding-house.

What was needed above all things was calm.

Knowing people and accepting company indiscriminately complicated the already far-from-simple task of living. There might be some truth in the sneer that monks and nuns were merely cowards who ran away from life's challenge, being content unto death to sleep, eat, pray, and mess about with some childishly useless 'work'. Was the monastery just a contrivance for isolation and insulation, not unlike a fever hospital? No, it was God's own house. Notions like that were nefarious in origin. What possible benefit had he derived from, for instance, his association with Hackett? Or, for that matter, with Mary? The one stimulated alcoholism, the other concupiscence. What of the dozens of people of both sexes he knew in the civil service? They were pathetic, futile nobodies, faceless creatures, and — worse — they were bores. Perhaps other people found himself a bore? What matter? Why should he worry about what other people thought? As an intending Trappist, he would have to turn his back on pleasure but that would not be so easy because he knew of practically nothing which could be called pleasure.

As his machine clattered to a final halt, he dimly discerned the Dalkey street below, early lights peeping in a few shops. As he stumbled down the stairs, he realized that he was in a bad temper. Why? Oh, nothing particular — nothing that a good decent drink (not gin) wouldn't fix before he took on Mary in the Colza. At the nearest licensed counter he studied the amber charm of a glass of whiskey and made up his mind once again that he must behave himself. *Finnegans Wake*, though, and all that line of incoherent trash be damned! What was the teaching of the Church on this question of literary depravity? He did not know but perhaps he could find out from one of those little Catholic Truth Society pamphlets, price tuppence.

Gradually an equanimity of mood descended on him. His mission was simple and honourable, his primary object the redemption of his soul. What was wrong with that? Nothing. But the necessary declarations could be made courteously, losing nothing of force for that. Bawling or rude manners impressed nobody, except possibly a member of the brute creation. What if Mary created a scene? It was quite unthinkable. Her attitude of poise, intellectual maturity and sophistication may have been all humbug but one cannot discard a life-long affectation as if it were an old jacket. There would be no scene and as if to register that prediction, he ordered a final glass of what might very remotely be called his pleasure, soon to be spurned forever. The Cistercians? Simple: a glance at a telephone directory on the morrow would locate those saintly men at their best proximity. He murmured to himself a wise Irish proverb: *God's help is nearer than the door.*

When he opened the door of the Colza Hotel, he sensed that he had stumbled on a special silence, sensing also that he himself had been under discussion. Mary and Hackett were alone together at the far end. It was clear from Hackett's lolling attitude and glossy eyes that he had been filling himself with drink for a long time. Mary was not drunk – he had never seen her go any real distance on that path – but her face looked pale and excited. Mrs Laverty was behind the counter, silent, looking strangely chastened. Mick nodded to all in a pleasant but impassive way, sat at the counter and murmured that he would like a whiskey.

– Enter the Prince of Denmark! Hackett said, a thickness in his loud voice.

Mick paid no attention. When he got his drink, he turned towards Mary.

– What sort of a day had you, Mary? he asked. Good, or dull, or just plain unremarkable?

– Oh, just so-so, she replied rather lifelessly.

– The evenings are drawing in, Mrs Laverty said.

– What have you been up to, divil? Hackett rasped.

– I have something to say, Mary . . .

– Is that so, Michael?

Michael! The word stunned him. His name was Mick. Even the ticket checker on the railway called him that, and so did many a barman. To be called Michael – by Mary! Well, well. This was certainly the queer prelude to the play he had composed.

– Did you hear me? Hackett said gruffly, sitting up. Quit this yapping for a few seconds. An explanation is called for. Confront him with the evening paper, Mrs Laverty.

The listless Mrs Laverty transferred the paper from her lap to the counter. The main headline meant nothing to Mick but across two other columns in big letters he read DISASTROUS DALKEY FIRE – Small Mansion Gutted. His startled eyes raced to the smaller print and soon verified that it was indeed De Selby's hide-away. It was understood, the report said, that the owner was in London. The Dunleary brigade had been severely hampered by poor water pressure and the inaccessibility of the conflagration. The building and its contents were totally destroyed and there was even fire damage to some trees. Almost without knowing, Mick swallowed the rest of his drink. Here was a how-do-you-do if there ever was one. Here was he sitting quietly at a counter, the far-seeing genius who had salvaged DMP. Lord!

— You might as well tell us all about it. Everybody here, Mary included, knows De Selby. Did he put you up to firing the house? Out with the truth, Mick, for goodness' sake. We're all friends here.

— Wasn't that a terrible thing? Mrs Laverty asked piously and quietly. Pushing his glass across to her, Mick asked when did this happen?

— Very early this morning.

— Tell us what sort of trickery has been going on, Hackett insisted rudely. I know finding out things will be a job for poor Sergeant Fottrell but let's have a few hints. Is this an old-fashioned insurance job?

Mick's reply was blunt.

— Shut up, Hackett. You're a drunken sleeveen.

There must have been real edge on his tone, for utter silence followed, or at least a brief interval filled by nothing but the sound of slobbering by Hackett at his glass. But Mary's penetrating tone came again.

— You said you had something to say?

— Yes.

Why not say it in front of Hackett, even though it was none of his business? Hackett was of no account, though having a witness was no harm.

— Yes, Mary, he said. I have something important to say to you but it's not confidential and I don't mind saying it here.

— You're very snooty tonight whatever you've been up to, Hackett muttered.

— Is that so, Michael, Mary said again, icily. Well, I have something substantial to say to you and I think I'd better say it first. A lady has precedence.

— Aw now, cut out these fireworks, you two, Hackett said. Cut it out.

— Yes, Mary?

— What I wanted to say is that tonight Hackett here has asked me to marry him. I told him I will. We are old friends.

Mick felt limp. He stared, slid off the stool, steadied himself, and then sat up again.

— That's right, Mick, Hackett blabbed, we're old, old friends and we're not getting younger. So we've decided to take the jump and be fluthered ever afterwards. No hard feelings, Mick, but you and Mary weren't engaged. You never gave her a ring.

– That wouldn't matter, Mary interposed.

– We've been going to shows and pubs and dances for weeks and weeks . . . and weeks. One thing about Mary – she's alive. You never suspected that or if you did, you kept the discovery secret.

Mary shook Hackett smartly.

– No need for that sort of talk, she said. His nature is different from yours and that's all. Let's have no clowning here.

– True enough, Hackett said, finishing his drink with a weak flourish. True enough. When you wanted to go out, he stayed at home to make stirabout for his poor mother.

Mick involuntarily again slipped from his stool.

– If you mention my mother again, he snarled, I'll smash your dirty mouth.

Mary frowned.

– Mrs L, Hackett called, give us a new drink on the double – all round. It's ridiculous for people like us to be quarrelling like babbies. All right, Mick, cool down.

Mick got back on his stool.

– What I wanted to say, Mary, he announced slowly, doesn't matter now. It doesn't matter.

Mary, he thought, blanched. It may have been a trick of the light, but her eyes sought the floor. Mick felt strangely touched.

– Tell us something, Hackett said with his greasy friendliness, about that James Joyce of yours if De Selby is barred as a subject of chat.

Mick felt neutralized, if that phrase makes sense. He even mutely accepted Hackett's new drink. What could he say? What *was* there to say?

– Yes, Mary's voice said. Let's talk about something else.

They drank uneasily in silence.

– Joyce, Mick said in the end, wherever he is and however he feels, was in his day a great writer. I'm wondering what sort of a job he would make of the story of Mary and me.

This speech of his own, as he heard it, sounded strange and pathetic. Mary was pale, preoccupied. Hackett was merely drunk. Hackett spoke again.

– Mick, you can keep your Mr Joyce. Know who could write a better book?

– Who?

– Mary here.

– Well, I know she's versatile.

– Ah, that's the word. Versatile.

Then she spoke.

– I don't think that's a story I'd like to try to write. One must write outside oneself. I'm fed up with writers who put a fictional gloss over their own squabbles and troubles. It's a form of conceit, and usually it's very tedious.

There was another considerable pause. Surely they were behaving absurdly – talking about books in a sort of study-circle calm immediately after a nasty flare-up in which personal feelings had been engaged, with the outside possibility of violence. It was artificial, bogus. Mick was beginning to be sorry he'd come, or spoken, or drunk so much. Hackett was now frowning; probably he had lost his way in the maze of his confused thinking. Mary kept her head down, her face a bit averted from Mick. The latter felt that everybody was uneasy. It was Hackett who broke the stillness, and he seemed to be talking mostly to himself.

– Mary, he muttered, let's forget this bargain of ours. We'd good times, but I'm no use. I'm drunk. I'm not your style at all.

She turned to look at him and said nothing.

– That damn fellow over there is all right, Hackett muttered on, and you know that very well. Look at him. He's blushing.

Very likely Mick was. He was upset, and felt a fool. Events seemed to have been perversely pulled inside out inasmuch as he felt he was to blame for making Mary feel like a pig. His ridiculous remedy was to ask Mrs Laverty to dish out another drink all round. He commandeered them, got a tray, and served them personally. His toast was loud:

– To us!

It was silently honoured.

– You didn't mean that, Mary? he murmured.

– No Mick. You're just a bloody fool.

– But the bloody fool you're going to marry?

– I suppose so. I like Hackett here, but not that much.

– Thanks, you cluck, Hackett smiled.

That is as much as need be told. The silence between them on the home-bound tram was mutually known and nursed. What had happened, after all? Nothing much. They had stupidly lost each other, but only for a matter of hours. Mary spoke:

– Mick, what was that awful thing you were going to say tonight?

The question was inevitable, Mick thought, but required care.

– Oh, about my mother, he said. She's getting feebler and has decided to go up to Drogheda and live with her sister.

Mary lightly gripped his wrist.

– Ah, the grand old lady! And the little house? I suppose we'll live there? There's nothing like a roof over your head. It's an old-fashioned idea, but a roof means security – for ourselves and the family.

– The family?

– Yes, Mick. I'm certain I'm going to have a baby.

ABOUT THE INTRODUCER

Novelist and speechwriter KEITH DONOHUE
is the author of *The Stolen Child* and *The Irish
Anatomist: A Study of Flann O'Brien.*

This book is set in BEMBO which was cut
by the punch-cutter Francesco Griffo
for the Venetian printer-publisher
Aldus Manutius in early 1495
and first used in a pamphlet
by a young scholar
named Pietro
Bembo.